"This book is fire. If you're into heists, sharp-tongued women with secrets, or rebellion served with banter and blood magic, you need to read this. Stolen Histories is perfect for fans of Leigh Bardugo, N.K. Jemisin, or anyone who ever rooted for the morally gray underdog. It's fun, it's furious, and it's got heart for days." — **Literary Titan Reviews**

"Michaels crafts a vivid world where elemental magic hums through every object and ritual, and where ambient power bleeds into city streets and backroom deals... The prose is rich and often lyrical, particularly in the worldbuilding: Castor pulses with life... A richly imagined, character-driven fantasy that's bursting with magic and mischief." — **Kirkus Reviews**

"If you like your heroes clever, your magic sharp, and your revolution just getting started, this one is definitely for you." — **The Prairies Book Review**

"Author B.R. Michaels has done an excellent job in creating an eclectic group of rogues who bring humor, personality, and gravitas to the dynamic narrative. This novel proved to be adrenaline-filled from start to finish." — **Philip Zozzaro, Portland Book Review**

Stolen Histories

By B.R. Michaels

Once Upon A Queer Publishing
LLC

To my mom, who spent many days trapped in a car with me, hearing about these characters.

"The thief, as will become apparent, was a special type of thief. This thief was an artist of theft. Other thieves merely stole everything that was not nailed down, but this thief stole the nails as well."

— Terry Pratchett

Magic System

The Written — Scribe

The Spoken — Singer

The Willed — Conjurer

The Forged — Artificer

~~*The Imbued* — Vessel~~

Magical Races

The Taos — Nightbloods

The Skorae — Sky Lords

The Andan — Forest Children

The Bera — Mountain Dwellers

The Ashan — Sun Eaters

The Osiyi — Sea Folk

~~*The Sonai* — Nullifiers~~

1

AMARI

Amari Kato should be dead. Anyone who knows or has even *heard* of her would likely agree, though not all for the same reasons. But Amari is the only one who knows her death had been Destined. It had been Foretold, and then it had been ignored.

In all her twenty-two years, Amari has never found anything quite as satisfying as watching the mighty fall. The wealthy and corrupt elite, the bullies in uniforms, and the magic users hoarding power built on others' sacrifices. Amari loves nothing more than seeing all that self-assured belief in their own invincibility crumble away.

"Here's your tea," a waitress named Jia, according to her name tag, says as she places Amari's order in front of her. Amari mentally pushes magic into her hearing enhancement runes so she can catch the words, and nods before the waitress walks away into the busy cafe. The cup is set on a folded-up newspaper, sporting headlines like *School Bans Fireballs in Dorms – 'Again'* and *WANTED: Apprentice. Not a Taos human. Must be okay with occasional frog transformations. Not a euphemism.* A drop of spilled tea bleeds onto one of the moving pictures, distorting the fangs of a local politician as he talks.

The seats outside the cafe aren't overly occupied, so Amari can clearly see a commotion erupting across the street. She smiles as she sips her tea, sharp purple eyes staying ever watchful.

This small cafe is notable not just for its lovely pastries, but because it is directly parallel to Castor City's Telas Bank, which is by far the most popular bank in the country of Esma. Since the rise of the neighboring Apolon Empire, the bank has consolidated incredible power over the past few centuries. Mostly due to their shareholders' willingness to bend to Empire authority.

People walking by or heading towards the bank's entrance suddenly jump back as the door swings open, as if a great force is pushing behind them. Castor police officers drag a struggling bank head out, his hoofs scraping the ground futilely. The shouting is easily heard, drawing the attention of every person on the street.

"There's been some mistake! You can't—UNHAND ME! This is unacceptable, you'll be hearing from my lawyers! I demand to speak with the police commissioner—" Telas Bank's *former* head is pushed roughly into a police transport, and the door closing muffles his further screeching.

A couple walking by Amari's table stops to gawk at the scene. One turns to the other. "What was that about?"

"You didn't hear? Someone leaked that he was shaving money off the top. Practically draining the Lower District dry."

"They all do that."

"But he took from Telas' shareholders, too, I guess, and you know they wouldn't accept being stolen *from*."

"I guess…" The couple's conversation trails off as they start walking again, moving on from the scene. Amari smiles to herself with a triumphant curl to her lips. Next to her seat, a bag nearly overflowing with folders is set on the ground, stamped with the official logo of Telas Bank.

She takes another sip of her tea, idly tapping the cup with her fingers. The black markings that stretch across her pale purple hands hum with dormant power, and she hums in satisfaction. A lovely end to a busy week.

After all that's left of the prison transport is dust, and she finishes her tea, Jia approaches her table again. "Is there anything else you need?"

"No, thank you. I'll just pay."

Amari rarely gets a peaceful moment to herself like this, so she drinks it in. The day's temperature is fair, a nice contrast to the chaotic weather that tends to hit the city. In the Upper District, the ambient magic is a touch calmer and flows around her like a fast-moving stream. The energy on the other side of Castor is much wilder, especially close to Kiyoshi Crater. Enough to make people who can afford it avoid the place at all costs.

Magic itself is everywhere and in everything. It's the energy behind every being's power and was given as a 'gift from the gods.' Amari isn't sure she agrees with this sentiment, except she must admit the usefulness of said gifts. Like right now.

Amari is hardly paying attention to her surroundings aside from a general awareness of potential threats when she senses danger. It's so minimal that she almost ignores it, but she decides to side with her intuition and turns to look at the café.

Her powers tend to give her a small warning when something violent is about to happen in her vicinity, and she'd rather avoid having to flee the scene of a crime right now. Inside the shop, her eyes immediately zero in on someone visibly agitated. A Skorae, or more commonly, a 'Sky Lord,' with large wings folded against his back and raptor-like talons for fingers. None of these traits is particularly alarming, but how the Sky Lord stares at Jia is. The waitress, for her part, is trying her best to ignore him.

Amari gets out of her seat and calmly strides into the cafe, the doorway tall enough that she doesn't have to worry about her ram horns brushing anything. She beelines for the Sky Lord, scanning the man as she does. Nothing about him tells her he's hiding any weapons, but that doesn't mean much if someone can throw tables with their mind. He startles when Amari walks in front of him, slightly bumping into his side. She pretends to be focused on the shop's counter.

The voice is muffled, but the outrage is clear. "What—"

"Sorry, I'm waiting for my bill. Did you see what happened outside?"

The attempt at conversation both irritates him and forces the Sky Lord to back off from his aggression. "Yeah. No excuse for the wait time here."

So that's why. What a ridiculous reason to get violent.

"Sure."

Jia arrives with the Sky Lord's packaged order, looking nervous. He snatches the bag roughly from her hands, hesitating as if he's about to yell, but not before glancing at Amari, then deciding against it, storming out of the café.

The waitress lets out a sigh of relief before seemingly catching herself. "Oh, your bill! Here."

Amari accepts it and pays while the waitress cleans several recently vacated tables. It takes work not to openly smirk as Amari pulls out the Sky Lord's wallet she swiped, leaving the money inside as a tip for Jia. She's smiling pleasantly as she steps out into the busy streets.

A train passes above her head, riding the waves of magical

energy that exist all around. It pulls into a floating station where transports take passengers up and down, adding to the bustle of the street. For a city with such a mixed reputation, Castor draws a lot of tourists, making it easy for Amari to hide in the crowds when she wishes. She makes her way home as countless people with a mix of wings, horns, antlers, tails, and more blend together into an indistinguishable mass.

Sitting on the northern coast of Esma and in the shadow of the imposing Apolon Empire, the city of Castor functions as both a popular port for trade and a haven for criminals.

It's a city of ghosts. Even the architecture reflects the blend of old Gothic spires with towering skyscrapers, juxtaposing remnants of the old world and modern innovation. The ambient magic leftover from ancient conflicts and turmoil still exists here, creating its own spaces in the city. Amari can see the flickers of the past if she looks closely enough, and glimpses of ancient monuments and temples appear from the corner of her eye as she wanders closer to the river.

East of the Kiyon River lies the Upper District, where the buildings of newly-made stone and gilded metal pierce the sky like jagged teeth. Here, affluent citizens reside in opulent mansions adorned with stained glass windows and other exotic imports. Marble statues of long-dead heroes stand sentinel in public gardens, their stoic faces watching over the citizens' daily lives.

Amari always breathes a sigh of relief when she leaves the suffocating streets behind, trading the carefully controlled environment for a place much more chaotic.

In contrast, the Merchant District has an atmosphere of bustling activity and desperate wishes. It lies on a small island parting the river that's connected to the rest of the city by stone bridges. She weaves through narrow streets that are packed with stalls of sellers trying to catch her attention. She passes people peddling food, love potions, and enchanted blades within the span of a second. This is perhaps the most diverse place in Castor, where people from multiple far-away cultures converge to try to make money. But it holds nothing for Amari today.

Beyond the bustling marketplace and artisan workshops, and just west of the river running through Castor, lies the sprawling expanse of the Lower District. Here, she watches the gothic spires give way to dilapidated tenements and labyrinthine alleys cloaked in perpetual shadow. In some places, the architecture is less cared for, just a patchwork of crumbling stone and timber, haphazardly patched with salvaged materials and adorned with graffiti artwork. Dark, twisting lanes wind between shops and makeshift homes, where the less fortunate people eke out a living amidst crime and dissent.

Regardless of where Amari is in Castor, the city itself seems alive —a silent guardian over its inhabitants, its ancient stones whispering tales of long-gone people and monsters. The past lingers here.

For someone who was born with the ability to see time outside of its natural progression, it's the perfect place to live. Amari almost feels normal knowing that everyone else in Castor is sensing the memory of a different time right alongside her.

The ambient magic gets less and less calm the closer she gets to her home. Naturally, her apartment building resides in the Lower District. As a career criminal, Amari can't very well live among the rich, can she? She wouldn't be able to stop herself from cleaning them out of all their valuables and getting caught for good measure. Her friend and roommate, Taliya, would never let her live it down unless she invited her friend with her, which was, admittedly, very likely.

She hoped Taliya was done collecting what they needed for tonight.

The Lower District welcomes her back like a stray cat that pretends it doesn't want your attention, and Amari slips through alleyways and side streets to get closer to the Kiyoshi Crater. Her natural affinity for sticking to the shadows helps as she expertly avoids a brewing gang fight, a mugging, and a violent game of rowdy kids involving a sphere of fire as the ball. Amari leaves the scene behind her none the worse for wear and smelling only faintly of smoke.

When she reaches the edge of the ancient and cavernous crater, she turns to follow the rim until she comes to an apartment building perilously close to a place most consider 'really fucking haunted.' A small sign nailed to the front entrance names the building as *The Hall* in swirling black calligraphy.

The Hall is a three-story structure, its exterior painted in a cheerful, light lavender that stands out starkly against the grittier surroundings of the neighborhood. She notes with pleasure that the paint still seems fresh and well-preserved, the occasional splashes of color coming from vibrant window boxes overflowing with various flowers. It had taken her days to paint the entire building. Taliya, naturally, had been of little help apart from loaning her some climbing gear and supplying her with snacks.

Once inside, Amari begins to let her situational awareness relax. This is the only place she can conceivably call 'safe' despite the strange location.

Each apartment has at least two to three bedrooms, two bathrooms, and a small living area attached to a small kitchen. Many of the apartments have small, personal gardens on their balconies or windowsills, filled with a mix of herbs, flowers, and unusual plants. By all measures, it's a nice place, but the proximity to Kiyoshi Crater means the prices are cheap, and the tenants are weird. Amari is self-aware enough to know she and Taliya follow this pattern.

She pulls out her keys as she approaches the door to apartment 2B, unlocking the many locks on the door with the ease of a long-held routine and stepping inside.

Amari shrugs off her jacket and collapses onto an armchair with the smile of a job well done. The ram horns that curl around her head dig into the soft material of the chair, but not uncomfortably so.

The figure sprawling in the only other armchair turns her attention to Amari with a sharp grin. Yellow eyes made for hunting in the dark peer at her out of a brown face framed by small braids left loose. "Hey, how was it?"

She uses sign language as she speaks aloud, knowing Amari likes to let her hearing enhancement runes depower at home. The runes drawn behind Amari's ears require only a small portion of magic to work, but they're a constant drain. When she's just in the apartment, it's not worth the effort when she could be relaxing. Their apartment is warded enough she'll know immediately if someone breaks in.

Amari's smile turns into a smirk. "Worked perfectly. Cops dragged out the bastard, I got to watch the whole thing."

"Sorry I missed it," Taliya snorts, hand movements exaggerated in her typical flippant manner.

After she lets her satisfaction over the victory fade, Amari gives her friend a searching look. "We're good for the plan tonight?"

The fellow thief scoffs. "I've only been prepping all day. All our gear has been checked over, *twice*, and the guard's schedules are on the worktable."

With what feels like a great effort, Amari forces herself up and toward the table. It's covered in documents and photos, with no real organization. Taliya says she leaves the arranging and labeling to the 'control freak,' which Amari is both irritated by and appreciates. Taliya always messes up her system.

Still, she sighs when she sees the mess but knows better than to mention it. "Okay, this looks good. We go with Plan Xcar."

"You and your ridiculous names."

"Hush."

The rest of the afternoon is mainly prep and conserving energy. The fun begins when the sun sets and two of the three moons rise.

She gets ready by changing into clothes that appear inconspicuous on the surface, but are reinforced with armorclothe and are equipped with many inner pockets. Amari hides her collapsible staff on her back, and other tools throughout her jacket. She wraps a dark scarf around her collar that she will pull up during the job to cover her face. Her hood will cover her horns well enough when she pulls it up, but the typical markings of a Taos — of a *Nightblood* — must also be covered. For one, the crescent moon on the side of her face is far too identifiable. She already has to be wary when she's out as a civilian, adding to her already substantial paranoia won't help her.

Finally, she ties her dark hair up in her usual style. It's a deceptively complicated style that is fundamentally still practical. Multiple small braids are woven along the sides, framing her face and adding texture and detail. She keeps these braids tight and precise to keep hair out of her eyes and untangled with her horns. At the back, the braids converge, usually gathered into a larger braid, twisted into a bun when she's on the job, or other times left loose with a half-up, half-down style.

This arrangement keeps hair out of the face and is practical for movement, but Amari also just enjoys the style. She can weave small metal rings or beads into the braids, which, done well enough, won't make a sound when she moves. Depending on what colors or patterns she uses, it adds a touch of decoration or a sense of nostalgia.

Taliya steps out of her room dressed similarly, no doubt with dozens of hidden blades on her person. She has no markings to be identified by, so her outfit is more straightforward. Twin swords are strapped to her back, something that won't draw as much attention as it perhaps should. Weapons are rather normal to see being carried openly. After all, when some people can light things on fire with a thought, what does it matter if others carry blades?

Their target is the Apolon Empire's Trade Center in Castor. It's not an easy mark.

The building is located on the east side of the city, in the Upper District, directly next to the Kiyon River that runs through Castor. The building is grand and aesthetically pleasing, as any official Empire Trade Center should be. Stone guardians sit atop the sloped roofs, over-watching entrances, and will awaken when the building's wards are breached.

Wards are one of Taliya's main specialties. She can work around the runes that power and control the wards better than anyone Amari knows. With enough time, she can get in anywhere. The problem will be the living guards—Empire soldiers who do rounds and are trained to catch wardbreakers like her roommate and friend.

Amari will use the schedule Taliya managed to copy and plan their heist to avoid the soldiers, preparing for the worst as well. No one knows better than the two of them how necessary an exit plan is.

"Ready?" Amari has thrown her jacket back on and waits for Taliya in front of the apartment's door. The thief grins and finishes packing her gear, then pulls all her braids into a haphazard bun. They both have the normal wardbreaking kit and some equipment for a more... explosive exit.

"Born ready."

The Hall, despite being uncomfortably close to Kiyoshi Crater, still has plenty of nice shops nearby and gets a lot of activity from the city's citizens that can't afford to go to the Merchant District every day. Yet, the presence of Castor law enforcement in the Lower District is low. It makes hiding illegal activities conveniently uncomplicated.

Amari and Taliya's route to the Trade Center will be by water. The Kiyon River always deals with more boats than it can keep track of. Sneaking a small craft across the water at night is a simple matter, even under the light of two moons. They're helped by Taliya's minor ability to control the river itself.

Her friend has never had any earthly idea who her parents are— not that the girl has ever cared—but Taliya does know she has Osiyi blood. The 'Sea Folk,' as many land folk call them, is an incredibly broad term, Amari knows. Taliya can never identify what kind of Osiyi she is, even if she wants to, that's how much variety the ocean contains.

Narrowing down the Osiyi to the ones that can spend time on land and have some form of hydrokinesis doesn't help. Unfortunately, abandoned children with unknown mixed ancestry are not uncommon in the Lower District. Right now, it's useful.

Taliya's method of controlling the water means she has to sing, so Amari makes sure to have some cover for the noise when they depart. It just so happens that at this time of year, the locals like setting off fireworks in reverence to the Dance of Ashes, which is a holiday based on an old myth surrounding remembrance and celebration of those lost. The point is that it gets loud at night, and even Amari can hear muffled, distant booms.

It helps them twofold, since a lot of officers will be posted around the festivities instead of near the Trade Center. If Amari and Taliya end up tripping an alarm, backup will take longer to get there.

Two broken and deformed moons hang over head, in different sizes and lunar phases because of their orbits. The third, and largest, moon will rise soon. Amari would like to be done before then. As they settle in their tiny boat, Taliya begins to softly sing. The distant cracking and roar of the festival drowns out any potential listeners.

Singers are always a wonder to witness, even when they're bringing calamity. For her part, Amari can't hold a note for her life, and she never could. Taliya's words aren't understandable by any human ear, speaking a language as ancient as magic itself. It's something instinctual to the ones who can speak magic into being. The air hums around her, deep notes resonating with every aspect of the environment.

Water moves under their boat, just ripples at first. Then, the song picks up, and with it, Taliya's control over her element. It never fails to remind Amari of the old stories about Sirens.

They glide across the water unnoticed, making hardly a sound. The boat arrives on the east bank just as a guard finishes checking the back of the building. Taliya waits until the soldier is out of sight to pull herself onto the bank and dash to the Trade Center. She has a few minutes before another guard makes it around, and Amari keeps watch.

Out of the corner of her eye, she can tell that the wards are typical for Empire security. Taliya has time to disable the alarm system that would go off if intruders touched the outside of the building, so no stone guardians are coming alive to rip them to shreds tonight. It takes careful precision, not undoing the ward itself while making it useless. Before the next patrol comes, she and Amari take advantage of the building's extravagant detailing, using it as grips to climb to the roof with practiced ease.

She eyes the stone guardians on the roof as they remain an ominous feature, but don't react to the thieves' presence. Light from the moons cast shifting shadows that the two women make a home in.

The Trade Center comprises multiple sections, each with its own security. The main trade floor takes up the most room, but nothing truly valuable is kept there. Taliya and Amari are targeting one of the vaults underground. Specifically, the one containing magical tokens, which are small disks that store energy for later use. They're easier to carry than jewels or coins due to their lightweight, and they can be scrubbed of their identification and sold easily on the black market.

"I'll give you as much Time as I can," Amari says, putting one hand on Taliya's shoulder and one on the roof. She closes her eyes and focuses on her ever-present sense of Time. It lies around her like a great blanket of swirling mist, and if she tries hard enough, she can manipulate it to an extent. As long as she can take the physical strain that comes with it.

Time moves along, sluggish and heavy like syrup to their senses.

Taking advantage of Amari's ability, Taliya begins wardbreaking in earnest, using her specialized runica to disrupt and rework runes. Truly *breaking* a ward inverts the magic and would trip an alarm, so what Taliya really does is more complicated. Normally, this would take up valuable time that would make their window of opportunity that much shorter before the tampering is discovered. Like this, the world seems like it's moving ten times slower while she and Taliya stay at the same pace.

Halfway through the wardbreaking, Amari's head starts to feel like someone is holding a hot poker against it, and she visibly winces. Catching this out of the corner of her eye, Taliya speeds up as fast as she can. When the wards are properly nullified, they slip in through a window that no guards can see. Amari palms some pain-relief medicine she keeps on her for exactly this scenario.

They enter above the main floor. Gilded balconies overlook the typically bustling trade floor, offering a vantage point. Some soldiers patrol here, too, so they move quickly towards the vaults. Doors to the stairs leading down are on every floor, making them easy to get to.

The gate to the vaults is where the lion's share of the Trade Center's security goes. Both Taliya and Amari work together to break the independent wards on the underground entrance so they stay ahead of the clock. With enough concentration, Amari's magic lets her see where the weakest point—where it will break first, where it will erode fastest, where it *changes*—in something is, which is, suffice to say, helpful. This ability works on gates, locks, weapons, and people.

Past the heavily warded gate, a hall full of vault doors is revealed. The passage curls around a corner, leading to what they know are the personal vaults for the wealthy donors who support the Empire. Amari heads directly to the third vault on the right. After everything else, getting past this lock is effortless.

Taliya swings the vault's door open with a grin. Inside, neatly organized stacks of magical tokens lie ready to be taken. Amari swings off the bag strapped to her back and begins packing it full. It was created to hold more than it should while keeping the weight manageable—a type of bag anyone can buy and essential for a heist. Taliya fills her own as well with tokens using haphazard movements.

They are maxing out the bag's admittedly large capacity when Amari pauses as her sense of future dangers rises. Something is rapidly approaching.

Taliya freezes, reacting to her with the experience of someone who's been in many situations where things went south fast. "What's wrong?"

Closing the bag abruptly, Amari swings it over her shoulder. "Be ready, I don't know what—"

Something big moves outside the vault door.

Amari's instincts scream at her to run moments before it appears. Her feelings are usually vague, giving at most an idea of where or when the danger might come. Never what.

She would have liked a better warning that a live *dragon* guards the vaults.

Damn! Amari and Taliya jump to the side to avoid a stream of fire. It doesn't affect the leftover magic tokens, which are all but indestructible when fully charged, though the flames leave scorch marks on the vault's walls. Luckily, the dragon has to be young and inexperienced, or it wouldn't fit in the hallway at all, except it's still a *dragon.*

"How did they keep this a secret?" Taliya's face contorts in disbelief as she yells, and Amari's runes barely catch the words past the noise of the dragon's frustrated growl. Amari sighs internally. *'Always prepare for the unexpected'* is a great slogan, but the unexpected can be really fucking unexpected in her experience.

"They probably don't let anyone down here unless they know about it or hide it around visitors," Amari says, then cuts off her train of thought to evade a giant claw. The dragon can't fit through the door and has taken to trying to catch them with one foreleg sticking into the vault like a cat.

"Plan?" Taliya wildly signs the word to make sure she sees it.

Amari drops to the ground to avoid her head being sliced off.

"Working on it!"

In a fit of frustration, the dragon retracts the appendage and goes back to trying to smoke them out. Literally.

Dragons… What does she know about dragons? Their fire has special properties, they're territorial, scales tougher than armor… Oh!

She swings off her bag when she has a moment of reprieve while the beast recharges its fire and tosses it to Taliya. The thief catches it and gives her a look of bafflement. Amari grins and runs toward the dragon.

It only takes a couple of seconds to reach the dragon's head — pressed up against the vault, snout opening to release more fire — and she uses her time wisely. She reaches into her inner jacket pocket and pulls out the small incendiary kept there in case of emergencies. With split-second timing, Amari hurls the explosive directly into the dragon's mouth.

She reasons that the fire won't hurt it permanently, but the blast will certainly be a nice distraction.

The dragon jerks back violently as the explosion detonates inside it, scrambling farther down the hallway as it writhes in pain while Amari is blown entirely off her feet. She hits the vault's back wall with a loud thump and crumples to the ground.

The world spins around her, and Amari briefly loses her consistently careful grip on her magic. All sounds soften and feel out of reach while her sense for danger stabs her between the eyes with an over-awareness of alarm. A flood of incoherent and unhelpful information is being sent to her before she reigns her power back in. The headache eases slightly as the real world retakes focus, and she can remember to use her hearing enhancement runes again.

This all happens in the span of a few painful seconds. "... Ow."

"Amari! You—you!" Taliya is there in a moment, dragging her to her feet. "We need to go!"

They run—or stumble, in her case—out of the vault and into the hall. Already, the dragon is recovering, turning its furious eyes on them. Taliya all but hurls Amari out the gate and slams it shut on the dragon. Fortunately, the gate automatically locks, so they don't have to test their strength against a dragon. It bangs uselessly against it, muffled roars echoing down the hall ahead of them.

For a moment, they just stare at each other.

"Well," Taliya says. "You really just... charged a dragon, huh?"

Amari keeps a straight face for a second before nearly collapsing in laughter. Taliya joins in, though not before punching her in the shoulder. Hard.

Their moment of humor is broken by the distant pounding of boots, hoofs, and whatever else from above, and they are fast approaching. Amari and Taliya's heads snap up at the same time, then they take off without a word.

There's no time for a quiet and quick exit anymore. As soon as they reach the ground floor, with the soldiers only moments away, Taliya places her own incendiary on a wall. They take cover in the stairwell as the blast rips through the building. Shouts erupt above them, and the two make their way through the new exit.

They emerge from the side of the building and race towards the river. As the yells get closer, Amari grabs Taliya's hand and focuses on her sense of Time again. The rest of the world slows down by centimeters while the thieves run off into the night.

When they reach the small boat, Taliya immediately begins singing, using her power to generate fog and make it thick enough to spread out across the river. Amari rows the craft and very slowly loosens her hold on Time. The drain of the night is worrying away at her, but she knows this is more important.

"Do you see them? Get over here!" Soldiers shouting reach Amari's enhanced hearing, and she can tell the moment they realize the river is the escape route the thieves are using.

"The fog! This came on too fast!"

"They're using the river!"

"Where's the Castor police?"

"Get a boat, you idiots!"

A small smirk makes its way onto the Nightblood's face.

When they reach the west bank, Taliya spends a precious minute creating as much of the fog as her abilities can. She draws directly from the water as a near-endless power source and channels it through her singing, but there's only so much she can do with that energy before it overwhelms her capabilities.

Either way, Taliya is strong enough to confuse the soldiers. No one sees them escape into the Lower District to go home. It won't be difficult for the Empire goons to guess, though, so Amari quickly goes over the best way to their apartment.

A straight shot leaves them likely of being followed, and considering the places in the Lower District Amari avoids on principle… Only a few routes come to her mind that aren't ridiculously long. In the sky, the third moon appears on the edges of the horizon.

Booker Road doesn't exist this time of year, but Amari knows an alleyway that starts a few blocks from the river here and leads out to the other side of the District. From there, they can cut through Kiyoshi Crater to the Hall.

Taliya immediately recognizes their route and groans even as she follows Amari down the alleyway. "I *hate* going through the crater, I always have dreams about other people's deaths afterward! And it's *steep*."

Amari laughs at her friend, who seems more grieved about the terrain of the Kiyoshi Crater than its status as the most haunted place in Esma, if not all of Avalon.

Coming out of the alleyway, the state of the buildings around them has changed drastically. Just proximity to the Upper District made the houses on the river better off than those farther away.

They slow to a casual walk now, no longer feeling desperate enough to get away over drawing less attention. Few people are out this late at night, but Amari would still rather be entirely forgettable.

It takes a few more minutes before the Kiyoshi Crater comes into view. Her eyes, much more suited for darkness than Taliya's, pick it up first.

"We're close."

"Ugh."

The crater dominates a significant portion of the Lower District, its presence standing out like a scar upon the urban landscape. Its sheer size and chilling ambiance make it an unmistakable landmark, casting a dark shadow over the surrounding areas.

Technically, access to the crater is restricted, with makeshift barriers and warnings posted to keep curious or unwary individuals away. However, those who are determined to explore or exploit the crater often find ways to bypass these obstacles, drawn by the promise of hidden secrets or arcane knowledge. Or just a convenient escape route, in their case.

Considering the other place they broke into tonight, getting past the crater's minimal security is child's play. Barely anyone even maintains the wards on the barriers.

Of course, the site itself is what keeps most people away.

Kiyoshi Crater is vast and irregular, stretching several miles across with jagged, uneven edges that rise and fall like the teeth of a monstrous beast. The rim of the crater is lined with a tangle of twisted, dead trees and overgrown, thorny vines that seem to reach out as if trying to pull anything nearby into the depths below. Amari and Taliya make sure to keep any thorns at a distance, not wanting to be pricked. The things that grow in places like this tend not to be friendly to human life. She doesn't like to tempt Fate more than she already does by existing.

The ground is uneven, with pockets of mist and shadow that cling to the edges and drift into the crater, creating an unsettling, ever-changing landscape. Amari always has to watch her step so carefully here, and it makes her beyond grateful for her natural affinity for darkness. Taliya, on the other hand, tends to be naturally graceful and able to keep her balance in the most treacherous places. It's the result of decades spent climbing through the rafters of buildings she planned to steal from and dangling off windows from her fingertips.

Their… *unique* affinities come in handy in moments like this, when the world seems to stand still without prompting from Amari, and everything feels like it is holding its breath. The hair on the back of her neck stands up, and she hesitantly approaches the center of Kiyoshi. They have to move past it to head in the direction of the Hall.

At the heart of the crater lies a deep, sunken depression that seems to absorb light rather than reflect it. The bottom of the crater is shrouded in perpetual twilight, where the sky appears to be eternally overcast, even on the clearest days. The air here is thick and heavy, carrying a chill that seeps into the bones of anyone who dares to come too close.

Naturally, Amari and Taliya have been here many times, in scenarios like this during an escape or for… stranger reasons. There might have been the one time Amari got conned into helping one of their crazy neighbors in The Hall with a research project. In her opinion, the people who live near the Kiyoshi Crater *on purpose* are perhaps the most unsettling.

The crater is known for its unnerving sounds and sights. Wind sweeps through, carrying whispers and murmurs that seem to come from nowhere and everywhere, creating an unsettling symphony of unintelligible voices. Amari knows, from unfortunate experience, that she'll be the only one to notice. These voices are being picked up by her mind, not her ears. The occasional glimpse of shadowy figures or ghostly apparitions flitting at the edges of her vision adds to the sense of dread.

Amari is always affected more than anyone in this place, but she's learned to block it out to a degree. She tries not to react to anything Taliya isn't sensing as well. She doesn't like to add fuel to that particular fire.

A general feeling of unease already marks the area surrounding the crater. Buildings close to the rim are often in disrepair, their foundations cracked, and their windows shattered, as if the very presence of the crater has a corrupting influence. The streets near the edge are frequently empty, with only the bravest or most desperate of souls daring to venture near. Like the people in The Hall, who are either there for the cheap apartments (Amari and Taliya) or specifically want to be close to the crater (crazy academics, mostly).

The crater has become a place of fear and superstition, with locals telling stories of disappearances and strange occurrences linked to the area. Most say it is cursed or haunted by ancient, malevolent spirits, while others believe it to be a rift to another realm entirely. From what she can tell, Amari thinks it's a little bit of both.

She feels a sharp warning before barely managing to dodge something striking out and grabbing her, which Amari recognizes as soon as she regains her balance. A root. Some of the plants here are proactive in getting resources; she just hadn't realized they had wandered so close to one.

It targets Taliya next, who effortlessly falls forward into a one-armed handstand, bending her elbow and spring-jumping out of danger. The thief lands near Amari, her stashed swords already out and ready to use.

They're dual tiger hook swords, which means Taliya tends to use them less for stabbing and more for blocking, swinging, or tripping whoever is unfortunate enough to face her. At three feet in length, the blades can be linked together to double the weapon's range, allowing for both close strikes and long-distance reach.

Her friend twirls them in her hands, showing off the ends of the handle. They're sharpened to a deadly point, like the edge of a spear. Along the handle itself are symbols engraved with care that pulse faintly with magical energy. These runes act as a conduit for each sword's enchantments, enhancing Taliya's already impressive agility and reflexes while using them.

Amari slowly pulls out her collapsible staff, the sleek, dark metal shimmering with intricate runes. She watches warily as dozens of roots the size of her torso start erupting from the ground in a frenzy. They've walked into a nest; she despairs before running through their options.

Doing any real damage to Kiyoshi Crater is considered wildly bad luck, and she doesn't want to draw attention to them anyway.

"Split up," Amari decides. "You go left, I go right. We get across the nest, no damage done to the roots."

"Why can't I go right, and you go left?" Taliya asks, her voice light, as Amari turns to give her friend an exasperated look.

"Do you actually have a preference, or are you just trying to mess with me?"

Despite her complaints, Taliya dodges to the left when a root zeroes in on them. "Maybe I do, you know? You never ask these things."

Amari weaves around a couple of the plants that are too slow to react, and swats away a few with her staff. She's channeling magic through some of the runes on her weapon, making the hits have much more of an impact than they would with just her strength behind them. "I'll be sure to fix that from now on."

"Oh?" Taliya asks, seeming curious as she hooks a blade around a stray tree branch and uses it to swing herself over some particularly aggressive roots.

"Yeah," Amari says as she slides under another root. "Before every job, I'll make sure to do a more thorough review of the plan for you."

Taliya nearly trips over nothing before the thief leaps over another attack. "Uh…."

"We'll go over every potential route," Amari can't help the small smirk that takes over her face as she spins around another plant's attempt to grab her. "Every. Single. Exit Strategy—"

"Okay, okay!" Taliya yells as she ducks under the last remaining root on her side of the nest. She rolls to her feet and turns to Amari with a finger pointed at her accusingly. "You don't have to go and ruin my fun like that!"

"What fun?" Amari deadpans while she runs out of the nest. She catches her breath, and her friend tries to hold back the laughter that has been building up.

Taliya's shoulders are trembling, and her lips twitch as she replies. "Fuck off."

Instead of verbally getting the last word, Amari merely smiles innocently at the thief and turns back to their path home. She can feel more than see her friend huff behind her before they both start heading in the same direction.

After the excitement, they only need a few more minutes to reach the side of the crater near their apartment building. Unfortunately, their last obstacle is a sheer cliff face dozens of yards tall. They technically have the equipment to get up it the normal way, but Amari honestly doesn't have the patience right now when there's a faster route.

There's a special art to climbing this cliff face. Physically, without the ability to fly or advanced climbing gear, it's impossible. Only races with extremely heightened strength or height can scale it barehanded. Luckily, Amari and Taliya don't need to worry about all of that.

A dead tree lies close to the cliff, not tall enough to reach the top, but close enough to climb. Carefully, mindful of where she puts her weight, Amari scales the barren branches. The tree groans under the burden, yet valiantly holds up. She reaches the highest branch that can support her and squares her feet as best she can. Amari sets her sights on a random spot in space a few feet away and above her, preparing to jump.

She bends her knees and leaps off the branch, airborne for a second, then gravity catches up, and she begins to fall. Thankfully, gravity only has Amari for a moment before reality shifts around her. The pocket of space she jumped into keeps her still, floating, before she slowly drifts up like an untethered balloon. The moment the top of the cliff is within reach, she grabs onto the earth with an iron grip and pulls herself out of the anti-gravity pocket.

Amari lies on the ground for a moment, trying to calm her breathing, and sees Taliya as the thief pulls herself onto the cliff. Getting up to help her friend, still catching her breath, they both stand, exhausted, wiping the dirt from their clothes.

"I hate using those," Taliya gripes, grimacing at the dirt on her gloves. Amari snorts but doesn't comment. Pockets where gravity doesn't work properly are rare in Castor and are too useful to ignore. Even information about one pocket's location sells high on the black market.

Still. "Get nauseous?"

"Shut up."

Both trudge along the short walk from the crater to their home, spent from the roller coaster of a night. Taliya starts yawning before they even see the building, forcing Amari to fight off an onslaught.

She's not too tired to feel the relief that envelops her when their home comes into view. Someone from the Upper District would probably call The Hall something snooty like 'quaint,' but Amari likes to think that the architecture is simple yet charming. A wrought-iron railing surrounds the small front porch, where residents have set up an eclectic array of potted plants, garden statues of all sorts, and handmade wind chimes that tinkle softly in the breeze.

Upon entering the building, she's greeted by a cozy, if somewhat whimsical, lobby. The walls are adorned with a patchwork of old-fashioned wallpaper in vibrant patterns that sometimes clash with each other, and the floor is covered with an assortment of mismatched rugs that create a warm, inviting atmosphere. The mailboxes are a curious sight, painted in bright, cheerful colors and covered in stickers and decals that reflect the eclectic nature of the building's tenants. Amari's mailbox has faded paint depicting the starry night sky, which she painted seven years ago after moving in when she was fifteen.

The hallways are lined with framed artwork created by residents, showcasing a range of styles from abstract to impressionistic. Many of the works are her own, and she can't help a small smile at the sight of them. Each door is uniquely decorated, with tenants adding personal touches such as hand-painted numbers, elaborate door knockers, and small, homemade wreaths.

After crashing into apartment 2B of The Hall, they dump their loot into a secret storage for illegal items that will eventually be sold or used. Then Taliya shambles off to collapse into her bed. Amari shamelessly laughs at the thief and goes to her room.

Inside, she contemplates the night's mixed success. Clearly, she had missed something when doing reconnaissance and while planning—an unacceptable misstep.

Amari lies down, staring at her ceiling and sighing.

One would think being the last seer in the world would mean something more. Maybe if she had paid more attention before everyone and everything were gone, she would have understood her own powers more, maybe she could have foreseen…

It doesn't matter.

The Future waits for Amari in her sleep. A glimpse of *what-might-*

be and *what-could-have-been* danced through her mind. She will remember little when she woke up, but in her dreams, Destiny stirred.

As the storm gathers

> *The mourner rages*

    The dead cry out for justice

> *A child turns on the parent*

    And the night falls

2

TALIYA

Taliya Camry is the greatest thief in the world.

Her roommate, best friend, and literal partner in crime would argue that this title is wildly subjective, except Taliya is. Amari can debate technicalities all day, but in the end, Taliya is just the best when it comes down to it.

Her power, her magic, doesn't automatically make her job easier. She can't break locks with her mind or go unnoticed by security. While her natural abilities might be as a Singer, she's a Scribe at heart. The power in the Written — in runes and sigils — is the most long-lasting yet easily broken kind of magic. She knows this well, as an expert wardbreaker.

Taliya's skills come from hard work and knowing how to do her job. Her magic is just another tool in her arsenal; she would prefer it that way any day. Thieves who rely solely on their innate power to get them in and out are the ones who get caught.

When things go wrong — and they always do — you have to be able to count on a solid foundation of skills. Amari says she would prefer to out-plan her opponents, but they both understand the importance of improvisation.

And now those hard-won instincts are telling Taliya she's being watched.

It's not a very malicious feeling or even an oppressive one. She barely notices it at first, that's how little bad energy she's getting from it. More worryingly, Taliya can't place where it is. Few beings are capable of escaping her surveillance skills.

So she's spent the last few hours wandering the Merchant District, waiting for the other shoe to drop. She even took to the roofs briefly to see if she could ditch her stalker, and the feeling remained.

Nothing has happened, just an ever-present sensation of being watched. If Taliya weren't having a decent time shopping, she'd be crawling out of her skin with nerves by hour two. For now, at least, the bags of new shoes and various knick-knacks that caught her eye are enough to appease her. Taliya's latest stop in the spontaneous shopping trip is a restaurant that caters to virtually every race in Avalon, even the ones less likely to be seen in a city.

The exterior is decorated with vibrant mosaics and murals depicting various magical creatures and their meals of cultural importance. A large sign announcing *The Enchanted Table* hangs above the entrance. Its door is framed with intricate carvings of recognizable ingredients and magical sigils that do nothing except make the store look interesting.

As she steps inside, Taliya is greeted by a restaurant organized into several sections, each dedicated to a different type of cuisine or palette. The menu is tailored to accommodate the diverse needs of its patrons. Dishes can be adjusted in flavor, texture, and magical effects based on the individual's species and preferences. It's a wildly effective marketing strategy, and she's not surprised to see the place is packed. Despite the expensive nature of the tailored experience, there's nothing formal about all the families and tourists hanging around.

She has to carefully weave through the seating areas, where every dining experience is customized to suit the unique dietary requirements of the guest. Chefs consult with patrons to ensure that their needs are met, whether they require specific magical properties or have particular dietary restrictions. Some dishes even come with interactive elements, such as edible enchantments or food that reacts to the consumer's emotions. Supposedly, this adds an extra layer of engagement to the dining experience.

Taliya remembers a time she and Amari went here with a few other residents from The Hall, everyone celebrating some special occasion years ago. The food was good, but she distinctly remembers the night ending with burnt tablecloths, a close case of poisoning, and not one but *two* dance-offs.

Ever since, Taliya has only come here to pick up takeout. Thankfully, there's plenty of ready-made food to buy, even as she has to contend with even more hungry patrons.

The first section features delicate, glowing flora and an intricately woven tapestry of the World Tree, an important symbol to the Andans, otherwise known as Forest Children. Taliya shoves past the display of fairy cakes, enchanted mushrooms, and fresh herbs with a passing glance.

Flames flare up suddenly from the Ashan section, nearly making Taliya jump and elbow a fellow shopper before she forces herself to relax. The Ashan are called Sun Eaters for a reason, and that reason is that everything they like to eat would burn anyone else's mouth for a minimum of two days. She hurries by and slips through the Bera's — Mountain Dwellers, they're accurately named as well — large area as well. There's enchanted bread that catches Taliya's eye, and she grabs some as she walks.

The food made to replenish magic is a must, so Taliya orders at a counter a colorful, floating salad made from fruits that change shape and flavor as you eat them. Some fruits may provide temporary enhancements to senses or magical abilities. The salad is presented in a delicate, shimmering bowl that keeps the fruits suspended in mid-air. Taliya pops a lid on it and packs it away for later. Another item meant to replenish magic she gets is an elixir that shimmers blue mixed into a smoothie. It's typically served in a crystal chalice for the theatrical effect, but she disappointedly gets it in a to-go cup instead. The flavor of it combines hints of exotic spices and extreme sweetness, which is really more Amari's kind of thing.

With Amari in her thoughts, Taliya heads to her friend's section with a touch of trepidation. The Taos, better known as Nightbloods, has a space that is dimly lit and has a more subdued ambiance. The decor includes dark, shimmering textures and subtle lighting. Much of the food offerings are locked away for other people's safety since they include items like shadowy fungi, abyssal fruits, and other outrageously poisonous things to anyone who's not a Nightblood. The shelves that are safe for everyone are lined with carefully arranged jars of treats like moonlit berries and starlight-infused pastries. Some of the highlighted items for Nightbloods are mooncakes, enchanted fruit preserves, and luminescent nectar. Taliya makes sure to get some of Amari's favorite mooncakes as she peruses the options.

Taliya likes to come to *The Enchanted Table* because it's one of the only places that actually serve Osiyin food. She has a particular taste for glimmer fish, a dish featuring a fish that glows with a bioluminescent light. It's both a delicacy and a source of vital energy she likes to have after a job has exhausted her.

Once everything's paid for, Taliya steps out into the Marketplace, the central hub of the Merchant District. She immediately feels the watchful eyes back on her, ever present as she moves through the Marketplace.

It's a sprawling maze of stalls and shops, each constructed with a mix of nautical and Castor's typical Gothic architecture. The structures are built from polished wood, carved stone, and shimmering enchantments that create a kaleidoscope of hues under the sunlight. The market's walkways are lined with glowing, stones that light up at dusk, casting a warm and inviting glow. Street performers, including illusionists and elemental manipulators, entertain crowds with their skills.

Taliya wrinkles her nose at the countless aromas that greet her out in the open — freshly cooked magical delicacies, fragrant potions, and the salty tang of the sea. It's an eclectic mix.

She glances around for anything that looks out of place, but only finds the splash of bright colors the district is known for. Directional signs and vendor advertisements float above their respective stalls, magically adjusting to follow visitors' movements and ensuring easy navigation through the crowded marketplace. The Marketplace hums with the chatter of merchants and customers, the clang of magical artifacts being traded, and the occasional burst of magical energy.

Since Castor is a port town, Taliya can hear the shouts from the docks. The Merchant District is on the river, where ships from distant lands unload their magical cargo. Down a street, she can see large crates and barrels stacked high, and vendors sell rare ingredients, exotic creatures, and enchanted artifacts. Floating platforms glide above the docks, transporting goods and visitors with ease. Taliya used to run wild there when she was a child, listening for whatever stories she could on the Osiyi.

Shaking her head, Taliya walks forward until the bustling marketplace transitions into a maze of winding alleys filled with colorful stalls and tented pavilions. This area is known for its magical curiosities, ranging from artifice components and enchanted trinkets to rare tomes and mystical artifacts. The air here is filled with the hum of arcane energy and the scent of exotic spices and incense. She stops at a stall Amari frequents to pick up some things they're running low on.

The eyes do not move a single inch away from her.

Further into the marketplace, stalls dedicated to elemental magics pop up. Here, vendors offer fire-forged weapons, water-based art, earth-enchanted tools, and air-infused charms. Taliya likes to look for interesting items when she passes through, but nothing catches her eye today.

Finally, Taliya reaches a narrow street lined with shops specializing in potions, elixirs, and ingredients for all manner of things. The air is thick with the scent of various brews, and colorful fumes drift from the alchemists' shops' open windows. Shelves are stocked with glass vials, mystical herbs, and bubbling cauldrons. Taliya doesn't hesitate to step into one store, the bell chiming as she walks in, and a familiar face peeks out from behind a counter.

Seeing her, they straighten up and smile pleasantly. Taliya holds back a scoff.

"Hello traveler, welcome to the—"

"Taylor, you've known me for five years, just let me buy something."

The assistant alchemist sulks briefly, sending Taliya a scowl. On the face of a fifteen-year-old, it looks more like a pout than anything. She fails at hiding her amusement, and the pout increases in intensity.

"Fine! What do you want?"

"What have you got for self-defense right now? Fast acting and non-lethal, preferably, but not a deal-breaker."

It probably says something that Taylor doesn't even blink at the request, just nods and starts going through a giant, worn-looking book with less care than it seems to deserve. "Right, I got an insta-knockout for you, and I can throw in something that paralyzes someone."

"Perfect."

After demanding a ludicrous price that takes five minutes to haggle down, Taylor hands Taliya a small bag, and she steps back out into the Marketplace. The feeling of being watched instantly returns.

No longer so casually, Taliya scans the market around her as she wanders through. She has a few options.

Some vendors are using illusions to showcase their products. Items that appear in their natural habitat or perform demonstrations to highlight their magical properties. Many also have protective wards and enchantments in place to ensure the safety of both merchants and customers. Those include barriers that prevent magical theft, safeguards against accidental outbursts of energy, and areas where magic use is limited to avoid chaos.

But those would all mean getting law enforcement involved, so…

The next thing that captures her attention makes Taliya grimace. Strategic locations throughout the marketplace are equipped with teleportation circles, allowing visitors to travel to and from other areas of the city quickly. These circles have intricate, glowing runes and are monitored by magical sentinels.

Taliya wouldn't trust those circles to transport a piece of a broken brick.

Amari has experienced her day-long rants; the teleportation circles are *not* up to code, and they mess up *constantly*. The Scribes cut corners on the safety measures to save on how much magical energy is used, and there are always flaws in the runes when she looks closely. That's why no circle has ever been publicly used to travel long distances. Why anyone would step into one in the first place after taking a single look at those circles is beyond Taliya.

It's perfect.

At a casual pace, she idles closer to a circle, trying to portray a sense of curiosity despite the grimace she's suppressing. Taliya feels no difference from the watchful eyes, but she keeps at it, acting like she's planning to use the circle.

All the while, she's glancing at any reflective surface around her —stray mirrors at stalls, water fountains, windows—to see if she can spot anyone trying to follow her.

Birds fly by, and tourists putter about, but she sees nothing of note. Holding back a scowl, Taliya decides to get a bit more proactive.

Of the stalls around her, quite a few have illusions…

Softly, almost non-verbal, Taliya starts singing.

When magic isn't cast right, a variety of reactions can happen. Most of them are deeply unpleasant. Illusion magic is relatively benign; it just kind of implodes. Except, being nonphysical as it is, implosions act more like a blanket of fog enveloping the nearby area, with strange and random illusions appearing and disappearing like ghosts.

Basically, sabotaging an illusion results in a decent enough distraction. Taliya sings under her breath, pushing the water molecules in the air around haphazardly, and the nearby magic implodes from the interference. The whole street is briefly covered in a mist that has the shapes of towering flowers popping up in random spots. Civilians begin screaming, some dashing away despite the fact that these illusions are harmless.

Quickly, while the mist conceals her, Taliya kicks a rock into the teleportation circle. It vanishes in a flash of light, leaving a small spiral of smoke that indicates it was just used. Then, she hides under a stall, giving her full view of the circle. She has her knock-out and paralyzing elixirs on hand, fully prepared to throw them at someone suspicious-looking.

The panicking traders soon get the illusion under control, profusely apologizing to any customers brave enough to stick around. Taliya doesn't feel the watchful eyes anymore, and she smiles grimly to herself.

To her confusion and frustration, no one approaches the teleportation circle. Nobody seems to even glance at it. Maybe her stalker ran off to find where the circle takes someone…

A bird lands next to the circle, drawing Taliya out of her thoughts. It has dark, regal-looking feathers and is fairly large, but it is not a species she can identify. Something vaguely hawk-ish. The bird hops around the circle, seemingly inspecting it.

Shamefully, Taliya can't help the gasp that escapes her as the realization hits her square in the chest. Her stalker is a shapeshifter!

Fucking Conjurers — they use magic with their minds, which makes it an incredibly difficult type of magic to master and risky to boot, but it is also a total cheat when it comes to stealth. No singing or written runes or gaudy artifices to give them away.

The bird's head snaps in her direction after her gasp, the movement both eerily human and very much not. Spotting her, it cocks its head, and she pulls her stoic facade over her face in an instant. Taliya slips out from under the stall, not desiring to be cornered if this leads to a fight. The elixirs are still clenched in her hands.

Woman and bird stare each other down, surely looking insane to anyone who could be looking. She doesn't look away even as a gust of wind whips through her braids and brushes against her dark skin. Thankfully, no one in the Marketplace stops to gawk at them, and Taliya keeps in her stare-off for a few minutes before finally breaking it.

"What do you want?"

Head still tilted, the bird naturally doesn't reply to her. Instead, it turns away from her after a moment and flies into a deserted alleyway.

Wow. Is Taliya about to get axe-murdered or something? Should she use a communication gem to contact Amari and tell her what flowers she wants at her funeral? This is ridiculous.

She keeps telling herself this as she follows her stalker into an alleyway, taking comfort in the elixirs as a means of self-defense.

While out of her sight, the bird has transformed back into a human. A man with long braided hair tied back and large antlers greets her with a polite nod. The contrast is almost unsettling.

The man — the Andan, Taliya easily identifies from his antlers and dark skin that takes on the appearance of tree bark in certain places — dresses in clothes that are nondescript and baggy in the right places, indicating a hidden weapon. The size of his antlers and the gray streaks peppering his hair reveal his age. He must be at least a few centuries old if Taliya has her Andan lifespans correct.

"I apologize for the subterfuge," the man starts, which is a new one. Taliya doesn't usually get an apology. "I'm looking to hire you and your partner for a dangerous job. It will pay very well, but secrecy is paramount."

Interesting. It is true; Taliya and Amari don't just steal on their own whims. They also take jobs from paying clients. They're just extremely picky about who they're willing to work for. Both refuse to be hired by the Apolon Empire or any of their allies. Most of the time, the two thieves are stealing *from* the Empire.

They've lost too much to ever work for those bastards.

So, no amount of money would make them do something they don't want to, which means she's inclined to hear him out before declining. Except she doesn't want to brush away the whole 'stalking me for hours' thing too quickly. "And that required you to follow me around all day?"

He chuckles, making Taliya's eye twitch. "This is a very important job. It's not just for me, you see."

Frowning, she stares him down, looking for any sign of deceit. He's old enough to be dangerous, and she refuses to bring him anywhere near Amari if this is some elaborate trap. Taliya already gets a kind of soldier-ish vibe from him, and its making her overcautious.

Seeing her conflicted feelings, the man sighs. "Let me explain. My name is Nuru, and I'm from a colony of shapeshifters that lives near Rowan. We prefer to stay off the radar, but we have recently found the location of an artifact of ours that was stolen centuries ago. I would like to hire you and your partner to steal it back."

Taliya crosses her arms, still trying to look for any lies in his words. She can't find any, and her hands tighten on her arms. "Fine, we'll listen. I'm not agreeing to anything."

"Of course," Nuru says, sounding all reasonable and calm. Taliya glares at him while she pulls out a communication gem and prepares to type a message with a sigh. Reluctantly, she packs away her elixirs.

Amari — who has been spending the day with a group of fellow deaf artists doing artist things — is not pleased to get the thief's message. After Amari chews her out for not contacting her *immediately, Taliya, what were you thinking,* they pick a random abandoned space to meet.

It's in the Lower District, away from the crowded streets of the Marketplace, and Taliya stores all her bought goods on a roof before going into the empty building with Nuru to wait for Amari. She keeps the knock-out and paralyzing elixirs in her pockets, though, just in case.

As soon as Amari enters the room Taliya and Nuru have been waiting in, they both straighten up. Even when her friend has splashes of paint on clothes, there's something about Amari's presence that demands attention. Might have something to do with her forbidden seer abilities.

"Who are you, why are you approaching us specifically, and what qualifies this job as 'dangerous'?" Amari immediately fires off, staring the man down. With the trademark black sclera and white pupils of a Nightblood, it's rather unnerving. For the man's part, he doesn't look phased.

"I'm Nuru, a shapeshifter from Rowan. I was referred to you by an information broker named Mia, and this job is… well, it's unique. I'd like to know if you're interested in taking it before going into more details."

Taliya and Amari share a speaking look.

Ah, *Mia.* Their friendly neighborhood information broker who is a bona fide rebel. Now, things are making sense. This guy wants them to steal from the imps. Those bastards in the Empire are always stealing from other people's cultures, so it's no surprise that Nuru's colony would be one of those victims. And where do you go looking for help against the assholes who stole from you? You go to their enemies.

Officially, there is no organized opposition to the Apolon Empire. The country Rowan is actively allied with it. The others, Esma, Ilved, and Dersuc, live in semi-peaceful coexistence until the Empire inevitably tries to take their homes from them, too. The oceans bordering the Empire are in a sort of cold war, neither side acknowledging the other as an enemy, but also definitely not as friends.

Unofficially, everyone knows about the Underground Resistance.

The Resistance is a mystery to the general public, a shadowy criminal underworld to Imperial loyalists, and a beacon of hope to anyone opposing the Empire. Taliya hadn't really cared about them until she met Amari years ago and began fighting the Empire the only way she knew how.

Neither of them are actually members of the Resistance. Amari and Taliya are freelancers, essentially. They're thieves who have taken jobs from very different groups of people—except the Empire. They've worked with the Resistance many times before, enough to start building up their own network of contacts—enough for some manner of familiarity and trust.

Through the Resistance, Taliya has ended up smuggling all kinds of objects and people from Imperials, sabotaging countless of the Empire's projects, and directly stealing money, information, and anything she could get her hands on.

This new job, as Nuru finally gets around to explaining in more detail, is something unprecedented.

At its core, it's a basic 'please steal this important item/person from the Empire.' Things get interesting when their potential client tells Amari and Taliya where their target is.

"You want us to go to the *Archive*?"

Nuru, the Andan shapeshifter looking to hire them, nods. His antlers are just short enough not to start being cumbersome in the small abandoned house. Those are also a sign that the person in front of them is very old. At least four hundred years, she thinks. Maybe even six hundred. "I'll be going with you, of course, but I can't do this alone. My Underground contact said that you two would be my best option."

Amari huffs. "Mia *would* say that."

"Why does the Empire keep your people's artifact in the Archive, anyway?" Taliya asks incredulously.

Most people would consider the Archive to be a myth. Concrete knowledge of the Ethereal Planes is always so difficult to find. Now that the Empire holds all the Portals out of Avalon, they can regulate any travel and information.

What is known is that the Ethereal Planes are the domains of the Divine. They comprise countless different realms, each more dangerous and absurd than the last. Avalon has few portals leading from their world to the Planes, and, even putting aside that they're controlled by Imperials, going through always carries high risk. Very little of the Planes is mapped out, and venturing into them is a death sentence.

Unless someone in this room has experience in the Planes. Taliya resists the urge to glance at Amari.

Nuru turns to her. "The Archive is supposed to be the collective of lost knowledge and forgotten memories. Its information is important to the Empire, but the Eindride royal family also uses the Archive as a safe place to keep their secrets and treasures. This includes information and artifacts they've stolen from people like mine."

Amari leans in. "The royal family have a portal directly to the Archive?"

Nothing else would make sense, Taliya thinks. Otherwise, the way to the Archive wouldn't be worth it for what the royal family would get in return for keeping their stuff there.

"Yes. Unfortunately, that portal is in the Royal Palace."

Of course.

"That would be a suicide mission for any thief," Amari states bluntly. Taliya feels compelled to challenge that declaration but knows her friend would bite her head off.

Nuru nods in tired agreement before he pulls out a scroll. He hands it to Amari, carefully. The seer opens it, scanning it quickly, before passing it to Taliya. She reads it, raising her eyebrows at the shapeshifter by the end of it.

"This is a list of everything the Eindrides put in the Archive in the last two decades?"

"Yes."

Taliya doesn't ask how he got it. Discretion is the name of the game for these kinds of things. "I assume if you came to us, you have a better idea of how to get to the Archive than trying to break into the Royal Palace."

Not that she would turn down the challenge necessarily…

Amari gives her a look like she knows exactly what Taliya is thinking.

"I have a lead," Nuru says, which isn't inspiring but is at least honest.

"What lead?" Amari asks, already absorbed by this mystery.

The shapeshifter gives them an assessing stare. "Does this mean you're accepting the job?"

They glance at each other. Amari is questioning, but likely invested already. Despite all her cynicism, the seer is always down to help inconvenience the Empire for a good cause. Or just in general. Taliya nods at her friend and then turns to the client.

"Sure, sounds fun," she grins. Nuru seems unsure whether to be reassured or wary of her easy agreement.

"The three of us might not be enough to make it through the Planes," Amari points out. "If your lead doesn't include a portal directly into the Archive."

"No, it doesn't. What kind of assistance are you thinking of?"

Taliya hopes Amari isn't even considering contacting Marina.

"I'll talk to Mia, and see if anyone is willing to help. Even temporary access to the Archive or the Eindride's collection is enough payment for some people," Amari says thoughtfully. Taliya breathes out a sigh of relief—no Marina.

"So, the lead?" Taliya turns to Nuru. The shapeshifter straightens and pulls a stone from one of his coat's many pockets.

"This is a thetamite crystal," Nuru tosses the small crystal to Taliya, who snatches it up greedily.

"A jewel only found outside of Avalon," Amari tilts her head to one side. "Why—"

Taliya cuts her off as she spots the mark. "Oh, this is marked as Imperial property!"

"Not just Imperial," Nuru corrects. Taliya focuses on every detail of the mark carefully carved into the crystal.

"It's the mark of one of the Imperial provinces' Governors, the Tera one."

"It's proof. His name is Vernon Jameson, and this Governor has been sponsoring expeditions into the Planes. One of them reached the Archive. Unfortunately, he's not sharing information with anyone lower than a General."

"Ah," Amari says, understanding. "So we steal the Governor's map, then."

Nuru nods, smiling. "Yes, though, of course, I can't guarantee the way will be easy."

"Easy's boring," Taliya states, rolling the crystal in her hand. Nuru continues to give her a wary look. "Do we need to worry about how much time this will take?"

The man almost grimaces, and she only catches it because she's watching for it. "I wish I could tell you to take as much time as you need, but this is an urgent issue."

"So we can't send someone to infiltrate ahead of time," Taliya reasons. "That would take too many months."

"Yes, I know."

"In that case, we need help even more," Amari states, with no room for argument in her voice. "I'll run any candidates Mia finds by you."

"Thank you," Nuru responds. "What do you know about the Planes?"

Taliya and her friend share a speaking look before her friend launches into a heavily edited discussion of what they know. It's a fair amount. Amari has had a few... misadventures over the years. And she's always had an affinity for sensing natural portals. Another side effect of being a seer.

There have always been portals between the Ethereal Planes and Avalon, but the Empire has managed to create stable gateways that they control. Natural portals will just show up and disappear at random intervals, and most go unnoticed.

If any of this information surprises Nuru, the man doesn't show it.

Taliya keeps studying the Andan carefully throughout the negotiation and discussion of details. While Amari and Taliya just agreed to take this job, she knows from experience that it's better to stay watchful in case of a betrayal. This could still be an elaborate trap, after all—if an increasingly less likely one.

The three of them discuss more details while Taliya also plans on collecting information on this governor. She would have to wait a few days before leaving to scope out the politician's stronghold, but that doesn't mean she can't start with the files kept in Castor's public library or copy some reports from the local Imperial Embassy.

The Andan gives Amari a contemplative look. Taliya wonders what he sees. She doesn't know much about shapeshifters, though everyone knows the much more widespread Andans.

Andans are known for their connection to nature and are native mostly to Rowan, yet Taliya is aware Nuru most likely identifies more as a shapeshifter. Amari always sees herself first as a Musei seer before one of the many Nightbloods that walk the streets. Even if the Empire swallowed the country formally known as Musei a long time ago.

A thought seems to come to Amari. "Once we have a proper team for this mission, Taliya and I know a place perfect for training. We have experience working in larger groups, but more practice is always good. Better to be prepared and all that."

"This is very generous," Nuru says. He sounds like he's trying to ask why they're being reckless in the most diplomatic way possible. Taliya can't help smirking, while her friend gives a small smile.

"We *are* getting paid. *Generously.*"

He gives Amari an unreadable look. "Even so. I was expecting more push-back, considering what is being asked of you both. The Ethereal Planes are not for the faint of heart. You have a personal investment in this."

Taliya holds back a wince for her friend's sake as Amari considers how much she can safely reveal. "My home and family are gone because of the Empire. There is nothing to take back and no reward that could make up for it."

It's moments like these that Taliya feels the divide between her and the seer so very clearly. She has only ever been in this to survive and to make money. Amari wants *vengeance*. She's just lucky her friend is pragmatic enough not to be too impulsive about it. Accepting insane jobs to spite the Empire aside.

Amari takes a deep breath. Nuru's expression softens but, thankfully, keeps quiet. "My people may never have justice, but I can help yours recover what was stolen. Does that answer your question?"

"It does," Nuru says gently. "Thank you. I know the risks you and Taliya are taking to help my people. It is not unacknowledged."

That does seem to make Amari feel better, actually. Taliya *can* understand that. They frequently take jobs that make them enemies of the Empire, but it's not often directly helping people like this. Amari clearly feels it's a good change of pace for once.

"Thanks," the moment of vulnerability begins to weigh on the room, so Amari switches gears. "What kind of recruits for this team would you consider? Any information is helpful for Mia."

Nuru graciously lets her blatantly change topics. "Ah, I was considering that..."

Later, Amari confides in Taliya once they're alone. "Maybe we can strike a real blow against the Empire."

"Imagine that."

"Oh," the seer smiles. "I am."

3

ERIKA

Erika Sinclair is somewhere she definitely shouldn't be when everything goes to shit. This is out of character for her, only because Erika has never had much interest in exploring outside of where she would be safe, not because she cares about following the rules.

Today, however, she nearly lost her best and only friend to entirely preventable circumstances. Something like that tends to make people act a bit uncharacteristically.

This does not imply Erika is making a logical decision right now. Mostly, she was feeling a lot of Intense Feelings and decided to run as far away as she could from the source of them. This plan was going okay until she came across a dead body.

At least now she has different problems.

Erika ignores the calls of her name as she runs away, dashing across the street into a crowded station and taking the chance to get on a bullet train right as the doors are closing. She sits down in a vacant seat, feeling like all her breath leaves her in one go. Dumping her backpack into the seat next to her, she fiddles with the book charms attached and traces worn patterns threaded in.

Her eyes sting fiercely, and she turns to look out the window, blinking furiously. The view from her glasses gets a bit blurry before it subsides. She measures her breaths until she doesn't have to anymore. *Four seconds in, hold for four, and another four out.*

Outside the train's window, the Haven Republic speeds by her, and she focuses on it as much as she can, forgetting everything else.

It's beautiful when she takes the time to appreciate it. The sprawling underground city extends deep beneath Avalon's surface, with multiple interconnected levels, each serving different functions. Architecture reflects the city's complex history and the ingenious adaptation of its inhabitants to a subterranean existence.

Towers of metal and glass catch her eye, the buildings accented by the trails of artificial light that are embedded everywhere. The lines run along buildings, streets, railways, and up to the city's ceiling. They dim during sleep hours to mimic night, and during the 'day' are meant to provide all the health benefits a real sun would have. Even though Erika has seen enough patients in her mom's office suffering from vitamin deficiency to know the system is imperfect.

There are more cities miles away, connected by tunnels, but this is the largest and capital city of the Haven Republic. It is structured into three primary levels, with smaller sub-levels scattered about, everything connected by a network of winding staircases, elevators, and bullet trains. The city's design tries to maximize its underground setting, blending natural caverns with intricate constructions.

The bottom level, known as the Hub, serves as the city's main space and is the farthest from the Upside—where the people born with magic live. Erika's people, whose ancestors were called the Sonai, were oppressed because of their lack of magic. Upsiders called them 'Nullifiers' because runes and the like didn't work on them. The stigma led to atrocities when the Apolon Empire rose, and the Sonai fled underground. No Nullifier has lived Upside in almost a thousand years.

Erika lives in the Hub, along with most of the Republic's citizens. This level's ceiling is covered with glowing fungi and enchanted crystals that provide a soft, natural light to counter the harsher artificial ones. Her home has a small garden of bioluminescent plants and a view of the glowing ceiling. Erika's mom is a doctor who likes to grow plants in her spare time, so their house is more colorful than most. The standard homes are in grays and whites, but her mom repainted almost the entire place, both inside and out, in bright colors. Everyone knows where the local doctor lives.

Her train passes through a thick layer of rock as it ascends to the Grottoes, the middle level, and the environment becomes more natural. Most of the space here is composed of expansive caverns and underground lakes. She sees that stalactites and stalagmites are common here and knows that natural rock formations are integrated into the architecture. Bridges and walkways connect different parts of the caverns.

The industrial area here handles mining and metalworking. Large, steam-powered machinery and forges are used to process ores and create goods Erika will find in shops in the Hub. Homes on this level are built into the cavern walls with sturdy, protective designs. They often feature large, panoramic windows that overlook underground lakes or glow with the light of embedded crystals. Erika's mom loves visiting the hidden gardens, which are cultivated using a mix of advanced botanical research and traditional farming methods preserved from the Sonai's time Upside. These gardens provide fresh produce and are maintained with an electric irrigation system.

Erika doesn't stay here today despite knowing she should. When her train stops in the Grottoes, she swings her backpack on and keeps walking farther into the tunnels, legs burning as she starts hiking *up* until she reaches a closed door.

It's the entrance to the highest level and is technically prohibited to unauthorized visitors due to how close to the surface it is. Truthfully, people sneak up all the time, and punishment is rather lax. She turns to the control panel on the metal door, smiling faintly as she recognizes the make of the work. Taking out her multi-tool from her backpack, Erika uses a screwdriver to remove the panel. Her hands are trembling subtly, so she tightens her grip and grits her teeth.

All her life, she's enjoyed taking machines apart to see how they work. Her mom has often despaired over her lack of interest in helping her garden. Erika hadn't realized before how useful that hobby would be when it comes to what is basically delinquency. The task of carefully disassembling before reattaching wires is a nice distraction, and the door opens in no time.

The highest level, known as the Old Town, is the closest to the surface and the most dangerous part of the city. Some advanced research facilities and laboratories are located here, focused on studying the surface and the unique properties of the magic Upsiders rely on. These facilities are heavily guarded and have strict security in place.

Erika avoids those completely, instead following the massive, subterranean rivers that flow through this level, the riverbank paved with cracked concrete. The water is dark and mysterious, and she occasionally catches flickers of fish swimming about. If it were a better day, she would be fascinated by what might lurk there. Right now, she just wants to keep moving until the pain in her chest stops.

Her paved path ends soon, and she trudges through uneven ground and into darker tunnels that clearly are not maintained. Erika's only light source is intermediate bioluminescent flora and the standard flashlight she had stuffed in her backpack. All there is to see is dirt and rock.

The stupidity of her impulsive actions begins to set in just as a distinct cry of pain makes her pause. It echoes down the tunnel, too far away for her to see the source with her meager lighting.

"What..." Erika trails off, uncertain. She feels like she has suddenly stepped into a horror movie. Whatever calmness her little escape and hike have given her vanishes in a sudden rush of fear.

Breathing in and out deeply, Erika quickly thinks over what could have caused that noise. She figures that the most likely situations are that a) an animal of some kind is hurt, or b) a person has wandered where they shouldn't and gotten hurt. If it's the latter, she really should check.

Erika musters up her courage and carefully walks forward, turning a sudden corner in the tunnel. She must have unintentionally entered the labyrinth of tunnels that twist around and above the Republic, and usually, anyone in it knows how to navigate it. Or they don't go too deep in, aside from her, apparently.

At least, this is probably some other idiot who snuck away.

As soon as she sees the dead body, she freezes in horror. It's not a Sonai body. No Nullifier has *horns*. It's not an animal, either.

"Who—" A voice that erupts into wheezing coughs startles her so hard she nearly trips on a loose rock. Erika sees another figure— seemingly Sonai, this time from their lack of fantastical features — slumped against a wall. "Are... You Re—Republic?"

Erika hesitates, casting a frightened glance at the dead body. But on closer inspection with her flashlight, she thinks the struggling Sonai is wearing the uniform of a Republic soldier. "Um, yeah—yes, I am. Fourth sub-floor in the Hub, student class."

They slumped further in what she can only figure is relief. Then they reach out a hand holding some kind of scroll that's hard to make out in the dim light. "Take it."

When Erika doesn't move, they repeat again, sharply. "Take it!"

Scrambling forward, she accepts the scroll while carefully

keeping out of grabbing distance as she shines her flashlight at it. It's dirty, like the man it came from, and bears an insignia Erika doesn't recognize. Of course, it doesn't, she reasons, even as some part of her freaks out. The Haven Republic doesn't use scrolls.

"Wha — what is this? I... I should get a doctor!" Common sense seems to have finally returned to Erika, and she's about to turn to run when the man yells again.

"NO!"

Erika freezes, some instinctual part of her stilling at being shouted at. "Why? You need..."

"I'll be dead in minutes," he rasps before nodding to the corpse Erika has been trying to block out of her mind. "The monster had poison blades."

This makes her startle again, for a worse reason. "Are you saying that's an Upsider?"

Erika feels sick. If the Haven Republic is discovered...

"Yes." He tries to sit up more, his breath heaving. Erika distantly feels like she should help, but overhearing her mom talk to patients about their weight issues in no way prepared her for someone being poisoned. "No one can know about this — the scroll — it's — everyone will be at risk!"

"Then... What am I supposed to do with this?" Erika looks at the scroll again for some kind of clue as to what it contains. Pushing up her glasses, she inspects the seal. It's made from some kind of wax with the symbol of an elaborate crown wreathed in flames on it. She feels like she's seen it before.

"Hide it! Don't let anyone... See it," another coughing fit hits him, making her wince in sympathy. She thinks for a moment she sees dark veins encroaching on his face, but it's difficult to tell in the terrible lighting and under all the dirt caking the soldier's face.

"What — why is an Upsider here?" Erika realizes she has very little time left to get information and tries to press for answers.

"Platoon chased me..." His voice is starting to go distant, to her horror. *I'm watching someone die,* she thinks hysterically. "Can't lead them further in, don't... Guardian, listen."

Does he think she's a soldier? A *guard-in-training?* "What? I'm not—"

"Can't let anyone see... If Haven sees this, it'll be war—" a terrible cough interrupts the ominous words. "We need the Accord o— of Jara to... the only hope."

His sentences become more broken up, and Erika panics. "Wait!"

"Only the Accord can stop... It now," he heaves a great final breath before stilling entirely. Her knees feel weak and nearly give out on her right as the realization that she's alone with two dead bodies hits her. *Fuck.*

And now she might be the only one who knows of a threat to the entire Haven Republic. One she doesn't even understand.

Erika blinks, while her train of thought mostly goes *oh my gods...oh my gods.* Over and over and over.

She probably could have stood there, frozen in looming terror, for hours. As it is, only a few minutes pass before Erika hears shouts.

Ice crashes through her body like a rock thrown into a stream. Didn't the soldier say an entire platoon had chased them? Erika didn't ask the right questions.

She can't lead the platoon to the Republic. That's the absolute worst-case scenario. Erika has to... trick them into leaving, none the wiser of what lies deeper within. Somehow.

Fuck, there are entire years dedicated to teaching guardians how to keep the tunnels clear, and she's supposed to figure it out now?

Finally unfrozen, Erika stuffs the scroll into the waistband of her jeans. She pauses, mind whirling, and turns to the dead soldier. If the platoon comes across the body...

That's nearly as bad as leading them directly to the Republic. The body of a Sonai cannot be discovered and taken by Upsiders. Without thinking more, Erika runs farther into the tunnel. Thankfully, her moment of utter recklessness works out.

These tunnels are a labyrinth. And the deeper underground, the harder it is for Upsiders to use magic. Something about the earth makes it more difficult to get a connection to their powers, or however her teacher had phrased it in class when she hadn't been paying attention.

Erika ends up at the mouth of three tunnels converging into one. She can lead the platoon away from the body and the Republic if she chooses correctly.

Looking at this rationally, if she feels airflow coming, it means the tunnel reaches the Upside, right? Focusing, she feels the slightest breeze from the right path, but she can't be sure. In the left tunnel, Erika hears a shout. It's incoherent, either from a distance or a language barrier; she isn't sure. She has no idea where these tunnels lead, but she has to choose. Now.

Taking another risk, Erika scrapes a chunk of earth off the right tunnel like she ran by in a hurry and disturbs the ground with her feet, leaving a trail to follow away from the bodies before she starts down the middle path. She has no idea if her gamble will work, but she doesn't hear the platoon anymore after a few minutes of moving as quietly as possible.

Sonai aren't born with heightened senses like some of the other human races. The only advantage Erika has is the sound traveling farther in the tunnels. She can hear them tromping through before they hear her frantic attempts at stealth.

She doesn't pray. No Sonai prays anymore, but Erika wishes, with all her will, that she made the correct choice.

The tunnel eventually reaches a familiar metal door made to blend into the tunnel. It's easily missed if you aren't looking. Only citizens of Haven are trained to recognize it. Erika breathes out in relief, and a strained smile graces her face. This is one of the Republic's doors. Technically, while regular citizens can identify them, they aren't supposed to know how to unlock the complex mechanisms, except it's kind of an open secret.

Guards regularly find teenagers and other fools trying to sneak out. Typically, they don't get very far without being found or getting very, very lost. Erika isn't sure if she is extremely lucky or unlucky to avoid these fates.

As she pushes the door open, she nearly grins in victory.

And freezes in terror for the third time in an hour.

Erika stares at the sky for the first time in her life. It hurts.

The tunnel didn't lead her back to the Haven Republic.

After the shock finally settles, Erika rips her eyes from the blinding sky and toward her surroundings. The entrance to the tunnels is carved into the side of a mountain, cleverly tucked away. If she didn't know that the shadowy corner hides a door, Erika's eyes would slip right by it.

She has to climb down part of the mountain and venture past countless trees to get a clear view of where she is. A vast field stretches out from her feet in a dizzying amount of colors. Erika has never seen this many plants in her life. She's only glimpsed some of them in pictures to be studied, not as part of the curated gardens that pop up in the Haven Republic. Not even her mom's garden...

It's... beautiful. The land swoops down into a valley before her, bright green grass swaying in the wind. More mountains rise in the distance, looking bigger than anything she's ever seen. Far to the left, she thinks she sees the beginning of water. Could that be an *ocean?*

She's in Esma. Erika is sure of it. That's where most of the Haven Republic resides under, and if she were asked to point at a specific spot on a map, she would be lost.

Far away, a cluster of shapes in the valley resembles a town.

Probably. Erika has only seen Upside towns and cities in pictures or art, but she thinks that's what it is.

Should she... go to it?

The reality of her situation sinks in. *Fuck.*

Erika sinks to sit on the grass with great gravitas. It's an interesting texture and slightly damp, yet she doesn't care enough to be bothered by it.

Okay, Erika thinks, *calm down. Focus on the facts... What are the facts?*

She saw a dead Upsider in the tunnels. She saw a Sonai—most likely a Republic scout or soldier, but she hadn't paid attention to any identifying insignias they were wearing—die. She heard a platoon of Upsiders and *hopefully* led them off course. The guards would deal with it. That's their job. Erika can't stress about it pointlessly.

She stresses pointlessly about it a little.

Another fact; the dead scout/soldier talked about war and great danger. Probably related to the Upsiders. Points to the dead Sonai being a Republic scout. They're the only ones who regularly go Upside.

And that scout gave her a scroll. Suddenly, the unfamiliar weight tucked into her pants pocket is at the front of her mind. Erika hastily pulls it out while trying to be careful with it. She's never seen a scroll before. It feels like she's holding some priceless heirloom or something.

It's not very big and rather plain, almost inconspicuous looking. Carved wood and an unfamiliar texture of paper, yet still rather simple. The symbol on the seal stands out to her again, though. A crown in flames... *Oh!*

The symbol of the Apolon Empire! That's what it is. Erika vaguely remembers seeing it in history class. Her teacher had just been teaching them the second most recent Age in Avalon, so the Empire had not come up much yet.

Hesitantly, she tries the seal. The scroll opens easily, like it had been opened before and had barely kept shut. Erika unrolls it, surprised by how long it is. The scroll's message is handwritten, in fancy script she feels makes her scraggly handwriting look illegible in comparison.

She can understand the words, which are unsurprisingly in Apolona — the Apolon Empire's language.

The Apolon Department of Archeology

*In a recent excavation, some discoveries of note are theorized to have belonged to a race known as 'Sonai.' They are said to have no access to magic and be all but immune to its powers. In our search, we found an artifact called the Accord of Jara. It is a **Divine Claim** that proves the Sonai's existence, their divine right to live in Avalon, and their inability to use magic.*

My team strongly believes the royal branch would be highly interested in this, and we are currently working on sending the Accord to the Empire's capital. My experts estimate that it will arrive within a fortnight.

Regarding the other Ashan artifacts found, I believe.......

She stops reading and skims to ensure no more mentions of Sonai or the Accord pop up. Once she's certain, Erika carefully rolls the report back up, tucks it away in her pocket, and very gracefully tries not to have a panic attack.

A Divine Claim...

Even as far removed from the gods as they are, the Haven Republic still teaches its children about them. If only so they don't forget to fear.

In the most basic of terms, a Divine Claim is a way to show that the gods approve of your race's existence in Avalon. It's an agreement, and the Sonais of the time traded their ability to access magic for being able to live in Avalon. When Erika first learned this bit of history, she thought it was ridiculous. And said so. Loudly.

"What does the gods' approval have anything to do with us living here?" Erika of ten years would ask.

"It shows that we deserve to be here to the rest of Avalon," her teacher would say with a slight grimace. "Every intelligent species has one: the Skorae, the Ashan, the Taos, the Andan, the Bera, the Osiyi, and even the dragons. Except ours was stolen and lost long ago. That was all the excuse the Apolon Empire needed to… go after Sonai. Only a few kind individuals helped us. To the rest of Avalon, we were on our own."

Erika firmly believes the Divine Claim is only as important as everyone else makes it. No one can truly deny her the right to call the world of Avalon her home.

But she does have to admit that the knowledge in this scroll would bring chaos to the Republic. Enough warmongers are calling for a war against the Upside as it is. They speak endlessly of the Sonai hiding in the shadows for long enough. Knowing that her people's Divine Claim is in the hands of the Empire? Shit.

With the Accord of Jara, though… Maybe a compromise could be made.

Erika shakes her head. That's fantasizing, she reasons. Who would steal from the Empire? It would be a fool's errand.

Yet, the idea is growing on her the more she considers it.

Logically, Erika should return to the Republic and leave this work to the professionals, but… It's much more likely this information would just cause needless internal and external war, as the scout said.

Am I really considering this? Erika questions herself and looks to the sky.

Its light blue hue stretches endlessly, punctuated by clouds dancing in the wind. The sun is blindingly bright and golden as it lights up the world. Each ray of sunshine wraps a gentle warmth around Erika. She can only vaguely identify creatures high in the air as (possibly) birds soaring gracefully across the sky, their wings outstretched. Time seems to stand still, and for a few minutes, all Erika can do is drink in the world around her.

The sun is a source of warmth on her back, somehow more intense yet softer than all the artificial lights back home. Erika smiles at the sky, something like laughter bubbling in her chest. Would she be burning right now if her mom hadn't been so militant over how much fake sunlight they needed for their health?

"Thanks, Mom," Erika whispers, her chest tightening.

She thinks of how many children and grown adults in Haven have never seen this. Entire lifetimes could pass before it's safe enough to leave the underground. How many more people will die from lack of sunlight when it's been right here all along?

I have to try. For myself, if nothing else.

Erika sighs and stands up, brushing the pieces of grass off her pants.

Well.

Time to see what the Upside is like.

Erika's first day Upside is an unmitigated disaster.

In the Haven Republic, she grew up learning three languages, as is the standard for students. The official language of the Haven Republic is Sonih, and no one outside of the Republic is supposed to know it. The other two languages taught—though fluency in them is generally considered optional—are Apolona and Esmesian. These are reportedly the most popular languages Upside.

When Erika stumbles into the closest town from the Republic's secret entrance, she expects to be at least able to understand most of what's being said.

Instead, she gets a crash course on how different dialects of the same language can be.

She's standing outside a store displaying brightly colored clothes, trying to listen in on people passing by, when someone stops. It's a being the size of a child but with a grown beard, and wings fluttering on their back as they angrily yell into a… watch?

No, some kind of bracelet. Erika worries about looking suspicious for a minute before leaning forward to get a better view. The bracelet is a simple design, with a spherical gem the size of a grape that's glowing a bright orange. A voice coming from the gem yells back.

Trying to put on an air of nonchalance, Erika goes over everything she knows about the Upside. They use magic for a lot of things the Sonia use electricity for. Is that gem the equivalent of a phone? Her phone is in her backpack, so far out of range it might as well be a brick for how communicative it is. It'll probably run out of battery in an hour anyway.

Unfortunately, she can't quite catch what the argument is about. She thinks she recognizes a few words thrown around, except the speech is too fast and too garbled for her to parse. The way they say their *r's* isn't the same as hers, she realizes belatedly.

Something *big* passes overhead, casting the entire street in shadows for a moment, and her head snaps up.

A flying train goes by, half a kilometer off the ground, and there are no tracks to speak of. No one else so much as glances upward.

"So this is normal," she mutters to herself, stuffing her hands in her pockets. The wind keeps catching her off guard at random intervals and sending a chill through her whole body.

Erika can't help but feel very small, being in a place entirely unfamiliar, with people who look strange and speak words she can't understand. She walks until she finally finds a public map and nearly bursts into tears. At least, she finds the writing here legible because she has a cursory knowledge of the two languages used in this area most often.

She tries to figure out where she is in Avalon once she's memorized the locations of the town library, public transportation, and some stores. Erika's right, at least. The town is in Esma, close to the border of the Apolon Empire. It's called Kilahn. It isn't considered a very large place, but it's a popular spot due to its closeness to the Kana Sea.

With the sun still high in the sky, Erika elects to keep wandering to get a better idea of what the Upside is like.

At first, she's worried it will be obvious that she's a Sonai. Thankfully, that fear is quickly absolved, since the range of what people look like is so wide, no one hardly gives her a second glance. There are people who look the same as her, with innocuous little things that out them as Upsiders like Nightblood markings, or pointed ears, or strangely colored eyes. They seem just as common as more in-your-face traits like wings, horns, and hooves. Erika runs cold, so she tends to wear large, baggy outfits, which could easily be hiding a tail or something. She doesn't raise any eyebrows.

Kilahn is a town of winding streets paved with cobblestones, their uneven surfaces giving the impression of a path worn smooth by countless footsteps over centuries. The buildings, none going higher than eight stories, are decorated with carvings and other whimsical details that Erika spends too much time staring at. Window shutters and balconies are adorned with bright flower boxes, which contrast nicely against the stonework.

It's very… touristy, Erika decides. She almost believes she's walked out of the Haven Republic and into an old painting of the Upside. This must be a common spot for people to pass through or visit. The sea is a standard method of travel, right? Maybe that's why.

Above, the city is alive with the hum of magical transportation. This, she tries not to look at for fear of her insides twisting themselves into knots at the sight. Trains and buses levitate gracefully on currents of enchanted air and glide effortlessly above the heads of pedestrians. From the glimpses she gets while they're resting on the streets, the aerial vehicles have glowing runes carved onto the surfaces and shimmering banners stuck on them. Their routes crisscross high above the city, casting shadows on the streets below that she still will jump at if she's not expecting it.

Most of all, she watches as helpful golems of various sizes and forms perform a range of tasks along the streets: from street cleaning and garbage collection to assisting merchants and guiding lost travelers. She's never seen an actual golem before. They're artificial beings made of natural elements — usually clay or stone — created to be assistants. With their friendly, animated faces and gentle movements, the golems blend harmoniously into the bustling cityscape.

Eventually, the rumbling of her stomach and the inviting smell of food draw her to a stand. She knows she can't pay, so she mainly just stands out of the way, looking longingly at the array of unfamiliar dishes.

"Hungry?" A voice calls in Esmesian. Erika reacts more out of surprise at being able to understand the word than at being addressed. One of the food stall workers is looking at her, large pointed ears poking out of a clumsily worn hair net.

"Oh — Yes." She feels the words come out stilted and winces. "I have no money. No, thank you."

The stall worker raises a pierced eyebrow at her. "Have some free samples, then, kiddo."

She's so intently studying how they pronounce their words that the actual meaning takes her a moment to register. "Oh! Is that alright?"

"Sure, that's why I said it."

The *t* sounds are different with this one, she notes. And Erika's Esmesian seems much stiffer in comparison. Hopefully, her Apolona will be better. Her mom had studied that one more since most older medical texts were in that language, mostly due to the Empire destroying or absorbing the competition.

Hesitantly, she approaches the stall and tries a few of the free samples the worker points out to her. Silently, she questions whether eating this much is actually allowed. She steps back as soon as her stomach no longer feels like it's going to eat itself, making sure to thank the generous stall worker.

They wave it off. "Come back anytime, kid."

"Yes," Erika says, heart lifting after hours of twisting in her chest. "I am very appreciative of your kindness."

She can tell her way of speaking is still awkward from the amused look she gets, but she can't bring herself to care too much.

Of course, then her spotty language skills are put to the test in the worst way possible, a few hours later.

She's ended up in the street with dozens of beautiful stalls set up and customers milling around in elaborate outfits when a large hand suddenly clamps down on her shoulder, pulling her around to face her assailant.

Heart in her throat, Erika looks up at the man with green skin, sharp-looking antlers, and dark, glaring eyes. He barks something at her, which, in her panic, she gets exactly zero of.

"What?" Erika tries to say in Esmesian. The man glares harder. Then she notices his clothes, which look worryingly like a uniform.

A shot of adrenaline hits her like a punch to the face. Is she getting arrested?

More words she doesn't understand are said in a tone of voice that sends its own messages.

"Sorry," she tries to say, unsure what she is apologizing for.

Esmesian is her worst language, apparently. She had done fine in class, but now her poor skills are becoming increasingly clear. Frustrated with the lack of progress, the man switches to Apolona, and the conversation is only marginally better. Erika can at least be more confident in what she's saying.

"This is a restricted area," is the gist of what she thinks he's saying. "How did you get here?"

"Um…" Had she just walked past a bunch of wards, completely unaware?

"She came in with me, officer," a new voice interrupts, words perfectly clear. Erika turns to look at her potential savior. It's a being with pale blonde hair, whose lithe frame feels like it towers over her. With no marking, wings, or other clear tells, she isn't sure what kind of human this person is.

"Are you sure?" The officer asks. Or, at least, she thinks that's what he says. His accent is giving her real trouble.

Thankfully, Erika can understand the new person just fine. "Of course. Would I lie?"

This assuages the officer, and Erika is quickly left alone with the blonde. She turns to thank them and finds she's being stared at.

The being looking down at her has such striking electric blue eyes that Erika almost forgets what she's saying. Then, the reality of the situation catches up with her. "Thank you, I… That could have been very bad."

"I imagine so," a smirk alights her savior's face. Erika feels strangely studied under their heavy gaze. "You need to take better care, little one."

Her face starts to burn. "I'm not *that* short!"

The smirk turns into a full-on grin. Head tilted back, a condescending look is directed at her, and the height difference is highlighted; Erika wishes the earth would open up and dump her back home.

"If you say so," their voice laced with amusement.

Erika tries to change the subject to something less embarrassing. "I'm Erika. I'm, uh, new here. Do you know where a good place to eat is?"

Not that she has money.

The blonde gives her a calculating look, still smiling. "Call me Karma. I'm here for business. Most of the restaurants on Fern Street are excellent, and not outrageously priced."

She isn't sure if Karma is pointing out the price specifically to her or not. "Alright, I'll check it out."

"What are you doing in Kilahn, Erika?"

Ah. "Research," she responds before she can think of a better explanation. Erika suppresses a wince while Karma raises an eyebrow, but doesn't call her answer into question.

"You must be heading to the library then."

"Yes!" Erika smiles, relieved beyond measure that she can be completely honest here. "I'm excited to see what it's like."

"That's good, what are you researching?"

Uh… "History!" Good enough. Erika has no idea if Karma believes her or is just humoring her.

"Here," Karma suddenly hands her a card she didn't see the blonde pull out. It's small and rectangular, with shimmering colors that actively swirl across the hard paper. Erika stares in awe before the actual words on the card catch her attention.

"Is this a business card?" She squints at the contact information, pushing up her glasses.

"Yes," Karma says, voice inscrutable. "For if you ever need help."

It's a generous offer. Too generous, Erika thinks. "Thanks."

"Of course," the blonde smiles before looking up as a bus stops yards above their heads and slowly lowers. The machine looks different than what she's used to, Erika notes. It has a visible power source, for one. And there's no wheels, it's just steadily hovering off the ground. "There, this one will stop in front of the library in five stops."

Her heart leaps, and Erika smiles appreciatively before climbing in. In a surprising show of kindness again, Karma pays for her pass without being asked. Deciding not to question the generosity, Erika simply thanks the blonde again.

"Of course, little one," Karma replies, the smile taking on a teasing edge. Erika's avoided embarrassment returns, looking away as the bus starts, and she studies the floor while her ears burn.

Well, Erika thinks as she ignores her emotions. *I'm never admitting this to anyone.*

Who would you even tell? You're all alone, another part of her mind cuts in ruthlessly.

Shut up, Erika replies. Then she sighs. "Great. Now I'm talking to myself."

Someone twice as tall as her, with big horns and large tusks, side eyes her weirdly from a few rows down, then quickly turns away. Erika sinks further into her seat and continues ignoring her burning face.

Things only get a little better after day one.

To her shame, she can't live off the kindness of strangers, so she manages to survive those first few days by stealing small bits of money and food and taking advantage of public water dispensers. None of the wards meant to act as security go off in her presence, something she takes an inappropriate amount of delight in. The currency takes hours of people-watching to figure out, but in the end, she walks away with some cheap food, so it works out.

Sleeping is a struggle. Because everything is so new and strange, even if Erika finds a place she considers safe enough to let down her guard, she can't actually fall asleep. The differences between Kilahn and the Haven Republic are disorientating. For one, Erika's used to houses all crammed together, every bit of space carefully utilized. There's so much free room to spread out and roam here.

Most nights, she finds a building that looks climbable and waits for no one to be looking to get to the roof. She will curl up in a corner with a stolen blanket and watch the stars until, eventually, sleep overtakes her exhausted mind. Other nights, water—*freezing, fast-falling, sock-dampening* water—will be pouring down from the skies, and she has to shelter. *Rain*, Erika knows it's called.

The first time it rains with her Upside, she admittedly freaks out. It's just so sudden, and she scrambles for cover like some kind of stray cat. Everyone else pushes a hood up or simply pulls out devices that shelter them from the rain. Erika has neither, so she has to either find a store willing to let her loiter inside the temperature-controlled space or try to make it to the library.

Now, on her fifth day Upside, she ducks into the library with her wet backpack clutched to her front and hair dripping. Ten minutes before, the clouds gathered and decided to send down not just gallons of water on her head, but also ice! Erika has never seen hail before and hopes never to see it again. It feels like the pellets of ice have left bruises on her shoulders.

Shoes squeaking annoyingly on the floor, she hurries off to a tucked-away corner of the library. The building isn't very big or extravagant, from what she can tell, yet it does the job. Erika is more interested in the books and the informational gems that work a bit like computers without the ability to talk to others. They're flat discs that appear to be mirrors until activated, and they store all publicly accessible information.

They also require magic to activate, so Erika has to get… creative about using them. Through trial and error, she learns that any item imbued with enough magic can activate the discs when they come into physical contact.

According to her research, long-distance communication is expensive. Small gems like the ones she sees people wear, like jewelry, are the most affordable. However, they come with restrictions like how much time can be used in a day or how far they can reach.

It explains why Erika keeps passing little booths on the street where people pay to call one another.

In the present, she wishes she had a decent amount of money. Or could at least apply for a library card. Erika sits in front of a large information disc and stares longingly at the cabinet of smaller gems locked away. With a library card, she could take one of those gems and download as much information as she wanted to take with her. Alas, she doesn't legally exist up here.

"Need help finding anything?"

Erika startles as a librarian stops next to her, so lost in her head that she completely forgets to be aware of her surroundings. Ducking her head, she pushes her glasses up on her nose before replying. *Stupid.*

"Uh…" She searches her head for the right words in Esmesian. "I am studying different cultures."

This is the right thing to say because the librarian beams, showing off rows of sharp teeth, before pulling out a notepad and pen from an unknown source. "Great! Let me write down some good journals and research to look into."

"Thank you."

After the librarian leaves her to her search, Erika resumes her study of how people live Upside. She wants to focus on the Divine Claim more, but how can she hope to find it if she knows nothing about the surface of Avalon?

Five days of watching and learning has made her more comfortable. She's been observing how people live and how things work without the inventions she's used to. Erika has taken apart many small devices and found no reasonable reason for why they work. Magic is a strange form of energy that she's never put much thought into understanding.

With immense effort, she leaves the beloved informational disc behind and begins initiating conversations with people. She tracks down the librarian to chat about book genres. For the rest of the day, she tries to better understand the languages spoken around her. Then, as she wades through the streets in her soaked-through shoes, she tries to understand the world.

It's all so… overwhelming.

Avalon is so much bigger than she knew.

From what Erika has seen in Kilahn, Osiyi living or even just visiting away from water is unusual, though people of mixed heritage are more common to see. She'll often see hands with webbed fingers and gills on the necks of Upsiders she passes by on the streets. The most surprising part is how different in size they can be. Despite their lack of appearance on land, the 'Sea Folk' are the most diverse group in Avalon.

In contrast, Erika can always spot a Mountain Dweller half a kilometer away. The shortest of them still tower a meter above her, and the tallest are too big to walk the streets at all. The Bera are a long-lived race, except they're few in number and tend to stick to their territories.

People with ram horns, markings, and black sclera — the Taos, better known as Nightbloods for their black blood — are more common in Avalon, even as they can be subject to harsher conditions than other races. Erika has seen more homeless Nightbloods than any other race. Apart from her initial caution, she's found them all to be incredibly helpful when she asks for directions or tips on where to sleep at night.

One even gives her an umbrella on her sixth day Upside after she's discovered shivering under a bridge to hide from another bout of rain. According to the kind lady with unnerving eyes — where the only speck of color to be had is the glowing white pupils — Erika looks like a *half-drowned puppy that's in dire need of a helping hand*. Despite not having much beyond a ratty duffel bag herself, the Nightblood graciously gives the teen a functional umbrella so she can travel through the bad weather to someplace warmer.

The disparity between how the Nightblood acts and how she's clearly treated leaves an ache in her chest.

So, largely, the population of Upsiders is made of a mix of Sky Lords, Forest Children, and Sun Eaters. It explains why she keeps almost running into giant wings and antlers more than extra limbs or fins.

Regarding her self-imposed mission and not just her general research, Erika feels she makes good progress until she very much doesn't.

In the library, Erika finds the most likely people to have the Accord of Jara quickly enough. The problem is those people are the royal family of the Apolon Empire. The Divine King—someone there is frustratingly few useful facts on other than he is 'the voice and sword of the gods'—and his four equally mysterious children are perhaps the most difficult people in the world to steal from.

Any actual personal information on the royal family is scarce, and knowledge of where they keep their treasures is even more so.

When Erika realized this, she spent hours staring at the sky, wondering if she should go home. Her mom is no doubt going insane trying to find her. Her best friend, Felicia, is probably feeling guilty for being the reason Erika was upset enough she ran off in the first place. There's a terrible ache in her chest every time she thinks of them.

How could she possibly steal from the *Apolon Empire?* From the *Divine King?* Is she crazy?

The stormy clouds part above her to reveal the bright blue sky and shining sun. It's a sight she always thought belonged in artwork, not in real life. The Upside felt so distant, like a different world entirely. Not like a place her people are *supposed* to live.

"I'll never forgive myself if I don't try," Erika softly says to herself. The sun shines down, so bright it chases away all the shadows. "I have to try."

She gets back into researching.

Her best lead is that the imperial family has an enemy known as the Underground Resistance, which is a name that makes Erika want to find them immediately. What are the chances Republic scouts have contacts in the Resistance?

Unfortunately, Erika can't just walk up to someone and ask how to contact an illegal organization. If only.

By the end of week two, she is lurking in shady bars and clubs to try and overhear something she can use. It's maybe not her best decision.

This is how the information broker finds her.

Erika is trying (badly) to blend into the crowd of a busy bar when a fight starts to break out. Now, normally, this isn't too terrible because she's usually sticking to the back wall of wherever she is and internally begging that no one notices her. This makes it easy for her to slip out just as things get violent.

It's deeply unfortunate she's not doing her usual routine of huddling in the corner and hoping no one tries to talk to her when it happens.

Regrettably, Erika is in the middle of trying to navigate the crowd to order a drink—something non-alcoholic that gives her an excuse to be in the bar—when the fight begins. She has no idea how or why, but the next moment, she's being swept up in the mass of people. Some are running for the exit, some are trying to join the fight, and some are just pushing around for no discernible reason. Erika nearly falls but desperately catches herself on a stray stool. It feels like how she imagines a survivor stranded in the ocean feels when they find a piece of driftwood.

She knows that being knocked to the floor could be potentially deadly with a crowd like this, and it worries her more than whatever fight is going on. Even if Erika only gets hurt, how will she pay for medicine? What is medicine like Upside? Damn, just another thing for her to research in the library.

Someone jostles her, and Erika pushes them away roughly. Sounds of angry shouting and fighting are getting closer. She considers how she'll get out of this as one of the shortest people here. It's useful for going unnoticed and is a pain in situations like these. The Nullifier also has no sharp horns, claws, hooves, or tails that could give her an advantage. No, she has to dodge *other* people's stray (and often deadly) appendages.

A large person, someone she couldn't hope to identify in the chaos, crashes into the table next to her. They take the furniture down with them, breaking it with a loud *crack!*

Erika tries to avoid the collateral damage, but someone charges the fallen fighter and knocks her down to the floor without a care. Scrambling, she crawls away from the wrestling match, which is taking place only a foot away, while dodging the heavy boots of people still trying to leave the bar. Fed up with it all, Erika grabs a wooden table leg that had snapped off at some point and uses it to whack away at someone who tries to grab her by her legs. She doesn't get a good look at them before they retreat, and she is forced to face off with the next assailant.

A hand grabs the back of Erika's jacket and lifts her up off the floor, high enough that her feet can't touch the ground. She doesn't hesitate to whip out the table leg at what she approximates must be a head. A strangled roar erupts behind her, and the hand lets her go. She drops to the ground, wobbles in her clumsy landing, and darts off as fast as possible.

Even at the edges of the main fighting, Erika has to keep ducking for cover from stray bottles and fireballs. At one point, a tentacle nearly clotheslines her.

She's cataloging every exit and trying to figure out how to reach them unharmed, when Erika is abruptly ripped out of her planning when an arm wraps around her waist and pulls her out of the fight. It takes a full three seconds for her to process that she's been drawn behind a turned-over table acting as a cover. The arm retracts before she can lash out, and Erika turns to look at her unexpected savior.

It's a Nightblood, she can instantly tell from the facial markings and eyes. Or, technically, a Taos, but the official names for species are seldom used in place of slang.

Seemingly female, the Nightblood has the tell-tale markings and curved horns of her kind. She's smaller, almost as short as Erika, and is dressed in a way that she has come to understand is common for Upsiders here. Lots of colors. Except, on closer inspection, Erika thinks some of the material is armorclothe.

That's mildly alarming. Armorclothe is, as the name implies, clothing that acts as armor. It's not quite as protective as the traditional metal plates soldiers still wear, but infinitely more flexible and discreet. AKA: the perfect invention for criminals trying to be lowkey.

The Nightblood smiles, and oh, she has some *very* sharp teeth. "Hi! So, I've been wondering what you're doing here?"

Erika stares at this complete stranger in bafflement. "I... what?"

"You know, skulking in every bar and club in the town for the past week?"

Ice instantly slides down her spine, and she leans away from the other without thinking. "Why...?

The smile turns less threatening and more something that could be considered charming. "I'm notoriously nosy. I see a random kid frequenting shady establishments and watching people; I get curious."

Not great. Erika spots nothing pointing to this Nightblood being

Empire-affiliated, which is better than what she immediately began fearing.

Someone is launched through the open door of the bar, taking most of the fight outside. Neither Erika nor her unexpected companion reacts.

"I'm not doing anything."

"Yeah, that's kind of the weird part," the Nightblood tilts her head, scanning Erika over with a curious glint in her eyes. Considering the eyes are bright red with white pupils and black sclera, it's a bit unnerving. "Who are you, kid?"

"Uh…" Erika has no idea how to answer that. So much time trying to find any information on who to talk to, zero time spent thinking over what to say. "No one important?"

The Nightblood snorts. "Okay, sure. I'm Mia."

"Nice to meet you. I'm—um," *fuck it*, she thinks. It's not like she legally exists up here anyway. "Erika. Just… Erika."

This makes Mia laugh outright. "Oh, I like you! Say, how about you tell me why you've been hanging around in places like these?"

Erika stiffens. Mia continues, unfazed.

"Because, see, there's only a couple of reasons a teenager would do that. You could be on some rebellious kick, but you really don't seem the type. You don't talk to anyone. You don't try to order anything fun. Someone could be paying you to spy because some kid's not the first thing people are wary of."

"No! No—I'm not…" Erika trails off, feeling unsettled. Mia smiles in a charming sort of way again.

"I'm not convinced of that one either. See, I think you're searching for something or someone. You got the vibe of a person with a clear personal goal, not someone only here for a paycheck."

She tries not to react, but Mia sees right through her. The Nightblood tips her head like she just confirmed a theory.

This might be her chance, Erika thinks. She tries to calm her nerves and stop her hands from fidgeting.

"I—I'm looking for something. I need to get it. It's… I'm nearly certain the Apolon Empire has it."

Mia tilts her head, not looking scared or disturbed at all. "Oh? They take a lot of things, kid. You're looking for a needle in the world's largest haystack."

Erika has never heard that turn of phrase before, and it nearly throws her off. "The Eindrides—I, well, I think the King would have it… Like, personally," she cringes at her poor explanation. For some reason, this makes Mia lean forward with interest.

"You think whatever you want is in the royal family's personal collection? And you want to steal it?"

She has to. "Yes."

Erika belatedly considers the ramifications of admitting intent to steal from the Apolon Empire's royal family, but Mia just grins.

"Oh, this is perfect."

"What?"

"Amari's gonna love this," Mia mutters under her breath. Erika stares, fingers fidgeting despite herself.

"Who—"

The Nightblood suddenly looks at her intensely, and she cuts herself off. "What would you do to get this thing?"

What would she do? Erika thinks of her mom, who's no doubt worried sick and demanding search parties for her. She thinks of her best friend, Felicia, and how she has dreams of leaving the Republic one day. How alone and isolated her best friend feels, being one of the only non-Sonai in the Haven Republic. She thinks of her classmates, teachers, neighbors, and every single person who has never seen the sky.

"Anything," Erika says.

Mia pats her hand serenely, a satisfied smile on her lips. "Then you've come to the right place. I know *just* the person to talk to."

4

NURU

Nuru sits in the hotel chair, smelling strongly of cleaning spells, and stares at the letter in his hands. The paper has worn slightly in some places despite only being delivered to him a month ago. His thumb rubs the edges, and he frowns at the obvious tell. Feeling anxious is one thing—showing it is another.

The words on the page stay the same. At this point, he has them memorized. They're burned into the back of his mind.

A month before, Nuru had been wasting away in his well-deserved retirement when an envelope arrived via Deliverance, which allows senders to mail anywhere. Size is irrelevant; the package can be as small as an acorn or as big as a house, and the delivery is instant. It costs a steep price. Nuru doesn't know many people who can afford it.

Obviously, the envelope was very suspicious. He had been excited to read it.

> *To my old friend,*
> *Nuru, dark times have been approaching, I fear. The need for our people*

82

to be united is more necessary than ever. You know I cannot give the details of how and why, but information regarding the Item has been discovered. It is in the hands of the Imperials, as we all suspected. They cannot be allowed to keep it. If they knew what the Item could do to us...

Unfortunately, the location brings us a whole new set of problems. The Divine King is clever in where he hides his treasures. The Ethereal Planes are impossible to reach without using a Portal, which are all under his control, and the Archive is treated as a myth by most. The Council refuses to order an official team to take this risk, but we both know this is a mission bigger than us.

I must ask you, as your friend and fellow soldier, please make this mission your own. You're the only one I can count on.

- H

The words are written with an enchantment so only the intended — Nuru — can read them. The page is charmed to burn itself to ashes in any other's hands. The message is clear: Nuru is to conduct this heist with the utmost secrecy. He needs to keep his cards close to his chest.

It's fortunate, then, that secrecy is what comes naturally to the shapeshifter. After all his years in service of the Mokeal community, he defaults toward being alone.

However, this mission also requires *help*.

Carefully folding the letter, he tucks it away in his jacket. The words stay with him, and he runs through all the risks the Ethereal Planes represent.

Yes, he will need a lot of help.

Nuru is reviewing Amari's information about the three potential recruits when Taliya climbs through the window. The thief is silent, but not making any particular effort to go unnoticed by him as she studies the hotel room.

"… Can I help you?" Nuru isn't quite sure how to interact with this one yet. Amari reminds him of a colleague or even a superior with whom he would get along. One with a sharp mind for strategy and the big picture, while also not treating their subordinates like tools.

Taliya is… strange. She's infamous in her field and dauntingly fearless. Moreover, she likes hanging off high places for fun and regularly walks around on her hands when bored. He's dealt with plenty of unusual people in his career and likely will encounter more, but he's not used to working with them for a longer mission like this. His usual coworkers in his old line of work tend to be more… reserved.

Except this mission will likely have them all end up in close quarters for days, if not weeks, in the Ethereal Planes. Amari is wise to suggest giving the team time to get used to one another.

Taliya finally turns to him after inspecting the hotel room. "How'd you get in touch with the Underground Resistance?"

He gives the thief his full attention, straightening up in his chair. "Is this the best place to discuss this?"

"You think Mia would recommend a hotel run by snitches? Nobody is listening."

Fair point. He checks over the room every time he comes back anyway.

Nuru holds back a sigh with great effort. "I've had occasional run-ins with them over the years. It took a while for there to be any trust, but we got there."

Taliya sits on the hotel coffee table and pulls her feet into a crossed-leg position. "We, as in some random members, or as in the actual organization?"

Ah.

"… Random members are the safe answer. But I think you already know the real answer, and I'd rather not foster distrust between us."

This makes Taliya smile. Nuru isn't sure if he finds it comforting.

"You're not just doing this for your people, right? Someone gave *you* this mission. You must be some kind of special agent to be trusted with this assignment."

Not inaccurate, though not the whole truth. Nuru elects to stay silent. The thief nods, seemingly confirming her theory.

The truth is that Nuru is supposed to be retired. He had earned it. But life rarely works out as he would like it to.

"Why did you come here?" Nuru hopes she'll get to the point eventually.

Taliya mercifully stops dancing around the subject. "Amari doesn't share personal information she knows or just deduces about clients and teammates unless it's vital to the mission. Or they're an asshole. But, the point is that if I want 'to be unnecessarily nosy,' as she would say, I have to figure it out on my own."

Huh. A good policy. "That's very reasonable of her."

"It's annoying."

Of course.

"What else do you want to know then? My family tree? How about my address and bank information?" Nuru barely stops himself from rolling his eyes. Taliya grins wide, revealing a mouth full of sharp teeth.

"I'll take the last one, for sure," she says. The smile dims to a less unnerving degree. "You have a lot of secrets, agent. Amari *and* I will keep them as long as we are allies. Will you do the same?"

Oh. "I'm well accustomed to keeping others' secrets, Taliya. You don't need to worry."

"That's good," the thief says. Taliya gets to her feet in a quick and graceful movement. She heads back to the window, only stopping once to finish speaking. "Loose mouths sink castles, or whatever the saying is."

Nuru sits in his hotel room alone, just thinking, for a long time.

5

AMARI

The Arcane Pages is Amari's favorite bookshop in Castor. It's nestled in a quiet corner of the Lower District, far enough from the crater for people from across the river to bravely venture inside. The shop's exterior exudes an old-world charm, with a slightly weathered facade and ivy creeping up its stone walls. A vintage sign swings gently above the entrance, engraved with elegant lettering that shifts subtly with the light. Inside, the Arcane Pages is a haven for book and magic enthusiasts alike, offering a selection of rare tomes, enchanted manuscripts, and intriguing curios.

Wind flows past her as she steps in, ruffling pages of open books while the door opens and closes behind her. Wood shifts underneath her feet, and the smell of the books nestled into dozens of shelves greets her. Amari smiles.

The shop's layout is cozy and inviting, with narrow aisles and reading nooks tucked into various corners. On the open shelves, books and scrolls are imbued with enchantments that allow them to float or rearrange themselves according to the reader's preferences. Shelves are lined with tomes that glow softly, their covers covered with shifting runes. There are also magical scrolls that unfurl themselves when touched, revealing their contents in a burst of light.

Amari wanders over to the rare manuscripts section, curious to see if anything new is on display. The aisle features glass-fronted cabinets showcasing rare and ancient books. Leather-bound volumes with ornate gold embossing are carefully displayed, and a few open books rest on velvet-lined stands. Some manuscripts are encased in enchanted glass that prevents them from aging or being damaged. Consider how often she visits, Amari isn't surprised by the lack of new items.

She glances away from the books, to a corner of the shop filled with magical curiosities and collectibles. Shelves have peculiar items such as enchanted quills, ancient inkpots, and a few more touristy items. Visitors can purchase enchanted bookmarks that help track their reading progress and provide brief summaries of the book's content when touched. Boxes hold rare artifacts like crystal balls, old maps with shifting landscapes, and magical relics from various realms.

When Amari has time, she likes to use the reading nooks scattered throughout the shop. She'll take advantage of the overstuffed armchairs and small wooden tables for hours at a time. Comfortable cushions and blankets are provided for visitors who wish to curl up with a book.

It's a shame she doesn't have the time today to choose a corner to spend the day away in.

"Amari!"

A young, delighted voice shouts, and small feet sprint across the old wood. Amari barely reacts in time as she catches the flying projectile launched at her.

Laughing, Amari spins around the little girl before setting her on the floor. "Little beast, are you trying to knock me over?"

"No, Tara would get mad if I messed up the books."

"Oh, is that why?" Amari sets the child down, looking her up and down. "Have you gotten shorter, Rajni?"

"No!" Rajni scowls fiercely up at her, dark eyes blazing and face scrunched. Her hair is in elaborate-looking braids — no doubt the work of her sister — that is barely managing to stay in place after all the trouble Rajni manages to fit into a day. "You've shrunk!"

Movement from the back of the shop catches her attention, and a new voice cuts in. "Rajni Nidarr, who are you terrorizing now?"

"No one, Mama!"

Cat pokes her head out anyway, her face lighting up as she spots Amari. "Oh, Amari! I should have known. Here for your usual?"

"Yeah."

"Alright, wait there. Rajni," Cat stares shrewdly at her daughter here. "Keep her company, and *don't* try to start any trouble. I don't want to find the shelves all in a mess again."

The girl scowls at Cat. "That was only one time!"

"*Three* times."

Amari can't suppress the grin on her face. "Don't worry, Cat, I'll keep her out of trouble."

"Oi!"

Cat gives her a look like she knows *exactly* how much trouble Amari gets into on the regular and huffs as she goes farther into the backroom, out of earshot.

Rajni crosses her arms and pouts, nearly making Amari snort.

"What's got you all in a mood?"

The little girl sighs like her life is a great burden, and Amari is making it all the worse for the asking. "Tara says I can't go on any adventures."

Amari, who knows what Rajni means when she says 'adventures,' nods. Rajni Nidarr barely understands the concept of fear or rules, which, as one can imagine, results in a lot of risky rule-breaking. She's sneaky enough to dodge any Castor officers yet predictable enough that her family can usually catch her trying to go off "exploring" like clockwork. This only stops Rajni half the time, in all truth. "Seems sensible. But your sister always says that. Why are you upset now?"

"Is it true all the portals to the Ethereal Plane belong to the imps?"

For a moment, this seemingly abrupt pivot catches Amari off guard. Her mind immediately turns to her current 'adventure' before correcting. "Yes and no. It's a bit complicated, little beast. Why do you ask?"

Rajni looks down, eyebrows furrowing. "Well, they're not gonna let me through, are they?"

Even the kids in Castor know the Empire isn't on anyone's side and only invested in their own interests. Amari sighs. "Not unless they believe you're going on their behalf or some other nonsense. Do you want to go to the Ethereal Planes so badly?"

This question, at last, makes Rajni light up. "I read there's a whole land of dragons! And there's a red town and the biggest library ever and castles in the clouds. Do you think I could fly there?"

Rajni has been trying to inexplicably gain the ability to fly despite being an Andan, not a Sky Lord, for nearly all nine years of her life. This is another great grievance for her family.

Amari can feel her lips twitching into a smile. "I don't know, little beast. But maybe that's something to try when you're older. The Planes are very dangerous, and Castor is interesting enough for now, yeah?"

"I *guess*," Rajni trails off, then brightens again. "Have you been there?"

"Well…"

"Have you been to a castle in the sky?"

"Rajni—"

"How many dragons are there? Have you met a god?"

Amari stops, opens her mouth, then shuts it. "Why would you ask that?"

Rajni grins up at her. "I want to meet a god one day. They live *forever!* Imagine all of the stories they can tell!"

Amari stills.

For a moment, the world splinters into a thousand million pieces and the Present is lost. The future manifested in front of her like a great big tree with infinite timelines branching off. One branch reached towards her. The feeling of *knowing* overwhelmed her briefly, and she opened her mouth.

"Light dawns at throne's end and deceit's remorse."

Then the vision and strange hold over her shatters.

The world refocuses around Amari, and she blinks stars out of her eyes with a bone-deep weariness she despises.

"... Amari?"

She looks down. Rajni stares up at her, eyes wide and a hand outstretched like she's going to help somehow. Amari feels herself fully settle into the Present and smiles as casually as she can. "Sorry, got a bit lost in my head. You were saying?"

Thank fuck it was just Rajni. Amari doesn't often go that out of time, but she has been dreading the day it happened involuntarily in front of someone other than Taliya. Not being in complete control of her power is a constant stressor.

After all, she can't use her seer magic publicly. It's one thing to be a criminal among a long list of the Empire's wanted, and another thing entirely to be specifically targeted by the entire religious branch of Apolon. The Order of the Flame can be more viscous than any soldier.

The girl in question tilts her head like a confused bird. "You okay? Tara has head pains, and she has stuff that helps."

The smile turns more genuine. "I'm good, thanks, Raj."

"Amari!" Cat calls as she pushes open the door of the backroom. She's carrying a small stack of books. "Got your order here. All pretty rare editions, too."

"Thanks, Cat." Amari internally begs Rajni not to mention her episode and walks up to the counter to pay. "You're brilliant, don't know how I'd get these without you."

"No worries, Amari, come back anytime!"

Fortunately, as Amari pays and collects her books, Rajni says nothing. She seems thoughtful, though, and keeps glancing at Amari.

Probably nothing. Amari decides to put the whole incident out of her mind. But the fact that Rajni had prompted such a disorientating episode tugs at her mind, not allowing her to push the memory away.

The very next day, Amari slides into a bar seat easily, nearly startling her contact. Luckily, the information broker is used to her by now. "Who do you have for me?"

She doesn't usually ask for assistance for a job. Taliya and maybe a client is all the backup Amari typically needs. This time is different. Even she can admit that multi-dimensional heists are reason enough to rely on more people for support.

"You're bloody insane, you know? I've got *maybe* four people willing to help you break into the fucking *Ethereal Planes*," Mia, Castor's best and trickiest information broker, hisses under her breath at Amari. She recovers her nonchalant mask quickly and shifts back in her seat at the bar. "Even with the chance of getting whatever they want from the Archive, it's so damned dangerous I got turned down by the *Ash Vanguard*."

The Ash Vanguard will usually do any job for the right price (which is always exceedingly high). Amari holds back a sigh.

"So, who's crazy enough to accept?"

"First, this ex-soldier—"

"No Empire."

"I said *ex*-soldier, and they aren't even Empire, so shut it. They're young, but you're not likely to find a better backup for any fight you get into. The second candidate is a mercenary from Dersuc who clearly is focused more on their own greed than their good sense, but is good with ward-breaking. And third, this kid who wants to go for his own reasons but has some of the strongest telekinesis abilities I've ever seen."

Amari considers the options. She immediately discards the mercenary. Greed isn't necessarily a bad motivator, but if Mia is going so far as to mention it in a negative context, the mercenary is likely too much of a wildcard to bring. Amari would rather have less backup than worry about being stabbed in the back because someone else has a better price.

"You said four people were willing to help."

"I said *maybe*." As she says this, Mia smirks and turns around to gesture to a table in a corner of the bar. Amari looks and sees a teenager hiding in the shadows, seemingly reading a book. "You should talk to her. I think you'll like her."

Amari raises an eyebrow at Mia, who just shrugs and returns to her drink. Well, then.

The girl looks strange and Amari can't quite pinpoint what she is. There are no identifying horns, talons, or markings of any kind. She has pale skin that's common enough and an average size, making her seem a bit like a blank slate. An unfamiliar artifice sits on her face, obviously designed to help her eyesight. It looks too simple for it to do anything impressive, and Amari wonders why the girls didn't just buy sight enhancement contacts.

Approaching the table, Amari can also tell this girl lacks situational awareness. She's so absorbed in her book that she doesn't notice the seer until Amari sits beside her.

"Oh!" Putting the text down, the teenager gives her a smile that doesn't look particularly genuine or fake either way. More nervous than anything else. "Uh, are you the one whose... You know?"

Okay. So, Mia brought Amari a civilian. "Depends what *you know* is."

The girl at least looks embarrassed by her own awkwardness. "Right, just, the Archive—you're going there."

"Yeah," Amari doesn't bother hiding it. Mia doesn't spread important information to people who will turn around and tell the Empire about them. "I'm Amari Kato."

"Miss Kato—"

"Just call me Amari," she leans closer. She doesn't use her real name on any legal documents, so the risk is minimal. "So, who are you, and why do you want to come with us?"

"I'm Erika," the girl answers automatically, then winces. Amari barely keeps her internal reaction to herself. *Very* civilian. "Um, well, I guess I need to come because I need documents that were hidden in the Archive by the Empire. I can't say what specifically."

Erika isn't good at keeping her emotions off her face. She naturally has her heart on her sleeve and is having difficulty changing that. Amari doesn't feel like she really needs to know the girl's story to understand her. But, realistically, that isn't true.

"If you're coming with my team on a mission into the Ethereal Planes, I need to know more about you and why you're coming. I don't care what you want as long as you stick with the team and the plan. You can't suddenly decide in the middle of a scary moment to abandon us."

Amari watches Erika's reaction. The teenager is nervous and easily startles, yet she has an edge of resolve that must be why Mia brought her. When it comes to working against the Empire, Amari prefers people who know who the real enemies are and why they're fighting.

"I can do that," Erika begins, carefully choosing her words. "I'm not really a fighter, but I know a lot about runes. I just… I have a secret, I guess, that if the Empire knew it would mean…"

Amari catches the distant look taking over the girl's eyes and lets the thought of her own secrets be tucked away. "I'm the one in charge of planning this trip. I need to know everything. Your secrets are your own, and I won't share them unnecessarily or take advantage. Trust me, we all have our own shit."

This time, Erika is the one studying her. She's pleasantly surprised to see a strong intelligence in those eyes. Maybe the girl just lacks experience.

"I'm—" Erika pauses, glancing around warily as if someone will overhear despite this whole bar being warded top to bottom, specifically for privacy's sake. She lowers her voice. "I'm a Sonai… a Nullifier."

Amari stares. Maybe her runes didn't catch that. "Speak up. This bar has privacy wards."

"Oh! I'm-I'm a Nullifier. Sonai."

Amari continues staring.

"That's all I'll say," Erika finishes anxiously, looking at the table like if she studies it hard enough, it will give her the answers to the universe. Amari takes a moment to reorder her thoughts, then nods decisively.

"Okay."

"*Okay?*" This is said rather noticeably, and Erika immediately shrinks even though no one else in the bar even glances their way. She turns back to the riveting content on the surface of the empty table.

"It will be useful for wards. You can basically walk right through most of them unharmed and undetected because they're supposed to sense magic, right?" Amari is already thinking of the possibilities. Yes, Erika could be very useful.

The Nullifier gawks at her. "I—yes? Um, is this—thank you?"

"Glad that's settled," Amari says, just to be irritating. From the look on Erika's face, it works. "Do you have accommodations?"

"Uh, kind of. I mean, Miss Mia has a room I'm kinda renting just for while this, uh, quest is going on."

'Quest.' Ha.

"Alright, I'll give you an address to meet tomorrow. We have some things to review before things are finalized," because Amari isn't just bringing strangers to the apartment now. "And you can meet the rest of the team."

The girl's face lights up. "Awesome! That's great. I'll meet you there! When should I show up?"

Amari gives Erika the details and heads back to Mia. She drops back into her seat with a world-weary sigh.

"You could have warned me." Having a kid from a species she previously thought didn't exist dropped in front of her isn't her favorite activity. Then a realization hits her. "Her 'room' is going to my tab, isn't it?"

Mia, the asshole, just laughs. "Sure is, and I have full faith in your ability to handle a few teenagers."

This reminder of Amari's other potential teammates makes her groan in despair. The young ex-soldier and the young telekinetic. "Tell me more about them before I make any commitments."

"Well," Mia starts with barely hidden glee. "The telekinetic is a runaway prince."

Amari drops her head into her arms, not bothering to reply to that statement.

"Prince isn't the official title, from what I understand, but it's basically the same. The Warlady's adopted son ran away from home a couple of months ago."

Not moving her head, Amari makes a questioning noise. The

Warlady is the sovereign of Ilved, well-known as a rather intimidating and unpleasant leader. She keeps an iron grip on her land, and Avalon is lucky that Ilved and the Empire are too far from each other to start any real trouble. Yet.

"Her son, Kol, apparently is looking for information on his birth mom or whatever," Mia explains, pausing to take a sip of her drink. She sets it down on the bar hard enough for Amari to feel it through her arms. "Kol believes this information might be in the Archive because the Warlady apparently told him his birth mom used to work for the Eindrides."

Amari slowly raises her head, giving Mia her best incredulous look. "Are you telling me that the Warlady stole a child from the Empire?"

Just the thought of what a political disaster this could be is already making her sick to her stomach. The information broker shrugs, finger trailing over the rim of her glass. The soft ringing sound is just the right pitch to be insanely irritating, so Amari adjusts her hearing runes to block it out. This is done with just a thought, but also a conscious use of magic. Her runes must work together in harmony, so any change has to be carefully calculated.

This thought reminds her that she should reapply her runes soon, before they start to naturally deteriorate from consistent use over time.

"I'm telling you what I know. Think what you want," Mia says, which isn't a definitive yes or no.

Sighing, Amari elects to let this go for now. Maybe they're wildly off-base. Maybe they're right, and the Warlady *rescued* this kid from the Empire. Both scenarios are equally likely. She'll just have to see if this 'Kol' is good enough for the team.

"And the ex-soldier?" Amari switches topics, straightening her back.

"A mysterious one. Silent and stoic type, but polite enough.

Definitely looks like a soldier."

"And they want to be paid how?"

"Something in the Archive," Mia confirms Amari's suspicion. "You were right that access to that place would be payment enough for some people. Think that's more reliable than mercenaries, anyway."

Amari raises an eyebrow.

"*Most* mercenaries," Mia says in a fake consoling voice, and pats her shoulder. "You and Taliya are fine."

Rolling her eyes, she asks for the name of this ex-soldier.

"Najaah. They're an Ashan. Almost as big as a Bera and has bright white hair with tall addax horns, so I'd say they're hard to miss, but I think stealth was part of their training."

A stealthy Sun Eater. Not something you come across every day. Amari and Mia's people are usually the ones stuck with the 'shadow fighter' cliches. The information broker slides her the folder on the three candidates for Amari to take with her.

"Anything else?"

"Nah, go tell Taliya," Mia waves her away, and Amari gets out of her seat at the bar. She gives Erika — who is again completely absorbed in her book — one last glance before leaving.

Fully intending to go straight home, she walks down the main street that eventually leads to roads less well-maintained the closer they are to the crater. However, her plans change when she finds herself turning down a street that she hadn't planned to go to. Why her seer abilities act up in this way, she has no idea.

Amari has enough experience with these sudden moments of purpose, allowing her to follow the feeling until she stops in front of a store selling artwork supplies.

Ah. She is running low.

When other seers were alive, she remembers being taught about visions and prophecies and how they should be recorded. Keeping these to yourself does no one any good. Amari doesn't mind writing down what she sees, but she loves to draw them.

Entering the store, Amari selects the pencils and paints she's out of, plus a new drawing pad and canvas. After paying, she walks home, unheeded by any more magical interruptions.

One of her and Taliya's neighbors sees her carrying art supplies into the Hall and fondly demands more paintings to be put on display. Amari ignores the darkening of her face and waves them off. She all but runs into the apartment and sighs as the wards kick on as soon as the door closes. The apartment is about the only space she feels safe enough to let down her guard, and she happily releases the magic powering her hearing runes.

Not wasting any more time, she sets up her tools on the coffee table, waiting for her feelings to guide her through the process of recording her vision.

Amari starts with a pencil on canvas, outlining what she recognizes as a throne. It looks like it's of Andan origin, which essentially means that the chair is half made of plants, like the throne is the natural shape of a great tree. It's also breaking in half, with great cracks splintering across and parts twisting away. Where someone would sit, a sword is buried in the seat of the throne.

Behind the throne, she starts sketching a sunrise breaking over an endless forest. It seems increasingly likely that this vision is connected to Rowan, where most Andans originate, and the site of the largest forest in Avalon. Beyond that, Amari has no idea what her vision is trying to communicate. 'Throne's end' plus the visual seems fairly obvious, but if her experiences with visions have taught her anything, it's that something that seems straightforward can have multiple meanings.

The bright side to all of this is the lack of urgency she feels. Amari has gotten visions before that she can't stop thinking about afterward, an impending sense of doom hanging over her head until the events come to pass. Those visions usually happen within a week of what they predict. That she doesn't feel that now means this vision is meant for something much farther down the line.

The destruction of the seers from the world meant an unfathomable amount of history was lost, and also a large amount of the future. Amari remembers the stores of prophecies and visions recorded in Musei, shelves going high above her head — so much information, just gone.

As a young girl, her mom took her to another seer community south of Esma. She was shocked by how different the people there were — not being Nightbloods or using the same customs as the residents of Musei. But seers are not a race. They're a calling of sorts. The original seers were chosen thousands of years ago, and now Amari is the only descendant.

After outlining the picture, she pulls out her paints. Depending on the type, some colors will move on the canvas or shift between other pigments. Amari is curious to see what the artwork will end up looking like.

Unsurprisingly, she pulls out a deep green to use for the forest and parts of the throne. The colors of the sunrise are a beautiful orange that fades into pinks and purples that bleed into the night sky. Amari uses brown and black to fill out the throne, and casts shadows in the forest. Streaks of moving gold weave through the chair, marred only by the swirling dark scars splintering the throne. The sword's blade is plain silver, but the hilt is black with a red handle.

As she adds details, Amari realizes the wrappings on the sword handle look suspiciously like dragon scales, and ice slides down her spine. She gives the forest shifting colors and twisting shadows, making it look alive. The stars she places in the night sky twinkle, and she recognizes some of the constellations. If she got her hands on a star map, she could probably figure out where this is.

The sunset glows, the light seemingly leaping off the canvas, and she smiles down at her finished work. It's very dramatic and mysterious, as all visions seem to be. Amari can't help wondering every time if seers are supposed to act on what they're shown. She's never been able to stop a vision from coming to fruition.

"The Divine King wouldn't have made our existence illegal if we could do nothing," Amari whispers to herself. Fate can be changed. It has to be.

"Did you say something?" Taliya practically jumps into view, signing exaggeratedly with her hands. Amari jolts, catching her paints just in time to stop them from spilling.

"What? No," Amari mutters as she rights her art supplies, heart still racing. She channels magic through her hearing enhancement runes, since she had let it go once she returned home. Taliya shrugs and heads into the kitchen.

"Sorry for jump-scaring you," her evil friend chuckles as she signs, before turning around starts raiding the cabinets for snacks.

"I was focused," the seer grumbles back as she packs away the brushes and paints. She writes in pencil on the back of the painting the words that accompanied the vision, just as a reminder.

"I noticed," Taliya replies with one hand as she walks over to the coffee table, a bowl and bags of snacks clutched in her other arm. She leans forward to see Amari's finished canvas before settling into her armchair, sitting upside down. "New vision?"

Amari swallows, eyes drawn back to the art. She senses no urgency, but the vision still leaves her off-balance. Her hands lift to sign along as she answers. "Yeah. I had it in the middle of a conversation with Rajni."

"What?" Taliya gapes. Reading sign language upside down is a strange skill Amari hadn't foreseen learning by being friends with the thief. "Did she notice?"

"Of course she noticed."

"Then—"

"But she didn't say anything," Amari reassures, slumping in her chair and dropping her head back to stare at the ceiling. "Rajni is nine. She's the best person I could have done it in front of, really."

"Alright…" Taliya signs when Amari looks back at her. She lets it go with a side look and a huff, tossing a chip in her mouth. "You still went to see Mia, right?"

"Yeah."

"…Well?"

"Teenagers." Her whole body conveys how tired Amari is as she signs.

It's worth it. She will treasure the baffled look on her friend's face forever. Taliya even moves to sit right side up to question her. "What?"

"All our possible teammates are teenagers. Three of them. I've only met one."

"…What?"

"Yeah."

Taliya drags a hand over her face, sighing theatrically. "No, seriously, Amari, what?"

"The kid I met is a civilian but has her own reasons for going; I'm inclined to let her. She'll be useful. The two we'll meet tomorrow are an ex-soldier—not an imp—and a runaway noble with strong telekinetic abilities."

"Do they all want something from the Archive?"

Amari nods and stands up to store her vision-inspired artwork with the rest of her works that she can't show publicly. It's a secret compartment under a floorboard covered by a rug, with a few wards etched into the underside of the wood to dissuade anyone from noticing. Older works are organized neatly, some on canvas, and others are simpler sketches. Most of the visions they depict have already occurred, so Amari sticks the newest painting with the small stack of unrealized visions.

"If we like them all, that makes a team of six," Taliya points out absently as soon as she's back, her fingers fiddling with one of her braids.

"A good amount for braving the Ethereal Planes," Amari says. She'd like them to take a healer with them, but Mia would have mentioned it if she could find one willing to come. We'll need to train together as a team, though."

"Ugh," Taliya wrinkles her nose and drops her head against the armchair with more melodrama than the situation calls for. "I don't like working with strangers."

"Exactly why we need to learn how to work together before we jump into the deep end, Tal."

"*Ugh.*"

Amari snorts, signing something along the lines of '*you lazy coward*' — you know, fondly — and Taliya responds by throwing a pillow at her head. This is obviously a declaration of war, thoroughly distracting them until they're both exhausted, the living room a mess from the impromptu fight.

Someone knocks on their door, and the wards automatically let them know of the presence outside. This makes Amari curse like a sailor as she tries to organize their apartment in under ten seconds. Taliya, who offers exactly zero help, laughs at her from where she's perched on a tall bookcase.

Amari finally opens the door after making sure her hair doesn't look like a bird's nest and powering up her runes in preparation for a conversation. Nuru stands on the other side, eyeing her like she's portraying odd behavior.

"I have the files from Mia about the potential recruits," Amari says, ignoring the state of her apartment as he steps in hesitantly. She hands him the folder Mia gave her, letting him come to his own conclusions from the information provided. Nuru gives Taliya a wary look—she's back on the bookcase, now standing on her hands, feet folded above her head—and sits down on the couch since the two armchairs are tipped over. Amari hastily rights them and sits in hers.

While the shapeshifter skims the folder, Amari has an intense but silent argument with Taliya about basic behaviors one should have around strangers. On her side, she would really prefer Nuru not to think they're out of their minds, and on Taliya's side, she sees no reason to act differently in her own home, regardless of company. Eventually, they compromise. Amari will not be 'a fucking nag' as Taliya signs, and her friend will not hang out on things two yards or more off the floor. The thief gets down from the bookcase with an air of sulkiness and collapses into their chair.

Once Nuru is done scanning the files, he puts them on the coffee table, a thoughtful look on his face. "An interesting bunch, to be sure."

"Teenagers," is all Taliya says, a wealth of emotions packed into the one word. The wrinkles around the shapeshifter's eyes crease, and his mouth twitches into the ghost of a smile.

"Quite."

Amari rolls her eyes and sighs. "Any that stand out to you?"

"That soldier will be good to have along," Nuru says. "The telekinetic will definitely be useful in the Planes, but I'm unsure about him and the other one. We will just have to see what they're like in person."

"'Mari likes the civilian girl," Taliya throws Amari under the carriage with zero remorse. "No idea why."

"She's the only one I've met," Amari defends, dodging the attempt for information on Erika. She means to keep the teen's secrets.

"Okaaaaay," Taliya replies, giving her a knowing glance while Nuru turns back to the folder.

"I'll keep that in mind," the shapeshifter comments absently.

Amari and Taliya share a look, silently debating something they haven't agreed on telling Nuru. Taliya is firmly against giving anything resembling personal information, distrusting anyone they haven't known for years. Amari is arguing for the practicality of it. She has relevant experience for this job, and hiding it won't do their team any favors.

After trading multiple glares and mouthed barbs, Amari finally turns to Nuru. If the man has noticed their silent argument, he kindly doesn't show it. "I have something to share."

Taliya throws up her hands before grabbing her snacks off the ground from where they had fallen in the earlier struggle. She chews angrily at Amari, who ignores it.

"I've been to the Ethereal Planes before," the seer reveals, watching the man's reaction carefully. His eyebrows jump up briefly, and his eyes widen a tad, but he doesn't show much emotion otherwise.

"Just you?" Abruptly thoughtful, he rubs a hand over his neatly trimmed beard.

Taliya scowls, practically throwing daggers with her eyes at Nuru.

"Yes," Amari answers honestly. "I've stumbled upon one or two natural portals. I've never been to the Archive, and I don't know if we'll go through any realms I have been to before, but I think my knowledge will be helpful regardless."

"Agreed," Nuru nods, a small, temporary smile lighting his face. Then he turns and gives her a scrutinizing look. "Have you ever met a god?"

"No," Amari lies. "Never."

6

ERIKA

There are no robots Upside, which is more jarring than Erika expected it to be. Seeing droids of all shapes and sizes go about keeping the streets clean, building things, and helping people is so what she is used to that the lack of it is unsettling. Eventually, she realizes that the surface does have something similar, though.

Golems made from rock or other unidentifiable materials can be found in shops, schools, and homes, helping where Erika might expect droids instead. If she had the two different creations in front of her, she wonders if she could catalog the differences. How does runework compare to programming? They are, she thinks, essentially the same thing with different methodologies.

At one point, she holds her flashlight and considers taking the battery out just to see how magic would interact with technology. She knows it is susceptibly small and mundane looking, but batteries in the Republic can hold a shocking amount of power. It would be interesting to see how magic reacts to that.

On the other hand, Erika will probably need that flashlight to be in working order at some point. So, she keeps it safe in her backpack.

The real tragedy is that Erika can't share any of these fascinating questions and observations with anyone around her. It's a reminder of her aloneness, and is enough to draw her back into the room she has rented from where she had ventured to explore. No one comments or notices.

Perhaps the isolation is getting to her. That's the only reason she can find the next morning for being *excited*, as well as extremely nervous, about meeting the team she will be working with. This is the most insane thing she's ever done, and she constantly oscillates between knee-shaking terror and heart-racing anticipation.

Erika stands for fifteen minutes in the hallway of the address Amari gave her before anyone comes. Or, at least, she thinks so.

From what she can tell, it's a pretty empty apartment building in a Lower District neighborhood that's very basic by Castor's standards. This means Erika has been jumping at shadows and watching for muggers the entire way here. It's far from the notable landmark, the Kiyoshi Crater, so the neighborhood is well-looked after. However, the apartment is locked, and the meeting time passed ten minutes ago.

The first person to show up is a boy about her age. He looks pretty normal by her standards, apart from the agitated feathery tail and pink cat eyes that glare at Erika as he walks up to the door. "Where's Amari? Mia said to meet her here."

"I don't know." She lets an awkward silence descend for a few moments. "I'm Erika."

"Kol. Why are you here?"

Every muscle in her body tenses involuntarily. "That's not really your business."

"*Excuse me —* "

Suddenly, there is a third.

They're in the hallway so abruptly that Erika feels her stomach trying to jump into her throat as soon as she sees them. It's absurd, too, because she has rarely seen someone so tall who isn't clearly at least part Bera.

The new person is almost two heads taller than her or Kol, and more, if one counts the vertical twisting horns on their head. Erika keeps using 'they' because she isn't sure about their gender, and makes an internal note to ask if she gets the chance underneath her sudden fright. Apart from that, she notes the *considerable* amount of obvious weapons they have, the silent footsteps despite their great stature, and the softly glowing red eyes to culminate in an intimidating image. Erika also gets the impression that they aren't much older than her either.

The slight rise in room temperature and the brightness of the newcomer's eyes point to them being an Ashan. A Sun Eater. Erika sincerely hopes she's not about to get a personal demonstration on how hot an Ashan's flames can get.

"Um, I—hi?"

"Who are you!?" Kol puffs up like a cat, nearly making Erika laugh before she catches herself in time.

The newcomer doesn't answer; they scan the two of them over before dismissing the two shorter beings and heading to the door. Erika moves out of their way as fast as she can. It's evident from how the Sun Eater moves that they know how to use their weapons. There is a kind of confidence only killers can have.

"Hi, look, did Amari send you here too?" Erika asks. For a moment, she thinks she has been ignored. Then the Ashan turns slightly towards her.

"Yes," they seem to pause thoughtfully, scanning her over again. "I'm... Najaah."

"Erika." She smiles as best she can, then remembers her earlier question. "Uh, she/her. You?"

"She/they. Use they/them right now."

"Okay, cool!"

From behind the two of them, Kol scoffs. "And I'm Kol, he/him. Great. I'm so glad we're getting introductions out of the way. Do either of you know when Amari's getting here?"

"She and two others are already inside," Najaah corrects as if they are commenting on the weather.

Kol straightens in alarm and agitation. "What?"

"How do you know?" Erika has been the only person outside the door for nearly twenty minutes…

"I scouted the neighborhood, I could spot them through the windows. They're not trying to hide."

Huh.

Is Erika supposed to have done some scouting or something? She probably should have done that.

Kol, reaching the end of his short patience, stalks past Erika and Najaah. He pounds on the door loudly. "Are you going to let us in?"

The entrance swings open after a tense moment. Amari stands in the doorway in all her annoyed glory.

"Do you know what the word discreet means? Are you trying to shake the whole building, you great idiot?"

"*Excuse me, I'm—*"

"Alright, enough." A short woman practically materializes next to Amari. Her dark hair is twisted into dozens of braids, all pulled into a bun, and she has the look of someone planning great mischief if crossed. There's a light in her eyes and a turn to her smirk that paints a story. Kol, apparently seeing the same thing as Erika, settles down. Slightly.

"Who are you?"

"Get. In."

The group hustles into the apartment, remaining silent until Amari and the mystery woman lead them into a large room with an occupant already inside. As far as Erika can tell, the newest person is a man with antlers that mark him as an Andan. He doesn't look pleased or displeased to see them, yet Erika swears she almost catches a smile before it disappears.

He has kind eyes, she thinks.

"Welcome. My name is Nuru, and I thank you for your assistance in this task."

Despite the amiable words, everyone is clearly tense. Only Amari lacks the wariness everyone else has in their gazes and body language. Erika is sure she doesn't come across any differently, unable to stop her hands from wringing. She itches for something solid to fiddle with and forcefully tamps down the feeling.

It's actually kind of funny, she admits to herself with grim amusement, watching so many people who plainly prioritize having a wall to their back and a clear path to an exit stuck in the same room. Taliya and Amari are leaning against a wall with a window between them, and Nuru refuses to stray too far from the door. There is only some basic furnishing, so at least Najaah can easily stand in the farthest corner by another window without being blocked by furniture. Only Kol and Erika are standing in the middle of the room, and she thinks he feels as uneasy about it as she does.

"Alright, you bunch of paranoid bastards," the woman with the braids starts. She ignores Amari's near-silent groan. "I'm Taliya, Amari's business partner. You've all met her before, and Nuru has already introduced himself. Let's get the awkwardness out of the way. We're all here to steal from the gods."

Erika gets the sense that watching four people become so incredibly uncomfortable is the highlight of Taliya's day.

"Isn't—I mean, I thought we were stealing from the Empire?" Erika is the first to respond. The sudden attention on her makes her hands clench tightly around her arms.

"Same thing."

"*Not* the same thing, but related," Amari corrects, giving Taliya a look. Erika glances between them, recognizing the air of familiarity they carry around each other. "The Archive is in the Ethereal Planes, which are the realms of the gods. The Empire also often keeps important information and artifacts there. The Eindrides work with the gods to have private access, so it's more secure than any vault in Avalon."

"Great," Kol mutters. "And you're sure the information on my real mother will be there?"

"Yes," Amari says, even as Erika does a double-take at the boy. Does he not care about keeping any secrets? "The Warlady told you your birth mother once worked for the Imperial's main branch in the Capital before escaping. Any information on the Eindride's personal Cabinet is kept in the Archive. And they're always very thorough, which is their only redeeming quality."

"And artifacts?" Najaah asks, their voice as neutral as it gets. They have their arms crossed and weapons blatantly displayed.

The Nightblood tips her head to the side like she's listening closer and then nods, pulling out a small scroll adorned with the imperial sigil and tossing it to the former soldier. "This is a copy of the objects in the Royal Treasury that have been transferred to the Archive in the last two decades. You can look it over and see if what you want is there."

Najaah scans the long list. Erika imagines it's mostly for show, so the rest of them can't guess what they want. Then, they nod curtly and toss the scroll back.

"So, what's the plan?" Erika doesn't ask for the scroll or for confirmation that what she wants is there because she is already certain the Accord *is* there. No other place makes sense.

"First, we need a way to the Ethereal Planes and then to the Archive specifically," Taliya says. "So we need to steal the information from the only group ever to reach the Archive and back without going through Eindride's Private Portal."

"Who was that?" Kol leans forward.

Taliya lets herself smile a little. "The Governor of Tera sponsored an expedition. We have to break into his fortress for the team's information."

This statement is met with silence.

To her own surprise, Erika doesn't feel any alarm in response to this statement, only furrowing her eyebrows. The irony of pulling a heist to pull off another heist is not lost on her.

"How exactly do you plan on getting past the extensive warding a Governor would have?" Najaah sounds only a little incredulous, to their credit. Kol, on the other hand, seems very skeptical.

"You're standing near one of the best ward-breakers in Avalon," Amari says, smirking and tipping her head at Taliya.

An offended noise escapes Taliya. "*One* of the best?"

"There was that time Miri beat you into the Magistrate's vault."

"She cheated, and that was *six years ago!*"

Nuru sighs, loudly. "So you can get all of us into the Governor's office, unnoticed?"

Taliya nearly scoffs. "Of course I can."

"We need to plan for multiple scenarios," Amari reminds them. "If someone gets separated from the group, if there's a security measure we don't predict, you get the idea."

"Mostly, we need to make sure you guys can work together," Taliya says bluntly. Erika thinks she can visibly see the egos getting ruffled. Kol seems seconds away from making some ridiculous argument.

"Oh," Erika speaks up suddenly, smiling faintly as she talks through her nerves. "That's good to hear. I've never done anything like this before."

This, thankfully, takes the wind from Kol's sails.

Najaah straightens more, somehow, and turns to her. "What

experience or training *do* you have?"

Erika feels her face start to heat up and does her best to ignore it. "Uh. I... Avoided a platoon of soldiers recently? But I don't really have experience—"

Mercifully, Amari cuts in. "Everyone here has something to bring to the table. But no one will be any use to the team if we can't work together."

This is said pointedly in Kol and Najaah's direction.

"You're right," Nuru agrees easily. "I have some ideas that might help. Do we know the layout of the Governor's office?"

"Yeah," Taliya nearly grins, and Erika glances between the two of them with a frown.

"Then we can simulate the break-in for a few days for practice. Is there a place where you can set up something like that?"

Amari and Taliya look at each other. They don't say anything, having a silent conversation. As one, they turn back. "We know a place."

"Telepathy will be one of our biggest advantages," Amari explains, leading Erika and the rest of her new team to the training area Amari insists they use. The busy streets have given way to more barren roads and silent buildings.

"Telepathy?" Erika asks, not able to keep an incredulous note out of her voice.

"Yes, I'm an experienced battle telepath. That means I can set up a group network so we can communicate with each other even if we're far apart," the Nightblood lets everyone absorb this before continuing as some worried faces emerge. "I won't be reading anyone's minds, and all of us will only hear or feel what the others purposefully send. Communication gems aren't reliable in the Ethereal Planes, so this is a must."

"What are the disadvantages?" Najaah cuts straight to the point. Even a Nullifier like Erika knows every magic has a price; something as simple as an overextended power limit can mean your brain melting. The thought sends a chill down her spine.

For her part, Amari does not hide from that. "As the anchor, the burden mainly falls on me, so the rest of you don't need to be concerned for yourselves. The downsides to my battle telepathy are that there's a twenty-four-hour limit to how long I can keep using it without stopping, and another twenty-four hours until I can safely use it again—"

"Though she should wait even longer," Taliya says. Amari gives her a look before finishing.

"There's also a limit to the amount of people I can form a network with, but the six of us will be fine. However, trust is the most important part of a battle telepathic network."

No one says anything, but everyone glances at each other.

Amari wraps up her explanation with an unphased tone. "That's why this is necessary. We need to be a team before we actually try to work as one. Does everyone understand?"

"Yes," Najaah replies first, and the rest follow shortly after. The remaining time it takes to reach Amari and Taliya's training spot is quiet.

The place, a perfect nondescript warehouse, looks completely benign from the outside. Erika would not be able to tell it apart from any of Castor's other warehouses. They're far from the part of the city that houses people and closer to where ships dock. It's a large space, a maze of storage spaces, and one could easily find oneself lost in it.

A good place to hide something.

Amari and Taliya apparently took advantage of this by turning the inside of their warehouse into a space specifically engineered to train individuals for any situation. According to a very smug Taliya, it has a fully functioning simulator set up inside, complete with the ability to create temporary solid illusions and runes designed to make the simulations as realistic as possible.

"How?" Erika asks Amari as soon as she steps inside. The Nightblood smirks, satisfied.

"Stole all of this from an Imperial garrison and set it up here."

This tracks with what she has learned about the two thieves.

It's a very large space, and everyone spreads out to investigate their new training ground. Erika lingers instead, periodically glancing at Amari.

As soon as she's sure the others are occupied, Erika walks up to the Nightblood. When Erika first heard Amari mention group telepathy, she nearly asked her burning questions in front of everyone. Thankfully, she has the self-control to wait until she catches the woman in a moment alone.

"Will I even be able to use the telepathic network? I'm—y'know…"

Amari gives Erika a reassuring smile as she leans against the warehouse's walls. "I know, I have theories about how you interact with magic. I think it will work."

"What do you mean?" Erika isn't sure if she feels comforted that she can use such an essential magical ability or worried that Amari is making *theories* about how magic affects her people.

"Well, most runes don't work on you because they're targeting magical signatures, right?"

"Yes?"

"And you don't have one, so a lot of magic that depends on that kind of system falls short, but if someone just threw a fireball at you, it would still hit you."

Erika *really* isn't sure she likes where this is going. "You're saying I'm affected by magic as long as it's not trying to attack my non-existent magical signature?"

Amari nods, looking pleased with herself. "Basically. An enchanted sword would still be a threat to you, after all. Going into someone's mind isn't all that different. Focusing on a magical signature when using mentalist magic is considered sloppy work. The best method is to go directly into someone's mind. Those well-trained in that kind of magic can sense different, uh… *auras* for different minds, so no magical signature is required."

It takes Erika over a minute to fully process this, which Amari patiently waits for. Eventually, she sorts through her thoughts to ask the most important question: "So you can sense my mind?"

"In simple words, yes. More accurately, it's… complicated. You're—how to say this—you're *hard to find*. Like I said, every mind has a different *glow* about it if I really try to look. Najaah is different from Taliya and Nuru, and Kol gives me a headache to look at. Yours is almost invisible, which I believe is due to you being what you are."

Amari taps Erika's forehead before continuing. "I'm not a mind reader. That requires a will to push past people's internal walls and violate their privacy, which I have no intention of trying. What I *can* do is I can establish a network for us all to *willingly* and *purposefully* communicate through. If you don't want to be a part of the network, it won't work regardless of whether or not you have magic. Do you understand?"

"Yes," Erika says. She looks at the floor, studying the concrete intently. "Can I think more about it before we try it?"

"Of course. This isn't something you should try unless you're sure in your feelings."

The Nightblood leaves her to her thoughts, and Erika takes the time to go over all the potentially alarming information she has learned.

She didn't know she could be tracked by magical means. No one in the Republic had ever mentioned mentalist magic like that—just as a tool for Upsiders to invade people's minds. Do people in the

Republic even know about this? Erika supposes she should be relieved that her mind is so hard for Amari to find.

The glaring differences between her home and the Upside feel more and more apparent each day.

Erika is still getting used to not being surrounded by Sonai.

Most of the people she sees have horns, tails, extra limbs, claws, fangs, everything! Amari has horns that curve around her head and sharp-nailed fingers covered in black markings before blending into her pale purple-tinted skin. If she didn't know the Nightblood was friendly, she would find her purple eyes with black sclera and white pupils much more unnerving. Kol, too, who can almost pass for a Nullifier with pink-colored eye holograms, has a tail!

Of course, she had met magical beings before going Upside. The Haven Republic does have citizens who aren't Sonai, but they're few and far between. Erika's best friend, Felicia Foster, is a Skorae—a Sky Lord. But the girl's only visible Upsider trait is her elongated ears and the unnaturally bright red of her hair. Felicia can barely even use magic underground!

It's disorienting at times. Erika is having a normal conversation with Najaah about the warehouse's simulations when she is abruptly reminded she's talking to a being with tall, pointy horns, sharp teeth, superhuman physical abilities, and the ability to potentially breathe fire. Not that Najaah has showcased her natural Ashan abilities much.

She likes to think she's adapting quickly, though. Erika barely hesitates before stepping up to Najaah to ask the question she's been wanting to bring up with the Sun Eater.

"Is there some way..." Erika feels embarrassed asking, but Najaah gives her an imploring look. The Ashan begins warm-up exercises before they are set to demonstrate their abilities, so Erika rushes her question out. "Is there some way you can show what pronouns you feel comfortable with at a given time? I don't want to get them wrong, but I feel like always asking would be—I don't know, irritating—or, uh—"

Najaah snorts, looking just as surprised by it as Erika. "Sure, I guess. That seems practical. Most people just choose one or the other and stick to it."

"But you implied it switches…?"

"Yeah," Najaah gives her an unreadable look. "Okay, how about this?"

Their hand reaches up to a pin with an insignia Erika doesn't recognize as they move it from the front of their armorclothe's collar and fasten it to the left side. "Left side means I prefer they/them, and right means she/her. Good?"

"That's perfect! I'll tell the others, so they know!"

"… Thanks."

Erika thinks she's getting more comfortable around Upsiders and finds she likes most of her team. Kol's attitude puts him on thin ice, and Taliya is a bit of a mystery.

A few hours after everyone familiarizes themselves with each other and the space, Amari calls everyone over to a workstation set up in a secluded corner of the large space. One table is covered in blueprints and different types of maps, all around the Governor's fortress, Erika assumes. The table Amari is standing next to has some books neatly stacked on it.

"I'm mostly deaf," the Nightblood reveals bluntly, taking only a second for that to sink in before continuing. "I use hearing enhancement runes when I'm working, but in the Ethereal Planes, they might not work reliably, so I'd like you all to learn some basic sign language in case we need to communicate. It's also useful in situations where we can't risk talking."

"I know some sign language, but I would love to learn more," Nuru says kindly, walking forward to inspect the books on the table. Textbooks, Erika recognizes once she looks closer. Najaah nods as well, signing something with firm yet stiff movements. Amari smirks, tipping her head at the Sun Eater.

Curiosity rises in her, and Erika moves to grab a book, gaping as she sees that the visual aids for learning signs *move*. It's like a book of videos! She can't take her eyes away from the pages as she flips through, enraptured by the moving artwork. It makes sign language look incredibly graceful and mesmerizing, and Erika's hands itch to try to copy the movements.

In the distance, she thinks she hears Kol grumbling about something, but she ignores him in favor of peeking at the other books, seeing if they're just like the one she's holding. The artwork varies, and the written instructions are in different languages — the book she's holding is Esmesian — but otherwise, they seem similar.

Kol is holding one with a script she doesn't recognize, while Najaah scans one written in what she thinks is Florish, the official language in Rowan.

To be honest, Erika did know some sign language, but as she flips through her book, she realizes that the signs used in the Haven Republic are different from the official ones Upside. Some gestures seem similar, like they were once the same, a long time ago, before evolving in opposite directions.

Her experience in nonverbal language comes entirely from her time working as her mom's assistant. As one of the best doctors in Haven, Ashley Sinclair gets all kinds of patients, and Erika pesters many of them to properly fill out the intake forms. There's a little boy whose parents bring in sometimes who was born completely deaf. After the first appointment, which left her feeling wrong-footed for not being able to communicate with the anxious kid, Erika tried to learn some basic conversational skills.

She's not sure if practicing with different signs will be detrimental to learning the ones Amari uses. Helpfully, the Nightblood hands out a list of basic words — things like 'stop,' 'duck,' and 'run, idiot' — to focus on. Najaah reveals they know military hand signals, asking if they should share any of them.

Shrugging, Amari answers. "Sure, why not? Could be useful."

The rest of the team seems eager to move on to spars afterward so everyone can get an idea of each other's skills. Erika feels absolutely no eagerness for this part. Probably having some idea of what she's feeling, Amari pairs Erika up with her. It's more of a relief than it should be.

There are multiple places for spars in the warehouse, and she watches as Nuru and Kol, plus Najaah and Taliya, pair off to test them out. Amari leads her to one sparring mat with a round borderline, reminding Erika of those stadiums for gladiators she's seen art of in history textbooks, but with no audience and on a much smaller scale.

"There's no need to be nervous, Erika," Amari says after she shows her how to wrap her hands to avoid potential injuries. "This is just to see what you need to learn."

Everything, Erika doesn't say. The most she knows about fighting is to tuck her thumb in when she punches, or she'll break it. With a glance around her, Erika tries to copy parts of the starting position others are using, keeping her hands up in front of her face and uncertainly widening her feet.

Amari says nothing, so the attempt can't be that bad. Still, her heart is in her throat as the Nightblood puts a foot back and brings open hands up in a guard position.

The spar, if you can even call it that, ends quickly. Erika is on her back before she even finishes sloppily throwing a punch. And so goes the next spar, and the next… It's only when Erika stands up after the fourth time being pinned to the floor that an idea occurs to her. So far, every time she enters a fight, her brain feels too overwhelmed to even keep track of what is happening around her, let alone actually form a plan.

Before the next spar starts, Erika takes a moment to take in some measured breaths as her mom has taught her and that she, in turn, has taught others who need the information. Some of the tension in her body leaves, and the world stops feeling like it's rushing past her at top speed.

She opens her eyes — not even remembering when she closed them — to see Amari watching her thoughtfully. The Nightblood gives her a small smile before she can respond as Erika raises her fists to guard her face, feet shoulder-width apart, just like her companions.

"Better stance," Amari comments, nodding and dropping into her own. Then she's rushing Erika, and the teen barely throws herself out of the way in time. It's nothing elegant, but she doesn't trip over her own feet, which is how low her bar is currently. Before the Nightblood spins around to attack again, Erika charges her, shoulder first.

It's something she's seen in sports before, and clearly lacks the power that athletes can use it with. Amari shoves her away rather easily, and Erika has to avoid a sudden kick. Taking advantage of the short moment where her opponent is not fully guarded, Erika tries to circle around the kick and hit Amari's unguarded side.

The Nightblood's center of gravity doesn't so much as waver, and she brings an arm down to redirect the punch easily. Before she can fully turn to face Erika, the teen tries to send another punch at Amari's face.

Memories of treating bloodied noses and broken fingers slam into Erika's mind, and her punch isn't as smooth as the first one. Her breath catches, and her eyes flinch shut instinctively in reaction to something that hasn't even happened yet.

Amari catches her arm in a lock, twisting it behind her and pushing her to the floor in a moment, with a knee digging into her spine. The pressure holds Erika down, trapping her other arm under her, and a few desperate kicks do nothing to help her escape the pin.

All movement adds to the force holding her arm, and a sharp pain starts to make itself known. Erika considers throwing her head back for a millisecond, then remembers her skull is more likely to break on Amari's horns before anything else would. If she pushes up with her whole body…

"If you keep moving in a pin like that, you'll end up with a broken arm. We'll work on grappling later," Amari says casually, not easing up in the slightest. "You did good, just don't hesitate so much. If you doubt yourself in the moment like that, you'll end up in a world of pain."

The weight is gone a second later, and Erika lies on the floor for the span of a breath before realizing she can move. Rolling over and sitting up, she sighs heavily as her mind goes over the spar.

"I don't know what I'm doing," Erika admits, because it really is the truth when you get down to it. To her surprise, Amari shrugs.

"You think everyone gets trained by professionals? You're getting back up and adapting fast, which is half the game. Just keep doing that. We'll show you how to survive."

Warmth spreads through Erika's chest, and she can't help the small grin that forms in response. "Thanks."

"Stand up. Let's go again."

7

TALIYA

Taliya feels immensely grateful that she and Amari decided to steal imperial training equipment on an impulse three years ago. She can't imagine how the weeks of preparation for this job would be going without that. Probably much less productive.

Logically, she knows that beginnings are always awkward. Working as a team with people you don't know is an adjustment and one that can be incredibly delicate, depending on the people and the mission. That they have to practice working together is a given.

But it would be a lie if Taliya claimed she wasn't worried.

For their first couple of days in the warehouse, they will mainly focus on better understanding each other's abilities. Amari, in particular, needs to know as much as possible since she's the one deciding everyone's part in this. It's vital she knows what everyone can and cannot do.

Some things are going better than others.

Taliya watches with unrestrained glee as Najaah fights simulated soldiers. The ex-soldier faces off against a never-ending wave of solid illusions manifesting as generic soldiers, simply to get a baseline for their abilities. Kol and Erika are both watching intently, meters away. They do not hear the commentary coming from Nuru, Amari, and her.

Amari sighs as Najaah double-flips over half a dozen illusions. "Yeah, you were right, Nuru. They were definitely not a regular soldier."

"Special ops?" Nuru suggests.

"Ooooh, assassin?" Taliya says excitedly.

"Not like you were, if so," Amari disagrees in a tone that shows she's considering the idea. Nuru is absolutely positive Najaah was special ops of some kind. Taliya admits it would explain a lot. Rowan's special forces are particularly brutal, both in training and outside of it.

"I think they've spent time at Ariza," Nuru says quietly as the Ashan executes a devastating move on an illusion. She nearly winces in sympathy for it.

"Makes sense," the seer agrees somberly. Taliya nods, containing a grimace and a pitying look. She's sure Najaah would not appreciate it.

All three of them can agree without saying anything that this theory is fucking depressing. It makes sense and is horrific to imagine in many ways. Ariza is the academy-slash-cult where killers dream of visiting, let alone attending. Many of the Empire's, Rowan's, Ilved's, and Esma's top enforcers are reportedly sent there for training. Perhaps it isn't so surprising for Najaah, except Taliya can't help wondering how young they must have been.

Amari clearly has a similar thought. "Not really our business, though. I imagine Najaah is a private person."

"Undoubtedly," Taliya says, though she feels a bit reluctant. Amari elbows her. She immediately tries to retaliate and can't because Amari has already put Nuru between them, looking far too smug for her to abide. The shapeshifter gives the two an incredibly exasperated look and raises an eyebrow judgmentally, which freezes Taliya in her tracks. Scowling, she slumps, and returns to watching Najaah with only mild pouting.

Up next, is Kol.

The boy is too powerful for his own good, is what Taliya mostly takes away from it. He is an immensely talented Conjurer for someone so young. Wielding such chaotic magic entirely with your mind takes a strong force of will. Yet, he obviously relies too heavily on his magic. Kol is casual with his use of telekinetic abilities — or gravity manipulation, as the boy insists — in a way that makes her uneasy. Even as a Singer, something that has very few ill side effects if overused, she is careful. Kol, at the very least, doesn't seem to need to be taught how to fight or how to control his powers. But as a Conjurer, his magic can take a steep toll if overused or used incorrectly. They will have to work on that.

Erika, on the other hand, desperately needs this training for more than just the sake of cohesive teamwork. Admittedly, Taliya thinks she has good instincts when it comes to knowing what kind of attack is coming and when to get space from an opponent, but that's about all she has right now. The girl even has to borrow a weapon.

It's nice to also see what Nuru is capable of, even if Taliya already had a small idea of what it would look like. He's said before that fighting has never been his preferred way of problem-solving. Especially in his first form. In his second, as a great hawk, Nuru has much more maneuverability.

Still, he's trained in hand-to-hand (or talon or claw or —) and tends to just take whatever weapon an opponent has and use it against them. Taliya thinks the others look suitably impressed by the time his run in the simulation is done.

In contrast, Amari and Taliya are a strange mix of skill and instinct. They both missed out on a formal education in fighting the way Nuru, Najaah, and Kol have, but they make up for it with years of experience and pure skill.

Amari primarily uses a staff when fighting. One that collapses down into a much more concealable size and has runes carved into it that Taliya knows for a fact are much more useful and deadly than they appear at first glance. With her handling of it and the sheer speed, she seems like a storm in motion.

In contrast, Taliya is small and fast and quiet. She has twin hooked tiger swords that she uses for maneuverability as often as she does for fighting, and hidden enchanted blades concealed in her sleeves that she brings out for quick take-downs.

"If I didn't already know about your former occupation, I would suspect it of you now," Nuru mutters under his breath as she exits the simulation. Taliya makes sure to send him her sharpest grin.

"Alright!" Amari says with a smirk. "Now that we've all seen what we can do on our own, let's see if any of us can work as a team!"

Everyone eyes each other with varying degrees of skepticism.

Great.

It goes about as well as can be expected, in the end. Najaah and Nuru are clearly used to specific protocols when working in a team, Kol has only ever led other people, and Erika has no idea what she's doing, but she is at least willing to learn. Amari and Taliya have their work cut out for them.

It doesn't help that Taliya has to speak in Apolona to the group. The language is the most widespread, and with so many team members from all over, it's the best choice.

When it comes to her native tongue, Esmesian, Taliya only feels comfortable talking in it with Amari and Nuru. Erika's dialect is so formal it sounds archaic, Kol's accent is atrocious, and Najaah is only at a conversational level. It makes the whole endeavor that much more frustrating.

Her friend gives her a look from beside her, as if she knows exactly what Taliya is thinking and doesn't appreciate it.

"*You* could be more helpful, you know," Amari says flatly, staring unblinkingly at her. Taliya shrugs, because while that's true, she doesn't have much experience with teamwork either. Good experiences with teamwork, anyway. The seer sighs like the weight of the world rests on her shoulders, and it would all go away if only her dear, dear friend would be willing to—

"Fine, I'll try to help," Taliya groans theatrically. Amari's expression immediately switches to cheerfulness, giving her a wide smile.

"Great! Go make Kol be cooperative."

Ugh.

Across the warehouse, Kol and Erika are trying to work together to defeat a simulated monster. Keyword here is *trying*. The monster isn't winning, but Erika doesn't seem to have anything to do with it despite her efforts to contribute. Instead, the boy is using his powers to hover high off the ground while hurling every object part of the simulated terrain at the monster. The girl is barely avoiding being a casualty of the assault.

Taliya storms over, purposefully stomping her feet to warn the teens of her presence. Only Erika turns, looking very harassed. She ignores her and turns to the flying annoyance. "Hey! Sky rat!"

Finally, Kol turns away from his lone monster attack to look at her, gaping for some reason. "*What* did you just call me?"

She scoffs derisively. "*What* do you think you're doing? This is a *team* exercise, not a let-me-ignore-my-partner-exercise!"

The rebuke might as well have flown over his head for how much attention he gives it. "You just called me a sky rat!"

"I did! Are you going to ignore my question?" Taliya asks, letting a measure of threat into her question. The brat finally registers the warning, scowling as he floats down to stand on the ground with the rest of the rabble.

"I was dealing with the threat. I didn't need help," Kol says, something like a whine peeking into his voice. Taliya bravely does not call him out on it.

"That's not the point of the exercise. *Teamwork*, remember?"

"But I don't need help!"

"Are you gonna make me repeat myself?" Taliya puts her hands on her hips, feeling strangely amused even as exasperation burns through her. Kol's hands tighten into fists and his tail swishes in agitation behind him.

"She can't do anything!"

Erika flinches minutely, and Taliya desperately wants to punch something. Whatever expression is on her face finally makes Kol back off, and his fingers start fidgeting nervously.

"She's willing to learn new skills, which at the moment is more than you seem to be capable of," Taliya grits out through clenched teeth.

Someone could be the most powerful magic user in Avalon and still be absolutely rubbish at fighting if it isn't something they are trained in. Battle magic is its own category. Outside of the military, people only learned bits and pieces for self-defense or just made it up as they went (aka street battle magic, which is wildly suspect but useful). Taliya was lucky enough as a child to get some lessons from a homeless veteran and built up her own style of fighting off that. Most street kids just work off instinct and what they've seen before. It can be the difference between death and survival. It can also build bad habits.

Erika, in contrast, has a blank slate as far as fighting skills go. Between that and her ability to be taught, Taliya is confident she'll be okay with enough training. Kol, on the other hand, needs to unlearn some things.

Something dark builds up in Kol before he deflates in a sudden sigh, scowling at the ground. As if it's been dragged out of him forcefully, he answers. *"Alright.* I'll… focus on teamwork. Whatever."

Taliya internally curses Mia out for setting them up with a host of teenagers, but externally just nods and watches as the two kids restart the simulation. Erika is hesitant and hopeful in the same breath, which is painful to see in so many ways. Kol is begrudging at every turn, yet slowly starts to get the hang of not being the sole powerhouse in a fight.

Eventually, the rest of the team wanders over because *they* didn't have any interpersonal problems with today's exercise. As soon as the two teens' simulation is done—successful with a few hiccups that nearly got one or both of them wiped out—Kol practically runs out of the training boundary line. Erika follows at a more sedate pace, looking exhausted but thrilled at the win.

"Not bad," Nuru praises because he's soft on kids. Najaah looks them over critically and doesn't say anything, which Taliya theorizes is probably some form of approval. Her friend, however, just gives her a small smirk, and she mouths the words *watch your back* at Amari. The other has the gall to roll her eyes before turning to the tired teens.

"I'm glad you both have made progress today. Do you have any questions?"

"Will there be monsters like that in Ethereal Planes?" Erika asks in a rush of breath, clearly having bottled up her curiosity until this very moment. Taliya hides a grin.

Amari nods, expression serene. "Sure. The one certain thing about the Planes is that we will find things that are extraordinary. Beautiful, dangerous, impossible—but extraordinary."

Taliya swears she sees stars in Erika's eyes. "Why haven't there been more expeditions?"

"Because they often don't come back, for one reason or another," Amari admits readily. "The Planes are fickle. Using anything but stable gateways is risky, and people often will get to a Plane and then can't get out."

Kol jumps in. "What happens if you get stuck in an Ethereal Plane?"

"You're fucked."

Amari elbows Taliya in the side before turning to face Kol. "The simplest answer is that it depends on which Plane.

"The longer one is that there are Ethereal Planes that have stable gateways set up, there are Travelers and Guides who you can ask for help, and there are natural portals that show up rarely. The issue that comes with these is that they're all relatively uncommon occurrences, and each Plane can be very difficult to survive if you don't know them well."

"So you're fucked," Taliya adds unhelpfully.

"Thankfully," Amari continues on, ignoring her. "The Archive is one of the most well-known Ethereal Planes to us. Information is not too hard to find. The Governor's past expedition will help guide us to it."

Erika and Kol both seem to accept this answer, while Najaah looks thoughtful. Taliya squints at the Ashan, but she is not forthcoming with answers. Nuru hums, a quiet concern flashing across his face before being shuffled behind careful neutrality.

"I'd like to go over the maps for the fortress again," Najaah says, not making it a question before she walks over to the other side of the warehouse where the table of maps sits. After an awkward beat, Erika runs after her, clearly looking to sate her own curiosity.

Kol seems like he's about to wander off, so Taliya holds out a hand to stop him. He jerks back from the almost touch, giving her a wary look.

"Hold on, kid," Taliya deadpans, not reaching out again. "I need to know if what happened today will be a repeat performance."

"I don't know what you mean," he says stubbornly, crossing his arms. Nuru and Amari stay silent, watching with knowing eyes.

"The solo fighter thing won't work out well for any of us if you keep it up," Taliya insists, suppressing the urge to roll her eyes dramatically.

"I am not a *coward*," Kol hisses, tail twitching wildly. Nuru sighs silently out of the corner of her eye, and she can tell Amari is barely resisting the desire to facepalm.

"And you not fighting alone means… what? That you're weak or something? Who cares? Do you think you're stronger than everyone else?"

"That's—" Kol splutters, outraged. "I'm the Warlady's son! That should be a given!"

"Yeah, I really wouldn't go advertising that, my guy," Taliya drawls and shares a tired look with Amari. "You're not in Ilved anymore. The Warlady doesn't have a lot of friends out here."

"So you would—"

"She's saying," Nuru interrupts with the ease of a diplomat. "That the way of life here is different from what you are used to, Kol, even for the Warlady's son. You would be served more by trying to learn how to adapt than by demanding we respect Ilved's ways."

After that, Kol seems to have the sense to take the cue to shut up and think it over rather than argue more. Taliya relaxes, not even noticing how much tension has invaded her body during the discussion. In times like these, she dearly misses jobs where only she and Amari work together.

"I'm going out," Taliya says under her breath, signing along discreetly. Her friend scans her over with a concerned frown.

"Alright. Take Erika with you and go the Nidarr's bookshop. They have a delivery for us."

And it's probably something illegal for civilians to have. Taliya snorts before nodding. She doesn't protest the tag-along, since Erika will no doubt be too enraptured by the books to be annoying.

The word 'bookshop' is all Taliya needs to drag the teen away from the maps, and they exit the warehouse into the biting cold of

Castor. With the scent of the sea on the wind, she finally lets the rest of the tension coiled in her spine dissipate and leads Erika through the twisting streets.

As soon as the storefront with the words *The Arcane Pages* printed on it appears, Taliya smirks. She's not disappointed when they step into the shop, and Erika gasps loud enough to wake the dead. Gaping, the girl scans the bookstore intently, taking in every worn tome and exotic curiosity that the Nidarr's have collected. She brushes her fingers against a book that passes through the air to be filed away, and Taliya leaves Erika to study every section of the place obsessively.

Tara is behind the counter, engrossed in a book, as Taliya approaches. The younger girl is huddled in her chair, still-growing wings folded up on her back. It takes a soft knock on the counter to draw the teen's attention away from whatever she's reading. Her eyebrows jump as soon as she sees Taliya before a grin takes over her face.

"Oh, hey, Taliya! Rare to see you without your partner, unless Amari is already lost in the manuscripts section."

"No, just a new kid," Taliya nods her tag-along. Tara catches a glimpse of Erika moving through the aisles and gives her a narrow look.

"Is she...?"

"New kid," Taliya repeats, stressing on the word *new*. Tara seems to get the message, before shrugging the worry away.

"Not my problem. You here for the stuff Amari ordered?"

"Yeah. I—"

"Taliya!"

If her instincts were any less sharp, Taliya might have been taken surprise by the small body that flies out of nowhere and launches herself at the thief. As it is, she barely manages to catch Rajni before the child takes them both down.

"Rey!" Tara scolds, using the girl's less common nickname.

"What have we said about doing that?"

"Don't do it to strangers," Rajni says innocently, even as she clutches at Taliya's jacket. The thief resists the urge to roll her eyes at the kid.

"Don't do it to *customers* either!"

"She doesn't mind!"

"That's not—"

Erika steps into view, holding a book to her chest that Taliya can't see the title of over Rajni's head. "Uh…?"

The Nidarr sisters still immediately, taken off guard by the stranger in their midst.

"My apologies," Tara says, straightening. Her voice has taken on the customer service tone that Taliya hasn't heard from her in years. It makes her wince involuntarily. "My sister can be energetic. How can I help you?"

Rajni's gone quiet, though hasn't made any move to get down from Taliya's arms.

Glancing at her uncertainly, Erika shifts her feet. "No—no worries. I, just, um…"

Mercy isn't one of Taliya's virtues, but she sighs all the same. "Erika, these two are the kids of the bookshop owners. Tara, Rajni, this is Erika. She's a new… colleague."

Tara's eyes widen imperceptibly before she goes back to professional mode. On the other hand, Rajni gives a small gasp of excitement. Taliya immediately feels dread shoot up her spine and decides to cut that at the root.

"Rajni, Erika is interested in learning about dragons, why don't you tell her what you know?"

Instantly, Tara facepalms, and Erika blinks at Taliya widely, mouth dropped open. Rajni does what she can only describe as *light up* and practically jumps out of her arms to get to Erika. The sacrificed teen recollects her wits as the kid grabs her shirt and drags the girl into an aisle, chattering about the book Rajni just *has* to show her.

"Brutal," Tara mutters, eyeing Taliya sideways. The thief shrugs in response. Huffing, Tara shakes her head and starts to walk toward the backroom. "*Your* problem now. I'll get Amari's new stuff."

Taliya can live with that, glancing at the excited child and captive teen briefly before looking away. After a few moments, they come back with a growing pile of books. It only takes a second to confirm that every single one of them is about dragons. Not just the fun stuff either, but the anatomical, boring historical books. Rajni doesn't obsess over things half-way.

Neither does Erika, though, as Taliya is learning. To her amusement, the teen is starting to look more intrigued than alarmed.

Unfortunately, her trick didn't completely put off Rajni. The kid looks between her and Erika with narrowed eyes. "So, what are you stealing?"

Erika sends very wide eyes at Taliya. The thief internally groans. "Not much. Don't worry about it."

"But where are you going?"

"Away."

"How away?"

"Away, away."

Eyes switching between them rapidly, Erika begins to look dumbfounded. Taliya ignores her.

"Can I come?"

"No."

"Can I *please* come?"

"No."

"Can you steal something for me, at least?" Rajni finally asks, looking sullen and earnest at the same time. Taliya actually stops and thinks this question over."

"Well, what do you want?"

"I want a dragon," Rajni says. She sounds so certain and firm that Taliya almost considers the request. Erika's eyes grow wider somehow, and her eyebrows jump up.

"Is — Is it possible to *have* dragons?"

Taliya snorts, mind going back to the vault. "No need to sound so alarmed. Rajni is just dreaming dreams again."

"Hey!"

"So, dragons...?" Erika trails off uncertainly. Rajni quickly forgets her offense and turns to the teen, eager to talk more about one of her favorite topics.

"Dragons are the best to have on your side! There's a long history of Dragonriders —"

"You want to *ride* a *dragon?*" Erika sounds so disbelieving that the thief can't stop the laughter bubbling up. The teen glares while Rajni continues to look very confident about everything she is saying.

"A Dragonrider, huh?" Taliya tries to contain her humor, feeling her mouth twitch into a smile anyway. "Any other notable achievements we should watch out for?"

Rajni's eyes brighten, having clearly been waiting for this very question. "I'm going to collect the best familiars — more than anyone's ever done! I bet I can get a bunch just in Rowan. And I'm going to be the best warrior, even better than Warsong!"

Taliya's brows try to escape into her hairline. "Those are some big goals."

"Warsong?" Erika mutters, sounding lost. The thief and the child both look at her.

"Do you not know who Warsong is?" Rajni asks. She stares at the teenager like she feels sorry for her and also wants to study her like a bug. "How can you not know?"

"Uhhh...."

Taliya decides to try mercy again, just this once if only so Amari doesn't complain to her about this later. "Warsong is what everyone calls this ancient warrior that randomly pops up in different places and starts fights. Some people write her off as a myth, but she's real. No one knows how old she is, and no one's beaten her in a fight."

Erika's face cycles between bafflement and alarm. "And no one's stopped her? Why is she fighting at all?"

Rajni jumps back into the conversation. "She's a warrior! Fighting is what she does! I read that she hunts down human traffickers and smugglers. Everyone's afraid of her, even the Empire. Some say she's immortal."

That's true enough. Taliya has seen Imperials shake and run away, fearing Warsong's wrath. The woman's full powers are unknown, but she's a legendary Singer and Conjurer. And even if she doesn't kill you, her singing can leave people insane, forever lost in their own minds.

Of course, she is just one woman. Warsong can go years without appearing on anyone's radar—decades. She's the equivalent of the scary bedtime stories parents tell their kids to make them behave. The thought of Rajni becoming like her is an amusing one.

Erika gapes. "Wow..."

Tara leaves the backroom, kicking the door open with her foot as she clutches some heavy tomes to her chest. Smirking, Taliya crosses her arms and waits in front of the counter as the teen struggles to carry the books. After sending her a glare, Tara dumps Amari's order—gently—on the counter.

Reaching out, Taliya turns the three hefty tomes to show their titles.

Oh, yeah, these look pretty illegal.

The first isn't so bad, called *The Art of Illusions: Creating and Breaking Spells*. Taliya knows the main issue with acquiring this work is that it requires a permit to have. Knowledge of complex spellwork, be it illusions or teleportation, is more restricted than enchanted weapons. This book provides methods for detecting and dismantling illusions.

"Useful," Taliya mutters, then focuses on the next book. This one is *Celestial Navigation*, and she wrinkles her nose at the imperial stamp on the inside of the cover. All works pertaining to the Ethereal Plane are considered Apolon Empire property. Cat must have had fun getting her hands on this. Flipping through, she scans the chapters on star mapping, astral travel, and gateways. The book includes detailed star charts, celestial alignments, and instructions for using cosmic energies. It focuses more on how travel between dimensions works over what the Planes are like for her comfort, but Taliya supposes Amari will figure it out.

She stills when the title of the third tome registers, something too complicated to parse rushing through her mind before Taliya shuts away any and all reactions.

Erika reads out the words over her shoulder before she can find an excuse to hide them. *"Temporal Enigmas: The Study of Time Magic.* Interesting."

Taliya waits for a response but doesn't get one. Logic finally reaches her, and she puts on a nonchalant front. Amari wouldn't have sent the teen with her if she were a risk. Turning back to the book, she runs her fingers over the cover, adorned with clockwork motifs and runes to preserve the accuracy of time-related information. A quick peek into the chapter titles shows the book delves into the complexities of time magic, including spells related to time manipulation, theories regarding time travel, and research on temporal distortions. It provides theoretical explanations, practical applications, and safety precautions for working with time-related magic. It includes diagrams of time loops and temporal fields. Taliya would put money on this being a book Amari has been interested in finding for a long time.

Is it a coincidence that it's uncovered now?

"Oh, here," Erika seems to remember the book she's been holding for minutes, and puts them on the counter away from Amari's order. "How much for this?"

Tara barely glances at the girl's order before calling out a price that Erika doesn't wince at. With no sense of propriety, Rajni walks up to the counter and looks at the item.

"Are you an Artificer?"

Curious about this herself, Taliya leans over to look. The book is about arcane constructs, referring to the building of constructs such as golems, animated objects, and other enchanted creations. The cover is embellished with intricate patterns representing various constructs, and she can see that the pages are protected with a charm to prevent unauthorized enchantments.

Face turning red, Erika splutters. "Well—No, I just was curious about how they work. This book talks about crafting, enchanting, and controlling magical constructs. And shows past case studies, too!"

Everyone stares at her. The girl's face steadily turns redder. Taliya reaches over and flips open the book. It's as academic as it sounds. There are diagrams and enchantment formulas, along with historical accounts of famous magical creations. It looks like a textbook.

"Are you a student, or something?" Taliya asks, the thought feeling deeply unsettling on some level.

"What? I mean, I go to school, yeah?"

Rajni grimaces and makes a sound of disgust. Tara sends her an exasperated look, no doubt remembering her sister's adventures in public school before her family had to start homeschooling her. Taliya, as far as she can recall, knows the Nidarrs are a pretty normal family, apart from the whole black-market-trade part of their work.

Taliya, who grew up on the streets dodging Esmesian child protective services and became a criminal, is feeling deeply thrown off by one of her teammates being so regular. "Right. Great. Awesome, let's pay and head back."

Now everyone's looking at her. Erika clears her throat and moves to pay. "Sure."

The Hall is a cheap apartment building hazardously close to the Kiyoshi Crater, which many stay far away from out of fear of it being really fucking haunted. Hence, the affordable apartments, even if the actual building is in pretty good condition by Taliya's standards.

The location isn't the only weird thing about the Hall. Everyone living here is weird, too. It starts with the nice couple who own the place and increases from there. The owners — two veterans who are very generous and take no shit — don't rent out to people who will cause trouble for the other residents. They take in anybody who is desperate enough to live close to Kiyoshi for a cheap price, and they're *friendly*.

As someone who grew up around criminals, Taliya has always found her current landlords disconcerting. The other residents can be downright terrifying.

Her and Amari's apartment is between a little old grandma who has a mystifying collection of antique daggers and an archeology major crazy enough to live near Kiyoshi *on purpose*. For *research*.

Just on their floor, there's also a freelance amateur necromancer, a chef who starts more fires than cooks with them, two runaway teens, a cartographer determined to get a coherent map of Castor, and finally, someone who Taliya is certain is a retired pirate.

This would all be fine if everyone kept to themselves and went about their lives, but *no*. The owners are friendly, so everyone else ends up acting friendly with each other, and the next thing Taliya knows, she's being invited to a 'housewarming' party for a new resident. Ridiculous.

The only positive is that the Hall isn't very large. There are only three floors, each with units A-H, which is still too many people, if you ask her.

It also means that when they briefly bring Erika to their apartment to get her outfitted in armorclothe and regular clothes, people notice. Not even a full day later, the kindly grandma next door —Ms. Hyde—asks after their 'young, scholarly-looking friend.'

Amari gives the noisy neighbor her patented 'nothing to see here, officer' smile and makes reasonable-sounding excuses while Taliya mentally prepares herself to be the main topic of the gossip mill for *weeks*. No doubt, everyone in the Hall knew about their visitor within a few hours of Erika's appearance.

" —looked so skinny, are you sure I can't make her any clothes? What about food? I've—"

"That's very kind of you to offer, Ms. Hyde," Amari says pleasantly, eyes screaming for help. Taliya looks away. "But we already—"

"Oh, call me Nona, dear. I've told you so many times."

"…Right, of course, Ms.—*Nona*, we have everything we need alre —"

"Nonsense! I'll make a basket for you to give her. It'll be ready in no time. I have some food for you two as well. You're both still so skinny."

"…Ah, thank you."

"No problem, dear!"

And that's just the start, Taliya thinks with a shiver. Soon, everyone will be putting in their two cents.

As soon as they enter their apartment to escape the neighborhood rumor mill, Taliya climbs the bookshelf and curls up in its shadowy corner. Amari just drops into her armchair, horns digging into the worn material, and sighs dramatically. "Moments like these, I wish I could just play the deaf card without consequences."

"Alas," Taliya says dryly. "Everyone knows you use hearing enhancements when you go outside. If only you were less paranoid."

"Haha."

Something she forgot slams to the front of her mind, and the thief rifles through her pockets without moving from her position on top of the bookshelf. Finding it takes her a moment, and she pulls it out with a triumphant noise.

"Here," Taliya throws over the improved runica to Amari. The rune-writing tool is a vaguely-pen looking thing that's clearly been messed with. Taliya will admit to some minor upgrades. The seer catches it with one hand, giving her an aggrieved look before seeing what it is. "This one should let your enhanced hearing runes last longer without maintenance. We don't know how much time to breathe we'll have in the Planes, after all."

"Thanks," Amari inspects the item, tracing a finger over some of the new runes. "Magic doesn't follow the same rules in the Ethereal Planes as it does in Avalon, so we need to prepare for the possibility of our abilities or runes not working, too."

"Okay... Does that mean you're packing an artifice?"

The seer sends her an amused look at the disdain in Taliya's tone. "No, if body enhancement runes don't work, the magic binding artifices will also suffer effects."

Makes sense. Of course, every artificer would disagree, saying their inventions are better than simple runes. But they're all a hypocritical tower of cards.

Body enhancement runes are illegal without a permit, pretty much all over Avalon. There are all sorts of reasonings about how random civilians shouldn't have access to runes that can give them super strength or what-have-you, but it's all bullshit. If that was the real reason, people like Amari should be able to easily get a permit for hearing enhancement runes The only people who are regularly afforded permits are soldiers and disciples of the Apolon Empire's religion, the Order of the Flame.

Instead of body enhancement runes, people turn to artifices for help if they need that kind of support. And it's expensive. *Incredibly* expensive. At this point, the companies that produce artifices for disabled folks have more people in their debt than the actual banks. It's… infuriating to think about for any length of time. She and Amari have stolen these artifices before, given them out for free, and still barely made a dent in anything.

Of course, there are still plenty of people who use body enhancement runes without a permit, but at great risk of being found out. Amari and Taliya are less concerned because illegal body enhancement runes are the least of their crimes.

"What's your plan if nothing works?"

Amari gives a distracted humming sound, looking deep in thought. She wonders if her friend is trying to divine answers from her seer abilities, for all of Amari's conflicting feelings toward them. Knowing the future in any respect, Taliya has come to understand, is far less helpful than it should be. Or maybe that's just Amari.

"The others learning sign language is good. Communication won't be a big issue. There's the telepathic network as a backup as well."

Taliya gives the seer a significant look. "And your plan for watching your back?"

"Isn't that what teamwork is for?" Amari answers sweetly, raising an eyebrow.

Scoffing, the thief glares at her friend. "Don't pretend you don't have a million exit strategies in place."

"I'm not," Amari says, humor fading away. Her eyes darken as she stares at the far wall, clearly focusing on something not visibly seen. Taliya is long used to stuffing down her curiosity and letting the seer sort through her thoughts. "Do you trust these people, Taliya?"

The thief gives a small sigh. She's never been one for deep

introspection, and the fact that her friend is leads to too many conversations like these. "As much as any ally in the past, I guess. I like Erika and Najaah well enough. Nuru is interesting. Kol is a pain but not malicious from what I've seen."

"And would you trust them to watch your back if you were injured?"

Ah.

"Probably, at least while we all have the same goal. I'd rather have you around, though."

"I'm not sure that will always be an option, Tal."

"Don't jinx us," Taliya grimaces, not liking the certainty in Amari's voice. "We have enough shitty luck."

"I think we can trust these people to do this job," Amari says, unheeded by Taliya's attempt to lighten the mood. "Just keep an eye out. Everyone has secrets."

Sighing louder than before, the thief reluctantly slunk down from the bookcase and met Amari's eyes levelly. It's a privilege in an around-about way. Amari only shares her honest opinions with people she trusts and knows will listen. "I promise to be careful if you do. Don't be reckless."

The ghost of a smile flashes across the seer's face. "I'll do my best. But I can already tell there's a lot of danger lying ahead of us."

"Of course there is," Taliya complains, slinking into the kitchen to make Amari's awful tea. She pulls out their mugs — black with moon motifs for Amari and yellow with explosion clip art for Taliya — and gets to brewing with minimal grumbling. "Nothing can ever be *easy*."

"You'd get bored," Amari calls from her armchair, smirking audibly. Taliya briefly considers throwing a spoon at the smug jerk before moving on with an aggrieved noise.

She goes through everything they've discussed as she brings over the steaming tea, a mug clutched in each hand. "So you've decided to trust these guys?"

"… Yes."

It doesn't sound easy to admit, and Taliya gets why. Amari and her — they're similar, by circumstances and bad choices that didn't really feel like choices at all. "If you're sure."

She sounds certain this time. "I am."

"Then we'll prepare for every worst-case scenario with that in mind."

Hopefully, none of it will be necessary. But Taliya and Amari don't have much trust in things going according to plan.

8

AMARI

The ground shifted under Amari's feet.

A god (one living fire, one time boundless bound, one empty as the void)
watched with sad eyes.

The future slipped through her fingers.

Somewhere far away, a man smiled and drank to victory.

The past greeted her with open arms.

Locked away where none could find her, a goddess cried.

Something terrible and unknowable looked her way.

The seers knew what awaited them.

Stolen Histories

Foresight did not save her people.

> *There is one who will die, one that will lie, and one that will rise.*

Blood on her hands.

> *All that awaits is what was behind you.*

Her dreams were filled with the throes of destruction and roars like thunder.

> *"Don't go where I can't follow."*

Amari was standing in the eye of a storm. It was not a normal storm and would, in fact, be more accurately described as a hurricane once it gained more power. If hurricanes were made of fire. Of flame and fury.

This was the wrath of the gods leashed to the Divine King. He brought this destruction here, and all Amari could do was watch.

It was terrible. It already happened.

When she first started having these dreams, Amari tried to do something. She was cold and desperate. Alone. But this was a vision, a dream of what had already been. It was a memory she wasn't allowed to forget.

Like every time before, the dream's details were sharp and hazy – the contradiction of a vision. And like before, Amari ran to the safety of her home. It was the only intact building left, though that wouldn't last.

The house was precisely as she remembered and horribly unfamiliar at the same time.

For the first time, something new happened in her vision.

Amari's mother stood in front of her. She was exactly as she was all those years ago, a piece of time frozen and preserved. It made Amari's heart *skip a beat and breath hitch, staring at this ghost.*

She smiled in the way she used to smile when she was sad and trying to hide it. "You've changed so much," she said.

The dream blurred around the edges of Amari's vision, like acknowledging this was a fantasy made it less real. "Everything has."

Her mother opened her mouth, but before she could say anything, the ground shook again. They both barely managed to keep standing in the wake of the destruction happening outside.

"Amari!" Her mother shouted, rushing close. She didn't reach out, which Amari couldn't decide if she was grateful for. "I have no time! Do you remember the day your brother was born?"

Already thrown off by this unscripted interaction, Amari couldn't bring herself to do anything but nod.

*"Good, **remember**. I – There were so many things I wish I had had the time to tell you, but – I'm so sorry." Her hand began toward Amari's face before jerking back. "So many things."*

The firestorm was increasing in power around their home with alarming speed now. Amari knew she was reaching the point where she woke up soon. Her mother seemed to realize this and took a deep breath.

*"Okay. Listen, if you need to know one thing, just listen," she leaned in, her voice gaining a strange echo – it was as if many voices were overlapping. **"Death is what you make of it."**

The wind ripped through their home, destroying the roof and decimating the walls. Amari caught one last glimpse of her mother before the dream world was ripped away.

Amari wakes up with a silent scream trapped in her throat. She jerks out of her bed in a single movement, years of being ready to defend herself in a moment's notice ingrained in her body.

The floor is freezing cold under her feet; thankfully, it's a strong enough sensation to draw her out of her mind, sending violent shivers up her spine and numbing her toes—a point for her apartment's terrible heating system. Chest heaving, Amari rushes to her bedside table. She desperately opens the drawer and the hidden compartment tucked away inside. Inside is a single, worn notebook and an enchanted pen.

Writing as fast as she's capable of, Amari describes her vision in as many details as she can. In her haste, she nearly rips the fragile paper with her pen a few times.

Finally, Amari can write no more and sinks to the floor with a heavy sigh.

The adrenaline feels like it takes all her energy with it as it leaves her, and she leans against her bed, exhausted. A growing, aching pain stabs at the back of her eyes. Visions are the fucking worst.

Despite her body's tiredness, her mind starts to race with the implications of her dream. As a seer, she often gets snatches of the past, present, and future sent to her sleeping mind. They're usually nonsensical without context or too abstract for anyone to understand. Recording helps, but it's easier with full visions. The details of dreams fade with time, though, so she has to be fast.

The firestorm—that's a recurring dream. Amari would consider it a normal nightmare if it wasn't so vivid and unchanging even after all these years—until tonight, apparently.

It is extraordinary. And annoying. Amari has never interacted with anyone in a vision like that, only as part of a scene in the past or future. But it's like her mother was… Actually there.

But that can't be possible. Amari refuses to believe it. If she goes down that road, Taliya would no doubt throw a fit over her researching anything necromancy-adjacent.

So. It's nothing. She looks down at the journal. Maybe she will at least try to make sense of what her mother said.

For now, the pen and journal go back into the hidden compartment.

Amari's seer abilities have never made much sense to her. As a child, being a seer was the norm—she was surrounded by seers, oracles, prophets, whatever name you prefer—so nothing seemed out of the ordinary. But now she's spent years around the rest of Avalon's people, and… To put it nicely, seer magic is confusing and wild in comparison to everything else.

It might have been easier if she had had the chance to finish her education with the seers, which is something Amari regularly thinks about.

Visions are at least more informative than the random moments of *knowing* she can be hit with. Sensing danger is one thing; sometimes, Amari feels compelled to do things outside of situations where she or someone else is in immediate danger. Not all these feelings make any sense now, either, but they will usually become clear down the road—occasionally, really far down the road.

Amari had one of these feelings when she was around ten years old. It was during a time when she had a temporary yet stable environment and had also been gaining access to more resources. She'd been staying at a safe house, and a place someone in the Underground Resistance had helped her rent. On a seemingly unimportant day, she wound up, rather inexplicably, having the urge to buy a stupidly large amount of yarn.

Bored and curious enough not to question it, Amari had followed the compulsion. She'd never used knitting needles before, but her hands were guided through the process. In the end, she had knitted four blankets, six pairs of gloves, a silly hat, and a long dark blue scarf. She was never able to knit anything again once the feeling left her.

Over the years since, Amari has given away the blankets and

gloves to people who desperately needed protection from the cold weather and the hat to trade for a book from Rajni, who adored the funny-looking thing.

The scarf, which had been determined during her initial shopping trip to be a specific shade of dark blue, had been waiting to be used for over a decade. Amari had forgotten all about it until Erika mentioned not having proper clothes for Castor's cold weather or the money to buy more. She's only planning on giving the Nullifier some money to get more clothes, until she suddenly feels the surprising urge to get that scarf.

When she looks for the old thing, it's in the closet, lying forgotten in a box. The scarf is just as she remembers it: soft, warm, and very blue.

Erika is silent when she passes it to the girl.

"Is this alright?" Amari doesn't think it's not, because she wouldn't have made it for Erika more than a decade before she met the teen if it weren't alright.

The girl's hands tighten briefly, and she holds the item closely. "I —Yeah, this is great. This blue is… It looks like my mom's eyes. Thank you, Amari."

Nodding, the seer doesn't mention the shine of tears to the teen. "No problem. Later, you can go shopping with Kol and Najaah for supplies and more clothes."

Erika agrees, and Amari expects more questions, but the human rather quickly excuses herself and leaves. Amari watches her go, thinking the interaction over before dismissing it. Sometimes a reminder of home is all one needs.

Amari's powers are weird. Her natural Nightblood abilities — mostly pertaining to manipulating shadows and feeling stronger at night—are completely nonexistent in comparison. It makes the differences between her and the rest of the Taos even more stark.

Maybe that's why she loves Castor so much. She isn't so strange here.

Castor is a city of lingering ghosts, dangerous secrets, and deadly tricks.

It hadn't always been, she knows. Not until a god was supposedly killed on its land thousands of years ago, and a gateway to a dark dimension was opened underneath the city. Now, time and space can get…*funny* in the right places and at the right moments.

There are streets whose existence depends on the year's season, along with buildings once demolished that remain like ghosts, and alleyways that lead to an entirely different part of the city. Some restaurants don't exist without a standing reservation, and hotels can have floors that were never built. At the right time of the day, there are pockets where gravity doesn't work properly if you know where they are. People have gotten lost in the underground, coming back after being missing for weeks but believing they've only been gone a few hours.

While human ghosts don't tend to haunt Castor (with some exceptions), the past *lingers*.

It's the only place since the destruction of Musei that feels like home. That lets her forget she's the last seer for a minute.

Not everyone feels so comforted by the eccentricities of this city, though. She can see it with her teammates. Najaah is watchful of every shadow, while Erika doesn't like to navigate the streets alone, and Kol prefers to skip past those steps entirely to instead fly between places. His powers let him control his own gravity but not any other living being's. Otherwise, Amari is sure Erika would be bartering for a free ride.

Nuru doesn't seem to let much bother him, but she can see his apprehension as he looks out her apartment's window. The crow's feet around his eyes are particularly pinched today.

"I've never been to a city like this before," Nuru admits over coffee as he stares out at the skyline. Amari gives a hum of acknowledgment.

She can theoretically understand the perspective of someone unused to it. The home of the seers would never have been called normal by outsiders, yet Castor is its own beast. Learning to live here as a non-native takes a great deal of adjustment. Amari remembers being eleven, alone, and so uncertain in the face of everything. Castor had been terrifying and comforting all at once in its familiarity.

On the surface, it appears to be a typical port city one can find on every coast. The Upper District is very much into acting the part. The illusion starts to break when entering the Lower District. The ambient magic here… is feral.

Looking at Nuru, she contains a wince. This is very different from what he must be used to. Rowan is known for its cities that have merged with nature — whole communities high in the trees, homes run over with plants, and animals of all sizes are free to roam. Except, even there, the magic is calm — tame, in a way. There's a balance between what's natural and unnatural.

Amari hardly sees any plants along the cold concrete streets here, and every home is built from stone, brick, and cement. The only plants are cultivated by aspiring individuals, not the city itself. Only some places outside the Upper District have been painted, and less so recently. All of this makes Castor look the opposite of the standard of Rowan cities.

Yet, the energy of this place is *wild*.

The magic affects the city unevenly. Some places are a step out of reality, as if the fabric of this dimension is thinner there. Other areas reek of barely suppressed violence or righteous rage. Amari recalls hearing Kol earlier this morning swear to Erika that he entered an alleyway that took him to an entirely different street and holds back a laugh at the memory.

Avalon's laws of magic are meant to be set in stone, so feeling this difference is alarming to those unfamiliar with it. When she was new, she would study every street corner and constantly question her directional skills.

It means something happened here or is still happening. Something that upset the natural balance so severely that other dimensions are leaking in and warping Avalon's laws of reality. Amari resists the urge to stare at the crater.

Naturally, Nuru isn't the only one to notice this discrepancy. Castor is a bit infamous for it, but the information is not as widespread as she thinks it should be.

The commonly held belief is that Kiyoshi Crater is the source of this unrest in the magic. It has a roughly 300-yard circumference that takes up a large chunk of the Lower District. It's the main reason the districts are so separate to begin with. Very few with the resources to afford it choose to stay near the crater. Because of this avoidance, the Lower District grew to be unmanageable by the other half of the city. The ambient magic's increased strangeness in proximity to the crater doesn't help.

"It is strange," Amari says, sipping at her mug. They head to the warehouse not long after, and she almost forgets about Nuru's interest when he eventually asks the obvious question.

"The ambient magic is because of the Kiyoshi Crater, right?"

"Everyone asks," she says, casting a glance at the shapeshifter. She's leaning against the work table while Taliya leads Kol and Erika through a simulation. Najaah has been forced to take a break after their earlier participation. "It's the local legend, you know? We used to get tourists looking to get scared, but the city itself seems to ward people off after a while. Upper District is trying to keep visitors on their side of the river or in the Merchant District, so the crater was made officially off-limits."

"Why does it frighten so many people?"

Amari shrugs. "Couple reasons. The crater was made over two thousand years ago when Castor was supposedly the site of this important temple."

"Ah," Nuru mutters, grimacing. "A god. That would do it."

"Not sure which god. There are a lot of debates over at the university and city library. A temperamental god is what everyone generally agrees on. Anyway, the temple is visited by a bunch of worshipers, offerings are made, sacrifices, etcetera, etcetera. Then, Kiyoshi arrives."

Nuru cuts in. "Who's Kiyoshi? I've never heard of them, but the crater is named after them, and no one has a straight answer."

The seer sighs, glancing at the ceiling for a moment. Wavers over telling a truth people like to hear and one that people shy away from. "There are multiple origins for her, but the common one is that Kiyoshi was a warrior from the north, seeking vengeance against the god of the temple. Some versions say she was a worshiper, and others claim Kiyoshi was a descendant of the god."

"A demigod?"

"Yeah," Amari says quietly. Demigods are... rare. All but forbidden, now, what with the gods no longer visiting Avalon. "Believe whichever version you want. When Kiyoshi reached Castor, she immediately entered the temple. No one's sure what happened inside, but we know that when she left the temple, the god was furious. The god said Kiyoshi had taken something of theirs and would curse the lands surrounding the temple until it was given back."

Gods raining wrath is a very common story. The area that was their target can be traumatized in the wake of it, but the ambient magic rarely is this disturbed thousands of years later. Amari can see how Nuru is confused over how this is so impactful even now. "What happened?"

"Apparently, there were twelve days of curses. Something new happened every day—plague, infestations, violence, fire, everything. For some reason, and there's a lot of debate over this, too, the city did not force Kiyoshi to return what was stolen. But after twelve days, they'd had enough of the god's wrath. Kiyoshi led an army of Castor citizens into the temple, and they killed the god."

"What?" Nuru's jaw almost drops open for a moment before the shock fully leaves. "How can a god *die?*"

Amari smiles, amusement rising despite herself. "They can't, according to everyone. It's just a story. But whatever fight did occur left the Kiyoshi Crater, and it's haunted — really haunted. Some believe the god was killed, and that's why the magic is how it is. Like I said, it's the subject of much debate. The reality, though, is that the story frightens people who hate being scared, so the Upper District tries its best to suppress the stories and avoid the crater altogether."

"If the Castor City government is trying to bury the story, then how can the university and library...?"

"Really?" Amari laughs, and her small smile turns into a grin. "You think some wealthy dustbags can stop the academics when they really get going? The students would riot. The scholars deal with all their documents. It's a mission in futility."

"Ah, right." Nuru clearly has enough experience with students and scholars to agree with that statement with little protest. "Wait, if there are so many bad rumors around the crater, why does anyone live near it?"

"It's cheap," the seer answers bluntly.

"...Right."

After giving her a look like *she's* weird, Nuru offers to spar against her. Interested, Amari agrees readily.

To avoid drawing attention, the shapeshifter tends not to carry weapons on them apart from smaller ones easily concealed. Because of this, Nuru focuses a lot on hand-to-hand combat forms. Amari doesn't often meet traditionally trained martial artists outside of fights, so the thought of a spar is enough to make her grin in anticipation.

"Weapons allowed?" She asks curiously.

"Sure," Nuru agrees casually, not looking phased at all when she pulls out her collapsible staff. Its cold metal casing feels familiar in her hands. "Just no magic."

"Got it." Amari doesn't want to fight a magically enhanced bird of prey anyway. She's dealt with enough asshole familiars to know that it isn't fun.

Amari strikes first with a sweeping arc of her staff, the weapon moving with practiced grace. Nuru deftly ducks under the initial strike, his agile movements undisturbed by the close call. As Amari follows up with a rapid series of jabs, he sidesteps and twists, his body a blur of motion as he avoids the staff's sharp thrusts. She's beginning to recognize he's practiced in a more defensive style of fighting. But it's likely not the only style he knows.

The first time her staff strikes Nuru's shoulder, it sends him stumbling back a few steps. Unperturbed, he quickly regains his balance before she can take advantage and launches forward, closing the distance between them. His movements are a blend of precision and speed, and his open-handed strikes aim for Amari's unprotected side.

Amari responds with a quick defensive maneuver, spinning the staff to create a protective barrier. As each of Nuru's attacks meets the staff, Amari can feel the strength behind them even as she expertly uses her weapon to redirect and deflect the blows. She speeds up the staff in a rapid circle, the metal shaft blurring before halting briefly as it blocks a powerful kick.

Despite the staff's formidable reach, Nuru's relentless assault begins to find gaps in Amari's defense. He slips past her guard, landing a series of quick strikes that force her to retreat a few steps. Thankfully, she's used to recovering fast. Recalibrating, she uses the staff to maintain more distance and create a defensive perimeter.

Both continue their high-paced dance, Amari's staff moving in sweeping arcs and precise thrusts, while Nuru's movements remain fluid and unpredictable while also disciplined. The warehouse echoes with the sound of the staff connecting with Nuru's forearms and the occasional soft thud of her strikes against his torso.

Amari executes a powerful sweeping strike that Nuru evades by ducking low and darting in close. This allows him to evade the staff's reach, and he lands a decisive kick that throws her off balance. She staggers a step before using her staff to catch her footing. By this point, they're both breathing heavily, but Amari sees the same thrill she feels reflected in the shapeshifter's eyes.

Despite the excitement, both fighters show signs of fatigue as the match progresses. Amari's movements, though still sharp, become more deliberate and calculated, while Nuru's strikes, though still precise, lack their initial speed. The staff whirls through the air with less force as Amari focuses on keeping her opponent at bay and getting a decisive hit.

She needs to switch things up a bit, she decides.

At a moment's notice, she pulls apart her staff into two escrima, dual-wielding with practiced ease. The surprise of the transformation buys her an opening, and Amari lands a solid hit on Nuru's shoulder before deflecting a grab. Going on the offensive, she rains down a series of blows that start to wear down his defenses until finally, she has an escrima pointed at his throat.

"Good game," she says wryly, mouth twitching into a smile. The shapeshifter looks like he wants to roll his eyes, but his tone is all good humor as he surrenders. Amari notices the four staring at them as she puts away her weapon.

Taliya looks smug, and the seer scoffs at her friend. Erika and Kol both seem varying shades of impressed and intimidated. She guesses from their perspectives, the skill gap must seem very wide and daunting. Najaah's face is too guarded to get a proper read on. To her own chagrin, Amari can't tell what the Sun Eater is thinking. It's more frustrating than she would like it to be.

"I'm going to focus on planning, everyone go back to simulations for now," Amari decides, keeping her tone light. Immediately, the younger group members begin arguing over who's on whose team. She walks over to her workspace with only a knowing look from Taliya, who doesn't chase her down.

Amari has been contemplating this team. It's a strange group of people: thieves, spies, soldiers, nobility, and a mythical Nullifier. Erika may be the strangest one among them, despite the girl's own beliefs. Amari has so many questions for every single one of them, and the effort to strangle them in her throat to avoid overstepping is mountainous.

Some of the edges she first noticed have been smoothing out. Teamwork comes easier to them after hours of joint exercises and simulations. Erika is finally comfortable enough to bite back when Kol is being particularly rude. Both teenagers respect Najaah, who is a good countermeasure to the other two's more strained relationship. Plus, Kol really seems to have imprinted on Nuru and tends to follow him around like a duckling.

Overall, she feels like she understands Nuru, is tentatively hopeful for Kol's possible development, and is beginning to trust Erika. However, there is one person she's still unsure about.

"Do you often sit in the dark and brood like this?"

Speak of a god, and they shall appear.

Amari turns to Najaah, who has approached the darkened corner of the warehouse she uses as a workplace with very little presence for the seer to sense. They are too good at blending into the shadows for someone with silver hair and is at least half a meter taller than everyone else, counting the horns. "I'm a Nightblood. And even if I wasn't, this is Castor; we like the aesthetic. If I brood in broad sunlight, it just wouldn't work."

Najaah snorts, seeming amused despite themself. "Well, don't let me ruin the mood for you."

They turn to leave, but Amari calls out to them. "Wait, I would like to discuss something with you."

Here, they tense like a bowstring being pulled. Amari keeps herself relaxed and neutral while observing.

"What about?"

"I'd like to know more about you. We're part of a team now, aren't we?" Amari has a feeling that lying won't work well for her here. Najaah is too easily spooked and likely very good at spotting lies.

They don't relax but sigh after a few moments of hesitation and sit in the chair across from Amari instead of the one next to her.

"What, exactly, do you want to know?"

"Well..." To be serious or to give an icebreaker? "What's your favorite color?"

Najaah stares. Amari smiles cheerfully, which isn't a common expression on her face. The Sun Eater looks like they can tell.

Finally, they roll their eyes. "Red, I guess. Or maybe orange. You?" This is asked in a mocking voice, making Amari smile more genuinely.

"Purple."

"Great," Najaah huffs, glancing away. Amari usually lets awkward silences stretch but doesn't prolong Najaah's discomfort this time.

"So," how to phrase this? "You said before that you wanted to join the team to find something in the Archive. For self-interest. Would you please explain that?"

Amari is trying to be more... tactile than usual as she says this, except she can see that Najaah does not want to explain anything to her. It's a familiar feeling—keeping your secrets close—and she sympathizes. She still needs to understand Najaah better than she does now.

"Why do you need to know?" They ask harshly, fingers clenching into fists on the table.

She holds back a sigh. Teenagers. How did she end up with so many teenagers?

"Because I'm going to be making the plans meant to keep us alive, successful or not. I can't make good plans if I'm not well-informed." Amari considers this situation from Najaah's perspective. "I swear I will not share anything from your past as long as it doesn't affect the team's safety. Not even with Taliya, alright?"

They stare at Amari warily for a long moment before turning to the window. The Sun Eater's fingers go to clench the table's rim, and she hopes they don't accidentally break it. She's not made of money. Both sit without speaking for a while before Najaah turns back and nods. "Alright."

"Good." Amari gives them a small smile that she hopes comes off as comforting. She's never completely sure. "Let's start with something easier. My first question would be about your skills and experience, then. I know you can fight and were previously a Rowanian soldier, but not anything more substantial than that."

Najaah hasn't relaxed precisely, but they immediately regain all the lost tension and straighten even further. Before Amari says anything more, though, they start talking. "I was... I was raised as a soldier in the Rowan Military."

Well, that sucks.

"I was sent to train for three years at Ariza, and I've been a part of many battles, including the Rowan-Menturai Conflict." They stop here, clearly unsure of how to explain more. The grip on the table is starting to look painful.

Amari nods, as if this is a perfectly normal background. "That would give you a lot of experience. Why are you no longer a part of the Rowan Military?"

The Apolon Empire and Rowan are tense allies. Both, along with Esma, are in an uneasy ceasefire, with everyone kind of expecting the day that Apolon makes a move. Amari hates politics on principle, except she constantly needs to stay current if she doesn't want to end up dead in a gutter. Rowan is run by an authoritarian tyrant who would probably get along with the Divine King like a house fire if the Empire didn't want to conquer their land.

Najaah doesn't notice the explosion of thoughts regarding politics that they have unleashed in Amari's mind. "I left half a year ago because… There was an ambush in Rose Valley, and most of my superiors were dead. I… After the raiders were defeated, I realized no one would notice if I left at that moment, so I took my chance to escape."

Well. Amari feels the last word sit between them for a minute. Then she breathes in and smiles reassuringly at Najaah again. "That must have taken a lot of courage. You want the Oathbreaker's Talisman, don't you? With that, you can break any contract Rowan has on you."

Rowan doesn't have slavery, in the classic way of it. It has contracts. Contracts, as the word implies, are agreements between two or more individuals. In Rowan and the other dark places in the world, they're as binding as blood. Contracts also don't need to necessarily be consensual. Or — more accurately — there's no way to verify whether both participants are willing before the magic sets in.

They just need some kind of signature made out of blood and the physical presence of both participants or a spokesperson in one's stead. This means many powerful residents in Rowan can force vulnerable people into any contract they like. There are rules and laws around the making of contracts in most countries, but Amari has never been naive enough to believe these laws are anything but steeped in one direction.

The Rowan Military, who rule the country, is the creator of most contracts. Najaah said they had been with them since they were young, and it's unfortunately not a rare story. Rowan is known for kidnapping children and forcing them into indentured service, which comes in many forms.

She won't ask what loophole Najaah must be exploiting to be sitting here at all, but she can respect the bravery it takes to walk that knife's edge.

"Yes," Najaah confirms quietly.

"Alright," Amari thinks over all the implications. "Alright. I'll help you get this. We all need to get to the Archive, so I'll ensure that we all do, okay?"

There were too many emotions for her to catch flashing through their eyes before they smile softly. It's an expression that clearly they're just as unused to using as Amari. "Thank you… I think I believe you."

"You better. We're gonna need all the belief we can get."

"Okay," Amari claps her hands, grabbing everyone's attention. The whole team is in the warehouse, spread out around the work table, studying maps and strategies. "We're testing the battle telepathy today."

She sends a pointed glance at the rafters above. Taliya has a book lying on her face, where she's sprawling on a metal beam. With one hand, she grabs the book as she rolls off the beam, catches herself on it with a leg, then flips down feet-first to a crouch on the floor. Less than a yard away from her, Erika nearly jumps out of her chair at her sudden descent.

"Right now?" Najaah asks, lips pursing. She doesn't show any signs of nerves, but Amari thinks if she hadn't had it trained out of her, the Sun Eater might be fidgeting right now.

Amari nods. "We've been training together for almost three

weeks now, and we have two weeks left to practice this before the fortress heist. No better time."

This seems to assuage the group's doubts, if not their wariness, at the prospect of sharing a mind space. *Great start,* the seer thinks.

With a carefully collected look, she leads everyone to the sparring area with the mats and instructs them to sit in a circle. Amari will readily admit it feels strange as fuck to sit on the floor with these people.

"So here's how it goes. I'm going to reach out to every one of you individually before establishing a telepathic network. There must be mutual trust for this to work, which means if anyone tries to force a connection, the harder it gets. If you feel uncomfortable, stop. Genuine consent is key to telepathic networks."

Erika raises her hand like a kid in a classroom. It isn't her first time doing it, which means Amari doesn't laugh. She just nods her head at the teen. "Does that mean we all won't be able to get into the telepathic network today?"

"That depends entirely on the individual," Amari says then, when the frown doesn't abate on the Nullifier's face, continues. "There's nothing wrong with how slow someone might be to join the network. As long as it works in the end."

A fire lights in the girl's eyes, and Amari suppresses a smile.

"I'll start with Taliya because we've done this before," she turns to her friend, who is next to her on the mat. The thief is relaxed and unphased by this whole process. Her biggest concern is how boring this might be for her to sit through.

Amari closes her eyes, focusing less on the Present and more on the flow of magic around her. There's a gap in it around Erika, and she would never have noticed if she didn't already know it would be there. Then, she detaches from the magical energy as much as she can. Finding Taliya's mind in the void that lays itself around her is as easy as breathing.

Hey, she establishes a gossamer thread connection with Taliya and gives a metaphorical knock on the thief's mind. Her friend immediately opens the channel between them.

This is going to be super long and boring, huh?

I think you're just going to have to deal with it, Tal.

Fuck me.

With some amusement, Amari brings herself a little back into the Present. "Alright, I've made a connection with Taliya. Nuru, are you okay with me trying with you next?"

She chooses who to ask instead of asking the general group to avoid forcing them to speak up. Predictably, Nuru is the most comfortable with this. He probably has some experience with battle telepathy.

"Yes."

Amari extends a new thread toward the shapeshifter. To her complete lack of surprise, Nuru has fully functional and intimidating shields protecting his mind from enemies. She makes no attempt to get past them, simply waiting outside. Her own shielding is half down in a display of trust that part of her recoils at instinctively.

He doesn't leave her waiting long. A door opens in the wall, anchoring the thread to Nuru's mind. His shields go back up while keeping the link and he begins to strengthen it.

It's all very professional. Amari is impressed.

In the Present, she says. "Connection established. Kol, how about you?"

"Yeah, okay."

In some ways, Amari wonders if this will be the most difficult one to work with.

The boy's shielding is a veritable mess. Oh, it works well enough — it would have to, for a child of the Warlady — but compared to Nuru's flawless wall, Kol has a barbed wire fence strung with broken glass. She has to work hard not to cut herself, leaving a thread outside his shields. She can feel power churning inside his walls, making no effort to go past them.

Part of the wall is ripped down, nearly forcing her to draw back in the wake of the shock. Amari can't help but tense and prepare for some kind of violence. Instead, Kol reaches out to the link.

It's like she stuck her hand in a magical generator.

With great control, she doesn't react and focuses only on the telepathic connection forming. Kol isn't familiar enough with how it works to speak coherently, and sends her a jumbled mess of thoughts, emotions, and intentions. She dampens the link so as not to flinch.

Carefully, Amari dials the link down enough that Kol isn't giving her a splitting headache. The teen seems confused about what's happening.

Kol, she starts. His mind jerks back like a startled cat, the mental image nearly making her laugh. She quickly collects herself and waits patiently, not letting any annoyance or other emotions be felt.

He – y⩽◊△⊥≳ –

Kol, Amari cuts into the screeching gibberish. *Calm down, it's alright. Just take your time to figure it out.*

Oka – △y

It's difficult to tell time when so disconnected from the Present. Amari gets bored anyway and discreetly checks in on her connections with Taliya and Nuru. Both are stable, with the shapeshifter's link becoming more familiar to her as she maintains it.

Hello?

Amari instantly pulls her attention back to Kol. The thread is less frayed now, and the power she senses from the teen is dampened to manageable levels. *Good job. Are you alright with keeping this as is?*

I think so. Kol hesitantly sends the message, the words feeling like they come through a wall of cotton. Amari figures that will fade with practice.

"Done," she says aloud. In the Present, Erika jolts after drifting off for however long Kol took. "Erika?"

"Yea — Yes."

She decides not to have the girl go last for the sake of Erika's nerves. Amari knows this is overwhelming enough as it is.

As she thought, finding the Nullifier's mind is a trial in and of itself. If she didn't know it *must* be there, Amari might never have found it. She has to be almost entirely immersed in her mindscape and detached from the Present, drifting through the void until she brushes against the faintest of presences.

Amari turns all her attention to Erika's mind and is fascinated by what she finds. Trying to focus on the girl feels like what she imagines people with poor eyesight deal with when they don't have their contacts. Fuzzy around the edges, details unclear and straining for a better view. It's incredible. Erika doesn't even need shields; this effect would put off all but the most powerful mentalists.

She stops trying to study Erika and instead leaves a thread for the girl to decide what to do with. Before this meeting, she instructed the Nullifier on what this experience would be like, and now she hopes Erika can adapt.

It takes a while — as much as 'a while' means in this state — before anything happens. Erika had told Amari that she had never done anything like this before. Nullifiers really don't use *any* kind of magic whatsoever. It's mildly unsettling to ponder for too long.

Finally, a blurry hand reaches out and grips the thread. A shaky connection forms and Amari sends a simple greeting to the girl.

Surprisingly, Erika adapts to the way of communication much faster than Kol. *Hello?*

The feel of the words is still unpleasant as she gets her bearings. Amari fights a mental wince. *Good job.*

I sound like I'm talking through a broken microphone, Erika projects the message. Amari isn't sure if that was something she meant to say or if it's an accidental thought that she sent. What's a microphone?

You'll get used to it with practice. Are you okay with me moving on to Najaah, or do you want more time?

Go to Najaah, Erika instantly replies, a sense of firm resolve radiating from her. It's easier to get a feeling of the girl with the link between them strengthening.

Alright.

Amari draws back, pulling herself back into the Present. She becomes aware of the growing headache making itself known and estimates she has enough energy to finish the network today. Once all the links are established, this will be much easier.

"Najaah, are you ready?"

"Yes," the Ashan's voice doesn't give away any emotions. Amari elects not to comment and just get into it, as she's sure the Sun Eater would prefer.

She has a lot of expectations going into this.

What she finds falls inside them.

Najaah's mind is a veritable fortress. Not the impassable, sleek wall that Nuru uses, or the jumbled mess of defiance that is Kol. There's a little of both. Amari can sense the formal training in the Sun Eater's shields while feeling their uniqueness. Despite Najaah's actual Ashan abilities — fire manipulation — being rather sub-par, being near her mind is like standing under the intolerable desert sun.

Hesitantly, not wanting to cause any undue stress, Amari leaves the barest thread of a link outside Najaah's shields.

Like Nuru, only a tiny door in the greet fortress opens to take the connection before snapping shut with more force than the shapeshifter's had. It's over and done with faster than any of the others. Amari can't pin down why that bothers her.

Instead, she turns her attention to the greater whole. Five

individual minds linked to her as different from each other as the elements themselves. She takes a moment to get a handle on it before sending the idea of establishing the telepathic network down each of these links.

Taliya instantly perks up mentally, a sense of *fucking finally, I was dying here* coming from her. Nuru and Erika simply reply with a clear agreement. Kol gives her a nonverbal acknowledgment that feels better than his earlier attempts, while Najaah sends the mental sensation of a nod.

Amari carefully fixes the bones of this network to her mind, not unlike how one fastens a fishing net to a boat. First, she takes Taliya's connection and makes links, tethering the thief to the other four. She gives them time to adjust, ignoring them as Taliya and Kol immediately begin a petty argument over something frivolous. Next, she connects Nuru, who tries to mediate the two. Najaah is third because she feels the former soldier has more experience with battle telepathy. Finally, she brings Kol and Erika fully into the new network.

For a moment, everything is quiet as everyone acclimates to the new presence in their minds.

Then, Kol speaks up. *Okay, this is kind of awesome.*

Wow, Erika projects her amazement and excitement into the group, followed by her embarrassment.

This will be extremely useful, is what Najaah admits, not giving much more ground than that.

Or extremely annoying, Nuru responds, giving off the sense of a kind of wry amusement. *I guess we'll see.*

I'm gonna vote for both. A feeling of mischief radiates off Taliya, who knows how to hide things telepathically if she wants to. Amari, for instance, doesn't let the group see her amusement.

Kol starts an argument back up, drawing in not just Talya but Erika this time. She lets the team relax and mess around, acting as a silent observer while studying the new structure.

The telepathic network anchored in her mind has a strong foundation, each individual shining in the interconnected web. For the first time, Amari feels excited at the prospect of this team working together.

9

TALIYA

As soon as they walk into the large dining hall-turned-meeting room, Taliya beelines for her favorite seat. It's in the back, where she can see everything going on, like who comes through the door, a clear view of the large dining table, and if anyone in the rest of the room is reacting to something. The setup is pretty simple, with the dining table being used by the building's owners and rows of cheap folding chairs facing toward it.

"I don't understand why you dragged me here," Kol mutters as the entire team finds seats around Taliya. He sits in the chair to her left, where they take up a whole row of the back audience. The room is filling up quickly, and they're getting many curious looks.

"It's a Hall meeting, you can't miss it! They're *hilarious*," Taliya insists. Someone from their floor — the retired pirate — walks by and waves at her. "I hear one of the building owners wants to propose a new policy. It'll be great."

Said owner — Jared Ortiz — stands up at the grand table while his husband, Kalsa, stays seated with an amused look, and the room's scattered conversations halt to give Jared their attention. "Alright, I'm glad you could all be here today to hear me out. I'd like to institute a yearly holiday based on the old festivals of light that took place in Esma a millennium ago. As you know—"

"What?" Kol whispers, sounding aghast. "What is he talking about?"

"He just likes making excuses to decorate the building and throw a party," Amari answers, leaning behind Taliya to whisper at the baffled teen. "Jared proposed to make the solstices a mandatory holiday, too, last year."

"—and the lights are released into the sky to honor our—"

With a frown, Najaah leans back from the other side of Kol to meet Amari's eyes. "A holiday for who?"

"—at the stroke of midnight—"

"Just the Hall. Everyone who lives in this apartment building," Amari explains with a ghost of a smile. "Who else?"

Taliya hasn't been watching Jared. Instead, she's been keeping an eye on one audience member. At the first signal that what she's been waiting is ready to erupt, she elbows Amari in the side as a grin grows on her face. "Grab the popcorn."

Automatically, the seer pulls the snacks hidden in her bag out and starts passing them around. There's no actual popcorn, but the sentiment is the same. Everyone takes them hesitantly, with varying levels of confusion.

"—a gathering meant to establish—"

"Enough!" One resident of the Hall abruptly stands up, tension in every line of his body. His tail twitches in annoyance, and his long ears refuse to keep still. Horns that jut upward make him appear taller than he is. "Are you seriously going to keep doing this every year?"

Jared puts on an expression of surprised offense, as if this conversation has never happened before. "Miles, I don't see what your issue is with celebrating something so—"

"My *issue* is that you try to make a new holiday so often that we're gonna have to throw half a dozen parties a month!" Miles Sadler—a first-floor resident whose most memorable quality for Taliya is his messy divorce with his ex—is nearly shaking with constrained frustration.

"That's an extreme exaggeration, we have a normal amount—"

"You once tried to make us all celebrate contraceptives!"

There's murmuring in the audience from people who distinctly remember the horrible events he's referencing. Taliya throws candy in her mouth as Amari snorts. Nuru watches the proceedings with fascination at the end of the row to her right.

"What's wrong with contraceptives?"

"Nothing! It's just not something I want to stand in a room talking about with people who use it as an excuse to drink shitty wine and stick streamers on the ceiling. *You* know exactly what I'm talking about!"

"Wow," Erika mutters from Amari's other side after tapping on the seer's shoulder. Taliya barely hears her over the show. "Can you yell at a landlord like that here?"

"Just Jared," Taliya says. "Because he does shit like this but is too nice to punish someone for having differing opinions."

"Oh, that is nice."

"Wait for it," Amari reaches into a bag of chips with a grin. "Miles is about to bring up the budget."

As she predicted, the man starts on about the limited amount of funds the building has for events like these. Taliya snorts.

Kol looks at her suspiciously. "Don't you guys have tons of money?"

Well...

Taliya and Amari *have* stolen a lot of shit. And they've gotten very good at turning any valuables around for a reasonable price on the black market. However, once you add up all that money and subtract the cost of equipment, bribes, travel, the occasional healing assistance, and just general life costs, you don't have all that much profit. Plus, Amari's side projects don't often come with any reward that can be calculated in the end in money.

They do have a considerable sum tucked away in what Taliya calls their 'everything's gone to shit' fund, though. So that's nice. Honestly, the fact that Amari is in charge of both their finances is the only reason they make any real, sustainable profit. Before then, they would just split their rewards between the two, and Taliya would usually spend it all in a week on useless things.

She debates with herself how best she can convey this to Kol. "Not enough to throw around for parties."

Just then, the room erupts into loud arguments. Aggressive debates like these can appear volatile from the outside when involving a mix of people who are all either powerful or scrappy in their own ways but also know each other well enough to know boundaries. Taliya watches an Ashan on the third floor burst into flames as they try to tackle her neighbor, who she's 98% certain is a pirate.

"Shit!" Erika screeches, hastily trying to escape the fighters who are completely ignoring her. Nuru places a calming hand on the panicking teen's shoulder. Taliya scoops out some more candy as Kalsa stands up to force order back into the room.

"Alright, everyone, sit back down! Let's just have a vote right now." Kalsa is of mixed Bera heritage, which means that he towers over even Najaah and has four arms, each individually capable of crushing a watermelon in one hand. He's one of the gentlest people Taliya knows, but everyone still quiets and sits down at record speed. "Are you all in favor of establishing a new holiday?"

Most of the room's hands raise. Miles facepalms while Jared grins.

"All opposed?"

Taliya raises her hand here, and Amari does too, yet they're clearly not in the majority. Kalsa nods, not looking pleased or displeased by the decision. "Motion passed, then. I'll see you all at the party."

Miles groans loudly before standing up and storming out in a fury of curses. Leaning back in his chair, Jared looks unbearably smug.

"Why did he leave? The meeting's still going on, right?" Kol asks quietly.

Snorting, Taliya pulls out a tiny folded-up flier from her jacket. It's a schedule of topics to be discussed at Hall meetings. "This is shoved under everyone's door the night before. I guess Miles didn't want to stick around for the next *debate*."

Kol scans the short list over. "The next thing just says 'loud or not loud?'"

"Yeah."

As soon as the audience settles, a beautiful woman in the front row stands up, grabbing everyone's attention. She is decked out in more glamorous clothes, jewelry, and makeup than anyone else in the room by a kilometer. Even at an event with people who have known her for years, Muna al-Faraj dresses to impress. "Hello, my wonderful neighbors. I'd like to once again bring attention to the *many* noise complaints made out to *certain residents* of our esteemed building."

A voice calls out before anyone else can react. "Just get to the point, Muna, we know who you're talking about!"

A group of circus performers mutters amongst themselves, taking up a whole row in the middle of the room. Taliya watches in fascination as one fiddles with a knife while another plays with fire in their hands. They show little interest in the pointed comments.

"Just let her talk, Clive!" A woman sitting next to Muna yells back. It's Cleo, a single mom who lives perilously close to the circus group's two rented apartments on the first floor. She's often a co-conspirator when it comes to noise complaints.

Muna's smile doesn't waver, an actress always on stage. "My *point* is that some of us sleep at reasonable hours and need to *stay* asleep to be able to go about our lives."

"Seconded!" A man calls out not far from Taliya's seat. She's unsurprised to see it's the diner owner on the first floor, Ali, who she knows gets little sleep as it is, since he is one of the only employees at his restaurant. "And it's not just the literal circus!"

"Hey!" The second floor's resident chef gasps in offense despite not being mentioned by name. Perhaps he's just paranoid after all the meetings specifically targeting his "experimental works of art." Taliya has no particular interest or talent in cooking, but she's pretty sure it doesn't involve as many sounds of explosions as this chef makes.

"Yeah, you," Ali says without remorse. "At least you're not in the apartment next to mine."

This is said pointedly in the direction of the woman, who has a snake wrapped around her shoulders, at least three birds perched on her antlers, and a sleeping bear cub in her lap. She's brought a restrained number of pets outside her apartment with her compared to past times. She looks away from Ali's gaze without a word. Taliya barely muffles the laughter that bubbles up, and Amari's shoulders are subtly shaking with the same effort.

"Woooow," Kol gapes. "Why are all your neighbors insane?"

"Proximity," Taliya answers with no hesitation. Najaah, to her surprise and delight, snorts quietly before quickly smothering all amusement.

"What about the noise-muffling runes?" Kalsa says, sounding reasonable. "Have they not helped?"

"Those require constant upkeep," Cleo scoffs. "Not everyone can just throw around magic like that carelessly."

The chef growls lowly, dog ears flat against his head in agitation. "If you hate the noise that much, you can find the magic to spare!"

"You—"

Nuru's voice speaks up suddenly, loud enough for most of the room to hear. "Why not have a communal rune system?"

Pretty much everyone turns to look at the newcomer who decided to participate in the meeting. Even Taliya and Amari are staring incredulously.

"What's a communal rune system?" Muna asks with a harsh voice. "And who are you?"

The expression that crosses Nuru's face as he stands to meet everyone's attention can only be called a diplomatic smile. It's a look Taliya has seen him pull out every time there's some kind of conflict. She can't bring herself to feel shocked by his response, but she doesn't have to like it.

"I'm someone who lives within many old and complex rune systems. My community often uses them for basic things like lighting, water, and temperature control because we have no magic generator."

This gets an energized reaction, with people becoming less argumentative and more curious about a new idea. Kalsa intercedes, eyes bright with interest. "Please describe what you mean."

"A communal rune system is what it sounds like," Nuru explains smoothly. "It's widespread sigil-work that covers a large space with many people. However, it's not powered by a generator or individual magical source. There are multiple places where residents donate small bits of magic to power the system. If everyone does this, then sustaining the runes won't be a problem."

"Why would we give away magic for something that doesn't matter to us?" Someone towards the front of the room calls out. Kalsa sends a sharp look in their direction, but Nuru continues before the giant can start scolding.

"You all care about living here peacefully, am I correct?" There's a quiet murmur but no disagreement with his words. "Then you can all help each other with this small thing. Together, the burden is not too much to bear for any individual."

Kalsa nods emphatically, moving to stand up with a small and genuine smile. "You're right. Do you know how we could create this communal rune system for the entire Hall?"

"Yes, of course. It's a simple process for any skilled Scribe."

"Good. Then I propose to bring this matter to a vote."

"Seconded," Amari backs her teammate up without pause. Taliya grins and throws in her support, mind already turning over how she could help set up the runes. Maybe down the line, they could create systems for more than just noise-muffling...

"All in favor of this new rune system?"

Immediately, every person who previously complained about the noise raises their hands. As Taliya and Amari join in, they notice most of the other residents hesitate before voting in favor. Only a few don't, and they're primarily people who decide to abstain.

"Proposal passed," Kalsa says with shining eyes and teeth bared in a facsimile of a smile. "Thank you, guest. I will want to discuss this with you more later."

"I look forward to it," Nuru responds, smiling pleasantly before sitting down. Taliya side-eyes him and his mask of politeness with heavy skepticism.

"What's the next topic —" Erika doesn't get to finish her question before someone new stands up abruptly, arms full of books and binders. Taliya recognizes the speaker instantly and is caught between the instinct to laugh or groan in despair.

"Here we go," Amari whispers, sounding thrilled. She loves it when Eliza requests to speak at Hall meetings.

Kol frowns, glancing at them. "Who's that?"

Eliza, a Nightblood-Ashan mixed being with bright red hair, dark crimson eyes, and impressive ram horns, doesn't pause before launching into her proposal. "My research has shown that the chthonic energy readings from the Kiyoshi Crater have spiked in recent weeks. I have found a correlation between..."

Taliya turns her stare to the ceiling, scanning aimlessly over cracked paint and suspicious-looking dents. The archeology major keeps talking, always sounding impassioned whenever the topic is about the haunted crater.

"I'm confused," Erika mutters. "Is she saying she wants to take stuff from the Kiyoshi Crater and store it in her apartment?"

"No," Amari answers. "She already does that. Eliza wants to use some of the public spaces as storage."

Muna makes a loud noise of dissatisfaction at the proposal. "There's no way you're keeping any of that haunted shit where I can see it!"

"What if my daughters find it?" Cleo, the single mom seated next to Muna, asks. Eliza doesn't blink at the interruptions before continuing about the fascinating discoveries she's making.

"In one ear and out the other," Najaah comments dryly, making Kol choke on laughter. Taliya smirks and leans over to the left to whisper.

"She technically never got permission to bring *any* samples to the Hall, Eliza just gets so focused on her work that she tunes out everything else. We're gonna have to start watching out for boxes of haunted dirt in the hallways now."

Shoulders shaking, Kol buries his face in his hands to muffle all sound. His tail curls around one of his ankles to keep from fidgeting. Eyebrows raised and mouth twitching, Najaah sends her an amused look. "So then why bring it to a vote at all?"

In the background, Kalsa has cut off Eliza's monologue as soon as she wanders off-topic into more obscure science, asking everyone to choose in favor of her proposal. It's almost a complete vote of *no*, but some people decide to abstain again. Taliya breathes out a sigh of relief even as she sees that Eliza is undaunted by the group's decision.

Turning back to the Sun Eater, Taliya gives a wry smile. "Basic courtesy, maybe? I'll be honest, I try not to guess what Eliza is thinking. Her mind must be a scary place."

Najaah snorts. Amari hums from the other side next to her, and the thief sends her friend a distrustful glance before sighing. At least the Hall meeting has no more proposals today. Kalsa moves on to announcements that are just about any events happening in the next month, anything about the physical building, or general important news for Castor citizens. He's one of those freaks who actually keep on top of local legislation. To her despair, Taliya usually knows whatever new laws or bills he's talking about because she, too, lives with another one of those freaks.

Most Hall residents use this part of the meeting to shamelessly gossip. Unsurprisingly, Taliya feels most of the stares turn their way. Amari and her don't bring many people around, so their teammates popping up in recent weeks is newsworthy by their neighbor's standards. It's why Amari suggested bringing them all to this meeting in the first place. Better to get it all behind them, and all that.

Taliya will admit that Nuru has made an interesting contribution to the discussion. She's curious about how communal rune systems work in real-world examples. The only ones she'd seen in person before, she didn't have the time mid-heist to pause and inspect the runework.

It doesn't take long for the meeting to officially end, and immediately, the room breaks into smaller groups. Incoherent chatter fills up the large space. One of the third-floor residents flits over toward Amari, and the seer stands up to meet them out of the way for a discreet conversation with fast-paced sign. Kalsa beelines for Nuru, with Jared trailing after him with contained, wary amusement on his face.

"I'm sorry, I didn't catch your name...?"

Even standing with his antlers, Nuru looks positively *small* next to Kalsa. Seemingly unbothered, the shapeshifter cranes his neck to make eye contact and introduces himself. "You may call me Nuru, I'm a colleague of Amari and Taliya. You are Kalsa Ortiz, correct?"

The giant beams, while Jared watches over the interaction with a bemused smile. "Well met, Nuru. Can you tell me more about this communal rune system? How would this be integrated into the building? Would noise-muffling be all it's capable of? What about…"

Taliya leans toward the chatting men to listen in on the details of this rune system. Meanwhile, the teens all gain a glazed look in their eyes as the conversation goes on. It doesn't take long before Kol gets up and walks away in boredom. Erika holds out for a few more minutes, then shares a glance with Najaah. The two teens leave to follow Kol.

In contrast, Taliya feels invested in the subject matter. The communal rune system is a fascinating concept, one she's been interested in exploring more. If enough people are part of the system, it can be used to a broader extent for security purposes. Her mind runs through all the ways a system in the Hall could be used.

What draws Taliya out of her train of thought is the subtle shift in conversation, away from discussing the specifics of rune systems to the workings of communities. From there, the conversation slowly evolves until Nuru is asking Kalsa and Jared about the functioning of Imperial communities.

It happens so naturally that she doesn't think anyone else realizes that the shapeshifter purposefully moved the discussion to this topic. It's a surprise, and not one at the same time — of course, Nuru noticed that the Ortiz's are former imperial soldiers.

Amari had noticed immediately, years ago. It put all her walls up instantly, and they almost never lived here if the two men hadn't explained their past in an effort to make an angry teenager comfortable. Taliya's always been glad they took the risk.

Anyone who knows anything about imperial soldiers can recognize the scarred brand on Kalsa's forearm. It's the symbol of one of their conscripted. The fact that there's a slashing scar through the brand shows that Kalsa has moved away from the Empire. Amari and Taliya know that the giant had to sacrifice a lot to get away, but to an outsider, it can look suspicious.

Less clear is the way both Kalsa and Jared hold themselves. It's reminiscent of Najaah, who struggles to relax out of a soldier mindset now that she's away from Rowan Military. The two older men obviously have had more practice in blending in, and yet it still shines through. People with no history of formal training rarely move in the same ways as these guys. Taliya is sure that Nuru notices all of this.

She wonders if the two owners even realize that the conversation has turned into a subtle interrogation. The teens certainly didn't catch it—though that might be because they've all tuned out the adults. Taliya probably only sees Nuru's real intentions because she knows the man and has an inkling of what his job is in his community.

Since Amari isn't here for her to share pointed looks with, the thief merely sits as she listens to the shapeshifter extract information about the dynamics between government officials and soldiers, the training of the Order of the Ash, and the types of wards the Empire prefers to use.

On some level, Taliya can't help but feel amused as she listens to all of this.

Eventually, the room begins to drain of occupants, and others wish to speak to the owners before they leave. Kalsa and Jared give Nuru a friendly goodbye before turning away.

The shapeshifter looks very content in the wake of all this. He raises an eyebrow at Taliya when he notices her stare. "Yes?"

Taliya scrutinizes the man intensely. "I'm not sure if you're nice or scary."

In the final days leading up to the Governor's fortress heist, Taliya leads the team through multiple simulations based on the layout of the place. She's staked out the fortress periodically over the past few weeks and can safely say that the security is pretty well-structured and unchanging—a thief's best friend.

The fortress is largely protected by layers of wards and a few patrols of human guards and sentinels, which are golems built with the express purpose of being foot soldiers. Having more sentinels than humans is great for them. The imps have a regimented schedule, but anything can happen due to human error. Artificial beings don't stray beyond what they're created for.

Past that, the Governor's place really does depend on the wards for protection. Even the sentinels don't react too much if the wards aren't breached. It's lazy security in Taliya's books.

For their apartment, Taliya and Amari have far more security measures than just wards. As expert wardbreakers, they know better than most that over-relying on them or even implicitly trusting them is foolish. Any ward enthusiast claiming otherwise doesn't know what they're talking about.

They tend to build their own equipment, too, or at least heavily modify what they likely stole. Taliya knows too much about the lack of care that goes into producing artifices to trust anything commercial. Despite not being Artificers, they get by well enough. At worst, they can find a reliable independent Artificer to commission.

The Governor's fortress doesn't have such well-thought-out innovations. The greatest difficulty the team faces is the anti-magic field. Any unauthorized magic that comes within the fortress's perimeter sends an alarm throughout the whole system. Disabling the field from the outside is nearly impossible, so Taliya, at the very least, has to get inside without using magic.

Wards against any unfamiliar magic signatures only begin past the inner walls, for the actual residences of the Governor, so that's where Taliya has to do the majority of her ward-breaking. The plan is for the other teammates to wait for her to bring down the wards, having already snuck past the outer walls.

Naturally, Amari has their movements scheduled down to the minute to take advantage of everything they know. They'll all be split into teams of two. Taliya has the pleasure of being Kol's partner.

It only takes a couple of hours of going through simulations with the Sky Lord before she gets sick of him and ditches him to watch Amari and Nuru coach Erika.

The girl has vastly improved since they started training a few weeks ago. While there's only so much someone can learn in that time, Taliya will admit the teen went beyond her admittedly meager expectations. Truthfully, all her teammates, including Kol, have exceeded the low bar she initially set. She might even like this group apart from the sky rat.

It's while she's thinking all this and listening to Amari teach Erika about fighting dirty — since they don't have time to train her properly — that Taliya notices the third teenager on their team watching the training session as well. As she eyes the Sun Eater, she sees Najaah fall into a parade rest, her hands clasped behind her back and feet shoulder-width apart. The former soldier doesn't appear to notice her actions until Taliya turns to look at the girl fully. Najaah visibly winces, no doubt self-conscious that she hasn't managed to break the habit yet.

She unclasps their hands in a seemingly casual motion and tries to… slouch. Najaah's body acts like it protests the very idea of not having perfect posture, making the whole endeavor look very awkward. It's achingly clear that Najaah is desperate not to seem too much like she wants the ground to open up and swallow her when Taliya walks over.

Instead of judging or whatever else Najaah clearly braces herself for, the thief simply stands next to the teen. The Ashan quickly catches onto how Taliya is wordlessly demonstrating a more casual posture, and Najaah mimics the thief's stance.

"Don't overthink it," Taliya advises softly. "The secret is to be confident, or at least assured that you belong where you are. If you don't want to come across as military, get different shoes and watch how normal people move. It's not economical, but not complicated either."

Najaah absorbs this, and Taliya says nothing else. Obviously, not being seen as a soldier for a long length of time is proving difficult for the Sun Eater, and she can't help the swell of sympathy that rises in her.

The thief stands with Najaah quietly until the next part of the simulation begins, and she starts to leave when the teen feels compelled to acknowledge what she did.

"Hey. Thanks."

Taliya gives a small smile. "Don't worry about it. We've all been there."

She leaves Najaah with that mysterious comment.

As she wanders by Amari, the seer practically jumps her and shoves her into a simulation with Erika now that she's ditched the sky rat. Taliya pauses and frowns when she realizes what simulation Amari wants the girl to undergo.

"She shouldn't be getting so close to the residences before I put down the wards," the thief points out. The simulation will place Erika right by the wards that specifically keep out unauthorized magical signatures. If Taliya hasn't dealt with the security yet, her presence will set off the whole system.

"This is good practice anyway," Amari says. The look on her face tells Taliya that the seer is aware of all of the potential risks and is deciding to do this anyway. "Please walk Erika through it."

Squinting narrowly at her friend, Taliya hesitates before answering. "… Right."

If Amari is using the word *please* with her, then there's some shit Taliya doesn't know going on in the background. She glances toward

Erika. The girl looks at her with big eyes, fingers fidgeting, and shoulders tense.

Taliya sighs, putting as much drama in it as she can. "*Fine,* I guess we can do it. Let's go before this drill captain gives us more work, Erika."

Amari looks like she barely suppresses an epic eye-roll while the teen's mouth twitches tellingly. As Taliya leads the girl to the simulation, she can see her shoulders slowly relax.

"Alright, so…" Explaining the setup for the training session is easy after so much practice, and Taliya tries to avoid considering why this particular exercise is suspicious. Erika listens to everything she says with rapt attention, which she admits is flattering. "You get it?"

"Yeah, I think so."

"Alright, I'll go through the first run with you before letting you have free rein."

Taliya might also want to see if she can spot why Amari has Erika doing this simulation. Does the seer plan for the teen to get close to the wards?

The illusions begin by imitating the fortress as accurately as Taliya can render it. The next step is adding realistic security measures before the environment starts reacting to their presence. Inside the simulation, it looks like they're actually there.

Ward-breaking is the goal of this simulation. The most challenging bit of ward-breaking, specifically. Only Taliya and Amari have gone through it. Others might be capable of eventually dealing with the wards, except there's a time limit of sorts. Only a few minutes before the defense measures kick in, the alarm sounds, and every illusionary guard starts attacking.

Already, Taliya can nullify every ward in under a minute, though she expects the real thing will be more difficult. Amari can finish without any security activating. She doesn't understand why Erika has to go through this.

Thankfully, the teen already has a basic grasp of ward-breaking. She would make a decent Scribe, but Taliya isn't sure what magic Erika gravitates toward. Frankly, she's beginning to think the girl just doesn't have a gift for magic at all, despite the fact that there has to be *some* reason Amari is insistent about her presence.

Either way, Erika isn't a fast enough ward-breaker to defeat the security before the defense measures start in. Taliya doesn't help with the runework and focuses on keeping the simulation off her back so the teen gets an idea of how everything works. She ends up fighting guard dogs with multiple heads and sentinels twice her size. Some things slip past her, and she whirls around in time to see Erika evade a sentient plant.

Soon, Taliya decides to start purposefully letting some enemies reach the teen so she can deal with them. The thief isn't disappointed by the results.

Erika has the potential to be something. She's certain of that. Taliya just isn't sure what that potential is for yet. The girl has a lot of drive under her anxiety and is good at thinking outside the box.

Right now, she's managing to outmaneuver the simulation well enough while still going after the wards. Amari is probably watching out of the system's zone, feeling smug or something. Erika doesn't notice, of course, hyper-focusing on the fake situation they're in. Surprisingly, the teen keeps up a running conversation with her.

"—so that works. If we do this, can we break through the wards without inverting them?"

Taliya thinks over her plan carefully.

"Yeah, I think that will work. Do you think you can fight if it comes to that?" The simulation's enemies and security measures are predictable by nature, except the girl already struggles in spars.

Erika pushes her glasses up her nose and fiddles with the handle of her short wooden sword, which she shows some promise in using. A new wave of sentinels approach. "Yeah, I think I can avoid getting too badly hurt."

"Good, that's your priority. Staying alive to fight future battles is more important than dying in a blaze of glory."

For some reason, the teen gives her a long look. "Okay. Okay, let's go."

Taliya successfully leads Erika through the first simulation, then steps outside to stand next to Amari as the teen goes at it alone. She fails, naturally, for the first few runs. As they watch, Erika begins to make more and more progress until she has the wards down before any security notices and before any defense measures can get to her. It's not nearly as quick as Taliya's record, but it's good.

She turns to Amari. "You think we're ready?"

"As much as we can be."

10

ERIKA

Erika likes to think that she is patient. However, this belief is challenged the longer she is forced to wait outside the walls of the governor's fortress.

Beside her, Nuru is sitting behind the bushes and trees that keep them out of view from human guards and stone sentinel golems. He looks perfectly at peace while everyone else moves into position. Erika might be losing her mind in real time.

Eventually, she gives in to the urge to do something and pulls out an OmniClockwork's Watch™ from her pocket. She had bought it a week ago from a vendor in the cheaper parts of Castor's Market District, not realizing at the time it was cheap because it was terribly made. The thing broke after a few days. It was an inconvenience in the moment, but now it's an interesting distraction.

The watch's dial appears surprisingly basic, despite supposedly giving lots of information, with faded numerals that are barely legible. Its hands move with a jarring, erratic tick, something she doesn't think is intentional, while the vibrant face is a tacky yellow shade, giving it a sickly appearance. A small, unremarkable gem sits within the heart of the watch as a magical battery, and it appears somewhat out of place, like an afterthought. The whole device seems to be built more for the appearance of utility than for any functional purpose.

She systematically takes it apart, carefully cataloging the placement of each tiny inner piece and studying what makes the magic watch tick. Inside, the gears are more interesting yet disappointing at the same time. As someone who grew up surrounded by amazing feats of engineering, Erika isn't sure what to feel when discovering the minimal number of gears. Everything Upside seems to run on magic and magic alone, which she can't see, feel, or take apart.

The signal comes as a welcome distraction from the twisting sensation in her chest.

Everyone in place? Amari's voice echoes through her mind, sending shivers up her spine. The telepathic network is incredibly useful. Erika will give it that, but having people in her mind is deeply unsettling, no matter how she slices it. Even if they can only hear and see the things she wants to share.

Ready, Taliya checks in. Erika wonders how she gets Kol to stop chattering on the network. He wouldn't shut up during practice.

In place, Nuru sends for their duo.

Amari continues. *Good. Remember, most of the human guards are asleep, and the sentinels have a regimented schedule, so we do this like clockwork. Nuru and Erika, you're first. Wait for the delivery, then get inside. Make sure to disable some of the systems that send out alarms throughout the wards.*

Got it, Erika pipes in. Her use of the telepathic network is still a bit clumsy, so she sounds like she's talking through a scratchy intercom. It makes her wince even though no one else reacts.

Everything goes quiet as she and Nuru wait for the delivery to arrive.

Erika stares up at the governor's stronghold, trying not to let her uneasiness show. Massive dark stone walls, impeccably crafted and maintained, encircle the hold in a way that she finds instinctively sinister. The fortress's surface is etched with arcane symbols that glow faintly in twilight, a clear signal to the powerful wards that shield it from external threats. Threats like Erika and the team.

Avalon's three broken moons shine enough light to catch glimpses of the sentinels patrolling the fortress and highlight the runes that feed off the ambient magic in the air. Of course, Erika also knows the placement of the fortress's magic generator. Thankfully, the team won't be going near that thing. Messing with such powerful and intricate magic would be incredibly dangerous.

She scans the fortress's battlements, which crown the walls, and sturdy watchtowers that rise every dozen or so meters. From her spot below, she can see that these towers are equipped with enchanted lanterns that cast a continuous glow, illuminating and alerting sentries to any approaching danger. Each of the towers serves various functions: some are observation posts, and others house the human guards or armories. According to the team's information, every tower is adorned with intricate runes and sigils, along with enchanted crystals on the tops that capture and redirect magical energy. These towers are connected by an elevated walkway that allows for quick movement and strategic defense. Sentinels patrol these paths, ever watchful for potential threats.

And Erika is going to be up there in a few minutes. Her palms start sweating as her eyes flick to the fortress's front entrance.

The entrance is a grand gatehouse flanked by stone watchtowers on either side, and a pair of sentinels stand on either side of the gate. A grand portcullis, with iron spikes and bearing the governor's sigil, can be lowered or raised to control access.

It's like something from a fairytale that Erika grew up hearing about, but always felt many steps removed from reality. She would never have guessed that one day she would be Upside, and about to help rob a stronghold.

Erika?

She nearly jumps out of her skin. Nuru has opened a direct channel solely to her so they can communicate freely.

Yeah…? Erika is not used to telepathy yet. She really isn't.

Ready?

As she'll ever be. She nods to Nuru, who hasn't moved an inch since they hid here.

At the gatehouse, the sentinels lurch to attention. A transport packed with crates of food and other supplies rolls down the main road, powered by a much smaller magic generator than what would be in the fortress. Altogether, it looks like some strange mix between a car and an old-fashioned carriage without horses. The storage inside contains so many varying types of food that Erika feels dizzy. Who knew so many kinds of food were growing and living above ground?

The gate is raised, and the driver waves at the human guard, who steps out to inspect the delivery. She waits with bated breath as the sentinels turn to oversee the transaction, no longer looking out into the forest.

As soon as the driver exits the transport, Erika moves while Nuru begins to shift.

Between Erika's status as a Nullifier protecting her against any wards and Nuru's ability to expertly mask his magical signature in his second form, they have the greatest chance of getting into the fortress without tripping any alarms. The rest of the team—apart from Amari—believes that Erika is not very powerful and can hide her own magic signature more easily than anyone else.

With the wards not being an issue, Erika needs to focus on staying out of sight and keeping her lessons on stealth in mind. She and Kol have been getting extensive lectures about stealth from the others since the beginning. It's the one topic they have a united dislike for.

Hyper-aware of where she places her feet and any sound she makes, Erika darts forward as the sentinels look elsewhere. The gate is only opened during delivery or when someone comes in or out, so they have to make it inside *now*.

Amari explained weeks ago that the senses of golems like these sentinels do not work like humans. They're more attuned to magical energy than any human could withstand without losing their mind. That means they work similarly to wards. If Erika is outside their field of vision, they don't notice her sneaking past them.

Nuru flies overhead, past the outer wall. *No one is looking. Get through the gate now, Erika.*

Despite doing what feels like a million simulations of this exact scenario, Erika's hands are still sweating, and her heart is beating like it's trying to jump out of her chest. The sentinels don't turn toward her as she edges around them, back against the fortress wall. Her pulse roars in her ears, and some small part of her is telling her to freeze.

Take a deep breath. Nuru's mental voice is calm as it interrupts her budding internal spiral.

Telepathy with a bird is not making this experience less weird.

Erika takes a deep breath, ignores every panicky thought attempting to invade her mind, and focuses on slipping through the gate without a sound. Sticking to the shadows like Taliya taught her, she makes for the door of one of the gatehouse's watchtowers before anyone can see her in the open courtyard. The first room has a door that leads directly to the stairs, and she climbs all five stories like her life depends on it. The change of sentinels is soon, so she needs to move very quickly.

When the team studied the fortress's security, Amari noticed the laziness of the human security forces here. The guards rely too much on their wards and golems. Someone walking freely in their watchtower is a completely insane concept to them.

Erika makes it to the walkway without trouble, apart from her heavy breathing after five flights of stairs, and waits out of sight for Nuru. She takes the short reprieve to look out at the fortress she's been studying for weeks in person.

An array of towers surrounds the entire place, each rising majestically against the sky. Each tower has intricate runes and sigils that pulse with soft, ambient light that Erika finds enchanting to watch.

Sentinels mostly stay in the towers, but every thirty minutes, a patrol uses a walkway. Erika has the schedule memorized. There won't be any sentinels in this section of the wall for another ten minutes.

She confirms, to her relief, that a few floating walkways connect to the second inner wall, designed to offer an additional layer of protection. This wall is slightly less formidable but equally magical from what she knows. It's constructed from lighter, more ornate stonework. From a distance, Erika is surprised to see that it's decorated with elaborate carvings depicting mythical creatures and legendary battles. This wall encloses the central courtyard and is equipped with defensive mechanisms to thwart any who might breach it.

Below the walkways, the fortress features expansive courtyards that serve as functional and ceremonial spaces. Outside the inner wall, the primary courtyard is a vast, open area surrounded by lush greenery and carefully manicured gardens, interspersed with magical fountains that produce water that routinely changes colors. According to what Erika has read, this courtyard is often used for grand events, gatherings, and magical demonstrations the governor hosts. Smaller courtyards near the towers and inner walls are dedicated to training and daily activities, everything designed to accommodate the needs of the fortress's human inhabitants.

Inside the inner walls, Erika knows the governor's personal tastes come more into play.

Nuru's voice speaks up in her mind again, directing her to the nearest written ward. It takes a bit of a climb up the tower's roof, but Erika soon rests on the hard tiles with a runica in hand. Glowing with magic, the runes protecting against outsiders stare back at her.

For a moment, doubt fills her entire being.

A bird lands next to her. *Can you do it?*

I can do it, Erika confirms, focusing on the task before her. It feels a bit like taking an exam, except the stakes are slightly more life-and-death.

The runica is specially made for her since she can't channel her nonexistent magic through it. Instead, the device has its own small magic supply that she simply uses at her discretion, like a standard pen with an ink cartridge. It was made by Amari and Taliya — the latter of whom did not know why these specifications were made. Erika uses it to strategically write a new set of runes in front of her, feeling like a toddler destroying a painting with a marker.

She doesn't try to destroy or deactivate any wards, since that would set off a whole different set of alarms and cause general chaos. Runes that are broken tend to invert, like a destroyed healing rune reopening the wounds previously fixed.

Instead, she adds on unnecessary auxiliary runes to the ward that detect magical signatures. This brings up the threshold of detection, meaning her teammates can enter the stronghold without setting off every alarm. Unfortunately, it's not enough for Kol to fly directly into the governor's office. They're weakened, so the alarms won't trip the moment he steps within a yard of the wall. The team will have to sneak past the sentinels and other defenses without a dramatic amount of magic.

Done?

Yeah, when's the patrol? Erika doesn't risk leaning over the tower's roof in case sentinels are about to pass below.

Four minutes. We need to move.

It feels like a swarm of butterflies is trapped in her stomach, and not in a good way. Nuru flies above, leading her down the walkways and to one that connects to an inner wall. All the while, she keeps ducking to remain out of sight. At one point, she has to backtrack around a corner to dodge a wandering human guard.

Eventually, they reach a shadowed corner of the inner wall. Erika turns to survey the governor's personal space.

At the heart of it all, nestled away from prying eyes, lies the main residence. This central building is grand, and its architecture is a blend of ornateness and an obvious show of strength. The residence is constructed from enchanted stones that Taliya says shimmer in the sun. Its design incorporates sprawling balconies, vast halls, and intricately decorated chambers, all imbued with protective wards and comfort-enhancing spells. The opulence is even more nauseating in person.

The main residence is surrounded by a private garden, much more audacious-looking than the ones in the more public space. Paths are only accessible through sealed entrances. Erika's eyes skip over the explosion of colors, certain she could not name even one of the plants there.

She rethinks her priorities as Nuru shifts back into human form, looking disturbingly alarmed.

What's wrong? Erika makes sure to keep her message just between her and the shapeshifter.

He doesn't answer immediately, increasing her own fears. His eyes are scanning the vast garden over and over.

Learning about nature is a requirement for anyone in Rowan, he finally says. This sentence does not fill her with confidence. *Whether you're under the military's rule or an independent people, you learn. Rowan is a country that knows the importance of telling the difference between a poisonous mushroom and a perfectly edible one. Many visitors who don't take such precautions wind up in a hospital. Or just dead.*

Erika shivers, wishing she could blame the weather. *Does the garden have dangerous plants?*

Nuru lets out a chuckle he quickly muffles. She knows she's staring, but can't stop as dread rises in her. Glancing at the garden, her stomach drops. The flora occupies about a few kilometers of space surrounding the governor's residence. Erika only recognizes the lantern-blossom trees dotting the twisting paths, bearing large, translucent blossoms emitting a soft, ghostly glow at night.

This garden is basically a nursery for some of Avalon's most dangerous plants. Nuru gestures down the wall they're standing on, directing her attention to the twisting, thin vines that escape the garden to climb up it, with small, glowing buds that look like drops of liquid starlight. *These buds exude an adhesive substance, capturing insects drawn to the light. They're also incredibly poisonous, but only when ingested, thankfully.*

He points to the garden's fields of grass. *The silvery grass littering the place also slowly steals energy from whatever it touches. Just growing them is considered highly dangerous... And those red vines, at the heart of the garden, a mere brush against the thorns can send someone into a coma. Forever.*

Scanning the garden with Nuru only shows more potential dangers. The governor's fascination with the Ethereal Planes makes more sense if this is the man's idea of a homely garden.

Nuru and Erika are trying to figure out the best way to the main keep that completely passes by the garden when the sound of boots stomping on stone suddenly can be heard from the nearest watchtower. Without any thought to the consequences, Erika pulls Nuru over the side of the wall.

She expects him to leave her and shift, but instead, he instinctively grabs the vines with her, which are sturdier than they appear. The adhesive material helps them keep their grip. Thanks to the time she spent training, Erika doesn't let panic overtake her. Instead, she clings to the vines, keeping quiet.

The human guards — Erika would remember if a patrol of sentinels was scheduled for now — exit the closest tower, and walk across the wall. Idle conversation passes them by, and she doesn't bother trying to eavesdrop. The guards don't look down toward the garden and see two intruders clinging to the vines. Erika's fingers ache with the strain of keeping her grip, and her arms start to tremble as the guards disappear into the next watchtower. Unable to help it, she sighs in relief.

She tries to climb back up.

Naturally, this is when the vines decide to fail them. Erika frantically reaches for the wall itself as the vines start to slip, but the one holding her up snaps —

— and they fall.

Right into the garden.

She lands hard, inches away from trumpet-shaped flowers that let out ear-splitting shrieks if brushed against, and scrambles away, taking care not to touch any of the plant life. Luckily, Nuru has fallen onto a path and is only a meter or two away. Some small part of her is still surprised the man hasn't simply shifted and left her behind.

Groaning, she staggers to her feet, swaying slightly before righting herself. Nothing is broken, thankfully. The silver field, while dangerous, makes a much nicer landing pad than regular grass. *Nuru, are you okay?*

He nods, distracted as he scans and catalogs every dangerous plant in their vicinity.

Just some bruises. Look, Erika, this garden is full of dangerous plants, we need to be very careful as we leave —

He cuts her off with an alarmed look as she walks closer and freezes, following his gaze as a patch of the orchids he warned against earlier reveals itself. They're so beautiful, she thinks, considering these flowers can apparently trap her in an eternal dreamscape.

Put on your mask right now!

Each member of the team has emergency supplies with them. Nuru has the medical supplies between him and Erika, but they both have masks in case of a gas attack, though Amari might not have predicted orchids as the source.

Since this is probably far from the first time he's been on a mission that required wearing a mask at one point or another, Nuru has his over his nose in record time. While Erika doesn't hesitate to listen, her movements are not as seamless. Many items fall out of Erika's pocket as she scrambles for the emergency mask. With luck, she finds it and straps it to her face before any of the orchid's magic can hit her. But with luck, there is usually a downside, and she notices a tiny fire starter has unintentionally fallen a short distance away, rolling further off the path. Right into the silver grass.

She moves to grab it, only to be stopped as Nuru takes hold of her arm and drags her away urgently. Ominous crackling sounds start up around the fire starter.

What's going on? The fire starter isn't even activated!

The grass will activate it.

Erika remembers Amari giving her different versions of most of the emergency supplies. *Most of the standard stuff is activated by magic,* the Nightblood had explained. *So I'm giving you the ones that are much easier to use. Barely need any energy to turn on. Be careful with them.*

The grass, she remembers distantly from Nuru's rundown on the garden, is full of unstable, stolen energy. This means when they interact with a highly flammable object or substance, they can spontaneously combust.

Her mind is suddenly pulled into a memory of science class, when her teacher had shown the class a similar reaction by pouring some oil on an unstable magic battery in a controlled environment. It was fascinating how quickly everything had gone aflame. The sample magical battery had to be kept secure because idiot students would regularly try to steal it for poorly thought-through home experiments or dares.

… Ah, Erika says, watching the fire spread. *Shame Najaah isn't here.*

Somewhere else in the hold, Amari and Najaah both get a strong sense that something stupid is going down. They can't decide which other team it's coming from.

(The answer is both.)

Run? Nuru suggests, already pulling her further away. Erika decides to stop staring, and instead turns to sprint down the path, away from the fire. He follows on her heels, trying to keep track of the new flora they pass by. They have to dodge around a few more of the trumpet-shaped flowers hanging into the path to avoid bursting their eardrums.

Erika is pathetically grateful for the lantern blossoms, realizing that otherwise, they would be making this dash in the dark with only the growing fire as a guiding light. The path splits up ahead, and she nearly skids to a halt if not for Nuru leading her down the left path.

Do you know where you're going?

I remember a little from when we were up above. The other way leads back around.

Huh… Wait. *Why don't you just shift and guide me out?*

There's no immediate answer, just the shapeshifter running ahead as they avoid stepping off the paved path.

I don't think it would be wise. This garden is as hostile to unfamiliar animals as it is to humans.

But you're a bird?

Instead of replying, Nuru points at the ferns dotting the edges of the path and on top of the many garden walls. Erika runs through her memory, bringing up what he said about them before. *They're known to respond to intruders by attempting to grab and absorb them.*

Oh.

As if by Fate itself, a fern a yard ahead unleashes a grasping vine to entangle them.

The weeks of training against environmental attacks allow Erika the skills necessary to jump over in time. She lands off balance, staggering with the excess momentum. The vine whips around and nearly gets her the second time, but Nuru drags her out of its reach.

They're very aggressive, he explains. There's no panic that Erika can feel coming from him, which makes it all her own. She tries not to scowl.

Would they attack you if you shifted and took off?

Without a doubt. I would likely survive one attempt through, but not one back. And I would rather not leave you stranded here alone.

… You don't have to do that, Erika says, trying to sound confident as she sends this message. She thinks none of her fears leak through, but he still doesn't leave.

Something warm fills her chest, until the adrenaline in her veins distracts her from it. They hear shouting.

Looks like someone has noticed our little distraction.

Erika takes her eyes off the path long enough to throw a look over her shoulder. There's nothing chasing them aside from the occasional fern, and the combination of darkness plus high-rising plants block them from view. *Do you think they'll realize there are intruders?*

It's definitely a possibility. But the fire starter will long be ashes by now, and I would wager that this garden is a well-spring of accidents waiting to happen. This can't be the first time something innocuous has caused a mess. Let's be careful either way.

Fate decides to step in again, this time through sickly yellow vines, some of the plants bigger than Erika's head. They weave together into a solid wall five meters high, blocking off the path.

They react to strong emotions, Nuru tells her, glancing behind them to make sure nothing is chasing. *Yellow, if my memory's right, is fear.*

Erika can't help the laugh that escapes her, and the vines' barrier rises. *I think it's a little hard not to be scared right now!*

Don't let it blot out everything else.

Dragging her hand down her face, she rolls over the problem in her mind, hearing her heartbeat thundering in her ears, an annoying distraction and wake-up call all in one.

Breathing exercises. That's where she starts. Erika goes through the familiar motions as the shapeshifter keeps an eye out for threats. It doesn't erase the panic in her veins, but it makes her thoughts feel clearer. She sorts through the fear until she reaches the reason why she came here.

Save her home. Make it so that Erika's people can live under the open sky.

The fear doesn't fall away so much as it is crushed under a fierce blend of righteous anger and love.

It's all pretty cliche, in the end. Erika opens her eyes — not even remembering when she closed them — to see the vines' sickly yellow color fade to a healthy green before untangling. The path lies open once more. She can't help the small grin that grows on her face as they move past the fallen barrier.

Of course, they're still hopelessly lost in the maze of magical indistinguishable vines. Erika resolves to not focus on her fear, which at least keeps the path from being closed off again.

As the sounds of shouts fade behind the mass of vines, Nuru reaches out to the other teams to inform them of their situation. They slow down their running to a stop so they can pay attention to the conversation. Erika elects to keep watch this time while Nuru gives the report.

Let me get this straight, Amari says in the telepathy network. Up until now, she has been wordlessly observing while the others have thrown out comments left and right. *You fell into a garden of the world's most dangerous plants, immediately set it on fire, and are now lost in a labyrinth with carnivorous flowers?*

...That's one way to summarize it, yes, Nuru admits grudgingly. Amari doesn't respond instantly, letting her silence speak for her.

Just use blades to cut your way out, Najaah adds helpfully. Erika has a feeling that strategy would actually work for the Sun Eater, instead of getting them eaten.

Amari starts up again, new energy in her mental voice. *Okay. Okay, this can work. The fire starter would have been consumed in seconds, and the intruder alarm hasn't have gone off. Let's use this distraction to our advantage. Nuru and Erika, do you need our help getting out of the garden?*

Erika shares a look with Nuru, neither of them having to use the network to communicate their intentions this time.

No, Nuru says. *We'll make it out in the next ten minutes and get inside the main residence.*

For her part, Amari doesn't question their decision. *Alright, then Taliya and Kol must head straight for the residence right now. Deactivate as many wards as needed. Najaah and I will secure our exit plan and then meet you four inside.*

There's a chorus of agreement before the network goes silent again, everyone focusing on their part. Erika and Nuru start down the path, not quite running at a dead sprint but not slowly either.

At a sharp corner, Erika nearly runs right into a towering plant resembling a snapdragon she saw in her school's garden. Weeks of honed instincts allow her to swerve out of the way just in time for the plant's great jaws to snap shut in the spot she just occupied.

Embarrassingly, an alarmed squeak escapes her mouth even as she gains a fair amount of distance between herself and the giant plant. A humming sound starts up behind her, and she turns to see more of the enormous snapdragons along the path, waiting for her to get close.

Erika almost jumps out of her skin when a hand rests on her shoulder. Nuru looks at her calmly, though she swears she can see his mouth twitching as he tilts his head toward an upcoming fork in the path. Erika frowns.

Do you know which way?

I think we should keep going left for now. Otherwise, we might end up turning ourselves around more.

Nodding, Erika follows him down the left path, noticing that more plants are intermingling with the walls of vines. Some are red and have thorns… Didn't Nuru mention that before?

Edging more into the center of the pathway, she determines it's better not to get close enough to find out why he had warned against them. This garden has already given her enough nightmare material.

Of course, that's when the situation becomes worse by orders of magnitude.

A low, earthy growl rips through the air, freezing Nuru and Erika in place. They turn to each other, eyes wide.

Erika nervously reaches out through the telepathy network. *Did you hear where that came from?*

…No, Nuru answers slowly, scanning their surroundings. It just looks like walls of vines to her; the lantern blossoms give them light to see where they step, but not enough to stop the shadows from looming around them.

Something behind Erika rustles in the foliage, and she startles so hard she bumps into Nuru, who catches her from tripping and falling on her face. This is all getting too horror movie-esque for her tastes.

She doesn't notice in time, so Nuru has to push her out of the way when a beast the size of a truck lunges for them out of the darkness. Powerful jaws snap close where they had been standing a moment before, and ice spreads through every inch of her body.

The details are difficult to make out in the low lighting. Erika is kind of glad for it. Even in the dim light, it looks like a mini dragon hybrid has come out to hunt them.

It's a drake, Nuru says. Erika has never heard of a drake. *They're people's failed attempts at making dragons. They're small, wingless, and there's no elemental breath to worry about.*

That sounds great, if not for the fact that the beast in front of her is still fully capable of ripping them apart. She can make out four powerful legs, sharp spines trailing down the spine, and the glint of fangs from a great maw. It's scales flash in the blossom light, sending her stomach into free-fall.

So what do we do?

She barely gets the question out before the drake charges them, and Erika instinctively splits from Nuru to give the beast two targets instead of one. The shapeshifter fearlessly rolls under and away from the drake's claws. In a flash of movement, he unsheathes a dagger she hadn't noticed and slashes a leg. He must have targeted a spot not covered in scales because it actually injures the beast, forcing a strangled cry of pain from the drake.

It turns on Nuru in a fury and she panics. Hastily, Erika leans to the ground grabs a stone from the side of the path and lobs it at the drake's head. The thunk of the stone hitting hard scales and then clattering to the ground echoes in the unsettling quiet of the night.

Teeth bared, the beast looks her way. Erika freezes.

Too fast for her to follow, Nuru dances around the drake and slashes another weak point she can't see. This instantly brings the attention back onto him, and he nearly ends up clawed for it.

Belatedly, Erika remembers the thorns.

"Hey!" She whisper-shouts at the beast, and it swings its great big head back in her direction as Nuru gets some needed space from it. The dim light reveals slitted toxic green eyes, full of a depthless hunger she can't begin to fathom, and her hands shake as she clears her throat. "Come and get me, you dragon knockoff!"

Erika has no idea if it can understand her, but her words do the trick. The drake bears its fangs and surges toward her in one great leap of its legs. Only her training with the simulated monsters lets her stand her ground for the right moment.

Just before she's ripped apart by claws as long as her legs, she hurls herself to the side. Even with all her strength, it's not enough to come out completely unscathed. The tail hits her side mid-air, crashing her to the ground and leaving what she knows will be some very painful bruises.

But the beast still manages to collide where she had been standing, momentum pushing it face-first into the wall of vines, and, miraculously, into the red thorns.

It staggers to its feet with another bone-shaking growl, looking for all the world like it's about to eat her alive. Nuru appears next to her to pull her up, face grim, when the drake sways precariously.

Erika stares, transfixed, as the great creature fights the thorn's magic before falling to the ground with a loud thud. The drake's eyes close, one final glimpse of its burning fury imprinted in her mind.

Silence reigns for a few seconds, then Nuru collects himself.

Good thinking, Erika.

Warmth spreads in her chest, and she stands back up with a little help. Her side burns as she moves and Nuru is already pulling out a healing salve. Amari says to always pack the best medical supplies, and Erika is really appreciating this advice as the pain immediately starts to numb.

A noise from ahead draws her attention, making her and Nuru look up to see the vines moving. Her heart stops momentarily, fearing what new obstacles await.

Stone flashes in her visions, and her spine straightens.

Is that—

It's opening an exit for us, Nuru says, something like awe slipping into his mental voice. *Let's hurry.*

She doesn't need to be told twice and breaks into a dead sprint for the way out. The exit has an ornate stone arch, a direct contrast to the barely contained wild the garden contains.

Erika sees activated wards on the archway and dismisses them with the intention of keeping going when Nuru holds a hand up in a signal to wait. She stumbles and has to take a moment to regain her balance.

The runes around the arch… A shudder seems to pass through Nuru as soon as he reads them. He grabs Erika by the arm quickly and drags her back from it. *Wait! I know what that is. It's an Ultimate Barrier. It destroys all magic that it doesn't recognize. It's an extreme deterrent, I can't believe a governor is allowed to have one…*

Erika's eyes widen, and she looks between him and the arch multiple times. *It destroys magic?*

Yes, Nuru answers firmly, giving her a narrow look. *Hiding magical signatures won't stop it. As long the magic **exists**, it can be destroyed.*

The arch doesn't look treacherous, yet Erika can feel the gravity in Nuru's mind. She takes a moment to absorb the idea and looks back at the shapeshifter. Clashing expectations weigh on her shoulders, digging into her bones. *So if I have no magic at all…?*

Taken aback, Nuru hesitates. *Then there would be no effect, I imagine. But everyone has—*

Erika doesn't give herself the time to doubt her decision. She runs through the Barrier. For a split second, she feels like the arch is going to simply evaporate her, when… nothing happens.

Nothing happens.

Her shoes slam to a halt on the stone ground, and she slowly turns around with her heart in her throat. Nuru stares at the unactivated runes with wide eyes, mouth partially hanging open. It's one of the most genuine expressions she's ever seen on his face.

As soon as he recovers, he shifts into his second form instead of addressing what just happened. Erika watches as the bird dodges a few persistent vines to escape the garden and heads toward her. He touches down next to the girl and shifts back so fast she misses the transformation in the blink of an eye.

Erika shifts on her feet, her limbs feeling sore as the adrenaline slowly leaves her system. The enormity of what she has revealed begins to settle in.

Unable to make eye contact or ask what she really wants to know, Erika tries a different route. *I think the distractions are still working.*

I would hope so. I don't like playing with fire for nothing.

He doesn't start in on interrogating her, which is more of a comfort than it should be. It allows her the time to appreciate the belated happiness at being free of the damn garden. The lack of vines enclosing them feels like a welcome relief. She looks up to the night sky, grinning at the unobstructed view above her.

Naturally, Nuru collects himself much quicker than she does and takes stock of their situation. *We don't have long. Let's get inside the main keep.*

Erika agrees but wants to know where they are in the fortress first. She eyes the large building in front of her, trying to recall the blueprints. *I think we're on the west side. Not too far from the governor's office.*

Nuru nods in acknowledgment, following her to the west entrance. It takes longer than they would like since they must be watchful of sentinels and human staff. Eventually, they find an inconspicuous servant door and hide among the (thankfully benign) foliage where it is in line of sight.

We're outside the main residence, Nuru reports to the whole network.

So am I, Amari replies. *East side. Najaah is guarding our exit.*

We're south. Dealing with the wards. Give us a minute, Taliya's message comes with a flicker of frustration, seeming very distracted.

Is there a problem? Amari asks, not sounding as alarmed as Erika would be in her situation. The Nightblood always seems so unphased by everything. It makes the Nullifier feel jealous at times.

No, no, no, everything's – Kol speaks up and then cuts off. The network is silent for a few seconds.

Got it! Taliya shouts suddenly. *Everyone get in.*

Erika and Nuru only wait to see if there are any patrols coming before entering the servant door. From the layout, she remembers they need to head a few floors up and a couple of halls down.

Between their unintentional distractions, the governor being away, and the late time, the hold is rather empty. Nuru and Erika can hear when someone is approaching, and both quickly hide as they make their way up. The closest call is when a door a few feet in front of them inexplicably opens, and Erika barely manages to duck into a strangely spacious closet with Nuru before they're caught.

They stay like that, hidden from any prying eyes, and wait for a small group of servants to pass. Erika sees Nuru lean his head back against the wall they're sitting against as their nerves finally calm down.

Erika, he begins, keeping his mental voice gentle and even. *Can you explain what happened back there?*

Erika hugs her knees and hides her face, mind a contained storm of fears and hopes.

I'm... I'm a Sonia. A Nullifier.

Ah. Yes, I suppose that would explain it. He appears to consider what to say next carefully, before asking a question. It's not quite the one she expects. *Are you here on behalf of your people or yourself?*

How much can she afford to say? She can't tell anyone about the Divine Claim, and the existence of Haven Republic is meant to be secret, except her being here is already a clue in that direction. So perhaps it's better for Erika to be in control of what information is being spread?

My… people. Nothing bad! Just, I can't really…

I understand, Nuru says. *I am in the same position. We both will work together to get back to our homes.*

She lifts her head and stares at him silently for a beat, emotions warring inside her. He waits patiently.

Why are you being — nobody is supposed to know, I mean —

Nuru nods, cutting off the mental stuttering as she tries to collect her thoughts. *My people and I know well what it is like to hide for fear of being hunted. The Sonia have done a remarkable job not revealing their existence to the wider world. I would not put that in danger.*

Shamefully, Erika's eyes start burning with vigor, and she rubs at them with her hand. *Thanks. Do you think I need to tell the others? Amari knows and said I could keep it secret, but…*

But the mission is proving that keeping this secret will be incredibly difficult and perhaps ill-advised.

He so easily puts her own thoughts into words. Erika wishes she could supplant all of his experience so she didn't have to make such a fool of herself all the time. *Yeah.*

Do you believe any of the others would take advantage of this knowledge?

From what she's seen, only Kol is likely to make a big deal of it. Taliya and Najaah certainly won't care; the two will just take it into account for the mission like Amari. The thought of the reveal still makes her hands shake, even after the relief Nuru's reaction brings.

What if she becomes the reason the Haven Republic falls?

Erika, the shapeshifter gently calls for her attention. *I'll help you tell the rest of the team, and I'm sure Amari will, too.*

Oh. ...Thanks, Nuru.

Of course. Now, let's hope we're not the last ones to reach the office.

11

TALIYA

On the other side of the fortress, at the bottom of the cliff, things are going… a little differently.

What do you mean you can't climb well? You can FLY. Taliya thinks as loudly and judgmentally as she can in Kol's direction. Despite this very logical fact pointed out, the boy stays on the ground. Without the ability to use his magic to a normal degree, he really is rather pathetic.

Arms crossed, he scowls back at her, not meeting her eyes. *I'm just not that great. It's not a big deal why —*

How have you NEVER mentioned this before while we were training?

You didn't say the climb would be this bad!

Did you look at the maps at all?

Kol looks at his feet, not answering. Taliya tips her head back towards the sky, internally curses teenage boys, not for the first time, and then starts pulling out her emergency rope a little more roughly than strictly necessary.

…What are you doing, Taliya?

Improvising.

She securely ties the rope in a makeshift harness around her before turning to Kol. He glances at her, the rope, then back to her.

Can I pass —

Nope!

Once he's fully tied up, Kol's face rapidly pales as he stares up at the cliff, looking for all the world like someone afraid of heights despite being a fucking Sky Lord.

To be fair to him, the cliff face could be considered intimidating if someone hasn't spent their whole life walking a razor's edge and dangling from barely visible grips by the tips of their fingers. Taliya knows this logically and yet can't quite get herself to feel very sympathetic to Kol's plight. Especially since he could have mentioned it at *any time before now.*

He swallows and turns to her. *If I fall, you'll catch me, right?*

That's what the rope's for, dumbass.

…Okay.

Once they start climbing, she privately tells Amari why they're a little behind schedule, and the seer sends Taliya her amusement over the link. The thief sends back the emotion everyone feels when giving someone a particularly rude gesture as she pulls herself up.

Kol is slow. Taliya has no other words for it. She is used to moving at a much faster pace, and right now, she is tied to someone currently moving at the speed of a lethargic snail. She carefully breathes in and out while one hand holds her whole body up on a small pocket in the rock.

I am going to carry you up. This is all the warning she gives.

*You're going to **what**—*

Taliya tightens the harness more, double-checks Kol is secure, and then climbs at a more normal speed. She reaches higher, even as the rope pulls taunt, and uses a foot against sheer rock to push herself up. A barely suppressed scream is left in her wake.

The strain tugs at her harshly, and her back muscles start to burn, but Taliya would be bored to tears if this was easy. She allows Kol to swing below her, looking like he is rappelling up.

Taliya… Do I weigh anything to you?

I've climbed higher places with stolen shit ten times as heavy as you strapped to my back. You're fine.

Great, Kol says, still seeming very frazzled. She ignores him and focuses on the last stretch of the climb, which becomes easier once it switches from the natural cliff to the southern walls of the fortress. She drags the two of them up onto a walkway facing the back of the main residence.

Once they're at the top, Taliya surveys the giant walls with distaste, packing away the rope while Kol lies down on the ground. Rising above the walls are turreted towers surrounding the governor's home and office. They are massive, cylindrical in shape as they punctuate the fortress's skyline, and they have arrow slits, showcasing their defensive capabilities.

Atop the parapets closest to the grand residence, stone gargoyles imbued with protective spells watch over the stronghold. They occasionally come to life to defend against threats. Best to watch out for those, Taliya reminds herself.

She nudges Kol with her foot. He groans but starts to move, acting ridiculously tired for someone who was carried the whole way here.

According to the schedule, the pair only has two minutes until a sentinel patrol passes by, catching them chilling on a walkway. One of the walks connecting the outer and inner walls is close, so she leads the two across it while keeping all of her senses attuned to their surroundings.

Before Taliya starts down the wall, Nuru and Erika's plight in a frankly nightmare-ish garden comes to light in the telepathic network. She now eyes the inner courtyard with a more wary eye. Instead of going down immediately, she pulls Kol onto the roof of a watchtower to avoid patrols.

Surveying the large garden, she maps out where it ends.

Okay, she directs Kol, who has been impatiently waiting this whole time. *The governor's garden of terrors is primarily to the north and stretches eastward and westward. If we go down to the right spot on the southern wall, we'll bypass it entirely.*

So, where are we going?

Let me figure it out.

Taliya pinpoints a good spot in between a few patrols to climb down, about to turn to tell Kol, when a thought occurs to her.

Hey, she privately connects to Amari in the network. *I know Najaah isn't coming into the inner courtyard yet, but how are you getting past the garden?*

An image appears of a cobbled path with clear protective material arching above and keeping out the dangerous fauna. *I found a hidden, safe path. This is probably where the governor takes guests through, so they can look but aren't threatened by the plants.*

Fucking seer powers.

Fortunately, for her and Kol, the way down the walls into the inner courtyard is much easier than climbing the outside. Taliya doesn't need to tell Kol what to do; he has better luck finding crawling vines he can use to descend than he did climbing up.

She touches down on the ground cautiously, knowing there likely aren't any motion sensors in this part of the stronghold, but she still feels wary. Never underestimate the weird shit paranoid rich people can pull. Nuru and Erika have certainly learned that lesson tonight.

Kol follows, less wary and not as quietly. Taliya resists the urge to glare and focuses again on their surroundings. They have a clear shot at the back door to the main building, except she doesn't like how open it is. Right now, the duo is in the shadows of a smaller building.

According to her mental map of the fortress, these should be... stables?

Peeking into the open window of the building, Taliya stills.

Kol looks in a moment after — and nearly gives himself a concussion, pushing himself away from the stable and into the wall.

The creature inside seems indifferent to them, except Taliya feels a touch of something like hunger, causing the hair on the back of her neck to stand up.

Vaguely horse-shaped, yet the similarities end there. Instead of a traditional mane, the creature sports a tattered, hazy wisp of shadows that seems to writhe and twist on its own accord. Its velvety, inky black coat is so dark that it seems to absorb light rather than reflect it. Massive wings that look more like they belong to bats than birds flare slightly at their presence.

Its legs are unnaturally elongated and angular, adding to its already skeletal appearance. The hooves are misshapen, with elongated, gnarled, and serrated edges, but the creature's eyes are its most unsettling feature. She feels like she's looking into a hungry abyss.

Taliya takes a careful step back and tries not to think about what's only a few feet away, separated by a wall that suddenly seems very flimsy.

This is, of course, when a surprise human patrol on the wall they just climbed down decides to start walking by them. Taliya quietly curses human spontaneity with great feeling. She hears them first, ears always listening for danger and catching the sounds seconds before they're going to walk into their sight lines.

The two thieves cannot be seen. The guards will not miss them out here, and somehow knocking them out or killing them from the courtyard would only keep the rest of the hold in the dark for a few minutes at most.

Fuck.

Taliya glances between the guards about to discover them and the dangerous-looking creature.

She grabs Kol by the arm and drags him with her as she opens the wide window, leaping into the stables. He tries to land gracefully but immediately jerks away from the creature into her, and she almost loses her balance. Taliya hastily closes the window, shoving the teen into a corner out of sight just as the guards pass.

While the heavy steps pass over them, she makes a point to keep strong eye contact with the creature. It stares back at her, almost as if it's deciding if she would be better served with or without salt. Taliya mentally projects *'we're really not that tasty'* as strongly as she can.

It doesn't leap across its enclosure to tear them apart, so maybe it works.

She resists the urge to nervously tug on her braids or fiddle with her concealed knives. Instead, she stays perfectly still, waiting.

As soon as the guards are gone, Taliya coaxes Kol out of his corner, and they edge out of the stables. The teen all but flings himself from the window as she follows, glancing back at the creature with wary looks.

She takes the lead as they sneak toward the main residence's back door. It's not the kind of entrance used for guests, but also not plain enough for regular servants. She figures it suits their mission fine.

At this point, Taliya would prefer to climb the building and break in through a window, but she and Amari decided the abundance of gargoyles outside the mansion was a risk they didn't want to take going inside. Leaving the building will be easier.

Thankfully, every servant is working elsewhere or on break, and the guards aren't timed to pass by in a while, making the coast clear. Just when she feels she can relax and things are going smoother, Taliya gets a good look at the wards.

She stares at the runes in disbelief, mouth slightly agape.

Oh, this is — this is absurd! How much money did the governor spend on this shit? What a —

What's wrong? Kol looks to be growing increasingly concerned.

The runes can't even be touched by anyone who doesn't have the right magical signature.

He stares blankly for a moment, then frowns as his brows furrow.

Can't you — I don't know, go around that? Kol manages to mentally project the idea of hissing these words. Taliya sends back her extreme irritation.

That's not how any of this works; wardbreaking doesn't look like it does in stories!

So we're stuck?

No!

Kol pauses, confused beyond words. Taliya has no pity.

It's locked to the governor's magical signature. I'm going to deactivate or delay as many of the alarms as I can, and then you're going to overload the wards until they're dead. Got it?

It's much more complicated than her simple order, but she doesn't think over-explaining will be helpful at this moment. Better to phrase it in a way that Kol will feel confident about.

Got it, Kol grins, small wisps of pink energy sparking around his fingers already. Taliya holds back a sigh before getting out her runica.

She turns to the wards with a laser-sharp focus. Not all the runes are physically in front of her, so she has to stretch her senses far out to get a feel for their structure. To her, the runes act like a lattice. Targeting one can still do damage, but because everything is interwoven, it will set off every single alarm.

Luckily, the way the fortress's lattice is set up isn't very efficient. Divided into sections — the main residence, the walls — focusing more on supporting those sections than the greater whole. This makes cutting the sections off from each other shamefully simple.

What makes Taliya the best ward-breaker is how quickly and smoothly she dismantles that lattice. She can scribe faster than most, channeling her magic into runes like it's second nature. And she's always been good at puzzles. Amari sees the big picture, but Taliya focuses on the problem in front of her and doesn't let anything else bother her.

The specific magical signature lock is an annoying hurdle that is easier to scale with Kol here. He essentially will put so much pressure on the lattice that it breaks all at once, while Taliya will ensure that he doesn't light up every alarm in the fortress.

The problem…

The magical signature lock means that the moment they mess with these wards, the governor will feel it. So Taliya has to do her very best to delay that realization. Mainly by layering as many signal blockers as she can over the alarm.

Suddenly, the telepathic network starts up in her mind.

We're outside the main residence, Nuru's mental voice says. Taliya holds back a curse, carefully speeding up her wardbreaking, motioning for Kol to start.

So am I, Amari speaks up. *East side. Najaah is guarding our exit.*

For final touches, she adds her own wards to prevent Kol's power from spreading beyond the runes in front of them. Or at least will let her know if he's using so much magic that her wards break.

Biting her lip and flicking her braids over her shoulder, Taliya gives a distracted report as she keeps almost all her attention on the wards. *We're south. Dealing with the wards. Give us a minute.*

Kol steps forward and rests his hands on the wards. Soft pink energy wraps around his hands, and the wards begin to glow. First, a standard white light, then changing to Kol's pink as his magic overwhelms the runes. She can feel power wafting off him in small waves and resists the urge to grimace.

Is there a problem? Amari asks, a hint of amusement in her message. Taliya privately sends her a mental kick.

No, no, no, everything's — Kol decides it's a grand idea to talk while doing incredibly fragile work. He cuts off as her wards go off, indicating he's putting too much power into it.

The teen pulls back, and after a few seconds, the wards slowly dissolve, leaving nothing behind.

Got it! Taliya grins and stashes her runica. *Everyone get in.*

Shoulders slumping, Kol gives her a small smile. Taliya elbows him in the ribs and heads inside the primary residence with a skip in her step. She can't help but feel the thrill that they managed to get inside without any major emergencies and with minimal scarring.

Taliya wrinkles her nose in distaste after she steps into the massive home of the governor. Kol whistles under his breath, and she resists the urge to stomp on his foot.

The hallway has polished marble floors that reflect the soft glow of crystal chandeliers hanging from the high, vaulted ceilings. Each wall is decorated with fancy tapestries depicting scenes that look appropriately pompous to Taliya. She can't imagine how Amari is reacting, considering the seer always has an opinion on the art people display in their homes.

She doesn't want to imagine how ornate the main entrance to the mansion must be if this is just what the back one looks like. On the plus side, Taliya won't lack in the amount of valuable items to pilfer along the way. And with the governor's clear fascination with unique magical trophies, she's sure to find something interesting.

Meters down, there's a grand staircase with polished wooden steps that curve gracefully upward. The balustrade is made of wrought iron and gold, its scrollwork painstakingly crafted to resemble vines and flowers. Enchantments are weaved into the very stonework of this building, but not for anything useful. Taliya internally scoffs at all the ways she sees magic being wasted so carelessly. If half the energy going into pointless aesthetic spells were used for security, she would have a much more difficult time breaking in.

Everything is so ornate and expensive that it crosses into gaudy. This governor is making up for *something*. Taliya scans the hallway for something useful. She finds it tucked away in shadows, above any reasonable person's reach.

Vent, Taliya sends Kol, expecting him to get the plan. He stares at her with raised eyebrows and a flitting tail. Rolling her eyes, she points to the ceiling. *We're moving through the vents. The office is three floors up and almost 300 meters northwest. It'll take us forever if we stay out in the open trying to dodge security. Those vents are big enough for you, too.*

From his grimace, she can see he wants to argue. Kol, Taliya has noticed, isn't a huge fan of getting dirty or going into small spaces. This is both. She waits for a protest that doesn't come.

….Fine. Lead the way. He waves his hand in a seemingly nonchalant manner. Taliya mentally shrugs and darts toward the vent. It's high up on the wall, just below the ceiling, but that doesn't mean anything to her. She jumps and uses her momentum to run up the wall until her fingers grab onto the metal pole holding an ugly tapestry. Taliya pulls herself higher and holds herself with one hand as the other removes the grate covering the vent in smooth, practiced motions. Catching the grate so it doesn't fall and make a noise, she looks to Kol and gestures at the open vent with her head.

The teen purses his lips before squaring his shoulders and running for the wall. His ascent is much less graceful without his magic lifting him, and Taliya has to extend a leg for him to grab so he doesn't fall back down. Without looking her in the eyes, Kol scrambles to pull himself into the vent.

He's unnecessarily loud about it, and she makes a low hushing sound before following him into the vent. She quickly gets the grate back on, leaving no evidence of their presence in the hallway.

Under her hands, the metal hums with the power of

enchantments that run throughout the whole mansion.

Vents like these play a crucial role in maintaining a building's internal climate. They are part of a sophisticated system that regulates airflow and temperature, ensuring that each room remains a comfortable temperature. With the money the governor likes throwing around, Taliya is sure no expense has been spared. She can practically feel the elemental magic in the metal under her fingertips. She can feel the water.

Functionally, controlling the moisture in the air prevents issues such as mold growth or damage to delicate furnishings and artwork. This is particularly important in areas like libraries or art galleries, where maintaining optimal humidity is crucial for preserving valuable collections.

The water being pulled and moved around just so happens to mean she has easy access to her Osiyi magic. Manipulating it wouldn't even trip the magic sensors.

However, the vents' magic also means Taliya has to be careful if she messes with the runes woven into them, or they'll end up in a metal box rapidly moving to extreme temperatures.

That's not the only risk. The vents are also equipped with air purification systems. Most of it is harmless — the system filters out dust, allergens, and unpleasant odors. Some of it isn't; with the governor's inclination for the strange and dangerous, she's wary.

Drawing herself back into the moment, Taliya squeezes past Kol and starts heading down the vent, keeping her mental map of the mansion in mind. She is mindful of actively slowing her pace to avoid leaving the Sky Lord behind. Mercifully, she doesn't comment on it.

It's lucky she insisted on leading the way because Kol would not have caught the first security measure they hit inside the vents. As it is, Taliya barely notices the discrepancy in the seams of the metal before a section slides to reveal a flamethrower. Only her instinct makes her hum an off-key note that sends every drop of moisture around them to douse the flame as it fires up and saves the thieves. After that, even Kol is on edge and watching every corner.

Taliya manages to disable most of the traps — runes meant to set off alarms if someone passes over them, blades that would jump out of the walls, little golems that patrol the vents for mainly maintenance reasons — even as a few stall them for a couple of minutes. She ends up with a large bruise starting to bloom on her shoulder after pushing against a wall that began to close in on them. The teen isn't much better off, having gained a cut above his eye from one of the little golems. She hopes it scars, just because it would be a hilarious story to tell.

Most of the journey is them looking at a seemingly endless metal chambers peppered with booby traps, but the grates they do pass are interesting.

There's a drawing room with a grand fireplace, its mantel decorated with priceless art pieces and rare artifacts that Taliya eyes with consideration. Crystal vases filled with exotic-looking flowers stand atop elegant side tables, their fragrance mingling with the subtle scent of polished wood and leather that filters through the grate. The second place she sees is a dining hall with an enormous, intricately carved oak table that stretches across the room, flanked by high-backed chairs upholstered in rich fabrics. Admittedly, she finds the room rather beautiful, if a bit over the top.

Taliya almost stops when she passes a grate showing a library with floor-to-ceiling bookshelves filled with rare tomes and antique volumes. The room is lit by a combination of enchanted sconces and large windows that let in natural light. Amari would love that room, she thinks.

After climbing a floor and heading down a long stretch of the vents, they come across a grate that shows people inside the room. At a glance, she identifies it as a kitchen. It's less ornate than the rest of the mansion, yet equally well-equipped, and she can tell it is maintained with the same level of attention to detail. The kitchen features state-of-the-art appliances she's seen only in ads and a large, polished marble island.

There are three sensibly dressed servants, one leaning against a giant fridge and the other two sitting on the island. From their relaxed posture, it's an easy guess that they're not working. Just people slacking off and chatting.

Taliya snorts softly to herself. Everyone's the same, even the ones in the Apolon Empire.

Kol nudges her, lips pursed. *Why are we stopped? What's going on?*

I want to see what they're talking about. I just wish I could hear what they're saying. It might be useful. The staff always knows all the secrets.

One of the downsides of being in the vents is that Taliya can't hear shit happening outside. The governor really went all out with his gaudy mansion. The vents contribute to the mansion's soundproofing, and they're designed to minimize noise transmission between rooms and floors, ensuring a 'peaceful and serene environment,' according to the manufacturers. The magical enchantments within the vents dampen external sounds and prevent echoes, allowing for a quiet and undisturbed experience throughout the mansion. Taliya thinks it has less to do with creating a peaceful environment and more to do with ensuring no one eavesdrops on something scandalous.

Rich people.

Kol sneezes behind her, the dust getting to him at the oddest times.

She's about to move on when a thought hits her, and she stills, her grin growing. The teen lying on his stomach next to her is staring at her warily. Ignoring him, Taliya pulls out her runica and gets to work.

In addition to everything else, the vents help distribute ambient magical energy throughout the mansion. If too much builds up in one place, things can get…weird. And she's certain that the governor has plenty of weird artifacts that need these kinds of regulations.

This energy helps power various enchantments and magical features within the home, while the vents ensure it's evenly distributed. So, if Taliya can manipulate the ambient magic, she can theoretically dampen the soundproofing. And because of Amari, she has more than enough experience with hearing enhancement runes to draw one behind her ear. The whole process takes less than a minute, and afterward, she can hear the servants talking.

" —telling you, it's true," the one leaning against the fridge says with a sly look on his face. Taliya mentally tags him as Horns due to the six medium-sized horns on his head that look like a crown.

"No way," the tallest of the trio is an Ashan with a tight bun of flaming orange hair, who she dubs Citrus because of the hair and the large bowl of fruit next to him on the island. The third servant has bark-like skin and small antlers that betray their youth. Horns, Citrus, and Junior—what secrets do they have for Taliya?

Horns doesn't appreciate his colleague's doubt. "*Yes* way, I overheard it from the governor's main secretary! You know she has all the dirty laundry."

"Doesn't mean you heard right," Junior speaks up, and Taliya catches a slight smirk on their face from her angled view.

"Hey! I can prove it, too, asshole. The new shipment arrives in a week."

Citrus wrinkles his nose in distaste. "The one with all the creepy artifacts? No thanks, we're already too close to where all that stuff is stored. I would rather be ordered to clean every single one of the mansion's bathrooms in a day with a toothbrush than go poking around that cursed shit."

"Gross," Junior mutters. "Don't manifest that."

However, Horns isn't willing to let go of his point. "But wouldn't it be so cool to know the future?"

Taliya thinks she stops breathing. It certainly feels like her lungs are empty of air.

"Isn't that, like, super illegal, though?" Junior asks, eyebrows furrowing. Citrus waves a hand in their direction as if to say, *see, they get it!*

"I don't think the governor cares," Horns snorts. "The mirror is supposed to give glimpses of the beholder's future. Some old seers made it before they became traitors."

Ignoring the blatant lies regarding certain historical events, Taliya's mind runs through the situation. An artifact made by seers... Amari has been trying to get as many as she can find, which are far and few in between. Most are, unsurprisingly, destroyed or lost.

She's suddenly very glad that Kol cannot hear the conversation without the body enhancement runes, even as he keeps nudging her impatiently for information. Her stomach feels like it's clawing up her throat, and the effort it takes not to react visibly is exhausting.

"That's wild," Junior admits, sounding more intrigued than before, and Citrus sighs heavily. "Think it gives good or bad fortunes? I heard seers liked to trick people into messing up their futures. Like a 'you get what you wished for in the most fucked up way possible' kind of thing."

Horns shrugs carelessly. "It'll be interesting either way, right?"

"You're an idiot," Citrus says.

The conversation moves away from anything useful at Horns' offended squawk, and Taliya's attention drifts. Her mind keeps coming back to the mirror. How many more seer artifacts are sitting in Imperial trophy rooms? Just the thought of Amari's face at this news makes her blood boil.

After heaving a world-weary sigh, Taliya deactivates the hearing enhancement runes and gives herself a minute to digest before focusing back on Kol, who is moments away from tackling her out of sheer frustration.

She sends him her best attempt at a wry smile. *The governor is up to some shady shit, surprise, surprise. We need to be more careful about security as we move forward because we're heading into the wing where he keeps his more dangerous artifacts.*

Does he have his office next to where he keeps his cursed objects? Kol frowns, brows furrowing. A smile graces Taliya's face.

I don't think common sense is something we can expect from him.

Kol snorts and looks pensive, which she takes as a signal that she can move past the eavesdropping session. *Let's keep going, or we won't make it in time.*

Taliya has been keeping an internal timer running in her mind the entire heist, with Amari occasionally giving her updates about the rest of the group. Right now, Nuru and Erika are close, while Najaah guards their exit strategy. Amari is focusing on her other objective, which is searching the governor's personal chambers for anything useful.

Luckily, Kol doesn't argue, and they start picking up the pace. She still has to be careful as she dismantles traps and other security measures, but the time running down motivates her to be as efficient as possible.

Instead of shutting off the alarm system entirely, she uses the simpler method of delaying it. There's no way they get in and out of the governor's office in the middle of his fortress without raising some kind of alarm, so Taliya focuses instead on giving them the time they need to pull this heist off.

Climbing the vents to other floors is easy for her, except apparently, the teen needs coaching to go up a metal shaft with no gear. It's moments when something she thinks of as so fundamental is foreign to someone else that she wonders what other kids learn growing up. At least the teen manages it with minimal grumbling.

Somehow, they still make it to the office first. Taliya wonders what could possibly be holding up Nuru and Erika.

The office's floor plan is large, so there are multiple routes through the vents to get inside. She scouts each one from a distance, sensing the greater security waiting as soon as they cross the threshold into the office.

Already, she can barely catch a glimpse of a transparent barrier that blocks each of the vents' routes. Once she chooses a path, she begins working on removing the barrier. Kol helps her by overloading some of the runes she points out to him while keeping a watchful eye in case he overdoes it.

She crawls forward, catching a little security golem that jumps out with one hand and sliding it down the vent for Kol to deal with. Other traps, like blades popping out of walls and targeted energy attacks, eat up precious seconds of her time. Eventually, she reaches a grate that overlooks a good portion of the governor's office.

Best of all, it's the closest grate to the desk. Set in the ceiling, it gives her an optimal view of the space.

Taking an important minute to scan over the room with her eyes, Taliya realizes what she must do. A ward wraps around every object in the office like a blanket. If she just drops to the ground, she'll set it off. The runework isn't in the walls, which is standard. She searches for the ward's anchor until she spots the small pyramid-shaped gem on the desk.

Perfect.

Shifting her bag so she can reach in, Taliya pulls out the rope for the second time tonight. She's always glad to be prepared.

What are you doing? Kol predictably makes a fuss when something he doesn't understand is happening. Without a word, she hands him one end of the rope before tying herself to the other.

I need to get to that pyramid on the desk without touching the ground. You're gonna hold this end of the rope and slowly lower me, got it?

From Kol's widened eyes and eyebrows trying to leave his forehead, she deduces he doesn't get it. Instead of explaining it more, she starts to secure his end of the rope to him while he blinks at her owlishly.

This seems like a bad idea.

Nonsense, sky rat, it'll be fun!

Using the nickname pulls him out of his head, and Kol sends a fiery glare at her. She grins back and resists the urge to piss him off more.

Alright, Kol, don't drop me. Taliya turns to work with the grate, ignoring the flash of panic she catches in his eyes. No time to hesitate. She straps the grate to her body as she pulls herself out of the vent to prevent it from falling to the ground, and then carefully descends into the office without touching anything.

She's suspended high up for a moment before Kol begins lowering her inch by inch. A part of Taliya wants to tell the teen to hurry it up, but knows the kid's nerves must be in tatters already. She can be merciful occasionally.

As a whole, the office exudes an air of wealth and the desperate need to be seen as powerful. The spacious layout is accentuated by high ceilings decorated with intricate moldings and a shimmering chandelier that catches the light of the moon in the dark. Rich mahogany furnishings are meticulously arranged, with the large, polished desk at the center, its surface strewn with elegant stationery, and the pyramid she is targeting. A wide window overlooking that perilous garden sits behind it.

The wall to the left has long bookshelves that are clearly there more for aesthetic purposes than for actual reading. Along the opposite wall, display cases made of reinforced glass showcase a collection of the governor's exotic artifacts, hopefully not as dangerous as the ones in his vault. Most of what Taliya feels is disgust at the sight of all this opulence, with a side of calculated greed. Everything is so obviously just for the sake of serving as status symbols. She'd love to see how much any of it is actually worth.

As soon as she is in grabbing distance of the pyramid, she tells Kol to stop. Taliya pulls out her runica with one hand while the other goes to a different tool in her metaphorical belt.

It looks like a small pair of metal tongs a blacksmith would use, but it's precisely for situations like this. When wards have a physical anchor like this pyramid, touching them sets off all sorts of alarms. The tongs Taliya has are designed to adapt to the energy of any ward, temporarily tricking the anchor into thinking the tool is a part of it.

She carefully lifts the pyramid with the tongs, hands steady as a rock. With the runica, Taliya starts to break the wards scribed into every surface of the pyramid.

The whole process takes her a good five minutes of their limited time, but it is worth it to avoid the no doubt intense traps this office is decked out with. On the pyramid, the runes fade away as soon as there's no more power running through them, and she nonchalantly lets the now-useless object fall to the floor.

All good now, sky rat, Taliya tells Kol, feeling his relief even as he bitches about the nickname. The way he carefully lets her down is telling in its own way.

Not even twenty whole seconds after the wards are down, the office door opens, and Amari waltzes in, followed by Nuru and Erika.

We're behind by seven minutes. Let's hurry up, the seer says to the telepathic network, not overly worried despite her words. Taliya rolls her eyes and turns to look at the office with an analytical gaze.

Something in the floor plans always seemed off to her.

There's probably some secret compartment or room. Look for a trigger to open it, she sends to the group. Erika's eyes light up in interest, and she immediately turns to the fancy-looking bookcase on the left wall of the office. Ignoring the girl's strange enthusiasm, Taliya looks at the other two with a raised eyebrow. *Why didn't you use the vents?*

Nuru gives her an inexplicably exhausted look. *We decided to simply use the halls.*

Kol throws his hands up from behind, where he had just jumped out of the vent.

Taliya shakes her head at the shapeshifter. *Well, that's why you're late, you had to dodge people constantly!*

Alright, let's move on, Amari cuts, her mental voice full of good humor. *Time is getting low, remember?*

Taliya muffles a surprise burst of laughter at the terrible pun. Then she returns to business, running her mind over where a secret compartment would be. The wall's dimensions are off, and if she narrows it down…

The whole right wall is too far forward for her liking. She inspects its length, doing her best to ignore the artifacts on display, which are often stolen treasures from conquered lands.

A click sounds out behind her, and she whirls around to see Erika with a book pulled out on one of the shelves. The hiss of the moving wall makes her turn back to the right wall, and a door reveals itself in front of her.

I can't believe that worked, Erika's mental voice is hushed in awe for some reason as she says this.

Ignoring the teen, Taliya studies the hidden door and scrunches her nose at its warding. Like always, security is focused too much on conventional wards and not much else. Admittedly, whoever did this runework isn't so bad. They must have outsourced the wardmaking—this is too good for the idiots on the Empire's payroll.

She pulls out her runica again. Light catches on it, even with it being the standard black, pen-shaped base. This time, others can clearly see there are obvious additions, mostly runes, that make the tool more effective.

She catches Nuru staring at her with astonishment on his face.

What?

That's the most illegal runica I have ever seen.

Erika squints at her runica before her eyes widen dramatically, and Kol tries to lean in to get a look.

Taliya snorts but doesn't comment. Her runica may have *some* homemade upgrades that aren't allowed. She turns back to breaking through the wards at ten times the speed a normal runica can accomplish with only a *smidge* of smugness.

Instead of her, Amari answers the shapeshifter's unspoken question with a proud smirk. *Taliya has been breaking the Empire's wards longer than most of their ward-writers have been employed.*

Nuru scoffs quietly, seeming impressed despite himself. He and Erika both look like they're thinking over how useful a tool Taliya's runica would be. Only Kol seems not to fully understand what's happening.

Erika, you do these ones while I finish here. Taliya starts directing Erika and then Amari to help her. Under their combined forces, the wards fade into dormancy in three minutes. Kol whistles lowly.

Taliya wastes no time basking in her accomplishment. She immediately begins checking for traps in the doorway before moving into the room itself.

The hidden room isn't very large. Easier to miss in the design of the building, she knows. With walls that seemed an alloy of iron and silver, no one can use magic to see inside or send any enchantments inside. A vault, essentially. The governor is more paranoid than Taliya had thought. She would approve if the bastard weren't a corrupt imperialist.

Interesting, Nuru notes in the network. *No Empire insignia in here.*

Yeah. Taliya isn't surprised. She expects the governor to care more about himself than even the empire he works for.

Shelves of books, scrolls, and folders line the walls, each reaching to the high ceiling. There is one large chest against a shelf, likely full of tangible valuables. With a grin, Taliya beelines for it while Amari focuses on the shelves. The Nightblood quickly assigns each of them a place to search.

Inside the chest, every manner of jewel sits inside. As tempting as it is simply to stuff as much as she can in her bag, she resists in search of anything interesting the chest might contain. There are some rare coins, a necklace that clearly costs a fortune, some enchanted metalworks…

Taliya holds up a dagger made of an unidentified alloy and features a blue, jewel-encrusted handle with fascination. This is —

Amari, Erika says, breaking the silence that has fallen. Taliya turns to see the girl give Amari an open folder. She catches a glimpse of the word 'exploratory' before it's passed over. Nuru and Kol abandon their search to get a look.

Is that it? Kol feels impatient, and his eyes glint with curiosity. Amari hums, not looking up from the document.

It's a report for a mission sent to explore the Ethereal Planes, Erika answers instead. *They mentioned 'a great library beyond anyone's wildest dreams.'*

Sounds like the right thing, Nuru smiles softly, wrinkling the creases around his eye. Kol grins in response as Taliya joins the group, her bag considerably more full than before they came here.

Show me where this was, Amari suddenly speaks up, catching Erika's attention. The teen nods, and they privately communicate in front of a shelf for a minute. Amari grabs five additional folders and turns back to the rest of the team.

If you want something else from here, get it right now. We're going.

On that cue, Nuru seizes some of the scrolls he had been searching through before. Taliya randomly stuffs more of what had caught her eye into her bag and snatches another expensive-looking trinket off a shelf while Kol just shrugs.

Okay, let's go. Remember, this time, no fires.

Nuru and Erika share a tired look.

Amari turns down Taliya's offer to lead them out through the vents, so they end up opening a window down the hall of the office and scaling down it after a patrol passes.

Why didn't we do this earlier? Kol asks since he apparently forgot to read about the gargoyles. He soon realizes why as they awaken one on their way down.

The great stone beast stirs as they pass by, attention zeroing in on Kol and making to lunge—

—only to be hit directly in the chest by a flaming arrow that shatters it instantly.

The poor kid jerks back so hard that he falls down the last ten feet to the ground. He just lies there for a minute as the rest of the group follows, the wind knocked out of his lungs.

Thank Najaah for the save, Amari tells him as she offers him a hand up. He takes it with a dazed look in his eyes. *She has our exit.*

By exit, the seer means their *ride.*

It doesn't dawn on Taliya what Najaah must have commandeered from the governor before the carriage led by the winged horses from someone's nightmare lands in front of the group.

Both Kol and Erika shriek, jumping back from the creatures like they're waiting for the beasts to lunge. Taliya is feeling somewhat sympathetic to their plight. Amari and Nuru are the only ones who have anything resembling a poker face.

The governor's absence and the fact that it's the dead of night are the only reasons they haven't been discovered yet. Wasting no time, Amari corrals the group and forces everyone—*yes, everyone, this is our best escape route, get your ass in the carriage*—into the death trap.

At least Taliya feels more secure sitting inside the carriage, away from the winged beasts. She has no idea why Najaah and Amari are so okay with sitting up front with the reins. Stuffed in the back with Nuru and the other two teens, everything is rather tense and quiet for the first few minutes.

Then, as the carriage takes off smoothly into the clouds, the group collectively realizes they have successfully pulled off their first heist, and everyone collapses in relief. Erika's eyes are dangerously teary, Kol grins in delight, and Nuru heaves a sigh like the world has been lifted off his shoulders.

They fly away from the fortress at top speeds, and Taliya doesn't look back.

12

ANNORA

Colonel Annora Bashkim watches the images flicker in front of her dispassionately. For all Sabina's fuss about rebels stirring trouble in Zie, Annora only sees evidence of desperate individuals, not organized efforts.

This is, of course, when she gets an urgent message that says suspected rebel terrorists robbed the personal office of the governor of the Tera Sector. The thieves broke into a heavily secured fortress and made off with highly sensitive material.

Annora closes her eyes, sighing as she waves the gem's message away. Governors are never pleasant to work with. They're always politicians who are motivated by profit or fame rather than duty. More than likely, this governor will be more interested in covering his own faults than anything else. She would bet real money that whatever information was stolen wasn't supposed to be in his personal office in the first place.

A new message pops up, containing a summary of everything taken by the thieves. She scans the list, eyebrows rising as she scrolls down.

Multidimensional travel.

If only Annora had made that bet, she would be making a killing.

She leaves her office unhurriedly, nodding at the soldiers stationed around the base as she passes them. The blue patches on their uniforms signal them as both Singers, different from her purple Conjurer's marker.

"Colonel!" A captain with a red Scribe patch salutes and lets Annora into the Portal Room.

She walks in and steps through the multidimensional doorway with familiar ease. Years of experience traveling between worlds make the process as simple as stepping through any other door. It takes her to an open field, gray grass swaying in a soft breeze, and a violet sky swirling above her.

The being that manifests before her is not very solid. It seems like smoke of varying and constantly shifting colors, trying to shape itself into something vaguely person-looking. Someone seeing it for the first time would likely be incredibly unnerved. Annora merely sends it a friendly smile.

"Greetings, Kera, how are you?"

Its mental voice is a poor imitation of a mortal, like the words don't fit quite right, but it manages to project Apolona well enough to Annora to be understood. *Colonel, you have a problem.*

Kera knowing that Annora has a task before she even asks is never a good sign. "Did someone tell you that, or did you See it?"

The being's form shifts in a way she has learned means it's feeling mischievous. *Fate is moving, Eternal One.*

She hates being called that.

"Can you explain?"

Nothing is set quite yet. What you do next will decide many things.

…Great.

"Thank you, Kera, your wisdom is always appreciated." Annora considers her next moves. She does still have a job for the being. "How do you feel about tracking down some thieves?"

13

ERIKA

Erika finally breathes a sigh of relief when the flying carriage touches down less than a mile outside Castor, out of sight but still close enough to reach on foot. While the multiple train rides it took to get within reach of the fortress were incredibly nerve-wracking, this flight somehow felt more stressful, despite only taking a few hours.

"Damn," Kol says, and the words spoken aloud startle her. The telepathic network has faded from her mind as it deactivates. "Those monsters got us here ten times faster than the trains could have."

"Yes, that was rather the point," Nuru says dryly. Next to Erika, Taliya is napping, her head resting against the window, and only wakes as the carriage rolls to a complete stop.

"Ugh," the thief mutters. "Now we have to *walk*."

Pursing her lips, Erika looks out her window to survey where they've landed. It seems to be a stretch of clear land blocked from view by a grove of trees, who knows how far away from any road.

She can't help the question that escapes her next, fingers digging into the cushions underneath her. "What happens to the horses and carriage?"

Taliya waves a hand carelessly. "Oh, Mia has some people who will take care of it."

Fingers tightening further, Erika frowns and debates saying more when Nuru sighs. She looks at the shapeshifter and finds a sympathetic smile on his face. "I think she means to ask if the winged horses will be alright?"

"Those things?" Kol mutters under his breath. Taliya blinks at her owlishly.

"Uh… Well, Mia will make sure they're alright. I mean, they're super useful, so the Underground Resistance will definitely take care of them. I could…ask her for specifics later?"

"Thanks," Erika smiles, fingers slackening. She can't even explain to herself why the thought loosens something in her chest. Then she notices Nuru's attention on her, and a question in his eyes makes her swallow. "I—uh, have something to share with the group."

A knock on the door cuts off any response to her words, and the carriage door on her side swings open to reveal Amari. "Everyone ready?"

"Erika wants to say something? Right, Erika?" Taliya informs the Nightblood, her voice sounding unsure. Purple eyes with black sclera and white pupils lock onto Erika. Without a word, Amari seems to understand her intentions instantly.

"Alright. Let me grab Najaah, and we can talk."

As the last two cram into the carriage, Erika tries to decide how to reveal her secret. The task is so daunting, even more than how she felt telling Amari and Nuru. Just as her nerves are about to shake her apart, a calm and cold hand rests on her shoulder. Amari looks at her evenly, a knowing expression on her face.

For a brief moment, the network winks back on between her and the Nightblood.

"*It will be okay,*" Amari sends her, projecting a wave of

reassurance. Erika feels a tension leave her that she didn't know she was carrying.

"So, what's this about?" Taliya asks, sprawling out in the small space the corner of the carriage provides. Between her and Amari, Erika feels a little boxed in. Across from her, Najaah, Kol, and Nuru watch her carefully with different emotions. The Sun Eater is too neutral for her to parse, while Kol seems expectant, and the shapeshifter simply gives her a comforting smile.

"Well, it's..." Erika has no idea how much she can explain without it being dangerous for her home. "I'm a Nullifier."

Silence. Amari is like a steady stone next to her as she sees a collection of emotions pass through the others. At least Nuru is calm.

"Is this a joke?" Kol questions, bafflement radiating off him. His brows are scrunched, and he's staring at her like she claimed to be from a different world. She might as well have, really. That might be more believable than a people long thought extinct or entirely non-existent.

"No, it's the truth," Amari backs her up, voice even but firm. "This isn't something to be shared with anyone outside of this group. We all have our secrets, and this one is just something we need to know because of our mission. Telling others will be Erika's choice."

Warmth fills her chest, and Erika ducks her head to hide a smile. *Thanks.*

Of course, the Nightblood sends back through the private link. Out loud, she continues. "We only need to know because this means Erika can cross most wards and get past security without issues. Ones we can't dismantle without taking too much time."

There's a moment of quiet as the new information sinks in.

"Explains a lot," is all Taliya says, nodding like this information is just par for the course. Kol's head swings at the thief, mouth gaping.

"Thank you for sharing this with us, Erika," Nuru says, eyes glinting. On the other side of his seat, Najaah's face flashes a ghost of a smile.

"It's good we know," the Sun Eater nods, ever practical. "You don't have to explain more."

"Hold on—" Kol starts and is cut off by Najaah lightly elbowing him in the ribs and Taliya kicking him in the shin. "Hey!"

"Don't be a fucking bigot, sky rat," the thief mocks, smirk lighting up her face with mischief.

"What? I'm not—I have questions, damn it, stop kicking me!"

The laughter bubbling up in Erika can't be suppressed, and she has to cover her face as her shoulders shake with mirth. Amari pats her shoulder in commiseration, not bothering to hide her own amusement.

"Alright, reveal's over. We need to ditch this thing and move," the Nightblood commands, not unkindly. The group stumbles out of the packed carriage, not entirely gracefully, and Erika breathes Esma's fresh air with a smile.

After tying the winged horses securely to a tree—and Amari confirming that Mia's people will come to collect them soon—they head off into the approaching morning. Apparently, they're only ten minutes from a road to Castor, and they march back to the city as the sun rises steadily on the horizon.

By the time they reach the city limits, Erika has remembered she's starving, and so has everyone else. Despite initial plans to head immediately to the two thieves' apartment, the group agrees on a detour. Then they argue over food options until everyone collectively throws up their hands and heads to a diner.

"A Hall resident owns this one," Amari explains as they invade the small restaurant. The owner gives them a tired look from behind the counter, but otherwise doesn't comment on their no doubt sketchy appearances. Erika is pretty sure she still has twigs in her hair.

The food is practically divine, though that might be more of a result of how tired she is than the actual flavor. Her full exhaustion hits her, and Erika has to steel her spine to get clean first before passing out as they leave the diner. The stairs up to the second-floor apartment have never seemed so mountainous.

Before she can call dibs on a shower, Taliya pulls her aside with force as they enter the apartment. Wistfully, she sees Kol commandeer one of the two bathrooms, while Najaah has already gone into the other.

Turning her attention away from her longing to be clean, Taliya grabs Erika's hand and places the dagger she stole from the governor's office in it. Even as someone who knows next to nothing about weapons, the Nullifier can tell it's a masterpiece of craftsmanship. The blade is forged from a silver metal that catches the light with an unnatural glow. Intricate engravings run along its length, with swirling patterns that seem to move as if alive.

At the pommel, a larger, oval sapphire sits with a soft internal light, pulsing gently, as if in sync with the wielder's heartbeat. Erika can tell this jewel is not just ornamental; it is a battery of sorts for magical energy. The grip is wrapped in fine leather, providing a secure hold, and is accented with tiny silver studs that add to the overall elegance.

Erika feels like if she touches this for too long, the value will drop. "Ummm."

"You need a weapon."

"Yeah, just—this is—I guess I want something I can't kill someone with?"

This, inexplicably, makes Taliya grin with sharp teeth. Erika is violently reminded that the thief in front of her could easily be related to the giant creatures categorized as Osiyi that hunt whales in the ocean. Every piece of art depicting them in Haven always looks terrifying.

"That's why I'm giving you this."

"Uh…huh?"

Taliya rolls her eyes and takes back the knife. Erika has no time to feel relieved or have any other emotions when the thief stabs a book lying on the closest table.

"HEY!"

A blinding flash of light makes Erika instinctively flinch and cover her eyes. When she finishes blinking the spots out of her vision, she notices the book is gone. Only the knife remains, and it clatters onto the table.

"What the..."

Sidling up to her, Taliya holds the knife up to show her the blade. Erika doesn't see herself in the reflection. Instead, to her great confusion, she sees the book. Without explanation, the thief moves away toward the table again and taps the handle's sapphire three times in a row.

The light flashes again, and the book appears on the table, completely unharmed.

Erika's mouth drops open, not caring about her dignity. "That... is so cool, how does it do that?"

Taliya hands the dagger back to her, and this time, Erika gladly takes it.

"It's a special kind of dagger that, clearly, stores objects and living things without harming them. They're in a kind of stasis in there, so any person stabbed wouldn't be hurt if captured or driven insane from isolation. The magic is self-contained, so anyone can use it as long as they keep it well-stocked with energy. This kind of enchanted item is tough to find and even more difficult to make, but it works perfectly for you, doesn't it?"

Erika has no idea how to express the warmth welling up in her chest. "Yeah. Yeah, this is perfect. Thank you, Taliya."

"I also have another idea," the thief says, steamrolling past the heartfelt gratitude, eyes lighting up. "Those things you wear on your face help your vision, right? *Only* your vision?"

"You mean... My glasses?" She can't help the bafflement leaking into her voice. "Yeah?"

Taliya nods along, grinning. "Well, I can put translation runes on them. They'll work as long as the magic doesn't depend on the wearer, right?"

"Oh, uh, yeah," Erika confirms, feeling a bit overwhelmed.

The wardbreaker is practically vibrating with excitement. "I'll have to update your equipment specifically for you then."

"Amari already—"

"I'm doing it!"

Erika feels she'll disappoint the woman if she turns her help down. "Alright... Thank you, Taliya."

The thief ruins the moment again by ruffling her hair with a little too much force. "It's fine, kid. Don't mention it."

Amari sits everyone down at a table in the warehouse a few days after the events at the fortress. She has the information they stole spread out in front of her, neatly organized, and with notes added in the margins in bright colors. Hand-drawn maps are scattered around the table for everyone to see, and Erika can't help but admire the artistry of the works despite their origin.

"Okay, so, I've gone over everything the Governor has," Amari says as she lays out a couple more pieces of parchment that showcase sigils that Erika is sure she will have to memorize. "There are only two Ethereal Planes we have to go through to reach the Archive, but they're both very dangerous. Luckily, I have been to one before, which gives us a better chance."

All of this is said so matter-of-fact that Erika almost breezes past the reveal. "Wait, you've been to the Ethereal Planes before?"

"Of course," Amari replies, sounding like *she's* the one being weird for asking. "That's why I'm the one who studied the expedition."

Erika blinks dumbly, not sure how to respond to this information. Kol, similarly, makes a strangled noise before everyone collectively moves on.

"Anyway, getting out of Avalon at all will be a challenge," the Nightblood continues like nothing happened. "The stable gateway we need to go through is under the control of the Order of the Flame."

Everyone grimaces. Erika wants to ask some clarifying questions, but feels it would be too revealing. The Order of the Flame, as far as she is aware, is the official religion of the Empire. She has no idea what that means beyond the obvious.

"A subtle approach would be best," Nuru suggests. Amari nods, and Taliya pulls out a map showing the layout of a large building—a church, Erika realizes belatedly. Or a cathedral might be a better word.

"We'll go over the details later," Taliya grins sharply, making Nuru eye her warily, yet he says nothing as Amari goes to the next part.

"The gate takes us to a spot a couple of kilometers away from the Red City, which is a Portal Nexus."

"A what?" Kol asks to Erika's relief. She really dislikes being out of the loop.

"That's what a realm is called when it has more than three stable gateways to other Ethereal Planes. Avalon is a Portal Nexus. The Red City has twelve gateways, and one leads to the Forsaken Forest."

Nuru leans forward and grabs a map that tracks a path through a long span of woods, going over the markers along the line leading to a symbol that looks vaguely like a door. "Why is it called that?"

Amari huffs, rolling her eyes at something only she knows. "Because imps are dramatic and bad at naming things. The Forest is a kind of a dumping ground for things that are lost to other worlds. Plants and animals that have gone extinct, legendary monsters that never truly existed, that kind of thing."

"Lovely," Nuru mutters. "And it has a portal to the Archive?"

"Yeah, a direct gate, but it's a trek through the forest from the Red City's portal to that one," Amari says wryly. "The way back to Avalon from the Archive is both easier and riskier."

Eyebrows rising, Erika gives her a baffled look. "How so?"

"Because the Archive is an Unstable Nexus. It has multiple portals to all kinds of worlds, but they're unstable. They come and go, and the destinations are constantly changing. According to the Expedition, though, there was always a portal to Avalon there. The placement just kept moving periodically. A gateway directly to the Empire's capital is the only portal they stabilized."

"So… we can leave the Archive and go directly back to Avalon, but where we land is a game of chance?"

Nodding, Amari pulls out a folder from one of her piles and passes it to Nuru. Najaah leans over to get a glimpse of it over the man's shoulder. "I think we should have plans for two main scenarios: one where we backtrack through the forest and Red City, and one where we use an unstable portal to return to Avalon."

"Good idea," Najaah speaks up, glancing at the maps with sharp eyes. Erika prepares herself for a long day of discussing mission logistics and gets comfortable in her chair. Under the table, she catches Kol sneaking candy like a student stuck in a long lecture. They make eye contact, and instead of snitching like she might have at school, Erika sticks her hand under the table. Smirking, Kol bribes her into secrecy as the rest of the team becomes absorbed in the mission details.

As soon as the discussion (and loud debates) about this and that are over, she hurries off to the local library, which, at that point, is hours later. Erika spends another hour wandering the shelves and leaves with a small stack of books. She argues with herself over returning to her tiny rented room before deciding to go to the Hall apartment, where there are comfortable chairs and snacks.

The apartment should be relatively empty when she arrives since, as far as Erika knows, Amari, Taliya, and Nuru are still going over plans. At the same time, Najaah tends to disappear in between group sessions to places unknown. So she's surprised to hear sounds from the kitchen area when she enters through the front door. What she finds nearly has her dropping her books in shock.

"What is this?" Erika pauses in the entryway, staring in horror. Kol has the audacity to look only slightly sheepish.

The kitchen is a wreck. No surface has escaped being covered in flour, with the bag lying miserably half-spilled on the floor. Various mystery sauces splatter the window behind the stove, black smoke rises from the oven, and the dish rack is inexplicably on top of the fridge. Burnt remains of what must have once been food smolder in the sink while the water runs, nearly overflowing. Random cupboards are open, yet nothing seems to be used for what they're meant for.

A gasp escapes her as she spots the overstuffed garbage bin. "Is that a pot in the trash?"

"Uhhhh….. I couldn't get it clean?"

Erika glares as harshly as she can and gets the satisfaction of seeing Kol wilt. She really has just one question. "...Why?"

Kol coughs awkwardly, not meeting her eyes. "I… thought it might be nice? I think? People are supposed to make food for… People they… work with, right?"

This is where Erika's mom might say, 'It's the thought that counts,' but Erika doesn't believe the kitchen deserves that injustice. "Sure, if they know how to cook. You clearly… don't."

Kol continues to look more like a kicked puppy than some not-prince of a faraway land or the devastating Conjurer he is. She refuses to be moved.

"Look," she starts, giving the kitchen a despairing glance. "Amari and the others will be back in like five hours for dinner. I'll help you clean this up as long as you promise to never use a kitchen unsupervised *ever* again."

He reluctantly agrees, clearly understanding the only other option is to deal with this alone and inevitably face Amari and Taliya's wrath over the egregious destruction of property.

It takes half a dozen enchanted sponges, two buckets of soap, and the better part of four hours to make the kitchen not appear like a band of gremlins had a full-on food war in it. Naturally, the other teen is a protégé at battle magic, but apparently can't perform a tidying-up spell for the life of him. They haven't spoken about anything other than who-wants-to-clean-what at first, and then Erika can't help getting more curious about Kol's sudden desire to do something for someone besides himself.

"It's just..." He begins, thankfully not pausing as he scrubs down another ruined pot. "You guys don't really have to put up with me, even if I can help, but instead, I'm here, and no one's even asked me to do anything in return except train. And in *team* exercises."

What a depressing thought. Erika shudders at the idea of going around thinking every nice thing someone does has to come at some kind of price, even if she is wary of excess kindness. "Not everything's a deal, you know. Amari's pretty kind under all that... intensity. Nuru, too."

"I know, I know, I just mean—I feel I should do something," Kol pauses, clearly embarrassed, then gives up altogether on what he was saying. Erika isn't sure what to say either.

"But you... You help with the team all the time! I—" She purses her lips, trapping words in her throat. "You're very helpful. I don't think anyone would believe you don't pull your weight around here."

Kol shrugs, not looking terribly convinced. Erika surveys the kitchen, which has reached some form of order. She looks back at the ridiculous boy, sighing like the world is weighing on her shoulders.

"Fine."

Kol looks up. "Fine, what?"

"Fine, I'll help you cook something!" Erika stomps over to the fridge and scans its contents for ideas. "We have ingredients for stir fry, I think. Enough for the whole group."

There's no reply for a moment, then, "Erika, you want to help me?"

She doesn't turn around. "I'm hungry." As she pulls out some meat options, she possibly catches a reflection of Kol grinning, but doesn't care either way.

It doesn't go as terribly as she fears. The whole process takes longer than usual, with Erika coaching the other teen through the entire thing and familiarizing herself with a new kitchen. The food is up to par by the time the rest of the team piles into the apartment.

Amari scans the whole kitchen with a raised eyebrow, like she can somehow see the uncooked rice that decorated the wall next to the fridge a few hours before. She doesn't comment on it, though, so Erika will take it as a win. Of course, Taliya proceeds to tease Kol relentlessly about helping cook for the team, and it takes a great deal of effort not to join in and reveal that this was his idea in the first place.

Dinner turns out to be good. Erika doesn't feel the yawning emptiness in her chest, something that had become the norm since coming Upside. Sitting at the table in the Hall apartment, eating homemade food with people she now considered friends, even with all of the good-natured bickering happening, everything felt right.

She settles in to read, as she initially planned, after dinner. The books from the library are stacked neatly on the coffee table, and Taliya threw a blanket for her at some point that ended up draped over her legs. Of course, she only gets twenty minutes or so to herself before being interrupted.

"Here," Amari says as she places a small box in front of Erika on the table, effectively yanking the teen from her reading. She has been bringing more and more books with her to study, and usually, the others don't bother her when her nose is in a book.

Erika leans forward to inspect the box, deciding it must be important if the Nightblood is interrupting her reading. The small chest is wooden, decorated with metalwork, and has careful runes carved into all sides. It's about as wide as her hand, and Erika pushes up her glasses to get a better look at the runes. "What is it?"

"These kinds of containers are used to store dangerous materials. Or, really, anything that might be prone to causing a mess if left unattended."

The teen leans back. "And why is it here?"

"I thought you might find what's inside helpful," Amari smirks before using a careless hand to undo the latch and open the box.

A vial sits inside, set into a soft cushion. The liquid is a shimmering teal that transfixes Erika if she stares too long. Despite being a relatively small amount of whatever it is, she stays wary and doesn't move closer. "What is it?"

"Eliza found it mucking about the Kiyoshi Crater," Amari explains as if this is supposed to be comforting. "You can consider it the residue of a ghost."

"A *what?*"

"A ghost."

"Ghosts aren't *real,*" Erika says, feeling hysterical. Ghosts cannot be real. The Nightblood gives her a terrifyingly contemplative look, as if something just occurred to her.

"Yes, I suppose your people don't have the magic to leave that kind of imprint behind..."

"Please stop saying terrifying things like that, Amari," she begs, moments away from giving up and going to bed.

"Anyway," the woman waves her hand carelessly, ignoring her words. "This will let anyone who ingests it see the flow of magic for a short time. It can be dangerous for people with too much access to magical energy already, but you'll be fine. I'm giving this to you in case of emergencies. Not sensing magic can be detrimental in the wrong circumstances."

"I'm not putting that in my backpack," Erika says point-blankly. The thought of *ghost residue* stuffed with her books, flashlight, and folded picture of her mom makes her sick.

Her lips turn into a smirk, and Amari's eyes glint as she looks down at her. Erika tries not to look away from them, as unsettling as they can be for someone unused to them. "That's what your dagger is for. Consider it free storage space."

That's… really cool, actually.

"Oh."

"Good?" The Nightblood stands smoothly, leaving the box with Erika as the girl nods hesitantly. "Then we should be ready soon."

Erika and most of the team are in the warehouse when Taliya bursts in. Everyone turns to her, some instantly ready for some kind of fight (Najaah), some looking like they just jumped out of their skin (Kol), and one watching calmly with a raised eyebrow (Amari).

"What's got you in a huff?" Amari asks, sounding like she's trying not to laugh. Taliya stalks forward into the great space to the table they're all sitting at, which is utterly covered in plans and takeout boxes.

"Mia gave me this," the thief throws a slip of paper onto the surface. Erika can make out a hastily written message in a coded language from her spot. Or maybe she just can't read the handwriting? Amari picks it up and casually scans the words.

"I see."

"It's them," Taliya says in a disgusted voice. Erika stares in confusion, as does everyone except Amari, who rolls her eyes.

"I know. Of course, it's them."

"Who is 'them?'" Najaah asks. She glances around the table to see if anyone else understands, to no avail. Sometimes, it's a little irritating for these two to be so in sync compared to the rest of the team.

"The Night Witches," Taliya answers with clear distaste. This makes Najaah and Nuru turn to the thief immediately, their bodies tense. Erika glances at Kol to see if he recognizes the name. From his furrowed brows, he's as in the dark as she is. "A trio of mercenaries, all extremely annoying."

"Annoying is not the word I would use for the Night Witches," Nuru mutters under his breath.

Najaah tilts her head in agreement. "Maybe 'deadly' or 'destructive.'"

Amari snorts, eyes on Taliya. "Tal's just not over that time Miri and Nadia pushed her into a lake."

"No, I'm not!" Taliya gestures dramatically. "They're menaces, and Marina is always trying to kill you!"

"I think she just likes the challenge," Amari shrugs, completely nonplussed by this. Now Taliya is the one to roll her eyes.

"So you're... Enemies?" Nuru asks, eyebrow raised. Erika is glad he voiced the question that everyone is thinking.

Taliya nearly shouts, the movements of her hands uncharacteristically aggressive as she waves them about, her braids whipping around dangerously. "Yes! They constantly take commissions hunting us or something equally ridiculous! They're the only reason we've had failed jobs! Marina literally said she considered Amari her 'nemesis!'"

Here, Amari scoffs. "She's just dramatic."

The thief throws her hands up. "Fine, don't blame me when that maniac finally succeeds at kidnapping you or something!"

"And they're coming after us now?" Erika cuts in, hoping to stop the budding argument. Taliya looks at the Nullifier like she forgot she was there.

"Yeah, definitely."

"What are their abilities and weaknesses?" Najaah switches quickly over into interrogation mode. Amari, for some reason, shoots her an amused look.

The Nightblood clears her throat. "Okay, well, Marina's the group's leader. She's smart and pragmatic, so it's usually better to avoid her altogether. Keep any advantage or disadvantage close to your chest. Marina is an Andan Conjurer; she can control animals and see through their eyes up to five miles away, so be aware of that. Her familiar, Bolek, is a Great Hystern Falcon, who she typically channels magic from. Thankfully, her mental magic is specialized towards familiars, but be careful of the tricks she can play on humans, too."

"Terrible bird," Taliya mutters. "Always tries to claw out my eyes."

"Miri is a scientist and scholar before a mercenary, which is both a blessing and a curse."

"She will do anything for research funding!" Taliya scowls at the roof like it's the source of all her troubles. "And loves blowing shit up!"

Amari sighs. "Basically. Obviously, she's an Artificer. Miri can tap into nearly every type of magic to a degree, though she usually sticks to elemental or nature-adjacent for her artifices."

Najaah's eyebrows go up. "Seriously?"

"…So she can make any type of artifice given the time and resources?" Erika tries to make sense of what Amari is saying.

"Yep!" The thief continues to look incredibly irritated.

"The last is Nadia," Amari looks at Najaah. "If we run into them, I think you should be the one to fight her. She's their primary fighter, though they can all be just as deadly. Nadia is a Bera and a Singer. She has some incredible control over earth-based elements and is very good with quad-wielding axes."

Najaah nods. "I've fought Bera before. Many lived in the

mountains of Rowan. The military usually had the common sense to leave them be, but I still have experience with defending against quad-wielders."

"Perfect," Amari smiles.

"She's a dirty fighter and a sadist," Taliya leans forward against the table, whispering to them. "Watch out for pepper being thrown at your face!"

Najaah stares at her, unsure if this is a joke.

Ignoring this exchange, Amari easily switches to the next part of her no doubt elaborate plan. "Nuru, can you be our eyes in the sky? Marina tends to stick with Bolek for fights since juggling multiple minds like that can be distracting."

The shape-shifter snorts. "Of course. No familiar stands a chance against a shapeshifter."

"Then, I'll deal with Marina while Taliya and Kol keep Miri from blowing us all up." Amari turns to Erika. "You will be helping secure our exit."

The human's eyes widen. "What? What can I do?"

"I'm glad you asked." The Nightblood's smile turns into a grin.

The view is beautiful for something so perilous. Erika has never been religious and hasn't researched much on the Order of the Flame, but she can admit their buildings are pretty if nothing else.

Amidst a bustling cityscape of marble and gold rises a grand cathedral dedicated to the Divine King. As her train approaches, she can spot the giant banners with the Imperial sigil on them from a kilometer away.

The exterior of the cathedral is a veritable symphony of flame and gold motifs woven into the facade's design. Gargoyles fashioned in the likeness of fierce dragons breathe imaginary flames, their scales shimmering with hints of gold leaf that catch in the afternoon sun. As the train moves closer, she can see the cathedral's entrance: twin solid oak doors with hammered gold reliefs depicting scenes of the king's heroic deeds and *benevolent* rule, each panel glowing in the sun's light.

It takes her breath away and leaves her feeling sick to her stomach. Erika wonders how many people suffered for this monument to the Divine King to be built? How many people lost their homes when this land was conquered?

The train pulling into the floating train station draws her from her mind, and she departs it with heavy steps. Erika is careful to be discreet as she searches for Taliya, the only one who took the same train as her. Everyone on the team traveled here alone, staggering their arrivals by hours. Amari and Najaah should already be at the meeting point.

When she spots Taliya getting off the train, she doesn't try to signal to her. Instead, Erika just heads for the transport that takes people down to the city streets and starts walking in the direction she knows the meeting point to be.

Only half an hour later, she turns a corner and suddenly Taliya is there, walking beside her like everything's fine.

"All good?" The thief asks, looking the epitome of casual with her loose braids and hands stuffed in a faded hoodie. Not trusting her voice at the moment, Erika nods. They walk silently up to a nondescript house up for rent that sits within easy view of the cathedral.

Taking a side entrance inside the house, they make sure they're out of sight of the Order's guardians posted around the twin oak doors. A great deal of tension leaves her body as soon as she sees Amari and Najaah camped on the third floor. Erika immediately gets to work helping them set up.

Less than an hour later, Nuru shows up in his second form, and she opens a window for him to come inside. He shifts to human as soon as she turns away. The only one left is Kol.

"Where is he?" Taliya asks, preparing an explosive. Erika watches anxiously from her corner of the room, unable to stop her fingers from fidgeting with the watch she's put back together a dozen times by now. It accurately tells time now, ironically deciding to work right before they leave every timezone it tracks.

"He said he'd be here on time," Nuru sighs. Scoffing, Najaah continues setting up the detonators.

"Kol was late two days ago, too, for the simulation!" Taliya huffs in irritation, but thankfully, she is still painstakingly careful. "You would think he'd make sure not to do it again for the real thing!"

"It'll be fine," Amari says, in that knowing way of hers. Erika gives her a frown from her spot closest to the Nightblood.

"You sound certain?"

"Call it faith."

Now, Erika really gives her a look. Amari doesn't strike her as the type to have unquestioning belief in anyone, especially in someone she has described before as 'annoying and knows it.' Amari ignores the questions written across the teen's face.

However, just like the Nightblood predicted, this is when Kol comes stumbling through the door looking harried.

"Don't say it!"

"You're late!" Taliya snaps.

"I said don't say it!"

"Oh, I'm gonna —"

"Enough," Najaah cuts in with a final tone. Their voice is so authoritative Erika instinctively straightens her posture, immediately feeling silly. At least it shuts the arguing duo up.

"Okay," Amari brings the room's attention to her. "We stick with the plan. The Night Witches are close behind, so we need to be coordinated if we all want to get through that portal. Got it?"

Everyone gives a nod (or, in Kol's case, a thumbs up), and they head out to do their parts. Following close behind Amari, Erika can't help but take in the grand architecture of the cathedral as they climb to the roofs. Once they're in position, Amari gives a mental tap to everyone's mind.

Everyone ready? The Nightblood asks, and Erika feels the team's connection snap into place. Being able to sense everyone is still incredibly bizarre, yet also becoming comforting at a rapid pace. Nuru, Najaah, and Amari's mental presences are the most professional, in her opinion. Taliya less so, but it's clearly not from a lack of experience. They've all obviously had training using telepathy, while Erika and Kol tend to either give off more than they intend to or too little.

At least Kol is better than when he started. He's no longer yelling as much. Erika is making progress in creating a shield between herself and everyone else. Amari and Najaah have been giving her lessons at different points over the past two weeks, which are full of boring advice like meditating and *visualizing*.

I overheard an Order guardian discussing the Night Witches' arrival, Najaah sends to the group, bringing back Erika's attention to the present. *The general consensus is that the guards don't like mercenaries but hate rebels more.*

Figures, Taliya mentally projects a scoff with extreme skill. Meanwhile, Erika's link is probably spilling over with her bafflement and curiosity.

ETA? Amari prompts.

Not enough time. Maybe ten minutes, they're coming by flying carriage, Najaah says, relaying the mental image of a sectioned landing area on the east side of the base.

Can you delay them? Maybe sabotage? Taliya asks Najaah. The Ashan responds with a *yes* and fades a bit from the group, indicating that they are focusing on the world around them.

Erika watches the skyline for a moment, waiting to see the flying carriage appear. She catches glimpses of Nuru in his second form flying above before something new arrives.

At first, it's only a speck in the far distance, but she registers that Nuru still warns the team. In the end, he's right as the flying carriage comes sailing in.

It's not a commercial one, Nuru notes. *This carriage has obviously been specialized for the Night Witches, and it's pulled by Air Spirits.*

These guys get paid more, or what? Kol asks, clearly appreciating the wealth showcased by the Witches. Taliya's disgust is particularly attention grabbing.

More like they don't care what they do for money, Amari corrects dryly.

Erika isn't very surprised from what she's heard of The Night Witches.

Amari leads her to a roof with a discreet view of the landing pad. The flying carriage touches down gracefully, looking like it didn't jostle the people inside at all.

Out steps three intimidating-looking women. None of them look alike, but something about each of them sets Erika on edge. The first to step out must be Marina. Her yellow hair is tucked neatly in a bun, shadowed by sharpened antlers, and a tan trench coat covers her golden skin. Erika thinks she sees the sun catch on some jewelry.

The Nullifier glances around and sees no sign of the Andan's familiar.

A slight woman with dark hair, a messy braid, and slightly scorched clothes steps out next. Miri, Erika identifies. She's carrying a heavy-looking bag.

The final member of the Night Witches makes Erika's mouth go dry and has her feeling *very* grateful that Najaah is assigned to the last mercenary. She's only met a few people with mixed Bera blood before, and they're always giant. This mercenary makes them seem small.

No wonder the carriage is so big, she realizes. Nadia, the Bera

Singer, and a woman with multiple axes strapped to her back, would tower at least a meter over *Najaah,* one of the tallest people Erika knows. Each of the woman's four arms looks like it could independently punch through a brick wall.

Remember, Amari says, looking over the Witches with a neutral gaze. *Miri is dangerous in any environment. Don't let her control the situation. Nadia isn't just brawn; she's a strong Singer who doesn't rely on magic. Her skill with blades is legendary, and she's a strategist at heart. Most of all, leave Marina to me. Alright?*

Okay, Erika agrees readily, not wanting to get involved with any of these enemies. The rest of the team chimes in with compliance, and Amari relaxes next to her as they watch a guardian of the Order greet the mercenaries.

It quickly escalates from a simple meeting to aggressive stances, and Nadia looms over the Order member.

What's happening? Kol asks, projecting his bewilderment. *They're arguing!*

Seems the Witches heard something they don't like, Najaah responds, mental voice full of mischief that is bizarre to sense from the former soldier. *Scheduling problems, perhaps?*

The guardian appears to be losing patience with the Witches. Even from this distance, Erika can see hands gesticulating wildly.

Najaah, what did you do? Nuru can't quite keep his amusement out of the mental link. Najaah sends the image of a fire breaking out in an office.

That would do it, Erika thinks.

Amari's chuckles rebound through the network. *The problem with having official processes is how frozen those systems get at the slightest inconvenience. Good work.*

One of the downsides to working alongside a government or people who are government-adjacent anyway. She has no idea how the Order fits into the Empire. Erika feels no pity whatsoever for the bureaucracy the Night Witches have to deal with.

Taliya and Kol approach the cathedral next, avoiding the guardians' eyes as they work on the building's wards. In training, the duo proved to be the best at wardbreaking between the thief's ability to cut through runes like a surgical blade and Kol's overwhelming amount of magic. At the signal, Amari pulls out an artifice that shoots a cable from their roof and digs into the cathedral's.

Giving the cable a dubious look, Erika wipes her sweaty hands on her pants as Amari takes out the pulleys next. The Nightblood turns to her with a raised eyebrow. *You first?*

... Sure.

Erika steps into the harness with practiced movements, willing herself not to look at the steep drop between her and the street below. As soon as Amari gives the all clear, she pushes off the roof before she can overthink it, her stomach in her throat. A scream wells up in Erika, and she has to strangle it in her throat as she passes over the empty street. Her feet hit the cathedral's roof with great force, nearly sending her flying again.

Hurriedly, she gets out of the harness with frantic fingers.

"Shit," she whispers to herself, the nerves needing some release. Amari goes next, and joins her with an iron poker face.

Nice job, the Nightblood says, patting Erika briefly on the shoulder. The cable retracts from the other side, being summoned back into the artifice as Amari checks their surroundings.

Erika turns her attention to the larger telepathic network. *Everyone inside?*

Following Nadia, Najaah reports.

Taliya's mental voice is full of disdain. *Miri is haranguing some poor workers about something. But, Amari, Marina has disappeared.*

She'll find me, Amari assures, which is actually not at all comforting. *Nuru, have you found her familiar?*

The shapeshifter responds immediately, his presence feeling distracted. *Yes. He's larger than I assumed, but I will keep him away.*

Everyone quickly goes back to their tasks, the network falling dormant. Erika takes a deep breath and steadies herself. Amari leads her to a window in an unused room on the top floor of the cathedral. Between the two of them, the remaining wards are a breeze.

Hopefully, Taliya and Kol won't have too much trouble on their end.

Erika and Amari slip inside the cathedral and out into an open walkway overlooking a giant hall. Before any guardians can spot them, the Nightblood leads her over the banister, up and into the rafters high above everything.

The vast nave unfolds below in a violent explosion of color and light, she has to blink frantically just to adjust. Stained glass windows, towering and enchanting, depict the life and triumphs of the Divine King. Even the air is perfumed with the soft fragrance of incense, which makes Erika want to sneeze. It mingles with the scent of the candles that flicker from ornate candelabras crafted from pure gold.

The centerpiece of the cathedral is an altar, clearly meant to showcase the Order's wealth, as if everything else doesn't do it already. The altar is decorated with intricate flame motifs wrought in precious metals. Above it hangs a grand tapestry depicting the king in regal splendor surrounded by celestial symbols of power and wisdom. Erika can't make out the Divine King's face despite the size of the tapestry and wonders if anyone even knows what he looks like.

Okay, Erika, Amari calls back her attention, and Erika looks at the Nightblood, who fits into the shadows of the rafters as if she belongs. *According to the reports, this should be right between a change of guardians. I'll draw the attention while you break into the altar, alright?*

Nodding, she sends a feeling of determination along and turns to the hidden entrance to the cathedral's sub-ground area.

As soon as a patrol of guardians exits the main hall, Amari uses a rope she had wrapped around a rafter to drop to the floor. In a room full of statues and benches meant for worship, she begins grabbing everything not nailed down to block the great doors, taking her time.

Erika slides down the rope much less gracefully and beelines for her target, ignoring the sound of shouting erupting outside the hall doors. Amari has started whistling.

The altar is even more gaudy up close, the gold shining so brightly it gives her a headache. Erika crouches behind it, out of sight of the rest of the room, and pulls out her runica. Since the fortress and subsequently her reveal as a Nullifier, Taliya has upgraded it a bit. It's easier to use than before, and with Erika's input, the runes are simpler for her to read.

Her teacher's warnings of inverted runes are running through her head. Erika had taken many elective classes about runes, but they were all textbook. She had never actually held a runica until she came Upside. Now, Erika is trying to keep all her lessons in mind as she works.

One of the reasons Taliya is so good is because she dances across the tightrope between disaster and stagnation. Runes are delicate in that they can blow up in someone's face if messed with. Erika is very aware of this fact as she tries to *change* an already active rune.

Power is flowing through it, which will explode at the wrong provocation. She is nudging the rune away from its intended purpose, which will cause a sort of domino effect on the rest of the wards. It won't nullify the security, but it will open the entrance without killing Erika.

It still takes a precious minute before the entrance opens without setting off anything. Slowly, the altar moves back on its base to reveal a hole with a ladder in it. She can't see the bottom and takes a second to pull out her flashlight to strap to her jacket.

Carefully, she descends into the darkness, not letting herself pause, even as the ladder goes on and *on*. She doesn't look down.

Finally, her feet hit stone, and Erika lets a small smile escape despite herself. She turns away to survey her new environment, finding a standard tunnel lit with the occasional torch, which casts a particularly threatening atmosphere. A few steps in, and she finds trouble.

The sound of air moving around a projectile is her only warning before something smashes into the floor next to her so hard the stone cracks. Erika jumps back so far that she almost trips over her own feet. Her back hits the bars of the ladder painfully, and she immediately jerks away at the realization she's cornered herself.

"This is a restricted area, little thief," a low voice growls, and Erika squints in the dim light of the torches to see an approaching form—a *big* one with horns centimeters from scraping the tunnel's ceiling. A guardian isn't supposed to be here, and she has no time to wonder why. To her growing alarm, the thing that almost took off her head is a spiked mace on the end of a long chain connecting back to the man.

The sound of the chain rattling sends chills down her spine and makes her palms sweat. Erika resists the urge to wipe them on her clothes, not wanting to give away her fright. As the guardian comes closer, her mind scrambles for a plan.

She doesn't get the time.

Mace flying, she barely dives under the arc of it, hearing the terrible crash behind her. The confined space means it takes a moment for the man to move freely, and he scowls at the realization. It's the only thing that makes that deadly aim miss her and allows Erika to run past the guardian, sprinting down the tunnel at a speed she thinks beats all her past records.

This is a small space, she reasons with herself. Her legs begin to burn as she tries to stay ahead of the man chasing her. He's the one at a disadvantage.

The guardian is catching up too quickly for her to think over a plan. As she runs down the tunnel, she realizes the wall to her left opens ahead. Stone underfoot turns to dirt, nearly tripping her, while the path she's using suddenly feels much less secure as one side now has a drop into a void that doesn't look like it ends.

Her attacker must have predicted this fear because the mace comes down to her right side just as she tries to edge closer to the wall, making her swerve dangerously close to the drop. Erika grabs onto one of the intermediate pillars that dot the left side with more strength than she knew she possessed.

Just as the guardian swings the mace at her again, she ducks and darts toward him, remembering Nuru and the drake in the garden. He's so tall that she can roll under his arms briefly.

The weapon goes down where she had been seconds ago with a furious crash, sending cracks out on impact. He harshly pulls the mace back, careless of any structural damage. Erika hysterically questions why the man is stationed underground before dodging an arm the width of a tree trunk as it swipes for her.

They dance like that for a handful of seconds, mace flying around while Erika is doing all she can to not be touched. She knows all it takes is one hit for her to be down for the count.

Amazingly, the guardian is the first one to fuck up. He must have put too much power in a swing because the mace buries itself in a pillar after Erika stoops low to avoid losing her head. The mace is stuck, even as he yanks the chain impatiently. Erika uses the moment to try to duck past him and fails miserably. Another swipe of the arm, and she jerks perilously close to the abyss.

Under their feet, an ominous fracturing sound echoes — both Erika and the guardian remain still, two humans caught in the sights of nature. Earth crumbles under her, and she can't stop the scream that rips out of her as gravity asserts itself. She can only think of leaping for the chain the man is clinging to now.

She makes it, holding onto the linked metal for her life, not daring to look down. Erika moves to climb up when she's interrupted in her desperation.

A hand wraps around her throat, squeezing to the degree that makes her vision swim, and her chest feels like it's caving in. On instinct, she tries to pull it away with her free hand with little to no success. She tries to kick in her panic, but the chain shakes under their scrambling movements. With one last thought of clarity, she grapples for her dagger.

The hand tightens at the sound of her blade being unsheathed.

"You little—"

Erika reacts with reflexes honed from weeks of drills and stabs him right in the chest. For a brief moment, a mind-numbing horror fills her, sending her heart plummeting. A flash of light nearly blinds her, and she suddenly recalls that her dagger isn't a normal weapon.

The man is gone in the next second, along with the chain, and she's free-falling.

14

AMARI

Amari watches the double doors shake from the impact of the Order's guardians trying to get in. Blocking their way is an impressive pile of miscellaneous materials she's stacked in front of the doors: benches, statues, and weird ceremonial-looking artifacts that she handles without care.

Before her veritable ransacking, the cathedral hall was dotted with statues of saints and martyrs standing sentinel in alcoves, flickering votive candles, and wreaths of fragrant flowers. Now, all items are in a sacrilegious pile against the doors. The irony is not lost on her.

She keeps her eyes on the vaulted ceiling overhead, its arches painted with celestial scenes and constellations that shimmer with enchantment. The top floor she and Erika came through is the only entrance now. Amari wonders if the guardians or the Witches will go first.

According to Taliya and Nuru's scattered reports, everyone's focused on their individual fights. Najaah has tracked down Nadia while Miri is being led into a trap by Kol. Amari awaits her own fight, but doesn't bother trying to set a trap.

She's right not to waste time. A presence enters through the same window she and Erika used after only a minute. Amari recognizes the being immediately, keeping all tension concealed as she turns to face her opponent, and the mercenary drops to the polished floor.

Marina Besat.

She's a dishonorably discharged Rowan soldier, a deadly Conjurer who specializes in taming familiars, and the leader of the Night Witches. Toxic green eyes dig into Amari, and her sharpened antlers cast shadows on the floor. The glint of gaudy jewelry contrasts the deadly grace of the mercenary.

"Kato, I didn't take you for a team player like this," Marina's voice echoes strangely in the grand hall. Internally, the seer adjusts her runes a touch to clear up the noise.

"Besat," Amari greets curtly. "Could I pay you to stay out of our way?"

Laughing, the Andan sweeps closer, coat brushing the floor in her wake. Her gloves are reinforced with metalwork to pack a mean punch. "You know we don't go back once a deal is struck."

Yeah, she thought the Witch would say that. "Worth a shot."

The tacky trench coat falls to the floor, revealing a sleeveless armorclothe vest. Marina's tattoos are on full display, and Amari pulls out her staff in a single motion in response. Of course, the woman can't do anything normal, so she must have more star-forged tattoos than any person Amari has seen before. There might even be a new one.

Star-forged tattoos are weapons—plain and simple. Scholars have argued about their use for other things, but there's little else people are willing to carve into their bodies and souls for. The tattoos work as a container for any manner of weapon, waiting dormant for the user to activate them. And the star-forged weapons, once manifested, are matched only by others of their kind. Amari's staff will hold just long enough against them, even with all the enchantments woven into it.

Unfortunately, the process of making star-forged anything is long, delicate, and expensive work. It's incredibly painful and magically taxing on whoever owns it. And it's permanent—once something is bound to a soul, it can't be unbound. Marina's dozen star-forged knives scattered over her arms are a testament to the lengths this woman will go to be the best.

Amari also catches glimpses of less deadly tattoos as she scans the Andan for any tells, namely a flickering candle, a small caricature of a nisse, and a world tree that clearly takes up a lot of space. More normal weapons are strategically placed in sheaths, which always feels ridiculous to see. As if the mercenary needs them.

"I'll admit," Marina says as she pulls a knife out of a wrist tattoo. The blade is made of bright green light, an energy construct deadlier than a steel broadsword. "I'm curious why you've taken a suicide mission. I mean, going to the Ethereal Planes, Kato? Have you finally lost it?"

"I'm not giving you information," Amari deadpans, not having the patience to deal with the back and forth.

Her senses alert her the moment before the knife flies at her, allowing her just enough time to dodge. The energy construct lands in the wall behind her with a thud, dissipates, and returns to Marina's tattoo.

Fucking star-forged weapons, Amari complains in the safety of her mind. If the magical strain hadn't been more likely to kill her than help her, she would have taken on the painful procedure years ago. Taliya, perhaps more sensibly, refuses to get one and deal with the downsides.

The mercenary is lunging forward the instant her knife is back, drawing out a second one to dual-wield with. Instead of outright blocking, Amari uses her staff to misdirect the energy constructs, allowing herself space to breathe. They fall into a familiar dance, neither making a significant blow to the other.

Her first signal that the battle is changing is the presence brushing against her mental shields. Gritting her teeth, Amari dodges a blade and tightens her defense, both in her mind and outside of it.

"Cut it out," she hisses at the mercenary. The Andan smiles sharply.

The thought of Marina reaching the others sends a chill up her spine despite the telepathic network being safe deep behind her shields.

"Afraid of what I'll find?"

Amari sweeps her staff low, making her opponent jump back to avoid being wiped off their feet. "It's just basic privacy, really."

"Because you have nothing to hide," Marina chuckles, and with her senses so heightened, Amari feels the sound reverberate throughout the hall. They swirl around columns and benches she hadn't gotten to stack in front of the doors yet.

No answer will do Amari's feelings justice about that response, so she doesn't bother replying. In her mind, the foreign presence starts attacking every perceivable weak point all at once.

Amari lets her legs stagger under her at the sudden mental assault, swaying dangerously. The mercenary takes the opening, sending a barrage of knives at the seer as she runs closer.

Internally, the seer smiles. Amari throws herself to the side to avoid the knives, rolling to her feet just as Marina reaches her. As the mercenary is in the middle of drawing out a new knife, Amari's mind snaps close like a bear trap, shattering Marina's efforts at infiltrating.

The shock manifests as a slight flinch, which the seer takes full advantage of. Her staff snaps up and slams into the Andan's solar plexus with as much magical force as Amari can channel through the runes. Marina is sent flying back through the hall, landing close to the doors where the guardians have given up trying to break down.

Satisfaction runs in her veins, and Amari lets a slight grin play on her lips while refusing to let her guard down even slightly. Before she can consider whether to try rushing forward to finish the fight, Marina groans, and an arm moves to push her up. Body of iron, that one.

"Stay out of my head," Amari says calmly, the warning clear in her voice. The mercenary chuckles as she staggers to her feet, meters away.

"Maybe this time," Marina replies with a wince as her damaged mental presence retreats entirely. "But I still have a job, y'know? Didn't work out to well for you last time we clashed, did it?"

Sighing, Amari twirls her staff into a standard block position, preparing for another bout. "I'd like to consider not being arrested that time a win all on its own. Seriously, one of these days, I'd like to just do rock-paper-scissors or something."

"As if either of us could accept losing," the mercenary points out immediately. She's unfortunately dead on the money.

"Well—"

The urgency that overtakes her in the next moment is such a head-rush that her vision almost blacks out. Desperately, Amari tries to pinpoint the source of the feeling. Who is in so much danger her seer abilities are reacting like this?

It would be far too convenient to be given a name or a summary of the situation, she thinks. Instead, she's overcome with the need to go down the altar entrance, which will have to be enough.

Marina notices something's changed, of course. Her sharp eyes watch Amari with an analytical look she's long familiar with. "Something wrong, Kato?"

Amari elects to ignore her entirely and dashes for the altar. The entrance is still open, and the ladder leading into darkness awaits. As a Nightblood, she can see that the climb down is over half a kilometer.

Too long. Amari jumps just in time to avoid a round of knives being thrown in her direction.

Marina's voice calls after her, filled with irritation. "This isn't over!"

For today, it is, Amari thinks.

The drop is fast and long at the same time, the seconds stretching into years as the alarm in the back of her mind grows ever more. Just as the ground comes up to meet her, Amari pulls her staff out and channels a burst of magic into a specific set of runes engraved on her weapon. Her momentum slows to a crawl moments before she would have crashed into the ground like a pancake.

Her feet move as soon as they touch the stone, following her sense of danger and ignoring her surroundings. She tries to slow Time down as much as she can around her, but it's difficult to tell how much this effort works in a tunnel. Stone turns to earth, and Amari feels the ground tremor underneath her.

The scene she comes upon is enough to send her heart to her throat. Evidence of a fight, a spiked mace wedged into a pillar, and two people dangling over an abyss. Before she can even open her mouth, a flash of bright light takes her by surprise, and she jerks back.

More instinctively than anything else, Amari leaps off the path. The drop is almost two kilometers, and the pit is too wide and sheer for her to cling to. Instead, she focuses on getting to Erika, who is falling at an alarming rate. Thankfully, it's easy to find the teen despite her vision still recovering from the light. Erika is screaming so loudly she doesn't even need her hearing enhancement runes.

It takes some expert timing and a kickoff from one side of the drop to finally get to the girl. Amari grabs her arm and instantly channels through her staff's runes again, bleeding out their momentum as the bottom of the pit approaches. Erika's still screaming as they float down to the ground.

The poor kid's legs give out immediately, and Amari has to hold her up to keep her from collapsing. Half-dragging her, she leads them down a small hidden side tunnel until they reach a set of torches for the Nullifier to see with. "Erika, you with me?"

She doesn't attempt to use the telepathic network at this moment, waiting for the teen to collect herself enough to respond. Erika is breathing fast before falling into a pattern that seems trained, but the shaking in her body persists.

"I...Yeah," Erika's voice is wrecked, and Amari finally notices the blossoming bruise on the girl's throat. The seer recognizes the shapes of the wound, making fury coil deep in her heart that she readily dismisses. Instead, she tucks away her staff and uses her free hand to rummage through her bag. Amari has one of the most stocked first aid kits of the team, mostly because Taliya doesn't have the patience to learn more than the basics.

"Here, let me put this salve on your throat. It'll heal the worst of the damage in under an hour, and you'll be able to talk without pain in ten minutes."

What she pulls out isn't a very large container because the salve is very potent. Amari only steals the good stuff to take on jobs. This is the kind of medicine that costs a fortune if you pay for it. Erika eyes it skeptically before leaning her head back, giving her a full few of the damage.

If she weren't a Nightblood, it would be too difficult for her to see properly in just the light of a few flickering torches. As it is, she doesn't need any help to understand how close the girl had been to something deadly.

Amari doesn't wait around and stare, moving on to opening the salve. During the quiet stretch of time as she applies it, the seer checks in with the rest of the team. In her urgency, she'd neglected to update them, and she left Marina behind, too, with no idea if the mercenary followed her or decided to go after the others.

Oh well. She holds back a heavy sigh, focusing back on Erika and putting away the salve after finishing up.

"So, the others are okay right now. The Witches split up as soon as they realized we were already here. Najaah is holding off Nadia, Nuru is dealing with Marina's familiar, and Kol is helping Taliya trap Miri. I may have left Marina up in the cathedral. We'll see what happens with her."

Erika stares at her wide-eyed, making Amari unsure if the kid is even registering what she's saying.

"You—How—How did you know?"

Her stomach sinks, and it takes work to keep her face neutral. "I learned there was more trouble than we suspected in the tunnel for you, and I followed. I got there just in time to see you fall."

It's a tense moment of silence as Amari waits to see if her omitted truths will be accepted. The Nullifier is looking down at the earth under their feet, short dark hair concealing her expression.

"Thank you."

The words are like a shock to the system, and Amari doesn't even know why. It hurts to smile, and she worries the strain will show. "Of course. Are you good, or do you need a minute?"

Erika straightens, a familiar light returning to her blue eyes. "Yeah, I'm ready."

It turns out they fell directly to the bottom of the sub-level where the gateway is. As soon as she tries to feel for it with her magic, Amari can sense the power radiating off the portal and wonders how she ever overlooked it. The tunnel they're in leads directly to a large door that appears it's made for the most impressive of vaults. A giant engraved Imperial seal stares back at the seer, and she takes great pleasure in unraveling every single ward on it.

Having a Nullifier makes every part of wardbreaking simpler.

The girl doesn't have to worry about most security measures, if at all. Amari is admittedly very jealous.

After the wards are down, the two wait for the rest of their motley crew to show up. In the telepathic network, Amari splits her time between giving directions to struggling teammates and despairing at others' problem-solving skills. This is the last time she's pairing Taliya and Kol together, she swears.

Nuru is first to meet up with them, sporting a viscous scratch on his cheek that has just started healing under the magic of a salve. He's very grumpy when Erika asks about it, muttering under his breath, and all Amari catches is *damned familiars.*

Next to appear is Najaah, who has no injuries but a suspiciously damaged vest. According to her, Nadia put up quite a fight but retreated in the end after the Sun Eater nearly cut off one of the Bera's hands. Amari is suitably impressed and worried over the lack of news regarding Marina. Silence is never a good thing when it comes to the mercenary.

Yet, Taliya and Kol arrive at the gateway without mention of the Night Witch's leader. Of course, they're still covered in scorch marks, bruises, and, inexplicably, flowers. When Erika tries to interrogate them, the two share a look and remain quiet on the subject. Amari decides she doesn't want to know.

The vault door opens with a push from the entire group, and everyone gapes at what's inside. Surveying their reactions, Amari can't help the twist in her chest at the thought of her first time seeing a portal.

Gateways are beautiful things. This one is set in a towering arch, energy swirling in a blend of every color. She can see glimpses of a different world if she focuses on the light. The air trembles with power. Amari is the first to move forward and into the portal.

Stepping through the gateway feels like slamming through a glass window into a wall of hard pudding and out a layer of cobwebs.

Amari remembers how she used to cringe at the sensation, and muses at being completely unbothered now. It's not very surprising, considering how many times she's been through a portal. Behind her, she sees Erika coming out frantically, patting herself down for multidimensional cobwebs, and finding herself completely fine.

"You okay?" Amari ends up ahead of them, looking back at the group with probably too much amusement on her face. Taliya just gives her an exasperated look. Scanning the team, she sees Najaah checking all her weapons like something might have happened to them. By her side, Kol is wildly checking his hair like Erika had done with her clothes.

"That," Nuru says as he walks past the teens, "Amari, was deeply unpleasant. I felt like I was falling with no way to fly."

Erika frowns. "Huh. Did everyone feel something different? What does that mean? Do portals all feel differently for whoever goes through them? Does that mean—"

"They're always unpleasant," Amari beams cheerily in the face of her unsettled companions. "But you get used to it, so don't worry!"

The collective looks on her team tell her exactly how comforting the words are.

Finally, someone turns their attention to where they arrived. "Oh."

It's a stunning place, Amari will admit. The sky is a deep purple stretching out as far as the eye can see as stars blink above them. Two red suns hang up high, both in different alignments. The group is standing on a hill and the beginning of a dark-bricked road leading to a distant city, or at least something city-shaped, barely more than a dot on the horizon from their spot.

On the right side, a forest of tall, gray and white trees with blue leaves tower over them, twisting into elaborate shapes that no one from Avalon has seen in trees before. Dark green grass, almost black, stretches from the other side of the road, cutting off at the end of a cliff.

She can see a red ocean just beyond it.

"Welcome to Cetybluscarof," Amari announces in a dramatic voice. She elects to drop the telepathic network for now. There are still many hours before the twenty-four-hour limit is up, but constant use is taxing. Better to save it for when it's needed.

Besides, her hearing runes work well in this world. She only needs to use a smidgen more power than usual. Amari was glad to learn they needed to come to this world for that fact alone. It's her silver lining.

"What?"

Amari smiles. "It's better known as the Redlands. And that in the distance, is the Red City."

"Certainly easier to pronounce," Kol scoffs. Najaah rolls her eyes.

"So the entrance to the Forsaken Forest will be in the middle of there?" Nuru confirms, gesturing to the distant dot of a city. Amari nods.

"Yeah, it's a bit of a walk, but it's early morning from what I can tell. We have time. And it's better to enter the city through the main entrance than to sneak inside."

Kol gives her a baffled look. "Why?"

"We need permission to reside in the city."

The boy looks more confused. "We're… criminals?" Taliya can't help but laugh loudly at this.

Erika, who also seems a bit confused, looks at the seer for some kind of explanation. She lets her smile turn into a smirk.

"Do you think we break into every place we go? Appearing out of nowhere would be even more suspicious," Amari tells them matter-of-factly, adding on. "Better to act like normal travelers. People don't usually question other people unless they act suspiciously, and the standards for tourists here are easy to pass."

"Oh." Erika pretends not to be embarrassed as Taliya continues to laugh. Even Nuru is chuckling. Kol scowls at everyone.

Eventually, everyone gets moving, even as some of them sulk while walking to the Red City. Everyone is enjoying the scenery until a loud shriek erupts from deep within the forest. It whines a bit in Amari's ear, and she holds back a wince. Then Erika nearly shrieks back.

"What was that?" Kol appears to be on the same wavelength. Taliya, who absolutely is not, shrugs. Amari doesn't even answer, interested in how everyone will react.

"Sounds like it's at least half a kilometer away," Najaah notes, though she doesn't sound very concerned. The Nullifier, from the look on her face, clearly does not feel this is enough distance to be unconcerned about, and walks faster.

"It isn't a bird," Nuru says helpfully. When Amari glances at him, his face is serious, but his eyes give his mirth away, and she ducks her head.

"What kind of animals live here?" Kol asks in Amari's general direction. She ignores them.

"Not many birds," Taliya answers with a straight face.

"I'm surrounded by assholes," Erika proclaims. Kol lets out a wordless sound of outrage, apparently having caught on to the teasing.

"Be serious! What if it's—some kind of relative of a dragon?"

The thought is too much, making Amari finally crack at this. Her chuckles echo around them, and Kol whirls toward her in a rage but keeps his distance as they walk.

"Really?"

She looks back at him, grinning outright. "It's a Tunycret. They're the size of your hand and have the voice of a dying hyena. Loud, scary sounds are their only form of defense, I promise you."

Kol doesn't talk to any of them for the next twenty minutes.

The Red City is… misleadingly mundane—at first. It's normal on the surface and waits for your guard to be let down. Amari learned that the hard way years ago and properly warned her teammates before they braved the city.

She still doesn't think they're completely prepared when they enter through the city's gates. At first glance, it appears like any other bustling urban center, teeming with life and energy. The streets are lined with ordinary buildings, their facades blending harmoniously with the surrounding architecture. People from all walks of life move about, their pace reflecting the cadence of a typical city. One would think they're still in Avalon.

Yet, as they delve deeper into the city, Amari notes the predominant red theme that subtly pervades every corner. Crimson banners flutter in the gentle breeze, and storefronts adorned with scarlet awnings beckon with an inviting charm. Even the street lamps emit a warm, ruby glow, casting a kind of romantic ambiance upon the city.

It's easy to believe that's why it's called the Red City.

She glances at the spiraling tower at the distant outline of the Heart of the city and looks away quickly.

"So," Kol says as he curiously looks around at the shops and homes they pass. "You said we have to wait to leave until the day of the week the moons align. When's that?"

From the positions of the suns, not long. "Tomorrow."

"Where are we staying tonight, then?"

Amari's mouth sets in a grim line. "Staying on the streets is not an option. We need to avoid the nicer hotels, too. Something cheap, but not… Criminal."

The others give her looks with varying levels of apprehension.

"That bad?" Nuru asks. Amari nods.

"How do we find…?" Erika trails off, stilling. Her gaze is locked on a figure in the distance. She's caught sight of the Heart. "What is that?"

"Don't look," Amari snaps. She needs to get them protections before they can do anything here. The Nullifier quickly turns away and resumes walking forward. "I know a place that should be safe. Just follow me and remember what I said: don't stare too long at anything or anyone. Don't let anyone touch you. And don't agree to anything without me there."

She gets various sounds and nods of agreement in response, which do little to ease the tension in her shoulders. Being in this place has her watching every corner and suspicious of every person.

Thankfully, the store is not very far from the gates. If it were, Amari would have been in even worse trouble the first time she came here. Seeing the place doesn't make her relax but is a relief.

Erika gently rubs her healing throat as she frowns at the sign above the unassuming door. "Aero Chambers? Like… air?"

"Yep," Amari pushes the door into the chamber, which is sealed off from the rest of the store, and first grabs the mandatory gas mask off the wall. Next to the masks are rows of goggles and various pieces of equipment to give customers of all shapes and sizes options. "Put these on, and do not take them off until we're back in a sealed-off chamber and the inner door has shut."

"Alright," Nuru says hesitantly, reaching for a mask. Najaah inspects the one she grabs closely before putting it on.

Once all the masks are securely on (and Amari double-checks them), they head inside the actual store, out of the compressed corridor.

In the shop, Aero Chambers has towering shelves reaching toward the ceiling, displaying a dazzling array of glass containers. Each container holds a different type of air—wisps of neon-green, sparkling silver, and azure swirl gently within its confines. The labels describe the unique properties of each air composition.

Amari doesn't look, yet knows that further into the store, there's The Wind Weaver's Workshop. A space dedicated to creating custom air compositions. In that place, an expert known as the Wind Weaver crafts personalized airs for clients. The room is filled with an array of glass instruments, each emitting a soft, iridescent light. The Wind Weaver, surrounded by swirling mists and vials of rare essences, works with focused precision to blend the perfect mixture. She remembers clearly how the workshop practically exudes the Weaver's reverence for the craft, where the magic of air is both an art and a science.

It is also incredibly poisonous to most who walk in. The Wind Weaver can survive in whatever atmosphere they create and does not regulate the air in the general area of the store. This makes shopping difficult, hence the sealed-off chamber and safety equipment.

As a Nightblood, Amari is immune to essentially every poison she has ever heard of. The Taos can — and will — eat anything, up to and including what everyone else in Avalon would consider deeply toxic. Unfortunately, this does not stop the Wind Weaver from creating fun new concoctions that still give Amari a splitting headache or a bad case of the suddenly-falling-unconscious. So, even she needs a gas mask and safety goggles.

She scans the store, not seeing the Wind Weaver at first glance, before heading to the Workshop. The door is slightly ajar, indicating a willingness to be interrupted, and pushes it open all the way.

Scattered about on two large tables are an array of instruments and apparatuses used often by alchemists. Glass orbs, vials, and containers of various sizes hold glowing gases in an array of colors and densities. Each vessel is meticulously labeled, detailing the unique properties and effects of its contained air. Elaborate alchemical contraptions adorned with runic symbols and brass tubing are used to distill, purify, and combine the essences of different gaseous elements.

At the heart of the workshop stands the Wind Weaver, a master alchemist, and elemental magic user. Cloaked in flowing robes adorned with intricate patterns of windswept clouds and swirling gusts, the Wind Weaver looks made from the very mist surrounding them—a being of shadows and smoke, not flesh and blood. Amari waits politely at the back of the workshop.

"Here to commission?" The Wind Weaver calls out after a few minutes.

"Yes, and something else," Amari says, voice coming out warped through the gas mask. The alchemist seems to recognize it anyway. They turn.

"Ah, Miss Kato. You were here just recently, weren't you?"

"Six and a half years ago, so it depends on your perspective."

"Right, of course. Here for the same? For you and your companions?"

Amari nods, thankful that the others have let her take the lead. The last thing the group needs right now is to say something unintentionally rude to an ally.

"I will have it ready in a few hours. Feel free to take your companions and show them through the side door."

"Thank you, Wind Weaver," Amari lays her flat hand over her heart, a gesture of deep thanks in the city. The alchemist nods and returns to their work.

She immediately turns and herds her group out of the workshop as quietly as possible before leading them to the discreet side door tucked away between the high shelves. At first glance, it appears to be a simple supply closet. Amari pushes past the mild illusion and into another sealed-off chamber. This one is smaller than the other and has very little equipment on the walls. She counts the masks—three—and then puts hers on the wall.

"Okay, follow me to the rooms, and I'll answer any questions," Amari states, cutting off Erika and Kol as they open their mouths to talk.

Minutes—and a steep walk up a spiraling staircase—later, she enters an empty room that mimics every standard inn she's ever been in and sits in a chair. Nuru claims the only other one, while the others quibble over which of the two beds to sit on.

Eventually, everyone is settled down enough to question Amari.

"So what was that? What is this place? Why is there—"

"One question at a time, Kol."

Najaah speaks up before he can again. "Explain what this place is."

Amari sighs, running a hand through her hair. Her braid is fraying from the day's activities. "Aero Chambers is one of the only places in the Red City that doesn't require the city's common currency—blood. I told you all that this place runs on sacrifices and violence. The Wind Weaver is one of the very few residents who doesn't have blood or care to use any in rituals. They have the rooms up here to rent for people who want to avoid sacrificing what they can't afford to lose to survive."

Silence descends for a good minute. Taliya falls backward and lies on her back on a bed, staring at the ceiling. She sees Erika out of the corner of her eye, fiddling with the broken clock piece she carries around again, and Kol seems to be having a small crisis by the look on his face. Taliya sighs. She's known about the Red City longer than anyone else besides Amari, but that's different than actually being here.

"Why?" Najaah asks. Amari raises an eyebrow. "Why is the Wind Weaver helping? What do they accept as currency if not blood?"

Ah, the real question. "Our payment for the rooms is air."

"What?" Erika looks alarmed.

"The air we're exhaling right now is being collected. The Red City's atmosphere is breathable for us, but our biologies are still different enough from any residents here that we're an uncommon commodity. It's completely safe. No air is removed in quantities that will affect us, and the room only empties out after we leave."

Najaah narrows their eyes. "What about the other thing you asked for? What are they making you?"

"Us."

"… What are they making us?"

She smiles. "Protection, if you will. The Wind Weaver is the best alchemist I've ever heard of when it comes to the atmospheric arts. They can create bottled luck in gas form, which is too pricey for us and is nearly impossible for other alchemists to make. What I asked for is a breath of… protection and health, you could say. Essentially, for a few days, our blood will be immune to contamination or manipulation by magic. It also has general restorative qualities, so if you get injured, you'll heal faster."

"Contaminate?" Kol's eyes widen dramatically. Inexplicably, Najaah has turned away from the conversation with a pinched look.

"I did say the city's full of residents and monsters who will try to take from you. There are worse ways they can go about it than to cut you. This city eats visitors alive."

Kol's skin has gone a very sickly pale.

"Is there an additional price for that?" Nuru questions perceptively.

"Yes. I brought samples of specific air compositions difficult to find outside of Avalon with me as a trade." Amari had a hell of a time tracking them down, too. Mia doesn't know a lot about alchemy, so the seer had gone traipsing through Castor's black markets for something suitable to trade. The biggest obstacle here was Marina nearly breaking the samples half a dozen times despite the sturdy containers Amari used.

Taliya sits up. "So we have somewhere safe to sleep, and in the morning, we can go scout the Gate's location?"

"Pretty much. You still need to be wary of the gangs in the

daytime, but scouting will have to finish before nightfall. The nightlife here is very different from what it looks like in the day."

From the look on Kol and Erika's faces, Amari doesn't think she needs to worry about them.

"The gangs? Remind me of them again, there are four, right?" Erika picks at a loose thread on her jacket. Najaah snaps back to attention at the mention of the potential enemies and allies in the city.

"There are three main groups, but also a few little ones we can mostly ignore. The Crimson Riders are the biggest gang and have been ruling over most of the city for a long time. They're honorable, in their own way, but can be pretty volatile. The gateway is in the Heart of the city, which is in the middle of their territory. Trying to barter with them would mean paying too high a price."

"So we need to fight them?" Kol asks. Amari attempts to smother a grimace.

"That's likely, regrettably. The two other gangs are always looking for a foothold in Rider spaces. The Damnation is the newer of the two and is *very* violent. They want to bring back the 'old ways,' which are just a fancy way of saying they want more blood magic in a city already overrun with it. We will be avoiding them. The Ravagers are the third group. I have a bit of history with them and will be approaching them tomorrow about a potential alliance."

This sets off twenty minutes of more questions while she valiantly tries to avoid giving the specifics of her history here. It's less of a secret, Amari reasons, and more of a personal matter. She's given all the warnings she can; it will be up to her team to follow them.

After finally moving past the questioning, they all settle into their rooms. The two rooms Amari has reserved are not particularly luxurious, with minimal furnishings aside from two beds in each room. For obvious reasons, she refuses to pay the price any better place would require. Also, she knows the only one on their team who would actually be bothered is Kol. Everyone else is either used to roughing it in worse environments (her, Nuru, Najaah, Taliya) or is not much of a complainer (Erika).

To avoid a squabble over who can share a room with whom, she simply divides them all by chosen gender and offers Najaah the choice of either one.

"Do you have a preference for which room you sleep in, Najaah?" Najaah looks at Nuru and Kol's assigned room. Despite only arriving twenty minutes ago, Kol has managed to spread all his belongings over his designated space and into others. Nuru watches over this with pained resignation.

"I'll stay with your group," Najaah says decisively. Amari carefully suppresses her amused reaction.

"Sounds good."

Taliya pairs up with her while Najaah and Erika take the other bed. Amari can't speak for the other room (and doesn't particularly want to), but hers seems much more motivated to rest than anything else. Taliya is curled up on the side closest to the window, braids splayed around her head like a halo. Erika is sitting on the other bed's covers, carefully going through and checking everything in her pack. Najaah, highlighting her training as a soldier, falls asleep on command as soon as she lies down.

"Why is she sleeping like that?" Erika is looking at Najaah in confusion from her side of the bed. Amari glances over. The ex-soldier is on top of the covers, fully dressed, armed, and with her boots on.

She answers, "Ashan don't need blankets to stay warm," leaving the rest unsaid. Erika seems like she wants to ask more, but thankfully, the teen prioritizes going to bed.

Hopefully, they'll all be able to sleep restfully. No one can be certain when they'll get a full night's rest next.

Amari and Taliya set out to find allies in this city the next day while the others scout.

From what she remembers and what the Weaver conveyed when she asked them over breakfast, Amari believes she knows where she can find their potential allies. The Ravagers are nomadic but have old boltholes spread throughout the city. Even dark arcana-using gangsters need a home.

The Bloody Clocktower is the site of many battles and atrocities. In the past, the clock tower was the city's crown jewel before the Heart was created. Nowadays, the tower's stone exterior is weathered and cracked, and black vines creep up its sides in nature's attempt to reclaim it. Despite the landmark's dilapidated state, Amari knows the Ravagers hold a strange pride in this foreboding monument, a symbol of their rich and dark heritage.

"Not sure about these groups, Amari," Taliya signs as they walk toward the clocktower. The seer sighs wearily.

"I know, but I think it's for the best. I don't want to bring Erika or Kol to this meeting, and Nuru needs to scout for us."

"Still," Taliya insists with exaggerated gestures, amusement creeping onto her face. "We did just let a bunch of teenagers loose in a hostile city."

Yeah. "I was younger when I came here," Amari protests weakly, grimacing even as she signs it. The look her friend gives her conveys everything she wants to say in reply.

Amari's time in the Red City... She had been very close to never leaving this place. The Wind Weaver is the only reason she managed to make it out intact, and the only reason she made it out as *herself*. There are worse things to lose than your life, she knows.

They turn a corner, and there it is, looming high above them. The grand entrance to the clocktower is marked by a pair of heavy wooden doors, their surfaces scarred and blackened by centuries of exposure. The doors, slightly ajar, creak ominously with the slightest breeze, inviting the brave and curious to step into the shadows within. Despite the unlocked entrance, Amari knows the wards don't allow those with malicious intent through.

Above the entrance, the clock face continues marking the time. The glass of the clock is shattered, with jagged shards still clinging stubbornly to the iron frame, but the Ravagers care for the tower enough for it to still tell time.

Stepping inside, the air is thick with the musty scent of decay and old blood, a lingering reminder of the tower's history. Cobwebs drape like tattered curtains over wards that look much newer in contrast to everything else. The Ravager's work, then. The wards don't follow the same rules as they do in Avalon, a different language entirely.

Ascending the spiral staircase, Amari and Taliya reach the heart of the clocktower—what was once the ritual chamber. It's an expansive room, dominated by a large, circular altar made of dark stone. In contrast to its bloody past, whoever spends time here clearly uses the altar as a regular table. Surrounding it are iron sconces, holding flickering flames that cast eerie shadows on the walls.

"Looks like nobody's home," Taliya says aloud, running a finger over the altar. A thin layer of dust comes away, and she wrinkles her nose at the dirt. Amari wanders over to the bookshelves to investigate.

"Don't be so sure."

Both women whip around to the staircase's door, finding a man lounging against the wooden frame. Amari narrows her eyes, suspicious of the sudden appearance but not willing to start a fight yet.

"And you are?"

The man isn't a very imposing sight, with one horn poking out of curly hair and another broken off halfway. He's dressed in what Amari would call 'apocalyptic chic' and grins at them with a mouth full of sharp teeth. His eyes, utterly blue with no sclera, are difficult to decipher emotion from. "Call me Sev. Now, what are your *names?*"

A test, of sorts. Amari is sure he can tell they're not from the Red City and is wondering if they're ignorant enough to give their names so freely. "You may call me Amari, and call my friend Taliya."

The smile turns sharp, and Sev leans forward. "And what's your business here, *Amari?*"

"We would like to meet with the Ravagers," Amari retorts, meeting Sev's stare squarely. She doesn't know *for sure* this man is one of them, but everything about him so far leads her to believe she's right. Sev settles back into a more casual position, feigning boredom.

"Oh, is that all? Maybe I can leave a message for you since I'm sure they're so very busy."

Taliya steps forward. "We want to propose a temporary alliance against the Riders. Do you think they'd be interested in *that?*"

Sev's eyes seem to darken in color, blue swirling in indecipherable patterns. Amari watches his body language, keeping a note of where any potential weapons could be.

"Might be. You know, I think I have a friend you should meet," Sev pushes off the door frame, then turns and heads down the stairs. Amari and Taliya share a mutually exasperated look before following the man at a safe distance.

Nuru chooses that moment to check in with Amari over the telepathic network. *I have news.*

What is it?

The shapeshifter sends over the image of a bloody scene set in an alleyway. There are no bodies, making the amount of blood on the ground and walls all the more ominous. From what Nuru conveys, it is remnants of an attack with ritualistic elements that he doesn't recognize. But he does know that the symbol of the Crimson Riders she drew for the team is written in blood on a dumpster.

This is not the only one, Nuru says grimly. *Every murder is on Rider territory. Someone is planning an attack on the Crimson Riders.*

The Ravagers are an unlikely suspect, Amari thinks. *They're not that bloodthirsty. It must be a rival gang, probably that up-and-coming one — the Damnation.*

That was my thought as well, Nuru replies.

Any idea of when the next attack will happen?

Soon, he says. *I'll look for more evidence as to when. This seems like more than random violence.*

Keep me updated, Amari ends the conversation and focuses on the present. The new information churns in her mind, and she goes over all the ways she can use it.

Sev leads them to a door that she is certain wasn't there before and opens it to reveal a room that does not fit the clocktower's floor plan. A minor pocket dimension is anchored to the tower. Amari reluctantly acknowledges its cleverness and its ability to make her feel jealous. Pocket dimensions are *expensive.*

Of course, this might just be a natural occurrence in the Planes.

The room is furnished with comfortable couches and armchairs, a homely fireplace set into a wall, and a long table on one side covered with papers and writing instruments. Naturally, there are no windows, so there is no clear view out into the infinite void of space. That's the kind of thing that makes people lose their minds from overthinking.

Three people are waiting inside, looking at her and Taliya warily. One is a woman with plant-like features and bright green eyes. Flowers grow from her hair, and vines snake around her limbs. She is studying them with mild curiosity, in contrast to a tall man wearing worn armor, and a pair of sharp horns that had seen many conflicts. He is standing by the fireplace and glaring at her and Taliya. In the center of the room is the group's clear leader, a woman with a shaved head and a multitude of tattoos starting on her head and continuing down, slightly hidden beneath her jacket. Amari recognizes some tattoos as runes or wards but is unfamiliar with the markings otherwise.

The leader's glowing red eyes rest on them even as she addresses Sev. "What's this about making a move against the Riders?"

Instead of answering, Sev simply turns to Amari and Taliya. The seer holds back a sigh but doesn't complain. "My team and I wish to use a gateway in the Heart. The Crimson Riders would demand an unreasonable sacrifice to use it if they let us at all, so we need them out of the way. We're asking for the Ravager's help in this."

"Oh?" The woman studies her while feigning disinterest. "And why would we do that?"

"Because we can also help you in the fight against the Riders. They don't know us and won't know how to fight against us if we have your support. The Riders have the home advantage as long as my team works alone," Amari adds meaningfully. There's a moment of silence as everyone digests this. Studying them, she can see that the leader is reluctantly interested. The woman with green eyes is excited at the idea of striking against the Riders, while the man is cautious, and Sev is strangely pleased.

"I don't know if you're aware, but the Riders aren't the only concern nowadays," the leader admits, watching her carefully. Amari suppresses a smile.

"The Damnation, right?"

"What do you know about them?"

As a seer, Amari can sometimes get very vague feelings about what actions she should take next in the moment. It took her years to parse it enough to be helpful, but now she can reap the benefits from years of frustration. This is all to say that when she does something that seems reckless and drives Taliya insane, there's usually a good reason for it.

"We know that they're attacking Riders and taking people to use as sacrifices." Giving away such information freely this early is something Amari often advises against, but again, she has a good feeling. What Nuru found tells her more than the shapeshifter realizes. Taliya, she can tell, is barely restraining herself from turning to her and shouting about her confusion.

The Ravagers act exactly as surprised as she imagined they would be. Clearly, the Damnation has been concealing their level of hostility towards the Riders from the rest of the city.

The leader of the group leans toward her. "And you're telling us this because...?"

"I think we can take advantage of the situation."

Red eyes lock onto Amari with a sharp intensity. "What's your plan, exactly?"

15

ERIKA-AMARI

Erika trails after Najaah and Kol down the twisting streets of the Red City. First thing in the morning, Amari wakes all of them up — even going as far as to throw a glass of water on a reluctant Kol — distributes them the vials the Wind Weaver made for them, and splits them up into three groups. Well, two groups and Nuru.

It was his idea, positing that he had more than enough experience of scouting alone and was in the best position to do it in his second form. They had a lot of ground to cover and not much time, so Amari had agreed.

Now, Erika is thankful she has both Najaah and Kol with her as they venture through streets that lose more and more of their polish. The trio is meant to get a feel for the energy of the city, which Amari claims is volatile and vital to know as visitors with an agenda. They are also supposed to scout out any potential paths to the Heart, where the gateway is. Nuru is flying closely above it to better understand the Crimson Riders' grip on the Heart and their security. Erika, Kol, and Najaah are finding the potential entryways, or in worse cases, the escape routes.

Simply wandering the streets hasn't gotten them much information, at least to Erika. That might be a different story for Najaah. Kol looks incredibly bored, hands in his jacket pocket, and barely paying attention to where he's going anymore.

"Do you have any idea how we can get 'the energy' of the city?" Erika asks Najaah. The instructions still strike her as way too vague. The soldier pauses walking and shrugs.

"I would usually go find whatever bar equivalent a place would have and listen to the residents."

Yeah, that's what Erika did in Kilahn, too. It took her over a week to get any results, and that was more due to some dumb luck meeting Mia than anything else. "We need something faster."

"Why can't we just ask?"

Erika and Najaah turn to Kol. He's standing a step ahead of them, hands still in his pockets. The casualness of the suggestion causes her brain to stutter over it.

"Isn't that—that's dangerous, right?" She looks at Najaah for support.

"We could just play up the tourist part. I shouldn't do the talking, though; I'm not trained for that kind of deception, and people rarely like talking to a soldier," Najaah is being sensible in suggesting this, but Erika can't help her mouth from gaping at the idea.

"It's—it's that easy?"

"Why would it need to be more complicated?"

With that endorsement, Kol beelines for the nearest person walking by. That person happened to be a woman with green skin, four horns curling around her straightened hair, and six arms, all in the process of doing something. She seems to be trying to write on two different clipboards while valiantly containing a squirming child in her top pair of arms.

Before she can stop him, Kol approaches the woman. "Hey! Can
—"

"No! I'm late enough as it is!" The woman yells, looking
harassed, and hurries on. Kol noticeably pouts at the rejection.

"I don't know what you expected from that," Erika deadpans.
Najaah is pinching the bridge of their nose. "But maybe try someone
with their hands less full next time."

Kol throws his hands in the air in a display of theatrical
frustration. "You try then!"

Erika pauses at his words, feeling nervous at the idea of walking
up to strangers *(from an entirely different world)* and starting a
conversation. The warnings Amari gave them all flashes through her
head. What if—

"Don't worry about the consequences, Erika," Najaah says
quietly. "We have your back if anything goes wrong."

Right. Right, Erika could do this. She takes a deep breath—four
seconds inhale, hold for two, exhale for eight, like her mom taught her
—and scans the street for potential targets. The woman wasn't the
only one in a rush, and Erika had to wonder if something was going
on or if this was a normal sense of urgency. Apart from that, a couple
strolls down the other side of the street, wrapped up in a conversation
with each other. Meters away, a teenager, Erika assumes but can't be
sure of anyone's age, is lingering outside a shop, looking at something
in their hand. Further down the street, a man is sitting on something
that only vaguely resembles a motorcycle and seems magnitudes more
dangerous to ride on.

Erika heads toward the teenager. As she walks closer, she
instantly recognizes that this is not someone descended from Avalon.
Beyond the youthful appearance, their skin is translucent, something
Erika isn't entirely sure how to process, so she doesn't. With a hood
over their heads, she didn't notice from afar that the eyes are
completely white, even the sclera, which she admits to herself is

deeply unnerving.

The teenager looks up from what Erika can see is some kind of flattened stone, its colors swirling over the surface in seemingly random patterns. "Hi! I have some questions. Are you busy?"

They open their mouth. "⫪⁕∴⌇ ⧴ᾱ⨪ ɥ⩹⫶ ◊△⊥⫶ ⟑Ꭹ∴⌐ ⸴⌐⌐¯∧ᵎ⫶⩾?"

"Thank you," Najaah says from behind her. "We're tourists."

"Ah, okay," the teen replies in what sounds like perfect Apolona.

For not the first time, Erika is incredibly grateful for the translation magic that so many people use. Sure, the Nullifier wishes *she* could use it, but with Najaah and Kol here and the support of the telepathic network, she can reap the benefits. "We're curious about what the best places to visit are? Places to avoid? What we need to know to be, you know, touristy."

The teen sighs, a universal signal of beleaguered exasperation. "I don't know, the shopping district is okay. You'll probably like the history museum if you're actually into that stuff. Places to avoid… Basically, everywhere after night falls, if you don't have the proper protections. You keep your head down, and the gangs will ignore you."

"Gangs?" Kol asks, a little too earnestly. Fortunately, the teen doesn't seem to care in the slightest.

"Yeah. Y'know."

Erika steps back into the conversation before Kol can get more suspicious. "Like the, uh, Damnation Riders?"

The teen visibly winces. "The *Crimson* Riders. The Damnation is their enemy. The Riders have owned the city for centuries, and now there are Damnations everywhere, and even the *Ravagers* are more out and about. Shit's gonna go down."

"Oh no!" Erika affected a concerned look. "Not in the whole city, right? They wouldn't be fighting in the streets!"

"Ha!" The teen lets out a harsh laugh and aims a sharp smirk at her. She suppresses a shiver, not liking those colorless eyes focusing on her. "The streets are gonna run with blood!"

"That's—"

The teen leans forward, smirk widening. "And you know what? It's exactly what this city needs. We've gotten complacent in our self-functioning systems. The City is stronger the more blood we pour into it."

Okaaaaay, she smothers the urge to lean away and grimace.

"That's very helpful," Erika says, trying for a polite tone that won't come across as condescending or dismissive. She thinks she nails it. "We'll be looking forward to it. Can you point us in the direction of that museum? We'd *love* to learn about when the city was stronger."

The smirk settles into a more normal-looking smile, and the tension Erika hadn't even noticed had risen vanishes as quickly as it appeared. Najaah and Kol are noticeably quiet behind her.

"Sure."

Once the directions are given, the trio leaves the teen behind as fast as they can without making it obvious. No one speaks for all of a minute.

"Well, that was fucking creepy," Kol comments. Najaah snorts, and Erika can't help chuckling nervously. The anxiety generated from that interaction alone is making her palms sweat and her heartbeat erratic.

"I agree. It was impressive, though," Najaah says.

"Huh?"

"Erika, I mean."

"*Me?*" She whips her head toward Najaah and tries not to show her shock. "What are you talking about?"

"You de-escalated the situation quickly and got us useful

information. I'm merely stating a fact."

Against her will, Erika feels heat rise in her cheeks and quickly turns her eyes forward. "I—um, yeah. Thanks."

"So, should we actually go to the museum?" Kol asks. Erika shares a look with Najaah, but neither answers immediately. "That'd be helpful, right?"

"Yeah," Erika concedes. "Even if the museum itself doesn't give a lot of information, which is unlikely, then we can use the tourist lie again."

The museum is only a fifteen-minute walk away, and once it comes into their line of vision, it becomes obvious why it's an actual tourist spot.

Erika is definitely feeling some mixed emotions as she takes in the building straight out of some dark fairytale. Its architecture is a striking monument to Gothic castles, with towering spires and intricate stonework. The exterior walls are constructed of dark, polished granite, reflecting a deep crimson hue, reminiscent of the lifeblood that is central to the museum's macabre exhibits.

Entering the museum, Erika is immediately enveloped in an atmosphere of solemn reverence. Even Kol doesn't dare break it as they walk through the foyer. The dim lighting casts long shadows across the room, and the more she walks, the more she feels like she's in a horror movie.

Erika feels a sudden rush of gratefulness towards Taliya for the translation runes the thief placed on her glasses. It makes the whole experience easier as she walks past displays. Though, some of what she sees almost makes her wish she couldn't read it.

After the foyer, the Hall of Rituals is the museum's centerpiece, a cavernous space lined with relics of blood magic from across the city's history. Ancient altars, stained with the remnants of countless sacrifices, stand proudly on display. Erika tries to absorb as much information as she can, but the creepiness of it all makes it hard for the facts to retain. It doesn't help that the other visitors milling around seem unphased by what they're learning.

In a smaller room, visitors can explore the genealogies of powerful blood mages. This is where Erika lingers the least, not much interested in the names and powers of long-dead monsters.

She moves on to one of the museum's most unsettling exhibits. The Vault of Vials is a darkened room where shelves of glass vials are displayed, each containing a preserved drop of blood from important rituals and sacrifices. The vials are arranged chronologically, offering a timeline of blood magic's evolution. Soft, red-tinted lighting illuminates each vial, casting an eerie glow that makes the blood within appear almost alive. Kol nearly gags as soon as he enters and speeds out of it without looking at any of the information. After sharing a look, Najaah decides to follow him while Erika stays behind to learn.

She completely ignores the part of the museum that features interactive exhibits, where visitors can experience holographic reenactments of historic blood magic ceremonies. The Nullifier can't even bring herself to even consider playing a part in it.

In the end, Erika settles inside the Alchemist's Alcove, the section that explores modern blood magic practices. Visitors are supposed to view contemporary art inspired by blood magic, read about ethical debates, and even see demonstrations of how blood is used in current magical practices. This section is designed to provoke thought and discussion, bridging the gap between ancient traditions and modern interpretations. But she can't help but think this part is for show, remembering what Amari told the group. Many of the practices 'debated' in this room are still very much used in day to day here.

The flow of other visitors has been an ever-present thing in the back of Erika's mind, so she notices instantly when she's all alone in the alcove. Silence blankets her, sending shivers up her spine and making the hair on the back of her neck stand up. Resolving to find

Najaah and Kol, she turns toward the exit just as someone new steps in.

A blood mage, Erika immediately recognizes. The man is wearing nothing that gives him away, but she just spent an hour seeing artwork and preserved examples of the tattoos sneaking their way down his arms and up his neck. Crimson eyes study her intently behind a common face and a lean fighter's body. Her heart drops to her stomach and she knows this man is here for her.

Still. "Hi, do you know the way to the exit?"

No reaction. Erika feels tension wind up her body and grabs the dagger strapped to her back.

She's not sure if that was a mistake, because he charges her the moment her fingers wrap around the blade.

Erika would like to say she puts up a good fight and gets some hits in. Truthfully, he disarms her immediately and shoves a vial at her face that gives her a nose full of something flowery. The dread in her doubles as she feels the effects of some kind of knockout drug kick in. Before she can scream for Najaah and Kol or consider sending a message in the network, the world goes quiet and black with a suddenness that sends one last jolt of terror through her.

Waking up is a gift; even if Erika is tied to what she is *praying* is not an altar. The ceiling she sees first is unfamiliar and completely unremarkable. Her first reaction is to try the telepathic network, and she feels a jolt of terror when she can't reach anyone. It takes her a moment to figure out the problem once she backs away from panicked idea everyone is dead.

Something is muffling her connection to the telepathic network. Amari had warned that this is possible, but a precaution most people don't partake in. Seems Erika is singularly unlucky today.

Whatever drug they used clings to her, making it difficult to focus, but she can still realize the danger of the situation. Bindings tie her hands and feet down, and a gag forces her to keep her cursing internally. Turning her head either way shows glimpses of a magical circle full of runes that send bile up her throat. The museum enthusiastically showcases many of its sacrificial circles, and Erika is in the middle of one right now.

Besides *that*, the room is largely nondescript, with a plain door covered in wards and a table with tools on it. Erika avoids looking at them for her own sanity until she realizes *her* dagger is on it.

She instantly closes her eyes and pretends to be asleep when she hears the door begin to open. At least three people walk inside, talking in hushed voices. Obviously, she can't understand a word without any way to piggyback on her friends' translations. It's nearly half an hour of torture waiting for the other shoe to drop when they leave her alone again.

Erika opens her eyes and realizes the problem. The ceremonial knife is being prepared for whatever ritual they want to perform. According to what she read earlier, binding this type of magic to objects can take some time to set in. But not long. If she's right... Then that means the door has shut, while Erika doesn't know how to get back to Najaah and Kol, and she has less than 10 minutes to figure it out. Elaborate and ridiculous plans swirl through her mind before she settles on a lesson Taliya gave her in case of capture.

She grabs hold of her left hand's thumb and takes a deep breath to psych herself up, then dislocates it as quickly and firmly as Taliya taught her. A cry of pain builds up in her throat that Erika barely manages to muffle, even as a low whine escapes. The pain is burning through her, and it takes another minute for her to work through it enough to slip out of the bindings. Every time something brushes against her left hand, the pain flares, making her escape a slow agony even as she reminds herself of the consequences of staying.

With the bindings no longer constraining her, Erika takes another deep breath and relocates her thumb. This time, she catches the pained scream and completely muffles it in her chest.

Erika staggers out of the sacrificial circle, eternally grateful that these runes have no effect on her. She grabs her dagger off the table and leans against the locked door to study the wards on it. These ones are more difficult. Slowly, she begins disrupting a few runes with the tip of the dagger. It causes an annoying scratching noise that reverberates through her teeth.

In her unstable state, Erika misses a rune. She has a split second to realize her mistake before a ward activates and releases a strong telekinetic force outward. It crumples the metal door and sends her flying across the room. Erika hits the altar with a bruising thud and falls to the floor as she groans.

Her world goes dark again.

Amari has just finished explaining her team's proposal and is waiting for the Ravagers to finish discussing it among themselves when the telepathic network activates. Amari smothers a wince at the headache it causes. Keeping the network up for the entire twenty-four hours of possible usage is doable, but painful. It's worth it to have communication in the Red City.

Erika has disappeared, Najaah reports immediately. There's no fear in the Ashan's voice, yet its carefully controlled manner hints at their concern. A scan of the network shows that Erika's end has not activated, though it hasn't vanished entirely, so she must still be alive. She's either unconscious or something is blocking her access to the network.

What? Taliya nearly yells down the network. Amari ignores Kol as he starts a rambling story filled with panic.

When? Amari asks and directs the question to Najaah. The former soldier does not disappoint.

Between 3 to 15 minutes ago. We were in the city's museum, which features their history of blood magic, and Kol got distressed halfway through. I followed him while Erika stayed behind to learn more. We agreed to meet at the museum's exit, and when she didn't show up, we scoured the building. She's gone without a trace.

Alright. A large time frame, but not the worst. *Anything happen before the museum?*

There was a pause, and then Najaah answered with an undercurrent of anger. *We acted as tourists and talked to a local, a teenager who recommended the museum. He expressed worrying views about how the city should return to the 'old ways.'*

Fucking— *How worrying?*

I know what fanaticism looks like. I would put money on the Damnation.

Great. So some local offered up a naive tourist to the most bloodthirsty gang in the city. Amari turns her attention to the whole network again. Kol is still freaking out as Taliya and now Nuru are trying to get him to calm down.

Erika has likely been kidnapped by one of the local gangs to be used as a sacrifice. The Damnation is the most obvious culprit. Amari sends this to the group and ignores the alarmed exclamations. *Nuru, check over the Riders to make sure it's not them. Then head to the museum to scout the area from above. Najaah and Kol, try to see if the building has any security that can give a clue as to what happened. Taliya and I are going to be there soon.*

Alright, Najaah says, while Kol has gone inexplicably quiet. Nuru agrees, and the network goes inactive as everyone focuses on their assignments. Amari keeps an ever-present watch over Erika's mental presence in the back of her mind.

She turns back towards the room's occupants, who are looking at her and Taliya curiously. "A team member of ours has been taken by the Damnation. Do you have any idea where they would take a potential sacrifice?"

The Ravagers share alarmed looks, except Sev, who looks thoughtful. "Depends where she was snatched."

"The city museum."

"Ah," Sev grimaces. "The tourist trap. Yeah, they have their own place under the museum."

Taliya's eyebrows try to escape to her hairline. "You're saying they use the museum as a hunting ground? How is that acceptable?"

"They keep the rate of missing persons down enough not to affect the profit margins too much. There are some secret passageways cause the museum was once a place where actual rituals took place."

"Makes an unfortunate amount of sense," Amari comments. She narrows her eyes at Sev. "Would you be willing to tell us about where these passages are?"

"I'll do you better," he smirks and stands straight. "I'll show you."

The museum is as theatrical as Amari imagined it to be. A gaudiness that borderlines on cheesy.

"Two of our friends are waiting inside. Where should we meet them?"

Sev runs a hand through his hair. "Vault of Vials would be best."

"Alright," Amari relays that to Najaah and Kol. The Sky Lord gives off waves of unease, but both agree to meet there.

Walking through the exhibits, Amari can't even pretend to be fascinated by the pain of past generations. All she can imagine is a museum in the distant future talking about the seers, displaying pieces of their lives and coldly laying out what happened to them. Taliya seems to notice something different about her mood and hurries them through the museum.

Najaah and Kol wait in a room that might be the worst one yet, but she forces herself to focus on the situation. Erika is more important.

Thankfully, Sev doesn't waste time before showing them that one of the display cases can be pulled out to reveal a secret entrance. The passage is shrouded in oppressive darkness, except the shadows have only ever been a comfort for Amari. She is the first one to step in.

Over a minute of walking later, the passageway opens to a space where three different routes branch out. A single torch illuminates the choices laid out for them.

"These all go to different levels. Left to right is higher to lower," Sev explains. "It could be any of them."

"We don't have time to search each one individually," Najaah says. "We'll need to split up."

Not ideal.

"Is that a good idea?" Kol mutters, clearly unhappy about being underground in a dark space. It must be messing with his natural Skorae sensibilities.

Amari doesn't think it's a good idea for Kol to go alone. "You two take the left route. I'll take the middle one, and Sev will lead Taliya down the right."

After all, Taliya will tell her if Sev says anything important, and Amari is the only one who's been to the Red City before. These dangers are as daunting as they are familiar. It was a memorable visit.

Heading down her path, Amari is sure to keep watch of the shadows. It doesn't take long for her first obstacle to show up directly ahead of her.

Like a flash of lightning, a creature appears between the beats of her heart. Amari blinks hard and is greeted by a powerful, cursed soul of ozone and heat. Two bitter eyes stare at her with an ancient hunger, while three jagged horns adorn its shapeless head, which is seemingly shifting constantly. A whistling snort escapes the creature's twisting nostrils, and its head sits atop a not entirely corporeal body.

Otherworldly faces bulge from what might be considered skin, and Amari can *feel* the echoes of pain from the souls it consumed in the past. Tendrils of lightning flicker around it like extra appendages, and she's sure this creature uses them as a weapon. The creature rushes toward her, unheeded by its lack of coherent legs.

Instinctively, she calls up a shield of pure magic before she even tries to dodge the speed with which lightning strikes out at her. The creature slams into her shield with the full force of its semi-corporeal body, and it shakes so badly she feels it reverberate through her staff.

What's the best counter for lightning?

Amari considers her options as she steadily pours magic into her shield. To her alarm, the creature starts *draining* her energy slowly. As if it's eating it.

"Gross," she mutters. It does give her an idea, though. Carefully, but quickly, she pulls out something from her bag with one hand. It's cold, empty of any power, and absolutely *perfect.*

Magic tokens—like the ones Amari and Taliya stole from the Empire before they got this absurd job—work in a very interesting way. Or, at least, interesting to her. Taliya fell asleep when she tried to explain in depth. The point is that, theoretically, when the tokens are empty of all magic and given the right conditions, they can pull magic from their surroundings.

Disregarding the lessons in caution that go hand-in-hand with lessons on messing around with magic tokens, Amari tries to multi-task by holding her staff *and* the token in one hand, while still feeding power into the defensive spell. Then, she pulls out her runica with her other hand and begins adding runes to the small surface. If she drops either the staff or the token, she might bring this tunnel down upon both their heads or just vaporize them completely.

There's a moment when the item nearly slips from the few fingers clutching it, and she feels like her heart nearly escapes her body before it's corrected. Thankfully, Amari has experience with slapdash magical solutions and manages to pull off her idea without any unwanted explosions.

Now that the token is suitably modified, she stows the runica and grabs the item in her free hand. Amari can't see beyond the lightning creature, but she tries to toss the token over what could be called a shoulder to land on the other side of it. The moment the token is in the air and about to hit her shield, she stops using magic entirely and leaps back from the creature.

In a moment, three things happen. Having been leaning against the shield, the creature stumbles now that the support is gone, which gives her the time to retreat from it. The second thing is she sees the token land on the ground behind the creature, glinting softly in the scattered light. Lastly, there is the feeling of a *pull* that activates with an intensity Amari didn't expect. It's like it's trying to reach into her very soul and drag her toward the token.

The lightning creature—not expecting this feeling like her and therefore has magic in abundance ready to be drained—is jerked back. The token's pull is stronger than the creature, and it begins to be sucked away at a worrying speed. Amari had designed the token to stop pulling in magic when the token was full, and now she's beginning to be concerned the creature might not be enough for it.

She starts backing away, keeping all her magic tightly wound within herself, as the creature seems to disintegrate in front of her. The token only takes a minute to completely absorb the monster, but it stretches out to an eternity.

Finally, the item sits on the ground, softly glowing. It's still taking in all the ambient magic in the air, but the pull is much less intense. Carefully, Amari walks around it to continue to explore her path. She figures that by the time she turns back this way, the token will finally be full.

The rest of the tunnel is much less exciting. It leads to an ample space filled with doors, and not a soul resides behind any of them.

Empty rooms are used for sleeping, for caged animals Amari feels bad for, and for storage (and not with anything interesting, either).

Nothing on my level, Amari reports to the network, feeling a little irritated by her lack of progress. Najaah and Kol respond with a vague acknowledgment. She wonders if they found something and decides to head towards their route.

Taliya checks in after a few minutes. Amari even has time to pick up the magic token, which is completely full of energy.

The lowest level is mostly just abandoned ruins, Taliya tells Amari over the network. *Pretty spooky, but no cultists have jumped out at us.*

Some good news.

Then, *Sev says there's an entrance to the old sewers here. Does that mean anything?*

Dread pools in Amari's stomach. She knows exactly what that means.

Beneath the bustling city streets lies a labyrinthine network of ancient sewers, as old as the city itself. It's a dark and foreboding place where past echoes of blood rituals and forgotten magic linger like ghosts in the shadows, especially to someone like Amari, who sometimes feels the past as something more real than the Present.

The entrances to this veritable maze tend to be hidden among crumbling stone walls and overgrown foliage, so they're easily passed over by those who don't already know they're there. It makes for a perfect way to sneak around the city, if you can survive venturing inside. Amari thought the Ravagers were the only gang insane enough to try it. But if the Damnation is using them…

This could be bad.

Stay away from the old sewers, Amari warns. *I'm heading to Najaah and Kol. They've been too quiet.*

Taliya sends the image of a thumbs up, and Amari doesn't fight the urge to roll her eyes.

Backtracking is annoying, yet necessary, and she tries to move quickly down Najaah and Kol's path. Thankfully, it doesn't take long for something to happen.

She sees shadows flitting down the tunnel before her hearing runes pick up the voices attached to them. As soon as she registers that the voices are unfamiliar, Amari presses against the side of the tunnel and stalks forward slowly. Closer, it's easier to tell that there's a fork at the end of the path, and around one of the corners, she catches glimpses of a few people loitering there.

Amari tries reaching out to Najaah and Kol again, but is alarmed to find the network has gone unresponsive. Her heartbeat rises and tries to climb into her throat before she shoves the feeling down. Logically, the answer is that Amari has entered an area warded against things like telepathic communication. The network's foundations remain untouched.

The most unnerving part is she didn't even notice, something she's not sure to blame on herself or the Ethereal Plane's weirdness.

The good news is that Erika is probably here.

Amari turns her attention back to the people lingering around the corner and holds back a smirk. If she can't ask Najaah and Kol what's going on, she might as well ask these people some questions.

Carefully, Amari slows down time around her and spreads her influence through the tunnel. She moves toward the fork in the path at what seems like a normal speed for her, but will look like a blur to everyone else, and slams her staff into the first unsuspecting person she encounters.

In slow motion, three other people start to react, giving her ample time to respond. She descends on the cultists—because creepy hideout + insular extremist group + bad outfits = cult—and knocks down every one of them with prejudice. She lets all but one go down in an unconscious heap, the cultist still awake and watching her with wide eyes as she holds her staff to their throat.

They weren't expecting an attack, meaning Najaah and Kol likely went undetected.

"I'll ask this nicely only once," Amari begins, staying cautious of any powers being used by her prisoner. "Where's the girl you people kidnapped earlier today?"

She can clearly see the fear in their eyes shift to anger and a sick sort of fanaticism before she channels more magic through her staff. The runes light up with power in an unspoken threat. They freeze in terror.

She zeros in on the weak link. "Where. Is. She?"

"It's-um-she's not-I," is the stuttered mess she gets in reply. Patiently, she waits for the words to become intelligible. "She's—we need her."

Amari suppresses a scoff. "So do I. And I'm going to find her. The question is if you're going to throw your life away pointlessly trying to stop me."

For a moment, the cultist just gawks at her with wide, wide eyes. Before their face crumples, and she can practically taste her victory. "The-the sacrifice preparation room. It's that way."

They jerk their head down the left path, and Amari studies the cultist's face for evidence of deceit. "How far down? How many guards?"

"It's after the next fork and past ten doors. They don't tel—I don't know how many guards there are."

Amari accepts the information and memorizes the directions. Then she presses *sleep* into the cultist's mind until they're unconscious. That trick only works because the target is trapped and vulnerable, and she can focus entirely on the mental command instead of on a fight.

She leaves, not giving the cultists a backward glance. It would be easier to kill them, she knows, but killing helpless prisoners has never been her style.

Amari is certain she's going in the right direction when she starts coming across a trail of bodies in more awful cult garb. Some are slashed, and others are bludgeoned by some force, clear signals that Najaah and Kol have passed through. Then she gets close enough to pick up snatches of fighting and runs to see Najaah locked in battle with three cultists.

The Ashan is the better fighter; she can tell immediately, but is at a disadvantage in these small tunnels. Najaah's head almost hits the ceiling, standing up; this space gives them little room to fight. Still, Amari has little worries for the former soldier, and, anyway, if she charged in, she'd probably just get in the way.

Behind them, she spots Kol carrying something large, which she assumes is Erika. Both relief at the girl's rescue and worry for her health war within Amari.

"Keep one alive and conscious!" Amari calls out to Najaah. The Ashan doesn't so much as pause in their fight, but Kol's head jerks in her direction. She can make out his wide-eyed face and barely resists the urge to scoff.

It's a minute before all but one of the cultists has fallen, and the remaining one has a blade to their neck. Amari approaches, a sharp scowl forming on her face as she takes in Erika's unconscious state. "What did you do to her?"

The cultist stubbornly keeps their lips sealed under her stare until Najaah pushes the blade closer and draws a line of blood. "Answer the question, or this will be a slow and pointless death."

It takes some more intimidation before the cultist finally chokes out an answer. "Nothing! There wasn't enough time to prep her! I swear! She activated one of the wards on her own!"

Turning to the unconscious teen, Amari begins to check her over for injuries. She can sense a temporary knockout drug leaving Erika's system, and a bunch of bruising that would line up with being thrown around by some wards. She nods at Najaah.

Satisfied, the Sun Eater slams the butt of her blade on the cultist's head and lets them fall to the ground in a heap. "Let's go."

Amari finishes her basic check-up on Erika as they hurry out of the level. She pours one of their most valuable healing potions down the teen's throat, prioritizing getting the Nullifier back on her feet as soon as possible. They can't afford to wait for a more natural healing process.

Erika wakes up just as they run into Taliya and Sev, where the tunnels split off. They have to stop trying to leave entirely to ensure she's feeling okay.

"Well," Erika says, looking weary. Her legs were a bit shaky after waking up, but she is standing up now after a minute. "That sucked. But it probably could have been worse. Nothing happened except me nearly getting myself killed."

Kol's shoulders relax, and Taliya smiles wryly. "Glad you're alright, kid."

"Did the Damnation say why they wanted a sacrifice?" Sev asks, barely taking the time to introduce himself when Erika stares in bafflement at the new person in their group.

"No, didn't want to stick around long enough to find out," Erika replies dryly, proving the experience hasn't affected her sense of humor. Her expression then turns thoughtful. "The runes I saw did look like some of the ones in the Gallery of Shadows."

Sev's face turns grim. "Which ones?"

Erika runs her right hand through her hair and adjusts her glasses. Amari is weirdly grateful the cultists didn't take those from her and frowns at the way the teen is careful with her other hand. The seer sees no visible wound and pushes the thought away for now. She knows the healing potion will deal with whatever damage is done.

"The ritual used at the Red Moon festival a thousand years ago, I think… Yeah, I'm sure. The circle had a similar patterning."

The Ravager scowls, glaring at a random spot on the tunnel's wall. "That means they're trying to recreate the rituals that summoned death gods to, and I quote, 'drink the blood of our enemies and bring fortune to our friends.' The Damnation has been after this for a while, but the complete rituals were lost to history. If they're doing this, that means they somehow found the rituals anyway. Or think they did."

Amari shares a look with Nuru, mentally going over their options.

"Death gods?" Kol murmurs, eyes wide.

"Minor death gods," Sev attempts to reassure before he grimaces and glances at Erika. "The only good news is that it requires a lot of sacrifices, so the fact you were the only one there means they're doing this slowly."

"Can we know how far along they are?" Amari questions, frowning. Sev shakes his head, scowling even fiercer.

"Not without questioning more of the Damnation themselves."

"I, for one, will welcome the chance to bust more cultist heads," Kol grins widely, showing off his teeth, tail swishing behind him in anticipation. Erika gives him a long-suffering look and pinches the bridge of her nose.

"Now I feel you're just being ridiculous."

Taliya nudges the teen's right side jokingly. "We'll let you get the first crack at them."

"Ow," Erika mutters, looking down at her right arm in surprise. Alarm races through Amari, and she grabs the teen's arm and rolls up the sleeve before the other can get another word out. In the crook of her elbow, above a big vein, there's the tell-tale evidence of where a needle was used. It's healing by the second as she looks at it, but it was definitely there.

"Do you feel strange at all?" Amari immediately questions, forcing herself to ease her grip and let go despite the desperate urge to examine further. Erika shakes her head, studying the spot on her arm.

"I think… they took blood rather than injected me with

anything."

That's better. Barely.

"They could be tracking Erika using her blood," Sev says, voicing Amari's own concerns.

Amari and Erika share a look. If this were Avalon, Amari would be confident in saying that wouldn't work on the teen's blood, except the Planes run on different rules. Blood magic in the Red City might trump whatever natural defenses Erika has as a Nullifier.

"What about the protections the Wind Weaver gave us?" Nuru points out, glancing at Amari.

"Only works for people trying to manipulate your blood in some way. Tracking is a simpler kind of magic, and the blood they have isn't even in her body anymore. The protections we already took won't do anything."

"How can we counter it?" Erika asks nervously, clearly seeing Amari's uncertainty over her other form of magical defense.

"The Wind Weaver can if we return to their shop," Amari assures. "We just need to get there without being followed."

Sev grimaces, raising a hand to rub the back of his neck. "Then the old sewers are your best bet. They're so chock full of other magical leftovers that nothing individually stands out. They'll get their wires crossed trying."

It's a good plan, except. "The sewers are extremely dangerous to travel through."

He gives her an assessing look. "But you've been before, right? You can take her."

Amari could. The sewers had become the only safe way to travel when she was last here. "And what will you be doing?"

A smirk that promises mischief creeps its way onto Sev's face. "I figure I can show your other friends how to stir up some trouble for those assholes."

Kol straightens, eyes brightening. "Like what?"

While the others gather around Sev, Erika edges closer to Amari, speaking quietly. "What did you mean? What is it about the old sewer systems that are dangerous?"

Amari can't help but snort. "This is the Red City. You've gotten acquainted with the people that live in it. What kind of things do you think live *under* it?"

The blood drains from the teen's face. Even as an unpleasant feeling rises in Amari in response to the fear on Erika's face, it's better for her to be aware than ignorant of the dangers. That's how you get killed.

"I thought magic gets weaker underground?" Erika says in a small voice, something flashing through her eyes before disappearing. The seer needs to lean in a bit to catch the words.

"Not here," Amari thinks that phenomenon is exclusively in Avalon, as far as she's aware. Plenty of other worlds have magical communities underground. This seems to ease Erika's concerns.

"You've been to these sewers before, right?"

Holding back a grimace, Amari nods curtly. "I'll get us through."

Erika's eyes rake over her face wordlessly. "… Alright. What do I need to be ready for?"

"Just keep that dagger ready."

The groups' plans are ironed out in only a few minutes, but Amari wishes they had lasted longer as she and Erika descend to the lowest level. They walk through the ruins of ancient ritual chambers, full of dried blood that was never washed away.

Every entrance to the old sewers Amari has seen feels unsettling. This one is no different. The door is a rusted, near-crumbling thing, with faded wards that are no longer illegible. In Avalon, ward maintenance is an important and highly competitive job. Runes left in disarray like this just highlight how far from home they are.

The first steps into the sewers take both a lifetime and not enough time, and Amari is immediately hit with the musty scent of damp earth and decay. The occasional drip of water echoes ominously, reverberating through corridors that twist and turn unpredictably into the darkness. Other noises are less clear: the scuttle of bugs, the scratch of claws, and the scrape of *something* against the sewer's stone. It's incredibly tempting to deactivate her hearing runes, but she resists the impulse.

"The smell is worse than I thought," Erika coughs into her elbow. Amari hadn't even noticed the smell so much as the *feeling* in the air. The ambient magic here reminds her of Castor in that it feels *alive,* but after that, the feel of it varies wildly. She's always found Castor's magic comforting. This place has no such thing.

"You'll get used to it," is all she says as they start walking down the westward tunnel. It's not a direct shot to the Wind Weaver's shop, Amari knows, yet it will get them close before the tunnels start forking off more aggressively.

"The most dangerous thing down here is tetanus," Erika mutters, surprising Amari so much that she laughs. It echoes down the tunnel, making her tense. She remains vigilant for any signal that something has heard them.

Amari knows well that navigating through this terrible place requires caution and nerve. Where there aren't living obstacles, parts of the sewers can be almost physically impossible to cross. Narrow bridges span chasms filled with stagnant water that could be lethal to fall into. Collapsed tunnels and debris-choked passages serve as reminders of the sewer's unstable and inhospitable nature. Amari tells Erika this.

"Then why do the Ravagers come here at all?"

"They have to. If you can brave its dangers, the sewers offer refuge to outcasts and fugitives. It's a hidden sanctuary beneath the city's civilized facade to people like that."

"…Like a safe haven?"

"I suppose," Amari says, glancing at the girl. She looks contemplative and goes quiet for a while. Then she feels the danger spike.

A roar signals the start of a hunt, and heavy footsteps give away their enemy before it appears in their line of sight. When Amari sees the hideous creation of bone and carnage, she nearly swears. Six hungry eyes stare at her with imminent violence, and another roar escapes from its gaping mouth as it gains its bearings. Twelve jagged horns sit on its chunky head, which itself is scarred all over. A whistling snort escapes the beast's tilted nostrils set within a serpentine nose. It features a compact, robust body made to win battles, with visible bones that act as armor.

A hunting familiar. They're creations summoned to hunt down targets. Someone in the Damnation must have sent this one after Erika.

The beast rushes them, its four legs steadily carrying its body with a threatening speed. A long, spiked tail snakes behind it, and runes cover it all across. It's aiming directly at Erika.

Amari yells to the girl. "Dodge!"

As Erika backs up, Amari decides to momentarily throw caution to the wind and purposefully draw the beast's attention to her. She tries to get a good grasp on the flow of time around her and reaches out for the familiar. Unfortunately, manipulating things in the sewers is an uphill battle of its own. The labyrinth is possessive of its domain and acts as a liminal space.

This means the beast shakes off her magical constraints easily, but it has turned to focus on her. So, it's a mixed success.

The thing is *fast*; it lunges at her before she has any time to think, and Amari reacts by holding her staff up defensively. Instead of doing something smart like using the runes inscribed on the staff to defend herself, she ends up using the actual staff to keep off the familiar. Powerful jaws clamp around her weapon, fighting to reach her. Drool drips from its mouth and looking into its eyes gives her a splitting headache, so she ends up focusing on its large, sharpened teeth and immediately regrets it.

Amari's mind scrambles for options that would work in such close proximity. Thankfully, years of close calls have prepared her for moments exactly like this.

Less carefully than she would like to admit, Amari pushes her magic into the runes on her staff meant to distract their target. Functionally, this means whoever ends up on the other side of this attack is gifted with an incessant ringing sound that slowly drives the target insane. With as much energy as she puts in it now, that descent is less slow and more instant.

The explanation for why Amari uses this spell is simple. This close, whatever magic she uses on the familiar is in danger of hitting her, too. So, for obvious reasons, a sound-based attack is her best bet.

She momentarily stops feeding magic to her hearing enhancement runes, and the annoying high-pitched note is barely noticeable. The beast, on the other hand, violently flinches away. It lets go of her staff to back off in a frenzied sort of panic, paws scrambling for its ears like it can block out the noise.

Taking advantage, Amari pulls out a throwing knife and aims for the beast's head.

A blast of wind rushes down the tunnel, knocking the weapon off track. It misses the familiar, hits a wall with a loud *clunk*, and falls to the floor in a noisy clatter. Amari's stomach drops to her feet, and she quickly starts activating her hearing runes again.

Backing up, Amari motions for Erika to get closer to her. "The familiar's owner is here!"

Gritting her teeth, Amari doesn't wait for the cultist to appear and uses her staff to create the second shield in a day. It holds against the wind, and the familiar bounces off it when it charges them again. The downside of shields is that it's all defense, but she isn't sure how else to protect Erika when she doesn't know the abilities of the cultist tracking them.

Being able to traverse the old sewers like this costs something, Amari knows. The Ravagers respect the natural order of things, and they're the kind to be drawn to in-between places like this. The Damnation, from what she's seen, wants both chaos and control. Conflicting elements like that in magic tend not to end well.

Whoever this cultist is, they must have paid a price to be here. She wonders what it was.

"Heretics, this is your last chance to surrender peacefully," a vaguely male-sounding voice says from the dark. Calm footsteps approach, and the beast recovers its wits to stand by its owner as the cultist emerges into the poor lighting the sewers provide.

Amari doesn't bother to hide her scoff at those words.

For their credit, the cultist doesn't pause before continuing. "You can be forgiven for being so new to our ways, but the ancient traditions of the—"

Oh, damn it all, it's a monologue. She goes through her options at a speed she can admittedly call 'frantic' before mentally throwing her hands up in the air. "Fuck it."

Making sure her grip on her staff is secure, Amari focuses intently on her shield. She pours more energy than she needs into it, slowly building up the pressure.

"—blood of the city runs through our veins, and—"

Erika gives her a weird look as she concentrates and ignores it.

"—accomplish something greater than your—"

Her shield is practically bursting with magic, and the hairs on the back of her neck stand up. She releases all the energy outward at once, creating a massive blast that throws the familiar and the summoner off their feet entirely. She sees the cultist fall in a way that indicates they are very much unconscious.

"Always the talkers," Amari mutters to herself, feeling the drain of energy in her bones. She has enough to keep going, she decides. They can't stop moving.

As soon as the cultist falls still, the familiar disintegrates into a pile of dust and bone.

The teen gasps audibly at the scene. "What—"

"That was a familiar summoned for one task: hunting you. It disappears as soon as that task is completed, or the summoner can't feed magic to it anymore."

"…Oh."

Amari and Erika move to stand over the unconscious gang member, neither speaking for a moment.

Finally, Amari sighs. "Okay, so you know we have to kill him, right?"

"We don't have to!"

"Do you really want to jeopardize the entire mission over someone part of the group who just tried to sacrifice you to a death spirit?"

Erika looks away, not agreeing or conceding. She bites her lips and seemingly attempts to keep the emotions whirling in her off her face. Amari tries very hard not to sigh again. Oh, to be so young.

"Alright. Compromise." Amari hates what she's about to offer, but she doesn't have it in her right now to force this issue with the teenager.

"What?"

"We won't kill him," Amari relents generously. "I will erase his memories of the last twenty minutes, so he doesn't know where we are or where we're going. Okay?"

Erika stares. Perhaps Amari did not explain this well enough.

"You can do that?"

"…Yes." She doesn't like to. It always feels violating on some level, but the guy would probably value his life over the last twenty minutes of memories, so.

The girl blinks, breathes in deeply, and tiredly rubs her forehead with a hand. "Okay. Okay, yeah, I need you to explain that one to me a bit more."

Amari was really hoping she wouldn't say that. Fuck. How to explain this ability without revealing the whole 'I'm a seer' thing? That's directly tied to her power!

"It's complicated. I don't directly go inside someone's mind if you're worried about that. It's also increasingly difficult the more you want to take and the further back you have to go. Since it just happened..."

"You can do it."

"Yeah."

Truthfully, Amari doesn't fully understand how she does it. Theoretically, her seer abilities can let her observe someone's timeline, past, present, and future. Theoretically, she can manipulate time. Realistically, she runs on instincts and no prayers.

At least she's done this before, so she's confident that this doesn't have any adverse effects on the victim except the memory loss itself. Which sucks but is sometimes necessary.

Crouching down, Amari places a hand lightly on the cultist's head. She focuses all her senses on this person, feeling as though she is looking at someone's life laid out all around her, like a city. Carefully, so carefully, she takes the threads that make up what has now been nearly thirty minutes. Once, years ago, she had absorbed those threads and ended up with some hellish nightmares. Now, Amari lets the threads drift away from whoever might pick them up.

Slowly, she draws her senses back. The Present always feels a little jarring after doing something like that.

Erika is watching intently, caught between looking concerned for Amari and for the cultist.

"We're good. Let's go meet up with the others," Amari says firmly as she stands up. It couldn't have taken her more than a few minutes to do that, yet it somehow felt like ages.

Hesitantly, Erika nods and leaves with her.

Obviously, things have to go wrong again before they can escape these damned sewers.

It's Amari's fault, truly. She should have recognized the territory they wandered into after all the time she spent here. But a tunnel in the more direct path to the Wind Weaver's shop was too collapsed to pass through, so they had to go out of the way.

Now, as she feels a suffocating presence approaching, she regrets not trying harder. Instinctively, Amari readies her staff and uses her free hand to grab Erika, hastily pushing the girl behind her in an insufficient form of protection.

"What's—"

Shh, Amari says through the network. *Don't speak aloud.*

What's going on? Erika asks, a thrum of fear to her thoughts. The seer would feel guilty for putting it there if she didn't think it was entirely warranted.

A spirit. A powerful one, Amari admits. A door in the sewers looms to the side of the tunnel, leading to a small room that was once used for maintenance. It doesn't lead anywhere, except that Amari doesn't need it to.

I'm going to draw it into that room, she tells Erika, who is gripping her arm tightly. *Wait out here and be ready to run.*

What? Are you sure I can't—

I know what to do, Amari tries to inject as much certainty as she can into her message, layering calm over their mental connection. Something must reassure Erika because the teen lets her go without more argument, even as she radiates anxiousness.

The moment Amari steps into the room and closes the door, she spreads her magical presence around the space. It acts as a beacon to those who would recognize her, and the spirit is there in less than five seconds.

"My old fri-end," the scratchy voice of the spirit resonates, sending chills down her spine that the seer ignores. She can see the cruel amusement in its form despite the spirit being little more than a malevolent black cloud.

She takes a deep breath and reminds herself she just needed to get it away from Erika. "I'm just passing through."

"Such thi-ngs have a price," it giggles sharply, sounding outright nightmare-ish.

"I don't have time for that."

"Don't you want to he-lp an old fri-end? My home has seen better days. So many up-starts trying to pick aw-ay at what is *mine*."

"Maybe you should have thought of that before you tried to bite off more than you can chew," she snaps, knowing even as she says it, she's stepping over a line. "I won't help you ever again. You can deal with your territory on your own."

The damned spirit's form twists into something distorted and furious, a low sound like a scream rising from it. Amari reacts before it can harm her or her friend.

With her hands out, she focuses on her sense of Time and the way it flows around the spirit. As pressure starts to build behind her eyes, Amari slows the spirit's perception of Time to a near standstill.

This maneuver is so precarious she's only done it a few times in her life. But the feeling of the sewers — the constant sense of death and decay — carries its own kind of power even if the liminal space resists her efforts. She channels the magic of the sewers through her, something she would never recommend anyone else ever do.

The moment it looks like the spirit is properly frozen, she flees.

She quickly opens the telepathic connection between her and the

Nullifier waiting outside. *Hey, Erika, you know how I said offending people here was a terrible idea?*

Yeah?

Well, Amari says. *I'm really good at picking fights. I'm so good that it often happens unintentionally. I should have mentioned it before, that's my bad.*

What?

This is the part where we run. She's booking it out of the room as she sends this message, snagging Erika's sleeve as she goes. The teen stumbles precariously for a moment, then regains her footing and tries to keep up with the seer.

For a few minutes, Amari leads them through the sewers entirely by her sixth sense of where danger lurks. As the feeling of oncoming doom dims in her mind, she eventually starts trying to direct them back to the Wind Weaver's shop again. Thankfully, their little detour didn't take them too far away.

"What was *that?*" Erika asks when they stop running, breathing heavily. Amari gently guides her around a section of collapsed pipes.

"An old, nasty spirit," the seer answers. Obfuscation is an art form. "We wandered into its territory. Stalling it and running was the best option."

"You're okay, though, right?"

"... Yeah," Amari says, staring into the depths of the sewers. The longer she stays down here, the more she feels like the touch of death sticks to her. "I'm fine. Just a bit drained, magic-wise. I can get something at the shop to help with that."

Erika doesn't respond, perhaps picking up that Amari is also drained social-wise. It's nice that she does not need to voice that feeling. Usually, only Taliya notices when the seer grows sick of people.

It takes them the better part of thirty minutes, but they head back to the Wind Weaver's shop without any more trouble. Amari's limbs feel like lead weights the whole way there.

16

TALIYA

As it turns out, Sev and Taliya's idea of trouble and how to cause it align spectacularly.

"You do this often?"

Taliya turns to the Ravager, who is watching her skillfully break into a building with amusement written all over his face. She raises an eyebrow at him. "This is your idea; shouldn't I be asking you that?"

"I would have thought the answer was obvious," Sev replies dryly. Taliya snorts, easing the newly unlocked door open. Inside, a room full of macabre furnishings and decorations sits ominously. She ignores the place's vibes and beelines for the most expensive object in the room. The gems she can sense are filled with magic, storing energy for future use. She checks them over for wards before dumping them in her bag.

Sev is staring at her. "What?"

He shakes his head, chuckling. "Nothing, nothing."

Since they're here for more than just stealing, Taliya goes back to scanning the room. This is supposedly some sort of safehouse for the

Damnation, and from the decorations, Taliya would agree. Sev claims there are also important rituals done here that they can sabotage.

"Here," he says, tugging out a trunk that was hidden inside a locked cabinet. He pulls out an object and raises it so Taliya can see. It isn't something she recognizes just by appearance, so she walks closer for a better look.

The item is similar to a piece of dice, she thinks. With twenty-four sides adorned by sigil carvings, made from a polished white material that's not stone, and being about the size of a watermelon, it's too weird an object to be for anything but magic. "What is that?"

"A Bone Pearl. The Damnation uses them as a channel to steal other people's life force through and use that energy as a sacrifice."

"Well," Taliya replies with clear distaste in her voice. "Let's make sure this one is out of commission."

They're not here just to steal. They're here to *sabotage*. She pulls out her runica, determined that the next time a cultist picks this thing up, they're the ones who will be on the other end of its powers.

Taliya and Sev leave the room in the same state when they found it before moving on to their next target. Najaah and Kol are doing a similar task in places that are more straightforward for people new to the city to access.

It takes them three hours before everyone regroups at the Wind Weaver's shop, and they return to an… interesting scene.

Amari, Erika, *and* Nuru beat them there, standing with safety gear next to the Wind Weaver himself. Half a dozen Ravagers are also in the room, including the three Taliya met at the clocktower.

The room descends into chaos the moment everyone is safely inside.

The Ravagers start arguing amongst themselves and with Sev. Kol ambushes Erika to make sure she is still here and conscious. Najaah ignores everyone else and starts questioning the Wind Weaver about something. In the midst of it all, Taliya tries not to start sighing in despair right out of the gate, and instead, she heads toward Amari so she can find out what's happening.

"Why do I feel like I just walked into a council meeting?" Taliya asks her friend, hands smoothly running through the signs. The mask probably muffles her speech too much, so she's disregarding it entirely. She's referring to the times they were present for a meeting of the Underground Resistance's top strategists. Grouping a bunch of paranoid, clever, desperate fugitives in one room and expecting a simple solution to present itself was too much of an ask then, and she feels the same way now.

Amari snorts as she leans against the wall next to her. "I see the similarities, but I'd like to think this is a touch less dire. No Imperial special forces or Order inquisitors are involved, for one. I believe we can get something worked out in time. Did your group run into any problems on the way here?"

"No. Stole some magic gems, sabotaged some creepy cult stuff, came back here. You?"

"We had a few problems. I needed to buy some magic replenishing vials when we arrived," Amari admits. "One of the Damnation summoned a hunting familiar and tracked us down in the sewers. Had an... eventful run-in with a native spirit. As soon as we returned, the Wind Weaver gave Erika something to stop all future attempts at tracking."

Taliya whistles lowly, eyebrows rising as she exaggerates her gestures. "Damn, those assholes really don't give up, huh?"

"They likely are paranoid that their plans to summon minor death gods will be released to the other gangs."

"A tragedy," Taliya signs, making sure her hands properly convey how sarcastic she is being. "Truly. By the way, what is the distinction between them summoning *minor* death gods?"

Amari's eyes sparkle in a way that means she is definitely smirking. "Would you rather them be summoning a *major* death god?"

"No, obviously, but what's the difference? Are the minor gods just less powerful?"

"Essentially," the seer answers with visible amusement. "It's a bit more intricate than that, though. What responsibilities a god has, the kind of death they represent, and the nature of the being all go into it."

"What," Taliya slashes her hands sharply. "Is there some kind of qualification process to becoming a *major* god?"

Shoulders shaking subtly, Amari briefly ducks her head. "Something like that."

The moment is broken by Sev clearing his throat loudly, instantly drawing the room's attention. "We need a plan of action, and not just for the distant future, for *today*. The Damnation's plans cannot be allowed to continue unheeded."

"Damn straight," Taliya agrees, making several Ravagers glance at her weirdly. "You got an idea?"

"I may," Sev says. He turns to Amari. "In your time here, did you hear about The Broker?"

The Nightblood leans forward to listen better as she grimaces under the mask and nods warily. "Yeah, I did. Are you suggesting we seek out his help?"

"He would be a useful ally, and I can't imagine he is any more pleased with the idea of unleashing death gods in his city."

"Who's The Broker?" Kol interrupts the back and forth, a scowl marring his face.

"A mob boss," Amari answers with a scornful tone.

"A landlord," Sev adds dryly.

"A neutral party," The Wind Weaver speaks up for the first time, drawing everyone's eyes. "He has no love for any particular gang. And he is a source of power and information. If you present your case, it is likely he will help stop the Damnation from changing the power dynamics in the city so drastically. For a price."

Sev sighs. "He also owns half the land in the city and knows everything that goes on in it."

"Exactly," Amari says. "A mob boss."

"Then are we sure he isn't already aware of the Damnation's plan?" Nuru questions, sounding very sensible.

The Ravager leader with red eyes Taliya had met before answers. "Probably, but he wouldn't make a move on his own and start a conflict between himself and the Damnation. If we make a good offer, he will help us."

"Then what can we offer?"

"I was hoping," Sev starts, looking directly at Amari. "As the dimensional travelers and ones who proposed this deal, you would have something."

Taliya wishes she could be irritated, except the Ravager has a point. "What kind of things does the Broker usually take?"

"Information, blood, land, money, anything of value, really. This situation will likely demand a high price."

"Blood, land, and money are out," Amari says thoughtfully, tapping her chin with her finger. "We don't have much information regarding the city apart from what the Broker would already know. Is there anything outside this world he would be interested in?"

Sev looks at the Ravager leader, frowning. They think it over for a moment before answering. "Anything that could affect this dimension or his business would be something he'd want to know."

"What about the governor?" Erika asks, shrinking as everyone's attention snaps to her.

"Governor?" Sev mutters.

"Ah," Amari says. "Governor Jameson. Yes, are you aware that the gate we used to come here is stable and under the control of a religious order from our world? Coupled with the multiple gateways in the Heart, your city could see a lot of activity from our dimension in the future."

The Ravagers exchange looks and quiet words, an energy of uneasiness coming over them. "No, but the Broker might be."

"If he does, I imagine there is only so much he can know about our world. We can trade that," Amari turns to Nuru, who has been listening intently. "Would you be willing to meet with him? I think we should split into two groups. One, for the Broker, and another to secure the gate."

Najaah asks their first question. "So one group will focus on getting support to stop the Damnation while you infiltrate the Riders?"

"Yes. I think the Damnation's plot is a good distraction from the gateways, don't you?" the seer muses wryly.

The Ravagers discuss the plan among themselves before their leader turns to Amari. "As long as members of your team are in both groups, we see no problem with this."

"Agreed."

Kol sends Taliya a baffled look, and she shrugs. Explaining the situation to the teen is so not her responsibility. He turns to Nuru, who sighs before launching into a quiet explanation about mutually assured destruction, or whatever you want to call it.

Everyone goes over the details, contingency plans, and where to make a fast exit if everything goes sideways. It's decided that Nuru, Najaah, Erika, and Sev, along with three extra Ravagers, will head to the Broker first. They will come to an agreement with the influential man and stop the Damnation's plan to rise to power in a way that draws attention away from group two.

Group two is Amari, Taliya, Kol, and the last three Ravagers, including their red-eyed leader. Everyone will be traveling through the old sewers — Amari and Erika make faces at the prospect but don't raise any complaints — to avoid early detection. However, Taliya's group will leave a full hour after the first.

Once everything is ironed out, everyone simply waits for dusk to fall before group one leaves. During the wait, Amari makes sure everyone in their group has the Heart's layout fully memorized. The dullness of the topic is countered by the anticipation of the future fight.

Taliya's group heads down to the old sewers as soon as the specified hour arrives. These unsettling tunnels aren't the worst place she's ever been, but they're pretty close. She ends up sticking close to her friend while Kol gets acquainted with the Ravagers ahead of them. At least the teen seems unbothered by the borderline hostile ambient magic of the sewers.

The walk is punctuated by random attacks from monsters lurking in the depths and traps, which Amari points out to Taliya to pick apart efficiently. Still, between the Ravagers' large amount of experience navigating these tunnels and Amari's senses, it's a rather dull journey.

At one point, Taliya gets fed up with keeping her questions under wraps and turns to her best friend with already moving hands.

"You never did tell me the whole story of what happened here last time," Taliya asks, glancing at Amari from the corner of her eye. Her friend is outwardly calm, projecting a sort of confidence that sets everyone at ease. The only evidence of inner turmoil is a small frown.

"It's not a pleasant one," Amari admits after careful contemplation, her gestures slow. Her brows furrow slightly. "You remember what I was like when I came back."

Taliya does. Amari was only seventeen then, and when she returned, she took her hypervigilance to a new level. She watched every shadow, was suspicious of every encounter, and only took the food and drinks she made herself or Taliya made for her. It was months before she loosened her grip on that feeling.

Worst of all were the nightmares.

"Tell me anyway," Taliya isn't usually one to pry. She knows Amari has secrets for a reason, even if that reason is fear.

The seer doesn't reply immediately, sorting through her thoughts. Then she signs with fast movements, like she's trying to get it out all at once. "I was stupid. I made a mistake. On my first night here, I got jumped by a group looking to harvest my blood, and I was injured in the fight. Badly injured. I barely made it to a clinic before passing out on their doorstep. But the clinics here don't trade in money."

Taliya swallows past the lump in her throat, trying to convey comfort. "What do they take?"

"Blood, of course. Plus, bone marrow, cells, and other things like that. Not enough to permanently damage, but enough to keep you weak and trapped. For healing the injuries from my fight, they said I would stay there for six months."

Amari was only gone a week, as far as Taliya remembers. But the Planes can run on a different timeline than Avalon. She feels a chill run up her spine.

"I couldn't do it. It was—I couldn't stay there..." Amari explains, expression edging toward shameful. Taliya wants to correct her, but feels if she interrupts Amari now, her friend will never finish the story. "I don't remember how I summoned it. I just know I wasn't alone in my room when I woke up from a harvesting. It wasn't a doctor or nurse, but some kind of spirit. Not a normal one—as normal as any spirit can be called. It was one native to the Red City. You could tell because it reeked of blood magic and decay and talked in the native language."

She doesn't ask her question, yet Amari must sense it. "The clinic undid my translation runes after telling me the price of my healing. It was a lucky break that they didn't recognize my hearing enhancement runes and left them be. I had to figure out the language to keep up with what was happening. That's how I knew the spirit was there to offer me a deal. A price in exchange for my escape.

"I was stupid. I would have done anything at that moment, and it asked for a steep price. It wanted my name."

Taliya didn't know she could feel like she was drenched in ice water despite being perfectly dry. "What does that mean?"

She doesn't like the far-off look that's overtaken Amari's eyes. Her friend's signs are getting a bit shaky. "Names are important. The more personal a name, the more your identity is tied to it. I almost lost my sense of self entirely when it took my name. I wandered the streets, confused about my purpose and who I was. Until I stumbled into the Wind Weaver. They offered me a simple deal: a safe place to sleep for the air I breathe with no harm to me."

"Do they offer that to everyone?" Taliya asks, a little baffled about what prompted the Weaver to offer help. Amari badly smothers a wince.

"I might have looked particularly homeless at the time," she admits with a wry smile. "I stayed for a couple of days. The Wind Weaver would always answer my questions patiently, and I figured out what had happened to me. I knew I had to get my name back.

"Things got a bit complicated after that. I ended up going to the Ravagers for help, then, too, because they have experience with spirits like the one I encountered. They told me the only way to get my name back was to bind the spirit and offer a new deal."

Amari frowns, flexing her hands for a minute before continuing. "I had to venture into the old sewers to find the spirit. Apparently, being on the surface was a rare occurrence for creatures like that one. It was… a harrowing journey. It took me a day and a half of interrogating every sentient creature down here, but I eventually found the spirit. I used my *unique* abilities and some warding the Ravagers taught me to bind it. It wasn't pleased by that. Brokering a deal that ended with my name returned to me *and* without the spirit taking revenge after it was freed proved to be difficult. I had to carve out space in the old sewers for the spirit to use as a territory. That means putting up wards, fighting off other monsters, and figuring out a cohesive pattern in these tunnels. It was incredibly tedious."

"Wow," Taliya mouths after Amari finishes her story.

"Yeah. Basically, it sucked. I'd like to avoid a giant delay like that. I'm not sure we can afford it."

Taliya barely resists sending the seer a *look*. She hopes her hands are suitably theatrical. "Oh, is *that* what you're worried about? I'm partial to avoiding treacherous spirits altogether myself."

She gets an elbow in her side for her attitude. Amari huffs, but a ghost of a smile appears on her face, so Taliya considers it a win.

They reach their destination not long after. The exit from the old sewers is a grate in the basement of an abandoned bar filled with rotting barrels of some unidentifiable liquor. Because Taliya likes to travel in style.

The bar is the closest they can get to the Heart without popping straight into a building or street occupied by Crimson Riders' patrols. Taliya follows Amari and the others up some precarious-looking stairs to the roof for a better view.

The Heart is aptly named.

From a distance, the Heart resembles an actual, colossal, organic heart, its contours marked by a network of flowing, vein-like structures that appear to pulse rhythmically. The building's surface is a macabrely beautiful blend of crimson and black, with walls that seem to beat with a life of their own. Taliya can feel the rhythm reverberating through the concrete underfoot even miles away. A network of arcane veins, wrought from twisted metal and enchanted crystal, snakes across the facade, their soft glow flickering in time with an unsettling pulse.

"Wow," Taliya says, impressed despite herself. "There's morbid, and then there's *this*."

"No kidding," Kol breathes, just a step away from openly gawking.

Amari hides a small smirk while the Ravagers give her weird looks. The red-eyed leader sighs. "It is a monument to the past. We don't need it anymore."

"Still, it seems a shame not to use it for something new," Taliya remarks, commenting even though she has no investment in the discussion. The Ravager hums thoughtfully.

Kol turns to Amari. "When will we know it's time?"

Right. Their telepathic time limit has run out, and gem comms don't work in the Planes very much, so they have to resort to other means.

"Well, the others are going to be a distraction. So we'll wait for something distracting to happen," Amari says. It wouldn't be apparent to anyone who doesn't know her as well as Taliya does, but the seer is laughing at them all internally.

The sky rat splutters in the face of that answer, looking like he's gearing up to start an argument, when a large explosion goes off in the distance. Everyone whips around to see a cloud of smoke rising above the rooftops on the horizon.

"That's by the Broker's casino," a Ravager points out.

"A good distraction," Amari comments. Kol sends her a look of disbelief. "We should head towards the Heart."

With some cajoling, the group is moving again across the roofs. In the waning light of the suns, the shadows stretch and cling to them like toddlers, giving them cover from the watchful eyes of the Crimson Riders. In all fairness, those eyes are turned toward the commotion picking up miles away.

Taliya discreetly scans the street as she passes over it, finding many citizens clumped together and talking. She's not close enough to discern any words, but the general vibe is clear from the frantic movements of their hands and the overall tension she can feel meters away. They're angry about something. Choosing to travel by roof is looking like more and more of a wise decision by the minute.

"What's going on?" Kol asks, having also noticed the strange behavior. The Ravagers, she notices, seem rather pleased as the group pauses their rooftop traveling to study the situation. The Heart is only a block away at this point, looming ominously over this whole scene.

"Someone's been riling them up," Amari mutters, eyes zeroing in on something one person is holding. She leans precariously over the edge of the building they're on, exposing herself to view but going unnoticed anyway. "The Damnation has been taking people from the Rider's territory to mess with the gang. I think they've underestimated how the rest of the public will react. With our interference, we might have a riot on our hands."

"And that would be... bad?" Kol says, eyeing the people with a frown.

"It would be chaotic," Amari clarifies. "Outside anyone's control at that point. That could be good for us, or it could be bad. Let's try to make it the first."

The clamor on the streets seems to reach a fever pitch, and Riders start to pour out of the Heart to try to gain control over the growing crowd. Taliya can immediately tell that it's the wrong choice, only firing up the people even further now that they have a physical target at which to aim their ire. Out of the commotion, a rock is thrown at a Crimson Rider. It misses by a wide margin, but it's the start of an avalanche.

"We need to keep going," Amari reminds everyone, pulling Taliya out of her staring. "This is our best chance to get into the Heart without much resistance."

"You heard her," the red-eyed Ravager says to their comrades, and the group starts moving again. Taliya catches Kol trying to watch the streets, despite Amari's order, and keeps a lookout for if anyone notices him.

Before she even realizes it, they're in front of the Heart, and she has to scale down a building to access the street entrance. No one is on guard, clearly responding to the hostile crowd so close by. She wonders how much security is left inside. According to the Ravagers, the Heart doesn't need many human guardians to begin with.

The main entrance to the Heart is an imposing pair of double doors fashioned from a dark, blood-red material that seems almost liquid in its fluidity. Above is a massive, pulsating glyph — etched into the very surface of the building — that serves as both a protective ward and a symbol of the blood magic that powers the structure. Despite the displays of grandeur, Taliya makes quick work of the wards. There are very few proactive measures that actually apply to her group. It's almost like the place is designed to keep people *in,* not out.

Once past the doors of the Heart, Taliya wishes she had taken her time with the wards. Something about the energy of the building makes the hair on the back of her neck stand up. The central atrium is vast and cavernous, dominated by a massive core that occupies the center of the space and beats in time with the rest of the building.

"At least they stay on theme," Taliya mutters.

As she follows the Ravagers into a corridor, the atmosphere grows heavier. Taliya warily watches the sigils on the walls, not wanting to step into some kind of trap unknowingly. She prefers to step into traps only when fully informed.

"Anyone else feel like they're being watched?" Taliya whispers to her friend, not wanting her voice to echo in these halls. Kol's eyebrows furrow, and he looks all around like an amateur.

"No?"

"Yes," Amari says, not reacting otherwise. "Whatever it is, it's not a Crimson Rider, so we should ignore it until it becomes a problem."

"I'm always down for ignoring my problems," Taliya agrees with a small smile, making her friend roll her eyes. Kol gives them both a look as if he's worried about their mental health.

"We're getting close," a Ravager tells them quietly, drawing them out of their side conversation.

The Heart's corridors have gradually been going upward, and Taliya estimates they're about 10 yards off street level by now. No windows to confirm this by, though. The wards and sigils on the walls have been slowly multiplying as well, almost as if in anticipation of something. Taliya really hopes it's just the gateways. According to the Ravagers, the Heart is built around *ten* stabilized gateways. In Avalon, where such things are sparse and rare occurrences, it's a bit mind-boggling to think about. She hopes the Broker realizes how important Nuru, Najaah, and Erika's information on the Empire and Order could be.

Thankfully, the runes on the wall haven't dipped into 'cursing all trespassers,' but Taliya is sure it's only a matter of time. In a place like this, assuming otherwise is less optimistic and more plain stupid.

"The energy of this place... is so weird," Kol mutters to himself, eyebrows furrowed. "I feel like it's trying to get inside my mind somehow."

"It is," Amari states, tone far too casual for her words. Both Taliya and Kol send her alarmed looks. The seer shrugs. "I told you before we arrived that you needed to keep your mental shields up."

"I thought you meant against actual people!" Kol hisses, trying to keep his voice down despite the strong urge to yell. Taliya turns her attention to the ambient magic of the Heart and immediately regrets it. She scrunches her nose in disgust, as if the energy has a smell to it.

"Those, too," Amari says.

The magic of the building feels like an oily, tar-like darkness that tries to cling and *take* from anything that gets close. As used to Castor as she is, Taliya has no trouble shrugging off the effects of ambient magic, but it's a great deal more unpleasant than her home. Strong emotions imprint on the magic around it, and nothing feels as strongly in the Heart as *greed*.

Taliya doesn't know what it says about her that she almost

didn't notice until Kol pointed it out.

"You're the most uncomforting person I know," Kol whispers viciously at Amari. The seer gives him a deadpan look, and the sky rat turns away with a huff. Taliya focuses back on the wards running along the wall, determined not to think about the Heart's ambient magic anymore.

As she suspected, it doesn't take long for the first wards that could do real harm to their team to appear. Taliya is in the back of the group, so she doesn't see it in time to warn the others, but Amari must sense it because she pulls a Ravager out of the way just in time to miss having their head removed by a blade that came out of the wall.

"Let Taliya deal with the wards," her friend suggests, glancing at Taliya to make sure she's alright with being volunteered. The Ravagers don't argue, likely relieved someone not a part of their gang must do the dangerous bit.

"How did you do that?" Kol asks Amari, just quiet enough that their allies don't hear.

"Do what?"

"Know the trap was there before it tripped?"

Amari gives him a flat look, giving off the air of someone exasperated, and only Taliya can see the tension in her body. "I know a bit about wards, too, Kol. Not like Taliya, but I can get by."

The seer turns away to watch the Ravagers closely while Taliya pulls out her runica and starts to move toward the wards. Kol frowns at Amari, something like suspicion flashing through his eyes before everyone collectively moves their attention back to getting to their destination.

After that brief foray into near misses, Taliya leads the group and dismantles wards as she goes. Or she tells the others how to avoid the trap. It brings their progress to all but a crawl, except they're so close to their goal it doesn't take too long before they reach a large set of doors.

"This is the entrance to the Gathering of Gateways. Half of the Heart's gates are in here, including the one to the Forsaken Forest," a Ravager confirms.

The doors are made of obsidian-like stone with intricate patterns carved into them. They're all very fancy-looking, and Taliya wishes there was something valuable behind them that she could actually steal.

Sigils line the doors, and she has to have a boost from Kol to get to the ones high up. It takes her over twenty minutes since Taliya wants to be as thorough as possible. Wardbreaking in the Planes, as she has learned, is also a lesson in adaptability.

There are rules in Avalon for magic. Rules are a joke in the Planes.

Essentially, Taliya is forced to be creative to ensure they don't all get blown up when they open the doors. So she's thorough. When the thief's finally done, Amari helps her open the doors, revealing a vast room.

The space itself is octagonal, with high vaulted ceilings that rise to an ornate, star-patterned dome. The walls are lined with an intricate mosaic of shimmering tiles, each depicting sigils and runes that pulse with the building's heartbeat. The floor is the same polished, black stone as the door, giving the impression that the room is floating in the void.

Positioned on the northern wall, a gateway is framed by an elaborate archway of intertwining silver vines. The portal within it is a swirling, translucent mist that shifts colors from iridescent blues to ethereal purples. Taliya can hear faint, melodic whispers coming from within the fog, and she feels as if it radiates dream magic. Best to keep her distance.

The second gate she registers is located on the western wall. This gateway is outlined by a luminous frame resembling a crescent moon. She glances at Amari, who is looking at the portal within—a swirling expanse of stars and galaxies — with curiosity. The light from the portal casts soft, twinkling reflections across the room, evoking a sense of infinite space and distant worlds.

In the southwest, another gateway is bordered by a dark, jagged rock that seems to absorb light. That goes on Taliya's list to avoid instantly. Located on the other side of the room, the northeastern space hosts the fifth gateway, encased in a crystalline frame resembling frost-covered glass. She marks this one under the 'safe enough' column since it's likely a realm of eternal winter.

Finally, Taliya's eyes fall on the gateway set into the eastern wall, framed by a lush arch of intertwining vines and flowering plants. The portal is a dark green expanse of dense foliage and towering trees, with a faint scent of earth and blooming flowers wafting through. The air around it is full of life, but not necessarily the inviting kind. It feels more like the energy of the untamed wilderness.

She notices that the large room is lit by a soft, ambient light that seems to emanate from the portals themselves, casting an ever-changing glow that shifts with the energy of each gateway. The air is thick with a faint, otherworldly hum that fluctuates with the presence of every portal, creating a harmonious yet eerie symphony of sounds.

"That one," Amari nods to the eastern gateway. Taliya glances at her, seeing the subtle tension in the seer's face. Taliya has no particularly special senses, and this room feels trippy to her, making her wonder what exactly her friend is sensing in this room.

The moment someone steps a foot in the room, it all goes to shit.

Shadows converge in the center of the giant room in a storm of darkness. Emerging from it is a monstrous abomination that feels like the concentration of all the ancient blood magic and ghosts of violence Taliya has sensed in this city. A grotesque form swirls into being from the shadows, a testament to the malevolent power that shapes it. It's a horrific fusion of emotion and decay.

"A Colossus," one of the Ravagers whispers in a trembling voice.

The Colossus fully stands up, towering above them, its hulking frame an amalgamation of twisted bone, corrupted flesh, and pulsating veins. Its skin, what once could have had a semblance of humanoid likeness to it, is now a mottled canvas of deep crimson and sickly gray, stretched taut over a framework of skeletal remnants. Jagged, necrotic patches pulse rhythmically, as if the blood that once coursed through its veins still lingers, driven by an unholy will.

Its face is a nightmare of contorted features, where hollow eye sockets burn with an unearthly glow. An unnatural light flickers within the empty voids, revealing glimpses of ancient runes and arcane symbols etched into the beast's corrupted flesh. These symbols writhe and shift as if alive, puppeted by the influence of residual magic. Taliya doesn't make a single attempt to read them.

The monster's limbs are gnarled and elongated, ending in clawed appendages that seem to be a grotesque parody of human hands. They're covered in intricate patterns of runes, and they drip with a dark, viscous substance that hisses and seethes with magical energy. She feels from the depths of her soul that no part of this thing should touch a human.

It's a miracle that no one in their group decides to say *fuck it* and run away at the sight of the Colossus. Taliya wouldn't even blame them if they did; she kind of feels like doing that right now.

"Don't let that thing touch any of you," Amari warns, staff out and fully extended in a split second. The thief almost scoffs at the obvious advice before the seer continues. "Its decay will spread to any living thing it touches."

Okay, now Taliya just feels nauseous and as if her heart's trying to escape her chest.

The Colossus takes a great lumbering step toward them, and everyone scatters. The Ravagers go left, Taliya and Amari go right, while Kol goes up. Surprisingly, no one books it out the doors before they shut with an ominous clang.

Everyone explodes into movement. Without discussing it, Kol begins acting as a flying distraction, Amari and Taliya mount a sort of hit-and-run offense tactic, and the Ravagers start darting around the room to scribe down symbols that drain the Colossus' blood magic. Unfortunately, the loss of power is far too slow and minor to deter the monster. They need something that will hurt this thing.

Taliya's swords leave little damage, no matter how much magic she channels into them, and none of Amari's offensive measures do more than irritate the thing. All the while, they're dodging swings of grotesque limbs and blocking tendrils of shadow that lash out from the Colossus.

"Cover me!" Amari shoves her staff into the thief's hands and turns away from the fight to pull off her bag. Taliya scrambles to do what she asks, hastily channeling magic through the staff's protective runes, ensuring no attacks reach the seer while she digs through her things. "Got it!"

"Got *what?*" Taliya has no memory of packing anything that would be helpful in this situation. Amari has pulled out a magic storage token, holding it in a careful way that baffles her. "What is that supposed to do?"

"Just buy me some more time!"

At that unsatisfying answer, Taliya blocks another attack from hitting Amari with a shield and keeps an eye out as her friend sets the token down on the floor with a caution that feels foreign to see. The seer starts drawing a rune circle around the token, and Taliya can't split her attention well enough to see what she's scribing.

Kol flies overhead, ensnaring the monster's focus away from them, and barely dodges a swing. The Sky Lord bumps into the ceiling for the third time Taliya has noticed, and he quickly drops to the floor to duck under another attack before kicking off a wall and flying up again.

Make that four times.

Taliya's just about to tell the kid to maybe stick to the ground when Amari abruptly stands up behind her and drags her away from the rune circle. She whips her head around to see and gets a glimpse of activated sigils before a shadowy presence, sparking with lightning, leaves the token and obscures her view.

"What the fuck is that?" Taliya gapes, watching some kind of spirit form. Everyone else in the room quickly gets some distance from the new player. "Amari, what the fuck is that? Did you trap a spirit in a *magic storage token?*"

The Nightblood, to her infuriation, just smirks in answer to her question. "We should keep our distance for now, but we can't let anything happen to the circle. That'll be what traps the spirit again."

"What, once captured wasn't good enough for you?"

The Colossus turns its attention to the pissed-off spirit, like two predators catching sight of each other.

Amari shrugs. "I figured we'd like to avoid it turning around and attacking us next."

A massive swing meant to flatten the spirit misses by a hair's breadth as the smaller creature lunges at the Colossus's throat.

"Fair enough, I guess," Taliya concedes. "Still, you could have mentioned that you had a random spirit bottled up in your bag."

"I thought it made a nice surprise," Amari smiles, eyes crinkling before her focus snaps back to the monsters. "And it's only been a few hours anyway."

Obviously. Taliya can't imagine a *token* containing a spirit for much longer than that.

The two monsters go at each other like rabid animals — all brutal violence and cornered fear and *hunger*. It takes everything the humans have not to become collateral damage as the room shakes.

Taliya can't help but notice that even as these two creatures of dreadful magic fight, they still avoid the five gateways like they're afraid to get close. It's a disquieting observation.

It takes a minute for the violent stalemate to come to a close. The Colossus sends a barrage of tendrils of darkness at the spirit, which prevents it from blocking a terrible strike of lightning across its face. Instead of bleeding like a living creature would, it seems like this attack damages the very integrity of the Colossus' form. A large part of the thing dissipates into shadows.

As the Colossus falls to its knees, Amari darts forward to the circle of runes she drew. With a few words, they light up again, and an invisible force begins to pull the spirit back. It lashes out angrily, a soul-chilling screech splitting the air. The seer doesn't waver as she seals the spirit away, leaving only a smoldering token.

"That's not going to last as a container," Taliya points out, keeping her eye on the wounded Colossus. Kol has decided to do the smart thing and channel his outrageous amount of magic into powering the Ravagers' runes, draining the monster. It starts disintegrating at a quicker rate, but still not fast enough to stop the thing permanently.

Her attention turns back to Amari as she picks up the spirit token with her gloved hands and then *throws it through the gateway of darkness.*

A strangled noise, so intense it hurts her throat, escapes from Taliya unintentionally. She reflexively pulls her swords back out. "Amari, *what –* "

"Most efficient solution," is all Amari says as she shrugs and turns her focus to the Colossus. Taliya wants to jump in front of the Nightblood and shake her until coherent answers pop out. That is, of course, when the remaining monster in the room makes a rumbling noise so full of rage it sends every hair on the back of Taliya's neck standing.

Darkness starts wafting off the Colossus like smoke, and she really doesn't like how the air is rippling around the thing.

"Shit," Amari mutters succinctly. "It's gathering ambient magic and planning to unleash its shadow attacks again. We need it still to deliver a final blow."

Taliya's stomach sinks. The seer doesn't ask her, but the Osiyi knows what her friend is alluding to anyway. This monster is too big and too powerful for any normal magic to contain it long enough to attack.

She refuses to hesitate. With a deep breath, Taliya opens her mouth to let out the beginning verse of a song in a long-forgotten language. The dark, haunting melody emerges, resonating at a spine-chilling timbre. The notes are low and rich, each word flowing like smoke. They curl and twist in the air, as the very essence of her voice becomes infused with ancient power.

Taliya slowly gains more and more awareness of every drop of water in the room, including the ones running through people's veins. She focuses on the dredges left in the Colossus, a being already fashioned from blood magic. With her power, she tries to grab as much of the monster as she can and *holds on.*

Blood magic isn't inherently malicious or cruel. In fact, healers use many smaller, more benign techniques all the time. Magic is a natural element of the universe. The people who use it decide whether it's good or evil.

Taliya knows this, academically. It still doesn't stop her from remembering times when reaching for the blood running in people's veins was as easy as breathing. Killing had been so easy, then.

The opening she gives is all Amari and Kol need, the seer using her staff to channel a blast of pure energy while the teen sends every piece of debris at the head of the Colossus with more force than any being would be able to throw. All the magic collides and implodes, sending everyone skidding back a few yards.

In the moments following, a tense silence lays over the room as the group collectively holds its breath. Seconds later, when the Colossus isn't moving, relief takes over. Kol cheers, a couple of

Ravagers hug, and even Amari smiles as the seer's shoulders relax. Taliya wordlessly stares at the fallen form for a long while after.

17

ERIKA

Erika grimaces as soon as the smell of the sewers hits her. Honesty, even on her second run, the smell doesn't get any better; it only makes her more aware.

Even if she can ignore the stains on the walls, the air is thick with the metallic scent of old blood, mingling with the damp, musty odor of decay. Faded sigils and runes are everywhere, remnants of the sewer's dark history. She recognizes some of the symbols from the museum and desperately avoids analyzing what took place here. Pools of stagnant water reflect the dim, flickering light from torches they carry, casting eerie shadows dancing along the damp corridors.

Erika decides to keep her flashlight in her backpack for now. Her worst-case scenario is ending up in a dark place like this and running out of battery. She may have grown up underground, but the Haven Republic never lacks light—whether from bioluminescence or man-made inventions.

There are more reminders of what went on as they walk deeper into the sewers and further into the larger chambers. Stone altars, now cracked and crumbling, stand as grim monuments to the past. Chains and manacles, rusted and broken, hang from the walls, their purpose unmistakable, causing Erika to want to heave, stomach twisting violently.

"Hey," Najaah is abruptly walking next to her, and the Nullifier nearly trips over a crack in the floor at the sudden presence. The Sun Eater stabilizes her quickly with one hand on her arm.

"Oh, uh, thanks. Sorry," Erika stumbles over her words, feeling stupider by the second. She thinks her ears are burning and is grateful for the poor lighting for once. The rest of the group trails ahead of them, watchful of traps.

"You're distracted," the Ashan says bluntly, tone irritatingly unfathomable. The Nullifier can't help the amused huff that escapes her.

"Yeah, I guess. This place doesn't help."

"What's bothering you?" Najaah asks, sounding rather awkward about asking. To be fair, she feels awkward about being asked. The answer eludes Erika for a moment, unsure how to convey the jumbled knot of emotions weighing on her.

"Do you —" She cuts herself off, not knowing how to phrase her question in a way that's not wildly insensitive. In the end, she goes about it a different way. "I… don't want to kill anyone. But we keep ending up in places where I might have to."

Najaah doesn't reply immediately, and it's too dark for her to see their reaction. The teen waits in unbearable silence for a minute before the former soldier responds.

"We know you don't want to hurt anyone. Everyone will do their best to avoid putting you in that position."

"No!" Erika surprises herself with how vehement she sounds. She takes a deep breath before continuing. "I don't want to be a burden. Please don't do that. I—I want to hold my own, you know?"

Najaah sends her a glance, eyes unreadable. "I understand the desire. But you can't have it both ways."

"…I know," she sighs, hands clenching together. "I guess I'm just having a hard time accepting it. Does it… get easier?"

Quiet falls over them again, and Erika fears she put her entire foot in her mouth when the Sun Eater replies. "Yes and no."

"What?"

"It can get easier, but you shouldn't let it. People who no longer care about the ones they kill become monsters," Najaah's words are full of a grim resoluteness that she has never heard from the former soldier in the past.

"Oh. Then what are your views on mercy?" Erika hesitates before asking, deciding to trudge onward anyway. She finds herself surprised by Najaah's opinion. Her worry had been that the team would expect her to be more ruthless for the sake of the mission. Now, she feels a bit silly and deeply relieved.

"Mercy is a matter of circumstance," the Sun Eater answers firmly. "Your circumstances, and the other's. Sometimes, death is a mercy. Sometimes, mercy is salvation… And sometimes mercy is not something you can afford."

After that, the conversation trails off into silence, both teenagers lost in their own thoughts.

The trip through the sewers ends eventually, though Erika feels it took hours instead of the thirty minutes Sev claims. This place could stretch on forever, every second taking a minute. If only there were someone who could make time run faster. That's definitely the kind of magic Erika would want to have if she weren't a Sonia.

After climbing out of a manhole into a side street, Sev leads three other Ravagers, Nuru, Najaah, and Erika, to a bar down the road. From the outside, the building looks very discreet, somewhere her eyes would glance over if she were walking by.

Alright, can you two hear me? Nuru sends to their minds. Since Amari has reached the limits of her mental abilities for the day, he volunteered to keep the connection between their half of the team open. Even with his experience, the quality of the smaller network is not as clear as the Nightblood's.

Najaah gives a subtle nod. They had also agreed it was important to have some special way to communicate when the trio is going into a potentially hostile diplomatic meeting. *Yes.*

Yeah, Erika confirms as they enter the bar.

Stepping inside tells a different story as a bell rings out at their entrance. The bar is a dimly lit haven for deals and secrets. Heavy, dark curtains drape the windows, blocking out prying eyes and casting the room in perpetual twilight. The air is thick with the smell of some kind of cigar smoke and the faint, lingering scent of expensive liquor. Patrons speak in hushed tones, their conversations punctuated by the occasional clink of glasses and the low hum of music from an unknown source. Erika catches many customers glancing their way before looking away quickly.

Sev motions to a private booth in the far corner that is evidently reserved for the Broker and his inner circle. A heavy, mahogany table dominates the space, surrounded by high-backed leather chairs that seem to swallow anyone who sits in them—apart from the man himself. The Broker is a blue-skinned man with a deadly crown of horns and gleaming golden eyes who seems larger than life even sitting down. The man's attention is firmly on them, and various members of his inner circle are seated around him, watching Erika's group warily.

According to the Ravagers, he holds court here, his sharp eyes observing every movement in the room. His lieutenants, always nearby, exude an air of menace, their expressions unreadable behind the haze of smoke and dim light. She is being very careful not to make eye contact with anyone in this establishment.

"Well," the Broker breaks the fraught silence that had fallen over the bar at their arrival. The man sneers in the group's direction. "Are you all just going to stand there waiting? You came for something, didn't you?"

Outwardly unfazed, Sev strides forward to the Broker's table but doesn't take a seat until the man motions for them to sit. Erika has to fight her inherent clumsiness so as not to make a fool of herself by the simple act of pulling out a chair. The palms of her hands are sweaty, making the endeavor unnecessarily difficult. Thankfully, she manages to sit down at the table without any mishaps.

"Broker, sir, we're here to represent the Ravagers and a third party," Sev sounds rather professional for a man who looks like Erika did when she had to sleep on roofs. "We have information about the Damnation you may already know that I hope we can agree is concerning."

"Oh?" The Broker's voice is a deep timbre that seems unreal, and she has to wonder what he actually sounds like without the translation assistance the telepathic connection between her, Nuru, and Najaah is giving her. "And what is that?"

Sev's face takes on a grim look, voice grave. "The Damnation is planning to bring back the minor death gods of old to our city. They've been taking people one at a time to achieve this."

Whispers erupt from the Broker's side of the table, his lieutenants trading hushed words and speaking glances. Erika tries to take it as a good signal, but the man in front of them appears unmoved.

"And?"

In the face of this disregard, Sev falters for a split second. Her heart rate ratchets up, and the next moment, Nuru enters the discussion calmly.

"We're asking for your help in stopping this threat to the Red City," Nuru states, facade just as unreadable as the Broker's when their eyes meet. Next to the shapeshifter, Najaah doesn't waver in the sudden attention. By the corner of the table, where there is thankfully less focus on her, Erika can't imagine how she looks compared to them. She feels like the entire bar can hear her heartbeat.

The Broker chuckles, sending a shiver up her spine. "Threat to the city, huh? And who are you representing?"

"Residents of Avalon," Nuru replies, gaze unwavering. His posture is confident but not confrontational. "A world with a direct portal to your home. We're a small group traveling through, and in the twenty-four hours we've been here, one of our members was almost sacrificed by the Damnation to these death gods."

More incoherent muttering from the inner circle while the man rubs his chin with a pensive expression on his face. The open mocking from earlier has faded a bit, to Erika's relief.

"That's unfortunate, but what those jumped-up bastards do isn't my responsibility."

"No," Nuru readily agrees. "However, it does make them a bold threat to your home. I understand that you value your neutrality, but is that worth letting these 'jumped-up bastards' run free and cause mayhem?"

The Broker breaks into loud laughter, the sudden noise startling everyone in the bar except the shapeshifter, who is watching the man evenly. "You have guts, Silver Tongue. What makes you think I am interested in working with you people? Maybe the Damnation will cut a better deal."

Not reacting to the mildly insulting name, Nuru tips his head in a small moment of acquiescence. The other man's words don't seem to dissuade him, though. "I think we can come to an agreement that you'll be satisfied with. My group has more information about our world that you should be made aware of."

"Do you, now? And you're not worried about betraying your world?" The Broker sends Nuru an unreadable look. Erika feels the hair on the back of her neck stand on end.

"We won't be betraying anyone," the shapeshifter refutes. "Our world has many differing factions, similar to your home. There is one faction we all see as an enemy, and it would be in your best interests to take our deal."

The boldness of his words seems to knock most of the listeners silent, and the Ravagers give Nuru several furtive side-eyes. Erika tries not to shrink in her seat, focusing on a random spot on the table, not moving her gaze.

"Ha," the Broker scoffs. His voice somehow becomes even deeper in reaction to Nuru's warning. "You sure have a lot of nerve, don't you?"

The bar's atmosphere is tense, and a palpable undercurrent of danger lurks beneath the surface. Deals are regularly made and secrets exchanged in this sanctuary of vice, but even those on the other side of the room can tell that this is no ordinary meeting.

"You're a gambling man, are you not?" Nuru abruptly says, making the Ravagers glance askance even more at him. The Broker snorts, a finger trailing around the rim of his drink.

"You're keen, I'll give you that, Silver Tongue. So what if I am?"

Nuru smiles. It's so different from the genuine ones Erika has become accustomed to that it appears alien. "Why don't we make a bet, then? Just between your people and mine."

The grin that alights the Broker's face is chilling, showcasing fangs in golden coverings with shimmering runes inscribed. She goes back to staring at her spot on the table, hands clenching on her lap.

"Alright, what bet are you proposing?"

"Why not a simple game?" Nuru motions with a hand to a large table set up in the back of the bar. No one's playing right now, but Erika is reminded of the pool tables she's seen in Avalon bars. "If you win, we'll give you all the information we have free of charge and leave without any trouble. If we win, you help us stop the Damnation and leave through our chosen gateway in exchange for the information."

It's not a bad stake for the Broker; Erika can see that, while not being devastating to them either.

Clearly, the Broker knows this too because the man laughs again, amused by the shapeshifter's continued audacity. He then turns to Nuru with a mean edge to his expression. "I think those stakes are too easy. Why not make them a real bet? If you lose, I get to keep you all here, forever."

The effort to keep rising panic off her face is one of the hardest things Erika has ever done. This mission has always been dangerous. She's known since the beginning that she might not make it home. But the thought of living the rest of her life *here*, never being allowed to see her mom again, never getting to *explain*…

To her mortification, her throat closes, and her eyes begin to sting against her will.

Nuru doesn't react negatively, just turning to look at her and Najaah. "If the rest of my group agrees to those terms."

Najaah? Erika? What do you think? Nuru confers with them in the network. *I've had similar experiences before, but I won't accept this without your agreement.*

Damn, Erika thinks. Damn.

Do it, Najaah says and nods to the Broker with a stern look. *I will kill every single one of the Broker's men before he can imprison us here.*

Let's call that Plan B, Nuru muses.

They're both so calm.

Erika? Najaah mentally brushes past her presence. Erika resists the urge to flinch away behind her shields.

She nods after what feels like an age, but it must be only a second. *Okay.*

Nuru turns back to the man watching them, smiling genially. "Then why don't we—"

"Not you," the Broker cuts him off, eyes glinting in the bar's dim light with a menacing light. His eyes skip over their group before landing on her. Erika swears her heart stops altogether. "Her. I'll play against her."

Najaah immediately shifts in their chair to be in front of the Nullifier, one hand drawing close to the blade strapped to their back. The only reaction Nuru shows is a slight frown.

In the telepathic network, he speaks to Erika directly. *You should politely turn him down, I can —*

"I'll do it," the words leave her mouth before she can stop them, and internally, she starts screaming incoherently. Najaah's head jerks to the side to look at her wide-eyed before returning to their guard position.

Erika…

Large hands with multiple rings and sharp claws clap together with a loud noise, and she stifles a flinch as the Broker grins again. He stands up in a single movement, unnervingly graceful for someone his size. It reminds her of Najaah. "Wonderful! Let's play…?"

"… Erika," she admits reluctantly. "Uh, good game."

The laughter that follows makes her ears burn as she gets out of her chair to follow the large man to the maybe-pool table. Nuru and Najaah bracket her, both tenser than she had ever seen before. It only makes her nerves worse until the shapeshifter puts a hand on her shoulder.

Remember Plan B, Nuru sends her feelings of comfort and firm resolve. Erika looks away when her eyes start stinging again.

She was right. The game in the back looks a great deal like pool. A coincidence? What does that mean?

One of the Broker's lieutenants steps up to her small group. The Ravagers have taken on the role of audience members since this bet doesn't include them, but the outcome still affects their people. The lieutenant grabs their collective attention as he launches into a lengthy explanation of the game's rules.

It's very similar to pool. The layout is nearly identical, with the cues and cue balls, though the patterns and numbers look different. Erika thinks she gets a basic grasp of the order in which the unfamiliar numbers go. Significant differences to the game include that more cue balls are used than in Avalon, and how you get a cue ball in a pocket earns you differing points. A straight shot is one point, hitting the cue ball off one side of the table into a pocket is two points, and any shot with more than one angle used is three points. The one who gets in the last cue ball earns five points.

"I understand," Erika says finally, going over the rules in her head, turning over the possibilities.

"Good, good!" The Broker cheers somewhat mockingly from where he has been waiting on the other side of the not-pool table. The game is called *treya*, which she assumes is a name that doesn't translate directly into anything for them. "Let's play!"

The *treya* space lights up, the table's accents bathing the thing in an eerie red light. Erika avoids looking at the old stains in some spots on the table too closely. She walks over to the rack of neatly organized cue sticks, pondering what would suit her best. Not something too tall or heavy, but with some force behind it…

Erika ends up with a pale white cue stick that feels comfortable in her hands and isn't too difficult to wield. The Broker watches her with interest as she readies herself. She does her ample best not to show how unnerved she is.

Naturally, the Broker goes first. He breaks the cluster of cue balls with one swing, having chosen one of the heaviest cue sticks. It looks more like a blunt spear than something meant for a game.

The Broker swiftly scores five points in just one turn, taking all the easy early pickings. His lieutenants are jeering from their spots, acting as an audience.

The thing is, Erika isn't sure how she wants to do this. Should she just do her best at *treya* and cross her fingers? She knows this game is only half of what's happening here. Nuru challenged the

Broker in more ways than one. What can she do to help?

"You're good," Erika compliments nervously, trying to emulate the same calm exterior Nuru always has. She probably misses by a kilometer. But her voice doesn't shake.

Smirking, the Broker sweeps a hand over the table. "Your turn."

Cue stick in hand, Erika rounds the *treya* table, targeting the few cue balls left that are simple to push into pockets. The fact that there are more cue balls here than in pool is a curse and a blessing. She is able to get more in the pockets early in the game. However, even if she beats the Broker at whittling down the cue balls, he could end up with more points.

Her opponent gets three points in his next turn — a straight shot and one angle. Eight points total. She has four. Erika clenches the cue stick in her hands, eyeing the *treya* table.

Erika steps up, taking a deep breath to settle her nerves. She thinks she's observed enough to understand the dynamics of the game. Hopefully, she'll get some pay off from her days lurking in Upside bars and watching pool games after boredom overtook her.

In the end, it's all math, right?

Lining up her cue stick, Erika shoots a ball down the table, hitting the table at two angles into a pocket at the other end. For a moment, there's quiet around her. Someone whistles softly in the back, and she feels her shoulder release its tension. She moves on to her next shot without acknowledging anyone. As long as she doesn't *look*, she can pretend no one's watching.

Erika earns nine points by the time she's done with her turn. Thirteen points total. The most someone can get is forty-five.

Finally, she risks a glance at the Broker. He's staring at her with a calculating look. She doesn't see outright anger there, which is a relief in and of itself.

Damn, kid, Nuru speaks in her mind. A warm glow of pride radiates from her, but she refuses to lean towards it. The Broker moves to do his turn, and she steps back from the table.

Thanks, she says back, feeling absurdly shy suddenly. *I wasn't sure that would work.*

What did you do? Najaah asks, face not betraying that they are communicating with each other.

I just mean that knowing the theory of something doesn't mean it works out that way in reality, Erika tries to explain, likely creating more confusion than giving clarity.

Najaah sounds uncharacteristically baffled in response. *The theory…?*

I see, Nuru doesn't visibly react, but she gets the sense he's smiling internally. *Good work.*

The Broker makes seven points in one turn, not giving away whether he's upset about this. Erika is blocking out the whispers coming from the audience section. She feels eyes on her anyway as she lines up her shot.

Six points. She has nineteen, and the Broker has fifteen. That fact feels surreal. She's *winning*.

"Have you played this before?" The Broker asks her after her turn, tone infuriatingly neutral. Erika nearly drops her cue stick, she's so startled.

"Oh, um, no. We do have a similar game, though. It's called pool. There are fewer cue balls and no points apart from getting them in the pocket."

He hums, the low sound resonating in the air. "You pick it up quick."

"Uh… Thank you," Erika has never wanted to fidget so badly in her life.

The Broker moves to take a shot, banking it off one side of the table into a pocket. Two points. He continues as he moves on to another target. "Why are you on this little trip through the Red City?"

Erika glances at Nuru quickly before looking away, unsure how much to share freely. "We're just here to use one of the stable gateways."

Another two-point shot. "Yes, I know that. Why are *you* on this ill-advised quest?"

"Oh." Erika clenches her cue stick again, mind scrambling for a suitable answer. "I'm… trying to reclaim something that was lost. It's important to, uh, me. And my home."

The Broker scores three more points before the turn is hers. "And this object is worth risking your life over?"

Maybe not the object *itself*… but what it means. Erika would do a lot to achieve the wish she made when she saw the sky for the first time. "Yes."

It's easier to admit than she thought. The subtle tremble in her hands abates, and she lines up a shot that sends the two cue balls into a pocket. Four points. Another shot. Two points.

Erika has twenty-five points and three cue balls left, while the Broker has twenty points and two cue balls remaining. The eight ball, or called the *triyan* here, is tucked away in a corner. Getting the finishing shot is five points, so the man still has a chance to get ahead of her.

Her fingers itch to do something, *fix* something, as the Broker steps up for his turn. She hopes she played this right. Please let her have played this right.

The Broker leans in for a shot, sending a cue ball into a pocket after banking it twice off the table. Three points. Erika's grip tightens past the threshold of being painful as she watches the man turn to his last cue ball before the *triyan*. There are two ways he could decide to score it. There's a fairly easy straight shot and a more risky two-point one.

Please let her have been right…

He lines up for the two-point shot and hits the cue ball, sending it toward a pocket. In a move that makes it look like he miscalculated, one of Erika's cue balls stops his before it scores. Her breath leaves her in one big sigh, and her fingers loosen. The Broker clicks his tongue in annoyance but doesn't otherwise react.

Erika didn't even realize how fast her heart was beating until it slowed down in the wake of her relief. Planting one of her cue balls in the way of his shot had been such a gamble.

Stalking forward, she narrows her focus to the table before her. She has one easy straight shot into a pocket, and then there are two remaining cue balls. One is in an awkward spot, and the other is dangerously close to pushing the Broker's last cue ball into a pocket.

Erika walks the length, eyes darting around the table, mind running through calculations. In the end, she sends the cue ball, practically touching her opponent away and into a pocket. For her last ball, she banks three times into a middle pocket.

In total, she has thirty points and no cue balls left. The Broker has one cue ball and twenty-five points. All Erika needs to win is to get the *triyan* into a pocket, and yet…

She can't make the *triyan* from where it is right now, Erika decides. So, she just needs to ensure the Broker can't make it in the next turn. With the cue stick, she sends the *triyan* into an awkward spot the Broker can't escape.

Across the table, the man chuckles at her bold maneuver. He doesn't try to start a conversation again as he scores his last cue ball. The Broker circles the *triyan*, eyeing the ball carefully. With a small smirk, he hits the *triyan* into another unplayable spot.

Erika fights a grimace. They could go back and forth like this indefinitely. The angle *is* bad, though. She tries to solve the problem backwards, choosing a pocket and backtracking how the cue ball would get into it. She does this for every single pocket until she's satisfied. Despite her quiet, no one is bothering her or hurrying her.

Finally, Erika takes her cue stick and lines up a shot, breath measured and hands steady. She hits the cue ball hard—and it banks all over the table, going up and down its length. Just as the momentum is fading, the *triyan* falls into a corner pocket.

—and the room erupts into chaos.

Erika is so focused that the sudden cacophony of noise startles her enough that she drops her cue stick, banging her hip into the treya table. At first, her panic rises to the forefront of her mind. Except when she looks, the expressions on her group's faces are positive. Nuru is smiling genuinely, and Najaah is even smirking, radiating an aura of smugness. Everyone, even random patrons of the bar and people who work for the Broker, is talking loudly and gesticulating excitedly.

She turns to the man himself, unsure of what she'll find, and sees the Broker looking far less upset than she feared.

"I'll accept the loss," he says to her, the sound strangely clear under the noise of the room. "I can respect someone who can win a bet without underhanded tricks."

"Really?" Erika breathes out with a growing grin. "And you'll help us?"

The Broker scoffs, voicing disdain at an invisible target. "No one has much love for the Riders or Ravagers, kid, but they're a sight better than those nutjobs in the Damnation. Getting one over on them will be entertaining."

…So, nothing about the whole 'releasing death gods' thing? At least they said they'll help.

Erika can't resist putting her incredulity into the telepathic network. *Why won't they just agree they want to save their city? It's their home.*

Nuru replies, wry amusement curling around his message. *Of course, they're not agreeing, Erika. Saying we're right would mean admitting they're wrong.*

Ugh.

The first thing the Broker does is tell the entire city what the Damnation is planning.

Okay, that's an exaggeration. He spreads information and discontent throughout the Red City's population in a frighteningly short amount of time. Erika feels she is finally getting a glimpse into the man's control over the city.

People are naturally upset over the news that a rising gang is the cause of a great deal of disappearances that were once blamed on sewer spirits and random harvesters. To know there's an organized effort to sacrifice citizens for the sake of their own power… well, Erika would be mad, too.

She's unceremoniously shoved with her friends into a group with Sev and one of the Broker's lieutenants. The rest of the Ravagers are working with the man to stir unrest among the people of the Red City. Even Sev says that a citywide protest of the Damnation is one of the only ways to force the Crimson Riders to break off their neutrality and use their superior numbers to take down the Damnation. And the general outrage will hinder the Damnation's plan.

"They'll get you where you need to go," the Broker says, nodding to his lieutenant and Sev, a newly lit pipe in between his fingers that's wafting out green smoke. Erika tries to discreetly bury her face in her hoodie to avoid the sickly sweet smell, and, to her embarrassment, amused glances are sent her way from all around.

"Thank you for your generosity," Nuru smiles serenely like they hadn't nearly become this man's prisoners. In contrast, Najaah is scowling in the Broker's direction, clearly not as keen to make nice after the close call.

The man himself smiles meanly at the shapeshifter. "Of course. Thanks for the details about that empire o' yours."

Nuru had gone over the details he thought pertinent for the Broker to know after Erika won the *treya* game. He gave a concise and clear report, with only the occasional addition from her or Najaah.

Mostly, Nuru told the man about the Order and the Governor of Tera — the people who guard the gateway and the imperial who has already carried out an expedition. The Apolon Empire was mentioned in broad strokes, and little else about Avalon was given.

While this was part of a trade, Erika is glad that the Red City was informed. From her history class, she knows what happens to people who aren't prepared for the Empire.

After tension-filled pleasantries, Nuru rounds their group up and out the door. Sev hustles them down the streets in the direction of the Heart. It's getting late, and the mood of the citizens is palpable. Erika looks up at a darkening sky, trying to calculate where Amari's group is. Probably close to leaving the sewers, if not out already.

As the first of the two suns begins to set, an uneasy stillness envelops the streets. The air is thick with anticipation, and Erika can hear whispers of unrest beginning to circulate among the residents as she walks by. People gather in small groups, their faces etched with concern and determination. News of the Damnation's brutal rituals — reports of missing individuals snatched for dark magic — spreads like wildfire, igniting a sense of urgency.

Over the course of the evening, more and more people begin to converge on the streets. Angry faces grow in number, united by shared stories of loss and fear — with the Broker's people fanning the flames. The crowd's energy swells as chants start to rise, slowly at first, a hesitant echo that builds momentum.

Erika and her group slip through shouting protesters, ignored entirely by the growing chaos around them. She can't stop the twisted ball of emotions in her chest at the sight of all this civil unrest. Did they only make things worse?

Crimson Rider patrols walk the outskirts of the people, their presence a silent threat to keep them in line. They observe from the shadows, sizing up the numbers, their expressions unreadable. Tension crackles in the air as gang members exchange glances, uncertain whether to intervene or watch the crowds grow bolder.

As night deepens, the energy shifts again. Fires are lit in barrels, providing warmth and illumination, casting flickering shadows that dance on the faces of the protesters. The smell of smoke mixes with the crisp night air, creating an intoxicating brew of rebellion. People begin to sing, their voices rising in unison, with words that aren't translating through the network for Erika. After glancing at her friends, she can tell from the open confusion on their faces that they don't understand either.

The chants grow louder, more fervent, drowning out the distant sounds of the city. There's no turning back now, Erika thinks.

As the situation reaches a tipping point, the once-quiet streets are charged with energy, and the promise of a confrontation looms. The anticipation is palpable, and the air is thick with a mix of fury and excitement as people prepare to take a stand against the gang that has hurt them.

It all comes to a head when an explosion goes off—

The ground shakes underfoot, and smoke rises in the distance, but only the sound wave reaches their group.

Erika covers her ears as the noise blots out her whole world for a minute, abruptly dropping her into a panic. She forgets entirely about the telepathic network, something primal scrambling for purchase inside her. A hand grabs her arm, and she clings before regaining her mental footing.

Nothing is broken on the street they're on, and the sound of the explosion has the most effect on the people there. Erika seems like one of the last ones to recover because protesters are already resuming their purpose.

That's our cue, Nuru says, ushering them away from the crowds.

A shout rings out, incoherent under the ringing in her ears, and Erika belatedly realizes that some of the Damnation have appeared somewhere in the city. Protesters spill into the streets, some clutching makeshift weapons — sticks, pipes, anything that could offer a semblance of defense against the gang responsible for the abductions — and others with magic flowing freely. Their faces are painted with determination, eyes alight with fervor as they march forward, pushing past barricades of debris hastily erected by the Riders. Erika and her group must hastily move to the sides of the road to avoid being caught up in the tide like leaves in a river.

Riots are breaking out now, Erika grimly thinks to herself. How violent will it get?

Nuru's hand rests on her shoulder as the group pauses to wait for a particularly rowdy throng of protesters to pass by. *The fate of this city is in their hands, not ours, as it should be.*

That's right, and yet... *Will anything change?*

Maybe, the shapeshifter sighs out loud. *There's always a chance.*

The teen reasons with herself that that is the most she can hope for. Trying to help these people more would put her own home at risk.

Eventually, they reach the middle of the Red City, and Erika gets a close look at what she caught a glimpse of yesterday when they first came.

The Heart is a disturbingly apt name for a building that stands as the pulsating center of a city enshrouded in enough bad vibes to make her want to turn around immediately. Except, even as disgust colors her emotions, Erika must admit the grand and grotesque immense edifice is an architectural marvel that defies conventional design and wisdom.

How did the builders manage to get the stonework to look so life-like? And the conduits acting as veins, the pulsing beat? Erika wants to get closer so she can study the runework —

"Erika?" Sev has a concerned expression on his rugged face. "If the Heart is too much for you —"

"No!" She cuts in quickly, not wanting to know the end of that sentence. "No, I'm good!"

At this point, the moon is rising, and the rioters are in full swing. The Crimson Riders have their hands full, making this no better time for sneaking into the Heart.

The architecture inside is as impressive as the outside, Erika marvels, a surreal feeling of horror warring with curiosity in her chest. She internally despairs over not being able to stop and examine the runes as Sev leads them through the hallways. Nuru laughs when they come across their first disabled trap.

"Taliya's work, no doubt," the shapeshifter muses.

Sev chuckles, a smile playing on his lips. "Yes, she has a gift for pulling apart traps at frightening speed."

Erika's lips twitch upward at the exchange, which abruptly stops the moment they reach their destination.

The room itself is large and has five incredible gateways to other worlds, but that's not what draws her or the rest of her group's attention. It's the gigantic, smoking form taking up half the space. Erika has no earthly idea what the creature is — or *was* — and she hopes to never see one moving around. It looks like a nightmare made of shadow and decay.

Scattered around are Amari's group. The Ravagers immediately leave their huddled corner and beeline for Sev, while Kol sets down on the ground in front of Najaah, from where he had been previously hovering high above.

"What happened?" Erika sounds aghast even to herself. Kol shrugs, which causes her to have the out-of-character impulse to *strangle him.*

"Security feature. We killed it."

That's seriously all he's going to say, isn't it? Erika gives up on him entirely and searches for Amari. The Nightblood is sitting next to Taliya on the other side of the room, and she makes her way over. She doesn't hesitate to put a wide gap between herself and the 'security feature' as she does it.

"What happened to you guys?"

Amari seems as even-keeled as ever, but something about Taliya seems… off. The thief's eyes are hooded and give away none of her thoughts. Erika notes that her body language is closed off, too.

"The Ravagers called it a Colossus," Amari says matter-of-factly. "It manifested as soon as we stepped inside. The fight took a while, but thankfully, no one was hurt."

"Oh, that's good…?" Erika trails off, unsure how to respond to positive news when the mood is so low.

"We should go," Taliya stands up suddenly, heading straight for one side of the room.

"What—"

"She's right," the Nightblood sighs, getting up and brushing off her clothes. "No time to waste. The situation outside will only get more volatile from here."

The reminder sends Erika's heart to her feet. "Oh."

Amari eyes her critically. "They'll be alright. This city has existed longer than most civilizations. Some punks stirring trouble are just another chapter in their history."

For some reason, the thought eases her chest. A form of relief courses through her veins, and Erika smiles wanly. "Thanks."

"Anytime. Let's go collect our strays," Amari muses, a ghost of a smile flashing across her face.

Saying goodbye to the Ravagers feels weirdly heart-wrenching for people Erika has only known for half a day. Maybe because this trip feels like a month crammed into a few hours. The Broker's lieutenant merely nods at them and leaves once it's confirmed they've reached their gateway.

Sev goes over their side of the mission with the rest of the Ravagers while Nuru and Najaah cut in with their own thoughts. Mainly about how Erika won the bet with the Broker. Her face is burning by the end of it, to the point that she's almost relieved when they part ways.

Then it's just her team and a stable portal wreathed in dark vines. A shiver runs down her spine at the sudden sense memory of the governor's garden she and Nuru had struggled through. Erika hopes this forest will be better, but everything she's read says it isn't.

Unsurprisingly, Amari is the first to step up and through the gateway's swirling portal. It doesn't look all that different than the one to the Red City's world, yet she feels more trepidation than she did yesterday.

Taliya steps up next, then Najaah and Kol, until Nuru is the only other one left. He's watching her with worried eyes.

"Ready?"

"Yeah," she whispers, heart beating fast. Erika measures her breath, balls her fists, and steps forward.

18

AMARI

Amari steps into the Forsaken Forest and immediately feels like it's a mistake. The portal deposits them onto a well-beaten path that leaves much to be desired compared to the surrounding forest.

The trees are towering giants, their trunks so immense that some even dwarf the mountains of Avalon. Amari feels dizzy, trying to imagine where it stops. Their dense and lush canopies form a ceiling that filters sunlight into a greenish twilight, casting a strange glow over the forest floor. She can see that the bark of these ancient trees is gnarled and twisted, crowned with mosses that emit an eerie light in the shadows. Roots thick and twisted snake through the underbrush and create natural tunnels and passageways that the path goes through in the distance.

The shadows around them feel alive, and Amari can sense eyes on her, yet she can't see anything. But no Nightblood should ever be scared of the dark. Still, this place has a feeling to it that makes her skin crawl.

She can't tell if it's due to her seer abilities, which is even more worrying.

Erika is the first one to speak up. "I feel like I just walked into a horror story, and considering a cult tried to sacrifice me to a death god this morning, that's saying something."

Taliya snorts, effectively breaking the sudden tension that had descended when they entered the forest. Even Najaah cracks a small smile.

Taking a deep breath, Amari focuses on the task ahead. According to the governor's expedition team, the gate leading to the Archive is a week's walk from the Red City's gateway. Navigation is unreliable at best in the Ethereal Planes, so the team used landmarks and pathways. Even in places like the Forsaken Forest, enough people or creatures have passed through over many millennia that trails have been worn into the ground.

"This path," Amari motions to the weathered footpath the gateway delivered them to. "According to the report, it will lead to a river. We follow that down until we hit a bridge and cross. After that, apparently, two paths end up at the Archive. One is longer, but the other skirts a cave system home to some monsters. The forest might have changed since this report, but it's a good start."

She gets a round of agreements with mixed enthusiasm. No one is thrilled at the prospect of such a dangerous hike.

Wisely, Nuru suggests they take some time to rest before starting. They've all already had a busy day. It gives Amari time to deal with some blossoming bruises from her earlier adventures that she had been neglecting.

The hair on the back of Amari's neck stands up, warning her of immediate danger, followed by Najaah whipping out their khopesh. Everyone follows the Ashan's example, but no one can see any threat. The cold air drops ten more degrees. Something is lurking.

"**How cute,**" a disembodied voice says. It sounds like it's whispering in her very ear, but Amari can sense it's being projected into her mind. Everyone else reacts as if they had been snuck up on. Out of the corner of her eye, Amari swears she can see the flickering form of something. A feeling of dread takes hold of her. **"Have you come to play?"**

It has to be some kind of spirit, she reasons. Anything weaker wouldn't be able to keep an intangible form for long, and anything stronger would feel more oppressive.

This deduction doesn't bring much comfort. Spirits come in a million different varieties, and they're all tricky. The one circling them isn't elemental, Amari can tell that much. The temperature lowered, but nothing else happened.

"Who's there?" Kol yells. Amari contains a wince and quickly shushes him.

"I am the thoughts that you don't speak," its voice is quiet but insidious. **"I am the wishes that are never fulfilled. I am the voice of the nameless."**

A spirit that knows the mind. Still too vague to truly categorize, and definitely a problem. Amari has little doubt this spirit could invade their heads without much effort. She can already feel a foreign presence encroaching on her shields.

"You're forsaken," Erika breathes, as if she hadn't intended to say it out loud at all. The spirit laughs, a creaky, raspy sound.

"Of course! Where do you think you are?"

"What do you want?" Nuru asks diplomatically. By this point, everyone has backed up together into a circle, waiting for the other shoe to drop.

"Oh, I'm just so bored, you see. No one visits anymore..."

"I wonder why," Kol mutters. Erika elbows him in the ribs, hard. Thankfully, the spirit keeps talking, unfazed.

"... So let's play a game!"

Amari's stomach drops. The kinds of games a spirit plays are often not meant for mortals.

"Let's not. We can't play your games," Najaah answers, fearless and bold.

"I don't take kindly to liars, oath breaker," the spirit snaps, not liking Najaah's answer.

The Ashan's breath stutters before replying in a quiet but furious tone. "What do you know, spirit?"

"Najaah," Amari says, trying her best to convey a warning. Before she gets a response, the spirit hisses angrily at them.

"I know you! I know every soul born and crafted that is here!"

"Stay back," Nuru advises Erika. He makes a fast motion with his hand, and Taliya nods. Amari pulls out her staff slowly.

"The one haunted by the ghosts of time yet to come!" It shrieks, its voice tearing all around their heads and rippling like wind. Amari flinches. **"The lost child! The traitor!"**

Najaah's skin starts to glow with an inner fire, and the temperature increases quickly. Red energy begins to swirl around Kol's hands while Taliya unsheathes her swords. **"The martyr! The eternal! The one meant for the void!"**

Having had enough, Amari lifts her staff high and slams it to the ground. The staff is carved with ancient runes designed to ward off enemies, but she pulls at her own power to be sure, even as she is careful not to let the others notice. Amari focuses entirely on the spirit she can just barely see and *pulls.*

Using her magic on other beings is harrowing, especially if they're not mortal. Trying to slow down the Time of the spirit is a whole other level. Surprisingly, Amari manages to stop the spirit completely, just for a heartbeat. Pulling this off twice in one day seemed impossible until this moment. There's a gasp behind her, and she realizes the spirit is fully visible now to the others. It's a mist-like, shadowy thing with burning eyes full of malicious glee.

Kol takes advantage of the moment to send every loose branch, leaf, and rock around them directly at the spirit. Without prompting,

Taliya drops her swords and starts drawing runes in the ground to contain it.

An enraged roar reverberates through everyone's heads, and the spirit charges the thief. The sound throws everyone off, making Kol's power slip briefly through his fingers, and gives the spirit time to reach Taliya.

Amari is moving faster than she thought possible, slamming her staff and directing as much power as she can against the spirit. It slows, but not before part of its form touches Taliya. The thief jerks back, then staggers away.

Taliya never loses her balance.

Taliya crumples to the ground with no warning, and Amari's heart drops into her stomach. It's only due to being long accustomed to moving past fear in the heat of the moment that lets her strike out against the spirit again. It freezes for a second, giving Najaah the time to slice a burning sword through it. It's not able to kill the spirit, but it moves like its energy is sapped, and a strangled whine leaves it.

Nuru and Erika quickly help finish the wards Taliya started while Najaah and Kol help Amari contain it long enough for the runes to take effect. The seer subtly adds her own power to the wards, sealing the spirit inside its bounds. Once they do, everyone watches the spirit writhe in fury and fear from inside the wards. Its words have deteriorated into garbled shrieks and hisses.

It's all very anticlimactic for something that's left Amari feeling like she wants to shake out of her skin.

"What did you do to her?" Amari steps forward to question it as she watches Kol throw pieces of rock toward the spirit in a show of unnecessary cruelty. Erika makes a noise of protest, but the rest of the group ignores her. Its pain means nothing to Amari right now. She subtly reaches out with her mind while it's weakened, putting further pressure on it.

Eventually, the spirit's strangled voice seeps out. **"You are** worried, night child?"

Najaah slashes at the spirit, receiving a pained whimper from it and a look of concern from Erika. Amari keeps her stare apathetic and even. She rapidly increases her mental assault from subtle to outright, and the spirit screams.

Throughout her career, Amari has been called a bleeding heart and a heartless bitch in equal turns. She's never particularly minded either label. If she's being honest, it mostly depends on her mood. Right now, she is concerned about the health of her best friend. Empathy can take a backseat.

"She... Will live," it admits finally, reluctantly continuing as Amari *pushes* with her mind. **"The Deep Sleep did not have enough time to take permanently."**

"Any ill effects?" Nuru asks, sounding calm and almost gentle.

"No... Takes more time to... keep their minds."

"Keep their minds?" Kol cries, voice rising. He starts to hurl stray forest debris again, and Nuru waves him off this time. The gravity manipulator scowls, reluctantly letting up on the spirit.

Najaah turns to Amari and tilts their head at Erika too. "We'll deal with containing this, go make sure Taliya is okay and watch the perimeter for more attacks."

Amari wants to grumble about being ordered away but concedes that the ex-soldier probably has a point in sending her out of any further interrogation. Najaah is likely used to regulations that include keeping emotionally compromised individuals off specific cases.

However... Amari increases the pressure on the spirit's mind, lashing out with a strength she wouldn't dare on a mortal mind. Its shrieks split the air. The spirit doesn't call out to her again, which she takes as proof it's been finally frightened.

"Amari," Nuru reminds her, and she reluctantly backs off.

"Fine."

Satisfied, she immediately beelines to check on Taliya. She kneels next to the crumpled form of her best friend, checking her pulse. It's steady and even, just slow due to being asleep. The seer has no time left for the telepathic network, but she risks causing a migraine checking her individual connection with Taliya to make sure the thief's mind is untouched. She dislikes doing it without explicit consent but her friend said a long time ago she was fine with it in an emergency.

Once her worries are assuaged, Amari pulls off her jacket to use as a makeshift pillow and shifts Taliya into a more comfortable position before looking out to the forest beyond. The trees are silent watchers, and the darkness between them is unnerving. Her senses don't pick up anything beyond the feeling of being observed.

"Amari," Erika says unsurely, standing close as she keeps watch too. "That was… taking things too far, I think."

The seer holds back a sigh. It's easy in moments like this to see who in their group grew up or worked surrounded by violence and who didn't.

"I'm sorry this made you uncomfortable. Finding out what happened was the priority, but I can see why this would worry you," Amari replies, even though the words taste like ashes in her mouth. Erika gives her a long look, and Amari isn't entirely sure if the Nullifier believes her either.

"I… get that Taliya's health is what's important. I just—what does it mean for us if we move so quickly to handing out pain like that to get our way?"

"I'm not sure any of us are the people to answer that question."

"You never wonder…?"

"Not really," Amari replies, and it's the truth. She believes wholeheartedly that the atrocities the Apolon Empire accomplishes through the system they set in place are far worse than anything she could do as a single individual. There are lines she's never felt the urge to cross, and that's as far as she thinks about it. Amari can't worry endlessly over morality when raging against a monster like the Empire. She wouldn't get anything done.

Her only regret is how Erika's discomfort might affect the team. They need this to work. And, on a more personal note, Amari doesn't want the girl scared of them.

"Oh."

Neither of them tries to continue the conversation, and Amari's mind starts to spiral as she stares at the slow rise of Taliya's chest. The thief's body is still and peaceful in a way it never is during real sleep. Taliya usually moves a lot and is a general hazard to whoever might be camping close by. She's also a light sleeper who wouldn't have been able to doze in such circumstances.

Amari fiddles with the ends of her sleeves, pulling on a loose thread with her sharp nails. A nameless anxiety is welling up in her, something separate yet confusing as it mixes with her powers of foresight. She recognizes it every time someone she cares about is in danger. It's a sensation she despises, and she doesn't often let people close enough to inspire it.

It's a prelude to grief. Except Taliya can't die. Not here, not now. There's little point to all this if Amari has to do this alone. Taliya is the only one who…

"Amari?" Nuru says gently as he approaches, catching her attention. He sits beside her on the ground, giving Taliya's unmoving form a concerned scan. "The spirit says she should be wake up in less than a day. We've got it secured now. Any thoughts?"

Kill it, she thinks.

"Don't waste too much magic, but make sure the runes will hold for at least a week. We want to put a lot of ground between us before they wear off."

"Alright. Should we stay here until she wakes up?"

Amari doesn't want to move. She can't even bring her eyes to look away from the proof that Taliya is still here. Nevertheless, she bullies herself into doing a quick sweep of the area with her powers. Nothing jumps out to her as alarming other than the baseline level of danger this forest exudes. And she gets no particular bad feeling at the idea of staying in this spot. "Yeah. We stay. We need to rest after today's activities, and we can make this place defensible while we wait."

"I'll take the first watch," Najaah calls out from a few meters away. "I haven't done much today."

"Sure," Amari nods easily, even if she doesn't necessarily agree with the sentiment. "I'm staying up too."

"Is that a good idea?" Nuru asks quietly as the three teens begin setting up a tent pulled from one of their bags.

"I'm staying up," Amari repeats, voice gaining an edge to it.

"… Alright. I'll take the second watch, then."

She'll be up for that, too, Amari doesn't say. He probably can guess, anyway. It's fine. She's done worse on less sleep. The seer knows her limits.

As the hours drag on, she eventually pulls out a sketchbook from her bag. It's blank, of course, because she's not stupid enough to bring already drawn artwork with her on a job. That happened once, years ago, and she nearly cried at the loss of work she had been doing for months. Now, Taliya will buy her a new sketchbook before every trip out of Castor as an apology for getting that old one vaporized.

Holding the compact book in one hand, Amari searches the stray contents of her bag for a pencil. After foraging for one, she unearths a worn, half-shaved thing that she loves using for quick sketches. It does its job well as she starts drawing the Colossus from earlier.

The monster isn't meant for human comprehension, Amari understands, yet she tries to nail down its appearance anyway. It doesn't come out quite right, but that's okay. In a moment of humor, she draws a small floating Kol trying to confuse the beast. He looks like a fly bothering a dragon.

Remembering the fight makes her think of how it ended, and the fact that Taliya used her blood magic for the first time in years. Amari glances at the unconscious woman beside her, eyes tracing over her face.

When they first met, years and years ago, Taliya used blood magic rather freely. Things changed, over time. She pulled away from that kind of work and focused on being a thief.

Amari reaches out a hand hesitantly and takes the thief's unmoving hand.

"Sorry, Tal," she whispers. Asking her friend to use blood magic had been necessary, and unfair, and might well be needed again.

She doesn't speak up again, and Amari stares out into the dark woods in heavy silence. The only spot of warmth is Taliya's hand in hers.

Fortunately, for Amari's sanity, Taliya wakes up after twelve hours of restful sleeping. Any longer, the seer might have done something ill-advised.

The camp they had set up around their sleeping friend is quickly packed up as Amari updates Taliya on what's happened. With some minor details left out. No need to bring up more conflict.

"So, you sealed the spirit in a temporary cage?" Groggy eyes stare at the seer over a mug of steaming coffee courtesy of Najaah. Taliya glances over at the hastily made box covered in runes and wrinkles her nose. It won't last long as a container made to trap a spirit, but it doesn't need to. It just needs to be long enough for them to get out of range for the thing to take revenge. "I could have done it better."

"Of course," Amari says, smiling for the first time since the thief collapsed. "How are you feeling?"

"Like I overslept," Taliya replies with audible disgust. "I hate it. When are we moving?"

Amari surveys the team, taking in Erika's subdued mood and Najaah's militant efficiency. The camp is all but packed up entirely now. "As soon as you finish that and have something to eat, I think."

Taliya practically leaps to her feet, mug not spilling a drop. "I can do both while walking!"

The sound of chuckling makes them turn around as Nuru approaches. "I'm glad to see your enthusiasm hasn't changed any, Taliya."

Wrinkling her nose again, the thief throws down the blanket that had been draped over her shoulders and pins her braids back with one hand while sipping at her coffee. "I just don't like being so *slow*. We've already lost time."

Her friend looks to Amari here, wide eyes imploring. The seer internally sighs. "We are a bit behind."

"Then—"

"But we did get through the Red City faster than I had thought," Amari adds without hesitation. "So, I think we're doing good. And, frankly, after the clusterfuck of yesterday, we probably needed the forced rest."

Taliya pouts at her, giving her an expression of mock betrayal. Nuru watches with amusement before Najaah announces to the whole group that they are *ready to go* and *burning daylight.*

Despite the former soldier's attitude, Taliya is still the first one moving down the path, bags packed, and mug drained.

Among the flora are familiar plants and ones so unique that everyone unanimously decides to avoid them. Some flowers they pass emit a faint, sweet fragrance that masks a subtle, entrancing potency, and Amari elects that it's best for the team to all have makeshift masks on hand.

It's not just the plants they need to worry about, however. The forest is home to creatures both mythical and terrifying. Massive beasts, long thought extinct or relegated to stories—or never known at all—roam freely through the dense foliage. Amari has read some of the reports on their current location. Great serpentine dragons will coil among the trees, their eyes watching travelers with a predatory intelligence. Phantasmal deer, their antlers adorned with glowing sigils, glide silently through the mist.

Amari is taking her group on a longer trail to the Archive specifically to avoid some of these creatures. Of course, if there were a completely accurate map of the Forsaken Forest, this would be easy. No map can be entirely reliable here. This forest itself will change on a whim, and creatures are not beholden to ink on paper. Because of this, more is left up to chance than she is comfortable with. It's been a long time since she's kept her senses as a seer this hyper-aware for so long.

It's tiring, even knowing how important it is for her to be alert.

They walk for hours, trying to use the filtered sunlight lighting their way. Days in the Forsaken Forest have no set rotation — daylight can last a few hours or up to forty hours. The night is the same way, so the group has decided to take advantage of any natural light. Kol volunteers to fly above the mountainous trees to investigate, but Amari shoots him down immediately. No one on the initial expedition could get through the canopy to see the sky, and the delay would not be worthwhile if it failed or drew the interest of some monster.

To the benefit of the group's morale, they come across the first landmark in the governor's reports before nightfall. Najaah picks up on the sound of rushing water far before they see it. From studying the expedition's sketches, Amari instantly recognizes the sight that greets them as Plomsade Falls.

It is a majestic waterfall cascading down a cliff shrouded in perpetual mist. The water is said to have magical properties that can either heal or cause harm, depending on the intent of the person who touches it. The falls are surrounded by dense, thorny underbrush and are closely guarded by territorial fey creatures that do not take kindly to intruders.

Amari makes sure they stick to the path that runs parallel to the river, ignoring the oppressive presence of the fey just yards away. The attention feels like hundreds of needles poking at her back.

However, her warning only stirs up curiosity among the group's teens. Erika is the first to ask. "What kind of animals live here?"

She's made them all read general reports of the monsters here, so Amari wonders what the girl is expecting to hear. "Anything that falls under the nebulous title of 'forsaken,' I guess."

"But what about creatures natural to this world? Or are they all… transplanted?"

A good question. Amari has no idea. "Probably some mix of both, knowing the Ethereal Planes."

"That's crazy," Kol comments idly, walking a bit ahead of the two. Taliya, still working off that extra energy, is leading the team and ignores the conversation to stay focused on the path ahead. "Aren't there, like, *ghosts* here?"

Amari nearly snorts aloud and coughs into her fist to cover the sound. Here, Taliya sends back an amused smirk.

"Why would there be ghosts?" Najaah questions, bringing up the rear of the group. "Ghosts of who?"

"Not ghosts, as in a piece of a soul left behind by someone who died," Amari finally corrects, adding on. "You're talking about wraiths. They're the manifestations of any type of negative energy that clusters together and stagnates after a time. Wraiths are ethereal beings that drain the life force from living creatures and definitely fall under the idea of 'forsaken.'"

"Creepy," Kol says. "Hope we don't run into those."

"Yes, let's try to avoid them. And other dangers the forest has to offer."

Of course, she doesn't get her wish. Their gas masks go from a caution to a life-or-death necessity at a moment's notice.

As soon as a mysterious fog starts gathering at her feet, she knows that they've run into a threat the expedition warned about. The path soon becomes thick with a moving cloud of magical miasma. It's a naturally occurring hazard in this world that can disorient and confuse those who venture too far off a path without proper protection. This miasma can warp reality, and many of the original expedition's members fell victim to it. Only a few survived.

It's one of the most insidious threats in the forest. This nearly translucent fog is a source of magical disorientation. It manipulates people's perception, making familiar landmarks seem distant or shifting, and creates illusions that lure travelers into traps. Breathing in the miasma can cause dizziness, hallucinations, and even madness in prolonged exposure. It's essential for anyone entering the forest to wear enchanted masks or protective wards to shield themselves from its effects.

Luckily, Amari stocked up, and even asked the Wind Weaver to check over their equipment before they left his shop.

She orders everyone to double-check they have their mask on correctly before they venture farther down the path. Najaah and Amari now lead the group forward, as the ones with the best eyesight and immunity to toxic substances. Kol and Nuru walk in the back because they're the ones who can fly out of range of the fog if needed. In times like this, the Sky Lord is cursing his inability to make other people float with him. Mainly, he can carry one of them with him if it comes down to it. Maybe two, if they don't weigh much.

It takes an hour of tense, silent, and fast-paced walking for the miasma to start thinning out again. Everyone breathes a sigh of relief —through masks that have stayed on out of due diligence—as soon as the mesmerizing fog clears from the path. With a better view, Amari can see that they're still following along the river, and that night has truly fallen now.

Hopefully, they haven't passed the bridge. When she searches her instincts for some kind of answer (*do they need to go back or keep moving forward?),* she gets the vague sense that something important awaits ahead. The idea of backtracking seems underwhelming in comparison to that feeling, so Amari assures herself they didn't already pass it.

Najaah — as one of the only ones here with any real experience traveling in the wilderness — decides a discreet grove only ten yards off the path works as their next campsite. Everyone, apart from Amari, is more than happy to settle down to rest.

This grove is a dense, dark area where the trees are so close together that their branches intertwine, forming a thick canopy. She can feel a presence as she brushes close to one of the trees, and Amari can sense whispered conversations if she pays attention. The seer makes sure to bolster her mental shields. They don't feel hostile, at least not yet.

The others don't react to the whispers at all.

For Amari, this forest is a constant source of paranoia. She's hyper-aware that she can sense things that others can't, and it makes her hesitant about what she's noticing. It's like being in the Kiyoshi Crater. The air is filled with distant whispers, rustling leaves, and occasional unsettling growls or screeches — and she doesn't know how much of it the rest of the team is picking up. Najaah has a spectacular sense of hearing, but the fact that *Amari* is picking up so much hints that they're more telepathic than anything else.

She makes sure either she or Taliya is always awake to watch out when the team decides who keeps watch and when. The thief doesn't have Amari's senses but knows when it's a good idea to wake her.

Suffice it to say, she doesn't sleep restfully in the Forsaken Forest. And they still have many days ahead of them.

Amari won't say it out loud if asked, but she's growing worried about the group.

Erika is the obvious contender, with the subdued mood that

seemed to overtake her in the wake of the rest of them interrogating the spirit who attacked Taliya. The seer understands why, academically. It must be disquieting to really see the glaring difference between the people the teen is stuck with in a dangerous new world and the people she grew up with.

That doesn't mean Amari can bring herself to regret her actions, not when Taliya was on the line.

It's not just Erika, though. Kol has also acted strangely since they left the Red City, for less apparent reasons. At least, Amari thinks the weirdness is centered on her. The boy keeps sending her suspicious glances anytime they're camped out, and she can always feel eyes on her when he's walking behind during the day.

Pinpointing the origin of the change in dynamic takes her a bit before she remembers a moment when her group was moving through the Heart. Amari had sensed a trap just before it activated and acted accordingly. Kol had seen the whole thing and questioned how she did it.

Amari had brushed off the questions and then completely forgotten the potential issue once the Colossus appeared. She withholds a sigh as the realization washes over her.

The problem is that any explanation she could give Kol that he would accept came treacherously close to the truth. And she can't allow that. Now, Amari feels it's too late to do much damage control, instead opting to be mindful about not being so openly suspect around the teen.

Avoiding him is easier than Erika is, not only because the girl is friendlier. Sometimes, the seer looks at Kol and sees a different boy, one who would have been about the same age now. Looking away is a relief.

More importantly, two out of three of the group's teens are acting weird, and it's mostly Amari's fault. Since any words from her are likely to make things worse, she elects to pair Kol off with Nuru and

Erika with Najaah for the time being.

Naturally, this is when Najaah begins to act suspiciously.

It's not enough that Amari is leading a team through a world not made for humans; they also have to have interpersonal drama as well.

There have always been 'strange' things about the Sun Eater, most of which Amari can explain away as her being a former child soldier forced into service. One of those quirks is Najaah's intense aversion to being seen in any state of undress. This never came up as an issue until the team found themselves in a hostile wilderness where they have to stick together to survive.

Kol and Nuru usually pair off when one of them needs some privacy, and Najaah could choose any group member as a partner without anyone minding. Amari is reluctant to let her go off on her own, and neither of the other teens seems to notice the former soldier's hesitancy.

It's not the seer's business to figure out where Najaah's hesitance comes from, so she tries to compromise by giving the Sun Eater space while insisting she stay close enough to the team so that someone can hear her if trouble appears.

Of course, no plan survives contact with dumb luck.

Amari is — perhaps unduly — unsurprised that the problem comes to a head because of Kol's blundering. Najaah isn't even undressed; she just hasn't put her coat and gear back on yet. Everyone's finishing up getting ready for another day of hiking through the forest after camping through a long night. Amari is sitting on a fallen tree log-turned-bench facing the former soldier, and the boy has walked up behind the Sun Eater.

"Are those tattoos?" Kol asks, oblivious to Najaah's sudden stillness. He's only the second after Amari to show up in the clearing where the group would regroup once they're done changing. Najaah has her shirt on, but apparently, it must have shifted enough to show something on her back when she reached down for her bag.

Najaah's face goes stony, and Amari winces even as the Ashan's ire isn't directed at her. The former soldier quickly forces herself into motion and puts her coat on before turning to give Kol a harsh look. "Were you ever taught manners, or have you simply been ignoring them?"

Yikes. Amari should probably say something, right? But she doesn't even know what sensitive spot Kol unintentionally poked at…

"Well, I—"

"That wasn't a serious question." Najaah slings the bag over her shoulder and tightens the straps. "Tattoos can be incredibly personal, you know."

The boy frowns. Amari will admit only to herself that she's unbearably curious and keeps quiet. "They didn't look ceremonial, they looked like—"

Najaah raises an eyebrow, her eyes colder than the seer has ever seen them, and her voice stays neutral. "And you are the judge of what ceremonial looks like?"

This finally makes Kol pause, face turning red. "Uh, no, probably not."

"Glad we agree."

This, to Amari's eternal gratitude, is when Taliya walks into the clearing and interrupts to ramble loudly about the inconvenience of nature, heedless of the tension she walked into. It makes the seer let out a silent sigh of relief despite the lingering concern.

After that morning, Najaah is more closed off to the group, and Kol's mood worsens in response. Erika seems stuck in the middle, trying to play peacemaker to something only Najaah understands. Nuru takes mercy on the girl and distracts Kol as best he can for the rest of the day.

Amari can only hope their differences don't interfere with the mission. She fears that if things get worse, she might not be able to properly hold together the telepathic network.

They finally reach the bridge on their fourth day in the forest. Amari feels the building stress in the back of her mind loosen a fraction as soon as she catches a glimpse of the landmark, but it's soon overtaken by wariness as she gets a better view.

Ahead, a drawbridge stretches precariously over the river that glimmers in the waning light. The bridge, crafted from weathered wood and bound with ivy and moss, blends seamlessly with its natural surroundings and bears the wear of countless ages. Its surface is uneven, worn smooth by the passage of time and the weight of many travelers. Amari eyes it with heavy skepticism.

Beneath the bridge, the river flows, shining golden. She can *feel* the magical energies that radiate from the river, like a gaping abyss; something about this area seems to enhance the water's power. The seer doesn't particularly want to discover what its magic does to humans. She can faintly make out strange runes etched into the stones along the riverbanks that pulse faintly, hinting at ancient protections and enchantments woven into the fabric of the forest itself.

Above the bridge, the forest canopy intertwines, casting dappled shadows that dance across the weathered planks. She realizes with some despair that the branches aren't sturdy enough to carry any of them.

An unsettling presence lingers near the bridge. She can sense something watching from the depths of the river, where the waters swirl with unseen currents. A creature of the old world, a myth made flesh in this realm. From the intent she can feel brushing against her shields, it's a guardian steeped in ancient magic and bound to protect the bridge from those who dare to trespass uninvited.

Even knowing it's there, she can't pin it down with her eyes. Its form is elusive, shifting between shadow and substance, its presence marked only by the faint rustling of leaves and the occasional ripple on the river's surface. As the group approaches the bridge, they all sense a warning in the air that they are not alone in this space and that passage across the drawbridge will come at a price.

Hopefully, nothing too big. She'll figure it out.

"Alright, I'm going first," Amari decides, ignoring the glance Taliya sends her way. "Kol, can you get in the air and watch over everyone who crosses?"

"Sure," the kid shrugs, already starting to hover off the forest floor, pink energy flickering around him.

"Good. Be cautious and only fight if you're attacked first."

Now, he looks a little alarmed. "Attacked by what?"

Amari smiles grimly, eyeing the elusive presence in the river. "I guess we'll see."

She thinks she hears something along the lines of *so not comforting* as the teen floats above her head. Instead of acknowledging him, she drops her bag to the ground to be moved later by their Sky Lord courier and scans the rest of the team. None of them seems particularly happy about the current situation, and she sighs internally.

"Look, we need to be careful. After me, Taliya can go, then Erika, then Najaah. Nuru, you stay here before shifting and crossing, alright?"

The shapeshifter, wordlessly understanding his job as a babysitter, nods seriously. Taliya says nothing despite looking like she's chewing on a lemon, and Najaah is getting everything conceivably heavy off Erika and themself.

In the end, Amari keeps her collapsible staff strapped to her back despite the added weight. The benefits of having it with her outweigh the risks. No pun intended.

Slowly, constantly alert for any shift in danger the bridge presents, she takes a step onto the worn wooden planks. Amari doesn't trust them a bit, even though she can feel remnants of the magic that went into making this structure. Perhaps it's something abandoned from another world, too.

Nothing immediately leaps out at her, which is a win in her books. It's not until Amari arrives at the middle point of the drawbridge—clutching at the ancient rope with white-knuckled hands the whole way—that she feels the presence in the river reaches out to her with purpose.

No understandable words are sent her way; instead, she gets a veritable storm of emotions and intent. Amari mainly gets *hunger* and *long-held patience* and *mine, mine, mine.*

Carefully, she presents a message in a similar package, telling the creature they are simply passing by and willing to pay a toll. She is very deliberate in how unobtrusive her response is, laying it out to be found in lieu of pushing it to the creature. It finds the message immediately, overtaking it and digesting it quickly. Amari tries not to let the mental sensation bother her so much.

The reply she gets is equal parts disheartening and alarming.

It can sense every single one of them, and the creature sends Amari its awareness of Kol, which is accompanied by a great deal of *greed.*

Instead of outright denying the creature, Amari turns to the teen. "I'm communicating with the presence in the river."

"We noticed when you stopped moving and started staring off into space," Kol says dryly, hovering above her. The rest of the team watches intently from dozens of yards away. Amari huffs, not willing to be amused at this moment.

"When I start moving, I need you to start ferrying people across as fast as you can, understand? This is going to get rough."

For his part, Kol just nods, not questioning her for once.

Mentally, Amari turns back to the waiting creature. She presents a mixture of *acceptance* and the idea that there is *something important to know.*

She can feel the thing's curiosity and its ravenous greed for knowledge. It lets her mental presence closer, past some of its shields, which feels like walking into a dragon's mouth unarmed. Amari doesn't let an ounce of her own emotions show.

Amari attacks the moment she is comfortably past some of the shields, but not so deep into the creature's mind that she loses her sanity.

Words fail to describe what happens next. The closest explanation she can dream up later is that the creature tries to *absorb* her mind and soul in response to her mental assault. Her attack distracts it, yet it attempts to consume her instinctively.

It's only her years of experience dealing with mindscapes that let Amari claw her way out, leaving her feeling numb. She pushes the feeling to the back of her consciousness with practiced ease.

At the same time as her attack, in the Present, she takes a step further down the bridge. Kol instantly darts back to the team, grabbing Taliya to move. With him, all their bags start glowing with his signature pink magic and follow him across the river.

Mentally, Amari has escaped the creature with her mind mostly intact. Physically, she watches with growing dread as small forms rise from the river — winged, viscous-looking things made from pieces of the beast that can't be bothered to leave its home. Like some unholy mix of rats and very small dragons, a horde of them flies directly at Amari.

Her staff practically teleports into her hand with the speed she unsheathes it, magic already channeling into the protective runes. The first deranged not-bat looking thing hits her hastily made shield with a shudder that nearly knocks her clean off the drawbridge.

In a not-panicking corner of her mind, Amari notes that Taliya has made it to the other side and has started fending off the small creatures with her hook swords. The thief links them together to get a longer range, while Kol dodges the winged monsters in an effort to get Erika. He's using forest debris as missiles.

Most of her focus is on warding off the mass of nightmare bats. They hit her shield without regard for personal damage, clearly a mindless horde that acts solely as vessels for the river creature's purpose. She channels her magic into bolstering her staff and swings the weapon at a random assailant. Amari feels a perfectly normal amount of satisfaction when the nightmare bat disappears in a cloud of ash as her staff hits it dead on.

The drawbridge wobbles precariously under her, and she desperately looks around for the source. To her despair, a pair of the creatures are chewing through a part of the rope that's barely holding this structure together. She doesn't even consider trying to save the bridge from the horde; instead, she works on moving closer to the side where Kol just deposited Erika with difficulty.

A flash of metal lashes into the edge of Amari's vision, and she looks forward, seeing something that makes her curse. Taliya is on the drawbridge but has decided to forgo the precarious wooden boards entirely. She's balancing on the drawbridge's rope a couple of yards closer than the seer wants her to be to get a better spot to hit nightmare bats. She appears to be performing the most treacherous circus act ever thought up.

To her increasing horror and bewilderment, Najaah joins her friend's insanity and jumps onto the rope on the other side of the bridge. Kol is batting away at any creatures that get close to him while he hovers unsurely around the Sun Eater, who is slicing away at the horde. Amari doesn't even notice Nuru until he is diving toward a nightmare bat trying to aim for her head. The shapeshifter in his second form barrels into the thing, talons first, turning it into ash.

Balance impeccable, Najaah runs along the unsteady rope to Amari, swinging her blade into every creature that gets within killing range. Altogether, the Ashan joins Nuru and Kol in helping Amari cross the drawbridge.

Since the majority of the horde is focusing on the seer, this effort becomes orders of magnitude easier with the support. Amari leans on her instincts, swinging her staff whenever her abilities alert her to danger, which is almost everything at this point. Slowly, she makes her way across the bridge.

As soon as she gets close enough to speak to Taliya, Amari curses the thief out fiercely. Her friend laughs sharply, sounding far too delighted about the situation.

At this point, the end of the drawbridge is within spitting distance, so the seer plants one end of her staff on a firm enough wooden board and launches herself to solid ground. Taliya joins her a second later, swords still snapping at anything that gets close.

She turns back to see if Najaah needs help, only to see the Sun Eater leap from the drawbridge and quickly close a distance that doesn't seem humanly possible. The former soldier lands softly next to them, and their two flying teammates aren't far behind.

Amari doesn't have to say anything before everyone grabs their bag off the ground and runs. Only Nuru doesn't take the extra time to shift back, and Kol picks up the shapeshifter's supplies without hesitation.

The group dashes down the path, chased by the remaining horde that shrieks in fury at their escaping prey. Amari is giving herself a splitting headache trying to sense every potential threat around them as everyone else is occupied with the small creatures hunting the team.

It takes a few minutes for the horde to lose steam, the magic controlling them straining at the growing distance between them and their master. Staff still out, Amari whips around and channels a burst of magic into the rune for *disruption*.

A tricky rune that can end in disaster if used incorrectly, it disrupts any active magic in the vicinity. She prefers to use it in cases like this when something is controlling a third party to attack them. Her magic corrupts the connection between the horde and master—

turning half of them to ash then and there.

This would never have worked so close to the bridge's guardian. Amari can snap the connection and destroy the horde now that they're far away.

In the aftermath, everyone on the team is breathing heavily, wearily watching their surroundings for more enemies. Nuru shifts back to his first form unceremoniously and immediately begins interrogating everyone over injuries. Most of them just have scratches that are mercifully not infected with anything. That could have been terrible.

She glances at Erika, who had defended all the supplies Kol dropped on this side while the others helped Amari cross the bridge. The teenager looks exhausted and sports a few scratches of her own, but otherwise, there are no extensive injuries. However, Erika won't look directly at Amari these days, so the seer doesn't try to reach out. Nuru approaches the kid not much later with the first aid kit.

Despite their tiredness, Amari doesn't let the team linger here long. No one has serious injuries, so she wants to put more distance between herself and the bridge.

The collective group lasts an hour more, hiking through the forest before people start to visibly droop. She's honestly impressed that Erika and Kol have lasted so long, and she instructs Najaah to find a safe place to camp out for the approaching night while the rest of them prepare some food.

The feeling of an incoming vision doesn't hit her all at once this time, but in a slow, building pressure in her head. As soon as Amari notices the sensation, she searches for Taliya urgently across the path, catching the thief's eyes after a moment. She doesn't need to say or sign anything to convey what's happening to her friend.

"Hey, guys!" Taliya calls out, instantly drawing the rest of the group's attention. "Last night, I had the *weirdest* dream that I—"

Amari felt the world fall away, leaving her falling through open air. Wind swept around her hair and made it difficult to see anything. The sky was a dark purple fading into darkness, and the shadows reached for her like desperate hands trying to grasp salvation.

Abruptly, the seer was standing on even ground, her mind scrambling to keep up with the shifting environment. Dead leaves littered the earth, crunching loudly under her golden slippers. An ornate monochrome ballgown trailed behind her as she looked around, taking in the mostly barren land.

Ahead of her, in the distance, rose a grand World Tree, branches twisting up into the sky. Avalon's three broken moons shone between the limbs, and she noticed with a shiver that the World Tree had lost all its leaves. She didn't think that was possible.

"What am I looking at?" Amari murmured, searching for *something* that would tell her what was happening. What was this vision supposed to tell her?

A gust of cold wind nearly knocked her down, and a great roaring echoed through her mind, making Amari cover her ears instinctively. It's a useless effort as the noise threatened to drown everything else out. For a moment, she almost thought she caught a glimpse of a dark shadow passing above before she was ripped away again.

The Present slowly comes back into view, the last dredges of her vision ripping through her. Body shaking, Amari realizes belatedly one hand is pressing hard against a tree for support, the bark digging into her palm.

" — grew into a giant shoe, flooding the whole street!"

"That's mad," Kol says, sounding fascinated. Nuru has his head in his hands while Erika whispers to Kol fervently. Najaah is picking a place to camp, ignoring Taliya entirely. No one looks at Amari as she slumps against the tree and takes a minute to catch her breath.

The pounding ache in her skull eases with every minute in the Present, and she uses her clear mind to go over her vision. Amari mulls over her fall and then the barren World Tree with a grim look. Ill omens don't cover it.

World Trees are remnants of the old world, when gods freely visited Avalon, handing out miracles and tragedies alike. They represent the land's history, the magical energy flowing through (almost) every living thing, and the diversity in life a world sustains. The branches of the World Tree hold different kinds of leaves and fruit on every limb, many of which are still being studied by scientists.

The fact that the tree in her vision was bare...

Amari suppresses a shudder, doing her best to focus and ground herself in the Present.

Thankfully, it doesn't take the Ashan long to find a suitable spot. As darkness takes over the forest, Amari ushers everyone else to sleep. After all, as a Nightblood, she's the only one who feels *more* awake when the sun sets. And considering the day she's had, the seer isn't sleeping any time soon.

She spends hours sensing every phantom noise of the forest, watching darkness hug the forest close.

19

ERIKA

"Damn, what did you pack? A bag of bricks?"

Erika squawks in outrage as Kol lifts her bag. She'd been reorganizing things while the team was camped out. But now it's getting dark faster than she anticipated, so the Nullifier needs to move everything into her tent for better lighting. "No! Just… some books."

"Have you been carrying this the whole time?" Kol asks, an insulting amount of disbelief in his tone. Face heating up, she glares as harshly as she can at the Sky Lord, who doesn't so much as blink.

"They've been sealed in my dagger," Erika admits begrudgingly after a few moments of expectant silence. She lugs her (much lighter) bag into the tent and points to where she wants her book bag to be set down.

Unfortunately, the light-hearted atmosphere is washed away the moment Amari straightens up in alarm from where she had previously organized her things.

As Erika has learned over the last few days, one of the most dangerous and unknowable dangers of the Forsaken Forest is not from its deadly plants or terrifying creatures.

Its unpredictable weather patterns pose perhaps the largest—and most tedious, according to Amari—threat. Sudden, violent storms can sweep through the forest, bringing torrents of acid rain or whirlwinds of fiery embers. These storms can cause severe burns and acid wounds or ignite the forest's flammable flora, creating an ever-present fire risk. The team's only fortune is that they are prepared for such weather and that their camping gear is made to withstand such attacks.

So when Amari tells the group to set up for a rough storm, everyone drops what they were doing and gets moving. Erika immediately begins helping Nuru secure the tents more, ensuring there are no potential leaks.

Taliya and Amari set up magical barriers while Najaah quickly scrounges food and wood for a fire in the surrounding area. Once the storm starts, they can't leave the campsite again until it stops. Kol is quickly organizing the rest of the camp with his power—his own tiny storm of floating supplies and bags whirling around him. Everything goes (somewhat) neatly into each person's assigned tent, or otherwise next to the fire pit Najaah had been working on.

Nailing down a corner of a tent, Erika fortifies the hastily built structure from being blown off by the wind. Her fingers trace over the edges of runes carved into the nail and feel for the magic woven into the very fibers of the tent. It's a strange sensation, like hovering her hand over a live socket and hoping it doesn't electrocute her. If she focuses too much, she almost thinks she could smother the magic.

With a shout of warning from Amari, Erika realizes that they have finished just in time, with Najaah being the only one outside the magical barrier when the storm hits. Luckily, as a Sun Eater, they have a natural immunity to the scorching rain of this world. The former soldier is inside the barrier in under a minute, and their clothes are damaged far worse than they are. Without any theatrics, the Ashan gets right into the business of making a fire after handing Nuru the food they foraged.

Acid rain falls outside their shield in thin, caustic droplets that can corrode metal and burn skin. Erika gets a full-body shiver watching a stray pen left outside the barrier melt in real-time. It's better than a fiery storm, she reasons with herself. Those bring swirling embers that can ignite the forest's flammable vegetation, creating dangerous forest fires.

Erika doesn't hesitate to huddle away in her tent until the food is ready and makes sure to stick close to the distracting warmth of the fire. Taliya drops down onto the tree log-turned-bench next to her, holding out a bowl of food. She takes it with a smile of thanks, more than happy to dig in.

The food is almost gone when the sky rumbles ominously, and Erika glances upwards briefly before looking away. Taliya notices from her seat next to her and questions her quietly. "Is something wrong?"

She flinches, hopefully not very overtly. "Uh, well, I guess, I just don't like the noise."

Thunder echoes above them to emphasize Erika's point. She's sure Taliya can easily read the stress in the lines on her face at the sound, and she curls into her jacket.

"You're afraid of storms."

It isn't phrased as a question, but the teenager takes it as one. "Oh, no, it's fine. Just loud."

Just to prove her wrong, lightning flashes in the far-off distance, and the wind seems to pick up. Erika flinches much more noticeably now, and her hands tighten. Taliya frowns thoughtfully.

"Have you always been afraid of storms?"

This was an easy question for most people, Erika is sure. Except she can't really explain how new she is to the concept of storms, now, can she? The team may know she's a Nullifier, but that doesn't mean she can just hand out information on the Haven Republic.

"Ummmm. Well, yeah, that, yeah." Erika groans and leans down to rest her head against her hands, clutching the bowl resting on her knees. "I'm not very good at this."

Taliya looks like she has no idea what 'this' is. Storms? Lying about her fear? General conversation?

"Everyone gets better with practice," the thief says, sounding a bit awkward. To be fair, it is typically true advice. Erika huffs, slumping more.

"I was kinda afraid of that."

Erika doesn't notice the contemplative look Taliya gives her, sinking into a spiral of half-formed fears and anxieties. Things like 'what if the Republic is discovered because of me?' Or 'what if this is all for nothing?' What if, what if, what if…

What if Erika doesn't recognize the person she is by the end of this?

"I wouldn't worry about it," Taliya remarks, throwing Erika off. Her train of thought crashes to a halt.

"What?"

"I know killers," the thief says wryly, something flashing across her face too fast for the teen to parse. In the end, the unreadable look fades, and Taliya gives her a small smile. "You're not one. It's a good thing, even surrounded by people like us. So, don't be too worried about it."

"Can you read minds?" Erika blurts out, then goes red in the face as the question registers. She doesn't know whether to feel thankful or resentful that the thief just laughs, eyes shining with amusement.

"Nah, just observant. And you've been rather obvious."

"…Right."

Taliya doesn't push her further on the topic and lets the teenager sit in her thoughts for a couple of minutes before turning the conversation over to the runes in the magical barrier protecting them all from being rained on with acid. Erika is more than content to listen to the thief ramble on about the art of intertwining wards and creating self-sustaining circuits of energy to power the thing.

Eventually, Amari calls for the team to break into those who will take the first watch of the night and those who will sleep. The Nightblood is always among the first on watch, so Erika doesn't push herself to volunteer. She stares at her empty bowl like it'll give the answers to all the conflicting emotions warring in her.

Surprisingly, Kol ends up on the first watch with Amari, who looks a little disgruntled at the prospect. Taliya is snickering at the Nightblood as she gets up and heads to her tent. Not interested in being left with Amari and Kol, Erika stands up quickly to go to her own tent. A not insignificant amount of tension leaves her as soon as she zips the tent closed, blocking out a great deal of the outside noise.

With the thunder and crackling of lightning muffled, it doesn't take long for Erika to fall into a fitful sleep. When her eyes open again, the night has given way to a very dim light.

More importantly, the rain has fizzled into a light sprinkle of acid by the time she wakes. It's still too dangerous to go outside the magical barrier, but it's a good omen that the storm will leave them entirely soon. Erika can already hear the tell-tale sounds of people moving around outside her tent. Most likely, it's Najaah, who wakes up as soon as dawn breaks because they're an Ashan and are always ready to work because they were raised as a soldier.

So imagine her surprise at seeing Amari restlessly moving around the campsite. Erika hesitates in the middle of unzipping her tent, feeling suddenly very unsure about everything. The Nightblood turns to her, face unreadable.

"Is something wrong?" Amari's voice is hushed in deference to the still slumbering members of their party. Fingers clenching around the tent's zipper, Erika debates what to say. She's not sure why she got up. The Nightblood continues before she can answer. "Najaah decided to go look for more wood for the fire if that's the problem."

"Oh," Erika says intelligently. "It's still raining. Are they okay?"

"They have an enchanted umbrella and coat," Amari assures. "It wouldn't be enough protection from the acid in the air for the rest of us, but Najaah will be more than fine."

"That's good..." Erika trails off awkwardly, not meeting the other's eyes. Even if the spirit hurt Taliya, its screams of pain still ring in her ears sometimes.

Amari sighs softly, then reaches into a bag and pulls out some of the rations they have packed. "Here, have something to eat. The rain should stop soon, and we'll need our strength."

Erika stares at the rations left neatly laid out for her on a tree stump as the Nightblood heads back to her own tent. Her fingers are hurting from how tightly she's holding the zipper, surely leaving indents in her palm. Finally, once an uncomfortable quiet has fallen over the empty campsite, she fully exits her tent.

The rations are good, even as they don't relieve the ache in her chest.

When Erika first stepped out of the Republic tunnels and onto Avalon's surface, she saw natural life in quantities she had never seen before. She remembers thinking that the governor's garden had more plants in one place than she would ever see again.

The flora of the Forsaken Forest knocks everything else out. Moreover, she's far more used to the man-made cities carved out in the Republic, so camping is a novel experience. And a dirty one.

Bioluminescent fungi and flowers flourish among the undergrowth, bringing nostalgia to the forefront of Erika's mind. These plants glow in various colors—sickly greens, fiery oranges, and midnight blues—casting an otherworldly light on the forest floor when the light from above dims. It's different from the plants native to the Haven Republic, most of which she can name off the top of her head after hours spent in school, having them drilled into every student.

She's constantly tempted to approach the glowing flora for a better sense of home. However, some of these fungi release spores that induce hallucinations or cause a debilitating fever if inhaled, while others exude a sticky, poisonous sap that can cause severe skin reactions. Amari ensures the group maintains their distance and keeps their masks close at hand.

As soon as acid levels outside the magical barrier are habitable for all humans, they set off again.

"Ugh," Kol complains as his boots sink into the mud. Mercifully, most of the paths in the forest have some paved stones or are very well-trodden. But it's not enough to save his shoes altogether. "Now the ground is *wet*. I don't see why I can't just fly."

"Suck it up, princeling," Taliya calls over her shoulder, not sounding the least bit sympathetic. Erika can't help feeling the thief is a little hypocritical for the comment after she spent the morning bitching about mud getting into her gear and leaving footprints everywhere.

"Save your magic for more important matters," Nuru says, not unkindly, giving Kol a wan smile. "Your boots are meant to get dirty."

The boy grumbles under his breath and grimaces in disgust just as there's a particularly loud squelch in the mud, thankfully keeping his silence. Erika enjoys the feel of damp earth under her feet as much as the other, but she ignores it in favor of keeping an eye out for any dangers. Path sloping downward, they end up in a small ravine, walls of packed earth and rock on either side, with tree roots peeking out. It makes the trees on top of the ravine walls look even more towering, even as they must weave around and climb over the occasional boulder.

Naturally, the group gets no warnings before the earth starts shaking around them. In fact, the only one to react in time so as not to be swept off their feet is Amari, which sends a thrill of alarm up Erika's spine that she has absolutely no time to examine.

The terrain in this forest is treacherous, as Erika has read about in the expedition's reports and now comes to learn this firsthand. With hidden pits and traps set by the forest's residents and a natural inclination for sowing chaos, it's a death sentence for anyone who wanders off a path.

Staying on the path isn't a guarantee of safety, however much she wishes it were. Some areas are prone to sudden shifts or collapse, creating sinkholes that can swallow an unwary traveler whole. Other parts of the ground may become a mass of animated roots and vines that wriggle and shift, ensnaring anyone who steps on them.

At this moment, the team is being violently educated about what it's like for the very earth to fight against your existence. The ground rolls underfoot, easily sweeping Erika off her feet and knocking the wind right out of her. As she wheezes on her back, she sees out of the corner of her eyes that Kol is already hovering up above the ravine but is waylaid from helping anyone by tree roots and low-hanging branches snapping out to grab him. He looks like a fly darting away from dozens of hands desperately trying to swat him.

Taliya is thrown hard into the air off the path and pulls out her hook swords to grab onto a stray crevice. She's reacting faster than anyone else who could attempt a rescue, only for the entire earth to shift back into a smooth cliff face. "What—"

Luckily, before the thief can take a nasty fall, Najaah leaps meters into the air after Taliya and catches her with one arm. The momentum takes them to a ravine wall, and the Sun Eater creates their own hold by brutally stabbing the khopesh clasped in their other hand into the earth.

Erika is so caught up in the chaos of what's happening to her friends that she misses a tree root sneaking up on her legs until it wraps around her in a tight hold. A cut-off scream escapes her as she's abruptly being pulled off her feet and down the ravine, away from the team. The hard slam to the ground knocks the wind out of her, leaving Erika gasping for breath from her burning lungs.

She thinks she hears someone call her name, but understandably, her attention is occupied elsewhere. Then suddenly, Amari is there, grabbing her by the straps of her backpack and slamming her staff down on the roots. Erika didn't even see her approach, as if she simply appeared at the perfect time to save the teen. Again.

The staff's runes glow a harsh red, and whatever they do seems to disperse the roots, letting Erika crawl away further. She shakily tries to get to her feet, only to stagger as pain shoots up her legs. They'll be bruises for sure, the Nullifier groans internally. A sigh of relief escapes her after feeling her legs carefully as she realizes she escaped a more severe injury, like a bone fracture.

Amari pushes her gently by the backpack toward the group, bringing Erika out of her head. The situation has calmed down somewhat with the rest of the group. It seems the movement of the earth was a violent but brief occurrence, and the others are having an easier time outmaneuvering the hostile trees now that the element of surprise has been lost.

"Thanks," Erika says, trying not to let the surge of anxiety in her chest show, and she feels like she fails spectacularly. Why does she have to be so gods-awful awkward all the time? Amari just saved her life! "It's—yeah, thank you."

The Nightblood gives a slight smile that doesn't reach her eyes and replies with stilted words. "Of course."

"Hey!" Kol calls out to the scattered members of the team from where he's hovering meters above them. "You guys should see this!"

Taliya scowls at the teen from the bottom of the ravine, standing next to Najaah, who is slicing every tree root that gets in their proximity. "See what?"

"There's something up ahead!"

Nuru shifts into his second form to scout without needing to be asked, and Amari gestures at Kol to come pick her up. With the teen carrying the Nightblood, all three teammates go to survey whatever Kol had seen from the air. They're out of view in a matter of seconds.

Legs and chest aching, Erika shuffles over to Taliya and Najaah. "What do you think Kol is showing them?"

"From that high up, and with his eyesight in the daytime, he could have seen something kilometers away," Najaah says thoughtfully, pausing afterward to swing their blade at another tree root that has the audacity to try to sneak up on them. "We shouldn't wait here. They'll come back along the path anyway."

"Yeah, definitely not keen on staying here," Taliya mutters, picking up Nuru's and Amari's bags in one swift move. Sticking close to the thief, Erika takes the time to get her breathing back in proper order as they walk down the path.

They're walking down the path for what feels like hours, but it is probably only half of one when Nuru comes swooping around a corner of the ravine. He turns back into his first form so quickly that his human feet touch down as he lands. "Wait!"

All three of them freeze at the shapeshifter's urgent shout. Erika doesn't think she's ever heard him raise his voice before. It makes the whole situation much more surreal.

"What's wrong?" Najaah is the first to start in on the questions, their posture straightening. Taliya shifts the bags on her shoulder, her free hand moving toward her sheathed swords, and making Erika reach for her dagger in solidarity.

"There's a mess of arcane flares and sigils up ahead," Nuru explains with a grimace, voice lowering as he walks closer. "It's like a minefield."

"That wasn't in the expedition's reports," Erika says, immediately feeling stupid for it a moment later. Hadn't they just reinforced the knowledge that this forest changes its terrain whenever it likes?

Nuru tips his head at her in acknowledgment. "Amari thinks earlier was a side effect of this field's migration through the forest. We need to be careful."

"What about the path?" Najaah asks with a tense frown on their face. The former soldier's hand is white-knuckling the handle of their sword. "Is it still intact?"

"Intact, yes," Nuru sighs, fingers brushing dirt off his coat. "Safe? Not so much. The path is now part of the minefield. We'll have to be extremely cautious moving forward. Kol is helping Amari map out the field, so we'll have to wait until they're back."

"Great," Taliya grumbled, plopping down to the ground without another word. "I *love* waiting."

"I'm sure Amari would love to hear that," Nuru gives the thief a slight smirk, but there isn't much energy in it. They're all rather tired after days of travel. Erika takes the opportunity to get off her aching legs — Najaah had already wrestled her down to apply some first aid, but even magical medicines take time to heal — and read a few more chapters of the book she's currently reading. It's a study of the Apolon Empire's effect on linguistics, told from the perspective of someone from one of their conquered territories who escaped the conquest to live in a different land. This makes it the kind of book that's banned in the Empire.

She doesn't notice Taliya side-eyeing her until Amari and Kol are almost back. "What?"

"Nothing. You're the type that went to school early, aren't you?"

"What?" Erika repeats, eyebrows furrowing. "I mean, I would go early to spend time in the library, I guess. Why are you aski—"

"They're here," Najaah straightens from a few yards away and calls out a full ten seconds before the two fly around the ravine corner into view.

Taliya gets up and turns away without clearing up Erika's

bafflement, and she begrudgingly lets the question go as Kol sets down. The boy looks a bit harried, but not the kind of tired someone should be after using so much magic for an extended period of time.

The ravine ends almost abruptly where the minefield begins, bringing them to an open and nearly endless stretch of devastated land. Erika's hands tighten on her backpack straps, and she decides to keep her eyes on the ground underneath her instead of looking at the wasteland.

With the obstacle up ahead, Amari is more exacting than usual. The team must walk in a strict formation that no one can deviate from, and she's very clear about how essential it is to listen to her instructions. Considering Erika doesn't want to get caught in an arcane flare or sigil — it's unlikely that every single one will be targeting magical signatures, after all, and it only takes one mistake — she doesn't put up an argument.

Minefields is an apt description of what Amari leads them through. The sigils are largely invisible to the human eye, so the Nightblood has been using magic detection and other tricks to find them before the team bumbles over a flare. If they did cross a sigil, a burst of harmful energy would explode in some nasty manner, setting off all the others around it. It's a truly vicious trap.

"Why is this even here?" Erika can't help voicing her thoughts as they carefully edge around an active sigil that Najaah has pointed out.

"Evidence of some old skirmishes," Amari murmurs, sounding strange. Erika glances at her face for an explanation and only sees the Nightblood with a very distant expression, as if she's looking at something none of them can see. The thought gives the teen a shiver that runs through her entire body before she forcibly moves past it. "This is most likely the remnants of some forgotten battle."

The group is quiet after that, and it takes them hours to progress. Light is fading by the time they finally make it to the edge of the minefield, but no one feels like finding a place to camp out yet, so they trudge forward. Erika knows she won't sleep well if they're still within a kilometer of the minefield. It doesn't help that she knows the field is prone to *moving*.

Before night falls completely, they see a hopeful sight in the waning light.

Another landmark from the expedition. Erika feels tension she didn't know she even had leave her in one sudden breath. Precisely as she read, the Wailing Peaks are a range of jagged, high rocks that rise above the canopy. These peaks are known for their haunting, wind-induced wails that echo through the forest. The wails are the result of ancient, trapped spirits or magical entities, according to one of the governor's researchers. This same man decided it would be a good idea to go searching for rare magical herbs that grow only in this high-altitude area, and somehow survived. Suffice it to say that the winds are dangerous, and the spirits can be hostile.

Thankfully, the Wailing Peaks aren't a stop on their journey or a detour they need to take. They're simply an ominous mark on the horizon, and Erika does her best to ignore them once the relief has left her system.

This resolve becomes increasingly difficult once the high rocks start living up to their name.

"Fuck," Kol curses. "I can't deal with this."

It truly is terrible, Erika agrees silently. The wails are shrill shrieks in the distance, like nails on a chalkboard. They carry a power with them, too, causing a subtle fear to root in her chest.

"What's wrong?" Amari asks, sounding concerned. Everyone looks at her except Taliya, who winces.

"You can't hear that?"

An unreadable emotion flashes in Amari's eyes too fast to identify, and then she raises an eyebrow at Kol. The boy's words catch up to him, and he flushes red all the way down his neck, making Taliya choke on a laugh.

Expression turning thoughtful, Amari taps the hearing enhancement runes behind her ear and purses her lips. "No, I guess I can't hear what you're listening to."

The wording makes Erika frown, and she considers voicing her confusion. Something stops her, and she goes back to trying to block out the wailing.

Another hour passes before the team feels a comfortable distance from the minefield to search for a place to set up camp. Night has truly fallen at this point, and Erika is flinching at every spot of darkness or rustle in the bushes. Now that they're back in the trees' depths, she misses the more open areas. In a weird twist of irony, Erika loves uncrowded spaces.

The ill-timed realization doesn't help the pensive mood that's overtaken her, sending her train of thought into disarray. She's distracted as she helps set up camp and quickly scurries away once the chore is done. Erika huddles against the least sinister-looking tree in view of their tents and broods. Half-formed theories and worries swirl through her mind, and she doesn't know how to feel about any of them.

In moments like this, she's violently reminded of how out of place she is. Now, Erika is in an entirely different world, with terrible dangers, and with teammates she likes and fears in equal measures. Somehow, she feels more alone now than she did in Kilahn, surviving on the streets and trying desperately to understand the world around her.

What will happen to her mom if she never makes it home? What will happen to her best friend, Felicia? Will the girl blame herself for Erika's disappearance?

These what-ifs are bad to contemplate, she knows, but her mind can't *stop*.

She's lost in her head until Kol drops down against the tree next to hers, joining her brooding corner. The pinched expression on his face tells Erika she's not the only one with a lot to think about. A quick scan of the camp shows that Nuru is going over the wards around his tent a couple of yards away, Amari is set up farther away around the fire, Najaah is walking close by, and Taliya is… somewhere, surely.

"You get the feeling that Amari's keeping secrets from us?" Kol asks after minutes of clearly wanting to say something. Erika glances at him askance as Najaah walks over to them. She can tell from the furrowed brows on the Ashan's face that they can hear Kol.

"Should you say that?"

"Why not? She's done some confusing things and then never explained! It's suspicious!"

It is, but does Erika have the right to be upset about that? On the other hand, she supposes she's feeling upset regardless.

"I think you should leave it be. Everyone is entitled to their secrets, Kol," Najaah cuts in and gives him a slightly judgmental look while Erika goes over her conflicted thoughts. "Would you like someone talking behind your back like you are right now?"

The Nullifier winces, but Kol scowls indignantly. "It's a—a safety risk! How can you trust someone who won't tell you the truth? What do we really know about Amari?"

"What do I know about you?"

"Plenty! I—"

Taliya is suddenly standing over Kol. He and Erika both startle hard, and the girl nearly flings herself into the dark abyss of the forest. Najaah doesn't even blink in surprise.

"Kol, Amari is the team's strategist. It's her job to plan for every outcome, and she's been to the Red City before, that's why she knew so much," Taliya, predictably, is defending her closest friend.

He stares. "How did you get here without making any noise? The ground's covered in dry leaves and sticks!"

The thief looks very unimpressed. "You're very paranoid for someone with terrible situational awareness, sky rat."

Najaah snorts, and Erika cracks a smile despite her mood.

"No, I don't! You're all just ridiculous. And I told you not to call me that!" He pauses to process what Taliya actually said when she almost killed him by her surprise drop-in. "I don't think being a strategist covers what Amari does."

Taliya narrows her eyes. "She's helping to keep you and everyone else alive, Kol. Why does this bother you so much?"

Kol's shoulders sag, and a guilty look crosses his face before disappearing. "I— Look, some of the things she's done are incredible. The bridge and the Colossus, especially, but she hasn't explained anything and still expects us all to trust her implicitly."

Taliya and Najaah share a speaking look. Erika continues to feel conflicted. She sympathizes with Kol, while well aware she's been the secret keeper before. She still is, in all honesty.

"That's kinda what you were signing up for, buddy," Taliya says, not unkindly.

"We don't need to know everything about each other," Najaah agrees. "You simply need to get through this mission. Will this get in the way of you trusting her to do her job?"

Kol sighs, then shakes his head. "No, it just bothers me, I guess. Forget it."

"Better to be honest about it," Nuru says, speaking up for the first time and showing he's been eavesdropping the entire time by his tent.

After the shapeshifter's comment, the conversation takes a more lighthearted turn, and the underlying tension slowly dissipates into the night.

Taliya soon abandons them to go do Taliya things. It's Kol's turn to cook, and Nuru goes to watch him carefully, with flame safety equipment on hand. This means Erika is left with just Najaah, eyes skyward to the few stars that peak out from the canopy above. They're a range of sizes and colors, making her all the more curious to see more.

"How are your legs?" Najaah asks, breaking the comfortable silence that has fallen between them.

"Huh? Oh, fine, I guess. Some bad road rash, but the healing cream is helping. Numbs the pain and keeps the wounds clean," Erika answers, fiddling with the hem of her sleeves. She pushes up her glasses and turns to look properly at the other teen. Questioning the Sun Eater's concern seems callous, but she can't help it.

"Good," they say shortly. Silence returns for a moment, and then. "You know a lot about first aid for someone with no combat training as of two months ago."

It's not an insult; Erika knows this, yet she still feels heat rush to her face and ducks her head to hide it. "Uh, well, my mom's a doctor."

"Hmm."

She's sure the Ashan means nothing by it, yet she's compelled to explain for some reason, falling into a rambling monologue. "Well, she's the *best* doctor, you know. I don't just mean that as a, uh, brag, or whatever. My mom is brilliant, and she teaches other doctors while also taking in a large number of patients. She's always in motion, always helping people... She's inspiring..."

The heaviness of all she said weighs down on Erika, bringing her embarrassment to new heights.

Najaah doesn't respond immediately. "That's... That must be nice. She must be a respected member of your community."

"Ah — Well, yes and no? She's a great doctor, yeah, but she doesn't like getting too much attention, so she's mostly well-known in the medical community; she's not, like, a household name. Mom and I don't live anywhere special, she likes to be where people need the most help."

"So, she does not care for money?"

Erika laughs quietly, wondering how to answer. People are so multi-layered, her mom just as much as anyone. "She cares, but not as something to hoard. She's ambitious, for sure, and is good with money. My mom just prefers to use it to create better ways to help people than for selfish reasons. It's not easy. She has her own expensive medical expenses to cover, but she's always helping other people, too."

"You look up to her a lot," the other teen observes.

"… Yeah," Erika says, swallowing hard. The lump in her throat doesn't abate, and an ache flares in her chest. "Yeah, I really do. She raised me on her own, you know? It was just her and me for a long time."

Najaah stares at her wordlessly for a moment, red eyes glowing softly in the dim light of the distant fire. The white curls that frame their face reflect the flames like streaks of moonlight. "I'm glad you were not alone."

"Thanks," she whispers, voice not rising above a hush. Her eyes burn, and she turns up to the stars again to stop tears from falling.

Eventually, the fire starts to die down, and Najaah gets up to tend to it. They appointed themself fire-keeper at the start of their journey into the Forsaken Forest, and no one argued with it. It's especially advantageous when they shelter the whole camp under a large tarp against rain. With an Ashan present, the dangers of having an open flame under a tarp are negligible.

With nothing else to do around camp, Erika retires to her tent to curl up in her sleeping bag. The sounds of fire crackling, hushed conversations, and distant animals lull her into a deep sleep, confident in the feeling of safety her friends bring.

Naturally, their good luck only lasts a few more days before everything turns upside down.

20

AMARI

Amari feels it first as inexplicable pressure, weighing oppressively down on her shoulders. Next, as the hair on the back of her neck rises, there is a growing pain behind her eyes and a sinking sensation in her stomach. She can taste the difference in the air, which is when Najaah stills in alarm. The rest of the team falls into battle-ready positions at their reaction without knowing what the threat is.

"What is it?" Nuru asks, eyes wary.

Amari and Najaah share a look. Amari hadn't been expecting the Ashan to recognize what has just arrived on this Plane, yet she's somehow not very surprised. The only other one who seems to pick up on the change is Kol, but he looks more confused than alarmed.

"A god is here," Najaah responds in a flat tone, poker face carved from stone. A hand hovers over her sheathed weapon.

No one likes that answer.

"I thought this was no specific god's domain?" Kol asks shakily. Erika has gone very still and looks smaller than Amari is used to seeing.

"That doesn't stop one from coming here," Nuru says grimly. He doesn't look resigned in this moment, but surely isn't far away from it.

"Do they know —"

"Sh!" Taliya hisses, which snaps Amari back into the present.

Stop talking, she quickly switches to the telepathic network, ignoring the strain the sudden activation presses on her mind after using it so much recently. It isn't a guarantee of privacy from a god, but at least she will know if something tries to listen in.

Could it hear us? Erika finally speaks up.

*It's a **god,*** Kol snaps back.

We need to leave now, Najaah cuts in before he can start an argument. *Move!*

The group breaks into a run, no longer carefully keeping track of their surroundings. Leaves crunch under feet, and branches snap loudly as they crash through the forest. Amari stretches her senses out to their limits to make up for it. The presence of the god is nearly too blinding to make out anything else. She's choking on the feeling of danger that permeates the air, and power so overwhelming it could blot out the sun.

There are moments when her precognitive warnings are more costly than helpful. This is usually because it's impossible for Amari to pinpoint a specific threat when there's trouble coming from every direction. She either doesn't have the time, which is laughable, to parse through a feeling or has so many feelings she's more inclined to keel over than react before it's too late.

Gods are like giant spotlights in her eyes. Their sheer power and aura are so distracting they can be impossible to work past. Even trying to track them doesn't work because it feels like they're everywhere. Amari has no idea how anyone fought these creatures before the Divine King rose.

If it's here for the team...

Or even if they run into it, the results would be disastrous.

Fighting a god straight on would never work, she knows. Amari flashes through strategies as the team runs.

Escape might be possible, depending on who the god is. Divine beings come in countless forms and tend to have wildly different affinities. This one is just as likely to be some minor flower god as a major death god.

They run for hours, only stopping when they have to for water breaks and the like. It's visibly hard on the less athletic members of the group, and Kol eventually takes to flying himself alongside them. Tellingly, he doesn't stray far from the team. There is little discussion over the network the whole time as they pass through the forest's shifting landscape. Amari would like to write it up to everyone being focused. She knows it's most likely not.

Trees change shape and color, while the path smoothes out from the bumpy hills of before. It is a bright spot swamped by the heavy tension in the air. No monsters pop up in their way, something she would consider a miracle if she didn't have a feeling every monster is hiding away in its den right now. The forest is frozen, and the snap of leaves and branches underfoot shakes the ground with distressing force.

Eventually, their luck runs out.

Impossibly, the weight of the god's presence worsens drastically, making her stumble. Taliya snaps out her hand to clutch Amari's arm and steadies her.

Amari, what —

It's here, is all Najaah says before the light goes out.

Amari's mind immediately catches on and tries to panic over the impossibility of turning off the lights when you're outside in the middle of the day, but she moves past it quickly. As a Nightblood, darkness has never been something she has feared.

Her eyes barely need a second to adjust, so she has the pleasure of clearly seeing the god that's materialized in front of them. In the dark, she can easily sense her companions around her, frozen in terror and preparation for a terrible fight.

The god is a kaleidoscope of shifting colors — deep indigos, toxic greens, and shimmering gold blend in a fluid display reminiscent of twilight skies and distant galaxies. Its form is ever-changing, sometimes resembling a graceful figure with elongated limbs that stretch and bend as if caught in an eternal dance. At other moments, it manifests as an amorphous cloud of light and shadow.

Two blazing jade eyes peer out at her, pinning her to her spot, yet Amari doesn't hesitate to remove her staff from its sheath. There's something unknowable in this being's gaze, and while its power isn't enough to make her give up in the face of it, even minor gods are still a calamitous force on their good days.

Surrounding the god are wisps of mist that ripple and pulse with a familiar energy, making Amari's hand clench painfully around her staff. The seer realizes with some apprehension that she sees flickering images in the tendrils of mist — fragments of distant places. There's the faint impression of landscapes, cities, and realms long past or yet to come. It pierces her senses, and Amari feels her dread build.

As the god moves toward them slowly, the mists swirl around it, leaving trails of sparkling light that shimmer like stars in a night sky. She thinks she catches a glimpse of Castor in ruins, smoldering in the wake of some great destruction. Amari nearly freezes as the image causes her heart to jump into her throat.

When the god speaks, its voice echoes like the gentle rustle of leaves, blended with the distant sounds of waves crashing, trains whistling, and winds howling through mountain passes. It resonates with ancient wisdom and a terrible warning. And it goes directly into Amari's mind.

"I am Kera," human language seems foreign to it. Amari would likely have a difficult time understanding if the being wasn't also mentally broadcasting its message. **"I am the god of travel, of past**

destinations, present destinations, and future destinations."

Fuck, she thinks succinctly.

Accompanying its voice, Amari can hear the whispers of travelers from ages past—fragments of conversations, laughter, and gasps of awe, each sound layered upon one another to create an ever-present hum of movement and exploration. From the way the others do not react to this particular sound, she's fairly sure the seer is the only one listening in.

"Greetings, Your Holiness," Nuru is the first to speak up, aiming for an awe-filled tone and landing somewhere closer to tensely diplomatic.

"Thieves," Kera replies, stating this more as a fact than an accusation. It still threatens to send Amari's mind into a tailspin. *The Eindrides,* the seer thinks.

"Ah…" Nuru doesn't quite stumble over his words, but it's a near thing. "Have we offended you, Your Holiness?"

Amari is the only one who understands what's happening right now. She scrambles for a solution while another part of her is screaming, the phantom heat of flames pressing against her back. A roaring storm engulfs her, moments away from destroying her whole world.

"Thieves dreaming of change," the minor god of travel continues unheeded. **"Thieves that have made powerful enemies."**

That confirms it.

She has a terrible idea.

Hesitantly, Amari reaches out with her senses, trying to get a better idea of how powerful this minor god is. Her hands shake, and sweat drips down her neck.

Kera is enveloped in a shimmering aura that ebbs and flows like a tide. This aura embodies the essence of time that Amari is so familiar with, streaks of silver and gold flowing through it, symbolizing the past, present, and future. As she gazes deeper into the god, the seer sees more distant places flickering within its form: ancient ruins, bustling marketplaces, serene landscapes, and strange cities built underground—each a testament to the infinite possibilities of travel.

"What have we stolen?" Najaah asks, and Nuru smothers a flinch from beside the seer.

Amari pushes all of it to the side, bile in her throat, searching for the god's core—the center of their power and identity. It's not a physical thing, but it's the closest thing to a heart that a being like Kera can have.

It notices, or perhaps the god knew what she was doing all along and simply didn't care to acknowledge it until now. In her mindscape, blazing jade eyes turn to her.

Let's place a bet, Amari projects to the god, hoping against hope that stories telling of the propensity of divine beings for games are true.

A bet? Kera asks, and abruptly the world fades away. Amari stands alone with the god in a grassy field the color of blood red. Random skeletal trees dot the otherwise empty horizon, and the wind whips through her braided hair. The sky is a blend of deep blues, purples, and pinks that fade into a sunset orange. No suns or moons are up above, telling Amari she's somewhere wholly unfamiliar.

An illusion, she thinks, and questions her own theory. The god of *travel,* the seer reminds herself. Panic is quickly smothered at the loss of her companions, and she hides her relief at being the sole focus of the divine being.

The god's form is even more fluid here, making Amari feel like she's talking to a cloud as it swirls around her. *If I win, you take me and my companions directly to the entrance of the Archive, unharmed.*

Hmm, Kera's thoughts are unreadable, something that is more disconcerting than she expected it to be. ***If I win, you and all your companions shall surrender immediately to be my prisoners.***

That's better than just killing them. Amari agrees to the terms, but thoughts of different bet parameters scramble through her mind – *a race.*

A race? The god of travel repeats, seeming awfully amused, and rightly so. She has to play this very carefully.

A treasure hunt, too, of sorts. The win condition is to find something of value within two hours, and whoever has the less powerful or famous object loses.

At this point, Amari is leaning heavily on her seer abilities to determine the best course of action. She's confident the best way to go about this is to appeal to Kera's odds of winning, but also ensure it's enticing enough of an offer.

And what are the parameters of this bet? Where would it be taking place?

Amari considers how to articulate her thoughts without the risk of offense. *The only parameters for you are that you can't use your powers to travel to the treasure instantly, and we can't directly interfere with each other. We start at the same place, at the same time.*

She's leaving a lot of room for interpretation, and they both know it.

I agree to those parameters, Kera projects, glee apparent in its mental voice.

Amari ruthlessly smothers the urge to sigh in relief. *Then, the location will be Batilinsorong. We start at the Gate of the Damned.*

For the first time, true surprise seems to dominate the god's feelings. ***Batilinsorong... How interesting.***

Yeah. Amari imagines it is.

In the next moment, the world Kera had brought her to fades away, and the overpowering smell of sulfur hits her. A veritable fortress looms high above in a pitch-black sky, with no light to be seen. Of course, what once was an impenetrable stronghold is now a broken ruin of what it was so very long ago.

Tall, crumbling stone walls loom ominously, covered in moss and creeping vines that twist and coil like tendrils of memory. The air is thick with ash, and she can hear the faint echoes of whispers bouncing through her surface-level thoughts, as if the ruins themselves hold the remnants of past conversations. The Gate of the Damned is a pair of bent and twisted iron doors, hanging ajar, set in a massive archway intricately carved with worn symbols.

We meet back here in two hours, Amari states, more to comfort herself than anything. She never wanted to come back here. *Whoever has the most powerful or famous treasure wins.*

The second she's done speaking, Kera moves at an incredible speed, in cloud-like form, unheeded by physical obstacles that Amari has to climb over. To her horror, the seer almost misses the god's presence now that she's alone in the ruins of Batilinsorong again.

Taking a deep breath to center herself, Amari pushes past the Gates of the Damned and carefully makes her way across the uneven stone to the doors of the fortress. They swing open easily for her, which doesn't make her feel any better about this decision.

Inside, the broken fortress is a labyrinth of corridors and chambers made from weathered stone, each more disorienting than the last. The walls seem to close in around her, and illusions attempt to distort her perception at every other turn. Amari catches flickers of people out of the corner of her eyes more times than she can count, and it makes her tense every time. Apparitions of monsters pop out of the woodwork every few minutes, and the lack of danger she feels from them is the only reason she doesn't react like a fool.

From her last visit, she knows that these illusions tend to corral or trip intruders right into the fortress's deadly traps. She'd like to avoid making a lethal mistake. Last time, she ended up stuck in an underground tunnel full of spikes coated in poison. Not an experience she wants to repeat. Not to mention that it would be a detour she doesn't have time for.

So, Amari is careful as she navigates the treacherous halls.

The ambient sounds her mind picks up—a blend of distant murmurs and the occasional roar of battle—add to the feeling of being some kind of ghost, making every step feel like a precarious venture into the unknown.

Amari knows many treasures lie hidden within, protected by ancient enchantments and traps designed to end intruders. The whispers that flicker past her mental shields are not merely echoes of another time; they're magical remnants, reflecting the fears and desires of those who once walked these corridors. And they can be directions if used accordingly.

As she ventures deeper, Amari encounters the first major illusion. She steps through an archway into a vast chamber that appears to be filled with shimmering treasures—gold coins, sparkling gems, and artifacts of immense power. The sight is meant to be intoxicating, tempting her to abandon her mission in favor of this illusory wealth.

Amari wrenches her eyes away until they catch on her reflection. Only the being the giant mirror shows her is a very different version of Amari Kato.

Predictably, she's draped in wealth and finery, but that's not what *really* calls to her. In the mirror, Amari sees Taliya behind her, wrapped in similar clothes. Her friend grins sharply as she wears a crown of gold that matches her eyes and holds a scepter that radiates magic through the mirror.

It suits the thief, she thinks distantly before she glances at the rest of the false reflection. In the background, the Divine King's castle lies in ruins.

Amari's breath catches, and she takes a few steps forward before she stops herself.

"An illusion," she reminds herself softly. It takes more effort than she will ever admit to tear her eyes from the image of the Apolon Empire torn asunder. The seer closes her eyes and reluctantly pulls her focus inward. Mentally, she turns her gaze to the illusion with a much more clinical mindset.

The illusion's draw is strong, and maybe it would have worked entirely if she were any less experienced in the art of discerning illusions and keeping up her mental shields. Amari takes one step at a time as she walks through the chamber, heading for the door leading to the next corridor. The pull of the illusion becomes stronger the closer she gets to leaving, and she stalks forward with purpose in defiant response. Opening the exit, she glimpses hungry eyes as the enchantment fades away behind her.

More traps lie ahead, each designed to impede her progress at best or kill her at worst. Some of the traps are physical, such as hidden pits and swinging blades that require precise timing to evade. Amari often has to duck or slide past sudden arrows and axes appearing. Her experience with traps is more helpful than her seer abilities in a place like this, where danger is ever-present and not always easy to discern.

When she reaches a fork in her path, Amari pauses to catch her breath. The fortress wouldn't be so bad if she hadn't spent so long running through the forest with a heavy pack. She's glad to have dropped it when Kera appeared.

That's when something grabs her ankles and drags her through the floor.

Amari is so surprised by phasing through solid stone like it's nothing but air, that she doesn't even react for a solid second. Her assailant pulls her down another floor before she lashes out with her magic in a brutal mental strike. She carefully times it for when she's *not* liable to get stuck in stone, and feels the presence holding her legs disappear.

The seer falls a few feet to the new, solid floor, and rolls to a standing position. Her staff is out and ready a moment later. Amari has a hunch for what just happened to her, and stretches out her senses, looking for a *specific* presence.

Out of all the echoes of the past lingering in these walls, she finally catches onto the one that is very angry. And capable of doing something about it.

A bona fide poltergeist. Avalon has so few, Amari wasn't expecting to come across one here. Foolish of her. Ghosts are drawn to her, probably because she is so good at sensing them. With her staff's runes, she puts out a subtle warning system since her seer abilities are easily overwhelmed in this environment. Between Kera and Batilinsorong itself, she's hard-pressed to sort out any individual threat.

It's not like she can rely on her eyes either. There's too many illusions and images flickering out of the corner of her vision. Too many ghosts here, but only one that can truly harm her.

"How conscious are you?" Amari's curiosity wins out and she asks aloud the question circulating her thoughts. "Just a malevolent spirit? A collection of anger made real? Or someone who can make decisions?"

As it often is, her curiosity is not appreciated. The ghost rises from the floor in front of her, features of what might have once been a person lost in a haze of mist. It likely doesn't remember anymore what it looked like when alive. The twisted snarl is apparent, though.

She prepares for an attack just as it comes, the force of the poltergeist's telekinesis hitting her shield like a wrecking ball. It doesn't break her staff's spell of defense, but her feet slide back on the floor and threaten to send the seer to her knees. That's a feat within itself.

"Shit," Amari mutters, feeling reluctantly impressed. The ghost launches itself against her shield, except she drops it a moment before it would hit and dodges out of the way. As its momentum flies the poltergeist past her, she swings her staff and hits it with a blast of pure magic power.

She can already feel the drain on her energy, yet the ghost screams in pain and darts through a wall. Amari cautiously pulls herself back into a battle-ready stance and waits.

It comes from above this time, and she doesn't move away in time. Her ghost flings her through the air, and she's worried about phasing through another wall when she hits it at full speed. The pain of stone being her cushion makes her rethink her priorities.

"… Ow."

Her vision swims, but Amari senses the moment the ghost charges again and snaps her staff up to meet it. This time, she uses the runes meant for capture. They're a simple set, the enchantment written to instill intense vertigo in the recipient.

Of course, such a spell would not ordinarily work on a ghost of all things. Amari has never been ordinary. One of the few positives to being so sensitive to ghosts is that ghosts are more sensitive to her and her magic.

The poltergeist freezes and sways, form twisting in what is likely confusion more than rage. She wastes no time pushing herself to her feet and pinning the ghost under her staff. A feeling she can't describe comes over her, and Amari's mouth opens as unfamiliar words tumble out.

"*You're released from this plane,*" the phrase comes to Amari as if it's been etched into her bones, waiting to be unearthed. "*No tether holds you. No memory anchors you. No love binds you.*"

It shrieks and writhes under her staff, the sounds blasting directly into Amari's mind. They shake her shields, threatening to burst past her defenses. She stands firm, gritting her teeth, and repeats the words.

Amari repeats them over and over until the ghost begins to fade, its fury and fear losing steam. Warmth grows in her chest as the poltergeist's struggles trail off, before vanishing entirely. Her pain from hitting the wall is just… gone.

It's like she drank twenty magic-replenishing potions —
something *very* unrecommended by any doctor with any common
sense. The exhaustion that had been nipping at her heels has
disappeared, and her magic is a warm feeling in her chest.

She wishes she had the time to try to understand. But only an
hour remains of her challenge.

The journey is longer now, and she can't afford to take a break.
Energy she doesn't fathom courses through her veins, giving her the
ability to keep running as she dodges more traps.

Finally, Amari finds herself challenged when a puzzle consisting
of ancient runes inscribed on a stone pedestal confronts her. The runes
appear to be a riddle; solving it will reveal the path to the treasure
she's searching for. The seer examines the symbols with a narrow
look, only vaguely recognizing the letters. They're foreign to Avalon,
she's sure.

It takes recalling stories she learned from her mother in Musei, so
long ago, it feels like a different life. The seers taught many stories from
other worlds, as one of the few people naturally inclined to travel
between dimensions. A great deal of knowledge was lost when they
were gone. With a heavy heart, Amari deciphers the riddle, aligning
the runes in the correct order, and with a resounding click, a hidden
door swings open, revealing a narrow passageway.

The hall continues that way for a few minutes — sprinkled with
traps that Amari has to stop to inch past or disable — until she enters a
grand chamber. It's untouched by time and destruction, a frozen
memory of what once was a great fortress. The ceiling arches high
above, decorated with glowing murals that depict the history of the
civilization that once thrived here. In the center of the room lies a stone
pedestal, bathed in soft light, upon which the original *Motion of Choice*
rests.

It's a small piece of artwork set in an elaborately carved frame
measuring 6.3 cm by 8.8 cm. The faint energy of protective

enchantments is all the magic that emanates from the completely normal painting. In neat brush strokes, it depicts a festive scene—a large street full of crowds bursting with excitement, fireworks going off, and music being played. Something is being celebrated, and even the small painting captures the feeling of triumph.

It's a commemorative artwork made following Batilinsorong's independence from an ancient enemy. Whoever made this artwork must have been famous because it was one of the few pieces saved when this fortress fell. A copy was brought back to Avalon by explorers a millennium ago as proof of culture from other worlds.

This painting has no power to it, but it's arguably the most famous work in Avalon. An entire world sees copies of this picture on the regular, and Amari knows some places that use the *Motion of Choice* as a stamp or as a symbol on their currency. Countless people have drawn homages, and scholars have studied every brush stroke.

More than any mortal, a god understands the innate power of being *known* and *revered*. Kera will have to acknowledge the painting's significance.

As she steps up to take the *Motion of Choice*, Amari senses the protections around the painting's pedestal activate. She doesn't feel the tell-tale pull to *move* or lose her head, so she stays still and waits with a hand poised to whip out her staff.

Between one moment and the next, she is no longer alone. A guardian spirit materializes before her—a shimmering figure made of light and shadow, embodying the essence of Batilinsorong. Its nothing like the poltergeist that attacked her. This spirit's intentions echo through her mind, questioning her goals and testing her mental shields.

Amari elects to stand tall, not sensing outright hostility from the otherworldly spirit. In a wordless message made up of memory fragments and emotions, she explains her quest, her motivations, and her journey through the ruins, emphasizing her commitment to keeping the *Motion of Choice* safe. The guardian listens intently, its form shifting as it assesses her sincerity.

As a final test, the guardian presents the seer with a vision — a glimpse of a potential future, one where the painting is taken and burned by oppressors like the ones who hurt Batilinsorong so long ago. Amari feels the weight of the moment, understanding the feeling behind the vision is very real even if the thing itself is a simple illusion compared to true moments of foresight. After a moment of contemplation, she reaffirms her desire to use the painting not just for personal gain, but to make sure it ends up somewhere it will be protected.

The guardian's form brightens, and she is granted access to the *Motion of Choice*, solidifying her win within Batilinsorong.

Amari makes her way out of the damaged stronghold with a lightness to her step even when the danger is far from over.

21

AMARI

Unsurprisingly, Kera waits for her outside of the Gate of the Damned. The strange, sphere-like artifact lying carelessly on the ground next to them wafts off divine magic like a bonfire gives off smoke, threatening to activate spontaneously and bring destruction to its surrounding area. Amari hopes she'll get enough warning if it does.

Almost missed the deadline, little thief, Kera comments, form swirling calmly. It's clear the god is assured of its victory.

My apologies, the seer decides to stay polite. No one likes an annoying winner. Carefully, Amari pulls the *Motion of Choice* out of her strapped bag, unwrapping the cloth she used to keep it undamaged. *This is my artifact.*

Kera moves closer, inspecting the small painting with an unimpressed air. ***I sense no magic from this thing.***

Don't look for magic, Amari states, keeping her face neutral and any conflicting emotions out of her mindscape. *Look for the level of renown.*

If the god is surprised she knows what renown means to a divine being, it doesn't show it. Instead, Kera reaches a thin tendril of its misty form to touch the paint. Instantly, a large ripple runs through the god's form, and Amari tries to take it as a good omen.

I see, Kera responds, mental voice unreadable even as their visible form doesn't seem so calm. ***You knew this would be here.***

Yes, Amari doesn't bother hiding it. Anything else would be insulting. *I put in my best effort.*

There's quiet for a moment. Then, a strange sound echoes through her mind. Like the ringing of an alarm in tune with roaring waves crashing against rocks. Belatedly, Amari realizes it's the god's version of a laugh. The seer has no idea if she finds that comforting or not.

Batilinsorong fades away in a split second, and a sigh of relief escapes her before she can help. Her surroundings come into focus.

Amari is definitely back in the Forsaken Forest, she recognizes, but not where she was before. For one, none of her teammates are on the path with her. Second, the massive gateway leading to the Archive looms above her and the god. It nearly distracts her entirely from the precarious situation.

I acknowledge your victory, Kera says, something akin to amusement flowing off it. Amari dips her head before turning her attention to the glaring detail.

And my companions?

Her teammates appear behind her abruptly, immediately generating lots of confused shouting, mostly from Kol. Amari wouldn't be surprised if no time passed at all for them.

My end of the bet has been met, Kera says, and the seer doesn't let any emotions show visibly. She can practically sense the alarmed bafflement exuding from the group. ***Now, all of you will be going to the Colonel.***

Colonel? Not the Divine King himself? Who else has the authority to command a god? Or is the King merely delegating?

That's not part of the deal, she says evenly.

I fulfilled your request. The god's form ripples in amusement. *I said nothing of letting you go.*

No, it hadn't.

Except, Amari knew this would happen. There's no way the Divine King would accept the excuse of a lost bet as the reason for the god's failure. The gamble was only ever supposed to get them here—to the Archive's grand gateway.

She's so close to the finish line that she can taste it. Now, all she needs to do is stop a god from taking it away.

Amari reaches back out to Kera with her magic, not using her staff as a channel. In this instance, doing so would hinder more than help, like trying to fill a lake with a faucet.

When it comes to Conjurers, they touch and manipulate magic in its most raw form instead of using an artifice—devices that have their own magic. And power always comes at a price. It's manageable within Avalon's natural restrictions, and most Conjurers use objects to channel magic through, like her staff. This doesn't stop people from trying to stretch their abilities further, often with horrible consequences.

For Amari, this means going beyond her limits can easily be a death sentence. It is like running to the point of death. Everyone has physical limitations, and keeping within them is important when using magic. Conjurers simply have steeper consequences than others.

Naturally, she is going to have to do exactly the opposite of staying within her limits anyway, despite the risks.

Amari brushes her presence over the god's overwhelming one and tries to assert her influence by trying to wrestle the other's ability to manipulate space-time away from it. It's like trying to grapple with a hurricane.

Kera is so taken aback by her sudden audacity that the god doesn't immediately smite them or transport them somewhere dastardly. With her attention divided, the seer taps into the team's telepathic network briefly. She can feel them moving in the physical world, and they need to stop.

Stay back! Amari yells as she struggles with Kera. She pushes her deep sense of urgency to Taliya, who, no doubt somehow knowing what she is about to do, tries to talk her out of it unsuccessfully. *I can block its power temporarily! You all need to run to the Archive as soon as I do!*

What—

How—

Don't be an idiot! Taliya sounds furious.

Ignoring all of them and the consequences, Amari brings all her focus toward stalling the god. A devastating pain starts up in the back of her mind, feeling like a scalpel digging into her brain, and only years of powering through headaches let her keep her fine control. She channels her seer abilities through it, calling up every bit of magic she can. Delving deeper into her wells of energy than ever before, Amari crosses lines she always feared toeing. Somehow, there's more magic for her to grasp than she previously realized.

Technically, seers have little to no control over Time itself. They can merely navigate it (somewhat successfully) or warp other's perceptions. Her ability to tap into it is something she has never fully understood. All she knows is that she can grapple with Time to do what she wants on occasion. And now, Amari is in a realm that already doesn't follow any strict rules of Time, and this god has time magic swirling all around it. She reaches out to it, feeling like she is trying to catch a storm in a bottle.

The world splintered around her, her focus scattered across timelines. She saw fragments of memories and visions and what-might-have-beens. Castor lay in ruins around her. Musei is a prospering land. The Apolon Empire seized control of the seas—and with them, all of Avalon. It could have only been a moment, or perhaps an eternity, before Amari returned to herself.

From an outside point of view, the god and her were locked in a frozen standoff. Time was settling, and the visions lost some of their realness. Amari dimly heard Taliya shouting at everyone to run. She was focusing everything on keeping a steady block to the god's power as it tried to reach out to capture them. Or maybe just kill them, at this point. It was costing her more in every breath. A nausea that signaled the beginnings of magical exhaustion was building, and her hands were trembling. Despite this, Amari pushed her abilities further. Time warped all around her.

Plants close by withered, died, and were reborn in moments. Weather changes by the second in their contained bubble, going from frozen ice to flowering fields.

Just as Amari nears the end of her rope (how long had it been? Seconds? Minutes? Hours? ~~Years?~~), something clicks in her mind, and her control over Time turns from grasping at the wind to more like knitting a pattern into the shape she desires.

Power rushes through her veins, banishing the rising exhaustion, and threatening to throw off her control entirely. Fright Amari has never felt before blossoms in her as she tries to adjust to the sudden change, unsure of what's going on. It's like the poltergeist again, but magnitudes worse.

Then, Taliya practically pops up next to her and throws something at the god. She immediately grabs Amari's arm and drags her down the path, bringing the seer out of her intense trance. Though her brain takes a moment to switch gears, Amari quickly catches on and starts running as fast as she can. Behind them, a blast of pure magic knocks down Kera and a few trees.

The thief overloaded a magical token with so much magic it turned into a bomb, she realizes, taken aback by her friend's gall. Taliya must have made Kol fill it with his power, since he's the only one with so much built-up energy.

However, no magic the team can muster could truly harm the thing. Amari knows this. Despite this, at that one moment when she had the god's power stifled, the blast stuns it—enough time for them to get to the entrance to the Archive.

It's a mad dash, and as the grand doors come upon them, they can all hear a great roar behind them. Kera is coming for them. The group runs to the doors, pushing them open. It takes a heart-stopping second for the great gates to shift, moving under the collective strength of all six team members.

Amari makes sure she's the last through the threshold, turning to see one last glimpse of a raging god before the heavy doors slam close behind them with a soul-rattling thud. There's a moment of frozen terror where they wait for the god to burst through the Archive's gate, but no such thing happens. Even divine beings can't simply barge into this realm. Outright malevolence is forbidden. Amari and her team are allowed in because they have no intent to harm the Archive itself.

A vast, ringing silence echoes, numbing her down to the marrow of her bones. Her runes sputter out, no amount of power activating them again. She clasps her hands to suppress their shaking and resists the desire to slide to the ground so she can unravel mentally over what just happened. Erika does not restrain herself from the same urge, and Kol plops on the elaborately tiled floor not long after her.

Movement from Taliya out of the corner of her eye alerts her to her friend approaching, and Amari watches uncomprehendingly as the thief's mouth moves, but the words are heavily muffled.

She blames the shock for her belated realization.

Immediately, she reaches out to the telepathic network, only to be met with an impenetrable fog blocking the connections. They're still there; she constantly feels the links as the network's anchor, but something is making communication impossible. The Archive is more protective of what it holds here than she thought.

"My hearing runes don't work here," Amari says, or tries to. She thinks she manages it based on the way the others react to her, but she can't hear it herself, so who knows? "And the network is down."

"Shit," Taliya signs, with great physical emphasis. "And we had been so lucky until now."

The sarcasm is as sharp as a blade.

"Yeah," Najaah agrees with a heavily visible sigh the seer feels on a spiritual level, then drags their hand down their face.

Amari pulls herself together first. Because she has to. The new obstacle the Archive brings will just have to be managed. She's been deaf most of her life, she can handle this without freaking out. They prepared for this.

The seer turns away from the doors to really take in the Archive. Her teammates wait another moment to gather themself before looking as well.

It defies imagination.

The Archive is incredibly difficult to describe in that it is full of every possible thing one can imagine—and what was never thought of at all. Every forgotten idea, every piece of lost knowledge, every erased history has a place in the Archive.

Amari could spend her entire life wandering the endless halls, learning all the universe's secrets. Her fingers itch to trail over book covers and scrolls, to lose herself in the search for answers. Unfortunately, she has a limited list of what to take from the Archive, and it's all in the Eindride's collection.

Knowing that there must be artifacts and knowledge of her people here in this place, and still leaving it behind, makes her heart *ache* with a pain greater than any magical consequences. But she can't afford to lose sight of why she's here.

None of them can.

"How do we...?" Erika asks with hesitant gestures, the question trailing off in the face of the infinite Archive. The door sits isolated from any wall in the middle of a large space before a grand circular staircase leading up and up beyond where any of their eyes can see, with countless floors and endless shelves in every direction.

Finding anything seems very intimidating suddenly.

Thankfully, Nuru knows the location of the Eindride Collection. As long as they can follow the Archive's organizational system... To be honest, Amari has little to no faith in a realm's natural inclination toward order.

Nuru explains the same thing to everyone else, and the group warily starts making their way up the large staircase. On the first level, they see it is marked simply as the 1st Floor.

"Which floor is it?" Kol signs slowly and looks like he's dreading the answer. Nuru, regrettably, doesn't assuage his fears.

"Floor 212."

Kol groans theatrically, and no one else even scolds him for it.

It's not a particularly fun climb.

For one, the Archive has traps. Amari, Taliya, and Najaah are hotly debating in fast sign language whether this is a natural phenomenon of the Archive or a result of someone specific (like the Eindrides). Nuru clearly thinks they're wasting their energy as he ignores them to trudge upward while the two remaining teens watch with wide eyes.

Before they even reach the 12th floor, the staircase under them flattens into a slide.

Amari whips her staff out and stops her fall by catching onto the railing, while Taliya has managed to stay in place, clinging to the slanted, smooth floor like a bug. Najaah snaps her left arm out to latch onto the railing, grabbing Erika with her right arm. Naturally, Kol uses his power to stop himself from falling, though not without nearly tumbling off the stairs entirely.

For Nuru, she can see him very nearly shift instinctively into his bird form. Instead, he course corrects and pushes off the smoothed stairs with his feet, jumping to the railing next to Amari. She can see his mouth moving and recognizes the shape of a curse in Florish before he signs with one hand about the unpleasantness of falling in his first form.

Amari sighs after a moment of frozen surprise, and they all take a second to catch their bearings.

With one arm wrapped around the railing, she uses her free hand to sign instructions. "Start climbing."

They all begin to climb using the railing for support, except Taliya — whose balance is unparalleled — and Kol — who floats. This causes Nuru to want to shift as well, but his vulnerable second shape in this world would only make him a target, so he stays as is.

Thankfully, the stairs revert to normal after a handful of meters, and they start carefully walking up again.

More traps await them, no more than fifteen floors apart, and each more treacherous than the last. The floor opens up beneath them next, and Amari has to use her staff again to leap across the sudden hole. A few minutes later, spikes erupt from the stairs, shaking the stairs enough for her to fall to her knees. Nuru pushes her out of the way of a particularly nasty spike. On the 100th floor, blades come out of the wall and nearly slice off their heads if not for the sudden warning her powers gave her. And, memorably, the stairs flatten again, and a boulder forms from ambient magic to roll down and flatten them. Kol has to grab both Erika and Nuru as he flies above the boulder, obviously struggling with the heavy load.

Approaching the 175th floor, Amari and Najaah spot the unpleasantly familiar sign of an arcane flare on a few steps. They collectively decide not to bother trying to wardbreak them, given how Amari's hearing runes are faring in the Archive. Clearly, this place plays by different rules. Instead, the team edges around a series of intricate, glowing sigils etched into the ground or walls, lest they suddenly flare to life when an intruder steps too close. The runes emit a pulsating, hypnotic light that attempts to disorient and mesmerize anyone who gazes at them, and Nuru has to lightly smack Kol's head more than once to draw the boy's eyes away.

An illusion covering multiple steps conceals a deep chasm filled with dangerous spikes that must be some kind of pocket dimension. Amari has a foot hovering over it when her senses blare, and she jerks back, arm going out to stop the nearest teammate, which happens to be Erika. The teen gives her a strange look as the seer investigates and discovers what she almost stepped into. They decide to have Kol quickly ferry them over the illusion one at a time.

This is all to say that by the time their group reaches Floor 212, they are—to every single teammate—exhausted.

The Archive is kind enough to provide benches outside the stairwell exit, and even Najaah is ready to take a break, though she is vigilant as she watches for more traps.

After twenty minutes of everyone catching their breath and no one making a move, Amari sighs. She straightens her posture on the bench, which seems to signal something to the rest of the group. Taliya stretches, standing on her hands, while Najaah goes over the team's weapons inventory. Erika immediately pulls out the group's rations and hands them out. Nuru tries to tell Kol to take his time with the food, but the boy scarfs it down like he hasn't eaten in days when it's only been a few hours.

"Do you have directions for where the royal family's collection is on this floor?" Amari signs without much enthusiasm at Nuru, who rubs his hand over his beard.

"A straight shot down the corridor, but it's a ways down, I believe," he nods to the large passageway leading away from the stairwell. There are rows of shelves on either side of them, but a seemingly endless corridor sits in front of them, dim lights sending shadows every which way.

"We'll just need to be careful," she ensures everyone looks at her when she says it, heavily emphasizing the *careful*. "Like we practiced."

This means that Amari and Najaah are at the front of the group, as they are the ones most likely to notice traps first. Erika and Nuru are in the middle, and Taliya and Kol guard their backs. The corridor looks innocent at first glance, but Amari can feel the hairs on the back of her neck standing on end. No specific danger jumps out yet, except that could mean there are too many to differentiate. Hopefully, Najaah's senses will be more helpful than hers are.

The first trap is pretty apparent as they walk forward. It's another collection of arcane flares, all innocuous-looking, where they're carved into the floor. Going around the sigils would mean going into the stacks bracketing the corridor, and Amari gets a strong feeling that's a bad idea. So, instead, she asks Kol to ferry them across the short distance again.

"These runes are a nasty piece of work," Taliya's hands move dismissively to her as they wait for the boy to bring Nuru across. "They're summoners, I think. When disturbed, they call on a magical guardian or creature to confront intruders. And the outer edges would also create an illusory barrier to stop escape."

Erika, standing on the side of the thief, grimaces. The team speedily moves on down the passageway away from the sigils, not looking back.

Along the way, Amari catches sight of more passive defenses — things that only activate when an intruder attacks first. Many bookshelves are warded with these protections. Often, a shield or barrier is set up to reflect or deflect any magical energy or projectiles directed at it. When an intruder attempts to use magic or a ranged weapon, the shield redirects the attack back at them or to a different part of the room. The shield may also absorb and store magical energy, releasing it in a powerful counter-attack when it reaches a certain threshold. She and Taliya have similar wards for their apartment or safehouses.

The next active trap is disconcerting even to Amari. At first glance, it looks like more arcane flares, but the purpose of these runes is much more sinister, in her opinion.

"I don't get it. What do they do then?" Kol asks as he stands before the trap, fingers visibly nervous in their movements. He's effortlessly channeling energy to overload the runes with magic instead of simply flying them over. Amari is working with him to make sure he doesn't accidentally cause the runes to backfire instead of going inert.

"When activated, these sigils cast a powerful enchantment that causes intruders to lose their memory of the area or the events leading up to their arrival," Amari explains quickly with fast movements, even as she needs to finger-spell some words. Almost all of her focus is on the runes in front of her. She wants them *gone.* It's a cruel trap meant to make the affected individual become disoriented, unable to recall the location of important objects or pathways, or even forget their own purpose for being there, effectively neutralizing their threat. This convinces her it was set by the Eindrides, not the Archive's natural defenses.

They must be getting close.

Amari has been keeping her senses open for the right moment and stops walking when it comes. Everyone looks at her in confusion, some more wary of potential traps than others.

"I need to do something. It will only take a minute," the seer says as she pulls out the *Motion of Choice.* To her great relief, the painting has remained unharmed despite all the excitement. Now, she can find a place in the Archive for it. Cautiously, she ventures down a line of shelves she feels calling to her.

Taliya and Kol follow close behind, clearly questioning her

common sense.

An empty display case waits for Amari, the Archive somehow preparing for its new artifact properly. She gently places the Motion of Choice in it and watches in admiration as the painting fits in perfectly, as the display clicks shut on its own.

Joining the group in the main corridor, Amari can tell they all have questions. With a sigh, she starts to give a polished explanation of the bet she made with Kera earlier, leaving out certain incriminating parts. It makes her strangely grateful for the beginner status of most of her group. She doesn't have to moderate how her voice sounds; instead, she simply signs the important parts.

The teenagers are full of pointed inquiries, and the seer weaves through them with the deftness of an experienced liar. In a terrible show of irony, she's relieved when the ominous doors decorated by the Empire's symbol appear before them.

They take another break once the doors to the Eindride collection finally come into view, knowing that more traps await inside. The younger members of the team show clear evidence of impatience, but Amari holds firm that they pace themselves. She's already tired from the day's events despite the strange surge in power she felt with Kera.

After over an hour of a watchful resting period, Taliya really starts inspecting the wards on the door.

"What the fuck," the thief's signs are emphatic. "I can't even read this."

"What?" Erika's confusion is written all over her face.

"These runes aren't from Avalon. They wouldn't even work in our world." Taliya's glare looks like it should be able to destroy the doors all on its own. She turns to the seer and signs grandly, "Amari, get the bomb."

"What?" Erika's confusion is quickly shifting to alarm, and Kol's eyes go very wide. Najaah skips past shock and goes straight to backing up far away, with Nuru not far behind her.

"Controlled explosives," Amari corrects, signing slowly so everyone catches the words. She wouldn't just carry around unstable bombs on her person.

"Oh, great, as long as the explosions are *controlled,"* Kol manages to express his sarcasm perfectly despite the shaky signs. His tail has started whipping around erratically.

Ignoring the teenagers, Amari goes to her bag and pulls out the *carefully stored* explosive devices. She and Taliya space them out around the edge of the doorway. By the time she turns back, all four teammates are standing very far down the hall. Kol is hiding behind Najaah.

Amari rolls her eyes, pulls out her staff and powers up the shield spell. As soon as Taliya joins her, she activates the explosives.

They go off as a chain reaction, shaking the floor beneath her feet. She locks her knees to stay steady, and Taliya is a warm weight against her back. The wards on the door go off, but without a clear target, they lash out randomly. Her shield takes the brunt of a fire attack and a nasty curse she's thankful to avoid.

It dies down after a minute, and the doors fall inward, crashing with a ground-shaking feeling. They wait for the dust to settle, then Taliya throws out a random pencil through the doorway. One last ward goes off and disintegrates the object.

Nothing moves for a moment. Then Amari releases her shield and turns to the others. Najaah has already begun walking forward, with the others trailing reluctantly behind.

"Is it... safe, now?" Erika asks anxiously, hands stuttering. Paces further back, Kol is eyeing the aftermath with a dubious expression.

"All good," Taliya grins and fearlessly steps into the Eindride Collection.

Beyond the doors, the rows of shelves reaching the tall ceiling loom ominously. There is little light she can see further into the Archive; the aisles are illuminated with soft floating lights that get fainter and fainter into the distance. As a Nightblood, the prospect of such darkness means nothing, but she can see the apprehension on her companions' faces.

"How big can the Eindride's collection be?" Kol asks, blatantly tempting fate. Taliya helpfully tells him to shut up. Heaving a great sigh, Amari starts investigating the archiving system.

"They're arranged by type of object—a relic, a document, a weapon—and then by level of danger."

Najaah scowls, her hand movements sharp. "The level of danger is decided by the Eindrides?"

"Yes, what fun," Amari mutters and pinches the bridge of her nose. "I always love a subjective filing system."

Taliya laughs as she approaches her friend, and the seer feels the thief's shoulders shake as Taliya bumps her fondly. Her gestures are characteristically theatrical. "That's one of the nerdiest things I've ever heard you say."

Amari sends her a rude gesture, and Najaah turns to Nuru. "We're splitting up, right?"

Frowning, Erika cuts in nervously with unsure hand movements. "Is that the best idea?"

"There are four objectives and an endless library," Taliya signs before she waves her hand at the infinite space. "It's kind of necessary."

"Alright..."

"I'll go alone," Najaah states, motions sharp and expression firm. It's not a suggestion, and no one argues.

"Me too," Kol says, which gets more side-eyes but no complaints. Amari and Taliya share a look, the seer trying to convey with only her eyes that the thief cannot leave her alone with Erika. Her friend stares back with mischief in her expression, and her heart sinks.

Abruptly, Taliya turns to grin at the team, hands already up and moving. "I'll go with Nuru. You're the one paying and all."

He rolls his eyes at the thief, then glances between Amari and Erika. He's undoubtedly noticing the slightly awkward energy radiating off their resident Nightblood and Nullifier.

Nuru agrees with a shrug and casually signs. "Alright, so I guess that means Amari will accompany Erika?"

"Yep!" Taliya answers before Amari can get a word in, fingers gesturing forcefully along with her words. Erika shifts a little uncomfortably, but in the end, just makes sure she has her hands free in case of traps.

"Meet back here?" Amari suggests after accepting her fate. Everyone agrees, even as Najaah adds that anyone who takes more than two hours to return will be searched for.

Amari, Erika, and Kol head into the dark of the documents section, the teens doing a poor job of masking their unease. One would think, how large could the collection of documents the Eindrides might want to hide away be? They would be fools.

In Amari's experience, the Empire is a mountain of secrets and bad cover-ups, and this section's vastness confirms this. Of course, complaining doesn't help them in their search.

Kol scowls at the differing classes, his hand scratching his neck before he signs. "How the fuck am I supposed to know the danger level?"

"Well," Amari starts reasonably. "What kind of information are you looking for? Consider, for example, how dangerous it might be if the general public got its hands on it."

This somehow makes him look more confused. Finally, he throws up his hands in a 'what the hell' gesture and storms down a random aisle in the number 7 division, which is a relatively low level of danger.

"Right, so I guess it's your turn," Amari turns to the Nullifier, who has been worriedly inexpressive this entire time. She can't tell what's going through Erika's head. The teen studies the sections thoughtfully before taking off without a word. Amari doesn't comment on it and simply matches the girl's pace. If the Nullifier wants to talk to her about something, she can.

More importantly, Amari doesn't know what specifically Erika is looking for, but the danger level they start at is number 1, which isn't a very auspicious start.

The girl suddenly stops walking. Her back is to the seer, tense in a way she hasn't seen before.

Amari maneuvers into her line of sight and signs, feeling strangely tentative. "Is something wrong?"

Erika takes a deep breath, then turns to face her fully with a stubborn resolve in her eyes. Her hands clench into fists at her sides, but the seer doesn't read any impending violence in her form. Erika's hands lift up into hurried movements, perfectly conveying the tone.

"I told you my secret when we met, and now, I'm bringing you with me to find something… incredibly important to my home. But you're keeping secrets too, and I don't know them, and that's your business! But it's unbalanced, and—"

"Erika," Amari voices to interrupt the girl's rambling before the teen spirals further. There's a moment of stillness while her mind races. She could offer to stay behind while Erika goes ahead and finds what she needs. She could insist there's no secret. She could do a lot of things.

Except Amari doesn't want to. "I'm a seer."

Erika stares at her wide-eyed, then her face twists in puzzlement.

"I'm," Amari pauses, hands spasming, before she clarifies. She has to finger-spell the word *seer*, knowing very few remember the sign for it. "I'm the last seer."

She gets no reply, and the tension doesn't abate between them before Erika finally breaks it with a subdued expression as she signs. "How can you be the last?"

The Nullifier could mean that in a bunch of different ways, and Amari doubts she has ill intent, except her mind can't help jumping to one thing she's heard so many say.

How can the seers be gone? What, did they not see it coming? How could they not have Seen this?

The truth is, they did.

Getting omens of incredible doom was like getting an unwelcome yet common sickness for seers. Mostly, they're vague, distant, and completely useless. The first confirmed foretelling of their end came five years before it happened.

From what Amari remembers, there was a lot of debate (read: petty academic arguments) over what the visions *really* meant. Naturally, security and general paranoia were increased in the wake of this news. But those first visions were the opening of the floodgates. Soon, everyone and their mother were predicting doom. Not just in Amari's home, Musei, but in every seer community in Avalon.

People fled, people hid, people prayed. A god's wrath is not meant to be escapable. Amari doesn't know why she is the only one left, just that she is. Amari has looked.

"There was a genocide, years ago," she says, hands shaking subtly. The word *genocide* has to be finger-spelled as well, and that makes the tremors worse, but she forges on. "It was a god. One called down by the Divine King. He decreed that every seer must die, and no one could stand in his way."

No one really knows why. There's the public story the Empire published—that the seers were plotting grave treason—there are conspiracy theories and rumors, but no truth.

If she looked, would she find the truth here? Or would she go mad looking in these endless halls for an answer that doesn't change anything?

"Oh," Erika's lips form, eyes wide and shining suspiciously. "I'm so sorry. I—I shouldn't have pushed."

"It's alright," Amari knows there had been no malicious intentions. She understands better than most what Erika must be feeling, being alone and so far away from everything she knew. "I'm glad we can be more balanced, like you said. I didn't think my secret would have any relevance to this job, but I should have prepared for it."

"No! You've done great! I mean—I don't know what I'm saying," Erika trails off, hands dropping and face flushing as she looks down at her feet. She takes a deep breath before looking back up to meet Amari's eyes. "It's the Sonia's Divine Claim. Proof that Nullifiers as a race have a right to Avalon, just like everyone else. It was found recently by the Empire."

Amari's eyes widen before she can school her face, and her next sign is more emphatic than she meant to make it. "What?"

The girl winces, gesturing in a shaky, sharp motion. "Yeah, it's a —a long story."

It must be. The implications, both in the short term and long term... If they didn't steal it, what is the Empire's plan? Hide it away where it can never be found, or use it for some nefarious purpose? And the Sonia, what will they do with their Divine Claim? As Amari understands, Erika's people are in hiding. Will this change the status quo?

"Probably best not to say it all here," Amari gestures to the Eindride collection around her. Erika nods sheepishly, and a wry smile lights her face. The seer feels herself soften fractionally. "But thank you for sharing. I understand the importance of this."

Finally, Erika grins at her, blue eyes bright, and turns all her focus on finding the Divine Claim instead of stewing in her emotions. The tension that had settled between the two of them since they entered the Forsaken Forest drains away until they're both more relaxed in each other's presence.

An invisible weight leaves Amari's shoulders, and her senses feel all the sharper for it. Now, she feels it clearly every time they approach a trap, and because the secret's out, she can be as transparent about her instincts with Erika as she is with Taliya. The teen doesn't hesitate to listen, and there are no questioning glances anymore or contemplative frowns.

They have a near miss with some hidden enchantments that cause the walls and partitions within the corridor they are walking down to move unpredictably when triggered. These moving walls attempted to close in on her and Erika, trying to separate them from each other and crush them in a confined space. The shifting nature of the trap can disorient and create a maze-like environment that's difficult to navigate.

Luckily, Amari can guide them through the shifting mini-labyrinth quickly, tugging Erika along so they don't get separated.

Some of the traps are more insidious, things that make her worry for the others. The cursed objects are chief among her concerns. In this section, they pass by scrolls with mysterious auras and books written in lost languages that all call out to those who pass by. Amari keeps a firm grip on Erika's arm, not trusting the girl's boundless curiosity. Any of these objects can lash out with a debilitating curse, an explosive reaction, or a summoned entity. The enchantment may cause hallucinations, weaken the victim's abilities, or even slowly drain their life force. Even if Erika has some natural protections as a Nullifier, it's better to avoid testing fate like that.

Of course, she can't stop the teen's inquiring mind entirely. At least the book that catches Erika's attention enough to stop walking doesn't send any thrills of alarm up Amari's spine.

"The Ethereal Atlas: Mapping the Unknown Realms," Amari reads over Erika's shoulder before the teen pulls the hefty tome out of a packed shelf. It appears to be something useful to the mission, and the girl grins at Amari, delighted by her find. As a seasoned thief, Amari doesn't even bother to chastise the teen for getting distracted by something that's not a mission target. It would be the height of hypocrisy; Amari was certainly doing stupider things at her age.

Not holding back a widening grin, Erika tucks the tome into her bag without hesitation. Amari muffles an amused snort. The girl pats her bag happily, fingers brushing over the runes that muffle the magical energy of the objects inside. A perfect mode for smuggling.

They walk ten more minutes in comfortable companionship until the teen breaks it, slowing to a halt.

The abrupt stop pulls Amari from her thoughts. She circles the girl to get face-to-face. "What is it?"

Erika pauses in front of another book, hand inches away from touching it. Amari tenses, just in case there is some kind of trap. She pulls away to answer the seer's question. "I think this is where they keep information on Nullifiers."

"What?" Amari pulls up close to catch a glimpse of the book's title. *A Defense of the Sonia*. Its faded green cover and yellowing pages portray the text's age. Time has little effect once something is inside the Archive, so this tome was old when it arrived. Next to it, a book titled *'The Nullifiers' Last Stand'* sits untouched. It seems far newer. "Huh."

After a minute of gazing, Erika must force herself to move on. Further down the aisle, Amari catches more titles and imagery that constrict her chest. Would she find the truth of the seer's annihilation here? Would it be worth it?

… Of course, it would. And Erika wouldn't argue—

"I found it," Erika announces softly, hand movements sharp and trembling. She stands before a rolled-out scroll hung on display, like some kind of fucked-up trophy. It has a powerful aura that gives away the nature of the document, even as the writing shines with the magic of the divine.

Amari shoves her selfish thoughts aside and turns to sign to Erika. "That scroll is too large for your messenger bag, use mine. It will fit, I promise. This can hold over a cubic meter of space and up to 200 kilograms."

"That's… a lot," Erika gives her an incredulous look. Amari grins sharply and shrugs.

"Sometimes you have to smuggle a cursed desk out of a military base."

"I don't even *want* to know," the teen rolls her eyes, putting emphasis on the sign *want*.

The wards take them a while to get around, and Amari has a close call with a particularly nasty curse that would have slowly made her lose feeling in her entire body.

Together, they carefully take down the scroll. It's a blessing in disguise that the Divine Claim is such a new addition to the Archive because the realm has been rumored to be… possessive of items that have been in it a long time. The scroll fits into the bag, and while the runes meant to hide smuggled objects don't completely muffle the divine energy wafting off the document, they make it manageable.

Unfortunately, as Erika is getting her side of the scroll down, she brushes a display next to the Divine Claim. A display they haven't done any wardbreaking on. Luckily, Erika doesn't spontaneously burst into flames. Less luckily, the display does.

"Fuck," Amari and Erika both say in unison, not needing to look at each other.

This is the moment the Archive shakes violently as, next to Amari, the teen's hands fly towards her ears to cover them. The combination makes the seer realize a massive explosion is happening in the distance.

"Fuck," she repeats.

22

TALIYA

After Amari's group splits off, Taliya and Nuru head off into the darkness. Najaah follows them for the first twenty minutes or so, also looking for a relic. Along the way, they debate the danger levels among themselves, while Nuru insists on starting with the most dangerous in Section 1. Taliya side-eyes him. The shapeshifter justifies his decision and stands firm, stating it makes the most sense to start at the most dangerous level and then make their way back.

Najaah takes the opposite route since the Oathbreaker's Talisman has no offensive or defensive capabilities, leaving them behind with a simple nod.

After a minute of silence between the pair, Taliya is the first one of the two to speak up. "So, can I know what the relic looks like, at least?"

"Well, you'll be seeing it anyway," Nuru admits with a sigh. "First of all, it's a plant."

"A plant? You crossed dimensions for *a plant?* One that counts as a relic?"

"Yes," the man huffs, except his mouth twitches into a smile with reluctant amusement. "It's the Mokeal Flower. There are fables surrounding it passed down through the generations, but the important part is that the flower is the only one of its kind. It has magic healing and spiritual properties."

The thief is quiet for a few minutes. "Cool. But if that's the case, why are we starting with the most dangerous relics?"

As if to emphasize her confusion, they pass a painting of some great battle on display that is two times bigger than a carriage and radiates dark magic. Similar objects line the aisles, like the inexplicable lamp Taliya passes that practically oozes bad vibes. Or the coin collection they walk by, which has a subtle yet insidious draw to it.

This collection holds everything from legendary jewels to cursed items to divine instruments. Very few traps are in this section of the Eindride's collection; the people who set them up are likely aware nothing they could make would stand up to the artifacts themselves.

He mulls over his response. "It is very important to my people, and all shapeshifters that live outside the sea. Centuries ago, it was lost, and the reclamation of it would be… significant. I imagine the Empire would like to prevent such a thing. And… while the primary abilities of the Mokeal Flower are benign, it has the potential to be exploited by the Empire in a way I can't allow to happen."

Silence falls for a few minutes, causing Nuru, in response, to begin to frown when Taliya takes pity and shrugs. He stares at her and stops walking, baffled for a moment too long. Taliya looks back and grins. "It's not really my business, so don't worry about it."

The poor man looks stupefied for a split second before his annoying, neutral expression returns. She moves on from the topic easily and points out any item they pass that appears even slightly plant-like, even ones that could not be more obviously not a flower. Nuru has to go into great detail about what the flower is supposed to look like before she stops.

They only pause once, when Nuru spots a relic that makes him halt in his tracks. She peers over his shoulder to see a small sphere on a pedestal, looking suspiciously innocent.

"Hey, you're not being hypnotized or something, right?"

Sighing, Nuru shakes his head. "Of course not. However, I think I know what that is."

"What?"

He reaches out carefully, searching for evidence of security, before grabbing the sphere. Taliya grimaces at the fact that she has to be the one to point out the common sense for once. "You probably shouldn't just pick stuff up here."

"This is a star map," Nuru says, ignoring her warning. The thief hums thoughtfully as she racks her brain for any recognition of that term, inspecting the sphere closer. Previously just a dark ball, it abruptly lights up with thousands of pricks of light, making her lurch back.

"What the—"

"Look!"

Blinking to help recover her vision, Taliya leans forward again more cautiously. Her eyes widen when she sees what Nuru is so excited over. "Is that... the Archive?"

The pricks of light on the sphere are connected by faint threads, and one dot is much bigger and brighter than the others. For some reason, she can sense the magic of the Archive radiating from that spot.

"Yes," the shapeshifter breathes. "And the lines represent the worlds directly connected to this one, like the Forsaken Forest."

"We're taking it with us," Taliya points out, obviously. Even if she isn't a thief, there's no way she's leaving such a useful tool behind. Nuru puts the star map in his bag without hesitation, taking the time to make sure it's placed carefully.

"A lucky find," the man smiles, scanning the area carefully for any traps.

"Surprised it's in this section," she mutters, brushing some braids back and glancing up at the sign above indicating they're still in level 1.

Nuru hums, considering the question seriously. "Maybe not so surprising since we're in the Ethereal Planes. After all, a map is how we were able to get here in the first place."

"I guess," the thief grumbles, not satisfied with the answer. She eyes the other objects in view, which mostly consist of random items like jewelry, art, and musical instruments. Some objects are subjectively beautiful — glass globes and elegant violins — while others seem out of place in these grand halls — specifically the worn banjo she eyes as they stroll by. Many radiate a cursed energy she steers clear of. Taliya even spots a broom hanging on a hook that has such foul magic pouring off it that she finds herself holding her breath as they walk past.

"If only we had more time," Nuru says with a wistful note in his voice. She looks at him with a raised eyebrow.

"What? You know it's only so long before someone notices we're here. If they haven't already."

"I know, I simply wish we weren't racing against the clock. The Eindride's collection on its own holds countless treasures, let alone the rest of the Archive."

Taliya wrinkles her nose. "Sounds like a hassle, we'd never leave trying to sort through all this."

The shapeshifter waves his hand dismissively. "I mean, how many other stolen artifacts are here? How many weapons could we take out of the Empire's hands? How much information could we take? Imagine…"

Amari would like that too, Taliya thinks. The thief almost wishes she could find something that belonged to her friend's people, as she's no doubt sure the seer longs for.

"We're not rebels."

This makes Nuru go quiet for a minute. "Aren't we? I don't think the Apolon Empire will care for the difference."

Ugh. He has a point. If Taliya's goal was to remain off the Empire's Most Wanted list, she's failed epically. "I don't really care what they think. Amari and I still only work with the Resistance on commission."

"And you want to keep it that way?"

Taliya pauses her walk and turns to Nuru, brows furrowed. "What do you mean?"

The man mulls over what to say. "I'm saying you and Amari seem rather aligned with the Underground Resistance for two freelancers."

He's... not wrong, damn him. "So?"

"It's not a criticism," Nuru assures, and Taliya rolls her eyes. Always the pacifier, this one. "I've been thinking about it myself. About responsibility."

Tilting her head, the thief frowns at him. "I have no idea what you're saying."

Sighing, the man runs a hand over his dreads. "After this mission is finished, I'm considering joining the Underground Resistance. I've only worked alongside them occasionally up until now, but I think it's time for that to change."

"...Okay."

"You could say I feel a responsibility to help," Nuru smiles wryly at her, eyes unreadable. "It's within my power to, after all."

"Within your power, huh?" Taliya repeats under her breath, gazing away. She starts walking again without a word, not wanting to stay in the moment of seriousness that had overtaken them.

The shapeshifter's assumption proves correct when they finally stumble on the true Mokeal Flower deep in Section 1.

Taliya stays back to give the shapeshifter space, noticing the amazement overtaking Nuru. She can understand his awe on some level despite having no prior knowledge of the plant. Even behind the runes suppressing the flower's magic and acting as security against thieves, she can feel its power brushing against her skin like a comforting touch. It's half a meter tall and inside a case to protect it from the elements. The funnel-shaped petals are a shiny black, but they gleam in different colors in the light, and the dark green leaves hide a few discreet thorns.

Nuru doesn't seem to notice that Taliya has given him space to have his moment; instead, he takes in the stolen treasure that the Empire had taken from his people. And now he can finally take it home. She wonders if every trouble and injury it took to get here feels worth it. The reverent way he reaches out suggests it does.

She turns away to inspect some other relics, beelining for the shiniest thing in her field of view. The pieces in this place are all meant to draw you in; whether to curse you or to help you is up for debate. Her fingers itch to study some of the runes she sees inscribed, but she holds herself back as she waits for Nuru to collect himself.

A diadem the Empire most certainly looted calls out to her via its glittering gems, and she leans in close to inspect it curiously. She feels the hairs on the back of her neck stand up before ducking as a blade passes above her, just missing her neck and slicing off one of her small braids. She vows then and there that Amari can never find out about this.

Dropping to the floor, she rolls between her attacker's legs, kicking at them as they jump back just in time. They swing around, readying their sword to act again, and give Taliya just enough time to get a good look at her opponent.

An Andan, one with strong tree attributes and smelling of battle magic. Between the proud Scribe's Patch, deadly blade, and the dark outline of the Empire's symbol carved into their armor, Taliya has a guess at what she's facing. It's an unwelcome surprise. *Now* would be a good time to be able to warn Amari telepathically.

"A member of Apolon's SPEAR," Nuru says for her. He takes the lull in the fight to grab the flower's container and safely store it in his bag. The soldier moves to stop him, but Taliya quickly pulls out and points her twin swords at them. Now, they're forced to focus on her.

"Where's the rest of your squad?" Taliya snaps, twists her weapons, and leaps at the soldier. The Andan throws up their sword to block her first strike, and the sound of enchanted steel meeting each other echoes loudly in the grand halls. "Don't you bastards travel in packs of four?"

All of SPEAR is equipped with specialized gear that enhances its combat capabilities. Each soldier carries a *Stormblade*, a sword imbued with elemental magic that can unleash bursts of energy upon striking, capable of stunning opponents or igniting flammable materials.

Luckily, Taliya's swords are designed to absorb much of the damage the Stormblade can dish out. She'll admit to taking some inspiration from the Empire's design.

Up close, Taliya can make out the details of the sword. It's a long, wide, barbed blade with runes carefully carved along the metal, held by a grip wrapped in expensive, jade green scaled leather. The blade has a broad, slightly curved cross-guard, which annoyingly ensures the blade is balanced and capable of protecting the owner's hands against any sliding weapons. She can also see that the cross-guard has an elaborate skull on each side, making her mentally calculate the cost of such an elaborate sword. She could probably sell it for a small fortune.

The Andan snarls back at her and swings their ridiculous blade around to make her back away. "I'm not answering to rebel scum like you."

Okay, so this is *definitely* a member of SPEAR. The Specialized Pursuit Elite Armed Regiment, or, as Taliya and Amari like to call them, a bunch of Imperial lap dogs.

If Taliya and her friends are being categorized as rebels instead of regular thieves, then the Empire takes this *very* seriously. Coming from a government that likes to pretend all criminals are beneath them and barely worth the effort of fighting, it's almost surprising.

Of course, what are the chances SPEAR's job *isn't* to quietly dispose of them?

Nuru seems like he's preparing to join the fight when a shadow jumps down from above onto his shoulders. He barely manages to roll with his fall and avoid being pinned in the maneuver. In a fast response, Taliya moves to help him escape the sudden attacker he's in danger of, but her own opponent charges at her.

In an up-close and personal fight—as this Andan clearly wants from her—Taliya prefers to rely on knives since her hook swords tend to just get in the way.

Ducking under a swinging blade, she replaces the long blades for a dagger she pulls out of her boot, and swipes at the Andan's legs. The armor has minimal weakness, but Taliya has always been good at aiming for the joints. She slices a line in the back of the Andan's knee and dances out of the way as the soldier rages.

The thief doesn't get another opening in the next minute of vicious clashing, and Taliya barely manages to keep the deadly Stormblade away from her. She can't win against a member of SPEAR in a straight fight like this.

In her periphery, she's aware of Nuru having a similar struggle. Neither of them is an expert fighter, even if they can usually get by fine, and it's showing against soldiers like SPEAR.

Taliya catches Nuru's eye as she pulls out something small from her bag, trying to put as much meaning as she can in one look. The thief thinks she gets the slightest of nods back before she throws her smoke bomb to the floor, keeping her mouth firmly shut as it detonates and fills the narrow passageway with a thick black smoke screen.

Without needing prior discussion, Taliya and Nuru take off in the direction they came, hoping to regroup with the team. There's every chance they're being ambushed as well, yet she would rather deal with SPEAR together than apart. At the very least, they should find Najaah.

"I'll admit," Nuru mutters as they dash around a corner. She barely hears him over the pounding of her heart and the distant sounds of the soldiers giving chase. "I wasn't expecting SPEAR."

Yeah, no shit. No one *expects* them. They're always an unpleasant surprise.

The presence of SPEAR is often enough to strike fear into the hearts of both enemies and those living under the Apolon Empire's rule. They are known to employ psychological tactics, often parading defeated foes through the streets as a demonstration of their might. Taliya remembers the one time they visited Castor ten years ago; soldiers marched in unison, their heavy boots thundering against the ground, creating a rhythmic sound that resonated through the streets like a war drum, sending a chilling message of power and dominance.

Their reputation is further amplified by the stories that circulate among the populace—tales of brutal raids, swift executions, and the unyielding grip of the Empire on any rebellion. This fear is strategically cultivated to discourage dissent and maintain control over the territories they occupy. Amari will go on an endless rant about it if you get enough drinks in her.

It's as they turn another corner that Taliya realizes she can hear sounds of fighting up ahead. She runs faster than Nuru with a burst of energy and comes upon Najaah holding off the other half of the SPEAR squad of four that came after them.

To her intense dismay, the Sun Eater isn't instantly wiping the floor with the soldiers. Instead, she seems to be facing a canny Sky Lord using gusts of wind to throw them off balance and a Nightblood with some manner of shadow manipulation. Both are armed with their own Stormblades and clearly know how to work together.

As Najaah avoids being trapped by twisting shadows, a strong gale of wind tries to push her over, and she has to work against it to block a blow. Both SPEAR members take turns approaching the Sun Eater, not letting up in attacks while getting out of range quickly when the other's khopesh lashes out.

Taliya can't help the surprise that shoots through her at the sight of Najaah's frustration. She knows that members of SPEAR undergo rigorous training, honing their skills in various forms of combat, but Najaah is the greatest fighter she's ever seen.

She reasons with herself that it must be because SPEAR is taught to work as a cohesive unit, and Najaah can only do so much as one individual. The knowledge still leaves a sour feeling in her stomach as the remainder of the squad runs up behind her and Nuru.

They'll have to deal with this now.

Just as Taliya reaches for one of her swords with one hand, she takes out her runica with another and starts scribbling body enhancement runes on her exposed arm. The rushed nature of her scribing is ill-advised but necessary in this situation. Nuru still gives her a disapproving look as they turn to meet their enemies again. As energy runs through her veins, giving her a needed power boost, Taliya grimaces against the sudden magic influx. It's like dropping into an ice bath, sending shivers through her body.

The hallway soon descends into further chaos. Taliya ends up back-to-back with Najaah one moment and is covering Nuru the next, and the four SPEAR soldiers don't seem to care about the priceless artifacts around them. In the corner of her mind, the thief can't help the annoyed feeling that arises, seeing the soldiers' carelessness.

Clearly, they weren't ordered to look after the Eindride's

collection. Taliya supposes she should be flattered that they're being treated as such a threat, if only it isn't so bothersome.

In a fight, the greatest disadvantage the thief has is also her biggest advantage—her lack of formal training. She's lucky to have a good foundation at all, but while Taliya struggles to keep the soldiers at bay, likewise, the SPEAR member has a difficult time following her movements. Between her informal way of fighting to the thief's spontaneous gymnastics, she manages to keep her head attached to her body and keep the soldier on edge.

Of course, such a stalemate doesn't last long in a real fight. Cartwheels can only get her so far. And their skirmish has distracted them all from the fact that they're in the *Archive*.

One second, Taliya is facing off against the Andan SPEAR member again, and the next second, the soldier is stepping on a discreet arcane flare. The sigil lights up the moment a boot touches it, and both of them look down in alarm.

"Flare!" Taliya yells immediately and throws herself away as the sigil lets out a giant energy burst.

The explosion rocks through the Archive, shaking shelves and display cases violently. She instinctively ducks down and covers her head as several objects fall to the floor around her. Her ears ring with the sounds of heavy thuds and shattering glass. Taliya's grateful they've left the most dangerous section behind in favor of the more harmless artifacts. At least she doesn't have to worry about cursed paintings or spheres falling on her head. That would be just what she needs today.

When she looks up, Najaah is standing over the bodies of the remaining SPEAR squad, clearly taking the flare's detonation as an opportunity. Nuru is off to the side, breathing heavily with his hands on his knees. She doesn't see any immediate injuries to address, so she doesn't hesitate to start jogging toward the spot to regroup with the rest of the team.

As she runs, Taliya looks to Najaah, who is easily keeping up while the shapeshifter trails a bit behind. "Do you think there's another squad?"

"Undoubtedly," the former soldier says, face set in stone. "They planned for us."

Not good. Where did they get information on —

"The Night Witches," Taliya hisses, teeth gritting as she balls her fists. Fucking *Miri*. And Marina probably happily spilled everything about them to the Empire.

"Yeah," Najaah agrees.

When they reach the front of the Eindride Collection, only Kol is already there. His clothes have a singed edge to them, and she wrinkles her nose as she smells the ash that sticks to him. The boy is scowling fiercely and crossing his arms, tapping his foot on the floor impatiently.

"What happened?" Nuru asks immediately, sounding concerned. "Were you ambushed?"

Kol's eyebrows furrow, and his expression shifts more into confusion. "Ambushed? By who?"

Taliya can't help the scoff that escapes her, giving the Sky Lord a pointed look. "Why do you look like you fought a pack of Sun Eaters if you weren't ambushed?"

Under the smudges of dirt and ash, she thinks she sees his pale face turn bright red. He kicks the tiles as he mumbles in reply. "I ran into some traps, that's all."

Some tension leaves her and the others at the answer, though the thief doesn't stop herself from rolling her eyes.

"Did you get what you wanted, at least?" Najaah asks. Glancing at them, Taliya realizes she forgot to ask the Sun Eater the same question. Considering the lack of alarm or despair she sees in the former soldier's face, she'll assume her search was successful.

"Yeah, but I didn't have time to look at it before having to get out of there," Kol complains as he pulls out a stack of folders from his singed jacket.

Erika's voice suddenly calls out to them as the Nullifier jogs out of the shelves toward them, followed by Amari. "What happened to your bag?"

Scanning the two new arrivals for injuries and finding none, Taliya feels more tension leave her in an abrupt rush.

Kol's face gets redder as the other teen approaches. "It got destroyed."

Sighing, Erika pulls open her smuggler's bag for him to dump his file into and gives the boy an exasperated look as he begrudgingly complies. Amari turns to Taliya, signing a question.

"We were ambushed by a squad of SPEAR," Taliya says with short, efficient motions, and watches the shock play across half the team's faces.

"Why weren't we?" Erika asks, face scrunched up. Amari waves to get her attention, then signs that the Empire likely doesn't know what she and Kol are in the Archive for. But the desires of a shapeshifter and a runaway Rowan soldier are easily deduced.

"Then there will be a trap set up ahead," Nuru confidently signs. "They know we need to go to the Portal Gallery. Should we head back through the Forsaken Forest, then?"

"No," Amari gestures firmly, shaking her head for emphasis. "We have a better chance against SPEAR than Kera."

The reminder of the god waiting outside the Archive doors sends a full-body shudder through Taliya, and the idea of SPEAR suddenly doesn't seem as bad as before. She quickly nods in agreement with the seer, though no one looks like they want to argue against that point anyway.

Erika fidgets with her sleeves and bites her lip out of anxiousness. "Then what do we do?"

"We don't need to win," Amari assures the teen. "All we need to do is escape through a portal going back to Avalon. And that's much simpler."

Outside the Eindride Collection and deep within the Archive lies the Portal Gallery, a space where reality blurs and countless gateways to other realms beckon. This vast chamber is an architectural wonder that Taliya has little to no time to marvel at as they run through, chased by a squad of SPEAR. Her eyes still catch on an arched ceiling soaring high above, decorated with celestial frescoes that depict the myriad worlds beyond. The air thrums with energy, a palpable sense of dimensions middling together as a kaleidoscope of portals flickers in and out of existence.

Getting to the Portal Gallery turned out to be the easy part; slipping past the traps SPEAR has set up is more difficult. Taliya isn't sure how many squads from the regiment are here in the Archive, but she knows it's overkill for a group of thieves. Amari's senses are one of the only reasons they're not all strung up right now.

At the forefront of the team, the seer takes another sharp turn in between the shelves, weaving them through traps like a serpent. Taliya wonders what the others must think of her when she's so blatantly using her powers like this.

Of course, they all have other things on their minds. As if on cue, an arrow embeds itself in a shelf where Taliya had just been moments ago, and she ducks instinctively, hissing at the near miss.

"They're catching up!" She calls out as they duck around another aisle of shelves. The Portal Gallery looms overhead, and around them, the artifacts on the shelves are remnants of different realms. Things she doesn't recognize fall off display cases as the squad chasing them throws projectiles.

Abruptly, Nuru stops in front of her, and Taliya skids to a halt to avoid plowing into him. She quickly ducks around the man to see that the group has frozen in the entrance to the Gallery's massive atrium, where the majority of the portals lie.

As soon as she looks, the reason for the sudden stop becomes obvious. A member of SPEAR is waiting for them in the middle of the atrium, standing at a casual parade rest with her eyes scanning the group. Taliya glances around, seeing only the single soldier and wondering what Amari must be sensing to block her so firmly.

"Greetings, thieves," the soldier says, face serious yet not severe. The SPEAR member is a tall female Sun Eater wearing the traditional uniform, a Conjurer badge, and stars on her shoulder that mark her as more than an ordinary foot soldier. "I am Colonel Annora Bashkim. You're all under arrest."

Amari—who can read lips to a degree but is likely just winging it at this point—flicks one hand out for the team. *Scatter.*

In one motion, Taliya draws her hook swords and swings herself up to a higher level, using the tops of some shelves for leverage as needed. Kol darts off on another path in the air, while Najaah and Erika split off from Amari and Nuru in opposite directions.

The squad chasing them enters the atrium a moment too late, looking at the colonel with harried expressions. For her part, Taliya doesn't see Bashkim so much as blink in response to their actions.

Taliya watches the colonel warily after finding a shadowed corner to disappear into for the time being. The woman knows she's in the perfect spot to stop them from going home and has no intention of letting them through.

She nods to her squad, and they split off into two to chase down Taliya's grounded friends. The thief's hands clench around her swords, settling in to wait for the right moment.

Surprisingly, Najaah is the first one to approach Bashkim directly, sword out and ready. Taliya was expecting Kol, but he seems to have the good sense to stay out of sight and out of reach.

The dim lights of the Archive reflect off golden hair and pale skin.

Intense red eyes stare each other down, and if Taliya didn't already know the colonel was an Ashan, the sheer heat rolling off the woman tells her more than enough. The thief can see the Colonel's Internal Flame roll under her skin, focusing on her hands as the sword she unsheathes lights up with a controlled fire.

Great. A flaming sword in a library. Just what Taliya needs to worry about.

The two Sun Eaters circle each other, reminding her startlingly of sharks in bloodied water. One moment, they're staring each other down, and the next, they're moving so fast that even Taliya is having difficulty keeping up.

Flame sparks every time their blades meet, and the enchanted metal sings in the atrium's echoing chamber. Both sword masters are aggressive fighters, with efficient, brutal movements. Taliya can see they both have the kind of economy of motion only two experienced warriors can have. The differences in styles are harder to see—Najaah relies more on their trained instincts and physicality than Bashkim, who has superb control over her magic. Fire dances around them, and the thief blinks past the waves of heat to be able to see the fight.

Of course, everyone else couldn't stay away for long. Kol is the first to intrude on the fight, smartly deciding to keep to the air as he throws projectiles at the colonel every chance he gets.

Bashkim nimbly dodges a glowing globe and slices through a bust without pause. Kol's efforts do more to help give Najaah room to breathe than harm the colonel. Taliya is considering how she can assist when Kol says *fuck it* and shoves a whole towering bookcase over at Bashkim.

The falling shelves are there one moment, and the next, they're not. It happens so fast that Taliya almost misses it in the blink of an eye. The colonel reaches out her hand and turns the tall, enchanted wooden shelves to ash in a split second.

Her heart drops to her feet, and a chill races up Taliya's spine.

She's never seen the advanced Sun Eater technique before. It's a rare ability to achieve — *Cremation*. And with barely a touch to the shelf, either.

Scrambling back as he hovers above, Kol gets as much distance as he can between himself and the walking calamity. Najaah doesn't visibly waver, yet Taliya can only imagine what the former soldier is thinking.

Just as it looks like the fighting is about to start up again, a yell erupts from the shelves, and half of the SPEAR squad comes out of the woodwork, dragging Erika. Taliya grimaces, her grip tightening on her swords.

One of the soldiers rips the Nullifier's bag off her, throwing it to the ground, making the thief thankful for all the charms woven into it that protect the items inside. Still, the situation is bad.

Najaah and Kol have regrouped and backed up, eyes watching Erika struggle against the soldiers holding her tightly.

"Let her go!" Kol snarls, teeth bared as his tail swishes in agitation.

"I think not," Bashkim says evenly. "In fact, I want all of you to come out of hiding and surrender, or my *hostage* will have to pay the price."

A tense moment of silence falls over the atrium, and Taliya fears they can hear her heart pounding in her ears. She swallows heavily before slinking out of hiding, not quite dropping into sight yet.

Her heart sinks further as Amari walks out of an aisle, staff stowed away, and arms raised in a casual surrender. Instead of walking over to the soldiers, however, she stands next to Najaah and Kol.

Nuru follows soon after, with a slight limp to his stride. Sighing, Taliya drops from her vantage point to hover next to her friends. Erika watches them all with wide eyes, mouth firmly shut, as the thief can see the blank panic on the teen's face.

"Where is the rest of the squad?" Bashkim asks, eyes narrowing in the first signal of irritation she's shown.

"Just unconscious," Nuru says, voice calm and level. His eyes implore you to trust him. Taliya glances at Amari with a raised eyebrow, discreetly signing the same question. The seer gives the barest of nods. So Nuru is telling the truth, then.

The thief turns her attention briefly to the portals themselves, not having a moment to pause and take it all in before. They're mesmerizing, each one a unique doorway to another world. Some are stable, their surfaces shimmering like liquid glass, while others flicker erratically, creating a disorienting dance of light. Each portal pulses gently, radiating an aura of inviting warmth, chilling cold, or whatever else, depending on the nature of the realm it leads to.

Taliya tries to see if any of the stable portals look like they lead to Avalon, but it feels impossible to tell when each one only gives a glimpse of the other side. Stable gateways are solid and seem reliable, framed in ornate archways of gold and silver. They glow softly, with intricate runes carved into the frame, indicating their destination. When stepped through, they will lead to well-defined places, like a bustling city, a tranquil forest, or an ancient temple, all shimmering just beyond the threshold.

Unstable gateways, in contrast, are elusive and unpredictable. Taliya watches many flicker in and out of existence in just a handful of seconds. They appear as swirling clouds of mist that shift in color and intensity, often vanishing and reappearing at random intervals. These portals are dangerous, leading to unknown destinations, realms that may not exist for long, or are in constant flux. Travelers who dare to step through must be prepared to be lost, as they could find themselves in a desert of endless sands or a realm where gravity shifts and reality bends.

Amari is the only one here who can say with certainty that she can find a portal leading home. Even if it's unstable.

Taliya looks away, not wanting to get so distracted by the gallery of dimensional portals that she neglects to pay attention to what's happening in front of her. All she seems to have missed is Colonel Bashkim launching into a speech.

" — you come quietly, no one needs to be hurt. I understand that desperation drove you here, and — "

Ugh. Taliya *hates* listening to imperial propaganda, especially the kind that tries to come off as so *sympathetic*. It's mind-numbing.

" — the Empire's mercy — "

Out of the corner of her eye, she sees Amari reach for one of her hook swords, the hand closing around it, hidden from view by Taliya's arm. The thief suppresses a smirk as her friend steals her weapon.

" — talk with the Warden — "

Taliya catches Erika's eye discreetly, her face unchanging from its neutral expression. The thief glances at her belt and looks away so quickly it shouldn't be noticed by anyone not watching for it.

The Nullifier's knife. Across from her, Taliya can see Erika using every bit of self-control she's learned not to let her revelation show and give her away. Her *knife*.

Bashkim is mid-sentence as Amari unleashes the hook sword, the metal elongating like a whip as she expertly lashes out at the soldiers holding Erika, forcing them to drop her. With all the speed she possesses, the teen pulls her knife out and throws it at the bag containing her and Kol's treasures.

Before the weapon even leaves her hand, everyone explodes into movement. Najaah, with reflexes unmatched by nearly everyone, is already leaping to attack Bashkim with her sword out. The colonel is the only person who reacts in time to block them. Both Taliya and Amari dodge out of the way of the fight while Nuru moves to disable the guards.

Erika's knife strikes the bag, and it disappears in a flash of light, safe from the threat of fire for the moment. The knife flies back toward the Nullifier, and Erika instinctively grabs it out of the suspended air as it stops just in front of her. Everyone looks in shock at the only person capable of such a thing. Kol grins sharply.

"Go!" Amari yells as she tosses Taliya her sword and pulls out her own weapon. She swings one side of her staff up toward the colonel without hesitation. Bashkim scowls and bats away the attack with a flick of her blade, clearly displeased at being interrupted and ganged up on. In tune with the seer, Najaah whips out a second, shorter blade to dual-wield with and covers Amari's back. The three clash together, and though Colonel Bashkim can likely manage to keep up with two opponents, she isn't prepared for another.

The thief rolls under a stray blade, hooks at the colonel's legs with both swords, and pulls the feet from under the soldier. Taken aback, the colonel rolls with the fall and kicks out at the thief's follow-up attack. After that, Bashkim flips onto her feet, and it's on.

Taliya, Amari, and Najaah fight like they've been working as a trio for years — the Sun Eater mounting an unstoppable offense with Taliya darting in and out while the seer covers their backs.

Distantly, she keeps track of the rest of the team fighting the other SPEAR soldiers, but the atrium is so big they manage not to trip over each other. The sounds echo violently all around, enchanted metal meeting each other alongside whatever the fuck Kol is throwing around.

Things come to a head as Kol sends multiple bookcases across the floor to wipe out the rest of the still-standing squad, and the Colonel cremates the shelves coming at her again. A scowl has marred her youthful face, red eyes blazing as she stares them down. Then she kneels on the atrium, a hand glowing from the power of *Cremation* on the floor's surface.

Instead of instantly disintegrating what she touches, this time, the colonel elects to turn the ground into bubbling *lava* at a worrying speed.

"Shit!" Taliya leaps backward while Amari slowly retreats warily from the spreading inferno. Najaah doesn't move, and the seer calls out to them.

"Let's go! We have what we came for!"

For a second, Taliya watches Najaah hesitate, staring down at Colonel Bashkim. The colonel looks back steadily. The thief couldn't say what was passed between them at that moment.

As Amari slams her staff to the floor, cracks radiate outward, making the colonel lose control of the lava as it surges up in a wave, pushing the enemy Sun Eater back. The seer grabs Najaah's arm and drags the former soldier towards a portal with incredible haste. Taliya scrambles to follow, quickly catching up with the group. Nuru, Erika, and Kol are booking it with her, all looking a bit worse for wear.

To her chagrin, Amari leads them to an unstable portal, one that looks like it's already starting to close. If she didn't know her friend so well, Taliya would question her sanity. She still might.

"What—" Kol starts to say, and Taliya pushes him forward before he can stop running.

"Go!"

Stepping through a portal is as unpleasant as she remembers. Taliya staggers into a room with a delightfully different architecture than the Archive, turning to watch the rest of the team hurry through. As soon as Amari comes through, she whirls around and watches the portal close behind them all. Erika slumps to the floor in relief.

"Well," Kol says from where he flops down onto the floor, "that was fun. Let's never do it again."

As much as Taliya wants not to move and simply bask in the fact that they made it out of the Ethereal Planes alive, she knows they're not safe yet.

The portal left them in a spacious room that clearly only served one purpose. No furniture or debris that would hamper multidimensional travel, very *specific* wards on the walls, and a pair of grand, ornate doors. This was an official site for travel between Planes. Or, attempts to travel, at least. Taliya recalls how unstable the portal was.

"Okay, everyone up! We need to get somewhere the Empire can't find us. I have no doubt they know where this portal sent us." Amari is looking perkier suddenly, fiddling with her hearing enhancement runes. Taliya sends her a questioning look, and the seer smiles. So, her runes are working again. They're back home.

Kol looks around the large room speculatively. "And… where did it send us?"

A good question.

Taliya is already at the doors, listening first, and then opening them when she hears nobody waiting outside. Of course, there could be countless other security measures, but they would just have to take that chance.

The day's — or night's by the lack of light outside — luck seems to be in their favor now because nothing is waiting outside the doors to jump them. Whoever owns this place really didn't expect anyone to use that portal. Perhaps it's a common phenomenon? If that's true, Amari is definitely right that the Empire will be on their trail.

Beyond the room, a hallway leads to an official-looking building that Taliya has no interest in investigating. The hallway outside has windows. They're leaving.

Once outside, it's immediately clear that the team is in an imperial city. Apolon flags hang from street lights, and the roads have the utilitarian layout the thief often sees in Empire-controlled places.

"We're in Lijah," Nuru announces to the group, holding a

newspaper he must have swiped when no one was looking.

"Lijah," Najaah says flatly, staring at the newspaper Nuru is holding. The front page is full of bright illustrations and moving pictures, but it is the location that captures their collective attention. "Lijah, as in a city in the middle of the Apolon Empire? That Lijah?"

"That's the one. It's in the region that used to be Nia before the Empire took over," Amari replies, tone tired. Her good mood after escaping the Archive and getting her hearing enhancement runes working again has long since left in the wake of exhaustion. "We need a safe house. Right now."

Yeah, Taliya glances around them. Sneaking around in alleyways will only work for so long. They're lucky they arrived back in Avalon in the middle of the night, the darkness covering their dramatic return to their world.

Nuru turns to Amari, eyes pinched at the corners. "Does the resistance have a hold here?"

She tries to search her memory for any mention of it, but doesn't find much. "I think I know of a resistance cell in the area, that's all."

"It's a good start. Do you know where they are?"

"No. I…" Amari goes through their options. They're going to need help. "I know how we can contact Mia. She'll know more. Come on."

Ducking into an alleyway, the seer feels is just enough out of the way, she pulls out a runica along with a piece of paper she had saved for a random occasion such as this. It only takes a moment for the runes to be drawn, and another few minutes for the runes to light up.

"What is that?" Erika asks, curiosity dripping from her voice.

"It's a way to communicate the resistance uses. Mia showed us," Taliya quietly explains. Kol gapes.

"Why is this the first time we're learning about it?"

"Because it doesn't work when we're not in Avalon, obviously,"

Taliya snarks back. Amari is too absorbed in writing out a message to Mia to keep track of the exchange. The thief sees her friend make sure to keep the words coded, while also giving them important information.

As she finishes writing, the words fade from the paper. Taliya waits in suspense with everyone for what feels like the longest five minutes of her life before new words appear.

Kol leans over the seer's shoulder and scoffs. "I can't understand any of that. Is that even a proper alphabet?"

Amari uses her shoulder to shove him away as she decodes Mia's message. "I have the address of a safe house. No active resistance members currently in Lijah, but Mia says she can set something up with enough time."

"How much time?" Erika demands. She's been tense since seeing the date in the newspaper. Despite being in the Ethereal Planes for less than two weeks, they've been gone a month.

"I don't know," Amari answers honestly. She frowns as a second message appears on the paper. "The Empire is already sending forces here. We need to get off the streets, now."

It's a harrowing experience, getting a large group to a specific location while trying to remain discreet without arousing suspicion, as the city goes on high alert for criminals. Some team members must learn how to blend in on the fly. Nuru is nice enough to whisper advice as they move through the city streets instead of simply abandoning them. Taliya itches to take to the roofs, but that's the first place the Empire will search today. Better to wait a day or two.

Eventually, the team arrives at a very innocent-looking suburb. The houses are packed together with narrow roads, so slipping into a quiet side street doesn't look so out of place. No door is visible from the main street, like Mia said, and there's a code for the side entrance only resistance members and allies have.

Inside, the safe house is set up like any other home, but Taliya is sure she'll find some interesting supplies when she goes looking.

Regrettably, as soon as they're in the safe house, the group's mood tanks after the adrenaline of the day leaves their systems. Technically, they've succeeded in their goals, except it doesn't feel that way with the Empire bearing down on them while trapped in enemy territory.

"It's too dangerous to leave right now," Nuru realizes. Sighing, Taliya slumps into an armchair, feet slung over the back and head almost touching the floor.

"I need to get this home," Erika says, clutching the sheathed knife to her body. Kol scowls.

"No one can go home if we're in a cell, or worse," Amari is scrambling for stray paper and writing utensils, very obviously going over every way out of Lijah she knows that the Empire could not be aware of. From what Taliya can think of, there are ways to get in and out, but nothing that doesn't carry its own risk. That's not even getting into the fact that the Empire will be descending on this city like a pack of dragons any moment now.

Into the Ethereal Planes, all the way to the Archive, and back, and they can't get out of a single city.

"But it's fine for you guys because your part is over," Erika snaps. "I have to go *now.*"

Amari doesn't say anything for a moment, glancing at Nuru. His jaw is clenched, and his face has a guilty edge to it.

Watching all this upside down takes the drama out of it. Taliya can tell that her friend knows more about the teen's situation than the rest of them, except that's not much of a surprise. It seems the weird tension from the forest has left them, at least.

"Hey," Kol responds before anyone else can think of what to say. "I don't want to be stuck here either, okay, but we—"

"That's not—"

"Enough!" Najaah cuts in harshly, startling the other teens. The ex-soldier had been very quiet up until this point. "Arguing solves nothing. Get a hold of yourselves. Erika, if we rush off without an actual plan, we are definitely getting caught, and this will have been for nothing."

The Nullifier stares at Najaah with an unreadable expression, hands clenched, then storms out of the unofficial meeting. A door down the hall slams shut loudly a moment later.

Taliya periodically forgets half her teammates are teenagers.

After a minute, Kol huffs and follows Erika's example.

Najaah turns and surveys the rest of them with a critical eye. The thief resists cringing, feeling strangely embarrassed.

"You three are the experts here, figure it out," the Ashan says decisively and sweeps out of the room.

The silence stretches for a few minutes.

"Well," Taliya finally speaks up, "that sucked."

Nuru and Amari both sigh.

"She's right," Nuru says. "If we were still on a countdown, we would be looking for another way regardless."

"Is that worth all our lives?"

"Taliya, I'm saying we should at least try."

"Because of one person? We don't even know what she got and why. Are you telling me you haven't at least thought about—"

"Okay," Amari cuts off Taliya before she can finish the thought. "Not appropriate, Tal. And there's no harm in *trying* to find another way right now. If there's too much risk, we'll discuss it again later."

The thief settles, still feeling prickly. "Fine, but I think we've already maxed out the amount of stupid risks we can take on this job."

"You just jinxed it," Amari says.

"Oh, shut up."

Amari lies down on the couch with a groan, throwing her arm over her eyes. After hours of going through maps of Lijah from different centuries, trading information on the criminal underbelly of the city, and throwing out increasingly bizarre ideas, she announces to everyone that she refuses to think about this for the next ten minutes, at least.

Around her, Taliya snorts from her chair that she is now sitting right side up in, and Nuru does a terrible job of not laughing as well.

"There's something we haven't thought of," Taliya insists, feeling certain yet exhausted. "Don't think the lack of sleep is helping, I'm afraid to admit."

"Perhaps a break would be good," Nuru concedes reluctantly. His whole demeanor still carries a sharp edge of guilt.

"I don't know, feels like every time we stop some new enemy is running ahead of us to block the way, you know? Someone like Miri or that colonel showing up is the last thing we need right now."

Amari sits up with such immediacy the other two startle back. She is staring at Taliya intently. "That's it."

The thief makes sure to give the seer a look that says *you've been up 72 hours locked in your conspiracy theory room, and I'm worried I need to grab a knock-out dart.* "... What is?"

"The way out—and home."

"Please expand a little."

Too caught up in her head, a thousand thoughts rushing past her, Amari scrambles for the table with countless documents, scrolls, and books strewn across it without replying. She rifles through and smiles when she finds what she's looking for. Finally, she turns back to her confused teammates.

"We're bringing the full attention of the Apolon Empire here."

Taliya and Nuru share a concerned look. The shape-shifter leans forward and says with a soft voice, "Amari, how about you explain your plan?"

23

AMARI

Nuru places a broken streetlight on the safehouse's dining table for Amari to inspect. The lights in Lijah are simple—floating spherical lamps connected through the invisible waves of magical energy in the air. They all connect back to the city's generator.

Standing next to her, Erika reaches out carefully and starts to take the lamp apart, piece by piece. The structure is bare, and most of the work is put into the runework that channels the light's power.

"So just one magic generator powers all of Lijah's lights?" Erika asks, frowning. Her voice sounds uncertain as she fiddles with a panel on the lamp. "That seems like a mistake."

"It's cheaper," Amari says. "Generators are expensive and costly to maintain. The city is lucky that they have multiple generators for different functions. I know places that can only afford to have one to power all public services. Lights, water, heat—everything."

"There has to be a better way."

"Yeah, probably," the seer admits. "But not one convenient enough to be implemented wide scale. Especially in a place that's all but an afterthought to the Empire."

"Better for us," Nuru comments, scanning the scattered pieces of the streetlight. "Do you think you understand the workings, Erika?"

The Nullifier fidgets, fingers running over the panel in her hands. Runes—the standard commercial kind that's mass-produced—are carved into it with uniform efficiency. They're easy to read and easier to disrupt.

"Yeah," Erika replies quietly, a thread of resolve in her thoughtful tone. "I can do it."

"Good, we start an hour before sunset," Amari claps her hands to signal the end of the discussion, leaving the dining room to check on the rest of the team.

Kol and Najaah are huddled in the kitchen, conversing about who knows what. Just as she's deciding whether or not it's worth it to investigate, Taliya slinks out of a hallway and catches her attention.

The thief has a hunted look about her that Amari empathizes with. Being wanted criminals isn't good for the nerves.

She interrupts her friend's walk to the kitchen and drags her into the living room to chat. Collapsing into an armchair that might as well be straight from the factory, Amari watches Taliya flip over the back of the couch to lie on it with her feet propped up by the armrest.

Her friend shoots her a look. "What's up?"

"I feel like I should be the one asking that," Amari says, scrutinizing the thief. Taliya's braids are as immaculate as always, but bags have begun to form under her eyes. They're not easy to see against her friend's dark skin unless you already know what to look for. "Did you get enough sleep?"

"Too keyed up, I guess," Taliya sighs, reluctantly divulging information since she knows from experience it's futile to hide from Amari. "You didn't sleep well either."

"I'm at my best at night," the seer argues. "And we're in a city that's landlocked."

Not just that, but in the valley of two massive mountain ranges. Of the two sides not blocked off, one leads into a wilderness few will brave, and the other is now under the control of the imperial army. The army searching for them, specifically.

"There's always water somewhere," Taliya responds, something unreadable passing over her face. Amari's eyebrows furrow, and she frowns at her friend.

"Is this about the blood magic you used in the Red City?"

"No, no, that's—it's fine."

"Convincing," Amari says dryly.

"Shut up."

Silence falls for a minute, the quiet surprisingly comfortable.

Taliya is the first to break it. "Do you really think that Colonel will show up again?"

Because she is gracious, Amari lets the obvious topic change slide. "She seemed determined, if rather polite for an imperial officer."

Scoffing, Taliya rolls her eyes theatrically. "Oh yeah, she may be an imperialist who unapologetically hunts people down and takes advantage of the public, but at least she's polite!"

"You know what I mean," Amari feels a smile ghost her face and doesn't fight it. "I know my hearing was shot at the time, but I don't think she called us criminal scum even once."

"It was a bit of a shock," Taliya mutters. "But she was preachy, which cancels any good out. I hate speeches."

Amari snorts, amusement curling through her voice. "Well, you're likely to avoid her if everything works out, so no more speeches."

Truthfully, the Specialized Pursuit Elite Armed Regiment—SPEAR—is a feared unit of soldiers serving the Empire, renowned for their ruthless efficiency and unwavering loyalty to the crown. Clad in dark, imposing armor that reflects the empire's austere aesthetics, they're a striking presence on the battlefield and in the streets of conquered territories. Their reputation is built on tales of merciless precision and the ability to instill terror in both foes and civilians alike.

From all that Amari remembers of SPEAR's time in Castor, the squadron specializes in shock tactics, employing sudden, overwhelming force to disrupt enemy lines. The seer knows the stories, and she recalls the terror in the streets the one time they visited. Things weren't as bad as they could have been, with regards to casualties, except SPEAR's presence alone was enough to spread fear and discord.

As if knowing the turn of her thoughts, Taliya abruptly grabs a pillow off the couch and throws it at her head. Amari sways after it nails her, and she scowls at her friend before launching it back.

The following commotion draws the attention of Najaah from the kitchen, who stares at them unblinkingly until they stop fooling around and get back to work.

Nuru is the first to leave, two hours before sunset. He departs out a window from the top floor of the safehouse in his second form, wings stretched out and taking him high into the sky in mere moments. Amari watches the dot in the distance fly eastward.

Lijah is not a very large city, has only two public ways in and out, with streets that are easy to navigate, and people accustomed to Empire soldiers, which altogether make the team's job incredibly difficult. Nuru by himself could easily leave in this form, but she is grateful he refuses to do that unless there are no other options remaining.

Entering the city is only publicly accessible through the eastern and western gates unless someone has the ability to fly. Because it's set in a steep valley surrounded by daunting and jagged cliffs on either side, no one is getting out on the ground. With the Empire crawling through every street and watching the skies, commandeering any kind of transport would only get them immediately shot down. Moreover, creating fake identities would take far too long, and they didn't have that kind of time.

Amari had considered the western gate as an exit briefly because it is not used much. It doesn't lead to a trade route like the eastern one, and the wilderness that stretches out west of Lijah for kilometers is infamously treacherous. In the end, Amari has decided to disregard this gate entirely. The entire team has had enough perilous forests.

In this moment, the main gate is surrounded by squads of soldiers who have taken control of all people going in or out. Nuru is the only one of them that can get close without being caught right now. The rest of them will steer clear of the eastern half of Lijah, for now.

Twenty minutes after the shapeshifter departs, Taliya slips out a different window, taking to the roofs of the city. The sky patrols are exhaustive and expensive on the imperial's resources, usually petering out after a day or two of surveillance with nothing to show for it. Now, only the occasional transport flies overhead, leaving the roofs the safest option.

That still doesn't take away the twist in the seer's chest watching her friend leave alone.

Amari stares out the window Taliya left through long after the thief disappears from sight, lost in her thoughts. Ways that today could go disastrously wrong bang around her head and disrupt her carefully constructed calm. The timing will be so important, and nearly everyone will be split up.

She can't stop feeling off-balance. Her seer abilities aren't helping either. There's too much noise to parse anything specific out.

"My turn," Erika says, voice hushed despite only the team being present. The Nullifier is dressed in unassuming clothes that hide armorclothe and her enchanted dagger. A backpack is hanging innocently from her shoulders. She looks like a student who stayed late after school. "Good luck to you guys."

"You, too," Amari responds, giving what she hopes is a comforting smile. It seems to work as the teen leaves the safehouse front door with her head held high.

Watching the girl walk the streets of an imperial city on her own leaves a bitter taste in her mouth, not quite in the same way seeing Taliya leave alone did.

Her idea had initially brought her mood up, before sleep came. The two nights they spent in Lijah, Amari's dreams were full of fire and thunder and darkness. She heard voices crying out for help, but she never finds anyone.

Foresight is often more of an obstacle than anything else. So, she ignores the dreams as best she can.

As the group that will be taking the brunt of the city's attention, Amari's team consists of Najaah and Kol—arguably their best combatants. She knows the other three are more than capable of looking after themselves, except she can't stop the slow creeping fear that something will happen. It's moments like this that make her question what the difference between her anxiety and her seer abilities is.

"It's been twenty minutes since Erika left. We have less than an hour until sunset now," Najaah says. The sound breaks the comfortable silence the trio had been waiting within, and the reality of the situation sets in. Amari has no time for doubt.

"Let's head out then," Amari scans her companions to make sure they're both suitably ready. "Kol, hide that knife in your boot better. We keep our distance from each other but head in the same direction, alright? Stop to window shop or something briefly if you need to sell the act."

Kol grumbles as he adjusts the knife Nuru forcible gave him, and Najaah makes sure the headscarf concealing her pale hair is on correctly. Amari leads the way out of the safe house, taking a side door into an alleyway as Najaah goes one way while Kol goes the other. Amari waits a few moments before trailing after the gravity manipulator.

The streets of Lijah aren't usually so busy, but the upheaval caused by the Empire's search for fugitives has people watching the police patrol with suspicion and rushing in between businesses. It's comforting for Amari to know that even this deep in the Apolon Empire, the populace is just as wary of what their government is up to. For all its corruption, Esma can't do anything in Castor without criticism from its citizens.

Since they tumbled through the Archive's Portal to Lijah, the Empire has been sweeping the city for them, conducting door-to-door searches. Their hideout has only gone undetected because the Empire doesn't know it exists, and the true entrance can't be seen from the street.

Eventually, Najaah pops up not far from Amari and Kol as the city streets become narrower and more crowded the closer to the government sector they get. They stay discreet, but the Ashan begins commenting quietly on the wisdom of building all of the important government buildings so close together. Amari knows in Rowan's capital, you're fucked if you want to get to two different buildings in an hour's time.

"Makes it easy for us," Amari says vaguely as a small smile graces her lips.

"And others like us," Najaah comments with veiled judgment as they eye the practicality of Lijah's architecture. "Very easy."

Kol does a poor job of not looking disconcerted by what he's overhearing them talk about. It makes Amari curious about what Ilved's cities look like. Perhaps they're built like targets as well.

And *their* target is the Lijah Center of Finance. While this isn't very useful to them functionally, it will be very stressful for the Empire when it goes up in flames. It will also undoubtedly bring all their enemies right to their doorstep. Which is the plan.

The group turns a street corner, the government sector looming ahead with plenty of people milling around to blend in. Normally, Amari would be concerned by Najaah's ability to be unnoticed due to the Ashan's white hair and countless weapons. But, to their credit, Najaah is very good at looking inconspicuous despite what their large stature and tall horns suggest. On the other hand, Kol is scowling at everything as the streets become more and more full of people.

"I could hear you whining from the other side of the street," Najaah says, their face not giving away any of the amusement evident in their voice. Kol glowers at them.

"I haven't said anything!"

"And yet, it's audible."

"Guys," Amari cuts in with an exasperated edge to her voice. "Can we save this for later? When we're not about to commit arson?"

Najaah gives her a look as if saying, *me? Not being completely professional? Ridiculous!* "Of course."

"Fine," Kol rolls his eyes and crosses his arms sourly.

This is when the situation stops being funny, as the environment around them starts to devolve into chaos soon after they arrive in the government sector.

The trio is immediately swept up into a crowd of distressed people who live in Lijah. Amari nearly loses Kol before Najaah grabs his arm and doesn't let go until they reach the front. Seeing what brought the crowd makes her heart drop to her feet.

"Shit," Amari says succinctly. Her head swims with the sudden overwhelming emotions warring for dominance in her mind.

Dozens of people are being shuffled roughly by soldiers and shoved into heavily fortified transports. The crowd is yelling and furious but is held back by a very severe-looking line of guards. Not SPEAR, thankfully, just normal imperial soldiers.

Amari watches a girl no older than eighteen being dragged by her shackled hands, kicking out at a passing soldier and being backhanded for her trouble. The scene brings the taste of bile to the back of her throat. Memories of imperial soldiers searching charred ruins for survivors flash before her eyes.

Kol splutters in shock, forcing Amari back into the present. "What...?"

"They're using us as an excuse to arrest anyone they deem as having 'rebel sympathies,'" Najaah explains dully. Their face could have been carved of stone for all the emotion it showed. Amari is certain she's doing a much worse job hiding her growing fury.

"Okay," the seer says, voice trembling before smoothing out. Her anger feels like a living thing humming under her skin. "Okay. Change of plan."

Najaah snaps their head to look at her. "What?"

"Change. Of. Plan."

"To what?"

Amari turns to them, a grin that perfectly highlights her sharp canines on her face. The telepathic network fires up in her mind with a flare of pain she resolutely ignores, and presumably everyone else feels it come on.

We're not setting the Center of Finance on fire.

Multiple voices chime in, professing confusion and concern. Amari continues unheeded.

We're doing a jailbreak.

After everyone stops using the telepathic network to yell at her, Amari explains her reasoning.

This is one of the most impulsive things I've ever heard, Nuru says, but in a resigned sort of way. Najaah sends a vague feeling of agreement down the connection.

You must be new, Taliya jokes, completely unrepentant.

So what do we need to do? Kol is surprisingly on board with her plan and hasn't said a word against it. Erika, very *unsurprisingly*, is also all for it.

The rest of you keep to your jobs, Amari says. *Kol, Najaah, and I can do this. Only come back us up when you're done.*

Will the timing still work? Erika asks, bringing some needed common sense to the discussion.

I'll make it work, Amari answers firmly.

Taliya speaks up first, sounding serious this time. *Okay, Amari, but how can you help these people in a way that won't be worse for them in the long run?*

It might not be, the seer admits. *Even if this plan goes perfectly, Lijah could face severe consequences. But the Empire is hurting them already, and I want to help. I'll do my best to focus all their wrath on me.*

*On **us**,* Erika corrects. A warm feeling erupts in Amari's chest, and she forces herself to concentrate on relaying the important parts of the plan. The group goes silent on the telepathic network as they all focus on their environments.

With a new resolve, Amari leads Najaah and Kol toward the city jail.

The building design is nothing fancy or even very secure, but the military and police swarming make breaking in a little difficult. It's clear Lijah isn't used to this much action going on at once and is having a difficult time keeping up with the imperial army's demands.

The basic layout means that there's one main entrance, a back door, a maintenance door, and dozens of windows that could be used to get inside. Her problem is that there aren't many options that would let Amari go unnoticed. In the end, she decides to slip through a narrow bathroom window while Kol uses his gravity manipulation abilities to cause chaos from a distance. The time for subtlety is over.

He's set up on a roof with the jail's main entrance in sight and is using his abilities to attack the military and police with debris. When

Amari left, he was using innocuous objects like stones and pieces of trash, but from the increase in yelling, he's escalated to much larger targets.

Najaah is currently watching Kol's back, before they'll move to the jail's back door to coral in the soldiers.

While they're being excellent distractions, Amari will break into the warden's office. Last she saw, the warden himself was out front trying to deal with the angry mob as the prisoners were escorted roughly inside the jail.

Inside the office, Amari plans to shut down the jail's wards that are keeping inmates caged, learn as much information as possible about the Empire's plans for Lijah, and destroy all their written records. The loss of information should cause enough of a nightmare to sort out that the new prisoners being out will be a low priority, and all but impossible to track down again.

Once Kol creates enough of a distraction, slipping through the jail's bathroom window and down a few empty halls to the warden's office is easy. Amari even slows Time down around her to give her an extra edge as she evades any guards lingering in the building.

Inside, the room is more luxurious than she would think any soldier would abide by. But, then again, the higher-ups in the military aren't all that different from the ones in any other field. Amari wonders where a warden from a smaller city like Lijah got the money for this level of comfort. The desk looks custom-made, with a chair that seems more expensive than Amari's rent. Posh artwork lines the walls and on bookshelves — any books there she would bet are only for show instead of being read — small military artifacts sit on display. She doesn't get any strong bad feelings from any of the objects as she does with cursed items or weapons still active, so she ignores them for the time being.

Finding the anchor for the jail's ward is fairly simple when one knows what they're searching for. The anchor is — to her horror — a stone bust of the Divine King. She knows it's the right thing because it radiates more energy than anything else in the office since it's connected to the jail's magic.

Of course, this terrible excuse for art isn't the main source of the jail's power. Amari knows there must be a genuine magic generator in this building, but she had bet on the warden having an override in his office. She's right, and now she can use his paranoia against him to release all the prisoners.

With a grimace, Amari approaches the bust with her runica out and gets to work unraveling the jail's wards. After the trials of navigating runes in the Planes, the straightforward rules of Avalon's magic are a breath of fresh air. Making her life simpler, she focuses on changing the wards instead of taking them apart entirely. Before her intervention, the runes were aimed at keeping all prisoners *in*. Now, the seer has flipped all that power to keep others *out*.

Prisoners are free to go, Amari lets her team know. *Najaah, break in and start escorting them out.*

On it, is all the Ashan replies.

Moving on to her other objectives, Amari finds that the office's filing system is old school, all handwritten. Standard for a military man of the warden's age, she reasons. The seer shuffles through the filing cabinet in the corner of the office quickly. When she's sure that it only holds standard jail forms and prisoner files, she uses the lighter on the warden's desk next to a gold gilded ashtray to set all the documents aflame.

Amari scans the custom-made desk next with a bit of magic, looking for any remnants of intent or clues to what might be kept there. The most likely place someone would set traps for thieves is a private desk like this. And sure enough, a drawer has a false bottom that, if opened incorrectly, would release acidic gas potent enough to make even a Nightblood back away. Nasty stuff, except Amari, could get around this bit of security in her sleep. The warden's her favorite kind of paranoid: the behind on current security measures kind.

The secret compartment holds a great deal of space and is a veritable jackpot. Documents with vague language that Amari can read between the lines on, and highly illegal trinkets sit innocently in the drawer. Bribes, smuggling, fraud, the usual. More interestingly, Amari finds communication from the Office of the Grand General.

The Grand General... Grand General Sabina Eindride is a terror but is also far too important to be communicating with a random warden. What could someone in the Divine King's Court want with Lijah's warden?

According to the evidence in her hands, the warden is meant to root out the Underground Resistance in Lijah. Except, Amari hasn't heard of a large presence of the Resistance here. Only a small cell in the general area of Nia, at best. It's possible she simply doesn't know, but it's a suspicious coincidence.

"Fuck," she mutters. This means that her team's arrival in Lijah was all the Empire needed to bring the full might of the military to the city in search of rebels. Without them, it would seem like the Empire had needed to launch such a large force against one of their own cities. They're just an excuse for all this violence.

A sharp pain of warning makes itself known and pulls Amari from her focus. Footsteps coming rapidly closer force her to hastily shove the rest of the documents into her coat just as the door slams open and the warden rushes in. A second later, he freezes, clearly startled by the state of his office and her presence there. Amari wastes no time using his desk as a springboard to launch herself at him.

Pulling out her staff mid-air, she swings her weapon down on him as he instinctively pulls his forearms up to block. The *crack* of metal hitting bone resonates through the room, and she jumps a few steps back to gain space.

He shakes out his arms with a furious wince, glaring fiercely at her. The warden is clearly a Sky Lord—which means she has the advantage indoors. He doesn't have a bulky pair of wings, but he sports some wicked talons, and a strong wind has already started swirling around the room in reaction to his anger.

Fire from the documents has spread to the rest of the desk, and the wind has only added to the flames. Amari stays mindful of the fire while sizing up the warden.

The warden glares at her like his gaze alone will force her to submit. He seems the type to take his wounded pride personally, so she likely doesn't have to worry as much about him trying to call for backup. "I'm going to throw you and all your rebel scum friends in a pit so deep you'll never see the sun again."

There, see? Amari mused. He's posturing instead of doing the smart thing and calling for help.

She can't help the small smirk that makes its way onto her face. The warden lets out an enraged noise and charges her, talons out as a gust of air tries to push her off her feet. She's able to stabilize herself using her staff to keep her balance. Amari rolls under his outstretched arm and whips her weapon at his legs.

He cries out as she hits the back of his knee and stumbles while she gets back to her feet. The warden's swirling wind has raised the flames, and smoke begins to permeate the room. Amari needs to finish this quickly or she might start choking on the smoke. Already, her throat is beginning to burn.

Coughing, the warden whirls on her and snarls. "Bitch!"

"How creative," Amari deadpans, then internally scolds herself for talking to an enemy while inside a room filling up with smoke.

An overwhelming burst of wind crashes against her, and Amari is flung against the closed office door. The pressure is intent on crushing her and is so forceful that her vision starts to go dark at the edges.

She realizes that her staff has fallen from her hands and curses. Time seems to slip through her fingers as she tries to grasp it, and a sudden increase in pressure slams her head back against the door when she tries to move. The air is knocked out of her, and ash fills her mouth as she tries to breathe.

Distantly, Amari can catch the sounds of chaos outside increasing, noting in some corner of her mind that she shouldn't be able to hear that physically. She thinks she registers Kol telepathically telling Najaah he's outright fighting a squad of soldiers outside the jail. Someone mentions SPEAR.

Her senses stretch out beyond her, and Amari can *see* Kol fighting off the Empire soldiers. She can *feel* their magic swirling and crashing against each other, struggling for dominance. She feels one, then another blink out in a way she immediately registers as *death*.

Awareness rushes back to Amari. The door's handle is digging into her side, and the wind is making her braid come undone. Her hands tingle with restrained power, and she swears the shadows have been inching towards her.

"—arrogant rebel bastards! Not so cocky now that—"

Amari realizes belatedly the warden has been monologuing for a minute or two while she got her bearings.

"—and you, missy—"

"Sorry, what were you saying? I wasn't listening." Amari cuts him off easily, carefully testing her mobility in the face of the wind's pressure. In the background, the fire has already spread to the back walls. The warden doesn't even seem to notice. "Something about rebel bastards?"

"*You*—"

Even though Time felt out of reach only moments ago, she latches onto it with a strength that surprises her, slowing the wind enough that she falls to the floor. Her legs take her weight unsteadily before she darts for her staff.

"What the—ARGH!"

Channeling her energy into the chosen runes, she slams the end of her staff into the shocked warden. From his perspective, it must have looked like she blinked in and out of existence.

Her magic floods him, and he collapses to the floor in a messy heap. She pushes the command to *sleep* into his mind just to be safe. In the wake of the warden's capture, the wind stops entirely, and the abrupt lack of pressure has Amari catching herself on the desk so she doesn't fall again.

The flames are beginning to smolder instead of spreading so quickly. Amari takes a moment to consider her options, then glances at the warden. She recalls all the crimes she saw contained in that desk. The Grand General's orders.

Her rage mirrors the fire around her, burning like a bonfire in her chest. The seer can't let this go.

Amari mentally reaches out toward the warden, trying to contain her disgust at the vileness that sits in his mind as she pulls out as much as she can. In the past, trying to wipe as many memories as possible from someone was never an easy or simple process. In some ways, being more precise takes less energy. But this time, Amari feels the warden's mind empty of memories with an ease that almost catches her off guard.

Once she's done, he slumps further into the floor. The office is strangely quiet in the aftermath, and the flames go out entirely. Numbly, she opens the office door to let out the smoke, distantly feeling the burning sensation in her throat.

Amari! Kol calls frantically to her from across the network. It's like a bucket of ice poured over her, and she runs out of the office.

What? I've finished with the warden, do you need backup?

YEAH, he practically shouts into her head. *COLONEL ANNORA AND THE NIGHT WITCHES ARE HERE!*

Well. That was quick of them. *Fuck. Najaah, stall the colonel. Kol, you just have to hold off the witches for a minute. I'm coming.*

Between the fight outside and Najaah previously freeing the

prisoners, the jail is barren as she climbs to the roof. It's the fastest way outside considering the warden's office is already on the top floor. She wants to get a better picture of what's going on and grimaces in preparation. Already, she can tell this is gonna be a mess.

Pure chaos awaits Amari outside the jail as she walks to the roof's edge.

Kol has his work cut out for him. He's a few meters off the ground, swirling red energy all around him in a constant state of defense. It looks amazing, but Amari doesn't have the time to waste gawking. The gravity manipulator is keeping off a dozen or so Empire soldiers at once, *plus* Miri. Physical attacks barely touch Kol when he has his power out like this. The closest anyone comes to hurting him is Miri, simply through sheer creative maneuvering.

Sky Lords rule open spaces. Projectiles fall into his orbit and become *his*. Weapons, or even fists, are either blocked by stray debris or countered with a gravity-empowered punch.

He's fine for now, Amari decides.

She looks for Najaah and nearly has a heart attack when she finds them. The ex-soldier is going all out against Nadia, not more than a kilometer away from Kol's battle. They look like they're trying to cut each other to pieces. Najaah's golden khopesh meets the mercenary's quad-wielding axes with such force that they're cracking the pavement beneath their boots. Neither is holding back—one moment, Nadia nearly beheads Najaah with an axe, and in the next moment, the younger almost impales the other.

It's clear to Amari that she would only be a burden to Najaah if she tried to insert herself into that fight. Simply following their movements is an ordeal, considering how fast they move. Most of the ground around them is scorched or sporting more suspicious craters.

Both her teammates have devastated the environment around them and scared the angry mob of Lijah civilians away to the edges of the square that lies in front of the jail. Distractions, indeed.

"Teenagers," Amari mutters. She hopes she wasn't this bad as a teen, but she doesn't have much confidence in that claim.

A loud voice breaks through the background noise of battles to reach Amari. "When did you become a babysitter, Kato?"

Fuck.

Amari slowly turns and internally groans when she sees Marina standing on the opposite side of the roof. The wind is ruffling the edges of her tacky trench coat and the last rays of sunset reflect off her jewelry directly into Amari's eyes. So dramatic.

"They not pay you enough to follow us into the Ethereal Planes, Besat?"

Marina scoffs, and her green eyes glow with the tell-tale evidence of magic. "You really are insane to not only go in but to come back out. Even the Divine King himself couldn't meet my price."

The Nightblood doesn't bother to hide how that statement makes her roll her eyes. She also searches the sky for a certain bird. "Guess all that arrogance is just fronting, then. Glad to have a long-held theory confirmed."

The Witch frowns at her, and Amari catches the reflection in another building's window of Bolek diving toward her from behind just in time to throw herself out of the way.

Amari curses internally and externally. It's moments like this — when so much chaos is happening around her — that her foresight is at its least useful and is more of a burden than anything. It's nearly impossible for her to differentiate between dangers in this situation.

After that near miss, she quickly rolls to her feet and sees Bolek land on Marina's outstretched arm. The familiar is completely healed from whatever damage it took from Nuru weeks ago and looks ready for some revenge.

"Careful there," Marina says in a false sympathetic voice. "Bolek nearly took your head off. You feeling okay?"

"The day I let your bird kill me is the day you suddenly quit mercenary work and enlist in the army," Amari snipes back, fully aware that Marina finds the idea of fighting without getting ludicrously paid offensive. Predictably, the Andan's nose wrinkles in disgust at the mere idea.

Bolek pushes off the Andan's arm and flies directly at Amari, talons outstretched and deadly. She uses her staff to shield herself, forming a minor bubble that emanates from the weapon. It dissipates quickly after a sharp impact, and she catches Bolek soaring away from her and off into the distance. Her fists tighten on her staff as her teeth clench.

Marina's familiar has left in the direction of the east gate, Amari quickly reports to the network. Nuru sends a small affirmative feeling to signal he got the message.

She focuses her sights on the mercenary and glares. "Where is he going, Besat?"

"Worry about yourself," Marina scoffs, flinging out her arms and muttering a word too quiet for Amari's runes to catch. She instinctively tries to throw herself off the roof before whatever trap Marina has set activates, but she's too late. Runes glow into existence around the perimeter of the building, and a translucent but visible forcefield appears.

Amari is secluded on the roof with Marina Besat.

What just happened? Kol suddenly asks, sounding alarmed in the telepathic network. *Something is happening on the roof.*

I'm trapped with Marina, for now, Amari admits freely. *Don't worry about it, everybody needs to focus on themselves.*

Good luck, Taliya chimes in, sounding suspiciously amused. Amari can't give her the hand gesture she wants to at this moment, so she sends the general feeling instead.

"I hope your adventures haven't left you too easy prey for us," Marina says smugly, staring the seer down intently. The energy of the forcefield shifts and Amari feels the magic reach into her mind. "I don't want to be bored."

"I'll try not to be disappointing," Amari replies as dryly as she can. Honestly, she doesn't have the *emotional* energy for Marina more than anything else. The world around them changes, and she realizes with a sinking heart that the Witch has trapped them both in an elaborate illusion. "Is it going to be another actual fight or an elaborate puzzle this time?"

"I'll let you figure it out."

So dramatic.

The illusion unfolds around them like a twisted landscape pulled from the minds of poets and nightmares. Shadows flit at the edges of vision, shapeless yet purposeful, as if watching, waiting, judging. The roof shifts and vanishes beneath Amari's feet, dark ground rising to meet her. It pulses like a living heartbeat, uncomfortably reminding her of the Red City.

These kinds of illusions only have a single goal: escape before the dreamscape consumes you entirely. Amari wishes she could be surprised that Marina decided to pull such an insane maneuver.

The Witch must have some kind of safety net for herself, but in the meantime, Amari has no choice but to compete against her as the rules of the illusion will be enforced.

"This is such bullshit," Amari mutters.

Marina smirks, but her form is fading. She's being pulled into a different part of the illusion. "Don't whine, it doesn't suit you. This dreamscape is going to be trying to keep both of us here. It's a perfectly fair trap, if I may say so. I even made sure your hearing runes would work properly."

"How sweet of you," the seer drawls, eyeing the shifting mist around her as it starts to solidify. Marina disappears entirely.

Better to get this over with.

She finds themselves in a corridor lined with mirrors. Amari can't tell where the dim light comes from, but it doesn't help the flickering of shadows in her reflection. Admittedly, the mercenary is likely having a more difficult time with her vision, wherever she is.

Amari hesitantly begins walking forward, waiting for a trap. She reaches out with her mind tentatively, double-checking that Marina was telling the truth. She doesn't feel the other woman's focus on her, so the other must really be facing her own challenge. It's a cold comfort. Whatever this illusion holds, Amari has no desire to find it out with that Witch hanging over her shoulder.

What Marina gets out of this is the real question. Amari keeps a hand out, not wanting to walk straight into a mirror. Just because her eyesight is good doesn't mean she can't be tricked.

Just then, the reflections start to shift. The seer stills, expectant as the mirrors warp, until she sees not herself but Taliya. Taliya running across rooftops, jumping far, missing a ledge, and falling…

"Fuck," Amari whispers as she closes her eyes to block out the illusion. "Marina, you bitch."

More mind games. What else should she have expected? The Witch knows Amari is hiding something, and she knows the only way to get answers is through trickery like this.

After that, it's a test of will to keep walking forward. She leans too heavily on her seer abilities to guide her. Each mirror now reflects not only her physical form, but also fragmented memories and images of possible futures, some bright, others dark. The reflections shift and distort, showing the faces of people Amari has known and lost.

Her hands are shaking at this point, and her eyes are burning as she walks past a mirror that shows her mother's last moments. She's already depowered her hearing runes, but the images don't abate. Only the knowledge that this is an illusion Marina has trapped her in keeps her going out of sheer spite.

She tries only once to break a mirror. Amari pulls out her staff, channeling magic for pure destructive power, and swings it with the limited space she has for a reflection showcasing a dying Taliya. The staff bounces harmlessly off the glass, and she forces herself to swallow the scream building in her throat.

This type of dreamscape is made of people's memories of failures, moments of triumph, and the shadows of doubt that linger in their hearts. It's a nasty surprise that Marina brought to the table. The mercenary might not be actively watching now, but how much of Amari's experiences will she see afterward when she goes over the enchantment?

Amari sees a mirror reflect Musei at its brightest, and another amid its destruction.

The seer must destroy this illusion so that Marina learns nothing. That's the only acceptable ending.

Stopping, Amari closes her eyes and takes deep breaths until her heart rate has slowed to a normal rhythm. Focusing her senses on the illusion around her, she tries to get a feel for it beyond the onslaught of memories and visions. It feels like a heavy fog draped over her shoulders, weighing her down.

Amari tries to look for the foundational enchantments of the illusion as her hand reaches out in front of her, anticipating the touch of a mirror. She obviously can't find the physical runes, but if she searches enough, she might be able to discover something that will let her bring this dreamscape crashing down.

Her mental connections to the rest of her team are a bit fuzzy through the illusion's fog, yet they act as an anchor to the outside. A reminder of what is real.

"Taliya's fine," she whispers, feeling the thief's link to her mind and knowing it's perfectly intact.

The anchor for this illusion is… Of course.

Marina. Amari holds back a scoff. The seer can't believe that woman had the gall to call *her* reckless when she pulls shit like this.

Making herself the anchor — the link grounding this illusion to the real world — and still stepping into the dreamscape with Amari?

Insane. She's lucky she didn't immediately lose her mind or leave them both detached from reality.

It also means she has to confront Marina to get out of this illusion, which is surely what she wanted the whole time. Amari, upset and off-balance from this maze of mirrors, would go to fight her.

Time is ticking in the back of the seer's head, and she's been keeping track of her team's progress subconsciously. She needs to get out of this illusion.

What would Marina not expect?

…Her team.

Amari surveys the telepathic network, taking note of the connections that seem fuzzier through the fog and what are clearer. Only Najaah and Kol are close enough to help her right now. The Ashan was locked in a death match last she saw, and the Sky Lord was dealing with a veritable mob.

She opens up a private link between the three of them, needing to expend more effort than usual to communicate through the illusion's fog. *Which one of you two can take a minute to help me?*

Nadia is with me, and the soldiers are trying to call for reinforcements, Najaah informs her curtly, telling Amari they're busy without outright saying it.

I think I can. Kol surprises her, and there's a strange excitement radiating from him. It makes Amari wonder if he's ever let his power loose like this before. *A lot of the escaped prisoners have joined the fight, and some rioters, too.*

Excellent, the thought of Lijah fighting back is a good one. *Kol, I need you to disrupt the runes that line the jail's roof. Don't completely overload it with magic, but break down part of the enchantment. I can use the opening to destroy this trap.*

Got it!

Amari mentally prepares for Kol to wreck the illusion, hoping he listens to her instructions. If he floods the runes with too much magic, it could kill Marina, and the seer would go down with her in this dreamscape. However, if the teen just makes enough of an opening for her...

The seer waits patiently, with her eyes closed and hearing runes off to block out the reflections. It takes a moment before anything happens. Slowly, she senses the fog shift, swirling in agitation at such blatant interference.

Enchantments like this one are terrible and intricate, making them elaborate traps that are all but impossible to escape from. But on the outside, they're delicate. Disrupting the runework is enough to poke holes and give Amari the chance to rip this place apart.

She feels it coming like the edge of a storm is threatening the careful balance of the fog. A slow smile takes over her face as she finds a hole in the illusion and wedges her magic into it, forcing it wider and wider until the enchantment is threatening to crumble.

A presence—who no doubt is Marina—tries to fight her and fix the illusion at the same time. Kol's magic practically bulldozes her out of the way.

That's enough. Thank you, Amari sends to Kol. She feels the wire Marina is walking on right now, keeping her head above the water and holding this enchantment together. Much more, and she'll collapse, taking the seer with her.

Kol projects a quick confirmation as his magic vanishes, a metaphorical trail of destruction in its wake.

Breaking the illusion is child's play after this. Amari cuts Marina away from the enchantment like scissors cutting paper, leaving the illusion with no anchor. Around her, mirrors shatter, and the dreamscape cracks open.

The fog lifts, leaving her and the mercenary stranded in reality, with no illusions between them.

They stand on the jail's roof again, facing each other like nothing had occurred. While the enchantment is gone, the forcefield that blocks her view and any noise remains. Marina scans the parameter, seeing the damage to the runework Kol caused. She looks like she's holding back a sneer.

"Such teamwork." Marina pulls out a star-forged Haladie knife from the tattoos winding around her shoulders. Its dual blades are long and as sharp as the day it was created. It looks wicked, and Amari endeavors to avoid it at all costs. "In fact, I have some questions about that."

"Ugh," Amari says, as she points her staff at Marina and readies for a fight. In the end, she prefers this to mind games. "Why can't you just try to kill me like a normal person? Why do we have to chat? Is it not obvious by now I'm not big on sharing?"

"The curiosity would kill me," Marina reluctantly reveals. She darts forward, blades aiming for her center mass. "You were so determined to be alone before you met Taliya eight years ago, and then it was just the two of you. Now, you have this group. What happened?"

Raising her staff to divert the Haladie's swipe, Amari uses the leverage to shove Marina away and gain distance again. "You've worked with people outside the Witches for a job before."

"Not like this," Marina grins sharply. "Don't lie to me, it doesn't work."

She uses her free hand to send a throwing knife at Amari's head. The seer ducks the blade by a second before it can kill her and keeps her staff in a guard position. This proves a wise decision as she barely has a moment to redirect the much larger Haladie Marina brings down over her.

Another attack comes, and Amari grimaces as she uses her staff to slide the blade down the length of it to unbalance the Andan. The risky move nearly takes her fingers, yet it gives her the moment to back away. She glances at the sky briefly and is pleased to note the sun has fully set now. Only a minute or two left. Marina *tsks* and twirls her

Haladie in preparation for a new assault.

"I'm not sure what to tell you, Marina, except that it's really none of your business."

This, predictably, irks the mercenary somewhat.

"You're so full of shit!" Marina swings at Amari with renewed energy, and the sounds of star-forged blades and enchanted staff clashing ring painfully in her ears. No one speaks as the next minute ticks by, a blur of blades and near misses.

Amari is calculating how she can get the chance to break away from the close fight when a feeling of *knowing* lance through her mind. The telepathic network soon confirms her intuition. Hiding any possible evidence of a grin, Amari waits for just the right moment.

The lights of Lijah abruptly go out, including the minimal lanterns on the jail's roof. With the sun entirely below the horizon and only one broken moon in the sky, shadows have been sweeping the city, only held at bay by the public lighting system. Now, that firewall is gone in the blink of an eye. Even through the forcefield, it's clear when darkness overtakes the city.

Even if she isn't a Nightblood, knowing ahead of time about the blackout gives Amari an advantage over Marina. Except she *is* a Nightblood, and she sees perfectly well how the mercenary stumbles in the wake of the sudden darkness. Grinning, the seer channels a burst of power into her staff and hits Marina square in the chest.

The Witch goes flying, landing hard a distance away on the roof. Stalking forward, Amari uses the mercenary's stunned state to handcuff her with a pair of cuffs she slipped from an officer years ago.

There's no way it will hold someone like Marina for long, but Amari doesn't need it to. Pulling out a knock-out potion from her bag, the seer smirks as she recalls that she purchased this potion specifically for this situation, considering how sturdy Marina's mental shields are. She carefully uncorks it and places it under the mercenary's nose for her to breathe in. The Witch is slumped over, unconscious, a moment later.

Amari doesn't hesitate to activate the emergency beacon on the mercenary's wrist. From experience, she knows it will alert Nadia and Miri of her location. They'll come immediately to her rescue.

Amari waits patiently, watching Marina for any indications of consciousness.

Moments later, Nadia's giant form leaps to the roof with the much smaller Miri clinging to her back. They pass through the forcefield without issue, causing the seer to roll her eyes. Their presences must have been keyed into the runes. Neither seems particularly surprised to see Amari standing over their sleeping leader.

"I told her this was a bad idea," Miri says cheerfully as she drops to the roof on agile feet. The Bera snorts, striding forward while keeping a wary eye on Amari.

"You should have been more convincing," the seer complains, eyeing the two for evidence of hostility. However, with one of their members passed out, the Night Witches are more likely to take a strategic retreat.

Nadia easily picks up the slumped form of Marina and gently slings the Andan over her shoulder, the Bera giving Amari a stern look. "This won't be the last time we meet."

"Of course not," the seer agrees. Nadia walks away from her, leaping through the forcefield again to a distant roof. Skipping after her, Miri sends Amari a friendly wave before following.

Alone now, Amari doesn't hold back the sigh building up inside her. What a disaster. Quickly getting over herself, she runs to the roof's edge to dismantle the forcefield. Without any distractions, the obstacle only takes a couple of minutes to take apart.

It dissipates with a hiss, and she gets a clear view of the mess she has been missing while distracted by Marina.

And what a mess it is.

24

ERIKA

Erika's ability to sneak into places guarded by soldiers has increased exponentially since meeting Amari and everyone else. She wonders if she should be concerned about going back to her normal life when all this is done. Something to consider later, Erika reminds herself as she travels across rooftops, her backpack weighing on her shoulders in a way that would have been more difficult to deal with just a few weeks ago.

Periodically, she finds herself stopping to hide when an Imperial Aerial Searcher flies overhead. The Empire's magical drone swings by and away from her more times than she's comfortable with.

Soon, she reaches her destination. It's a small clothing store that looks unimpressive and seems unimportant unless one knows that, inside, there is a secret entrance to the city's underground maintenance tunnels. And that the store is less than a block away from one of Lijah's public power stations, where the city government manages things like temperature regulation, transportation, and lighting for the community with magic. This one, specifically, powers most of the lights used in the city. Many buildings have backup stores of magic just in case of a hijack or attack, but having control of this station will still be a huge asset.

Because of this, the security of power stations is insane. Unless the team wanted Kol to alert the whole city of the break-in or have Taliya spend hours working, Erika is the only one who can walk through most wards undetected. Taliya upgraded her runica for everything else.

At least the security will be at its most lax during the daytime.

Careful not to be seen, she climbs down from the store's roof and drops onto the balcony on the third floor. The store isn't open today, but the Empire is still doing door-to-door searches, so she doesn't have much time to dawdle. She only knows for sure what Mia told the team: that the secret entrance is on the ground floor.

Erika easily picks the lock of the balcony door and slips into the silent building. Inside, piles and boxes of clothes litter the open space, some of nicer quality than others. She walks down the stairs until she reaches the first floor. Even though the variety in clothing styles and sizes is unfamiliar, it looks like a stereotypical clothing store. Some things are universal.

Erika reasons the secret entrance wouldn't be in a public space, and she scans the area, taking in the floor plan and mentally contrasting it to the blueprints Taliya gave her. Except it appears that the store is too small for the measurements that were given to her... Ah, that way.

She finds a locked door tucked away in the back and opens it with little trouble. It reveals the space she noted was missing from the store's overall blueprint size.

It's clearly a staff-only area. The organization is rather haphazard, making her step around articles of clothing that have fallen to the ground. Scanning the tiled walls, she immediately notices the discrepancy. There's a pattern to the monochrome walls, and a disruption in that design jumps out to her. Mindful of how fucked she would be if this is secured in a way that affects her non-magical self, Erika presses the tile that doesn't match the wall's pattern.

A large number of tiles in front of her suddenly begin shifting, and she startles back as a small space opens up for her. It's the size of a closet, except the floor is gone in favor of a hole. There's no light further down the drop, making it look even more ominous. As she peers inside with hesitation, she sees a rung ladder leading the way toward the tunnels, the bottom only vaguely visible in the consuming darkness of the underground.

Erika hadn't thought to ask Taliya why a clothing store has direct access to Lijah's maintenance tunnels—too wrapped up in the bigger picture—but now she kind of wishes she had.

She pulls off and opens her backpack, revealing the carefully stored first aid supplies, snacks, a water bottle, a roll of thin yet durable rope, a book, and her flashlight lying on top. Erika clutches the flashlight tightly now, internally grateful she's been so careful with the battery life. After closing the bag, she secures the device to her backpack's shoulder strap before slowly climbing down the ladder. Only a few rungs down, and the secret entrance closes above her, leaving her in darkness, only held back by her own light.

It's oddly comforting. Being underground again, and not in the Red City, where everything was so steeped in blood. Her joy at being underground and her anxiousness over being on her own are now conflicting with each other.

Doing this part of the mission with no help ironically reminds Erika of all the horror stories Felicia was delighted to tell her growing up. People who got lost in the Haven Republic's labyrinth and never came out, or if they do, they're not the same. Her friend loved those kinds of tales, while she never had much of a stomach for them.

Now, Erika has definitely faced worse over the past few weeks. Except it seems so much worse when she's alone, without her new friends as support. She didn't realize before how much more she had begun to rely on them than just as a means to make up for her lack of fighting experience. Reluctantly, she continues down toward the tunnel.

When she touches the ground, it's a hard metal floor.

Her mind brings her back to earlier that day, when her friends had been going over the mission again. *Amari gave Erika a concerned look. "Remember, this isn't like any place you're used to. It's run by magic but not imbued with wild magic like in the Red City or Castor. This place is carefully made and run by people. Some would argue that this means you won't encounter any monsters, but I disagree. So, be cautious, okay? This isn't worth your life."*

"I will," Erika promised.

Breathing out as she focuses on the present, Erika gets her bearings both physically and mentally. She's only a block away from the station, and she knows the direction to take. Any traps or guards in her way will be a problem she deals with when she finds them.

Analyzing the tunnel as she walks, moving at a watchful but steady pace, she can see her environment is mostly a collection of metal and more metal with runes carved into the walls at intervals. She thinks they might say something like, 'No Unauthorized Sentients Allowed,' which makes her wonder how the runes differentiate between those who are authorized and those who aren't. Clearly, she doesn't even register to them.

After walking interrupted for a good two minutes, Erika is hopeful she can reach the station without any problems. Her steps almost feel lighter as she strides forward, thinking how lucky she just might be.

Then she hears voices.

" —forcing us to work overtime. Are you getting paid for it? I'm sure fucking not," a young male voice complains just loud enough for Erika to pick up the end of his statement as she cautiously slinks forward. There's a bend in the tunnel ahead that hides the person speaking from view and echoes his words. As she comes closer, she flicks off her flashlight in favor of using the dim lighting coming from around the bend.

"It's because of the military setting up camp, Gabe," another voice says, older and much wearier. "You know they've been turning the city upside down looking for some rebels."

"And that means we get shaken down, our homes ransacked, and now being worked with no pay? How's that *fair*, Torrin?"

A gusty sigh. "Fair's got nothing to do with it. Just be glad we still have our jobs with how things have been going."

What does that mean? Erika stops moving entirely, absorbed in the conversation she's overhearing. She knows the Empire has been combing through Lijah for them, and Kol came back the night before and told her what he saw. Hearing about the arrests was disquieting and only made her more determined to get the team out of Lijah as fast as possible. Even now, she's discovering more of the consequences of their actions.

How many people in this city are paying for their crimes?

Back against the tunnel wall, Erika slides up to the turn in the passageway and quickly sneaks a peek beyond the bend. A lantern resting on the cement floor is the only source of illumination in the tunnel. About ten meters away is a ladder leading up to the power station's entrance. Two people are guarding it, with one lanky figure leaning against the tunnel with their arms crossed and a smaller but broader person sitting on the ground.

Erika can easily tell that the person standing is Gabe, the younger employee, while the one sitting is the tired Torrin.

"But did you hear what happened last night downtown? They're dragging people out of their homes over nothing!"

"We shouldn't assume," Torrin sighs, the wary tone to his voice contradicting his words.

"And what have these rebels even done? How can we be sure they're real?" Gabe mutters bitterly, leaning his head back against the wall. Torrin abruptly leans toward him and swats the younger one on the leg. "Hey!"

"Don't say such things where others can hear you," Torrin warns, and Erika ducks back around when he scans his surroundings for eavesdroppers. "You never know who is listening."

If only he knew. She wonders how he would react to the fact that one of those rebels is listening in.

Erika stills. There's a thought.

Before she can overthink it, Erika walks around the tunnel's bend into full view of the two guards.

Torrin, unsurprisingly, reacts first and lurches to his feet. Gabe straightens but seems more confused by her sudden appearance than anything else. With a clear view, Erika can now see that the older of the two is an Ashan with graying hair, sturdy clothes, and a steady glow of heat underneath his skin. One of his horns has snapped at one point, leaving him with less than half of what the other is. Gabe, on the other hand, is a Sky Lord, which strikes her as a poor choice of who to assign a guard job *underground*. The younger has small wings, dull brown and gray, that look like they need some care.

"Who are you?" Torrin asks suspiciously, only relaxing a little when Erika gets close enough for the light to show her young age.

"A rebel," Erika blurts out. The two guards share a brief, incredulous look before turning their full attention to her.

"That's a bad joke, kid."

"Not a joke," Erika smiles. All or nothing now. "And I need your help."

"With what?" Gabe laughs, seemingly still convinced she's playing a prank. Torrin has gone silent and narrows his eyes at her.

"Sabotaging this power station," Erika says. The Sky Lord's good mood evaporates. "Only temporarily. The military has swarmed Lijah, and they'll leave after we escape."

"This is ridiculous," Torrin scowls and takes a cautious step forward. Gabe is all but hiding behind the older guard, eyes widened in a way that makes her heart clench. "Go home while you still can."

"That's what I'm trying to do." Erika slowly reaches for her backpack and pulls out the runica Talya upgraded for her. So many adjustments have been made to it that are illegal throughout Esma and Apolon. She holds it up to the light as proof of her status as a criminal. The runes reflect and shine silver in the dark. "Believe me yet?"

"What the fuck," Gabe whispers, leaning forward despite the older man's sharp look of warning. "That's so... cool!"

"Gabe! Shut up," Torrin snaps at the other and then glares at her. "If you're really one of the rebels the soldiers are hunting, why haven't you just attacked us? We're technically government workers."

Erika doesn't know how to put all her feelings into words. The ordinary people who act as a cog in the wheel for great and terrible machines like the Empire are not much better off than anyone else. They were just talking about being negatively impacted because of her team's presence. Thinking about everything she's learned about the Empire makes her want to *fight*, and she knows fighting these two wouldn't amount to anything. So now Erika's doing something wildly impulsive and trying to talk instead of starting pointless battles.

"I don't like violence," Erika easily admits. "We just want to go home. You can work with me now and not have to deal with the military anymore."

"Why would we risk everything to help you?" Torrin demands gruffly, arms crossed. Gabe glances between the two of them, wings twitching and feathers puffing up.

That's when the telepathic network turns on in Erika's mind, and Amari drops the news that there's been a change of plans.

We're not setting the Center of Finance on fire.

Erika isn't the only one on the team to voice her surprise in the network, and she remembers belatedly to keep her mind in the present as well. Torrin is looking at her suspiciously, so the Nullifier reveals the existence of the telepathic network as Amari explains her new plan.

"What are they saying?" Gabe asks curiously.

"Our leader has decided to break out the people the imperial soldiers have been rounding up," Erika says haltingly, having difficulty keeping track of two conversations simultaneously.

Will the timing still work? She double-checks with the team.

Getting confirmation, she turns to Torrin and Gabe. "I still need your help sabotaging the power station."

They gawk at her, stuck on the idea of a jailbreak happening downtown.

In the network, the prospect of this hurting Lijah more than helping comes up. Erika's stomach swoops, even as a steady feeling of resolve fills her.

It might not be, Amari concedes to this possibility. *Even if this plan goes perfectly, Lijah could face severe consequences. But the Empire is hurting them already, and I want to help. I'll do my best to focus all their wrath on me.*

On us, Erika says, something solidifying in her heart.

Out loud, she tells the two men exactly what her team is planning to do. Namely, stage a jailbreak, cause chaos for the imperial soldiers, and escape the city. They say nothing and stare wide-eyed for a solid minute. She lets them have their understandable moment of disbelief.

"Does that answer your question on what you get for helping me?"

"…Yeah," Gabe says, shock slowly turning to awe. Torrin is unsurprisingly more reserved.

"Why risk yourselves to help these prisoners?"

Erika smiles, her heart lighter since hearing Amari's firm

conviction to help Lijah's citizens. "My mom always says, '*It's better to be kind than to be successful, but there's no reason you can't be both.*' We're the reason this is happening, I don't want to see that be for nothing."

"Alright," Torrin gives her a look she can't quite read. "Tell us your plan, kid."

Erika breaks down the new plan as best she can, pausing between what she feels is a lot of her own nervousness to see their reactions. When she's done, and much to her relief, they both chime in, helping her adjust the parts they believe will work better, or would have gotten her into trouble.

"When there is a city-wide threat, there are protocols in place to protect what's most valuable—like the magic generators," Gabe tells her. "Normally, there are about fifteen to twenty guards in the building, but with the threat alert, there have to be well over thirty."

"They're spread out, though," Torrin says, gesturing with a hand. "Only a few on each floor and less than a dozen around the magic generator. I can think of a few ways to throw them off your scent, but you'll still have to deal with some of them."

"Leave that to me," Erika replies. She sounds more confident than she feels. All Erika knows is that she *has* to do this.

Climbing out of the tunnels and into the building reveals pristine and sparse halls, with security wards she scans and dismisses. After so much training, Erika can instantly recognize when runes simply track magical signatures.

"Don't know how you're fooling the wards, but it's impressive," Torrin admits, eyeing the runes warily. Erika just gives him a small smile instead of an answer. The man huffs in amusement while Gabe climbs in after them.

"Okay," the younger man starts, tone tinged with nervous excitement. "The generator is three floors up, let's head for the stairs. Guards don't shift for another half hour, and we want to miss them, right?"

"Right."

The stairs on this floor are unguarded, like her companions said they would be. They creep up the steps, careful not to tip off anyone on the other floors that they're here.

On floor three, Erika stops in front of the door. Torrin and Gabe have confirmed there would be a guard posted here, so she needs to use her element of surprise wisely.

The door opens her way, so…

Erika motions for Torrin and Gabe to hide themselves, and then knocks on the door when they're out of sight. She moves to the side, so when the door opens out, it blocks her from view.

Like she thought, the guard opens the door to investigate the noise. "Hey, Fresco, is that yo—"

As soon as the guard enters her field of vision, Erika pounces. Their back is turned, so she's able to easily put her unsheathed, not-enchanted knife up against their throat. Silence falls instantly, and the guard freezes.

For a moment, the world stills, and all Erika can feel is the knife in her hand and the heartbeat it threatens. Everything narrows down to those two feelings, and she refuses to let herself hesitate.

Hesitation kills.

She brings the butt of her knife up and slams it into the guard's throat, knocking the breath out of them, causing their knees to give out as she swings the handle of the knife down on their head a final time. They collapse to the ground, unconscious.

Now Erika pauses, stunned by her own actions. Taliya was right. She is not a killer, and she will not become one.

The sounds of more guards approaching pull her out of her head and remind her that now is not the time for revelations.

It must be a patrol, she reasons. Erika leaves the unconscious guard in the stairwell and quietly closes the door behind her. The patrol is about to turn the corner and see her, so she moves fast.

Taliya ensured Erika's runica had enough stored magic to work for her, meaning she could technically write her own wards right now instead of just disrupting already written ones. She crouches to the hallway floor to scribe on the polished tile and begins to stand just as the first guard turns the corner.

Erika sees the guard stall, imagining his brain trying to process the scene before alarm takes over and their hand can reach for a weapon.

They stagger as the ward she wrote activates.

"What—" More guards arrive, reacting with alarm at the sudden assault on their senses. Erika marvels as every single one who reaches for a weapon or tries for a magical attack is abruptly subjected to an intense round of dizziness.

Dashing forward, Erika slams the handle of her knife down on the closest guard with a good burst of momentum, knocking them to the ground. She dodges someone trying to seize her, though the uncoordinated efforts make it easier than it should be. Still, her knife isn't gonna cut it with a group like this.

Spying a baton on the downed guard's belt, she grabs it. It's much heavier than she expects, but this works in her favor as she swings it at every soldier she can.

Najaah would probably be weeping internally if they saw her uncoordinated fighting. By the end of it, she's surrounded by unconscious or stunned guards as she tries to catch her breath. Deciding to play it safe, Erika takes all the communication devices they have, just in case.

She finally returns to the stairwell and calls out softly for Torrin and Gabe. They both gape at her once she shows them the aftermath of her fights.

"Is that a ward for *dizziness?*"

"Yeah," Erika confirms, somewhat sheepishly. "My, uh, friends tell me it's better to use low energy-depleting wards like this in a fight that still have great effects than to drain a bunch of magic trying to end the fight instantly."

Both men stare at her with wide eyes before Torrin chuckles, and Gabe smiles widely. Erika relaxes at the unspoken approval, then focuses back on the mission.

Their plan involved Torrin staying behind to play the part of the panicked employee who points the authorities in the wrong direction while Gabe helps Erika break into the generator room. It's down a few halls, and when the next patrol passes, the duo hides from them until they're gone.

The two guards blocking the generator room are easy work, in Erika's opinion. She reuses the ward that inflicts dizzy spells, but because she has more time, uses it to greater effectiveness from a distance. Now, she lets the feeling come slowly onto the guards until they collapse on the ground, where she can hit them with the baton.

And then it's just them and the door to the generator room.

Not all the wards are so simple here, so she keeps the runica out, which Gabe gawks at once he gets a closer look at it. Erika is careful not to repeat the disaster in the Ethereal Planes. Even though the rules of magic are more straightforward in Avalon, she takes the time to study how the runes interact. They layer over each other and weave together, barring entrance from all. The door opening would set off alarms, regardless of her lack of magic.

She needs to change that. Instead of trying to break the wards or overwhelming them, she tries to shift a few of the auxiliary runes to focus more on magical signatures. It takes a few minutes of cautious drawing, all the while she glances nervously around the hallway, but she manages it. Erika won't be sensed by the wards, and the door won't automatically set off every alarm.

Gabe stays outside to watch for security, and she opens the door as quietly as she can. Erika slips inside, closing it gently and turning to face her target.

Her first thought is: *That is way bigger than I thought it would be.*

Thankfully, Erika's time spent studying and playing with devices that are made Upside pays off. If she had entered this room with no knowledge beforehand, she would have failed her mission just from her lack of familiarity with the engineering. She recognizes the parts at work here and can read the runes with an ease that surprises even her.

The magic generator is a beautiful thing. It's surrounded by protective wards etched into its surface that Erika would have a tougher time navigating if she hadn't spent the two months with a master wardbreaker. The magic generator itself appears as a spire, crafted from a seamless fusion of enchanted metals and crystalline conduits.

But the grand device in front of her looks like an empty shell, and Erika does not see the pure magical energy being harvested. She'll need to fix this, too.

Unsheathing her enchanted dagger, she activates the spell and takes the box Amari had given her after the heist on the governor's fortress. That felt so long ago, now. The idea of *ghost residue* had been the grossest and creepiest thing she could imagine existing, let alone carrying some around in her knife.

That had been before the Red City. And the Forsaken Forest.

Now, she unlatches the box, reaches for the vial, and tips it back without a thought. It tastes foul, but she's honestly had worse herbal shots made in her mom's office. A second later, she nearly drops the vial and scrambles to stop it from falling to the floor.

The room is *glowing*.

Erika had always wondered what magic looked like. As a Nullifier, she had hardly seen any before coming Upside. On the surface, Avalon is full of magic, but she can only see when that magic is manipulating something else—runes, fire, Kol's strange brand of telekinesis.

Now, everything is so bright, her eyes are blinking against the strain. It takes a minute for her vision to adjust. The ghost residue took effect much faster than she had expected. And what she sees now… Erika stares in awe.

Magic is light made tangible. It's like lightning in a bottle, except with none of the frantic energy. There's something almost serene about the currents she sees all around her.

In front of her, the generator is like a beacon banishing all the world's darkness. The core is a swirling vortex of elemental forces that spin endlessly, harnessed through intricate channels that amplify and stabilize the raw magical energies. Erika wants to reach out and touch despite knowing how bad of an idea it is.

Recalling Amari's lesson, the seer had explained that these energies are drawn not just from the air, but from ley lines that crisscross beneath the city. They tap into Avalon's natural magic reserves with a precise balance. Radiating outward from the central core, a network of enchanted conduits distributes the generated magic throughout the city. These conduits wind like snakes through the tunnels and into the sides of buildings, providing the city with its power.

And Erika needs to sabotage it.

The great thing about sabotage is that it's much easier than fixing anything. Erika's biggest hurdle is making sure the generator doesn't work *and* doesn't blow up. This much magic built up could make things go south very quickly.

Forcibly shaking herself, Erika pulls out a toolbox she had stored in the dagger for this part of the mission. Even with her own initiative in the Upside's mechanics, Taliya had still given her a rundown of what all the tools were and how they worked. It makes it easier to use them without overthinking their purpose.

Being able to see magic in its raw form is a huge relief. Trying to do this without blowing herself up will be difficult enough with the Sight. Carefully, the Nullifier starts by disconnecting and breaking the generator's access to Avalon's natural energy, effectively cutting it off from gaining more power. She then begins doing the equivalent of 'poking holes' in the core, so magic starts seeping out. In a controlled manner, most of the ambient magic is pulled back into the air or the ley lines themselves. It takes time to drain the core of a significant amount of magic, but that build-up was the most dangerous part of the generator.

Erika knows the next part is tricky. She could systematically disconnect all the city's conduits from the generator, but that would take out the lights one sector at a time. Erika is meant to turn them all off at once.

She begins by writing runes. A chain reaction meant to activate all at once whenever she desires.

"What time is it?" Erika checks in with Gabe as she finishes with the scribework. There's no point in continuing the activation if the sun's still in the sky.

"8:36 pm," Gabe says, eyes watchful of both ends of the hallway. "Should be plenty dark by now."

It's later than she thought it was. In the telepathic network, Erika isn't sure if anyone's listening, but she sends out the signal anyway. She's turning off the lights.

Erika starts off the chain reaction, and the city's conduits all dim. The lights in the room flicker out, and their only light source is the remaining magic in the core churning away.

Relief for her success nearly brings her to her knees before she mechanically makes herself move to the door. It opens easily, the core's light showing Gabe's amazed expression.

"Okay. Okay, wow. Thank you, Gabe. Tell Torrin thank you as well when you see him," Erika processes her mission's win and barely stops a wild grin from overtaking her face. Her hands might be shaking. "I have to go now, I think. They're gonna know someone's here."

Gabe breaks out of his shock at the darkness and hastily leads the way out of the hallway. They both go back to the stairs, just as the sounds of boots and hoofs start pounding toward the generator room.

Standing in the stairwell, Erika thanks Gabe for his help again. "This was a huge risk, so thank you. Go back to the tunnels, avoid the soldiers, and just tell them you were down there the whole time. You wouldn't even know that the lights went out."

"I'm glad that—that I helped," Gabe says with a smile, something burning in his eyes, before racing down the stairs.

Erika heads up. She narrowly misses a patrol storming down from the roof to the fifth floor, but waits out of view before she keeps going. The sounds of soldiers outside converging on the building are something even she can hear from inside. It's a miracle she manages to keep out of the way long enough to make it to the roof.

Burying a rising panic that has washed away her sense of victory, she turns her attention back to the telepathic network.

There are a bunch of soldiers here now. I'm on the roof, but I think I'm going to need some help.

As soon as she starts moving, *someone* will spot her, and the chase begins.

The response is quick. *I'm on my way,* says Najaah. Erika can't help the immediate relief, yet focuses on the present.

Someone speaks up behind her, destroying all her carefully curated calm. "I should have followed up on my hunch sooner."

Erika's stomach drops to her feet, and she stumbles to a halt. That voice is familiar.

Slowly, she turns to see the tall figure standing a dozen yards behind her. Colonel Annora Bashkim, decked out in full SPEAR armor and with her formidable sword strapped to her back. The woman gazes at Erika with some kind of amusement, like a cat watching a mouse.

Her mind becomes utterly blank with panic, and Erika does the only thing she can think of. She runs, her fear of the gaping chasm between buildings forgotten as she makes to jump between roofs.

The Colonel underestimates Erika. That's the only possible explanation for what happens next. Instead of chasing the teen down and forcefully stopping her, Annora calls out an order.

"Activate the net!"

A ring of runes lights up on the roof, and Erika catches a few as she runs. They all seemed geared towards nonviolent capture, with a heavy emphasis on magical binding.

Her panicked mind barely feels her own relief as she dashes right through them, completely unaffected by the wards. On instinct, the teen grabs one of the little grenades Taliya has started stuffing in her jacket and throws it back. Erika is just as surprised as the Colonel when it creates a giant cloud of smoke.

She jumps to the next roof and doesn't stop. The free-running makes her stomach drop and her palms sweat, but she knows she can't afford the luxury of hesitating. The smoke helps as much as it terrifies her, further obscuring her view in the dark.

Soon enough, she hears a shout that sounds suspiciously like "There they are!" and more shouts and yells start as soldiers on the ground and spilling onto the roof begin chasing her.

Erika doesn't have much experience with free-running. If this is a chase, she will be caught up here quickly. Her flashlight both gives her away and is the only reason she doesn't fall to her death. She begins looking for a way down as best she can in the darkness. Eventually, after an excruciating few minutes where her rooftop chasers slowly catch up, she finds a roof access that's unlocked, and she heads down into some kind of empty office building.

The intention is to find some side or back door that she can make a run out of, but before she even makes it to the fourth floor, the building begins to shake.

Is someone *destroying a building to get to her?* Erika knew the Empire soldiers were intense, but this level of property damage for one person could not be efficient.

She tries to run down the stairs as quickly as possible, even as the shaking and cracks creeping up the infrastructure force her to flee the cramped space. The floors themselves are hardly better and get increasingly worse as she races down halls searching for a window. The ceiling splinters violently, and she dodges a piece of it, slamming to the floor.

"Fuck," Erika mutters as she dashes away through the falling debris. The building is breaking at an alarming rate, foundations crumbling under pressure in a way that looks horrifyingly like crumpling paper. *That can't be up to any kind of building regulation,* a distant part of her brain notes.

Above her, an ominous cracking sound splits the air, and she realizes she won't make it out in time. Erika doesn't stop running, a part of her refusing to give up even as she knows —

Arms suddenly grab her around the waist and lift her up. Erika barely registers the fact she is abruptly moving at an incredibly fast speed over her surprise at being picked up at all.

Her rescuer leaps out of a window just as the ceiling caves in, taking everything with it. Erika watches the ground rise, feeling like she left her stomach behind, except the person carrying her lands with a seemingly casual grace despite falling four floors. It's Najaah, she recognizes belatedly.

Of course, Erika remembers as the fact she survived sinks in, Najaah had been coming to help her. She twists her head to thank the Ashan, stopping only when she catches sight of blood dripping down their arm.

"You're hurt?" Erika startles, the statement coming out as more of a question than she intended. Najaah stills, then huffs and swiftly places Erika on the ground. She feels like a doll being set down more than anything else.

"I'm fine."

"I don't think we have the same definition of—"

Najaah rolls their eyes and pulls back their armorclothe to reveal the wound. Or where it would have been if there was one. Instead, all Erika sees is smooth, dark brown skin, without an injury or scar in sight. She even points her flashlight to get a better visual and frowns at the discrepancy. The teen stares for a second too long before looking up.

The Ashan gives her a pointed expression. "See?"

"But. Then why…"

They pull the sleeve down roughly, scowling. Despite the flashlight, the dark clothing and bad lighting make it difficult to see clearly, but the blood still looks far too fresh for Erika's peace of mind. And, she thinks, a strange shade of red. Like, there are flecks of gold—

"It's not mine. There was a circle of Singers outside, bringing down the building. They're all dead now, but the damage was done," Najaah says, and then whirls around in time to cut an arrow in half with their khopesh. Erika stumbles back in shock, her mind having trouble processing how quickly it happened.

"It's clear I should deal with you myself," Colonel Annora walks down the street at a leisurely pace toward them. She waves her hand in some kind of signal, and Erika spots a few archers on nearby roofs disengaging. The Nullifier isn't sure whether to take that as a good omen or not.

Stay behind me, Najaah says directly to Erika, who sends a wordless affirmative. She has no intention of getting between the two Sun Eaters. They both look like they could individually bench press her.

The next second, Annora's blade is out and coming down to meet Najaah's. Erika is pushed back in the same moment, nearly tripping over a loose piece of rubble as she retreats. Her eyes are wide as she tries to track the two sword fighters in front of her. Each one moves so fast, she can't keep up. The heavy darkness of the night doesn't help, only illuminated by her flashlight and Colonel Annora's fiery powers.

Flames flicker off her blade, though not in the same way as in the Archive. She must not see the point in using those abilities against Najaah, another Sun Eater. Erika imagines Lijah will be grateful for the small amount of restraint when this is all over. Then she glances at the demolished building behind her and winces.

Annora suddenly speaks up as she locks blades with Najaah. "You've trained at Ariza, haven't you? Were you one of the conscripted or sent there to train by someone?"

Instead of answering, the younger Ashan scowls, brows furrowing intensely as their khopesh tries to hack off Annora's arms. She steps out of the way, and the blade skims just past her. Erika feels like she has stopped breathing.

"Not very happy memories, I take it? That's alright. I wasn't fond of the place either," Annora smiles wryly as something akin to anger flashes over Najaah's face. The force in the other teen's strikes takes even Erika aback. "Let's see what you learned."

Anyone watching the following fight without enhanced eyesight would be unable to follow what happens, so Erika doesn't stand a chance. All she knows is the sound of clashing metal, the sight of damaged concrete, and the smell of ash. The street cracks under their feet from the force of their blows as enchanted swords meet.

They break apart suddenly, and Erika doesn't know why until she sees Annora draw back in surprise. A quick glance down shows a thin but strategic cut between her armor plates. The silence that follows is heavy and pervasive.

"Huh," Annora says, tone unreadable. She backs away from the younger Ashan, mouth in a thoughtful downturn. Najaah stares at her warily, eyes narrowed. "I apologize. It's clear I've underestimated you."

"What?"

Erika feels a chill up her spine.

"I'll rectify this immediately."

The sword in Annora's hands—already a large, sharp-looking blade—lights up with power. There must be some leftover effect of the ghost residue, because the sheer glow of the sword makes Erika turn away to cover her eyes. Out of sight, she hears the crackle of electricity and swears loudly. *Stormblade.*

Lightning!

Even a Sun Eater's natural immunity to heat is diminished in the face of a storm's power. Erika feels herself backing further away before she can think about it, the ringing of thunder beating in her ears. Her heart is in her throat, echoing the terrible sound.

Her friend doesn't do anything as cowardly or undignified as *retreat,* but even Erika can tell the tides have turned. Annora moves with an unshakable confidence and doesn't hesitate to use her Sun Eater abilities to further destabilize the ground. Superheated concrete doesn't burn Najaah, but it's just another environmental factor not in their favor.

Erika grits her teeth and takes a step forward despite her every instinct. Najaah needs *help.*

The Nullifier's mind flies over every tool in her arsenal, every weapon the team has recommended, every little thing that was snuck into her backpack. What can she use to help? She pulls off her bag, hand stopping at the flashlight still strapped to it.

Her flashlight… The battery!

With quick, efficient movements, Erika unscrews the bottom and carefully pushes the battery out of place. It pops out easily, a warm weight in her hand.

Looking up, she sees Annora forcing Najaah to give ground

under the threat of her electrified blade. Erika reaches out hesitantly in the telepathic network, worried about breaking her friend's focus.

Najaah, I have an idea. Maneuver her within throwing distance for me, and then back away very quickly.

The Sun Eater doesn't answer, and Erika fears they couldn't pay attention, when Najaah suddenly leaps far from Annora. Even the Colonel pauses, eyebrows shooting up at the abrupt move.

"What—"

Erika doesn't let the woman finish her question. She lobs the battery directly at the Colonel, or more accurately, her *sword*.

Annora easily moves out of the way of the projectile, but doesn't think to guard her blade. As soon as the battery is within a foot of the lightning sparking from the sword, everything explodes. Erika is knocked onto her ass at the blast, ears ringing faintly even as she still hears shouting in the distance.

In the corner of her eyes, she sees Annora holding onto her blade with shocking stubbornness, even as the once-controlled lightning is unleashed. It strikes out against the wielder and everything else around it. Burn marks are left on the street, yet the Colonel doesn't falter as it hits her.

Technology mixing with magic is more volatile than she expected. Erika would sit up and take notes if her head wouldn't stop spinning.

She doesn't have the time to recover before Najaah appears again to pick her up and carry her away at high speeds. The rush doesn't help the dizziness she feels, and it takes a few minutes for Erika's mind to come back online. She dimly registers the surrounding neighborhoods and taps for Najaah to let her down when she recognizes the government district.

It looks different than the day before.

In the time it took Erika to complete the task given to her, Lijah had changed a great deal.

The city itself is drenched in darkness, yet Najaah easily navigates the streets littered with debris and the remnants of shattered glass. Buildings still standing are marked with evidence of a fight. Windows are broken, and doors hang ajar, offering glimpses into the ransacked interiors. The air is thick with the acrid smell of smoke and the faint, lingering scent of burning flesh. All the usual sounds of city life are replaced by the din of distant conflict and the wails of sirens.

It's only when Najaah leads her to the jail that she sees the epicenter of the fight. The scene awaiting her instantly sears into her brain and reminds her a great deal of the rioting in the Red City.

Someone has enchanted working lights that levitate harmlessly around the open space, which might be the only silver lining.

The jail has collapsed inward, looking like a veritable mountain of rubble. People on both sides are avoiding it at all costs, and she wonders what happened with fierce curiosity.

Bodies of the dead or perhaps just unconscious are strewn throughout the plaza in front of the jail. She drags her eyes away with a lump in her throat, considering pulling out her first aid supplies to help the first responders already running around with medical equipment.

The very pavement is cracked and shattered, with remnants of written runes and broken artifices scattered about. On the outskirts, random civilians and escaped prisoners seem to be taking their frustrations out on the soldiers trying to get some kind of order. Half of the surrounding buildings' walls look scorched.

In the eye of the storm is Kol. He floats meters above the ground, still in a swirling hurricane of debris he controls. A dozen or so soldiers are trying to get to him to no avail. They're barely keeping off the onslaught of projectiles at Kol's disposal or woefully failing at doing any damage to him.

"It's less chaotic now," Najaah comments. The words are so

incomprehensible to Erika that she can't even bring herself to reply. *Less* chaotic?

A voice calls out to them from above. "What took you both so long?"

Erika whips her head up to the sky to where Kol levitates in the air, so far above their heads. He doesn't seem very injured, from what she can tell, but incredibly dusty for some reason. Did someone throw flour at him or something? Regardless, she can't believe he's talking to them while in the middle of a battle.

"A building collapsed and we ran into the Colonel," is all the Ashan says. "Are things wrapping up now?"

"… You could say that," Kol replies, sounding uncertain. He's about to explain all that has happened in Najaah's short absence when Taliya drops from the roof of a nearby building.

"You guys took your time."

Erika will swear to the day she dies that the thief's sudden appearance gives her a mini heart attack. As it is, she startles so hard she nearly stumbles over a crack in the pavement as Najaah catches her shoulder, stabilizing her without even looking at Erika.

"We had to ditch a great deal of soldiers," the Sun Eater says. "Is everything ready?"

"Just about. Everyone is making sure that, you know…" Taliya eyes the collapsed building pointedly. Frowning, Erika looks between her friends. What aren't they saying?

"Of course," Najaah nods like the thief's words make perfect sense.

The words burst out of Erika then, her curiosity demanding to be answered. "What happened here?"

"Well…"

25

TALIYA

The rooftops of Lijah are quickly becoming familiar to Taliya. Even if she is forced to be more careful than she would in Castor because of the Empire's sky watchers.

Taliya heads toward the northern part of Lijah as Nuru goes east, Erika disappears into the south, and the others plan to create a mess in the government district. She's prioritizing stealth over speed, which is how she avoids the surprise squad of soldiers that pop up around a corner just as she is about to vault over to the next roof.

Taliya drops to the ground quickly and rolls behind a chimney, hoping no one catches a glimpse of her, straining her ears to listen for any indication she's been spotted.

" —just saying, I hate those bloody paper pushers that have never left their desks to work the field a day in their lives but think they can tell *us* what to do."

"Someone needs to be doing it, I guess. Are you volunteering to do some paperwork?"

A shrill, outraged noise erupts, signaling Taliya that at least one of the soldiers is a Sky Lord with bird attributes. Only their unique vocal cords can make that kind of sound. "Don't fucking joke about that! You're not funny, asshole. What, did someone wake up on the wrong side of the *tree*?"

And an Andan, Taliya notes, likely with tree characteristics. In her short glimpse, she only saw four soldiers, so that's just two she hasn't heard speak.

"Fuck off. Can you never—"

"Will you idiots shut up already?" A new voice. "Being awake in the daytime is annoying enough without you two yapping my fucking ears off."

… And a Nightblood. Interesting. The Taos don't often enlist in the Apolon Empire's army, so this one was likely drafted.

Taliya nearly snorts at the soldier's words, though. Spending so much time with Amari—who never has and never will subscribe to anything resembling a functioning sleep schedule—makes Taliya forget that Nightbloods naturally loathe being awake when the sun's fully out.

There's muffled grumbling that she can hear, and then the fourth voice speaks up. "Hey, do you guys sense anything? I swear I sensed somebody's blood nearby."

Taliya stills.

"Why do you have to say it like that? You're so creepy."

"What way exactly would be better? Hey, I think I felt a *body of water* large enough to be a person and close enough to be concerning?"

Huh. So, if they can sense water to that degree, the fourth soldier is someone with mixed Osiyi heritage. That's… unexpected. Taliya shouldn't be surprised, really; it's not rare for the Sea Folk to make a trip out of the ocean, have an affair or two, and then leave their bastard with the land dwellers. Only *true* Osiyi can reside in the sea kingdoms full-time. So they say.

"How close?"

"Uh, up? To the left a few meters?"

Okay, time to go. Obscured from any view by the chimney, Taliya rises to her feet and takes off in a different direction. She wants to backtrack as little as she wants to lead them to her final destination, so to the west, it is.

"H-hey! It's moving!" She catches a few sounds of alarm before moving quickly out of range to listen. Taliya tries to maximize her speed while not attracting attention, jumping over rooftops as little as possible and staying in the setting sun's growing shadows. Only an hour until the night can hide her better, then even more so when Erika turns off the lights.

Lijah is a city of stone and concrete, the hard material solid under her feet. Its structure is not the conveniently anarchic and packed-together architecture of Castor, but Taliya finds her way nonetheless.

The rooftops are a patchwork of weathered shingles and ancient tiles, stretched out like a mosaic. Taliya needs to be mindful of noise as well as mossy patches and ivy tendrils trying to climb to new heights. Ducking under a weather-vane twisting lazily in the breeze, she watches for her reflections in dormer windows peeking out from sloping roofs. She registers and avoids enemy patrols moving through the cobblestone streets with methodical precision, the sound of their boots on the stone echoing faintly. Most of all, she listens for the footsteps chasing her.

After minutes pass of her free-running in no discernible pattern, she starts to cautiously head northward again. Taliya passes more patrols on her way, and no one notices her like the first squad of soldiers. Yet the reprieve doesn't settle her nerves as it should.

She wouldn't admit it to anyone, but the Osiyi's presence is unbalancing her more than she likes. It's not just that they're working for the Empire, Taliya reasons to herself; it's that an Apolon Osiyi soldier is posted in the middle of the gods damned continent. They could not be farther from the sea. Taliya, on her part, did not intend to end up here. The soldier is a different case.

That concern, together with the fact that the Osiyi had sensed her *blood* from that distance, is… worrying.

As the northern edge of the city comes into view, Taliya pushes the issue away from her thoughts. She needs to focus on the job, not on random Empire soldiers. The worry is relegated to an annoying itch at the back of her mind.

Ahead, the buildings line up against the northern wall surrounding Lijah, all dwarfed by the cliff they're set in front of. The rock slashes into the sky above her, setting all below it in shadow. All the better for her.

Most of the properties are non-residential, from what Taliya knows. Company headquarters, factories, storage, and some other services. She scans the buildings from a nearby roof that gives her a bird's eye view.

The wall itself is dozens of meters higher than her, even from her elevated perch, and she keeps a careful watch for any guards or security that might spot her. Thankfully, with the mountains imposing behind the city walls north and south of Lijah, the gates get the most attention. Out here, Taliya is nothing but another shadow in the corner of the eye.

She's looking at her target when the telepathy network comes to life in her mind.

It's — predictably — about how the mission has gotten a change of plans and will be even more difficult than before, but she can't bring herself to be upset about it. The thief will just have to trust Amari to pull it off until she can go help.

Taliya waits for the shadows to shift and stretch until she's confident the night is only minutes away.

The lights of Lijah are still on, but that's fine by her. Everyone's attention is already away from this part of the city. She can hear alarms in the distance and smells ash in the wind.

Her target is a fabric manufacturer factory. Not her most daring heist, she knows. Except it's necessary, so the ease with which she bypasses the wards and heads inside is negligible.

The factory's schedule starts early and ends early, which means Taliya has the whole building to herself, excluding the random security guard half-asleep at their desk. She walks the halls, careful of any recording devices, and opens the door to the factory floor.

The machines are of varying shapes and sizes, with metal conduits snaking along the floors and walls. This factory specializes in clothing materials that can stand up to anything; of course, the place looks elaborate. Taliya has no earthly idea how any of these things work, but she can probably use plain common sense to find what she's looking for.

It's not the only fabric manufacturer in the city, but it's the only one with what she needs. Taliya studies the machines with a critical eye, the—

The feeling of every cell in her body freezing, a paralysis overtaking her so suddenly she almost thinks she's making it up. But an overwhelming power presses around her, *trapping her.*

Taliya does not get trapped, she doesn't, *she doesn't—*

"So *this* is where you ran," a voice speaks from outside the factory room. The door swings open, and the Osiyi soldier, who Taliya thought she had slipped, stalks in. A formless terror strikes through her, before she crushes it and tucks it away to never think of it again. She still can't move, and the urgency of her position settles into her bones.

Breathing feels like a herculean effort, and she's not entirely sure it's due to his magic. Still, her mind turns over the situation, heedless of the rising dread.

He's not singing, and she would be able to tell if the soldier was using runes or an artifice to channel magic. A Conjurer, then.

A Conjurer using blood magic. That's why he's posted in Lijah, despite being so far from any large pools of water. This Osiyi is so incredibly skilled in blood magic that he doesn't *need* any normal water to be an effective soldier.

"You came all this way for little old me?" Taliya doesn't even have to think before a snarky response slips out. The soldier circles her so she can see him as he frowns at her, clearly disappointed she is not quaking in fear before his power.

"You're one of the rebels, I'm sure of it. Bringing you in will be all I need to get promoted, but I want you to tell me," he clenches his fist, and the pressure trapping Taliya quickly goes from unpleasant to borderline agony. "What are your plans? Where are the locations of the other rebels in the city? When—"

"Fuck," it takes great effort to speak coherently. "You."

The pressure tightens even more, before easing enough for her to still breathe. She's feeling lightheaded in a way that is distantly alarming, and her vision swims a bit.

"Clearly, you do not understand the severity of your situation."

Taliya laughs. "No, pretty clear. I'd just rather be tortured than give away information to an imp."

Gritting his teeth, the Osiyi tries to squeeze her again. Taliya is internally scrambling for escape plans. Even though she knows blood magic too, she can feel this soldier's power vastly outmatches her own. *And* he's a Conjurer. She can barely talk, let alone sing.

Her thoughts turn back to the Red City, where she used more blood magic than she ever had before. She thinks of Najaah, whose natural Sun Eater powers pale in comparison to others but still manages to be a force of nature.

She can do this. Taliya doesn't have great power—she can't see the future or move mountains. How she uses it crosses that great divide.

The pressure is still intense, so she screws her face up in a pained expression and plays up her difficulty to speak. "Wai—wait, I—I—"

Smirking, the soldier lets her breathe easily again, looking far too smug for her liking.

Until she starts singing.

The first thing Taliya must do, above all else, is protect her ability to sing. If he tries to choke her again, he will fail. Slowly, she lightens his pressure as the blood in her limbs constricts, almost allowing herself to become distracted by the shocked look on his face.

Due to… past job requirements, Taliya knows the exact part of the brain that deals with controlling magic. It's a risky, risky move to use if you care at all about the person's continued existence, which, at this point, she no longer does.

Conjurers can be mighty magic users, but their power takes incredible focus and an understanding of how their powers work. It's an indication of a terrifyingly capable Conjurer if they can still talk casually and do other things while using their magic. AKA Kol.

This soldier is nothing like Kol. His magic dissipates entirely as soon as she messes up his focus. She takes the chance to paralyze him, too. Taliya would be using up too much power if she controlled all his blood as he did to her, so she chooses to utilize key points to great effect. Like squeezing his lungs.

Her song tapers off, but the magic she laid will last for a few minutes.

"Where's the rest of your squad?" Taliya presses immediately. The soldier lets out a choked-off wheeze, and she sings a note to loosen her grip on his lungs a bit. Internal organs are so delicate.

"They—they didn't want to chase a ghost," he coughs violently, then struggles to continue. "I told them I—I would get all the credit any—anyway."

Taliya can't help the laugh that escapes her. "So you came *alone?* Well, you certainly did find me. Are you pleased?"

She ignores the strangled sound she gets in response, mind turning to what she must do next. It's been a long time since Taliya's killed anyone using blood magic, and it isn't a sensation she's particularly missed. This soldier cannot report back to his superiors about where he found her.

Well, she can at least be nice about it. He wouldn't do the same for her, but Taliya likes to think she's better than an imp. Singing a high note, she uses the blood in his brain to kill him instantly, painlessly.

Taliya leaves the body with a sigh, hands clenched painfully at her sides. Her heartbeat eventually goes back to normal while she returns to her search for what the team needs. The factory is like a maze from her perspective, and it nearly takes her half an hour to find the finished products.

Newly-made Emergency Healing Service uniforms are neatly folded on a table, waiting to be sent to the local medical centers. They'll be stored in hospitals and clinics and, most importantly, *ambulances*. A vehicle people unanimously get out of the way for and don't overly question. Especially during a crisis.

She grabs six uniforms, checking over the sizes before packing them away in her bag. Having what she needs, Taliya quickly heads out of the building after hiding the body to put off the discovery of their plan.

Now, she heads to the jail and to see what chaos her friends have made.

Night truly has fallen outside, to her great relief. The three broken moons shine overhead, and Taliya basks in the familiar light. She didn't realize how much she would miss something so intrinsic to her world until she had to live without it.

Checking the time, the thief notes it's a quarter to 8pm.

She makes it back to the rooftops and starts moving away from the north much quicker than she approached it. Before she gets into the government district, Taliya can already tell that no one will notice her sneaking around. Amari, Najaah, and Kol have caused such a commotion that every soldier is rushing toward them, with only a few left to guard certain areas. The largest groups of soldiers not heading to the jail are the ones converging on places essential to Lijah for it to function. Basically, magic generators that power the city. Erika must be having a fun time with that.

No one is watching as she free-runs across Lijah. The night is here now to cover her anyway, and she keeps an eye on the roads for any ambulances to hijack.

When she finally reaches the jail, Taliya is coming from the back of it, so she can only see flashes of Kol's battle at the front entrance.

A pale dome encases the jail's roof, where Amari is trapped with Marina. The thief frowns at the eyesore, tempted to reach out to her friend in the network. It's better not to interrupt her, Taliya reminds herself. The less distractions for the seer when facing off against someone like Marina, the better.

And, if she looks closer, the thief can spot pale red cracks in the dome. She smirks as the realization that Amari is already in the process of escaping sets in.

Other than the roof, the jail is taking the brunt of the damage from all the fighting. Spots in the building's walls give way to gaping holes and scorch marks. Multiple groups of rioters, prisoners, and soldiers clash violently, and Taliya can only tell the Empire soldiers apart by their uniforms. Shouts and cries of pain fill the air, mingling with the harsh sounds of magic being thrown around haphazardly and the clash of metal on metal. Many of the escaped prisoners gang up on their former guards, moving with desperate energy. Others are ducking behind makeshift barriers and overturned vehicles, their faces grim and determined.

Civilians, caught in the crossfire, flee in all directions, seeking shelter from the madness. Some huddle in alleyways, their eyes wide with fear, while others dash across open streets, hoping to find safety amidst the chaos. The once-bustling district is now a battleground, with overturned stalls and scattered goods trampled underfoot.

Taliya catches sight of one group of escaped prisoners and leans forward to get a better look. They're having a difficult time making it through the chaos, clearly trying to grab a hold of the chance to take back their freedom.

Dropping down onto a fire escape, Taliya considers her options. She doesn't want to draw attention to the protesters, yet magic is about the only way to help them out. Scanning the cracked and scorched plaza, she catalogs which imps are in their way. Then softly, she begins singing.

Using blood magic on multiple people at once is too much for her meager skills. As a child, she had learned to puppet a single person, but that takes too much work. So instead, she focuses on whoever is closest to the protesters. Of course, Taliya doesn't go overboard and paralyze them like a fool. She gently lightens the blood flow to the brain, not enough to do serious harm, but enough to make the soldiers tired and dizzy. She's always been better at precise uses of magic rather than grand shows anyway.

It works like a charm, and the protesters are off the battlefield within a few minutes.

Taliya drops down to the ground near them, startling many of the protesters. "You all should consider getting out of Lijah. This is the best time to escape through the eastern gate."

The protesters stare at her like she's inexplicably turned into a dragon and told them to take her hoard.

"Who are you?" Someone finally speaks up.

"Not an enemy," Taliya says. It's the most truthful she can be that doesn't tell too much. "I'm serious, though."

A slender woman with twisting horns and bright blue skin steps forward. "No, I don't understand, why are you helping us? That was you with the soldiers back there, wasn't it?"

Someone's observant. What a pain. "Does it really matter?"

"We have nothing to give you in return."

Taliya suppresses the instinct to scowl. She's irritated at being told this and irritated at herself for not understanding the protester's more pragmatic desires. "Don't need anything you have. Just go before the imps catch up."

Many of the protesters do start hurrying eastward then, but the woman remains for another moment. She stares Taliya down with sharp and conflicted eyes.

"You're a rebel," she says, quietly enough for it not to be alarming. Taliya still glances around to see if anyone hears her, just in case.

"You have to know I'm gonna say no to that either way."

The woman ignores Taliya's attitude and blurts out, "I want to join the Underground Resistance."

Oh boy. Is Taliya a recruiter now? A recruiter for a group she's not even a part of? Is that what's happening? Mia is never going to let her live this down if she hears about it.

"Yeah, not sure I'm the right person to ask. Are you sure that's what you want anyway? You literally *just* got out of jail."

She hesitates, shuffling her hooves and clasping her hands. "I— It's important, I should…"

Taliya sighs, already knowing that what she's about to say would get her eternal shit from Mia. *And* Amari. "Look, you don't have to decide right in this moment. But you do have to choose. No doubts, no regrets. Pick a choice and *commit*."

Just call her Taliya the Life Coach. Taliya the Therapist. Taliya the—

"That… I can do that. Thank you for your help!" The woman smiles, showing sharpened teeth, and gives her a small bow before running to catch up with the other protesters.

Sighing again, Taliya tips her head back to face the sky and rethinks all her life choices. Then she shoves her mini-crisis to the back of her mind and walks onto the battlefield waiting for her.

Nothing like tripping and smashing some imps to take her mind off something.

Within a few minutes of ambushing a small squad of soldiers, her audacity for assuming things bites her in the ass.

An ear-splitting roar sweeps through the area, and absolutely everyone freezes. Taliya scans the sky as best she can in the darkness, dread pooling in her stomach.

Did you see what that was? Taliya directs her question at Kol and Najaah, knowing the others are nowhere near (Nuru & Erika) or currently trapped with their nemesis-they-refuse-to-call-a-nemesis (Amari).

No, Najaah answers immediately.

Uhhhh, Kol says. *I just helped Amari, so I'm flying higher and… I think I see a dragon coming at us.*

Fuuuuck.

Najaah responds to him while Taliya rethinks her life choices for the second time in twenty minutes. *You **think,** or you **know?***

I mean, there's a large dragon-like shape flying right at me, so — fuck! Okay, okay, definitely a dragon!

Taliya hears a boom that feels like miles above her head and knows that Kol is in some deep shit right now. She racks her head for an answer while wishing Amari wasn't dealing with her own problem at the moment. The fact that this is the second dragon she has seen the Apolon Empire use as a weapon does not escape her. *One of you wouldn't happen to know how to trap or knock out a dragon, would you?*

No? Kol sends back as another large clap of sound resonates. *I'm barely able to dodge this thing!*

I don't think fighting fire with fire is wise in this scenario, Najaah says.

Alright, so it's up to Taliya to figure this out. Great. *Kol, please keep it off the ground as long as you can.*

Fine!

The battlefield has unfrozen. Imperial soldiers have gotten a pretty large morale boost and are starting to turn the tide back in their favor. Taliya wants to deal with that, but the dragon is a much bigger problem.

Najaah, clear the area as best you can. I'm coming over to your side.

The Ashan sends an affirmative, and Taliya makes a break for it while trying to injure any imp she passes by. It's pure luck that none of them seem to be able to both see her well in the night *and* keep up with her speed.

A great shadow passes over her, and Taliya does her level best to ignore it and not start running away like most of the other people in the plaza. By the time she makes it over to Najaah, she feels calmer about the situation. In a 'this might as well happen' sort of way.

"SPEAR is here. They must have brought the dragon with them."

Taliya stares at Najaah, unable to stop the yell building up in her. "Are you serious?"

"Yes. Nadia told me."

"… I need you to give me more than that, dude," Taliya sighs, pinching the bridge of her nose in a way that feels reminiscent of Amari. "Why did she tell you at all?"

"I almost defeated her in close combat. She retreated."

Is this a soldier thing? Is Taliya just missing some context here?

The dragon flies overhead, effectively bringing her back to the present.

"Where are Nadia and Miri now?" Last thing Taliya needs is those two swooping in to cause problems while trying to fight off a dragon. She is still annoyed, remembering her encounter with Miri a few weeks ago. The witch had nearly vaporized her with an experimental grenade!

Najaah points behind her, and the thief whirls around to see Nadia single-handedly taking on a group of golems. Miri darts in between the towering figures, looking like a cat as she does damage while dancing out of the way of any blows. Taliya gawks at the scene for a moment before turning to the Sun Eater, silently demanding an explanation.

"A lot of the locals set their golems on the guards once the riots really picked up. A high-ranking soldier ordered those two to deal with it."

Well, at least Taliya doesn't have to deal with Miri again. "Okay, never mind that. How strong are you?"

The Ashan tilts her head. "As in, how much weight can I lift?"

"Yeah. Would it hold up against a dragon at all?"

"Not by myself," Najaah answers honestly. "Maybe if I have body enhancement runes and ward-support."

Ah, soldiers and their permits to have whatever magic they like. "Yeah, okay. I can do that. I'm familiar with body enhancement runes."

"Because Amari is deaf?"

The words are said with no judgment, which is why Taliya makes no move to clock her. Instead, she shrugs because it's not really an explanation for her to give. Najaah doesn't question further and rolls up their sleeves for Taliya to begin scribing. The thief goes over her idea while carefully using her runica to enhance and fortify the Ashan's natural strength.

Until a loud *boom* and a following *crash* shake the plaza, making her still instinctively.

"What was that?" Taliya turns to Najaah, knowing the other has the better eyesight of the two.

"Kol just got slapped out of the sky and into a building."

"…Ah."

The dragon — now unheeded by a flying pest — turns its attention to the little creatures on the ground. Taliya really wishes it didn't.

"This will have to be enough." Taliya hides away her runica before going to her bag and pulling out the enchanted rope. She hands one end to Najaah. "Here."

"You're sure this will work?"

"Well, we're fucked if it doesn't."

"…Fair enough."

Quick as lightning, Taliya starts tying her end of the long rope to everything nailed to the ground and reinforcing it with more wards as Najaah waits. The dragon scans the plaza for a moment, seemingly ignoring those wearing Empire uniforms, before focusing on them; the only not-imps who aren't cowering in fear. Maybe the dragon just knows who its enemies are, because it dives at Taliya and Najaah with a terrifying grace.

"Scatter!" Taliya yells and runs for a gaping hole in a nearby building. She throws herself through just as the great beast lands on the ground, cracking stone underneath its claws and carelessly causing damage with its spiked tail.

This thing is nothing like what she and Amari saw in the imperial vault months ago. This dragon is fully grown with eyes that speak of tortured intelligence. It must be three stories high at least, and nearly as long as a ship. From the ground, it feels like the divine wrath of the gods everyone grows up hearing. At the back of her mind, Taliya wonders if this is what it was like for Amari.

Then, seemingly unheeded by silly things like mortal terror, Najaah runs into view. They hold the other end of the enchanted rope that runs under the dragon's great big head, and, to everyone's shock, Najaah uses a wall to springboard onto *the dragon's snout, running across it* towards Taliya. The dragon is so taken aback by the teenager's audacity that it doesn't move for a critical second. The rope Najaah is carrying circles the dragon's snout. They drop down to the ground and run back the other way under the its jaw, effectively trapping the dragon's head and keeping its maw shut.

The dragon recovers from its shock and nearly rips Najaah off the ground in a rage as it jerks away from the rope. This creature has never been held down by a single human before, and a shock of panic lights in the dragon's eyes. With the enchantments on the rope itself and Najaah's body enhancements, it's a narrow victory for Taliya's group.

She runs out of the building, dodges a claw that is as tall as her, and defends Najaah from a few Imperial soldiers who try to free the dragon. Luckily, Nadia and Miri seem entirely uninterested in getting close to the dragon, staying with the golems they were specifically ordered to deal with. Taliya is glad she can rely on their sense of self-preservation, if nothing else. "Najaah, when I said the rope could be used to constrain part of it, I didn't mean the *gods-damned mouth.* Are you insane?"

"Then you should have been more specific," the former soldier deadpans.

Taliya's being sassed by a toddler. That's what's happening now. Every time she thinks the Ashan has no sense of fun, they pull shit like this. Najaah, she decides, might have the darkest humor of the entire group, which is an achievement in its own right. "Alright, smartass. What's your step two?"

The dragon is starting a game of fucked up tug of war with

Najaah. Neither side seems to be having any fun.

"I thought you would know, as this was originally your idea," the Sun Eater grits out as their muscles strain. Boots dig into uneven pavement, refusing to slide.

This kid.

"Fine. Keep holding it. I'm going to try to see if there are any weak spots." Taliya very much does not want to do this, but it is necessary. At night, she can't just hope to spot something from a distance. It's better to look now while the streetlights still work, at least.

Dragon scales are one of the toughest materials in Avalon, and the known Planes beyond this one, so piercing the dragon's hide is a no-go unless it has a weak spot in its scale patterns or maybe previous damage done to it.

The beast is fighting against the rope wildly, claws scratching at its own face in an effort to dislodge the enchanted rope. Taliya moves fast while the thing's distracted, ducking under the dragon like the way she had criticized Najaah for doing minutes before.

Taliya has to admit it's terrifying. The dragon doesn't notice her as it's jerking itself around, so she has to constantly dodge a massive leg and claws that could slice her into pieces instantly. At one point, it crouches down, and she is nearly crushed underneath the giant thing.

And yet, she finds no weak points. No convenient spots where the scales do not perfectly armor the dragon, or damage from a previous battle. Taliya isn't sure if that says this particular dragon is new or just undefeated. With her luck, it'll be the second option.

She turns back in Najaah's direction just in time to see an Imperial sneaking up on them, and she's throwing a knife that was stored in her jacket before she even fully processes it.

More imps are flooding into the plaza, and Taliya tries to calculate the best way to defend Najaah's back, when the dragon's claws finally begin to fray the rope. Bit by bit, the enchanted rope gives, and Taliya scrambles for a plan.

A sharp, piercing whistle splits through the chaos in the plaza, and a small blur shoots through the air directly at the dragon. Before the great serpent can react, it ruthlessly hits the dragon's right eye and darts away. Now blinded on one side, a pained roar wretches out of the dragon, sending shivers down everyone's spines.

Everyone—rebels, soldiers, mercenaries, civilians, and prisoners alike—is immediately distracted by this wild turn of events, imps running around frantically searching for the source of the attack.

Taliya tries to trace the small blur as best she can and realizes it's a kind of bird as it slows to land on someone's outstretched arm. She wastes no time putting distance between her and the giant beast, approaching the individual. She's ready for a fight but hoping for an ally.

"Who are you?"

In the shadows, it's hard to make out the person's features. She can see the outline of curly hair and straight horns jutting out, put together with a striking leather jacket. *Dramatic,* she thinks.

"I'm reinforcements. Mia says hello."

Oh. So Mia really did send some help from the Underground Resistance in time. Huh.

"Thanks for the help. Is it just you?"

"Nope," they turn, and Taliya sees a group of five emerging from an alleyway not blocked by rumble, clearly aiming for the imps in the plaza. Najaah looks over to her, and she gives a small nod to signal the newcomers are allies.

Unfortunately, the dragon recovers from its blow and starts pulling at the rope again. It won't last much longer.

"Don't suppose you have a plan for that?" Taliya asks without much hope.

"Didn't even know that was here until a minute ago," her new ally says.

Figures.

"Okay, we need a way to permanently disable it, or at least long enough for us all to escape," Taliya mutters, mind running through options.

"Obviously," the Resistance member snorts. "Killing a dragon isn't an option, even if this one is a pet of the imps."

That's right. You can't kill a dragon.

Well, Taliya is aware that it's *possible*, it's just highly inadvisable. And illegal in most countries. Which makes the way that the Apolon Empire uses them as weapons all the more despicable.

Dragons are connected to magic and to *Avalon* in a way no human could ever be, and their deaths leave a mark on the world. Their bodies don't decay in the same way humans do, and the results are unlivable for people. Additionally, the more violent the cause of death, the greater the mark left behind on the earth. Some sites of a dragon's death are left uninhabitable for centuries, not unlike Kiyoshi Crater in Castor.

So they're pretty fucked if they don't find a way to subdue this beast without killing it. A delicate balance Taliya isn't sure they have time to walk.

This is when Kol reappears, like a dusty and bruised savior sent to save them. He's floating down from the roof he was batted away into, looking at the scene with an expression Taliya can only describe as baffled.

"What the fuck?" He says, gawking. Taliya supposes that between Najaah lassoing a dragon and the new reinforcements fighting the influx of imps, the plaza looks a bit chaotic.

"Hey, sky rat, are you still able to chuck rocks, or do you need to go lie down?"

Kol gives her a disgruntled look, fingers running through his unfixable messy and dirty hair. "Yeah, whatever."

Taliya's new friend laughs aloud from beside her. "I'll have my familiar help distract the beastie. It's blinded in its right eye, so it's got a big weakness now."

The runaway prince seems reluctantly impressed and nods in agreement with the plan. After some internal debate, Taliya decides to inform their new allies of the city-wide blackout plan, so to prepare them for when it happens. Erika should be done any minute now.

The sky rat and bird take off just in time, as the rope frays to the point of breaking, and Taliya signals for Najaah to drop it and get to cover. Kol and the familiar keep the dragon occupied for a few precious minutes. All the while, Taliya has a terrible idea brewing in the back of her mind.

Then all the lights in Lijah go out.

Taliya huffs. "Right on time."

Kol swears excessively, barely managing to dodge a spiked tail in the sudden darkness. It takes a while for everyone's eyes to adjust, and Taliya plus allies use the time to ambush as many unprepared imps as they can.

After a few minutes of fighting alongside Najaah, she stops to breathe and tries to think of an actual *solution*.

Then Amari drops down next to her from the jail's roof. Taliya almost screams. The smug bastard just gives her a knowing look. "Seems some things have happened while I was trapped."

"Just a few."

"Need my help?"

Taliya shrugs, braids falling into her line of vision that she has to brush back "*Nah*, who needs you? We got this handled fine."

Amari snorts and shoves her shoulder. "So, seriously, tell me what's happening."

"You first. Where's Marina?"

The ghost of a smirk makes its way onto Amari's face. "Unconscious and with her retreating friends."

Taliya belatedly looks around and sees that, yes, Nadia and Miri *are* gone. "Nice."

"And you?"

"Mia sends her regards."

The seer smiles genuinely this time. "She sent the calvary?"

"Something like that."

"And the dragon?"

"Colonel Bashkim also sends *her* regards."

"… Ah. Fantastic."

The telepathic network activates in the back of Taliya's mind, but she focuses on the fight in front of her, trusting the others will handle it if it's serious.

"Erika needs help," Amari says, glancing between the dragon and the jail. Then she turns to Najaah. "Najaah, you go."

"Alright."

"Can we spare them?" Taliya asks quietly, even as the Ashan is already moving quickly toward Erika's last known location.

"We have to."

Kol narrowly avoids a lunge, and the dragon partly crashes into a building. The building takes far more damage, but the beast seems to wobble before flying after Kol again.

"The jail," Amari says with a certainty that preludes her most insane plans.

"Oh?"

"It's empty now, every prisoner escaped, and every guard is chasing after them. Just a great big building, whose bottom floors are already busted."

Taliya sees the shape of the plan and whistles quietly. "If you're sure. How are we getting it back on the ground?"

"Bait."

Great. Three guesses who is acting as the bait. "That's a bad idea."

"Do you have a better one?"

Sighing, Taliya admits, at least to herself, that her only idea is arguably worse. "Okay, well you're not doing it alone, at least."

Amari stares at her with an assessing gaze for a moment, then smiles. "Yeah, alright. Let's go set a trap for a dragon."

The actual trap—the jail—takes many volunteers, since the building must collapse at just the right moment, and it has to be all at once. Taliya writes runes on specific points around the jail to set up a chain reaction so that when activated all at the same time, the place goes down at once. Mia's reinforcements are spread out around the perimeter of the jail, waiting for the signal to activate the rune. They also keep civilians and imps away from the building.

Amari relays the plan to Kol through the network, and he, plus the familiar, has been slowly leading the dragon towards them in the sky. Once the trap is set, Kol lands on the ground in front of the jail, running over to where Amari and Taliya stand before what is left of the main entrance. After the breakout, it's more of a massive hole in the wall.

The dragon crashes to the ground in front of them, cement taking even more abuse. Its spiked tail flicks behind it, carelessly smashing into things. The claws dig into the pavement like it's dirt.

Disregarding the original layout of the building, Amari has created a route that leads directly to a giant magic circle at the center of the jail, which will bind the dragon to it. There's a bulldozed path large enough for the creature that leads straight to it and a small exit for them to escape through. Once the circle activates, the reinforcements will collapse the whole building.

Running through the jail is both simple and one of the most nerve-wracking things Taliya has ever done. Amari made sure to make the path easy, but the large dragon chasing them—head smashing through the ceiling to the next floor, body creating an even bigger gap in the building—makes the whole experience mind-numbingly terrifying. Everything shakes around them, and would no doubt already be falling on their heads if not for the reinforcements holding off collapse outside.

They finally reach the magic circle and slow down just a bit after passing it, wanting to make sure the trap works.

The dragon skids to a stop in front of the edge of the magic circle that's meant to bind it in place and lets out a roar that shakes the building down to its foundations. It must sense the large amount of energy it takes to power a circle, something that usually means a group effort. If they don't get the creature in that circle, they're pretty fucked.

Taliya recalls her extremely bad idea. "Might as well," she mutters to herself.

Quietly, unnoticed by everyone else, she begins to sing. The song she barely remembers being sung to her as a child, the one meant to send someone to sleep. It's a mix of blood and siren magic, a psychological and biological push to *sleep*.

Naturally, Amari catches on first—more out of feeling than anything else—and quickly deactivates her hearing runes. She motions to Kol to cover his ears and start backing out towards the exit as quickly as he can. The seer turns to Taliya, hand reaching out and clasping their hands. A powerful rush of energy fills the thief, and she grins at the support.

Taliya sings, and the dragon sways slightly. The next roar is less powerful, more subdued.

Her throat begins to ache as more magic than she's ever felt before runs through her veins, and the dragon snarls. She can feel it fighting against her enchantment, feral and furious.

Sleep, Taliya sings, again and again, Amari standing like an unmovable guardian next to her. She doesn't stop, even as she stands in front of the exit. She doesn't leave and keeps singing. Singing until both she and the dragon are unable to move anymore. The beast's great legs buckle beneath it, falling partway into the magic circle. It activates, and a rush of adrenaline hits Taliya like a punch to the chest. She needs to get *out*.

With all the energy she has left, she and her friend dash out the exit, barely making it out as the building collapses, trapping the dragon in it. She can taste blood in the back of her mouth, but Taliya disregards it, stumbling out of the rubble.

Amari catches her immediately, eyes scanning her narrowly. "You alright?"

Sending her a shaky thumbs up, the thief lets out a slightly hysterical laugh. The seer snorts at that reaction before focusing her attention on monitoring the dragon's status. It should stay unconscious and bound, for now. Taliya watches tiredly as Amari turns her runes back on so she can go order some of the Underground's people.

Exhausted, Taliya staggers away to go lean against a wall that's still standing. She isn't sure how long she just stares off into space before checking back into the world again.

As soon as she feels well enough, Taliya climbs to the nearest stable roof to survey the situation.

From her spot, she can see that Kol's dealing with some leftover imps, and the Underground Resistance members are helping Amari monitor the dragon, just in case.

She's considering helping Kol when Taliya spots Najaah and Erika arriving and heads over to them. The poor kids were apparently in their own collapsing building, and Erika's looking at the jail's rubble warily.

"What happened here?" Erika asks, eyes wide. The teen's brown hair is covered in dust, but otherwise, she seems fine.

"Well..." Taliya grimaces.

"There's a dragon trapped under the collapsed jail," Najaah says bluntly. Erika whips her head over to the Ashan, mouth gaping.

"A *what?!*"

"Yeah," Taliya answers, putting as much casualness in the words as she can. Watching Erika flounder in the face of their calm might be the best part of this day. She eventually decides to have mercy. "It's fine, Erika. The imps had a dragon in their arsenal, it came after us, and now it's trapped under that mountain of rubble."

"*What?*"

Okay, maybe Taliya doesn't have much mercy at all.

"It's still alive?" Najaah comments, tone neutral but with an underlying urgent question. Taliya nods while her mind goes over the problem.

"Of course it is."

She leaves Najaah to deal with the explanation for an alarmed Erika, who doesn't seem to know many facts about dragons over the myths. Amari eventually joins her in standing apart from the others.

"The dragon didn't speak at any point, did it?" Amari questions softly from beside Taliya. She turns to the seer.

"Yeah. What do you think that means?"

"They might not know how to speak at all. The Empire would see no need for it as long as they followed commands."

That's fucking depressing. Now, Taliya is starting to feel guilty toward a giant lizard.

"So what do we do?"

"Well, we obviously can't kill it," Amari says. Her voice is firm in the way it gets when she is certain about something. "That would be devastating for Lijah, and, I feel, worse in the long run for us. We should just leave it trapped and escape. The Empire will take it back, but we'll all escape with our lives."

"Is that a feeling or a Feeling?"

Amari pauses to consider it. "Both."

"Then we keep it sleeping until everyone's gone."

"I'll relay it to the others," Amari walks away to where the team's teenagers and Mia's reinforcements are in discussion.

Taliya stands around for another minute thinking before she notices a bird flying toward her. It takes her a second to realize it's Nuru's second form. He must have finished putting knock-out drugs in all the food and drinks in the imp's camp outside the main gate. Nuru's mission was to secure their exit, so if he's back, things should be over soon.

He lands close to her and shifts so quickly that Taliya feels like she misses the transformation just by blinking.

She smirks at him. "Finished terrorizing the imps?"

Nuru seems like he is barely restraining himself from rolling his eyes at her. "I've done all I can. Have you got the uniforms?"

"Yeah, no ambulance, though."

"That's alright, I saw a few on the way. I'll ask Kol to follow me and help me commandeer one."

"He's a bit banged up, maybe ask Najaah. They're fast enough to keep up with you."

Nuru nods. "Alright… Just one question, Taliya. Since you don't seem to be mentioning it."

She tilts her head. "What?"

"I have a very good sense of animals, you know."

"And?"

"And… Is there… a dragon under that pile of rubble?"

Taliya can't help the laughter that overtakes her, loud and unrestrained. Nuru looks miffed in the face of her breaking down laughing in front of him, but she can't bring herself to care. Eventually, the shapeshifter gets sick of her and goes to find Najaah so he can 'talk to someone with common sense,' or whatever that means.

Left alone, Taliya finds an unbroken bench to sit on and sinks back into her thoughts as soon as the hysterical laughter leaves her. One thing has been at the back of her mind for a while.

What Nuru said in the Archive about responsibilities had been sticking with Taliya as this job played out. Amari and Taliya aren't full members of the Underground Resistance, yet they regularly work with them. Independent while staying in the organization's orbit. Maybe that needs to change.

Taliya definitely hadn't been in a place to consider it when she first met Amari, who already carried a large grudge against the Empire, but she had told herself she didn't care for so long. Even now, Taliya didn't fight Imperials without getting something out of it. Without her hangups, she's sure Amari would be taking charity cases left and right.

That core of practicality will never leave Taliya, and Amari will never ask her to disregard it, but maybe she can stop holding back. With the Underground's support, they might be able to do real damage to the Empire and make real change for the people suffering under its control.

Or maybe Taliya is spending too much time around idealists.

"I can hear you brooding from the other side of the plaza," Amari says as she sits down next to Taliya on the bench. "Is it something to do with the job?"

"Not exactly."

"So, it's related, but not something to do with all the people trying to kill us."

Taliya snorts and tips her head to Amari, conceding the point. "Pretty much."

"Any plans on sharing or going to keep staring at the walls like they owe you money?"

Hiding a smile, Taliya huffs. "Okay, okay. Been thinking about the Underground Resistance."

Unsurprisingly, Amari straightens at the mention of an Apolon

Empire-related topic. "In what way?"

"In a 'maybe we should make it official' way."

The seer says nothing, waiting for Taliya to explain more, even as she feels Amari's body thrum with barely repressed interest.

Taliya sighs deeply, making it as put-upon as she can. "It might be nice to make this fuck-the-Empire thing a full-time gig. I mean, half our jobs are basically from or through the Underground now, anyway. Nuru's thinking about joining after this. It might be worth looking into."

"That's," Amari seems pleasantly surprised, with an undercurrent of excitement. "That sounds great, Taliya. With Mia and the others in Nisha, we could start getting direct lines to the Underground's information on the Empire. We could pick our own missions!"

Despite being unable to hide her smile this time, Taliya attempts to give Amari a look. "You sound like you've been planning this awhile."

"No! I'm just saying, this is great!" Amari grins and leans into Taliya's side briefly in a burst of affection. "You could really find out who's the best wardbreaker now."

"Oi, I already know!"

They both laugh for a minute, excitement at the new possibilities before them at the front of their minds. Taliya settles back on the bench, feeling more resolved than she's felt in a long time. Even if their efforts end in a blaze of glory, she doesn't think she would regret going out fighting against the Empire with Amari.

A few minutes later, Nuru signals that everything's ready for them to go. It takes another minute of hasty movement before everyone is changed into first responder's uniforms and clambers into the emergency vehicle. Nuru is driving, as he is the only one who has gone unseen by any soldiers in Lijah while the rest of them sit in the back. He turns on the emergency lights, which signal the rest of the city to stay out of the way.

There's a tense moment at the checkpoint before the gate where they're almost stopped, but the sheer chaos of the situation, coupled with the army being spread too thin, is in their favor. No one is really prepared to stop an ambulance right now.

They leave Lijah behind, no one looking back.

26

ERIKA-AMARI

The trip from Lijah to Castor is anticlimactic.

After all the excitement in the Planes and in the city itself, Erika was sure that dozens of obstacles would pop up. That seems to be the theme of this whole trip.

Yet, nothing. The ambulance takes them far enough away from Lijah that they can safely switch vehicles and change into normal clothing. The next day, they meet with a contact from the Underground and are on a flying carriage to Esma within the hour. From there, Castor is just a boring two-hour train ride. She gets to finish the book she's currently reading.

Erika doesn't know what it says about herself that she finds the whole ordeal of waiting for the other shoe to drop more taxing than her mission to sabotage the generator. By the time they're all gathered in Amari and Taliya's apartment, she's *exhausted*.

The speed at which things are happening makes Erika's head spin, but she doesn't point this out to Amari. After all, she's the one who insisted on a sped-up timetable. It feels like only yesterday she saw the sky for the first time, and at the same moment, she feels like it's been years since she was last home. In actuality, it's been over two months. Or maybe more, since time passed differently in the Planes?

The sun is sinking below the horizon, the sky painted in pinks and purples. The bustling of everyone in the apartment goes down as the light fades, and eventually, Erika can't hold out against her rising exhaustion.

As soon as her head hits the pillow on the hastily prepared couch, she's out.

After waking up to the sun fully above the horizon, Erika goes to find Kol, but he's gone.

At first, she's more confused than anything else. Then, as she looks around, Erika realizes what most likely happened. In all the drama and fighting, none of them had had time to look closer at what they had brought back from the Archive. Everyone else, at least, had a good idea of what they were getting.

But Kol had no idea what those files about his birth family would contain. He must have read them when they were finally safe. When everyone was exhausted and finally resting.

Why would he run? What did he find? Erika sits in an armchair, staring out the window. Maybe she's overthinking, and Kol only left temporarily.

Someone walks out of the hallway, and she jerks to look over at them. Najaah is eyeing Erika curiously as the Sun Eater makes her way to the kitchen. The former soldier has been consciously trying to be a bit louder when she moves so as not to sneak up so much on everyone else, though Erika cannot tell if the fact that she's wearing house slippers helps or not.

"Hey, Najaah," Erika says. She hesitates briefly before continuing. "Have you seen Kol? His stuff's gone too, I think he…"

Najaah doesn't reply immediately, instead focusing on making tea. "He left the building in the middle of the night. He seemed in a hurry."

Erika nods, absorbing this. She doesn't ask why Najaah didn't stop or question him. She wouldn't expect the former soldier to insert herself into someone else's decisions like that.

The Ashan brings her a cup of tea, and the two sit in silence for a few minutes before Erika breaks it.

"Do you think—do you think he'll be alright?" She feels ridiculous as she asks this, yet Najaah doesn't seem to mind.

"Kol has proved he can take care of himself." Najaah and Erika both recall the kitchen disaster simultaneously. "To a degree."

"Yeah…" Erika doesn't know what else she wants to say when Amari walks in next.

The seer seems to catch some of the tension in the room, then dismisses it. "So, what are your plans?"

Erika straightens, surprised at being asked. "Uh, well, I need to go home, you know, to bring the artifact back."

She doesn't understand why she feels so awkward. Najaah is giving her an unreadable look before turning to Amari. "I will break my contract."

Erika opens her mouth to ask a question, thinks better of it, and stays silent.

Amari nods as if it makes perfect sense. "Good luck, both of you. When do you plan on leaving the apartment?"

The cup in Erika's hands feels so cold now for no discernible reason. "I don't know. I guess as soon as the way out of the city is safe."

Humming, Amari ponders this and then smiles. "Well, the Hall has a celebration this afternoon, no idea what for, so maybe stick around for that. The people here know how to throw a party if nothing else."

"Oh! Cool, I'll go," Erika isn't sure where the sudden relief coursing through her veins comes from, and fiddles with the sleeves of her hoodie. Isn't she supposed to be missing home right now?

Najaah drains her tea. "I'm leaving today as well, but I'll stay for the afternoon." She gets up and heads back to the office, where hers, Nuru's, and Erika's belongings are dumped.

Amari watches the Sun Eater go with a thoughtful expression before focusing on Erika. "You okay?"

"What? Oh, yeah, I'm good," Erika hesitates. "Everyone's leaving. Did you know Kol left in the middle of the night?"

Amari sits in the chair Najaah vacated with all the grace of someone who doesn't care about appearances. Her horns dig into worn indentations on the back of the armchair. "I'm not surprised."

"Why?"

She gestures around the apartment. "We aren't a group made out of people who typically stay in one place long."

Erika stares. "You and Taliya live here."

"It was years before we did, and even now, we don't stay for long before running off on jobs. Taliya would start climbing the walls if we didn't," Amari smiles wryly. Then the seer gives Erika a look she can't decipher. It seems sympathetic, but she doesn't know why. "It's okay to be sad."

"About what?"

"Nothing lasts."

She feels a shiver run down her spine. Amari's eyes look too knowing, sometimes. At least now the Nullifier has an idea why.

"I don't want to leave so soon," Erika whispers, not wanting to speak the words too loudly. There's a lump in her throat and a stinging in her eyes. Her friend looks at her, eyes softening, and smiles wryly. "But it has to be today."

"Well, better to leave under the cover of dark," Amari says gently.

"Mia and I can get you safe transportation to wherever you need to go."

"Kilahn," Erika answers, because that's as close to a location as she can give. The seer nods thoughtfully and seems to come to a decision. She gets up and grabs a book off the shelf that lines the side wall. It's a medium-sized tome yet large in width, with a hefty weight to it. The cover is blue with silver accents, and as Amari passes it to her, she stares at the title printed in swirling font.

"*The Fabric of the Arcane: Understanding Magical Theory and Energy Flow,*" Erika reads aloud, tracing the lettering with her fingers. It's in Esmesian, which she's better at reading than speaking.

"It's yours," Amari says, making the teen rip her eyes away from the book. "Since you have to return all the library books you got. And I know you're interested in this kind of thing. I think it will do you a lot of good in the future."

"You're sure?"

Erika winces at the double meaning of her question, feeling hesitant to reference the seer's powers.

Amari just smiles. "Yeah. Even when things end, it doesn't erase what happened. You're different than when you started, and that's not something to reject."

Tears sting her eyes, and Erika hastily wipes them away. How did her friend know she'd been so worried about what her return home would be like?

The seer continues. "Endings mean the start of something new. You can mourn the end of something while celebrating the beginning of something else."

Erika swallows, looking away but feeling warmer than she did before. "Can I—I might need to contact you again. If—"

"Sure," Amari interrupts, giving her a small grin. "Taliya, Nuru, and I are thinking of officially joining the Underground Resistance."

"Really?" She leans in, feeling excited despite herself. "That's great!"

"Yeah, and don't worry, Erika," Amari has that look about her again. "I have a feeling this is far from the last time we'll meet."

This time, the premonition is comforting, and Erika smiles widely. "I hope so."

They sit in a comfortable silence until Taliya bursts from her room, wearing a bedazzled jacket. Erika blinks furiously as the sunlight reflects violently into her eyes.

"Why is everyone sitting around? I hear Trasary is bringing the fountain and the homemade fireworks again!"

Amari chuckles and stands up with a stretch of her arms while the Nullifier turns the words 'homemade fireworks' over in her head. She tries to imagine what such a thing is. Nope. Still doesn't make sense.

"Go get Nuru and Najaah if you're so impatient," the Nightblood retorts, snorting and waving at her friend to go collect them. Taliya practically breaks down the door to the office, and they can hear muffled yelling from the living room.

A thought occurs to Erika, making her frown. "Where does the Hall host parties? You're right next to the most haunted site in the city."

A slow grin grows on the seer's face, purple eyes shining. "I'll show you, come on."

Not waiting for Taliya to get the others, Amari drags Erika out of the apartment and to the Hall's stairwell. They climb up, past the third floor to the access door to the roof.

"Seriously?"

"Yep!"

Being pushed out the door, Erika nearly stumbles and then proceeds to gape at what she finds.

The roof's structure seems reasonably basic for a building like the

Hall, which has clearly seen better days. But what makes Erika stare is the apparent love that goes into making it beautiful. Plants litter every other spot, filling the otherwise dull gray building in every color she can name. The ground is painted in swirling patterns of purple, silver, and gold beneath her feet.

Under a canvas to defend against the elements are comfortable-looking chairs and benches, along with tables to sit around and a fire pit that can be wheeled out into the open on clear nights.

She can't tell if the floating lanterns, dance floor, and fountain are always there or are for events. The snack table and music setup have to be temporary, right?

Scattered clusters of people are already there, many of whom Erika recognizes from the Hall meeting she went to. The teen is surprised by how long ago that time feels now.

"Okay, really," Erika mutters furiously to Amari. "Why is there a party today?"

"Isn't it obvious?" A new voice answers, turning her attention away from her friend. Walking toward her is Kalsa Ortiz, the large man dressed in a hilariously soft and colorful sweater. If the purpose is to make the giant seem less intimidating, it works. "We're celebrating the theft of the Eindrides and the thieves who escaped getting caught."

"What?" Erika's mouth drops open again. She sends an alarmed glance in Amari's direction, except the seer looks unbothered. Does he know about them?

"The news has been breaking rather explosively," Amari comments, stealing her focus. "I wonder who leaked the information to the public?"

The giant shrugs, uncaring. "Better not to know, but I'm certainly thankful for the good news."

Erika is standing between them, still processing. So their actions are now known publicly? What does that mean for them? Does that mean the giant does or doesn't know that they're the thieves? "Why celebrate this?"

"Because no one here likes the Empire," Kalsa smirks faintly at the teen, eyes twinkling. "And Jared wanted an excuse to use the chocolate fountain."

"Ah…" Whatever Erika might say in response to that is interrupted by a loud shout, and she turns to see a woman with blue skin set off a device labeled firework in big letters. Instinctively, she tenses in preparation for something bad to happen next.

The noise is loud, but the teen watches in awe as the colorful sparks shooting into the sky turn into hundreds of tiny birds that fly all around. A pair of young twin boys start chasing the small constructs, laughing in delight while adults watch on the sidelines.

The scene is such a contrast to the chaos she last saw in Lijah and the Red City that Erika feels her mind has trouble grasping it. How can the people be so calm here?

A shoulder bumps into hers, and the teen turns to look at Amari, who is giving her a sad smile. Erika hadn't realized how piercing the seer's eyes were before, and now she feels stripped of all secrets.

"You good?"

"Yeah," Erika says quietly, glancing back toward the party. The circus troupe she remembers from the Hall meeting is lounging on some of the furniture with an avid audience as they spin entertaining stories. While a few teens about her age are mobbing the snack table as they loudly discuss something, she spots the woman who brought a ton of animals with her to the meeting surrounded by even more concerning creatures. None of them seem burdened by the events that have taken place in the last month because they don't directly affect them.

Something about that drains the tension from Erika's frame, relieving an anxiety she didn't even know she had.

Behind her, the door to the roof opens, and the rest of her friends tumble out. Taliya is still in her eye-straining get-up, and Nuru even seems to be dressed nicely, while Najaah seems more toned down yet surprisingly casual. The thief beelines for the snack table, hooking an arm through Amari as she passes by to drag the seer with her. A laugh bubbles up in Erika at the affronted look on the Nightblood's face.

Kalsa lights up at the sight of Nuru and goes to greet the shapeshifter, leaving Erika with Najaah as they survey the partygoers.

"I'm not sure what I expected," the Sun Eater huffs, looking out at the controlled chaos. "This city seems full of eccentric characters."

"It's nice," Erika smiles, and belatedly processes the words 'chocolate fountain.' She gasps, frantically searching the roof. It's at the end of the snack table and is the greatest thing she's ever seen.

It's only later—once she's made some unwise choices and given herself a stomachache—that her dread at leaving everything behind creeps up on her again. Erika throws herself into conversations with her friends and with complete strangers to distract herself.

She learns more about seafaring than she ever considered before, just standing within earshot of one man. Not long after, the teen is regaled by epic nights performed by members of the strange circus troupe that lives in the Hall. Briefly, Erika is in-between two residents arguing over the price of groceries. In the midst of the partygoers, she acquires more knowledge about living Upside than she did her entire time in Kilahn.

The twin boys she first spotted—Link and West—nearly bowl her over as they run by holding sticks that have a crackling fire on the ends, delighted laughter echoing behind them. Erika marvels at whoever decided it was a good idea to let children barely bigger than toddlers hold what amounts to tiny, violently sputtering flames. She wonders if these are like the fireworks Taliya mentioned earlier. The prospect is a bit alien to her, as most forms of open flame are considered a hazard when everything is underground.

Her mind blanks of everything except amazement when the *real* fireworks are set off. It makes the one from earlier seem more akin to the small poppers the twins held. They're loud blasts of color that threaten to overwhelm her, and yet, she can't step away. The lights move in unnatural ways in the sky, taking the shape of plants and animals that chase each other through the air. Erika is only pulled back to earth when, ironically, a firework takes the form of a dragon that slashes across the horizon.

Goosebumps rise on her arms, and she looks discreetly for her friends. Najaah is standing nearby, face strangely impassive, while Nuru openly grimaces. Amid the cheers of the party, she thinks she sees Taliya and Amari duck away from the sight.

Eventually, Erika exhausts herself from social interaction and retreats to the sidelines of the party. She leans against the railing lining the roof's edge and looks toward the sky.

It will never get old to her, the Nullifier thinks. The endlessness of it, the limitless space around her. It's a greater freedom than she had ever dreamed of.

"I can't wait for everyone back home to see this," Erika whispers to herself as a breeze whistles by. Her hair moves with it, and she can't help smiling.

Erika is taken by the view overlooking Castor as the sun sets behind the horizon, casting deep purples and fiery oranges across the sky. Even the city itself is a wonder. The skyline is dominated by towering spires and intricate archways, each structure adorned with ornate carvings and gargoyle-like sentinels that seem to watch over the bustling streets below. The tallest buildings, constructed from dark stone and shimmering glass, reflect the twilight in a kaleidoscope of colors, giving the entire city an otherworldly glow.

Despite the lack of support the Lower District has, she can so clearly see the care that goes into keeping this place livable. And beautiful, too. Tall, narrow structures twist up high, their facades embellished with delicate filigree and intricate stained-glass windows that depict scenes of ancient legends and magical lore. Balconies decorated with lush greenery and blooming flowers protrude from every level, adding vibrant splashes of color against the darkened backdrop.

She's still surveying Castor City's Lower District sprawled below them when Amari walks up next to her. The sun is sinking below the horizon, lit up like the colors of the fireworks she just witnessed.

"Have you enjoyed staying in the city?" There is a note of slyness to her question, and Erika can see a small smirk on the other's face when she glances at Amari out of the corner of her eye.

"Is it always like this?"

"Like what?"

Erika gives Amari her most Unamused Look. It must not be very impressive because the Nightblood chuckles in response.

"Seriously, is it always… so miraculous?" Castor City is constantly changing, infested by the eccentric and defiant.

"Miracles are for the gods. We have magic and the sacrifices it demands."

She knows, in a distant way, that the perception of magic to Upsiders and Nullifiers is different, but it's still surprising to hear. "There's really a difference?"

"Our magic is our life. Think of it like this: the abilities we are born with and the energy we can bend are our ordinary, Erika. Miracles are for the unbelievable, not the everyday."

She considers this. It makes sense, in a way. To call Kol's ability to fly and make things float anything but a miracle is incredibly strange, though.

A thought occurs to Erika. "If magic is life, does that mean anything with enough magic is technically alive? Even things like stone?"

"Close enough."

"... So the city is alive?"

Amari shrugs. Erika very much does not appreciate the vagueness of this reply.

Having sympathy, the Nightblood gives another answer. "It depends on your definition of alive."

"My definition? Can it think?"

"... That depends on your —"

"Okay! I get it," Erika says, crossing her arms. "You don't get it either, do you?"

In response, Amari decides to smile mysteriously. Erika valiantly resists the urge to stick out her tongue.

"Castor protects its own," is what the seer says eventually. None of these replies are very helpful.

"What happens when people in the city fight each other then? Can't be all good."

"No, it isn't. I guess you could say Castor is the closest thing to a neutral party we have here. Wealth, power, status — they all mean nothing in the end. There were protests once, decades ago, over labor conditions, I think. As far as I can see, the laborers were completely justified, but the city didn't do a thing when the corporations suppressed the protests. I think Castor expects us to sort ourselves out when it comes to each other."

Erika really isn't fond of Amari talking about the city she's currently standing in like it's a sentient being.

"Sounds difficult."

"Everything has a price when it comes to magic. You can't make something out of nothing, you can't bring back what's gone, and you can't push past your limits without consequences."

"I feel like that defeats the point of magic."

Amari laughs. "That's why we say miracles belong to the divine.

The rest of us have to struggle and deal with each other. No place in Avalon can be perfect. Not in the sea, on the surface, or above the ground."

"Or under," Erika mutters, then goes completely stiff. Amari smiles wryly.

"My hearing runes suddenly powered off," she says. "The future voices were very loud just now, and I heard nothing."

Erika's shoulders slump despite herself, like the strings holding her up cut without warning. She gives a small, grateful smile and gladly turns the conversation around to less secret-filled topics.

The party starts to disperse as the first, then the second moon rises. Eventually, the remaining members of the team congregate around the now-lit fire pit. She's curled up on a loveseat when Najaah decides it's time for the former soldier to go.

No one can fault her for hurrying out the door. Erika can't imagine how long the Sun Eater has been waiting for this opportunity.

"Goodbye," Najaah says, looking unsure for a moment before the emotion is tucked away. Resolving to be brave, Erika takes the initiative and hugs her friend. The other teen towers over her, so when she hugs back hesitantly, the Nullifier feels like she's being held by a giant. It's surprisingly nice.

"Take care of yourself," Erika tells the Sun Eater firmly, trying to put as much authority as she can in the words. Logically, she knows Najaah is perfectly capable of taking care of herself, but she's allowed to worry.

"… I will."

Leaving is bittersweet. Since night has fallen and Najaah has already left, Erika stops stalling. She goes back to the apartment to pack, taking the time to be careful with all the new possessions and treasures she has. From clothes to the Divine Claim itself.

Despite her best efforts, Erika ends up shedding a few tears. It's embarrassing and makes her whole face heat up, except no one bothers her about it. Nuru hugs her goodbye, telling her firmly that she shouldn't worry about Kol, and that he hopes she enjoys going home. Erika will admit to tearing up even more after that, just a little.

Mia even drops by to say goodbye.

The red-eyed Nightblood is unsentimental yet generous with her help. She has a train ticket for Erika that will take her directly to Kilahn and some simple identification papers to use to get past security without a problem. Taliya insists on stuffing a purse of cash in her backpack anyway, saying it's better to have funds 'just in case.'

Along with the book, Amari gives her a bracelet made of the gems Erika recalls seeing when she first came Upside. The ones that let you communicate long-distance like a phone.

"But I'm—"

"I stored some magic in the gems already," Amari cuts her off, smirking faintly. "So you can make at least one call without needing any magic yourself."

It's so thoughtful that Erika hugs her, too, making the seer stiffen reflectively. Then she relaxes and hugs back tightly.

"Good luck, Erika."

"Thank you," Erika says. "For everything."

The older woman waves her off with an amused look. "Don't mention it. It'll ruin my reputation."

Taliya walks up next to the seer after showing Mia out, rolling her eyes. "What reputation? You're the biggest softy around."

Retaliating immediately, Amari elbows her partner in the side, making the thief wheeze.

"Anyway, don't forget to be careful, Erika."

The teen smiles as Taliya tries to wrestle Amari to the ground. "I will as long as you guys do too."

"We'll try," Nuru drawls with a dry tone, watching in

exasperation as the two thieves break out into a full-on wrestling match.

Erika leaves her friends in the apartment like that; smiling and laughter trailing off. She steps out of the Hall into the dark streets of Castor, so unafraid of something that would have had her shaking months ago.

The trip is simple, after everything. She knows where the train station is by now and gets on without the nervousness that had permeated her first trip. Her wonder at flying mechanics hasn't changed, and the realization is a pleasant one.

She falls asleep on the journey and wakes up an hour before her arrival. It's enough time to eat a small breakfast and steel herself for the day that awaits her.

The train station of Kilahn is smaller than Castor's and better maintained. Staring around, she's amazed to find the town completely unchanged from when she was last here.

The town that started it all for her.

She takes the time to walk the streets, remembering spots where she hid away from the rain — something she thought so scary, but now pales in comparison to the storms of the Forsaken Forest — or stole to get enough money to eat or fitfully slept away the nights.

Then she walks out of Kilahn to the grassy fields and rolling hills that were her first glimpses of the Upside. She's seen so much since then.

The hidden entrance is difficult to find, but Erika had predicted this problem when she first left and wrote down some small notes on the location before the memories faded with time. It still takes her over an hour of traipsing through the forest and rocky areas to re-discover it.

Opening the entrance, she remembers the door being heavier than it feels now. The scent of damp earth hits her, and the dark tunnels greet her like a long-lost friend. Erika briefly misses her flashlight and heads into the dark, trying to retrace her steps as best as she can.

Honestly, she has no idea if she's going the right way. Except it doesn't matter as she turns a corner and runs into the first other Nullifier she's seen in months.

A guard of Haven Republic stares at her, surprised to find her this close to an entrance to the Upside. Erika's eyes drink in the familiar uniform, the rounded ears, and the hornless head. She can't help the wry smile that overtakes her face.

"Hi," Erika greets. Her first language is a balm and a discomfort on her tongue. "I'm Erika Sinclair. I've been Upside for two months and I have something important that the Republic Council needs to see immediately."

As night falls completely, the city transforms into a realm of shadows and shimmering light. The glowing windows of homes and shops illuminate the streets, and the sound of soft music wafts through the air. She usually loves this time, but all she can feel now is a tired sadness.

Amari watches Erika leave from apartment 2B's window. There's an ache in her heart seeing the people she's spent so much time with recently leave. Najaah, she knows, will look after herself. Erika is going home. Kol… The seer supposes she will have to have faith in Kol.

"What about you?" Amari asks a few minutes later, breaking the silence that has fallen.

"I need to head home as well," Nuru says. The Mokeal Flower must be an ever-present concern at the back of his mind. "My people have been waiting long enough."

Amari nods, making sure her face reads as calm, while Taliya scowls softly as she's slumped in her armchair. "Right."

"However, I think I will return here after the flower is in its rightful place," Nuru announces abruptly. Amari and Taliya look just as surprised as he seems to feel at his words.

The thief sits up in her chair. "Back *here?* Really? Don't you have work?"

"I'm supposed to be retired, actually," he admits. The look on both girl's faces shows precisely how they feel regarding that sentiment. Amari finds the idea rather absurd, considering what she knows of the man. "I know. It doesn't suit me, does it? I think I will have to do something else."

"You actually mean…?" Taliya trails off, a slow grin taking over her face while Amari's eyes light up.

"The Underground Resistance is always looking for volunteers," Nuru says, smiling. "And I think we make a good team."

"Yes!" Taliya cheers while Amari laughs, the skin around her eyes crinkling with the force of her joy. The enthusiasm makes Nuru chuckle, and the ache in the seer's chest eases.

"When I finish my business back home, I will come back, and we can talk to Mia about the Resistance," he pulls out the sphere that Taliya told her had caught his eye all the way back in the Archive. "And we can show them this."

Amari leans forward, focusing intensively on the small sphere. "Is that really…?"

"A star map? Yes. This is an old artifact I recognized in the Archive. It was once used to find natural gates and pathways between worlds. It wasn't as efficient of a method once people learned how to stabilize gateways, but I think the Resistance could find a use for it, don't you?"

"I think they'll be thrilled," Amari breathes, not caring as her grin gives away her excitement. Taliya holds a hand out, and Nuru gives it to her to study. The thief traces the patterns in fascination before passing it to Amari. The seer stares at it intently, feeling it with her magic. Something... "This will definitely be useful. I think it's meant for you, though."

Nuru takes back the star map with a raised eyebrow. "What makes you think that?"

Amari smirks. "Just a feeling."

He harrumphes. "Fine, keep your secrets, but I'm still showing this to the Resistance."

"Of course. Do you need any help getting back home or for the trip back?"

Accepting the change in subject, Nuru launches into the details of his (comparatively short) journey. It only takes a couple hours to iron out his travel plans and for him to be all packed up.

Watching their friend leave is easier this time with the knowledge he will not be gone long.

"Did Mia get it?" Taliya asks the next day, hand movements exaggerated so Amari can see from the kitchen and breaking the calm that had settled in the apartment. Despite this home being meant for two, it feels strangely empty in the wake of everyone else leaving.

"Yeah," Amari signs and abandons her attempt at breakfast in the kitchen to go to her room. She pries open a hidden compartment in the floor and pulls out a wrapped package. Bringing it to Taliya in the living room, she sets it gently on the coffee table.

This is her first time looking at it since Mia discreetly slipped the package to her yesterday, and Amari carefully undoes the wrapping. In her armchair, Taliya leans forward curiously.

A hand-held mirror lies on the table, looking elegant and innocuous at first glance. The handle is iron molded into patterns reminiscent of baroque leaves and the silver metal gleams. That's as far as one would get before the illusion of normalcy falls apart. The mirror's reflection appears almost liquid, rippling and shifting as though it were a surface of water disturbed by a gentle breeze.

"Don't look into the mirror," Amari idly warns her friend, hands snapping quickly. Logically, she knows the thief is likely cautious enough to heed the danger without the seer having even mentioned it.

When Taliya told her that she overheard servants of Governor Jameson talk about a fortune-telling mirror being shipped to the fortress, she thought it was too good to be true. Finding artifacts that belonged to her people is a trial in disappointment. Rarely, she finds anything. Most of the seer's work was destroyed in the wake of the god's wrath, but Amari has always kept an eye out for them.

Resisting the urge to scour the Archive for anything had been intense. Nothing of note had been on Nuru's list, so she had resigned herself to being satisfied with a job well done and administering a blow against the Empire. To have found an actual artifact, if in another way... It makes Amari smile.

Truthfully, objects like this one are a threat to non-seers. Navigating Time magic isn't for the unprepared and inexperienced. That's why relics like this mirror are considered dangerous or cursed, even though the original intention behind their creation was likely benign.

This mirror, specifically, is a novel find. With focused intention, any viewer can catch glimpses of possible futures swirling within the glass. Images flicker like shadows, sometimes clear and vivid, other times hazy and indistinct. Visions may range from mundane moments —a cup of coffee being poured or a child playing in the sun—to monumental events like a grand celebration or the scene of a battle.

The real problem comes from people resisting the temptation to over-rely on such a gift, see something they wildly misinterpret, or become obsessed with getting the future they want. For Amari, the risk is null and void. She has visions of greater significance all the time.

This mirror was likely used as an assistive training tool for young seers.

"Neat," Taliya signs with casual motions, breaking the seer from her musings. "Glad Mia pulled through on that favor."

Yes, the informant had done a good job getting the information on the mirror and sending someone to hit the delivery midway to the fortress since Amari was too busy to go herself. Now that they will be officially joining the Underground Resistance, it will be easy to repay the favor for Mia. Hopefully, the fellow Nightblood doesn't ask for anything exorbitant.

"Hey, is this just a keepsake, or do you think it'll be useful?" Taliya waves her hand at the mirror, genuine curiosity on her face. The seer hums, turning the question over.

"I think it will come into play at some point," she signs, not getting a premonition but making an educated guess. "For now, we keep it safe."

The mirror still calls out to her as she puts it away, making sure to place wards that mask the artifact's power. Nostalgia is a more powerful force of persuasion for her, and she still needs to be careful not to get too caught up in the mirror's magic, even as a seer.

As a kid, Amari remembers reading about seers who trained that connection to be open constantly, people who erased the line between *self* and *Time.*

From what she learned, there were mixed results. Which is to be expected when someone decides to become a permanent conduit for a fundamental cosmic force. Amari has absolutely no desire to follow their example. She doesn't want to move out into a hut in the mountains and be the crazy old oracle heroes go to for unhelpful advice. Amari likes coffee and wandering the streets of Castor at three in the morning, thank you very much.

Mirror safely stowed away, she returns to her quest to scrounge up a suitable breakfast. After weeks away and hosting so many people at once, the kitchen is rather barren. She mentally adds things to a grocery list, debating whether she wants to foist the chore onto Taliya or do it herself to ensure everything is done correctly.

Surprisingly, when she mentions the issue to her friend, the thief jumps at the opportunity to stretch her legs, leaving her in a flurry of jackets and shoes.

All alone in the apartment, the silence rings in her ears, adding a metaphorical weight to her shoulders with Taliya's absence. Sighing, Amari settles in her armchair and tips her head back to stare at the ceiling.

In the wake of everyone leaving Castor, even if Nuru is soon returning, Amari finds herself feeling oddly lonely. Life is too quiet in more ways than one. She has not entertained this feeling often since Taliya came into her life unless her mind is particularly stuck in the past. Now, the apartment is silent in a way that should be familiar and comfortable, except it isn't.

Erika has left Castor and is going to wherever her home is — someplace Amari has no idea the location except for the girl's slip, which implies it is underground. With the Divine Claim, Erika will no doubt have her hands full when she arrives. Amari isn't sure the teen understands the enormity of what she has done for her people, and how much her life will change in the aftermath.

Moreover, Amari hasn't met anyone more independent than Najaah. The Ashan must have been forced to rely only on themself growing up, and Amari has no idea how to begin closing that gap. She doesn't know if she should. Najaah is already on the road to Rowan, in a bid to destroy their Contract. The only help they accepted from Amari was to contact her if they needed a thief.

According to her contacts in the shipyards, Kol safely left Castor a few hours ago and was on a boat heading to the western coast of the Apolon Empire. Amari has no earthly idea why he would go there, but she hopes it works out for him. There's not much more she can do for the Sky Lord now, so she tries to push the subject from her mind.

She pushes all of them from her mind. Gaining a new friend and colleague in Nuru is more than she ever expected from this suicidal mission.

Amari needs to focus on her Present because their actions will affect things — that she knows. It's not a matter of *if* but *when.* She's just wary of how much effect and what or *who* it affects.

Lijah will no doubt face backlash. She and the Resistance have done their best to stymie it as much as possible, but the Empire is not run by sane and reasonable people. Someone there will face the consequences. Amari simply hopes they've done enough to ensure that someone is not every civilian in Lijah.

The Underground Resistance has shown more of itself in the past month and a half than it has in years. The crackdown on rebel activity will spike dramatically if the Grand General's response to the Resistance hasn't changed in the past few years of quiet. And the communication Amari found in the warden's desk clearly implies that it has not.

Depending on how much information the Night Witches are willing to give, Amari and Taliya could be in some hot water. The mercenaries don't know that Castor is their home, but they are well aware that they live in Esma. They could easily give the Empire Amari and Taliya's names, (known) powers, and criminal history. One of the only upsides is that Amari knows the Night Witches aren't allying with the Empire for any reason except money. And Marina doesn't want Amari dead — or, more accurately, doesn't want Amari dead by anyone else's hand. She likely won't give the Empire enough to hunt them down.

The rest of Avalon's reactions are up in the air. The only predictions Amari is comfortable assuming (without her seer magic to back it up) is that Rowan will likely comply with whatever requests Apolon makes in the search for rebels, and the Osiyi will remain neutral. Other than that, Esma, Ilved, Dersuc, and *the Sonai*, apparently? Amari has no idea what they will do or if they'll do anything at all.

Her anxiety looms in the back of her mind like a foreboding shadow at the uncertainty of it all, yet part of her is excited. The world has needed some shaking up for some time. Avalon has become stagnant in its delicate balance of oppression and peace. And nothing good comes from stagnation.

One part of this whole dramatic saga has bothered her, though.

The colonel. Colonel Annora Bashkim, leader of SPEAR.

According to what Mia and Amari's sources in the Apolon Empire can scrounge up, Bashkim is a bit of a mystery. The talented soldier who rose through the ranks at a phenomenal speed before stopping at colonel and, by all accounts, deciding to stay there. No one is sure why. It could be a punishment for something, some incentive behind Bashkim's decision, simple sentiment, or none of the above.

The lack of history pokes at Amari, a feeling of dread attached to the sensation. A past wiped away can mean so many things, most of them not good for her friends. She'd like to believe that they've seen the last of the colonel as well as SPEAR, except she knows better. Amari doesn't need to be a seer to understand the Apolon Empire cannot afford to look weak in the face of their brazen crimes.

Resolved to do something useful, Amari gets up and heads into the office that she technically shares with Taliya, even though the thief rarely uses it. She sits at the desk and starts writing letters — that, with the magic of Deliverance, is a better form of communication than by gem, which can be easily monitored. The written word can be encoded and enchanted so only the recipient can read the message.

Even with these safety measures, Amari writes in double-speak, never clearly stating her intentions. For one, she writes about the smattering of storms hitting the Empire's east coast that seems suspiciously reminiscent of what an ocean's monarch can call up when irked. To another correspondent, she goes on a rambling account of a rare art piece discovered in a dig out in No Man's Land. One letter talks only of the magical properties of mushrooms. More follow this pattern. By the time she's done, she feels rather satisfied.

Of course, Amari doesn't use her real name for any of the letters. Marina and the Night Witches have surely shared her name, at the very least. It's not much of a loss since Amari doesn't work under an alias. The lease for the apartment, her clean bank accounts, her library card — those she has under different names. A long time ago, she decided not to force 'Amari Kato' to be a civilian separated from her criminal adventures.

Amari has to do enough pretending as it is.

For the letters, however, she doesn't even use the same fake name for each; instead, she gets creative as she comes up with aliases the recipients will see through and no one else. Honestly, it's a bit of fun.

The expensive cost of using Deliverance is worth her peace of mind, and Amari sends the letters with a grim smile.

The seer is still trying to resist wasting away in an empty apartment, younger visitors gone and Taliya out in the city, by reading a book, when it hits her.

The feeling of receiving premonitions versus prophecies is vastly different. It's like comparing being punched to getting shot by an explosive energy blast. One is bracing, and the other is debilitating.

It's fortunate, then, that she's at home when it happens.

Throughout the whole job, Amari has felt Fate weighing on her. Has seen Destiny out of the corner of her eye. The Future a step before and behind her.

Now, Time itself flowed around her like smoke, suffocating her.

Amari's mind fought to stay present, to stay grounded in an onslaught of undecipherable glimpses of the future too fast for anyone to process.

The Words suddenly reached through the fog of Time and gripped her by the throat. Without her consent, the prophecy was seared into her memory. Never to be forgotten.

There will be six thieves, renowned
Fighting against the wrongly crowned
All destined for war and secrets buried deep below the ground

One for death, one to pay the cost
One who rests, one trapped by waters never crossed
One cursed, and one condemned to darkness, forever lost

Amari felt herself drift in Time, like she was drowning in the sea with no idea which way was the way to the surface.

Eventually, she began feeling pulled to the Present.

"—ari! Amari, wake up!"

That was…

"Amari!"

She opens her eyes. Taliya is on one knee in front of her, hands on Amari's shoulders. The thief looks worried and shakes her forcefully. The Present crystallizes around her.

"Hey, are you with me?"

When did it get dark outside?

"I…" Amari's always so fucking groggy after these things. She focuses on the grounding feeling of Taliya's hands and tries to answer. The hearing enhancement runes are being forcibly activated by her friend, the only one allowed to do this. "Yeah, yeah."

"What happened?"

Taliya, of course, basically knows what happened. But it's good for Amari to put it into words.

"Prophecy. I—Shit," she sits up, more aware now. "Shit. It was intense, and the Words…"

"Amari?" Taliya asks and reminds her again to stay in the Present.

Amari tells her the prophecy. She can't bring herself to write it down. It's not like she'll forget, anyway. Prophecies are carved into reality in a way that regular visions just aren't. Taliya starts swearing too.

"What do we do?"

That is the question, isn't it?

Amari has long since learned the hard way what fighting a prophecy entails. That doesn't mean she intends to do nothing. "We do what we were planning to. We get more allies, and we fight the Empire any way we can."

Taliya is watching her closely. "Okay. Do we tell anyone?"

The notion almost startles Amari. Someone else knowing what she is is as unnerving as it is a relief. Erika is one thing, they're both not meant to exist in Avalon anymore, but anyone else…?

She considers it. "Nuru, maybe. The others… They left. I won't put Destiny on their shoulders like that if I can help it."

It's one thing to have a dangerous future ahead of you; it's an entirely different thing to know it. Taliya nods in understanding.

"Great. So, basically, it's you and me against Fate?" Amari focuses back on her friend, only to see Taliya grin. "Can't wait."

"You're not funny."

"Shut up, I'm hilarious. *Hil-ar-i-ous.*"

"The *worst*," Amari mutters as the remaining tension drains from her frame. "Just for that, you can have dish duty tonight."

"Bitch," Taliya replies brightly, not saying that the thief wouldn't let Amari do it anyway after such an intense prophecy. The pain dulls to an ache, spreads all over her body, and is accompanied by a pounding in her skull. In the next moment, seemingly in the blink of an eye, Taliya hands her some pain relief pills and a glass of water.

Amari signs a lazy thanks before throwing back the pills and drinking them down. The relief isn't instant, but a part of her relaxes at the mundaneness of their routine. Her friend helps her into her chair—when did she fall out of it—with an exaggerated wheeze at Amari's weight. Elbowing the thief, the seer collapses in exhaustion.

"I think I've had enough excitement for a month," Amari announces, feeling the tiredness of her drained magic draw at her while, at the same time, the oncoming night tries to revive her. It's a very unpleasant sensation.

Back in the kitchen, brewing tea and pulling out a pan, Taliya snorts without restraint. "You would die of boredom within the first week. Just take a day before you start overthinking everything. We have enough clean cash now to last us a while without trouble."

And plenty of side projects, Amari thinks, remembering Nuru's idea for a communal rune system for the Hall and her preparations for future clashes with SPEAR. "Fine."

Tomorrow, she'll look ahead to the future again. The seer will track global politics with a fever matched only by the most diligent scholars. She'll scour informant networks for information on Colonel Annora Bashkim, prepare to join a rebel group formally, and answer letters—all before lunch.

But that's tomorrow.

For now, Amari and Taliya will rest.

27

NARRATOR

All around the world of Avalon, people who knew more than they should and hid behind masks observed the aftermath of the thieves' deed with rapt attention. Six thieves did what many have failed to do for centuries: catch the attention of the immortals left in Avalon.

The Warlady paced the halls of her grand fortress in the rocky mountains of Ilved, stewing in frustration.

Adam Wright, the Prime Minister of Esma, sent spies searching his cities for word of talented thieves. He won't waste the chance to gain an upper hand over the blasted Empire.

The monarchs of the Eight Seas met to discuss the potential fallout of land dwellers. An ancient and worn ceasefire cracked further.

A shadow with electric blue eyes laughed and laughed and laughed. They had been waiting for this for a long, long time.

Queen General Elvira of Rowan sat on her throne, built on bones and ash, and planned.

The Divine King — Niklaus Eindride, to so few (and fewer every moment) — read reports and listened to his Cabinet members scream at each other. He let his Grand General deal with the problem and said nothing of it except to one. A cold fury burned in his soul.

Acknowledgments

Writing a book is never a solitary effort, even if much of it happens alone at a desk, staring at a blinking cursor. This story would not have made it to the page, let alone into readers' hands, without the encouragement, patience, and brilliance of so many people.

First, to Hillary Leftwich, thank you for your sharp insights, keen eye for detail, and the gentle but firm way you nudged this book into its best possible form. Your ability to see both the big picture and the smallest sentence-level improvements is truly a gift. To my beta readers—Michelle, Blair, Helen, and Amber from Beta Reader Bookings—you braved the early drafts, pointed out my plot holes, and never let me settle for *good enough*. Your feedback made this story stronger, and your enthusiasm kept me going when doubt threatened to creep in.

To my friends and family, who listened patiently as I talked (and talked… and talked) about this book, its characters, and all the messy twists I was trying to untangle—thank you. Your support means everything. A special shoutout to my mom for always reminding me to take a break, eat something, and trust myself even when I was convinced this book was a disaster. You kept me sane through every rewrite.

To the team at Once Upon A Queer Publishing, your passion and dedication to bringing new stories into the world is truly inspiring. Thank you for believing in this book and for all the work you put into making it shine.

And most of all, to you, the reader—thank you for picking up this book, for stepping into this world, and for taking a chance on these characters. Whether this is your first book of mine or one of many, I'm so grateful to share this adventure with you. Books don't just exist on the page—they come alive in the hands of readers, and I'm honored that you chose to spend time in this one.

This book was a journey, and I couldn't have done it alone. Thank you, all of you, for walking this path with me.

About the Author

B.R. Michaels writes fantasy stories filled with creative worlds, eccentric characters, and humor while tackling real-world issues. They are a lifelong lover of speculative fiction, and they mostly spend their time holed up in their library or getting lost in bookstores.

When not writing, B.R. Michaels can be found watching comedy with their mom and playing with their dogs. Their work often explores themes of found family, moral ambiguity, and the cost of power, and they love crafting stories that blend adventure, heart, and a touch of the unexpected.

You can find them at brmichaels.com/home.

Also by B.R. Michaels

The World of Avalon
Shatterpoint: An Amari Kato Novella